Wallace, Irving
The three sirens

By Irving Wallace

THE THREE SIRENS

THE PRIZE

THE TWENTY-SEVENTH WIFE

THE CHAPMAN REPORT

THE FABULOUS SHOWMAN

THE SINS OF PHILIP FLEMING

THE SQUARE PEGS

THE FABULOUS ORIGINALS

The
Three Sirens

a novel by

IRVING WALLACE

Simon and Schuster · New York

1963

Library of Congress Catalog Card Number: 63–17727
Manufactured in the United States of America
By H. Wolff, New York

Dedicated to the memory of
my beloved friends
Zachary Gold
(1918–1953)
Jacques Kapralik
(1906–1960)

There is a scale in dissolute sensuality, which these people have ascended, wholly unknown to every other nation whose manners have been recorded from the beginning of the world to the present hour, and which no imagination could possibly conceive.

> JAMES COOK
> *Account of a Voyage round the World*
> 1773

At last we are isolated from the outside world. Here, on these coral isles, which I have christened The Three Sirens, I will undertake my experiment . . . to prove, for once, that marriage as practiced in the West is antagonistic to human nature, whereas my System, blended with the Polynesian System, can produce a radically new form of matrimony infinitely superior to any known on earth. It will work. It must work. Here, far from the bigoted Throne and Censor, far from the accursed Peeping Toms of Coventry . . . here, amidst naked and unfettered Freedom . . . and with infinite Blessings of the Lord . . . my compleat System shall face the Test, at last.

> DANIEL WRIGHT, Esq.
> *Journal*
> Entry June 3, 1796

I

It was the first of the letters that Maud Hayden had taken from the morning's pile on her desk blotter. What had attracted her to it, she sheepishly admitted to herself, was the exotic row of stamps across the top of the envelope. They were stamps bearing the reproduction of Gauguin's "The White Horse," in green, red, and indigo, and the imprint "Polynésie Française . . . Poste Aérienne."

From the summit of her mountain of years, Maud was painfully aware that her pleasures had become less and less visible and distinct with each new autumn. The Great Pleasures remained defiantly clear: her scholarly accomplishments with Adley (still respected); her absorption in work (unflagging); her son, Marc (in his father's footsteps—somewhat); her recent daughter-in-law, Claire (quiet, lovely, too good to be true). It was the Small Pleasures that were becoming as elusive and invisible as youth. The brisk early morning walk in the California sun, especially when Adley was alive, had been a conscious celebration of each day's birth. Now, it reminded her only of her arthritis. The view, especially from her upstairs study window, of the soft ribbon of highway leading from Los Angeles to San Francisco, with the Santa Barbara beach and whitecaps of the ocean beyond, had always been esthetically exciting. But now, glancing out of the window and below, she saw only the dots of speeding monster automobiles and her memory smelled the gas fumes and the rotted weeds and kelp of the sea on the other side of the coastal road. Breakfast had always been another of the certain Small Pleasures, the folded newspaper opening to her its daily recital of the follies and wonders of Man, the hearty repast of cereal, eggs, bacon, potatoes, steaming coffee, heavily sugared, stacked toast, heavily buttered. Now, the hosts of breakfast had been decimated by ominous talk about high cholesterol and low-fat diet and all the linguistics (skimmed milk, margarine, broccoli, rice puddings) of the Age of Misery. And then, finally, among the Small Pleasures of each morning, there had been the pile of mail—and this delight, Maud could see, remained a constant delight, uneroded by her mountain of years.

The fun of the mail, for Maud Hayden, was that it gave her Christmas every morning, or so it seemed. She was a prolific correspondent. Her anthropology colleagues and disciples, afar, were tireless letter writers. And then, too, she was a minor oracle, to whom many came with their enigmas, hopes, and inquiries. No week's grab bag of letters was without some distant curiosity— the one from a graduate student on his first field trip to India, reporting how the Baiga tribe nailed down the turf again after every earthquake; the one from an eminent French anthropologist in Japan, who had found that the Ainu people did not consider a bride truly married until she had delivered a child, and who had asked if it was exactly this that Maud had discovered among the Siamese; the one from a New York television network, offering Maud a meager fee if she would verify the information, to be used in a New Britain travelogue, that a native suitor purchased his bride from her uncle, and that when the couple produced an off-spring, the infant was held over a bonfire to assure its future growth.

At first look, this morning's mail, with its glued-in secrets, had appeared less promising. Going through the various envelopes, Maud had found the postmarks were from New York City, London, Kansas City, Houston, and similar unwonderful places, until her hand had been stayed by the envelope featuring the stamps with the Gauguin painting and the imprint of "Polynésie Française."

She realized that she still held the elongated, thick, battered envelope between her stubby fingers, and then she realized that more often, in these last few years, her habit of direct action had been bogged down in musings and mind-wanderings clouded by a vague self-pity.

Annoyed with herself, Maud Hayden turned the long envelope

over, and on the pasted backflap she found the name and return
address of the sender, spelled out in a swirling, old-fashioned European calligraphy. It read: "A. Easterday, Hotel Temehami, Rue
du Commandant Destremau, Papeete, Tahiti."

She tried to match the name "A. Easterday" to a face. In the
present, none. In the past—the efficient file of her mind flipped
backwards—so many, so many . . . until the face captioned by
the name was found. The impression was faded and foxed. She
closed her eyes, and concentrated hard, and by degrees the impression became more definable.

Alexander Easterday. Papeete, yes. They were strolling on the
shady side of the street toward his shop at 147, Rue Jeanne d'Arc.
He was short, and as pudgy as if he had been mechanically com-
pressed, and he had been born in Memel or Danzig or some port
quickly erased by the storm troopers—and he had had many names
and passports—and en route, the long way to America as a refugee,
he had come to a standstill, and finally a residence and business,
in Tahiti. He claimed to have been an archeologist in other years,
accompanying several German expeditions in happier days, and
had modeled himself after Heinrich Schliemann, testy and eccentric excavator of Troy. Easterday was too soft and grubby, too
anxious to please, too unsuccessful, to play Schliemann, she had
thought then. Alexander Easterday, yes. She could see him better:
ridiculously perched linen hat, bow tie (in the South Seas),
wrinkled gray tropical suit stretched by a potbelly. And yet
better: pince-nez high on a long nose, an inch of mustache, cold
dribbling pipe, and warped pockets bulging with knickknacks,
notes, calling cards.

It was coming back fully now. She had spent the afternoon
poking through his shop cluttered with Polynesian artifacts, all
reasonably priced, and had come away with a pair of Balinese
bamboo clappers, a carved Marquesan war club, a Samoan tapa-
cloth skirt, an Ellice Island mat, and an ancient Tonga wooden
feast bowl that now graced the sideboard of her living room downstairs. Before their departure, she recalled, she and Adley—for she
had wanted Adley to meet him—had entertained Easterday at the
rooftop restaurant of the Grand Hotel. Their guest had proved
an encyclopedia of information—tidbits illuminating the lesser
puzzles of their half-year in Melanesia—and that had been eight
years ago, closer to nine, when Marc had been in his last year at

the university (and being contrary about Alfred Kroeber's influence there simply, she had been sure, because she and Adley worshiped Kroeber).

Sorting the dead years now, Maud recollected that her last contact with Easterday had been a year or two after their meeting in Tahiti. It was at the time their study of the people of Bau, in Fiji, had been published, and Adley had reminded her to send Easterday an inscribed copy. She had done so, and months later Easterday had acknowledged their gift in a brief letter of formal appreciation mingled with genuine delight at being remembered at all by such august acquaintances—he had used the word "august," and then she had possessed fewer doubts that he had been schooled at the University of Göttingen.

That was the last that Maud had heard of "A. Easterday"—the thank-you note of six or seven years ago—until this moment. She considered Easterday's return address. What could that dim, half-forgotten face want of her now, across so many leagues: money? recommendation? data? She weighed the envelope in her palm. No, it was too heavy for a request. More likely, it was an offering. The man inside the envelope, she decided, had something to get off his chest.

She took the Ashanti dagger—a souvenir of the African field trip in those pre-Ghana days between the World Wars—from her desk, and in a single practiced stroke she slit the envelope open.

She unfolded the fragile airmail sheets. The letter was neatly typed on a defective ancient machine, so that many of the words were marred by holes—instead of an *e* or an *o* there was most often a puncture—but still all neatly, laboriously, efficiently single-spaced. She riffled through the rice-paper pages, counting twenty-two. They would take time. There was the other mail, and certain lecture notes to be reviewed before her late-morning class. Still, she felt the curious and old familiar nagging from the second self, the unintellectual and nonobjective second Maud Hayden, who dwelt hidden inside her and was kept hidden for being her unscientific, intuitive, and female self. Now this second self nudged, reminded her of mysteries and excitements that had often, in the past, come from faraway lands. Her second self only rarely asked to be heard, but when it did, she could not ignore it. Her best moments had come from such obedience.

Brushing aside good sense, and the pressure of time, she succumbed. She settled back heavily, disregarding the metallic protest of the swivel chair, held the letter high and close to her eyes, and slowly she began to read to herself from what she hoped might be the best of the day's Small Pleasures:

PROFESSOR ALEXANDER EASTERDAY
HOTEL TEMEHAMI
PAPEETE, TAHITI

Dr. Maud Hayden
Chairman, Department of Anthropology
Social Science Building, Room 309
Raynor College
Santa Barbara, California
U.S.A.

DEAR DR. HAYDEN:

I am sure this letter will be a surprise to you, and I can only hope that you will be kind enough to remember my name. I had the great honor of meeting you and your illustrious husband ten years ago, when you stopped over in Papeete several days, en route from the Fiji Islands to California. I trust you will recall that you visited my Polynesian shop in the Rue Jeanne d'Arc and were generous enough to compliment me on my collection of primitive archeological pieces. Also, it was a memorable moment of my life to be the guest of your husband and yourself to dinner.

Although I am out of the main track of life, I have managed to keep in touch with the outside world by subscribing to several archeology and anthropology journals as well as *Der Spiegel* of Hamburg. As such, I have read of your activities from time to time, and not without pride, I must admit, for having encountered you once. Also, through the recent years, I have acquired some of your earlier books in the more accessible paperbound editions, and I have read them with burning interest. Truly, I believe, and not I alone, that your brilliant husband and yourself have made the greatest of contributions to modern-day ethnology.

Therefore, it was with shock and dismay that I read—it was three or four years ago, I believe—in our local weekly, *Les Debats*, of your husband's decease. I was too moved and awkward to write to you at the time, but now that the years have passed I tender my sincerest condolences. I can only hope that you have withstood the loss, and are now recovered and in strong health, and teaching, writing, and traveling again.

I pray this letter reaches you, for I have only your old card with this address, but if you have gone elsewhere, I am sure that the postal authorities will locate one of your renown. The reason I say that "I pray this letter reaches you" is because I feel that the subsequent contents may interest you deeply, and may have a profound effect on the course of your work.

Before I inform you of the remarkable curiosity that has come to my attention, I must refresh your memory—if it is necessary—on a portion of our conversation ten years ago. It was after the dinner in Papeete, when we were having our liqueurs, that you and your beloved husband thanked me for the minor anecdotes and histories I was able to relate. We drank in silence for some minutes, and then you spoke to me the following, and I base my remembrance of your words not on faulty memory but on passages of a journal I have faithfully kept for years. You said:

"Professor Easterday, our field trip to Fiji, our side trips throughout the Melanesia area, and now our brief visits to Tonga, the Cooks, the Marquesas, and here to Tahiti, have been so productive and stimulating, that my husband and I feel we must return. We want to come back to Polynesia, specifically Polynesia, in the near future. However, there must be a reason, a purpose, for such a visit. This is where you come in, Professor Easterday. We make this request of you: if ever you learn of a Polynesian people, on an unknown atoll, whose culture remains uncontaminated by outside contact and has not been subjected to scientific scrutiny, I want you to be certain to let us know of this discovery at once. If the people and their atoll are worthy of a study in the field, if they can teach us something about human behavior, we would undertake an investigation. For your part, you would be amply rewarded."

When I heard this, Dr. Hayden, I was moved by your faith in me. At the same time, if you recollect, I had to admit that I doubted if I could be of any help to you. I told you that, to the best of my knowledge, there were no important islands—that is, populated islands—that were not already known, charted, visited, investigated. I told you, frankly, that the explorers, missionaries, whalers, traders

—and since then the militarists, tourists, beachcombers, anthropologists—had seen all there was to be seen in these parts, and it was unlikely that there was anything new or virginal left.

Despite my firm statement, if I recollect accurately, you were undiscouraged. I have since learned that this was typical of you, that your perceptions, optimism, persistence are some of the characteristics of your fame. And so, at the time, you were able to say to me:

"Professor Easterday, while you know Oceania better than we ever shall, I must tell you that our experience in many places has taught us that all is not discovered, all is not known, and nature has its way of withholding its little surprises. As a matter of fact, I have personally met several anthropologists who served in the Pacific during World War II and who confessed to me that they had come across at least a half-dozen obscure islands, inhabited by primitive tribes, that were not on any existing maps. These anthropologists are being very secretive about their previously undiscovered islands—are not mentioning their location to anyone—for fear that they might be placed on public maps and charts. These anthropologists are hoarding their little atolls against the day when they have time and funds to make their exclusive studies. As you surely understand, exclusivity—that is, new ground to be covered —often counts for much in the social sciences. Now, I have a feeling that, among the more than ten thousand atolls, coral islands, volcanic islands in Oceania, there must be some so-called lost islands worthy of study in depth. I repeat, Professor, if ever you should hear of one such island, with a people whose customs are yet unknown to the outside world, please remember the Haydens and their deep interest. Do not forget what I speak of tonight, Professor Easterday. Do not forget. I promise, you will not regret your trouble."

I have never forgotten what you spoke of that night, Dr. Hayden. You may have long forgotten, after these many years, but I have not. Your request was always in the back part of my mind. True, in recent years, especially as Western jet civilization encroached more and more upon the South Pacific, I thought your hope, and my quest on your behalf, an impossible chimera. We are both aware that the world map still displays unexplored areas —the interior of Dutch New Guinea, portions of the China-Burma-India range, the upper part of the Amazon River Basin—with tribes

never seen by outside eyes. But your dream of a previously un-
visited, populated island in Oceania? I confess that I had finally
almost abandoned listening to any rumor or gossip that might sub-
stantiate your dream. Then, suddenly, last week, by accident, when
I had all but given up thinking about the matter, your old request
bore fruit.

Yes, Dr. Hayden, I have found your lost island.

Forgive me, if my stiff English belies the thrill within me as
I put these words to paper. How I wish for eloquence in your
language, this moment of fulfillment. Handicapped as I am, I will
do my best to convey to you my enthusiastic emotions.

After a decade of years, I have found, among the thousands of
islets of Oceania, the hitherto unknown island and unknown people
that you once sought. This is not hearsay or native gossip, Dr.
Hayden. I address you with the authority of firsthand evidence.
For, I have walked on the soil of this minute high island. I have
consorted briefly with its inhabitants, a mixture half-Polynesian
and half-English, as in the instance of Pitcairn Island. I have observed, and since heard more of, the customs of this tribe, and
these customs reveal one of the most peculiar and strange isolated
civilizations on the earth today. I try to see this find of mine
through your expert and experienced eyes, and I see a study that
might be of great importance in your work and a useful contribution to every man and woman alive.

The name of this overlooked South Sea island group—one small
but lush volcanic isle, and two tiny atolls—is The Three Sirens.

Do not attempt to locate The Three Sirens on any map. They
are not there. They have not been officially discovered for the
authorities or the public. Do not attempt to research The Three
Sirens in any learned books on Oceania. As far as history and
geography are concerned, they do not exist. You must trust my
scholar sense: The Three Sirens, if microscopic by comparison,
are as real as Tahiti or Rarotonga or Easter Island or, for that
matter, Pitcairn Island. As to the populace of the Sirens, no more
than two hundred I should venture, they are also as real as you and
I. With the exception of myself and two other Caucasians, they
have not been seen by anyone alive on earth today.

What is most unique about these people on The Three Sirens—
I must state this as a preliminary, for if this does not interest you,

then you need not trouble to read further, and I shall reluctantly turn elsewhere—what is most unusual about these people is their advanced (I might add *amazing*) attitude toward the practice of love and marriage. I am sure there is nothing similar to their historic behavior in any other society on the globe.

I cannot comment if the sexual and marital customs on The Three Sirens are good or bad. I can only remark, without equivocation, that they astound me. And I, Dr. Hayden, speak not as an ignorant, inexperienced undergraduate, but as a scientist and a man of the world.

If I have piqued your interest, as I pray I have, you must read on. Remember, as you read, that I am no teller of tales, that I speak with the cold objectivity of a German-trained archeologist. Remember, too, the words of the immortal Hamlet, "There are more things in heaven and earth, Horatio, than are dreamt of in your philosophy."

I will discuss, chronologically, my own involvement in this accidental discovery, as well as what I found, what I observed, what I heard, and, as it may concern you, what may be done about this, in a practical way.

About six weeks ago, there came to my shop a tall, aristocratic, middle-aged Australian gentleman, who introduced himself as Mr. Trevor, of Canberra. He said that he had just completed a tour that encompassed Western Samoa, the Marquesas, the Cooks, and that he could not return to his homeland without bringing some souvenirs. He had heard of my stock, and my reputation for honesty, and he wanted to purchase several small artifacts. I led him about the shop, explaining this item and that, its origin, its history, its uses and meaning, and soon he was so taken by my broad knowledge of the South Seas that he began to question me about many of the islands and my travels and buying trips among them. Eventually, his stay extended to several hours—I served him tea—and although he departed with purchases amounting to no more than 1,800 Pacific francs, I regretted his leaving. It is rare one finds literate listeners in this lonely place.

I thought that was the last of Mr. Trevor, of Canberra, Australia, so you can imagine my surprise when, shortly after I had opened my shop the following morning, he reappeared. He had not come for artifacts, he said, or to listen to my stories, but rather to receive my answer to a business proposition he was about to offer me. He had been impressed, he said, by my acquaintance with the many islands and natives of Polynesia. He had been hunting for such a one as myself, he said, and in his entire tour he had found no one reliable as well as knowledgeable, until he had chanced upon me. Because he thought me too good to be true, he had made inquiries among prominent officials the night before, and they had supported and recommended me.

Without further prologue, Mr. Trevor revealed his mission. He represented a syndicate of Canberra businessmen who believed in the future of Polynesia and desired to invest hard pounds in it. The projects were many, and diversified, but among the first was to be a fleet of small passenger airplanes to carry tourists between the lesser but most picturesque islands and the larger ones. The company, Intra-Oceania Flights, would undercut, in fares and freight charges, Qantas, the French TAI, South Pacific Air Lines, New Zealand's TEAL, and several others. Essentially, it expected to offer a shuttle or ferry service, giving it greater mobility and latitude than the larger companies. Because light aircraft would be employed, small and cheap landing fields and inexpensive facilities could be used, and rates could be kept low. Mr. Trevor explained that arrangements had been made throughout Polynesia, in cooperation with foreign home governments, but the site for one more airfield was still missing.

Mr. Trevor could remain no longer to locate this last elusive airfield. He needed someone to act in his stead. That was why he had come to me. His proposition was the following: he wanted me to take several aerial surveys, by private plane, in two directions. First, he wished me to study the corridor between Tahiti and the Marquesas Islands. If that provided no adequate site, he suggested I range southward from Tahiti, covering the broad triangle formed by the Tubuai Islands, Pitcairn Island, and Rapa Island, and if necessary to go even further south and away from the traffic lanes.

What was wanted by Intra-Oceania Flights was an uninhabited small island, with a plateau or level area that could be bulldozed, on which to erect an airfield no more than a mile and a half long. An uninhabited isle was preferred, because then the land could be leased cheaply from the neglecting government that had possession.

On the other hand, if the appropriate island showed itself to me, but happened to be inhabited by a single tribe or a mere handful of natives, exclusive of whites, that would do, too. The natives could be removed or, indeed, bought off and segregated, and the land would still be cheap.

It would be my task, said Mr. Trevor, to locate three or four such islands from the air, and then land and visit them, and then submit a fully detailed report to Canberra. Mr. Trevor's experts would sift my report, narrow focus on one or two islands, and send their specialists to make the final decision. For my scouting expenses, I could have $500. For my completed report, if successful, I could have $3,000 additional.

Despite my joy of travel among these islands, this was not an undertaking to my liking. For one thing, I have an aversion toward flying. For another, I have little energy left for trampling over barren or nearly barren and remote tracts of land. Still, Dr. Hayden, I keep no pride from you that lately my pecuniary fortunes have been low. I do not make myself out more than I am. My day-to-day life now is a struggle to make ends meet. I have growing competition from native dealers. Valuable artifacts are increasingly difficult to come by. Therefore, whenever there is an opportunity to supplement my meager income from the shop, I cannot disdain accepting it. Even though Mr. Trevor's expense budget was limited, his final payment was considerable, certainly more than I profit in an entire year from my shop and other enterprises. I had no choice but to accept the assignment.

After I had received my full instructions, and Mr. Trevor had flown back to Australia, I immediately set out to charter a private seaplane. The number that were available in Papeete—for example, the two flying boats of the RAI which taxi tourists to Bora Bora —were all far too expensive for private use. I continued making inquiries, and when I mentioned my problem to the bartender in Quinn's, he told me that he knew just the man for me. He said that one of his customers, Captain Ollie Rasmussen, whom I remembered hearing about, owned an old amphibian flying boat that he had bought from an American firm after World War II. The bartender said that Rasmussen owned a cottage and Polynesian wife on Moorea—which, you know, is a stone's throw away from us—and that he had a warehouse just below the Quai Commerce.

Rasmussen was an importer, the bartender thought, and he used his seaplane for freighting. In any case, he came into Papeete at least once a week, and I would have no trouble seeing him.

Within a few days I had met Captain Rasmussen and his copilot, a native in his twenties named Richard Hapai. Rasmussen had whiskey on his breath, and also profanity, and his appearance was disreputable, and I had some misgivings. He did own an aged Vought-Sikorsky—a clumsy, creaky twin-engined plane with a maximum cruising speed of 170 miles an hour—and I found it clean and well cared for, and this engaged my respect again. Rasmussen was colorful and voluble, deploring at length the necessity of giving up his old pearl schooner in 1947 for a flying boat, but I think he liked the flying boat more than he would admit. He took trips through the islands every week, for two days at a time, yet he had spare time enough and had no objections to chartering his seaplane and services to me. We haggled for an hour, and at last he agreed to take me on three scouting flights, two short ones and one longer one, and to land no more than three times, for $400.

Two weeks ago, with Rasmussen and Hapai in the nose cockpit, we took our first exploratory trip. Captain Rasmussen, I must say, knew the area between Samoa and the Marquesas better than I did, and he directed me to a fair number of uninhabited atolls, which you had always suspected might exist but were on no maps. However, not one was suitable for Intra-Oceania Flights. A few days later, a second scouting expedition proved equally unprofitable, although I directed Rasmussen to one landing and visit ashore. I was disheartened—I saw that I might not earn the $3,000 offered me—but still retained hope that the third and longest flight might uncover what I wanted. Then, for a number of days, this final trip was delayed. Rasmussen was absent from Papeete, and was nowhere to be found. At last, he presented himself at my hotel, five days ago, ready to take off at dawn for what was to be a two-day survey, interrupted only by fueling stops, an overnight stay on Rapa, and my own orders to land whenever I sighted a good possibility.

There is no need, Dr. Hayden, to have you suffer the desperation of that last empty excursion aloft. The first day was fruitless. The second day, leaving Rapa at dawn, we ventured south, flying high and low for hours, far afield from the beaten ocean paths, examining coral islands one after the other. None was suitable for Mr.

Trevor's purposes, and there was no use in deluding myself. It was midafternoon when Rasmussen switched to the auxiliary gas tanks, and turned his ship for home, already grumbling that we had gone too far to return to Tahiti by any reasonable hour of the night. I suggested that he pilot the seaplane back by a northeasterly route, so that eventually we would skirt the Tubuai Islands as we headed for Tahiti. Rasmussen complained about this, and about his diminishing fuel supply, but then he took pity on my dejection and obliged me between swigs of Scotch.

Hapai was at the controls, and Rasmussen well on his way to total inebriation, and I was crouched behind them, peering beyond the window, when I saw a vague hump of land, coruscating in the setting sun, far off in the distance. Except for the Tubuai group, which we were yet nowhere near, I was not familiar with the area, yet I sensed that this hump of land was no traveled or major island.

"What is that, way out there?" I inquired of Captain Rasmussen.

Until this moment, despite his uncouth aspect, I had found Rasmussen the most congenial and cooperative of companions. Certain vulgarities of his speech I considered disagreeable, and I overlooked them, yet I shall attempt to reproduce his locution from the life, so that you may experience what I experienced in the air that late afternoon.

To my inquiry about the hump of land in the distance, Captain Rasmussen replied, with a snort, "What is it? It ain't nothin'— some lousy atoll—deserted—a little grass—guano maybe—no water, no life, 'cept albatrosses an' terns an' plovers—it's for the birds, not for airplanes."

I was not satisfied with this explanation. I have had some knowledge of the islands, I remind you. "It does not appear to be a small atoll," I persisted. "It seems to me to resemble a somewhat larger island with a coral plateau, or even a volcanic island. If you do not mind, I should like to inspect it more closely."

With this, I recall, Captain Rasmussen sobered, and a hint of asperity crept into his voice. "I do mind wastin' time on a detour. Anyways, I done my job—it's almost comin' on night—I'm low on fuel—an' we still got a long ways to go. We gotta skip it."

Something about his tone, his manner, the evasiveness of his eyes, made me suddenly suspicious of his integrity. I decided not to surrender. "You told me it was uninhabited," I said.

"Yup, that's what I told you."

"Then I must insist upon seeing it more closely. As long as we are in this plane under my charter, I suggest you accommodate me."

His eyes, watery with drink, seemed to clear and harden. He glared at me. "You tryin' to cause trouble, Professor?"

I felt uncomfortable, but I took a gamble. There was too much at stake for me to be timid. I replied to him in kind. "Are you trying to conceal something from me, Captain?"

This angered him. I was sure that he would curse me. Instead, his body lurched toward his native copilot. "Awright, let's get him off my neck—take him in a little closer, Hapai, show him there's nothin' on the Sirens but cliffs an' stone an' a few hills."

"Sirens?" I said quickly. "Is that the name of the island?"

"It's got no chart name." He had become extremely surly.

By now the seaplane had swung about in an arc and was laboring toward the distant speck of land, which gradually became more distinct, so that I could make out the definition of steep seaward cliffs and what might be a plateau with a mountain crater beyond.

"Okay, far enough," Rasmussen was saying to his copilot. Then he said to me, "You can see for yourself, Professor—no landin' place."

This was true, if there was no plateau, but I suspected that there was a plateau, and I told Rasmussen what I thought. I demanded that he fly in even closer and lower, so that I could satisfy myself one way or the other. Once more, Rasmussen, fulminating under his breath, was about to object aloud, when I interrupted him with all the severity I could muster. "Captain," I said, "I have a fair idea where we are. If you refuse to give me a proper look at this island, I shall find someone else who will, and I shall return tomorrow." This was sheer bravado, for I was nearly out of Mr. Trevor's money, and I was not sure of our exact location, but I almost believed my threat.

Rasmussen was silent a moment, blinking his eyes at me, licking his cracked lips. When he spoke, at last, his voice was faintly insinuating and sinister. "I would not do that if I was you, Professor. This has been a friendly arrangement, a quiet, private-like trip. I've been pretty generous with you. I never took no one in this area before. I wouldn't want you takin' advantage of the captain."

I was a little frightened of Rasmussen, but I was equally frightened of failing on my assignment. I prayed that I could maintain my note of bravado. "It is a free sky and a free ocean," I said. Then I repeated, "No one can keep me from returning here, especially now, when I am positive you have something to hide."

"You're talkin' through your hat," Rasmussen growled. "There's a million barren islands like that one. You won't never know which one. You won't never find it."

"I *will* find it, if it takes me a year," I said emphatically. "I'll enlist my Canberra backers and their entire air fleet. I have some idea of the general area. I've observed certain landmarks." I made my final gamble. "If you are going to obstruct me, very well. Take me right back to Tahiti. I shall handle this matter with charter pilots who will perform what they are paid to perform."

I feared that Rasmussen would explode or do me violence, but he was sodden with drink and his reactions were slow. Muttering to himself, he gestured in disgust at me, and turned to his partner. "Take the sonofa—— over the Sirens, Hapai. Maybe that'll shut him up."

The next ten minutes of ocean were traversed in prickly silence, and then we came over the island, which I now observed was not one island but three. I had a glimpse of two miniature atolls, each less than one-quarter mile in circumference. These were coral, hardly above sea level, each with dry land, some grass and brush, and coconut palm trees. One had a tiny but lovely lagoon. Relative to these, the main island was large, but actually, as compared to other islands in Polynesia, it was small, I should guess no more than four miles in length and three miles in breadth. In the speed of our passage, I could make out the high volcanic crater, steep slopes, thickly covered with green foliage, screw pines, hardwood forests, several valleys heavy with vegetation, a brilliant, copper-colored lagoon, countless gullies and ravines, with enormous rocky cliffs guarding the land.

And then I saw my plateau. Green vegetation covered it like a massive carpet, and it was flat and straight, unbroken by boulders or ravines. Blurring before my eyes, the plateau dipped into almost jungle slopes that led down a ridge to a narrow band of sandy beach.

"No anchorage for ships," Rasmussen was saying, with satisfaction. "Shallow—submerged reef—boulders—north winds would smash any vessel. That's why I never touched the place when I had a schooner. Only possible when I got this plane."

"There is a plateau," I said, hardly suppressing my enthusiasm. "It is perfect."

So entranced and absorbed had Rasmussen been by the sight of the larger island, that he seemed to have forgotten my purpose. My words brought him up sharply.

"I want you to put down," I said. I think I repeated this several times, like a chanting child who has found a sweet. "I want to see it for myself." My heart was swelling with hope, for I knew this was suitable land. I would fulfill my assignment for Mr. Trevor and Intra-Oceania Flights. I would have my payment.

"No," said Captain Rasmussen.

"No?" I said incredulously. "What do you mean?"

We had eased around for another pass over the main island. Rasmussen gestured vaguely toward the window. "Surf's runnin'—poundin' hard—bad wind—we'd pile up."

I looked below. "The sea is glass. It is perfect."

"I don't know," Rasmussen mumbled. "There's other things. It's dangerous. There's head-hunters—cannibals—"

"You said it was uninhabited," I reminded him sternly.

"I forgot."

I knew there were no cannibals in this area. Yet, I could not brand him a liar. I said, "I'll take my chances, Captain. Please request Mr. Hapai to land. I shall only require an hour or two."

Rasmussen remained strangely adamant. "I can't do it," he said weakly. "I'm responsible for you."

"I am responsible for me," I said firmly. "I have said this twice and I will say it a third time—if you continue to prevent me from seeing this island, I shall return tomorrow with someone more co-operative."

Rasmussen stared at me for many seconds, and we could only hear the hammer of the monoplane's two engines. His Nordic countenance, wrinkled and stubbled, was a portrait of consternation. Finally, almost without emotion, he said, "I should open the hatch an' heave you in the ocean."

I could not discern if he was jesting, but there was no humor in his face. "People know I am with you," I said. "You would be guillotined for it."

He glanced out of the window. "I don't like this at all," he said. "Why'd I ever get mixed up with you? If I go takin' you down . . ." His voice trailed off, and he shook his head. "You're causin' me an awful lot of grief, Professor. I made my pledge never to bring no one to The Three Sirens."

I felt the blood throb in my temples. So these lost islands were likely inhabited. To whom had Rasmussen made his pledge? What was Rasmussen shielding about the patch of land below? The mystery excited me as much as the potential airfield.

"Are you going to take me down?" I demanded.

"You're givin' me no choice," said Rasmussen, with evident despair. "If I was you, I'd wear blinkers ashore. Look for your damn airstrip, an' nothin' more."

"That is all I am interested in."

"We'll see," said Rasmussen, enigmatically. He glanced at Hapai. "Let them know I'm comin' down. Then retract—cut her slowly to sixty-five miles per hour—sea's good enough to bring her in half a mile from the beach. I'll untie the dinghy."

As the seaplane turned, Rasmussen lifted himself from his seat with a sigh and went aft to the portside. Immediately, I took his place in the pilot's compartment. Hapai had brought the flying boat back over the center of the main island. He came in low across what I made out to be a deep valley hidden in shadows. Unexpectedly, he rolled the plane, dipping the wings, once, twice, almost throwing me from my seat. Then he appeared to gun the plane upward, soaring over the volcanic crater, and easing around in the direction of the cliffs and beach.

The descent was rapid and even, and when we perched on the water offshore, Hapai left his place. I found him opening the main entrance hatch on the portside. After that, he helped Rasmussen move the dinghy free, and lower it into the water.

Rasmussen preceded me into the bobbing dinghy, and reached up to help me down beside him. He called to Hapai, "You stay put. We'll be back in two hours. If we're longer, I'll have Paoti or Tom Courtney send someone."

My mind held on the curious pair of names—Paoti—Tom Courtney—provocative because of their juxtaposition, although one was obviously Polynesian and the other sounded Anglo-Saxon, despite the fact that Courtney is of French derivation. Before I could remark upon this oddity, Rasmussen gruffly ordered me to take up a paddle and go to work.

Even with the smoothness of the sea, the exertion of rowing—combined with the discomfort of the almost airless, muggy afternoon, unrelieved by any stir of breeze—had me soaked through with perspiration by the time we had made the beach. The stretch of sandy beach, the crags behind, met us in silence. When I alighted, it was as if I had stepped on the earth of Eden the fourth day after Genesis. (Forgive my eloquence, Dr. Hayden, but this was how I felt.)

After Rasmussen had secured the craft, he lost no time. "It'll take a half-hour's stiff climb, if we keep movin', to reach your god—plateau."

I was at his heels as he led the way to a narrow, winding footpath that ascended gradually along the slope of a cliff. "Are there people here?" I wanted to know. "Who are Paoti and Courtney?"

"Don't go wastin' your breath," growled Rasmussen, " 'cause you'll be needin' it."

Lest I weary you with the details of my adventure, Dr. Hayden, I will be as concise as possible about our climb to the plateau. The path was not steep, but constantly rising, and the rock walls on either side hoarded the stifling heat of the early day and was suffocating. Because I called a halt, several times, to ease the stitch in my side, our ascension took nearly three-quarters of an hour. In that period, Rasmussen uttered not one word to me. His lined, burned face was grim, and he turned aside my inquiries with cross grumbles and snarls.

At last, the rock formations reached the summit of a broad boulder, which led to verdant hillocks, and these slowly merged into the long, level plateau.

"Here you are," were the first words Rasmussen had spoken in all this while. "What you goin' to do now?"

"Examine it."

I went deeper across the plateau, estimating its length and width, judging its evenness, studying the vegetation, testing the consistency of the soil, attentive even to the direction of the winds. I did all that Mr. Trevor had instructed me to do. It was during my absorbed examination—we could have been on this plain no longer than an hour, and I was on my hands and knees testing the grass and topsoil—that I first heard the voices. I lifted my head with surprise to realize that Rasmussen was not behind me. I quickly cast about, and then I saw him and saw that he was not alone.

I leaped to my feet. I could make out that Rasmussen was in the company of two towering, lean, fair-skinned native males, one carrying a short stone adze. As far as I could judge, from my distance, and with Rasmussen blocking a full view, both native men were naked. They were in stances of repose, listening, as Rasmussen spoke to them, gesticulating broadly. Once, he half pivoted, to indicate me, and when I mistook this as an invitation to approach them, Rasmussen quickly waved me to remain where I stood. The conversation, out of earshot, went on for perhaps another five minutes, and then suddenly the three of them came toward me.

As they advanced, I could make out the features of the two native men, and I could see that one was possibly Polynesian while the other was definitely Caucasian, although both were of the same color. They were each naked, head to toe, except for one concession to modesty. Both men wore white pubic bags—like the medieval codpieces—around their genitals, loosely held up by thin coconut fiber strands around their waists. I must confess I was disconcerted, for though I had seen these supporters in Melanesia some years ago, they are no longer the fashion in civilized Polynesia, where Western trousers or native kilts are favored. I had the impression that these men, or whomever they represented, were adhering to the old ways and had been untouched by modern influences.

"Professor Easterday," Rasmussen was saying, "these gentlemen were huntin' near here when they saw my signal an' came up to meet us. This is Mr. Thomas Courtney, an American who is an honorary member of the Sirens tribe. And this is Moreturi, oldest son of Paoti Wright, Chief of the tribe."

Courtney offered his hand and I shook it. Moreturi did not offer his hand, but only a forbidding aspect.

A brief smile was on Courtney's face, no doubt at the astonishment unsuppressed upon my own. I asked myself then, and for a short time later, what a naked American, garmented in such a fashion, was doing on an island called The Three Sirens, which existed on no map? Even as the puzzle teased me, I could definitely distinguish the two men now.

Moreturi was the younger, no more than thirty years of age, and possibly an inch shy of six feet in height. We know that Polynesians are light-skinned enough to tan, but he appeared to be a dark white man who had tanned. His hair was black and wavy, but his entire body was devoid of any hair at all. His face was broader and more handsome, with its straight and correct features, than

Courtney's face. All that indicated "native" was the slight slant of his eyes and fullness of his lips. His chest was powerful, his bicep muscles enormous, all tapering down sharply to slender hips and legs.

Courtney was, as I have said, the older of the pair. I should guess nearly forty years of age, but of superb condition and physique. I estimated him to be six feet two inches in height, with sandy, uncombed hair not recently barbered. His face was longer, more angular than that of his Polynesian friend, with deep-set brown eyes, a nose that appeared to have once been broken and imperfectly set, narrower lips and wider mouth. He was the leaner of the two, but rangy and also muscular, with moderate hair on his chest and legs.

My descriptions of these persons may not be completely accurate, for all this I observed in short seconds, and only supplemented later when there was darkness and scrutiny was more difficult.

I was aware that Courtney was addressing me. "Captain Rasmussen is, in effect, our ambassador and lifeline to the outside world. He has, as best he could, told us something of you, Professor, and of your assignment for Intra-Oceanic Flights." His voice was low, well-modulated, and his speech cultivated, indicating that he was an educated man. "You are the first stranger to come here since my own arrival, several years ago. The chief and villagers will be quite concerned. Strangers are held tabu."

"You are an American, not one of them," I said boldly. "Why are you tolerated?"

"I came by accident," said Courtney, "I remained by the grace of the Chief. Now I am one of them. No one else would be welcomed. The privacy of the village and islands is holy."

"I saw no village when we flew over the islands," I said.

Courtney nodded. "That's right, you saw no village. But it exists, and there is a population of over two hundred, the survivors of both white and brown forebears."

"Descendants of the *Bounty* mutineers?" I inquired.

"No. This all came about quite differently. There is no time for further explanation. I think it would be wise, Professor Easterday, if you left here at once and forgot that you ever laid eyes upon us or the islands. The fact is, your arrival has imperiled the entire population. If your disappearance did not endanger Captain Rasmussen's position in Tahiti, I am sure Moreturi would not let you leave at all. As it is, you can depart unharmed."

Unnerved though I was, I determined to stand my ground. The speech was less ominous coming from an American turned native than from a Polynesian. "This plateau is a perfect airstrip," I said. "It is my duty to report it to Canberra."

Moreturi stirred, but Courtney touched his arm without looking at him. "Professor Easterday," Courtney said softly, "you have no idea what you are doing. This seemingly inaccessible, rarely visited island, uninhabited to the eye, has remained impervious to outsiders —the corruptions of modern civilization—since 1796, when the present village was built and the present culture begun."

I think, Dr. Hayden, it was his use of the word "culture" that first put my mind on anthropology, and your request of a decade ago. However, my conscious mind was still on Mr. Trevor.

"It is my job," I said.

"Have you considered what your job will lead to?" Courtney asked. "Your associates in Canberra will send surveyors. They will approve of the terrain. Your friends will then seek permission of an outside government that owns Polynesian colonies or holds mandates. They will appeal to France, Great Britain, New Zealand, the United States, and other nations who possess islands and bases in the Pacific. What will be the result of their inquiries? Consternation. If no outside power is even aware that this minor island exists, how can they claim it? No discoverer ever waded ashore. I shall have to fight the cause of these people in some international court, to prove their independence. Suppose I even win my case? All will still be lost, for the Sirens would have become a romantic public cause. Its present society could not be preserved. And suppose I lose my case, and some foreign government is awarded claim to this place? The French, let us say. What will happen then? The French administrators and petty bureaucrats will come, followed by your business friends with their freighters. They will unload their bulldozers and prefabricated buildings and drunken laborers. And when the field is ready, the commercial airplanes will fly in and leave daily with their jabbering, gawking tourists. The island will be a public terminal. What do you suppose will happen to the Sirens tribe?"

"They will no longer be savages. They will become civilized, enjoy improvement and progress, become part of the living world. Is that so bad?"

Courtney turned to Moreturi. "You heard the Professor, my friend. Is that so bad?"

"We will not permit it," said Moreturi in perfect English.

I fear that I gaped at him.

"You see, they are not savages," said Courtney. "In fact, they have more to offer your so-called civilization than you have to offer them. But if your exploiters and commercial drummers appear, they are lost to us forever. Why is it so important for you to destroy them, Professor? What are you getting out of it? Are you a part of that Canberra company?"

"No. I am merely a merchant, and my vocation has made me a student of the South Seas. I have affection for all these people, and their ancestral ways. Nevertheless, I know they cannot continue to hide from progress."

"Then progress is your motive? Or is it money?"

"A man must live, Mr. Courtney."

"Yes," Courtney said, slowly, "I suppose that is so. You must have your pieces of silver, in the name of progress, and a most remarkable, a most wonderful tiny culture must die."

I could no longer repress my curiosity. "You keep praising these people. What is so remarkable about them?"

"Their mode of life," said Courtney. "It is like none on earth. Compared to the way you and I have lived, this life is near perfect."

"I'd like to see for myself," I said. "Show me the village."

Moreturi turned to Courtney. "Paoti Wright will not allow it."

Courtney agreed, and addressed me. "It is impossible. I cannot speak for your safety if I take you there. You must accept my word that the preservation of these people is more important than any money you may earn from that syndicate. You must go back with Captain Rasmussen and keep your silence."

"Suppose I do go back now," I said. "How do you know you can trust me? What if I speak of this to Canberra—or to others?"

Courtney was quiet a moment. "I cannot say you will suffer more than a bad conscience. Yet, I cannot guarantee that alone. You have met the Captain's copilot, Richard Hapai? He is one of us, one of the Sirens. If you break the tribal tabu, ruin his people, then it is possible that he, or one of his kin, may one day hunt you out, and kill you. This is not a threat. I am in no position to mete out revenge by vendetta. This is only a practical warning derived from my knowledge of these people. I mention the possibility."

"I am not afraid," I said. "I will leave now—"

"And make your report on The Three Sirens to Canberra?"

"Yes. You have not convinced me that I should not, Mr. Courtney. You have tried to lull me with words—a remarkable culture, a wonderful people, something incredible and different—and I say those are empty words. You will not take me to the village to see for myself. You will not tell me precisely what you mean. You have not given me a single reason why the Sirens tribe should survive in its present primitive state."

"And if I did tell you the truth—at least some of it—would you believe what I tell you?"

"I think so."

"Would you refrain from reporting to the Canberra syndicate?"

"I do not know," I said, truthfully. "I might. It depends upon what you tell me."

Courtney glanced at Moreturi. "What do you think, my friend?"

Moreturi nodded. "It is necessary to speak the truth."

"Very well," said Courtney. He faced Rasmussen, who had been listening all this while. "Captain, I propose we return to the beach. You can get Hapai to come from the plane and bring us food. We will build a fire, and we will eat, and I will spend an hour or two informing our visitor of what goes on here."

"Why all that kinda nonsense?" demanded Rasmussen. "I don't trust the Professor. I say lemme leave him here for good. You can put him with the criminals an'—"

"No, I don't like that," said Courtney. "It's not fair to him, and it wouldn't be fair to you. I can't take the risk, Captain. It'll endanger your life—Hapai's, too—and in the end the authorities might find out what happened to Professor Easterday. No, I prefer it to be handled on the basis of reason. I'll take my chances on the Professor's basic decency."

I liked Courtney after that.

Well, Dr. Hayden, we all trooped down to the beach. When we arrived there, it was dark, except for the light from a small part of the moon. Captain Rasmussen took the dinghy back to his flying boat, and soon returned with a supply of food. Moreturi had already gathered twigs and built a fire. Rasmussen cooked—efficiently, I must say—and while he cooked, we all sat on the sand, around the fire, and Courtney began his story of The Three Sirens.

Courtney prefaced his narrative by saying that he could not reveal every detail of the history and practices of the Sirens group. What he promised was the barest outline. Speaking quietly, casually, he went back to the beginnings of the experiment. As he proceeded to modern times, he became more intense and earnest. For my part, I was so immediately engaged by the wonder of what I heard, that I hardly knew my food was before me.

There was a brief interlude, as we ate in silence, and it was interrupted only when I told Courtney that I could not contain my thirst for more knowledge. I begged him to oblige me. Gradually, he began speaking again, and went on at length. I never took my eyes from him. We all consider ourselves judges of men, and I, too, consider myself perceptive in this respect, and it was my judgment that Courtney did not lie, did not embellish or exaggerate, that what he told was as factual as the best scientific papers. So intrigued was I by his account, that when it was done I thought no more than several minutes had passed. Actually, Courtney had been addressing me for one hour and a half. Now that Courtney had presented his case on behalf of his tribe—and I realized that part of his skill as storyteller was based on his experience as an attorney in Chicago, part on his love of the Sirens people—I was bursting with a hundred questions. I was civil enough to ask only the most pertinent ones. Some he replied to candidly, others he turned aside as being, in his words, "too personal, an invasion of privacy."

It was late evening, still warm but cooling slightly, when Courtney said to me, "Well, Professor Easterday, you have had the most elemental briefing on The Three Sirens. You have heard enough to know what it is in your power to destroy. What is your decision?"

All through the latter part of Courtney's recital, I had begun to entertain thoughts about you, Dr. Hayden. Every bizarre fact made me tell myself: ah, if only Dr. Maud Hayden were here, how much she would relish this. As Courtney continued, and I listened, I recollected your old request. I realized what a visit to The Three Sirens might mean to you, and, through you, to the entire world. Several times, I had heard you say that primitive cultures must be rescued, the old ways preserved, before they died out or were wiped out. You felt, you always said and wrote, that isolated

primitive cultures could teach us every variety of human behavior
and, in so doing, be applied to help us improve our own behavior.
Clearly then, the odd and miniscule society on The Three Sirens
deserved to be saved before I, or someone like myself, assisted
modern technological society in obliterating it. I was gravely
moved by my power for good or evil, and my responsibility to
those who might be capable of using this island society as a laboratory for the better welfare of our society. Suddenly, the importance of your work—of which I am a poor and minor ally—made
my duty to Mr. Trevor and the Canberra syndicate seem insignificant.

Courtney had asked for my decision. Across the blaze, he
awaited my reply.

"I would like to make a deal with you," I said, abruptly. "It
would be, in effect, a trade."

"What kind of trade?" Courtney wanted to know.

"Have you ever heard of Dr. Maud Hayden, the famous anthropologist?"

"Of course I have," said Courtney. "I've read most of her books."

"What do you think of them?"

"Brilliant," said Courtney.

"That is the trade I offer," I said, "the price of my refraining to
mention The Three Sirens to Canberra."

"I'm not sure I understand you," said Courtney.

I spoke slowly, with great emphasis on each word. "If you will
permit Dr. Hayden, with her colleagues, to come here for a field
trip in the next year, if you will allow her to make a record of this
society for all time, I will guarantee my future silence and your
future privacy."

Courtney allowed the proposal to sink in. After several reflective
minutes, he exchanged glances with Moreturi and Rasmussen.
Finally, he returned his gaze to me, as if appraising my good intentions. "Professor," he said, "how can you vouch for the silence of
Dr. Hayden and her staff?"

My mind had anticipated this, and I was ready with an answer.
"Of course," I said, "Dr. Hayden and her colleagues will be sworn
to absolute secrecy about the destination of the field trip. But human beings are frail, and I know that oral promises may not be
enough to satisfy you. Therefore, I would suggest that Dr. Hayden
and her colleagues be literally kept in the dark about where they

are going. She and her group could come to Tahiti, and be brought to The Three Sirens by Captain Rasmussen in the middle of the night. None of the anthropologists will know latitude or longitude. Nor will they know if they are flying north or south, east or west. They will know only that they are somewhere in the South Pacific, on some dot in a maze of ten thousand or more islands. You will accommodate them, within the boundaries of your own restrictions. They will observe and hear what your Chief permits them to observe and hear. They will photograph what you wish them to photograph, and no more. When their study is concluded, they will leave as they came, in utter darkness. They will never know exactly where they had been. Yet they will possess their full scientific report of this society for the benefit of mankind. Thus, though the Sirens may one day become extinct, the record of its marvels, and excesses, too, will remain behind. These are my suggestions. I believe them to be fair."

"And no airfield," said Courtney.

"None, upon my word."

Courtney pursed his lips, thinking, then signaled to Moreturi. The pair lifted their naked bodies off the sand, and walked down the beach, along the water's edge, deep in conversation until they disappeared in the night. After a while, Rasmussen flipped his cigar butt in the fire, rose, and went off in their direction.

Within ten minutes, they had all returned, and I stood up to hear their verdict.

"You have a deal," said Courtney, briskly. "You are empowered by Chief Paoti Wright, on the pledge of his son, to inform Dr. Maud Hayden that she may come here, under the exact conditions you outlined, for no more than six weeks in June and July. You will employ Captain Rasmussen as your intermediary with us. Through him you will let us know if she is coming and exactly when she is coming and any modifications of this agreement. Captain Rasmussen drops down here one day every two weeks to pick up our exports in return for supplies we require. So he is constantly in touch with us. Now then, Professor, is everything understood?"

"Everything," I said.

I shook hands with Courtney, bade Moreturi good-by, and accompanied Captain Rasmussen back to the seaplane, where Hapai was waiting.

As we took off in the darkness for Papeete, I saw the fire on the beach extinguished. Soon, even the silhouette of The Three Sirens was lost to sight. During our journey homeward, I sat in the main cabin, alone, undisturbed, and with my notepaper and pen I jotted down what I could remember of that stimulating evening on the beach. Largely, I devoted myself to hastily recording the highlights of Courtney's recital of the history and practices of The Three Sirens tribe.

Reviewing my notes as I write you this long letter, Dr. Hayden, I see there is more detail omitted than I had imagined. Whether this is the fault of my memory or Courtney's deliberate omissions, I cannot say. Nevertheless, this unorganized outline should be more than sufficient for you to determine if you want to make this field trip.

Briefly, then—

In 1795, there lived on Skinner Street in London a struggling philosopher and pamphleteer named Daniel Wright, Esq., supported by a private income left him by his late father. Daniel Wright, Esq., had a wife, a son, and two daughters, and an obsession to improve or reform English society. He was much in the company of his neighbor, friend, and idol, William Godwin, then thirty-nine years old. Godwin, as certainly you will recall, was the author and bookseller who eventually married Mary Wollstonecraft and who later suffered Shelley for his son-in-law. The important fact is that in 1793, Godwin published *An Enquiry Concerning Political Justice*, in which he advocated, among other things, doing away with marriage, penal punishments, and private property. Not only this work, but Godwin's whole personality, had influence on the radical thinking of Daniel Wright, Esq. However, Daniel Wright was not so much interested in political reform as in matrimonial reform. He had been writing, with Godwin's encouragement, a book entitled *Eden Resurrected*. The idea was that, through the Grace of God, Adam and Eve were given a second chance, an opportunity to return to Eden and start over again. Disenchanted with the state of connubiality as inherited and promulgated by them, they determined to practice, teach, and promote a new system of love, cohabitation, courtship, and marriage. An intriguing concept, I must admit.

Wright's book violently attacked the marital system and customs of love then prevailing in England, and went on to advocate an entirely different system. Wright drew not only from his own imagination, and Godwin's ideas, but also upon ideas advocated earlier in Plato's *The Republic*, Sir Thomas More's *Utopia*, Tommaso Campanella's *The City of the Sun*, Francis Bacon's *New Atlantis*, and James Harrington's *The Rota*. Along the way, Wright could not resist striking out at prevailing practices of government, law, education, public welfare, and religion. Wright found a courageous publisher, and by 1795 the first copies of the slender and explosive volume had come from the press. Before these copies could be distributed, Wright learned, through Godwin, that members of George III's court had become informed of the contents of the radical book. Charges were being drawn to declare Wright's marital utopia as "youth-corrupting" and "subversive." Confiscation of the book and imprisonment of its author were inevitable. Heeding the advice of Godwin and other friends, Wright packed a copy of his book, the most portable of his household goods, his savings, and, with his wife, family of three, and three disciples, rushed in the night to the Irish port of Kinsale. There, the party boarded a 180-ton vessel bound for Botany Bay, New Holland, later known as Sydney, Australia.

According to Courtney's story, based on original papers in the native village of The Three Sirens, Daniel Wright would not have fled England merely to save his skin. In truth, he was martyr-minded, and, on trial, would have enjoyed trumpeting his ideas to the authorities and the kingdom. What made him escape, as he did, was a motive more affirmative. For several years, he had toyed with the idea of going off to the young sixteen states in the New World, or to the recently explored Southern Seas, to practice what he preached, so to speak. That is, instead of merely writing about his visionary ideas on matrimony, he considered traveling to some remote place and putting them into actual practice. However, he was a sedentary scholar, a thinker not a doer, and he had the day-to-day responsibility of growing youngsters, and he could not rouse himself to make so dramatic a revolution in his life. The suppression of his book and the impending prison sentence in Newgate inflamed him, not only at the injustice of the government, but at the narrowness of the society in which he dwelled. It was this, then, that incited him to go off and do what he had always wanted to do anyway.

During his long, weary voyage to Australia, he had the time to convert the utopian fancies of his book into practical measures, at least on paper. All that was needed was a free place to try them out. Daniel Wright hoped Australia might prove such a place. No sooner had he and his company landed in Botany Bay than he knew that he was mistaken. The area, great morasses and mud, abandoned by the first colonists to naked blacks with spears and convicts with cutlasses, was a hell on earth. Hastily, Wright and his company moved on to Sydney Cove, the main colony of the English felons, established eight years before. Within a month, Wright knew that he must move on even further. Life in the convict colony was too harsh, violent, unwholesome, and there was no tolerance for an English crackpot reformer and zealot to live under His Majesty's Governor.

Possessing the romantic writings of both Louis Antoine de Bougainville and James Cook, who had explored the South Seas, Wright decided that this unsullied paradise was exactly where he belonged. After all, had not Bougainville written of the Tahiti of 1768 in his log: "The canoes were filled with women whose pleasing faces need concede nothing to the majority of Europeans and, for beauty of body, could rival any. Most of these nymphs were naked, for the men and old women with them removed the loincloths in which they usually wrapped themselves. At first they made from their canoes little teasing gestures. The men, simpler, or else freer, made matters clearer; they urged us to choose a girl, follow her to shore, and their unequivocal gestures showed the fashion in which we were to make their acquaintance"? And once ashore, had not Bougainville added: "It was like being in the garden of Eden . . . Everything is reminiscent and suggestive of love. The native girls have no complex about it. Everything around them invites them to follow their heart's inclination or the call of nature"?

This was enough for Daniel Wright, Esq. Beyond Australia lay a new and uninhibited civilization, practicing love and marriage in a manner compatible with his own best ideas. There, far from the wretched, restrictive practices of the West, he would combine his ideals with the similar practices of the Polynesians, and develop his perfect world in microcosm.

Wright bought passage for his company on a small but seaworthy brig that was heading into the South Seas for trading purposes, with Otaheite, as the English then called Tahiti, its final destination. Wright asked the captain of the vessel if, for additional payment above the fares, he would journey beyond Tahiti, touching on half a dozen obscure, uncharted isles, until one was found where Wright, his family, and followers might remain. The captain was agreeable.

The captain of the brig kept to his word. After the voyage to Tahiti, and an anchorage of two weeks, the captain continued far southward through Polynesia. Three times the brig lay offshore, while Wright and two male companions explored the small islands. One was made useless by mangrove forests, another lacked springs for drinking water and had not any fertile soil, and the third was infested with head-hunters. Wright urged the captain to resume his search. Two days later they sighted the island group shortly to be christened The Three Sirens.

A day's exploration of the main island convinced Wright that he had found his earthly Eden. The situation of a haven, which was off the trade routes and which possessed no natural harbor or deep anchorage, gave high promise of privacy. The interior of the island had abundant flora and fauna, clear streams, and other natural resources. Above all, Wright had come upon a village of forty Polynesians, and they proved gracious and hospitable.

Through a native interpreter brought from Tahiti, Wright was able to speak at length with Tefaunni, Chief of the tribe. Wright learned the villagers were descendants of a Polynesian kin group of long ago who had gone colonizing in deep sea canoes and had found a refuge in this place. The Chief, who had never encountered a white man before or been the recipient of such magical gifts (a metal hatchet, for one thing, a whale oil lamp, for another), was in complete awe of Wright. He considered it great *mana*—a word Wright learned to mean, among many meanings, "prestige" —to have his visitor share the island and its rule with him. Taking Wright on a tour of the village, Tefaunni explained the habits of his people. In his journal, Wright would note that the people were "gay, free, sensible yet joyous of life and loving" and that their attitudes and manners would have "gladdened Bougainville's heart." The following day, Wright's family and disciples, eight in all, himself included, were set ashore with their possessions, consisting also of several dogs, goats, chickens, and sheep. The brig sailed away, and Wright joined Tefaunni to set into being *Eden Resurrected*.

There is much, much more to this unusual history, Dr. Hayden, but the details you will learn for yourself, if you are of that frame of mind. Within the limitations of this letter, I should prefer to devote the remainder of it to the customs of the society that ultimately developed from 1796 to the present day.

A month after Wright and his company had physically settled into the Polynesian community, he undertook a serious study of their tribal traditions, rites, and practices. He noted these carefully, and alongside these he committed to paper his own ideas on how life should be lived on The Three Sirens. In the matter of government, the Polynesians believed in a hereditary chief. Wright believed in a committee of three men or women, who had been trained for leadership, and had survived all tests. It was a modification of Plato's idea, as you know. Wright saw that his own system would not work on this lonely isle—where and how to set up a school to train universal-minded men in leadership?—and he conceded to the Polynesian idea of a hereditary chief.

As to labor and property, each Polynesian kin group of relatives, while individually building and possessing its own home and furnishings, worked as a unit to grow or pick food and store it in a common family pool. Wright preferred a more stringent system, and one more communal. The Chief, he felt, should control all real property, and dole it out according to the size of each family. As a family expanded in size, so might the property. If a family contracted, so would the property. Furthermore, Wright felt, each adult male on The Three Sirens should labor four hours a day, at what best suited him, be it agriculture or fishing or carpentry or any other occupations found necessary. The products of these labors would go into a large community storehouse. Weekly, each family would take out of the storehouse a minimum amount of food and other supplies. This minimum amount would be equal for all. However, the more productive laborers of the village would exceed their minimum supplies with bonus amounts of what they preferred. In short, absolute equality, no poverty, yet a certain degree of incentive. Tefaunni readily gave in to this reform, and it was introduced in 1799.

According to my jottings taken from Courtney's explanation, similar compromises were effected all down the line—the best of the Polynesian system here, the best of Wright's visionary ideas there, and sometimes two ideas were blended. Compromises were reached on education, religion, recreation, and other important matters. Wright would permit no two systems, pertaining to one subject, to exist side by side. He felt that this might invite conflict. Always, it had to be the Polynesian practice for all, or his own practice.

There was much bargaining, of course. To control population against future famine, the Polynesians practiced infanticide. If a woman had more than one child in three years, the other children were drowned at birth. Wright found this abhorrent and got Tefaunni to make the practice tabu. On the other hand, in return Wright had to make certain concessions. He had hoped to impose halters and skirts on women, trousers only on men, but was forced to forego modesty for the more sensible Polynesian short grass skirt, without any undergarment, and bare breasts, for women, and the penis-wrappers or pubic bags, and nothing else, for the men. Only on special occasions did the women wear tapa skirts and the men wear loincloths. Courtney spoke with amusement of passages in Wright's old journal when he recorded the embarrassment of his wife and daughters on their first appearance in the village compound, with their breasts uncovered and their twelve-inch grass skirts lifted high by the wind.

There were numerous other compromises. The Polynesians defecated wherever they might be in the brush. Wright opposed this as unsanitary, and sought to introduce communal toilet huts, two on either side of the village. The Polynesians considered this innovation as elaborate foolishness, but humored Wright by permitting it. In turn, Tefaunni demanded that his system of punishment for crime prevail. Wright had desired to introduce banishment to a restricted ravine for all crimes. The Polynesians would not have it. For the crime of murder, they sentenced the lawbreaker to menial slavery. This meant the criminal had to become a servant in the home of the victim's family for the difference of years between the victim's age at the time of death and seventy years. Wright had some misgivings about the harshness of the punishment, yet saw the justice of it also, and submitted. I might add that, according to Courtney, this punishment is still being practiced on The Three Sirens.

However, all that I have outlined heretofore are relatively minor practices as compared to the customs of sex and love and marriage that were agreed upon by Tefaunni, and his tribe of forty, and Daniel Wright, on behalf of his eight. Here, the Polynesians and the progressive English had less to disagree about, and compromises were few. Wright found the sexual practices of this tribe not only unique but superior to any that he had ever learned or imagined. They suited his own philosophy in almost every way. Above all, they were practical. They worked. Since many of these ideas represented almost exactly what Wright had dreamed to introduce, little readjustment or modification was necessary. It was Courtney's estimate that of the sexual customs practiced on The Three Sirens today, about seventy percent were predominately Polynesian in origin, and about thirty percent were dictated by Wright.

I might interject here that the present-day descendants of Tefaunni and Wright are one people, one race. For some years, Tefaunni and Wright ruled jointly. When Tefaunni died, Wright became the sole Chief. When he died at an advanced age—his son had already passed on—his eldest grandson, the product of an English and Polynesian marriage, became the new Chief. Through the years, intermarriages continued. Today, there is no division between Caucasian and Polynesian. There survive only the people of the Sirens. These people, without dissent, practice the exact system of love agreed upon by the founders more than a century and a half ago.

As to this system of love, I am sorry to say that Courtney would not elaborate on many of the current customs, but what he volunteered to tell me seemed provocative enough for any anthropological study. Some of the practices he reported are as follows:

Adolescents between the ages of fourteen and sixteen are given practical sex education. As I understand it, they learn about sexual intercourse in theory. Before graduation, they observe and participate in actual love-making. The approach, Courtney insisted, is entirely wholesome.

In adolescence, the Sirens male undergoes an incision of the penis, similar to circumcision, in order to expose the glans. When this has healed, he loses the scab by enjoying his first intercourse with a slightly older female, who guides him and teaches him sexual technique. The adolescent female, on the other hand, has her clitoris stretched over a period of years. When it is extended at least one inch, she is considered ready to be taught sexual intercourse by actual participation. This enlargement of the clitoris has no magical connotation. The motive is simply to increase pleasure. Virginity, I might add, is regarded on the Sirens as an infirmity and a defect. However, from my own observations in the Society Islands and the Austral Islands, these practices are not unfamiliar.

There is a great house on the Sirens called the Social Aid Hut. Its function is twofold. It is used by bachelors, widowers, and un-attached women for courtship and love. The second function, merely hinted at, is one that I can only deduce to be more unique, even startling. It concerns some means of—I repeat Courtney's exact words from my notes—"providing fulfillment, at all times, for married men or women who request it." Whatever this implies, it is, apparently, not as abandoned and orgiastic as one might imagine. Courtney said this "service" of the Social Aid Hut was sensible, logical, and that there were strict rules. He would not expand upon the subject, except to remark that on The Three Sirens there were no physically repressed or unhappy men or women.

Marriages are arranged by common consent of the individuals involved. The ceremony is performed by the Chief. The groom invites the male and female guests. On entrance to the ceremony, the groom steps over his mother-in-law, who is prostrated, sym-bolic of his ascendency over her. After the ceremony, the bride lies down in her husband's arms, and each male guest invited by the groom, except a blood relative, is solicited to enjoy sexual inter-course with the bride. The groom is the last to participate. This latter rite of incorporation, if memory serves me, is also practiced on several other islands of Polynesia, especially in the Marquesas group.

The initiation of divorce, according to Courtney, is among the most progressive of practices on The Three Sirens. Courtney was extremely reticent to give me any details. He did mention, how-ever, that a panel of elders called the Hierarchy did not grant divorce merely on request of either party or on hearsay evidence. He said only that divorce was permitted after "long observation" of the parties concerned. My interest was aroused, but Courtney would go no further.

Courtney and Moreturi both spoke of an annual festival held in late June for one week. Although both men referred to sport com-petition, a ceremonial dance, a nude beauty contest, neither would speak at length of the primary purpose of the festival. Courtney said, "The ancient Romans had their annual Saturnalia, just as the natives of Upolu, in Samoa, still do. The festival on the Sirens is not precisely the same. Still, it is a form of release, in certain areas, affording license to long-married couples as well as unmarried people. There is simply too much adultery and divorce in America and Europe, don't you think? There is hardly any on the Sirens. Back home, married people are often too miserable and restless and bored. That is not so here. The so-called civilized world outside might learn a lot from these supposed primitives." That was his only oblique reference to the enigmatic festival.

More about love customs on the Sirens neither Courtney nor Moreturi would tell me. In summing up, Courtney said that nowhere else on earth, as far as he knew, was love practiced with less embarrassment, tension, fear.

There you have all that I have learned, Dr. Hayden. You may be curious to know more about this Thomas Courtney, but I cannot oblige you. Except for admitting that he had been an attorney in Chicago, and had come to the Sirens by accident, and had chosen to remain and been allowed to remain, he would say nothing. I found him attractive, learned, often cynical about society on the outside, and devoted to his adopted people. It is a great advantage, I think, that he knows of you and your work and respects it. I felt that he would trust you, and I believe he himself is sincere and honorable, although our meeting was of short duration and I cannot be positive.

This is the lengthiest letter that I have ever written. I can only hope the cause justifies its length. I do not know your present situation, Dr. Hayden, but if you are still active, then the door to a fresh and daring culture is wide open to you, within the limitations stated.

Please reply at your earliest convenience, but do not delay. You have four months for preparations, yet on this end, apparently, the time is all too short. If you intend to come here, tell me so and inform me of the approximate date. Let me know, also, the size of your staff. All of this I will promptly relay to Captain Rasmussen, who will transmit it to Courtney and the present Chief, Paoti Wright. They will then make arrangements for your arrival and accommodation. If circumstances make this undertaking impossible, let me know this, too. For I shall then attempt, with reluctance, believe me, to pass this information on to another anthropologist or two of my acquaintance.

The cost of this expedition, excepting transportation, should not be excessive. The people of the Sirens will furnish you both lodgings and food. The fee for Rasmussen's services will be minor. For my part, I ask nothing of you, except your good will, and, of course, reimbursement of the $3,000 fee I forfeited by not passing this information on to Mr. Trevor of Canberra.

Hoping this finds you in good health and high enthusiasm, and looking forward to your reply, I remain as ever,

Yours sincerely,

ALEXANDER EASTERDAY

Maud Hayden lowered the letter slowly, as if hypnotized by it and left in a trance, so absorbed had she been through the reading. Yet, inside herself she felt the heat of rising anticipation and excitement, and close to the skin her nerve ends tingled and vibrated. It was the feeling of aliveness—all senses engaged—that she had not known in the four years since the death of her husband and collaborator.

The Three Sirens!

The lush green words, as wondrous as "Open sesame," and the imagery they evoked, required no acceptance and approval from her intuitive second self. Her outer self, that was cold logic (with its invisible scale weighing what is good for you, what is bad for you), knowledge, experience, and was objectively professional, embraced the invitation in one enormous hug.

Presently, when she had calmed down, she lay back in the swivel chair and thought about the contents of the letter, especially of the practices that Courtney had related to Easterday. Marriage behavior in other societies had always held a fascination for her. The only field trip that she had even considered, since Adley's death, had been one to South India to live with the Nayar tribe. The Nayar woman, after formally marrying a man, sent him from their house a few days following the ceremony, and then took on a host of nonresident lovers, one after the other, depositing subsequent children with kinfolk. The custom had appealed briefly to Maud, but when she realized that she would have to be interested in the whole pattern of the Nayar's social behavior, not just in their marital ways, she had dropped the project. But then, she knew, that was not why she had dropped it, really, not really. She had not wanted to travel as a mourning widow to the remoteness of South India.

Yet, here was Easterday's letter, and she was alive, and there was a caroling inside her. Why? The Gauguin stamps on his envelope sent her memory to *Noa Noa* and its author's reminder, "Yes, indeed, the savages have taught many things to the man of an old civilization; these ignorant men have taught him much in the art of living and happiness." Yes, that was part of it, the easy ways in the South Seas. Her visit there had been one of the happiest periods of her entire life. She thought of the place: the temperate trade winds, the tall, sinewy, bronze people, the oral legends, the orgiastic rites, the smell of green coconuts and red hibiscus, the soft Italian-like intonation of the Polynesian tongue.

Nostalgia was what was moving her so, these moments, and immediately she swept sentiment aside. There was a higher purpose, as Gauguin had indicated. Savages could teach the civilized visitor much. Yet, in truth, how much? The curious beachcomber in Easterday's letter, Courtney, had made life on The Three Sirens sound idyllic to the point of utopia. Could there be a utopia on earth? The word *utopia* was derived from the Greek, and it meant, literally, "not a place." Promptly, Maud's ruthless anthropological discipline cautioned her that the regarding of any single society as utopian involved a set of value judgments based on one's own preconceived conceptions of what is an ideal state of affairs. No real anthropologist could pretend to seek a utopia. As an anthropologist, she might come up with some prescription of what might be a good way of life, or what might be a most satisfying culture, but she could not define one place as utopia and another as not.

No, she told herself, she was not after some questionable Graustark. It was something else then. Her colleague, Margaret Mead, when in her early twenties, had gone to Pago Pago, briefly stayed in the very hotel where W. Somerset Maugham had written "Rain," lived with the Samoan women, and reported to the world how absence of sexual restraint among those people eliminated sexual hostility, aggression, tension. Overnight, Margaret Mead had made a success, for the Western world was always curious about the forbidden and held forth a begging hand. And that was it, finally, Maud told herself. The Western world wanted self-help and Instant Wisdom. Whether or not the Sirens represented utopia was not the point. Whether the Sirens society could teach civilized man anything or not was not the point, either. The real point was now illuminated for Maud: it was not what the world needed that was exciting her, but what she, herself, desperately needed.

She recalled a letter Edward Sapir had written to Ruth Benedict, when Ruth was planning to apply to the Social Science Research Council for money. Sapir had warned Ruth about her subject: "For God's sake, don't make it so remote and technical as last year. Pueblo mythology doesn't excite people any more than Athabaskan verbs would . . . come across with a live project—and you'll get what you ask for."

Come across with a live project—and you'll get what you ask for.

Maud sat up sharply, the leather soles of her flat shoes thudding on the floor beneath her desk. She dropped the letter on the blotter in front of her, and, hands clasped before it, she considered the remarkable find in the light of her present situation.

She had not been handed an opportunity like this since she had been on her own. It was like a gift of years. The culture of The Three Sirens—some of it known to her from other field trips, some refreshingly new—was precisely her kind of subject. She had always avoided the worn, the used, the mauled-over. She had always rejected the dull familiarity of parallel studies. She had—she would admit this to no one but herself—a nose for the extraordinary, the marvelous, the fantastic. And here it lay at her fingertips, known to no anthropologist but herself. Everything about it was favorable: instead of the usual year in the field, the limitations were six weeks, so she could have no uneasy conscience about deliberate superficiality; a subject, by its nature, that begged to be written and published, not only scientifically but popularly; and—yes—an easy solution to the problem that had vaguely oppressed her so long.

Her mind went to the letter that Dr. Walter Scott Macintosh had sent her two months ago. He had been her late husband's college companion and her own good friend in the years after. Now, he was a Gray Eminence, an influence, less for his physical anthropology attainments than for political power as president of the

American Anthropological League. He had written her, as trustworthy friend, as admirer, and as strictly between them, to whisper of a magnificent, well-paying position that would be open in a year and a half. The job was that of executive editor of *Culture*, the international voice of the American Anthropological League. The present executive editor, in his eighties and ailing, would be retired. The lifetime post would be open, with its unmatched prestige and security.

Macintosh had made it clear that he would like to nominate Maud for the job. On the other hand, several of his colleagues on the Board leaned toward a younger person, Dr. David Rogerson, whose recent papers had spectacularly reflected two field trips to Africa. Since seething Africa was in the news, so too was Dr. Rogerson. At the same time, Macintosh had written, he personally did not feel Rogerson had Maud's wide experience in many cultures or her contacts with those in the field around the world. Macintosh felt that she was right for the position. The problem, he intimated, was to make the Board members also feel she was right, more capable to fill the job than Dr. Rogerson.

Macintosh, in his delicate way, had hinted at the obstacle. Since Adley's death, Maud had done little on her own. She had remained stationary while the younger Turks moved ahead. Beyond several papers, rehashing old field trips, she had not published at all in four years. Macintosh had urged Maud to go once more, one last time, into the field, and to return with a new study, an original paper, that she might read before the League at its next three-day convention. It would be in Detroit, shortly after the Thanksgiving holiday, and would precede the Board meeting to select the new executive editor of *Culture*. If Maud had any plan for a trip and a fresh paper, Macintosh had written hopefully, he wanted her to advise him promptly so that he might schedule her to address the conclave.

Macintosh's letter had given her a great lift, a hope, for the position was exactly the one she needed in this time of her life. With such a position, at her age, she need no longer suffer the rigors of toil in the field, she need not exhaust herself in the monotony of teaching callow students, she need not suffer the demands of writing papers, she need not worry about security or worry about any dependence, in years to come, on Marc.

With this position, she would have a salary of twenty thousand dollars a year, offices in Washington, D.C., a cottage in Virginia, and be the nation's anthropologist emeritus. Yet, for all this reward, for the temporary stimulation given by Macintosh's letter, she had been unable to act decisively. She had sunk back into her spiritless rut, too inert to conceive a new study, too tired to propel herself into motion. Finally, after some delay, she had replied gratefully but ambiguously to Macintosh's kind suggestion. Thank you, thank you, she would see, she would think, she would let him know. And, in the two months since, she had done no more about it. But *now*. She touched Easterday's letter lovingly.

Yes, she was alive. She stared at the bookshelves across the room where ranged the colorful volumes on the Fijians, the Ashantis, the Minoans, the Jivaros, the Lapps, that she and Adley had written. She could visualize one more monument: the Sirens Islanders.

She heard footsteps, and knew them to belong to Claire descending the staircase. There was that, too—her daughter-in-law, Claire, and Marc. Maud did not belong in the same house with Marc, now that he was married. She suspected that he chafed to be free of her, socially as well as professionally. The Three Sirens would make that possible. Her freedom might be Marc's liberation, also. It would help the marriage, she knew, and then she wondered why she thought the marriage needed any help at all. But this was not the morning for that. Another time.

The electric walnut-framed desk clock told her that she still had fifty minutes to her class. While it was all bursting in her mind, she had better make notes. Nothing must be overlooked. Time was of the greatest importance.

She took up Easterday's bulky letter, handling it as if it were a fragment of the Scriptures, and laid it to one side. She placed her large yellow pad before her, found a ball-point pen, and hastily began to scribble:

"Number 1. Rough out a colorful project statement for Cyrus Hackfeld re obtaining sizable grant.

"Number 2. Consult Marc and Claire—several graduate students, too—on research clues in Easterday's letter to build up presentation for Hackfeld. Research area of 3 Sirens—any mention in history of anything resembling it?—research Daniel Wright and Godwin —research parallel customs elsewhere to 3 Sirens—look into Courtney background, etc.

"Number 3. Narrow down list of names for possible team to accompany us. Hackfeld likes big flash ones. Possibilities—Sam Karpowicz, botany and photography—Rachel DeJong, psychiatry—Walter Zegner, medical—Orville Pence, comparative sex studies—and others. Once Hackfeld okays, then dictate letters to Claire for all team personnel to inquire if available and interested.

"Number 4. Write Macintosh if time still open to read new paper to League symposium on Polynesian Ethnology. Tell him about Sirens. Don't write him. Telephone."

She sat back, studied the yellow pad, and felt that she had covered about all that was to be done immediately. Then she realized that she had omitted one task, perhaps the most important of all. She bent over the pad once more.

"Number 5. Write and airmail letter to Alexander Easterday—Tahiti—*tonight*. Tell him yes—absolutely *yes, yes, yes!*"

II

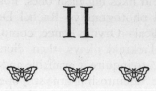

OF THE four members of the Hayden household—four members, that is, if you recognized Suzu, Maud's continually smiling Japanese day helper—Claire Emerson Hayden, she told herself, had been the least affected in the matter of daily routine by the arrival of the Easterday letter some five weeks before.

The transformation of her mother-in-law, Maud (Claire still found her too formidable, after almost two years, to call her Matty), had been the most marked. Maud had always been busy, of course, and efficient, too, but in the past five weeks she had become a dervish of activity, doing the work of ten people. More than that, before Claire's very eyes, she had become increasingly youthful, energetic, creative. Claire imagined that she was now as she must have been at her physical peak, when Adley was her collaborator.

Thinking all of this, Claire, this moment immersed to the shoulders in her luxurious bubble bath, lazily fanned a path through the foam with one palm. She permitted her mind to travel to her sketchy memories of Dr. Adley R. Hayden. She had met him twice before her marriage, when Marc had brought her up to Santa Barbara for social functions, and she had been much impressed by the tall, stooped, slightly paunched scholar, with his dry wit and broad knowledge and understanding. Even as Marc had stammered in his father's presence, challenging him too often and being turned aside too easily with good-natured ridicule, she had found herself stupefied by Adley's authority. She had always felt that she had made a sorry impression, although Marc had reassured her that his father found her "a mighty pretty young thing." She frequently wished that she could have been more to Adley, but a week after their second meeting he had suddenly died of a heart attack, and in his Valhalla, she was sure, she was still regarded by him as no more than a mighty pretty young thing.

The soap bubbles had formed again before Claire's body, and absently she began to smooth them. Her mind had wandered, she knew, and she tried to remember what she had been thinking. She remembered: the Easterday letter five weeks ago, and its effect on all of them. Maud had become a dervish, yes. And Marc, he was busier now, more intense (if that was possible), more nervous, more complaining about petty annoyances but above all about the questionable wisdom of the field trip. "Your Easterday sounds like a romancer," he had told Maud just two nights before. "A thing like this ought to be investigated properly before wasting all this time and money." Maud had treated him as she always treated him, with the infinite patience and affection of all mothers with their precocious little boys. Maud had defended Easterday's solidity and explained that the circumstances permitted no investigation and reminded him of her infallible ear for a good thing, the result of instinct as well as experience. As usual, once overruled, Marc had retreated, and submerged himself in the burden of extra work.

Only Claire's routine had seemed unaffected by the recent event. There was more typing and filing to do now, but these did not appreciably fill her hours. Every morning, still, she could linger in her warm, soapy bath, read at breakfast, consult with Maud, do her customary work, then participate with the other young faculty wives in tennis or tea or attendance at a lecture. And the nights when Marc was too busy to take her to a movie or out for a drive, or when there was no party, she would let him pore over his notes, do his research, correct his papers—man's work—while she read novels or watched, with sleepy boredom, the portable television's screen. None of this had been changed by Easterday and The Three Sirens.

Yet, Claire was positive, something had changed for her. It had nothing to do with daily routine. It had to do with a feeling— almost a tangible effervescent sac of emotion—inside her being. She had been Mrs. Marc Hayden, officially, legally, for better, for worse, forever, for one year and nine months now. With the marriage—"a good one," her mother and stepfather had decided—the sac of feeling within had been buoyant and fun, like a bubble that carried you up, up, up, and all below was marvelous. But gradually, in the aging of her marriage, the bubble of buoyancy had subsided, settled, flattened into a dreary little puddle that represented nothing at all. That was the look of the bubble: nothing. That was her feeling toward everything: nothing. It was as if all excitement and possibility of joy had fled. It was as if all of life was predictable, every day ahead, even to the last day, and there was no hope of wonder. This was the feeling, and when she heard new mothers discuss post-baby blues, she wondered if there were post-marriage blues, also. There was no one to blame for the disappointment— surely not Marc, not Marc at all—except possibly the inexperienced bride herself, with her wilting bouquet of over-romantic and great expectations. If she had the money, she thought, she would finance a team of experts to find out what happened to Cinderellas *after* they-lived-happily-ever-after.

But five weeks ago, or thereabouts, something good had happened to Claire. Its effect on her whole person was immediate, but hidden from those around her. She felt awakened. She had a feeling of well-being. She felt that there was going to be more to life than unfulfillment. And she knew that the inspiring element had been the Easterday letter. She had lovingly typed abridged copies, double-spaced, of this letter. All that Easterday promised, she knew by heart.

Except for one week-long trip to Acapulco and Mexico City, with her mother and stepfather when she was fifteen (she remembered the Pyramids, the Floating Gardens, Chapultepec, she remembered not being alone one instant), Claire had never been outside the United States. And now, almost overnight, she would be transported to an unknown and exotic place in the South Seas. The promise of change was unbearably stimulating. The actual details of The Three Sirens had little reality, and therefore little meaning to her. They resembled too closely the thousands of words in Maud's books, in countless other anthropological volumes she had perused, and they seemed like mere history and the ancient past and no part of her present life. Yet, the date was drawing nearer and nearer, and if Easterday was not the "romancer" that Marc had labeled him, if these things were real things and not word things, she would soon be in a sweltering hut, among almost naked men and women, who took food from a common storehouse, who regarded virginity as a defect and practical education in sex a necessity, who practiced love in a Social Aid Hut and at an uninhibited festival (with a nude beauty contest, no less!).

Claire glanced at the enameled clock beside the wash basin. It was nine-fifteen. Marc's early class would be over. Today, he would have four hours before his next class. She wondered if he would return home or go on to the library. She decided that she had better dress. Reaching out, she spun the lever beneath the faucet, and the outlet clanged open and the water and suds began to gurgle down the drain.

She pulled herself erect, gingerly stepped over the side of the tub, and stood dripping on the thick white mat. As the rivulets of water rolled downward across the curves of her glistening flesh, her mind returned again to the Easterday letter. What was it that he had said of the mode of dress on The Three Sirens? The men wore pubic bags held loosely in place by strings. Of course, that wasn't really shocking, considering how men dressed on the beach every summer. Still, just those little bags and nothing else. Yet, they were natives and that made it decent, almost clinical. She had seen hundreds of pictures of natives, some of them without even pubic bags, and it had seemed quite natural for *them*.

The thought occurred to her, standing as she was now in the middle of the bathroom without a stitch on, that this was the way she might be expected to appear in public on The Three Sirens. No, that could not be quite true. Easterday had written: the women wore short grass skirts "without any undergarment" and with breasts bare. But heavens, that was next to naked.

Claire swung around to face the full-length mirror on the door. She tried to imagine how she would look, this way, naked, to the natives on The Three Sirens. She was five feet four and weighed 112 pounds on the scale this morning. Her hair was dark and shiny, cut short, with the ends clustering against her cheeks. Her almond eyes were of a vague Far Eastern cast, evoking the submissive and demure girls of ancient Cathay, and yet the effect was contradicted by their color, smoke blue, "sexy," Marc had once said. Her nose was small, with overdelicate nostrils, her lips deep red and her mouth generous, too generous. From the slope of her shoulders and chest, her breasts developed gradually. Her breasts were large—how she had hated that in adolescence—but still high and young, which was a source of gratification in her twenty-fifth year. Her ribs showed somewhat—what would the natives think?

—but her abdomen was almost flat, only slightly rounded, and the proportions of her thighs and slender legs were not too bad, not really. Still, you could not tell what other people in other cultures would feel—the Polynesians might consider her skinny, except for her bosom.

Then she remembered the grass skirt. Twelve inches. She could see that twelve inches permitted only four inches of extra modesty. Forgetting any breeze—My God—what happened when you bent over or lifted your leg to ascend a step, or, for that matter, how did you sit down? She determined to discuss the whole business of dress with Maud. In fact, since this was her first field trip, she must ask Maud what would be required of her on The Three Sirens.

As she dried, she saw herself in the mirror once more. How would she look when she was pregnant? Her belly was so small, really. Where would there be room for another person, her child? Well, there always was, and nature had its way, but it seemed absolutely impossible at this moment. Thinking of the child she would have, but did not have, her brow automatically creased. From the first she had spoken wistfully, later practically, of bearing a child, and from the first Marc had been against it. That is, he was against it for the time, he always said. His reasons seemed important when he stated them to her, but when she was alone, and free to think, they always seemed puny. They must adjust to marriage first, he once said. They must have some free years together, without added responsibilities, he said another time. And lately it had been that they must get Maud settled, apart from them, and be on their own, before having a family.

Now, rubbing the towel along her legs, she wondered if any of these reasons was honest, let alone valid, or if they concealed the truth: that Marc did not want a child, dreaded having one, because he was still a child himself, a grown child who was too dependent to take on responsibility. She did not like the momentary suspicion, and determined not to speculate further.

There was a rap on the door behind the mirror. "Claire?" It was Marc's voice. She started with surprise, and felt guilty with her thoughts now that Marc was so near.

"Good morning!" she called out, cheerfully.

"Did you have breakfast yet?"

"Not yet. I'm just dressing."

"I'll wait for you then. I had to miss it this morning. Overslept. What should I tell Suzu? Anything special?"

"The usual."

"Okay . . . By the way, the last of the research came in from Los Angeles."

"Anything exciting?"

"Haven't had time to look at it yet. We'll go over it together at breakfast."

"Fine."

After she heard Marc leave, she hurriedly fastened on her brassière, then pulled on her panties, garter belt, rolled on her sheer stockings and secured them, and got into the pink slip. Emerging from the warm bathroom into the cooler, sunny upstairs bedroom, she wondered if the final research had turned up anything more. In minutes she would know. Quickly, she combed her hair, made up her lips, but used no cosmetics on the rest of her face, then stepped into her light cocoa-colored wool skirt, drew on the beige cashmere sweater, buttoned it, found some low-heeled shoes, shoved her feet into them, and hastened into the hall and descended the stairs.

Suzu, grinning, was putting down the breakfast, and Marc was at the kitchen table, bent over an open folder, when Claire entered. She hailed Suzu, and then brushed her palm over Marc's crewcut as she pecked a kiss at his cheek.

She slid into a chair, gulped her grapefruit juice, grimaced, having forgotten to sweeten it. She looked across the table. "Isn't Maud back yet?"

"Still hiking across the moors," said Marc, without looking up.

Claire broke off the corner from a piece of toast. "Well," she said, indicating the research, "does our Polynesian Disneyland really exist?"

Marc lifted his head, then shrugged. "Maybe yes, maybe no. I wish I could be as sure as Matty." He tapped the papers in front of him. "Our graduate students seem to have done a thorough job, even at the Library of Congress, combed South Seas literature, published and unpublished. No mention of The Three Sirens anywhere. Absolutely not a word—"

"That shouldn't be surprising. Easterday said it was an unknown group."

"I'd feel more comfortable if there was something in print. Of course—" He began to leaf through the notes again. "—certain other findings tend to support Easterday a little."

"Like what?" asked Claire, her mouth full.

"There actually was a Daniel Wright, and he did live in Skinner Street in London before 1795. Also, there was an attorney named Thomas Courtney practicing in Chicago—"

"Really? . . . Anything more about him?"

"Dates, mostly. He's thirty-eight. Degrees from Northwestern and the University of Chicago. Junior partner in some old-line firm. Flew for the Air Force in Korea in 1952. Then back in practice in Chicago. The listings stop in 1957."

"That's when he went to the South Seas," said Claire, flatly.

"Could be," said Marc. "We'll know soon enough." He closed the folder, and devoted himself to his cereal and milk.

"Eleven shopping weeks left to Christmas," said Claire.

"I don't think The Three Sirens will quite be Christmas," said Marc. "It's no place for a woman, among those primitives. If I could leave you behind, I would."

"Don't you dare try," said Claire, indignantly. "Besides, they're not entirely primitives. Easterday said the Chief's son spoke in perfect English."

"Plenty of primitives speak English," said Marc. He smiled suddenly. "Including some of our best friends. I wouldn't want you to spend too much time with them, either."

Pleased by his unusual concern, Claire touched his hand. "You mean you really care?"

"Male duty and instinct," said Marc. "Protect one's mate . . . But seriously, field trips are not picnics. I've told you how much I hated the ones I've been on. They're never as idyllic in real life as they sound when they're glossed over in print. You usually find you don't have much in common with the natives, aside from working with them. You miss all the amenities of life. Inevitably, you get laid low by dysentery or malaria or some damn fever thing. I don't like exposing a woman to all that hardship, even for a short time."

Claire squeezed his hand. "You are a darling. But I'm sure it won't be as bad as you expect. After all, I'll have you and Maud—"

"We may be very busy."

"I'll see that I'm very busy, too. I just want the whole experience."

"Don't say you weren't warned."

Claire withdrew her hand, picked up her fork, and poked at her fried eggs thoughtfully. Knowing Marc as she did, she began to wonder if he was really concerned about her welfare, or just projecting his own private fears of an undertaking new and strange. Was Marc, like so many males, two separate men, constantly embattled, each determined to win his kind of peace? Did he secretly chafe at dull routine, yet all the while find his security in it? He was as steady, in his movements through a day, as the hands of a flawless clock. At the same time, despite the comfort of this treadmill existence, he might want to escape it. Behind his surface adjustment, Claire felt, could lurk another Marc, one who went off on journeys she would never share, voyages to secret Monte Cristos that temporarily freed him from budget prisons and nonentity dungeons. For him, perhaps, The Three Sirens offered no personal advance, only an uncomfortable tagging along. And so he would transform his dislike of his own uprooting into a worry about the one closest him. Claire could not be sure, of course, but this was her guess.

Finishing her fried eggs, Claire looked up and watched her husband as he ate. No person should ever watch another person eat, she told herself. People do not look their best when they eat. They look foolish, distorted, and they look self-indulgent. She separated Marc from his food. He always seems shorter than he is, she told herself. He is five feet ten, but there is something inside him, some perverse and uncertain hormone, that shrinks him. Yet she found him physically attractive. His features and physique were right, regular, balanced. The crewcut seemed an anachronism on a face so rigid and so often brooding, although it belonged to him when he smiled or teased or was pleased and hopeful. The eyes, opaque gray, were deep but set well apart. The nose was aquiline. The lips thin. But the general aspect was handsome, sincere, sometimes amiable, one of rugged scholarship. He had the compact, overmuscular body of an athlete who always came in second. He wore his suits loose, smart, and well. If looks were only everything, she told herself, he would be happier and she would reflect his happiness. But his inner self, she knew, too often wore different clothes, and resented their poor fit. She did not mean to sigh aloud, but she did.

Marc looked up inquiringly.

She must say something. She said, "I'm a little nervous about the dinner party tonight."

"What's there to be nervous about? Hackfeld has already agreed to a grant."

"You know Maud says we need more. How can Hackfeld insist on such a big team, and then be so stingy?"

"That's why he's rich. Anyway, he's got a lot of other irons in the fire."

"I wonder how Maud'll bring it up?" said Claire.

"You leave it to her. That's her specialty."

Claire's eyes followed Suzu to the stove. "Suzu, what's it going to be tonight?"

"Chicken Teriyaki."

"The way to a man's purse is through his stomach. Brilliant, Suzu."

"You bet," said Suzu, grinning.

"Whose purse? Whose stomach?" It was Maud Hayden in the dining room doorway. Her gray hair was indescribably tangled, apparently from the wind. Her wide old face was outdoor red. Her squat, stout body was shapeless in muffler, pea jacket, navy blue flannel skirt, and therapeutically customed, cloddish shoes. She waved her gnarled walking stick, a product of Ecuador and Jivaro country. "Who were you discussing?" she demanded to know.

"Cyrus Hackfeld, keeper of our money," said Claire. "Did you have breakfast?"

"Hours ago," said Maud, unwinding her muffler. "Brrr. Cold out. Sun and palm trees and still you nearly freeze to death."

"What do you expect in March?" said Marc.

"I expect California weather, my son." She smiled at Claire. "Anyway, in not so many weeks we'll have all the tropical weather we can stand."

Marc stood up and handed his mother the folder. "The rest of the research just came in. Not a word on the Sirens. There was a Daniel Wright in London. And, until recently, there was a Thomas Courtney practicing law in Chicago."

"Wonderful!" exclaimed Maud, removing her pea jacket with Marc's help. "Courtney is the one I'm depending upon. You have no idea what a timesaver he can be." She was addressing herself to Claire now. "Any decent field trip should take half a year or a year, even two years. Why, the shortest one I've ever been on took three months. But here we have a ridiculous six weeks. Sometimes it takes that long to locate your key informant, a person in the village who is relatively reliable, knowledgeable of the legends and history, willing to talk. You just can't find him in a week, and then establish rapport overnight. You have to play a waiting game, let them all get used to you, learn to trust you, eventually come to you. Then you find the right man, and often he puts the whole village into perspective for you. Well, here we have great luck. We have Courtney. If he is what Easterday says he is, he is the perfect go-between. He has prepared the Sirens people for us. He understands them and their problems and, being one of us also, he understands us and our needs. He should be a mine of information. And he should get us to our informants at once. Believe me—" She had turned back to Marc. "—I'm terribly pleased we have independent evidence this Courtney exists." She wagged the folder. "I'm going up to the study to look into this right now."

Claire rose. "I'll be with you in a minute."

After Maud had gone, and Marc had taken the morning newspaper into the living room, Claire cleared the kitchen table. Despite Suzu's protestations, Claire began to wash the dishes.

"It's no work at all," she told Suzu. "You have your hands full doing all the cooking for tonight."

"Only four come tonight besides us," said Suzu.

"Except that Mr. Hackfeld eats for eight, so that makes it a big dinner."

Suzu giggled, and returned to her basting.

When Claire had finished the dishes, and dried her hands, she clucked her admiration over Suzu's chicken and then she went upstairs to learn what she could do for her mother-in-law.

She found Maud, swivel chair turned away from the desk, rocking gently as she pored over the researchers' notes. Accepting Maud's acknowledging nod, Claire went to the coffee table to take a cigarette from the ever-present pack and light it. Then, puffing contentedly, she wandered about the familiar room. She gazed at the sepia and white tapa cloth hanging on the wall, at the framed, signed photographs of Franz Boas, Bronislaw Malinowski, Alfred Kroeber nearby, at the electric typewriter beside her own small desk, then she came to a halt before the bookshelves. She studied the bound copies of *Culture*, mouthpiece of the American Anthropological League, and *Man,* the publication of the Royal Anthropology Institute, and the *American Journal of Physical Sciences.*

"Fine, fine," she heard Maud say. "I wish I had had all of this when I prepared the project statement and expenditures for Hackfeld. No matter, I'll feed him some of the supplementary material tonight."

Claire moved to the large desk and sat down across from Maud. "Will there be any more research?" Claire asked.

Maud smiled. "It never ceases. In fact, yesterday I was up past midnight trying to trace some of the practices Easterday reported on the Sirens. Many are carry-overs from other islands. The old civilization on Easter Island despised virginity as much as the Sirens now do. And the rite where all male wedding guests enjoy the pleasure of the bride—Easterday is correct—that is also practiced in Samoa and the Marquesas Islands. As to the mysterious Social Aid Hut, I located something similar, a pleasure house or *are popi*, in Peter Buck's study of Mangareva. But some of the practices on the Sirens seem absolutely original. For one thing, Easterday's comments about a Hierarchy investigating divorce. I tell you, Claire, I can't wait to look into all this, get there and see for myself."

Claire felt that this was the moment to speak of what had been on her mind earlier, after her bath.

"I can't wait either," Claire said. She ground out the stub of her cigarette. "Except, I will confess, I'm a little apprehensive—"

"There's nothing to be apprehensive about."

"I mean—I've never been on anything like this—how am I supposed to behave?"

Maud seemed surprised. "Behave? Absolutely as you've always behaved, Claire. Be yourself—friendly, modest, courteous, interested—be your natural self." She reflected on this a moment, and added, "As a matter of fact, I suppose there are a few pointers someone inexperienced in field life might keep in mind. You can't ever be squeamish, aloof, or condescending. You've got to adapt yourself to the environment in the field and the new social situation. You've got to appear to enjoy yourself. You have to have respect for the so-called natives—and, before them, show that you respect your husband. Very probably you are going into a patriarchal society. In this situation the Polynesian woman always defers to a man in public, however much she may lay down the law at home and in private. Whenever possible, if you are invited to participate in a feast or work or play, you do so, you try to be one of them. It's all a matter of degree. Ordinarily, the things to avoid as a woman are getting drunk and foolish in public, being overaggressive, and, as a married woman, cohabiting with the Polynesian men."

Claire blushed, and then saw that Maud had been joking about cohabitation. Claire smiled. "I think I can manage to be faithful," she said.

"Yes," said Maud, and she added seriously, "Of course, there's no absolute right or wrong about that, either. Often it depends on the nature of the tribe you work with. There have been many instances where natives appreciated an anthropologist cohabiting with one of their own. They considered it an expression of acceptance. A woman in the field—if she had no outside attachments —might easily enter into a relationship with a male native, and be applauded since, as an outsider, she is surrounded with an aura of wealth, power, prestige."

"Well, you needn't discuss it seriously," said Claire.

"The important thing for you to recognize," said Maud, "is that those people on the Sirens—let us say they are predominately Polynesian—are not low primitives. You know, old man K—" Claire understood her to mean Kroeber, "—used to say that ants have a society, but no culture—culture meaning, in this context, not refinement but rather verbally derived customs, techniques, traditional beliefs to which they subscribe. Well, Polynesians are neither ants nor primitives. They have many solid and old cultures. When I hear laymen speak of primitives, I know they mean people who are nonliterate brutes of undeveloped mentality. And, of course, in sections of Africa or Ecuador or Brazil, in Australia, too, you can meet such people. Real aborigines. Don't expect that on the Sirens, especially since they are Polynesians crossed with Caucasians. Those people probably have a time depth as great as we have. They may not have a complex material culture, but they will have a complex social structure. They may be primitives only in the technological sense. You can be sure that socially they will be extremely advanced."

This was the exact moment, Claire knew, to bring it up. "It's hard to think of them as being civilized when the men run around all day wearing less than athletic supporters and the women are naked except for twelve inches of grass below."

"I'm sure they dress quite sensibly for their climate and their attitudes toward one another," said Maud, placidly.

"Will we be expected to go native?" asked Claire.

Maud seemed startled. "What do you mean?"

"I mean—will you and I have to take off our clothes and—"

"Heavens, no, Claire. Picture me in a grass skirt, with all my flab and authority at the mercy of the breeze. Heavens, has that been on your mind? You'll dress just as you'd dress here in California. The usual summer clothes, but of a lighter weight, and plenty of drip-drys. In fact, we must both do some shopping soon. The one tabu would be to wear blue jeans or slacks. To the natives you'd look like a man, and that might confuse and upset them. Rather than jeans or slacks, it would be better to go stark naked. They'd pay less attention. No, you can stay with comfortable blouses and skirts, or sleeveless prints. That will be acceptable. The main thing will be to show interest in those people, to show empathy. None of us can behave like the aristocratic young English anthropologist that Robert Lowie used to tell about. This English anthropologist went out among the natives, and returned with the following report, no more, no less—'Customs scarce, manners vile, morals lacking'!"

Claire laughed with her mother-in-law, and felt better. As she went to the coffee table for the cigarettes, she saw Maud take a sheaf of papers from a desk drawer.

"Are these the carbons of the letters to our potential team members?" Maud asked.

Claire looked over her shoulder, nodded, and returned to her seat. "I typed four of them. I excerpted the parts of Easterday's letter you suggested and enclosed them. I signed your name."

"When did they go out?"

"Yesterday afternoon, in time to catch the pickup. They were all airmail, except the one to Dr. Rachel DeJong since her address was in Los Angeles."

"Yes—let me see—yes, here's the letter to her. I think I had better glance over these, in case I omitted something. It'll give me an excuse to follow up. I hope they are all available. Hackfeld was quite impressed. I'd hate to go back to him with substitutes—"

"They should have their letters sometime today," said Claire. "I imagine we'll have answers over the weekend."

"Ummm," murmured Maud, scanning the first letter. "I certainly hope Rachel has the six weeks."

"Is that the woman psychoanalyst? I've been wondering, Maud. What made you choose her?"

"I once saw a paper that Rachel wrote—'The Effects of Courtship and Engagement upon Marriage'—and it was a superior piece of work. I decided that she would do wonderfully on the Sirens. Besides, she's type-cast for a field trip—absolutely cool, unemotional, thoroughly objective, not maddeningly Freudian, and very poised for a person so young. I have a strong preference for colleagues who are in control of themselves as well as any new situations that may arise. Rachel's for me. I just hope I'm for her."

"She won't be able to resist," said Claire with confidence.

* * *

It was eleven forty-one in the morning. In the dim psychiatric office high above Wilshire Boulevard in Los Angeles, Dr. Rachel DeJong sat in her chair beside the patient, grinding the pencil between her fingers, and telling herself that if this continued one minute beyond the nine minutes of the session left, she would scream.

The patient's voice had trailed off, and Rachel had a moment's professional panic. Had the patient sensed her own hostility? Uncrossing her legs, Rachel bent toward the couch, observing the patient, and then realized that the patient was staring ahead, lost in thought and oblivious of Rachel's analytic presence.

Poised over the couch as she was, Rachel realized another thing. The tableau that she and the patient presented, in these fleeting seconds, resembled an old-fashioned painting that she had once seen—in an advertisement, possibly—of beautiful Narcissus bent over the fountain, mesmerized by his own reflection in the water. The image was accurate as to appearance: she, Rachel DeJong, was Narcissus, and the leather couch was the fountain, and Miss Mitchell, prone, was the very reflection of herself. The image was inaccurate in only one respect: Narcissus pined away from love of his reflection, whereas Rachel disintegrated from hatred of her reflection.

Considering Miss Mitchell, she tried to analyze the emotional turmoil inside herself. She did not hate Miss Mitchell as a person.

What she hated was what she saw of herself, so mockingly exact, in the problem of Miss Mitchell. Rachel's hatred, via her patient, was self-hatred.

In her short, busy years as a practicing analyst, this had never happened to her before, at least not in this manifestation. Until two months ago, when Miss Mitchell had come into her life on a referral, Rachel DeJong had been relatively composed and dispassionate, everything fastidiously balanced. She knew her personal problem was there, had always been there, had survived her own analysis, and that Miss Mitchell had not brought the problem to her. What Miss Mitchell had done was to bring into the open, expose and dramatize Rachel's problem, identical twin to Miss Mitchell's problem.

Rachel settled back in her chair, fingers still angrily working her pencil. She should, she knew, have dismissed the patient after the fourth week, when the patient had been sufficiently liberated to begin to discuss her problem. Instead, Rachel had suffered hearing it, and now heard it over and over, agonizing with it, masochistically absorbing it, and by night examining it and hating herself. She should have gone to Dr. Ernst Beham, her own training analyst, from the beginning. This, she knew, would have been the professional solution, and yet she had failed to do so. It was as if she had wanted to preserve the self-flagellation longer, to endure it, as if to deny weakness, to prove that she was solved and strong. But there was more that restrained her from visiting the training analyst. Rachel realized that he would not have permitted the relationship with Miss Mitchell to continue. Of this, she was positive. And somehow, Rachel wanted it to continue. It was as if, three times a week, for 150 minutes, she was tuning in on a to-be-continued story about herself, and she dared not miss an episode, for she must know the outcome of the miserable plot.

Today was the worst yet. Perhaps because her own situation, in her private life, was at its worst. Today's session was unendurable. She cast a sidelong glance at her desk clock. Seven minutes of the fifty remained. They would be terrible. Should she cut it short?

"—don't you agree, Doctor?" the patient had asked.

Rachel DeJong coughed, and wore the hood of sagacity, and when she had her bearings, she spoke. "We'll go into my opinions later, Miss Mitchell," she said. "Right now, as I have told you before, the important thing is that you have the source of this disturbance out in the open, where you can see it clearly. Soon, I think you will not require my opinion. You will acquire your own insight. You will see what must be done yourself."

Miss Mitchell revealed displeasure, and turned her head on the doily so that her eyes were directed to the cool aquamarine ceiling. "I don't know why I keep coming here or paying you," she complained. "You hardly ever give me advice."

"When advice is necessary, I shall give it," said Rachel crisply. "Right now, the important thing is that you tell me all you can. Please try to go on."

Miss Mitchell brooded in hurt silence a moment. At last she said, "Well, if you insist," and she resumed her free association.

Rachel, as she had done several times in the past, secretly examined the person of Miss Mitchell. The patient was in her late twenties, the only offspring of an illustrious society family, its wealth inherited. Miss Mitchell had been well educated before and after Radcliffe, and had been well traveled and well attended by young swains. She was glacially attractive, from her impeccable blond bouffant hair-do to her long slanted face (so like the ancient Egyptian bust of Nefertiti) to her straight mannequin figure. Physically, she was desired by men, and never in want of attention from them, yet she had deliberately shied away from any attachment until recently.

Rachel tore her gaze from her patient, and stared at the carpet and at herself. If Rachel had a problem, it was not one of false modesty. She knew that she was, in her own way, as attractive to the opposite sex as was her patient. If she was not so tall or thin, if she was not so well groomed, she was still her patient's equal in comeliness. In fact, this had always been a difficulty of hers with male patients. Their transference was often total, and on several occasions, aggressive. She wondered how Miss Mitchell saw her as female, not therapist. Rachel's severe dark suits and high-necked blouses—the ensemble she wore today—did not entirely detract femininity from her appearance. Like Miss Mitchell's hair-do, her own light chestnut-colored hair was bouffant, although less so. Her lynx-eyes were small and lively, her nose classically straight, her cheekbones high and full so that her face tapered to a firm triangular chin. Rachel's body was long and bony, with broad shoulders, large but not deep breasts, wasp waist and boyish hips. Possibly her calves were too straight. But all in all, physically, she was not inferior to her patient or, indeed, to most of her friends. Yet, at thirty-one, she was still unmarried.

Her problem, then, like her problem's twin possessed by Miss Mitchell, was not that of lack of appeal to the opposite sex. Rather, the malady of the twins was an interior one, a malady of fear, fear of the opposite sex. For both of them, the damage and crippling had occurred in early childhood, and for both of them the adult symptom was a withdrawal from all emotional involvements. Both cultivated an extreme independence, evading obligations to other human beings.

The patient's voice intruded, and with its complaints and tortures, there came to Rachel a twinge of guilt, and she forced herself to direct her attention to Miss Mitchell.

Miss Mitchell was speaking. "I keep remembering, it keeps coming back, those first weeks after I met him." Miss Mitchell paused, shook her head, closed her eyes, and resumed. "He was absolutely different from all the others, or maybe he wasn't different but I was, that is, my feelings about him as a man were different. When the others tried to neck with me or pet, or when they proposed, I could always say no and not be sorry. I didn't give a damn about any of them. They were children, spoiled children. But when he came along, I positively flipped. I wanted him. I mean I really wanted him. I was afraid I would lose him. Can you imagine me being afraid to lose a man? Well, he felt the same way about me— I've told you that a dozen times—but I was sure—still am sure—he loved me, too. Why in the devil would he want to marry me, if he didn't? He had almost as much money as Dad, so that couldn't be it. No, he wanted me for his wife. And I wanted to be his wife. But the night I was to go out with him—I mean hours before—I knew he was going to propose that night, I simply knew—and then I got sick—conveniently, you'll say—go ahead—conveniently . . . I guess you're right. I wanted to be wanted, and I wanted him, and wanted our kind of childish suspended engagement to go on and on, like a fairy tale, a nice fairy tale where there's no sex—only platonic love—where there is no realness—no responsibility to meet—no adult contact—no having to give and give good, expose yourself, depend on another instead of just yourself—I know, Doctor, we've been there—I know—"

Rachel listened, wincing inwardly, and she thought: the hell you know, Miss Mitchell.

Rachel's mind stumbled backwards, her twin joining Miss Mitchell's twin in the not too distant past. All through medical school, and after, there had been men, sometimes students, sometimes older men. There had been proposals, too, nice ones, appealing ones. *It'll be perfect, Rachel, you'll have your work and I'll have mine. We can hire someone for the kids. We can buy two couches at once, and get a discount, ha-ha. Come on, Rachel, say the good word. Remember, the family that works together, stays together.* And always she had had one stenciled reply. *You're a darling, Al* (or *Billy* or *Dick* or *John*), *but you see . . . and besides that . . . and so . . . and that's why I'm afraid I can't, I really can't.*

She had always tried to reduce passion and fervor to grayest friendship, and she had always succeeded. Only twice, in the year after she had made up her mind to specialize, to become a psychoanalyst, had she permitted a super-relationship to exceed friendship. One subject was a fellow student, an awkward, lanky boy from Minnesota. The setting had been his cheap bachelor apartment, the place his couch (they had made the joke about that simultaneously). She had come prepared for it, and endured it as stoically as having a tooth filled. She had given nothing, and he little more. That had played one performance. Still in quest of Experience—how could one guide others, in the future, without firsthand knowledge in one's past?—she had flirted with a foolish young professor, husband and father, and managed a weekend with him in a hotel bungalow on Catalina Island. This provided a higher degree of professionalism, but no joy. She had kept her privacy, even when he was locked within her. Her role had been innocent bystander, impartial observer, and as far as she was concerned, he might have been masturbating. That one closed after three performances. He could not understand why she had cut the idyllic weekend short. It was the last of Rachel's firsthand Experience. Thereafter, Rachel's knowledge of the function came from lectures, reading, and, eventually, from her patients. She reassured herself that her libido rested in peace, a sleeping princess, and when the proper prince came along, she and her passion would awaken normally.

Fourteen months before this day, the right man had come along. And she and her passion had, indeed, awakened. All was on schedule. He was then forty years old, now forty-one, she then thirty, now thirty-one. He was a big, tender man, darling oxlike eyes, vigorous physique, a bachelor of sound education, the best instincts, the widest interests, the highest income. He was the Morgen of the brokerage firm of Jaggers, Ulm, and Morgen. Joseph E. Morgen. Fine family, too. She was awakened, and happy, and he was netted and liked it.

The chronology of the first ten months, condensed book version, was simple. Chapter I. Art galleries, museums. Chapter II. Theaters, movies. Chapter III. Nightclubs, assorted bars, come-by-for-a-drink. Chapter IV. His family's house, his family, lovely people. Chapter V. Her friends' houses, her friends, wonderful people. Chapter VI. Parties, lots of parties. Chapter VII. Parked car at Laguna, Newport, Malibu, Trancas, kissing, kissing. Chapter VIII. Her apartment, petting, petting. Chapter IX. Carmel weekend, the walk along the water at night . . .

Miss Mitchell had sobbed, and Rachel did not regret leaving that walk along the water at night. The moment that Miss Mitchell began to speak again, Rachel wanted to retreat, for she knew what was coming, had heard it before.

"All that day, on the Riviera, I felt it was right," Miss Mitchell was saying. "I had rushed off like a frightened schoolgirl and he had the love to follow me, still determined to spring his question. But I was more settled, and when we drove back to Cannes, I was sure it was solved and I would say yes—I would say yes, and Christ, get it over with, get on with the happy ending. But the sun was still out and he wanted us to dress for the beach, get some of it, have cocktails on the beach. So I changed in the cabaña, and then he did, and when he came out I felt I was going to become ill, upchuck, I mean it. The sonofabitch was wearing bikini trunks —I'd never seen him like that before—so gross—so animal—he, as a person, was no different, he was the same—but that other made it different. I couldn't look at him, and then he sprawled out next to me, and right there he blurted it out—proposed—get married right away—and I knew what that meant—and I started to cry, and ran off to the hotel. The doctors kept him out—but what could I say? —and anyway, look at my condition—that was the breakdown, as you damn well know—that started it, that thing—that was the beginning—"

The end, that was the end, Rachel thought to herself.

They had found the lonely stretch of beach north of Carmel, and parked among the trees, and he had helped her down the steep slope to the sand. It was warm on the beach, and the water rippled gently in the moonlight. They kicked off their shoes, and padded along the surf, hand in hand. She knew that he would propose, this big sensitive man, so in love with her, and she with him, and she kept her silence, and he proposed. She had gone into his arms, thinking at last, at last, thinking not a second beyond this bliss, only nodding her head as he whispered endearments.

He wanted to celebrate. He wanted to go into the water with her. She wondered how that was possible. They had no suits. And he had said gayly that they needed no suits now that they were practically married. Bewildered at what was happening within her, she had dumbly assented, and wandered off behind the jutting rock to undress, and had unbuttoned one blouse button, and frozen, and stood there trembling, chilled and trembling for more than five hundred seconds. And then she had heard her name and heard the movement of him, and rushed around the rock to explain, somehow explain, and found him in nature's state as he had expected her to be. The look of sheer horror on her face had instantly wiped the carefree smile from his own. She had stared at the massive hairy chest, and involuntarily, as if in a dream, had lowered her gaze . . . yes, Miss Mitchell, yes . . . and she had run off through the sand, falling, rising, running, with his shouts pursuing her.

When he had returned to the car, clothed, she was waiting, dry-eyed and controlled, and all the way home, the long, long way home, they were terribly reasonable and intellectual about it, so that by the time morning came, and Los Angeles appeared through the smog, it was understood that the fault had been his own. He should have known better, you see. Women are different, more highly strung, more emotional, you see. Men tend to barge ahead, be impetuous, forgetting. Her profession had nothing to do with her frail womanhood. She had given a pledge of marriage, and had been overwhelmed and overwrought. Agreed? They would be married, everything would iron itself out. It always does. I love you, Rachel. I love you, Joe. It'll work out, Rachel. I know, Joe. Better start thinking of the date, Rachel. I will, I will, Joe. Tomorrow night, then? Tomorrow night.

There followed a period of four months of tomorrow nights, some appointments kept, some not kept. Joseph Morgen had pressed for the wedding date. Rachel had used every device known in the annals of femininity to avoid any date. Her defenses were built on emergency cases, a burden of free clinic work, psychiatric papers to write, conventions to attend, relatives to entertain, sicknesses to recover from, and suddenly it was last week. A fight. She was making a fool of him, he said. If she didn't love him, why didn't she say so? But she did love him, she said, she loved him very much. Then why was she evading him, tricking him, really refusing to marry him? It would work out, she said, it would work out soon. And then he said and she said, and he said the last words, which were that he would not press her any more, but his desire was the same and his offer stood, and when she was ready she must come to him and tell him.

All that ruinous haggling was last week.

Last night she had read in a Hollywood column that Joseph Morgen had been seen dining in Perino's with an Italian film starlet.

She had not slept three hours in the night.

She became time-conscious. She noted the clock on her desk, and shifted in her chair. "Well, Miss Mitchell, I'm afraid our time is up," Rachel announced. "This has been a most useful meeting. While you may not feel it, you are making progress."

Miss Mitchell had sat up, smoothing her coiffure, and at last she stood, her face more relaxed than previously.

Rachel rose. "Have a pleasant weekend, and I hope to see you Monday, same time."

"Yes," said Miss Mitchell. She went to the door, Rachel behind her, and then she hesitated, and turned her head. "I—I wish I could be like you, Dr. DeJong. Will I ever?"

"No, nor would you want to be. One day, soon, you will be yourself, a self you will value highly, and that will be sufficient.

"I'll take your word for it. Good-by."

After the patient had left, Rachel DeJong leaned against the doorway arch, feeling oddly disoriented. It was with effort that she realized the hour was noon, and that she would have no other patient until four. Why was that? Suddenly, it came to her. She was to participate in a panel discussion, with Dr. Samuelson and Dr. Lynd, on the stage of Beverly Hills High School. There would be a discussion on adolescents and early marriage, and afterward the meeting would be thrown open to the parents and teachers in attendance for questions from the floor. This had all been arranged several months ago, and it was to occupy her from one to three this afternoon. When it had come up, she had accepted the invitation readily. She had always enjoyed the give and take, the mental challenge and stimulation, of such events. Now she felt weak and weary, unhappy about Joe, disgusted with herself, and soggy with low self-esteem. She was not in the mood for flourishes and wit and psychiatric wisdom. She wanted to be alone to recuperate, to think, to solve herself. Yet, she knew that she could not default on the panel. She had never done so, and she could not do so now. It was too late for a substitute. She would have to go through with it, as best she could.

After coming out of the washroom, she made up her face, tugged on her coat, and left her office. Passing through the reception room, she saw her morning's mail on the lamp table. There were half a dozen letters. She stuffed them into her pocket, locked the office door, and took the elevator down to the lobby of the building.

Outside, the air was chilly and the day as somber and weighted as her heart. She had intended to get her convertible, drive into Beverly Hills, have a drink and a quiet meal at one of the better restaurants, and hurry to catch the panel by one o'clock. Now she was too preoccupied for either a drink or a real lunch, and so she turned up Wilshire Boulevard and made her way, by foot, to the snack shop on the corner.

The counter was almost filled, but there were still two booths empty. She took her place in the nearer, for she wanted privacy. After ordering a bowl of bean soup, a cheeseburger medium well, and coffee, she sat, hands folded on the table, trying to construct something out of the wreckage of recent months.

She could not blame Joe for the date with the starlet, or for further dates in the future, that was clear. He had his life, too, and he had to live it. His date did not necessarily mean he was becoming emotionally involved elsewhere. It probably had no more depth than fornication. Joe had last said he wanted to marry her, and it was up to her. Well, dammit, she wanted to marry him, and it *was* up to her. The sensible thing, she saw, would be to go to him and simply lay it on the line, bare herself, expose the degree of her inhibition. He was psychiatrically oriented. He would understand. With his understanding and support, she would return to her training analyst, and work it out. At last, she would be able to marry Joe.

To her psychiatrist self this was simple and the only procedure. Yet, her female self—her utter female self—dissented. She did not want to reveal to him her basic problem. It spoiled things a little, a very little. The bride has a problem; she cannot shed her veil. This was foolishness, sick foolishness, but it was there. She was confused again, and what had been briefly simple now knelt to encompassing complexity.

The lunchroom was steamy, stifling, and as she began to remove her coat, she felt her morning's mail. She folded the coat and put it on the seat next to her, and took her mail from the pocket.

Spooning her soup, she sorted the mail. None of it interested her until she reached the last envelope. The return address read: "Dr. Maud Hayden, Raynor College, Santa Barbara, California." This was surprising. While Rachel knew Maud Hayden fairly well, she considered Maud as no more than an acquaintance-friend, whom one always met professionally. She had never been to Maud Hayden's house, nor had Maud ever visited her apartment. Never before had either of them written the other. She could not imagine why Maud Hayden would write to her, but her admiration for the elderly woman whom she considered among the peers of anthropology was so great that she quickly ripped open the envelope. The letter lay before her, and the next moment she entered the distant world of The Three Sirens.

Finishing her soup, slowly munching her cheeseburger and sipping her coffee, Rachel DeJong read on. As she read one page, then two, and went eagerly to the extracts from the Easterday report, her private world—so filled with her problem self, with Joseph Morgen, with Miss Mitchell—was populated by Alexander Easterday, Captain Rasmussen, Thomas Courtney, a Polynesian named Moreturi, and his father and Chief, Paoti Wright.

The impact of Maud Hayden's letter and enclosure jolted her into space and landed her, vibrating, on a serene, foundationless, weird planet, a blend of Malinowski's Boyawa, Tully's South Sea dreamland in *A Bird of Paradise*, and D. H. Lawrence's Wragby Hall. She tried to project herself into the picture of The Three Sirens, and found her sensible self fascinated by the culture but repelled by the evident eroticism of that culture. At an earlier time, when her nerves had been less raw and repressions comfortably buried, she would have been interested, she knew, and she would have telephoned Maud Hayden instantly.

Rachel remembered, as Maud reminded her in the letter, that a year ago she had volunteered for a field trip under a director and mentor capable of teaching her so much. She had been interested in the mores of marriage, extremely interested. That was at another time, when her mind and her work and her social life (she had just started going out with Joe then) were organized and controlled. Today, such a trip would be folly. A study of uninhibited sexual play and successful marriage would be unbearably painful. She no longer had the objectivity or poise for it. Besides, how could she leave her relationship with Joe unresolved? How could she leave Miss Mitchell and thirty other patients for six weeks? Of course, several times in the past she had left her patients for protracted periods, and there was no indication that her remaining here would resolve anything with Joe. Still, at a time like this The Three Sirens was pure fantasy, impossible self-indulgence, and she must forget it.

The appearance of the waitress with the bill brought her out of never-never land. She consulted her watch. Eighteen minutes to one. She would have to speed to make the panel.

Hurrying out of the snack shop to her car, and then in her car to Beverly Hills High School, she arrived backstage just as the moderator was putting in a call for her. The audience was waiting, a filled auditorium, and presently—all activity had a detached, somnambulant quality for her this afternoon—she found herself behind the table, between Dr. Samuelson and Dr. Lynd, participating in a lively discussion of teen-age marriages.

The minutes fled, and she knew that she was playing a passive role in the debate, allowing Dr. Samuelson and Dr. Lynd to dominate the floor, hold the strong exchanges, and speaking herself only when spoken to. Usually, she did well in these public polemics. This afternoon, she knew, she was doing poorly—jargon, banalities, quotations by rote—and she didn't give a damn.

Rachel was dimly aware that the panel discussion had ended, and questions from the floor were being flung at the three of them. She was the target of two, and her colleagues the other dozen or more. The wall clock told her that the ordeal was almost over. She settled back, considering a possible showdown with Joe.

Suddenly, she heard her name, which meant a question was being directed at her. She stiffened in her wooden chair, and tried to comprehend it fully.

After the question mark, her countenance assumed the expression of thoughtfulness—Joe would have seen through this—and she began to reply.

"Yes, I understand, Madam," she said. "I have not read this popular piece of his you mention. But if the content is what you say, I can honestly state that I would not touch that popular penis of his for anything—"

Her voice halted, bewildered. Puncturing the hush of the audience had come a squeal, followed by giggles, and now a low breaker of tittering and voices buzzing.

Rachel hesitated, lost, and concluded lamely, "—well, I'm sure you get the point I'm making."

Unaccountably, the entire audience broke into a roar of laughter.

In the hubbub, Rachel turned helplessly to Dr. Lynd, whose cheeks were flushed, and who was staring straight ahead, as if he had to pretend not to have overheard a scene of indiscretion. Rachel whirled toward Dr. Samuelson, whose lips were curled in a smile, he too looking directly at the audience.

"What's got into them?" Rachel whispered against the noise. "Why are they laughing?" She tried to remember what she had said, something about not touching that magazine article for anything—for anything—that article—that popular piece—piece—thing— Suddenly, she gasped, and whispered to Dr. Samuelson, "Did I—?"

And he, gaze still directed ahead of him, replied from the corner of his mouth in a cheerful undertone, "I'm afraid, Dr. DeJong, your Freudian slip is showing."

"Oh, God," Rachel groaned, "you mean I *did*."

The moderator rapped his gavel, and quickly order was restored, so that the slip was soon lost in the questions and answers that followed. Rachel trusted herself to speak no more. It was a test of character to brazen it out, to sit there on exhibit, wooden and unsmiling. As the words built their fence about her, her mind went back to her student days and her reading on "speech-blunders" in Sigmund Freud's *Psychopathology of Everyday Life:* "A lady once expressed herself in society—the very words show that they were uttered with fervor and under the pressure of a great many secret emotions: 'Yes, a woman must be pretty if she is to please men. A man is much better off. As long as he has *five* straight limbs, he needs no more!' . . . In the psychotherapeutic procedure which I employ in the solution and removal of neurotic symptoms, I am often confronted with the task of discovering from the accidental utterances and fancies of the patient the thought contents, which, though striving for concealment, nevertheless unintentionally betray themselves."

Rachel had been dwelling on this, and her own "speech-blunder," for some seconds, when she realized that the discussion was over and that the meeting had been adjourned. Rising and walking off the stage, slightly apart from the others, she knew that she would be writing two letters tonight. One would be to Joseph Morgen, confiding in him the truth of her problem and letting him decide if he was willing to wait until she worked it out, for better or for worse. The other would be to Maud Hayden, informing her that Rachel DeJong would have her affairs in order and be ready to accompany a team to The Three Sirens for six weeks in June and July.

* * *

Maud Hayden had taken up the carbon copy of the letter Claire had typed and sent to Dr. Sam Karpowicz, in Albuquerque, New Mexico. Before reading it, she turned to Claire.

"I hope this dazzles him," she said. "We've simply got to have Sam. Not only is he an excellent free-lance botanist, but he's a brilliant photographer, one of the few creative ones. The only thing that worries me is—well, Sam's such a family man, and I pointedly ignored inviting his wife and daughter along. Maybe they'd be no problem, but I'm trying to keep the field team small."

"What if he insists upon bringing his family?" asked Claire.

"Then I don't know, I really don't know. Of course, Sam's so important to me that I suppose I should accept him under any conditions, even if I had to take along his grandfather, pet poodles, and hothouse. . . . Well, let's hold a good thought, and cross that bridge when we come to it. Let's see what Sam has to say."

* * *

It was after ten o'clock in the evening when Sam Karpowicz locked the door of his darkroom shed and crossed the few yards of wet green lawn to the flagstone steps, wearily ascending them to the constricted patio. Beside the outdoor wicker lounge he halted, inhaling the cooling, dry night air, and clearing his head of the darkroom fumes. The intake of air was as delicious as any intoxicant. He closed his eyes and inhaled and exhaled several times, then opened his eyes and momentarily enjoyed the distinct rows of street lights and scattered residential lights off toward the Rio

Grande. The street lights seemed to shimmer and move, with yellow grandeur, like the torchlights of a nighttime religious procession he had seen last year between Saltillo and Monterey, Mexico.

He stood quietly in the patio, reluctant to give up the pleasures of the place and its scenes. His affection for this suburban neighborhood, for the dusty pueblos of Acoma and San Felipe nearby, the flat grazing land and irrigated chili pepper fields, the blue spruce mountains, was deep and unshakable.

He remembered, with a pang, what had brought him here, so unlikely a place for one who knew nothing but New York's Bronx from birth to early manhood. During the war—the Hitler war—he had come to know Ernie Pyle very well. Sam had been a press officer and Signal Corps photographer, despite his university degree in botany, and Pyle had been a battle correspondent. In their long hikes together, on three Pacific islands, Sam would discourse on the wonders of Pacific plant ecology, and Pyle, at Sam's urging, would speak of his passion for the peace of his New Mexico. Some months after Pyle's death in action, Sam had been sent to California for discharge from the service. He had purchased a beaten-up old car and driven through the Southwest toward New York, determined to have one look at this country before burying himself in the monotony of metropolitan teaching.

His route had taken him through Albuquerque, and once in the city, he knew that he could not leave it without visiting Mrs. Pyle, and Ernie's cottage, and the neighborhood his late friend had so often discussed with such love. Sam had put up in a four-dollar single at the Alvarado Hotel, next to the Santa Fe station. After cleaning up and dining, and making inquiries at the desk, he had driven through the hot, quiet business district, past the pueblo-styled University, until he had come upon Girard Drive. He had turned right on the paved street, so familiar and friendly after his dead friend's descriptions, and had cruised onward for a mile, between Spanish adobe homes, until the street became gravel, and after several blocks he had arrived at the corner of Girard Drive and Santa Monica Drive. Ernie Pyle had said that his cottage was at 700 South Girard Drive, a corner house with shrubbery, cement patio, a dog named Cheeta, a green-shingle roofed white house made for peace.

Sam had parked and gone to the house and knocked. The door had been opened by a nurse, and he had identified himself and explained his mission. The nurse had told him that Mrs. Pyle was too ill to see anyone, but suggested that if he was a friend of Ernie's, he might like to see Ernie's room, untouched since the day he had left it forever. In his mind's eye, Sam had seen the room often, and it held no surprises. Somehow, it was more his own room than the one in the apartment in the Bronx where Estelle waited for him. Slowly, he had circled the room—the open dictionary on the stand, the autographed drawing by Low, the two walls of books, the framed photograph of Ernie chatting with Eisenhower and Bradley, the dirty green baseball cap hanging from a peg—and finally, with thanks and regards for Mrs. Pyle, Sam had left.

Once outside, Sam had wandered along the gravel road, nodding to a neighbor mowing his lawn, observing the University buildings some distance off, poking about several empty lots, often halting to stare at the faraway hills, and at last he had returned to his car and to the city.

He did not remain in Albuquerque overnight. He remained a week. In that week he applied for a post at the University of New Mexico, and after that he resumed his cross-country journey.

One year later, he was an instructor at the University, with a private laboratory and shining new compound microscope, and two years later he had his own adobe on South Girard Drive.

And here, on the patio of this cottage, he stood tonight. Not one day had he ever regretted the move, nor had Estelle regretted it either. The only occasions that he had ever known regret had been those occasions when he had found it necessary to leave Albuquerque on work trips.

One last time, he breathed the invigorating air, letting it fill his thin chest, and, partially revived, he went into the house through the open glass doors of the dining room. Securing the doors, he shouted, "Estelle, how about some coffee?"

"Ready and waiting!" she called back. "In the living room!"

He found Estelle curled in the wide armchair. Her purplish-gray hair was done up in curlers, and her large loose bathrobe was flung out to cover both her ample frame and the sides of the chair. She resembled, he decided, a comfortable teepee. She was reading, with the dogged intentness that denotes self-improvement, Riesman's *Individualism Reconsidered*, and now she laid the book aside to rise and take the coffee pot from the portable hot plate. Sam made for the opposite armchair and, as if being lowered by a derrick, settled his lengthy skeleton frame creakingly into the chair. Once seated, spindly legs outstretched, he groaned pleasantly.

"You're making sounds like an old man," said Estelle, pouring coffee into the cup that rested on the lacquered table.

"The Torah says when a man is forty-nine, he has the license to groan with equanimity."

"So groan then. Did you accomplish much?"

"I printed some of the stuff I shot around Little Falls. That Mexican sun is so bright you have to work like a dog to get true definition. Anyway, the *pitahaya* turned out beautifully. I'm almost at the end. I think I can wind it up in a few weeks. How's the typing going?"

"I'm caught up to you," said Estelle, returning to her place. "When you write the rest of the captions, I'll do them."

Sam tasted his coffee, noisily blew at it, and finally drank with enjoyment and set down the half-filled cup. He removed his rimless square glasses—"the Schubert glasses," his daughter called them—because they had steamed, and then, feeling untidy, he smoothed down his mussed saffron-gray hair, ran a finger across each of his peaked eyebrows, and finally searched for and found a cigar. As he prepared it, he suddenly glanced around. "Where's Mary? Is she back yet?"

"Sam, it's only ten-fifteen."

"I thought it was later. My legs feel like it's later." He started his cigar glowing, and drank his coffee again. "I hardly saw her today—"

"We hardly saw you, hour after hour in that black hole in the back. A human being at least comes in for dinner. Did you eat the sandwiches?"

"Darnit, I forgot to bring in the tray and dishes." He put down his empty cup. "Yes, I cleaned the tray." He sucked at the cigar again, erupted a cloud of smoke, and asked, "What time did she go out?"

"What?" Estelle had gone back to her reading.

"Mary. What time did she leave here?"

"Sevenish."

"Who was it tonight—the Schaffer boy again?"

"Yes, Neal Schaffer. He took her to a birthday party at the Brophys'. Imagine, Leona Brophy is seventeen."

"Imagine, Mary Karpowicz is sixteen. What I can't imagine is what Mary sees in that Brophy girl. She's absolutely vacuous, and the way she dresses—"

Estelle dropped the book to her lap. "Leona is perfectly all right. What you object to is her parents."

Sam snorted. "Anyone who puts Americanism stickers on his car —God, how often I try to think what's in the minds of those people. Why would anyone have to go around billboarding the fact that they are Americans in America? Of course, they're Americans, and so are we, and so is almost everyone in this country. It's so damn suspect. What are they trying to say—that they're super-Americans, special Americans, more American than ordinary Americans? Do they want to prove that everyone else might want to overthrow the government some day or sell secrets to a foreign power, whereas the stickers prove that they guarantee they will not, as long as they live? What crazy dark things are inside those people, that they have to *prove* their citizenship and loyalty? Why doesn't old man Brophy also wear a lapel button saying Marriedism or Manism or Godism?"

Estelle accepted her husband's outburst patiently—the truth was, she secretly adored him in these moments of indignation— and when she saw that Sam was done, she returned with practicality to the central point. "All of which has nothing to do with Leona or her birthday party or Mary going there."

Sam smiled. "Right you are," he said. He studied the cigar. "This Schaffer kid—Mary ever discuss him with you?"

Estelle shook her head. "Sam, you're not going to pick on him, are you?"

Sam smiled again. "In fact, I was, but only mildly. I don't have much more than an impression of him, but he seems too smart and old for her."

"They'll all be too smart and old for her, as long as you're her father and she's growing up."

Sam was tempted to make a wisecrack, but he did not. Instead, he nodded placid agreement. "That's right, I suppose you're right and Mother knows best—"

"—about Father. She sure does."

"The subject is changed." He surveyed the lacquered table. "Any calls today—visitors—mail?"

"All quiet—nothing in the mail except an invitation to a dinner dance at the Sandia Base—some bills—a report from the Civil

Liberties Union—*The New Republic*—more bills—and that's about—" She suddenly straightened. "Oh, dear, I almost forgot—there's a letter for you from Maud Hayden. It's on the dining room table."

"Maud Hayden? I wonder where the old girl is now? Maybe she's coming out this way again."

"I'll get it for you." Estelle was already on her feet and, bedroom slippers plopping, on her way to the dining room. She came back with a long envelope and handed it to Sam. "It's from Santa Barbara."

"She's becoming sedentary," said Sam, opening the envelope.

As he began to read the letter, Estelle stood beside him, stifling a yawn, but unable to leave until she knew what it was all about. "Anything important?"

"As far as I can make out . . ." His voice trailed off, as he read on, absorbed. "She's going on a field trip to the South Pacific in June. She wants company." He handed her the page he had finished, absently groped for his spectacles and hooked them on and continued to read.

Five minutes later, he had finished the letter, and waited thoughtfully, looking up at his wife, as she read to the end of the Easter-day enclosure.

"What do you think, Estelle?"

"Fascinating, of course—but Sam, you promised we'd stay put this summer—and I don't want you trotting off without us—"

"I never said I would."

"There are a hundred things to be done to the house, and work you have to catch up on, and we've promised my family that this year they could come out and—"

"Estelle, relax, we're not going anywhere. From my standpoint, I can't see that The Three Sirens would offer anything different than the rest of Polynesia. It's just that—well, first of all, it's fun to be with old Maud, and it's good to be associated with her—secondly, you've got to admit, sounds like a real odd place, those customs—I'd have the camera—might give me a picture book that, for a change, would sell."

"We're doing all right. We don't need it. I'm sick of being either a nomad or a botanical widow. For one summer let's be a family in a home in a place where we belong."

"Look, I'm worn out, too. I love it here as much as you do. I was only speculating. I have no intention of budging an inch out of here."

"Good, Sam." She bent over and kissed him. "I can hardly keep my eyes open. Don't stay up too late."

"Just until Mary—"

"I gave her permission until midnight. What are you—Grover Whalen to welcome her? She has a key and she knows the way. Get some sleep, you need it."

"Okay. Soon as you're through with the bathroom."

After Estelle had gone up the hallway to the bedroom, Sam Karpowicz took Maud's letter and leisurely reread it. Aside from the war, he had visited the South Seas only once, for a short time, collecting specimens on the Fijis, the year after Maud had been there. He had collected a wonderful assortment of wild yams, several of a species unknown to him, but after painstakingly measuring them, learning their names and histories, he had done something wrong in their preservation, and they had all deteriorated on the way home. It would be valuable to have another set again, that is, if they grew on The Three Sirens. Also, there was the possibility of the picture book to supplement, even profit by, the bestseller that Maud would inevitably write. It was tempting, but Sam knew that it was not enough. Estelle was right. The family must come first, allow its own roots to grow and flourish. It would be a good summer in Albuquerque, he decided, and he did not mind; in fact, he was glad. Neatly, he folded Maud's letter and returned it to its envelope. He turned down the lamps, leaving one on, and the front porch light on as well, for Mary.

The bedroom was already darkened when he reached it. By squinting, he could make out the mound that was Estelle in her bed. He felt his way to the bathroom, closed the door, turned up the shaving light, and prepared for the night. When he was done, he was surprised that it was already ten minutes after midnight. He pulled his faded blue robe over his pajamas, having decided to say good night to Mary.

Crossing to her bedroom, he could see that her door was open. When he reached it, he could also see that the bed was still made. Disappointed, he trudged to the cramped study, relighted the student lamp on the desk, and parted the Venetian blinds. Outside, Girard Drive was empty and desolate. This was unlike Mary, and Sam turned away troubled. He considered another cigar, but he had already brushed his teeth and so he vetoed the cigar. He sat down at his desk, puttered restlessly, leafing through some botanical journals.

After a while, he heard the approaching sound of an automobile. The mantel clock told him it was twelve thirty-four. Quickly, he jumped up, turned off the student lamp, and opened the Venetian blinds. He could make out Neal Schaffer's Studebaker compact. It came past the house, made a U-turn, and drew up at the curb directly ahead. The engine died. Sam released the blinds as if they had burned him. A concerned parent, yes, but a spy, never.

Slowly, his heron legs carried his tall, concave person to bed. He jerked off the robe, and crawled between the covers. He lay on his back, and thought of Mary, and of her infancy, and allowed his mind to revolve to Maud, and back to the field trip that he had made with her, and then back to the war and after, and suddenly he was back to Mary, and still wide awake. He had been listening all the while and had not heard her enter. And then, as if to chastize him, he heard the metallic rattle of the key, the squeak of the hinges, the contact of wood against wood as the door closed. He felt his face smile in the darkness. He waited to hear her footsteps go from the living room to her bedroom.

He waited for the automatic tread, and did not hear it. More awake than ever, he listened harder. Still, no sound of footsteps. Strange. He contained himself, and turned on his left side, and pretended to try to sleep, but his eardrums waited. Silence. This was unusual, and he was nervous now. At least five minutes had passed since her entrance, he was positive. He could stand the mystery no longer. Throwing off his blanket, he stuck his feet into his slippers, pulled on his robe, and went into the hallway.

Again, he went to her room. It was not occupied. He went to the living room. It was quiet, and appeared empty, and then he saw her in his chair. She had kicked off her high-heeled pumps—which he could never get used to—and she sat straight in the chair, unaware of him, staring blankly ahead.

Curiouser and curiouser, he thought, and he came around to confront her. "Mary—"

She lifted her head, and her narrow peach face was so lovely and fresh, so young, that he could see it had been marred about the eyes, as if she had been crying. "Hi, Dad," she said in a low voice. "I thought you were sleeping."

"I heard you come in," he said, carefully. "When I didn't hear you go to bed, I got worried. Are you all right?"

"Yes, I guess so."

"This is not like you. What were you doing here, alone, like this? It's late."

"Thinking a little. I don't know what."

"You're sure nothing happened tonight? Did you have a good time?"

"Sorta. The same as always."

"Did young Schaffer bring you home?"

"He sure did—" She came alive, and pushed herself forward in the chair, readying to rise.

"What does that mean?"

"Oh—nothing, Dad, please—"

"Well, if you don't want to tell me—"

"There's nothing to tell you, really. He was just unpleasant."

"Unpleasant. Does that mean fresh?"

"It means unpleasant. A little kissing is one thing, but when they think they own you—"

"I'm afraid I don't understand. Or maybe I do."

She stood up all at once. "Please, *Pa*—" Sam knew she only used *Pa* when she was exasperated with him, when he was being an ice cube, which in her parlance was very square, indeed. "Don't make a mountain out of a molehill," she was saying. "It's embarrassing."

He was not sure what else he should say. He was nudged by the necessity of preserving parental authority and the father image, and yet she was maturing, and deserved some privacy. As she retrieved her purse, he watched her, brown hair groomed, beautiful dark eyes set in an unblemished sweet face, new red going-out dress clinging to a slender body that revealed nearing womanhood only in the surprisingly protruding and firm bosom. What was there to say to this half-child, half-woman, who did not want to be embarrassed? "Well, if you ever want to talk—" Sam said lamely, and quit.

She had her purse and her shoes, and she said, "I'm going to bed, Dad."

She had put one foot before the other, and started to walk past him, when she seemed to stumble—one knee collapsing like a broken joint under her—and she started to go down, fighting for balance. He was beside her in a stride, catching her in time, and helping her upright. As he did so, her face brushed his, and the smell on her breath was unmistakable.

She tried to go on, murmuring thanks, but he blocked her path. He had kicked indecision out of the room. He knew what was right and he knew what was wrong.

"You've been drinking, Mary."

Beneath the quiet disapproval, Mary's poise melted away. The transformation was instantaneous. She was no longer twenty-six but sixteen—or maybe six. She tried to brazen it out for only a second, averted her eyes, and stood there, his young child, with her Oedipal guilt. "Yes," she admitted, almost indistinctly.

"But you've never—" he said. "I thought we had an understanding about that. What's got into you? How many did you have?"

"Two or three, I can't remember. I'm sorry. I had to."

"You had to? That's something new. Who twisted your arm?"

"I can't explain it, Dad, but I had to do something to be there. You can't be a squeep, spoil everything. Anyway, I figured it's better than the other thing—"

Sam felt the constriction in his bony chest. "What other thing?"

"You *know*," she said, one hand working her purse handle. "They all want you to do it. If you don't, you don't belong. Everybody does it."

"Does *it?* Does what?" he demanded relentlessly. "Are you referring to sexual intercourse?"

"Yes."

He could hardly hear her. "And everybody does it?" he persisted.

"Yes. Almost."

"Almost, you say. You mean some girls don't."

"Well, yes, but they won't be around long."

"Your friends—this Leona—does she do it?"

"It's not fair, Dad, I can't—"

"Then she does," he said. "And that was the unpleasantness with the Schaffer boy. That's what he wanted you to do out there?"

Her eyes were downcast. She said nothing. And seeing her thus, this fair and innocent part of him, he had no more stomach for playing stern judge. His heart went out to her, with pity and love, and he wanted only to care for her, protect her, banish all unpleasantness from her pure white kingdom.

He took her by the elbow. His voice was gentle. "Come, Mary, let's sit down in the kitchen and have some milk—no, better make it tea—let's have some tea and crackers." When she was six and eight and ten, and wandering awake with heavy-lidded eyes and tangled curls and rumpled pajamas, carrying a felt pony, he had often brought her to the kitchen to join him in milk and crackers, and tell her a good-night fable, and lead her back to the youth bed.

He went into the kitchen, turned on the light, set the tea kettle on the burner, and got out the crackers. She sat at the dinette table, woozily following his every move. He readied the cups with their tea bags and sugar lumps, and poured the hot water over the bags.

At last, he was seated across from her, watching from over the rim of his cup as she nibbled at a cracker and sipped her tea. They had not exchanged a word since the living room.

"Mary—" he said.

Her eyes met his, and waited.

"—you drank because you wanted to be part of the crowd, to be doing something, since you wouldn't do the other. Isn't that so?"

"I suppose," said Mary.

"But the other is still expected?"

"Yes."

"So why don't you leave that crowd, join up with some other kids who have better values?"

"Dad, these are my friends. I grew up with them. You can't go around shopping for friends every time something annoys you. I like all of them—they're the best kids—it's been fun up to now—and still would be—if not for this."

Sam hesitated a moment, and then he said, "Do your girl friends ever discuss with you what they're doing?"

"Oh, sure, all the time."

"Are they—do they feel—well, troubled or guilty? What I mean to say is, are they bothered by this activity or do they find it fun?"

"Fun? Of course not. What can be fun about a dirty thing like that—I mean, a thing like that being forced on you? I think most of the girls don't care one way or the other. They don't think it's fun and they don't think it's wrong or worry about it. They think it's just one of those boring things you put up with to keep the fellows happy."

"Why is it so important to keep the fellows happy, as you put it?

If this is a bore, unpleasant, why not say no and keep yourself happy?"

"*Pa*—you don't understand. It's one of those things you put up with to make yourself ultimately happier. I mean, then you belong to the group and you can have real fun, all the dates you want, and lots of laughs, and going driving and to movies."

"But first you pay the admission price."

"Well, if you want to put it that way. Most of the girls think it's a pretty low price for all the rest. I mean, as long as your girl friends are doing it, what can be so—?"

"Mary," he interrupted, "why didn't you do it tonight? I assume it was proposed?"

"Yes, he tried to—to talk me into it."

Sam winced. His little trundle-bundle girl in baggy pink pajamas. "But you didn't go for it. Why?"

"I—I was scared."

"Of what? Your mother and myself—?"

"Oh no. I mean, that wouldn't be the main thing. After all, I wouldn't have had to tell you." She sipped her tea absently, her shiny brow furrowed. "I can't say exactly—"

"Were you scared of becoming pregnant? Or maybe catching a venereal disease?"

"Please, *Pa*. Most of the girls don't even think of such things. Anyway, I heard the fellows use contraceptives."

Again, Sam winced. It was as if Gainsborough's Blue Boy had uttered a four-letter word. He stared with incredulity at his little Blue Girl.

Mary was deep in thought. "I guess I was scared because I'd never done such a thing. It was one of the mysteries. I mean talking and doing are two different things."

"They certainly are."

"I think all the girls my age are curious, but I don't think we want to go all the way. I mean, the idea doesn't arouse us. I kept thinking, at the party, later in the car, when I kept pulling his hands away, that it would be horrible, it would soil me, I would never be the same again."

"I'm not sure I understand, Mary."

"I—I can't explain."

"We've always been—well, fairly open-minded about sexual matters—sensible—so you can't be repelled by that part of it."

"No. It's something else."

"Could it be that the coldness of the approach—the sort of barter involved—the sort of saying that if you want to be with them and have friends and kicks, you've got to pay rent—?"

"I don't know, Dad, I really don't."

Sam nodded, took her cup and saucer, and his own, and stood up and carried them to the sink. He went back to her slowly. "What's next, Mary?"

"Next?"

"Are you going to see Neal Schaffer again?"

"Of course I am!" She came to her feet. "I like him."

"Despite his busy hands and propositions?"

"I shouldn't have told you. Somehow you make it sound even nastier. Neal's no different from the others in the gang. He's a normal American boy. His family—"

"How do you intend to handle him next time? What if he won't take no. What if the gang threatens to drop you?"

Mary bit her lower lip. "They won't, I mean not really. I'll manage. I've always managed up to now. I can find ways to stall him and the others. I think they like me well enough to—" She stopped abruptly.

"Like you enough to what?" Sam demanded. "To wait until you finally give in?"

"No! To respect my wishes. They know I'm not a complete squeep. I don't mind a kiss now and then and—well, you know, having a little fun."

"And now they know you'll drink."

"Dad, you make it sound like I'm going to become a falling-down alcoholic. I'm not. Tonight was—well, it was an exception—and I won't disappoint you—"

She had taken up her purse and shoes again, and was starting for the hallway.

"Mary, I just want to say this. Perhaps you're too old for lectures. And I accept the fact that you are an individual with a mind of your own. But you're still very young. Things that seem important to you this minute will seem far less important in a few years, when really important things come up for decisions. I can only say this and hope you are impressed. I cannot hold your hand when you go out with your friends. You're a decent, intelligent girl, and you are respected by everyone, and Mother and I are proud of you. I'd hate you to behave in a way that would disappoint us, and, in the end, take my word, disappoint you in yourself."

"You take everything too seriously, Dad." She went to him, on tiptoes kissed his cheek, and smiled up at him. "I feel much better now. You can trust me. Good night."

After she had gone to bed, Sam Karpowicz lingered in the kitchen, leaning against a cupboard, arms folded across his robe, examining the whole problem of his sixteen-year-old daughter and her fast crowd. He knew that there was no running from her present environment. If he took her to Phoenix or Miami or Memphis or Pittsburgh or Dallas or St. Paul, she would gravitate to the same friends, the same fast crowd with different faces. It was the condition of adolescent society today, not all of it, but much of it, and Sam hated it (accepting some of the blame for its existence) and hated his daughter growing up in it.

He could see the near future, and he could see it plainly. What he dreaded was the crucial summer ahead. In the next few months, the gang would still be absorbed with schoolwork and finals and intramural activities, and they would not see each other so much or have complete leisure on their hands. With summer and the school vacation, that would change. The gang would be on the loose, and Mary with it, daily, nightly. She might, as she intended, fend off the Neal Schaffers the next few months. But summer was the prime time for love. Neal would grow impatient and annoyed with being stopped at her lips, at her bosom, with having his hands removed from under Mary's skirt. He would insist upon consummation, and if refused, take his arousal and his social offerings elsewhere. Mary would be left out. The mark of the leper would be upon her. Was she strong enough to face this? Sam doubted it, he honestly doubted it. Who, after all, could withstand the threat of ostracism or deliberately embrace loneliness?

And the drinking. Another danger. Then, suddenly, Sam pushed himself from the cupboard, as it came to him why she may have drunk. At first he had thought she had done it to prove that, despite an affection for virginity, she was still a good sport. Now he saw her drinking in another light, with a different motivation. She *had* wanted to belong. And she *had* been afraid of intercourse. And so, probably at someone's suggestion—Leona? Neal?—she had drunk twice to shed her inhibitions and make capitulation possible. Tonight, she had not succeeded in overcoming her fears. But another time, not two drinks but four or five . . .

Sam felt ill and helpless. He clicked off the kitchen light. He started toward the hall, detoured to turn down the living room lamp. As he did so, he saw Maud Hayden's letter. In the darkness, he stared at it, and then he started for his bedroom.

Flinging the robe aside, he fell into bed.

"Sam—" It was Estelle whispering.

He turned his head on the pillow. "Aren't you—?"

"Sam, I heard almost all. I got up and listened." Her voice was tremulous and worried. "What are we going to do?"

"We're going to do our best," said Sam firmly. "I'm writing Maud Hayden in the morning. I'll tell her it's all of us or none of us. If she says yes, we'll have Mary out of here, on some peaceful small island where she won't be tempted."

"That's this summer, Sam. What'll we do after that?"

"After that she'll be older. I only want her older. So let's start with first things first. And the first thing is to take care of this summer. . . ."

* * *

Maud Hayden raised her eyes from the carbon copy of the letter to Dr. Walter Zegner, in San Francisco, California.

"What was that, Claire? Why am I inviting a physician on this trip? Well, now—" She hesitated, then said solemnly, "I'd like to tell you it is because Dr. Zegner specializes in geriatrics, and I've enjoyed my long correspondence with him, and the Sirens might be a valuable laboratory for his work."

She paused once more, and permitted her face to break into a smile. "I'd like to tell you all that, but this is strictly family and four walls, so I won't. I've invited a physician, my dear, because of politics, pure politics. I know Cyrus Hackfeld's mind *and* his business. He owns a great chain of cut-rate drugstores, and is a major shareholder in the pharmaceutical house that supplies those drugstores. Hackfeld is always interested in any simple medication or herb that primitive tribes use—some exotic nonsense that might be converted into a harmless stimulant or wrinkle cream or appetite killer. So whenever any scientists apply for grants, he is inclined to inquire whether a medical person is going along. I anticipated this would come up again."

"What about Dr. Rachel DeJong?" Claire wanted to know. "She's a graduate M.D. as well as an analyst, isn't she? Wouldn't she satisfy Hackfeld?"

"I thought of that, too, Claire, and then I vetoed it," said Maud. "I decided Rachel might be rusty in the M.D. department, and over-worked taking on two jobs, and in the end, Hackfeld might feel shortchanged. So that's why I took no chances with our sponsor. There's simply got to be a full-time medical person along, and if that's the way it is, then that's the way it is, and I can only hope the person is Walter Zegner."

* * *

It was twenty minutes to eight in the evening, and Walter Zegner had said that he would be by for her at eight o'clock. In the ten weeks that she had known him, and the nine weeks and six days since she had known him intimately, Harriet Bleaska had never once been kept waiting by Walter Zegner. In fact, on three occasions that she could remember—and even now the remembrance brought a smile to her lips—he had arrived fifteen minutes to a half-hour early, motivated by what he explained to be "an uncontrollable desire."

Yes, he would be on time, especially tonight when there was so much to celebrate, and she must be ready.

One last tug and she had her newly purchased dark bottle-green silk cocktail dress on straight, and now, working the zipper up her spiny back, and fumbling for the hooks and loops, she walked over to the window. From the height of her apartment on the hill, she could make out the great claws of fog, animated gray against black night and yellow lights, creeping across the city below. Soon, all of San Francisco would be obscured, and only the girders of the Golden Gate Bridge, like distant detached bars in the sky, would remain visible.

She knew that Walter detested the fog, and although he had spoken of a night on the town, she suspected that they would get no further than the restaurant at Fisherman's Wharf. After the drinks and meal, if the old pattern prevailed, they would return directly to the comfort and warmth of this one room and the wide daybed that Walter would help her prepare for them. She did not mind. It made her happy to see him—with all his outside reputation, wealth, connections, power (and now high position)—reduced to equality by her flesh, which was that of an uncomplicated sensuous animal. This talent to so disarm him of worldly prides, to diminish him to his unadorned, essential self (the best part of him, she thought), was her ace in the hole and her greatest hope.

From the window, she had gone to the dresser to find, in the cheap scuffed jewel box, some becoming combination with which to ornament herself. She tried to match several pairs of costume earrings with several costume necklaces—inexplicably, her men always gave her large art books or small liqueur glasses (she *did* have one theory that she would not accept because she believed it: that, in common, her fiancés felt jewelry would be wasted on her)—and settled, at last, on the plainest pearl earrings and necklace because they would be the least obtrusive.

Harriet Bleaska did not look in the mirror above the dresser to see if the costume jewelry enhanced her appearance. She knew very well that it did not, and had no wish to be reminded of Nature's heartlessness. If she had any self-esteem, and she had considerable, it gained support neither from her countenance nor, indeed, from any visible attraction of her body. Like one born a cripple, Harriet had learned early that her appearance automatically barred her from certain satisfactions of life.

Now, breaking her rule, her eyes did meet her reflection in the mirror, only to be sure that her make-up was still fresh. The familiar face in the glass—The Mask, she secretly had named this face, for it hid from everyone her true beauty and virtue—stared solemnly back at her. If the predicament had only been one of plainness, of being unbeautiful, or anything neutral, it would not have been so bad. This was not the predicament at all. For almost forever, meaning all her twenty-six years, Harriet had lived with the fact that she was outstandingly homely. Her features seemed to drive males away from her path like a foghorn. Even the best of her features, which was her hair, would have been the worst feature on any pretty woman. Harriet's hair was shoulder-length and stringy, and the color of a cinnamon mouse. It was hopelessly straight. In an effort to achieve some style, she wore the front in stiff bangs. From the hair down, everything worsened. Her eyes were too small and too close together. Her nose was pugged to an extremity beyond cuteness. Her mouth was a vast gash, almost devoid of upper lip and overabundant of lower. Her chin was long and sharp. She imagined that people said she had the physiognomy of a Belgian mare.

The rest of her person offered no alleviating compensations. Her neck had the grace of a plumbing fixture; her shoulders seemed fitted with football pads; her breasts did not fill size "A" cups; her hips and ankles were as thick as those of a prize Percheron, or so they seemed to her. In short, as Harriet had once thought, when God had made women, he had used the scraps and bits that didn't fit for the creation of Harriet Bleaska.

With a shrug of resignation—she was too sensible and practical ever to be bitter—Harriet turned from the dresser, found a filtered cigarette, lighted it with the silver-plated lighter in the shape of a galleon (which Walter had given her), and returned the lighter to its place on the large and glossy art book (which Walter had given her). There were still twelve empty minutes, and no way to fill them. She determined to fill them by counting her blessings.

Smoking steadily, as she paced the room, she decided that she had not done too badly for an ugly duckling. Certainly, based on their personal research, a handful of handsome gentlemen in the land would testify, in unison, that no female on earth was more beautiful than Harriet Bleaska—in bed.

Thank God for this blessing, she thought, and weep for all her sisters who were emotionally homely, deformed and wanting below the waist.

Still, her pleasure in this major superiority of hers was clouded by the harsh facts of life. In the marketplace of her time, men bought beautiful façades. What lay behind the façades was less important, at least at the outset. A whole age of males was oriented by poetry, romantic fiction, radio, television, motion pictures, billboards, theater, and magazine and newspaper advertising, into believing that if a girl's face was lovely, her bust prodigious, her figure otherwise well proportioned, her manner in some way provocative (lips parted, voice husky, walk undulating), she would automatically make the best bed partner and life partner in the world. When a girl had this exterior, she had her choice of buyers—the handsome, the aristocratic, the wealthy, the renowned. The second-best exteriors attracted lesser buyers, and so it went on downward, spiraling downward, toward the lonely place where you reached Harriet Bleaska.

The idiocy of it, while not embittering, made her sometimes

want to scream sense at the stupid males. Couldn't they see, realize, understand, that beauty is only skin-deep? Couldn't they see that too often, behind the beautiful façades, lay selfishness, coldness, psychoses? Couldn't they see that other qualities gave better guarantees of marital happiness in the living room, kitchen, and bedroom? No, they could not see, they were raised not to see, and that was Harriet's Cross.

Men equated The Mask—her unattractiveness—with an unattractive marriage and unattractive sex life. Rarely, they would give her a chance to prove that she was more; and when, infrequently, they did, it was still not enough. For, in this society, marrying beauty, even when it was known to be wrong, was right because it was part of the public success symbol. Conversely, marrying ugliness, even when it was known to be right, was wrong because it was part of the failure symbol. Men were fools, and life was foolish, and yet there had been times when both held more promise.

She had been born in Dayton, Ohio, of decent, simple, outgoing, loving Lithuanian parents of the laboring lower middle class. She had not known that she was different in her early years, because she had received such lavish attention and praise from her parents and their extensive family. She grew to puberty feeling important and special and wanted.

Not until her father, employed in a printing firm, followed a promotion to Cleveland, and she entered Cleveland Heights High School there, did she have her first inkling of what stood between her and the normal social life. It was The Mask. Her homeliness had reached its maturity. She was a cactus among camellias. Her friends were many, but mainly of her own sex. Girls liked her because of an unconscious motive. She was a perfect foil to set off, contrastingly, their own endowments. And, the first semester, boys liked her, in the corridors, in intramural activities, as they might like another boy. To exploit and retain even this limited acceptance from them, she became, for several ensuing semesters, more tomboyish.

With the advent of her upper junior year at Cleveland Heights, the tomboyish act palled on her. The boys were older now, and they did not like other boys. They wanted girls. Dismayed, Harriet scrambled back to maidenhood. Since she could not give the boys what the other girls could, she decided to give them more. Her female friends were as conservative as their parents had been, in all matters, and the Cleveland boys of the crowd were made to understand boundaries very early. Kissing was agreeable, even French kissing. Petting could be engaged in excessively, but only above the waist. Dancing could be body to body, with considerable stimulation induced by contact and movement, but that was the end of it. Harriet, because of her handicap and the license of her up-bringing, because of her need and her outgoing spirit, but mostly because of her handicap—creating the necessity to go twice as far to get half as much—was the first to break the unwritten rule.

One late afternoon, after school hours, in the dark back row of the balcony of the empty auditorium, Harriet permitted a pimply, clever boy who had recently transferred from University Heights to reach under her skirt. When she offered no resistance, only a closed-eyed murmur of anticipation, he was almost too over-whelmed to continue. But continue he did, and when her convul-sive response to his manual love excited him beyond restraint, she quite naturally repaid him in kind. The exchange had been brief, hot, mindless, and it served Harriet well. It gave her status as a girl, at last.

In her senior year in high school, Harriet progressed to the ulti-mate form of mutual excitation. The boys considered her a sport; the girls considered her cheap. Harriet was satisfied by the accept-ance from those she regarded as her better halves. Also, in her occa-sional acrobatics—she did not go all the way all the time; she had her standards—she found a release for her warm, embracing, loving nature. She found it a deep source of satisfaction to please. In those embryonic grapplings, inexperienced on both sides, she was never called upon to please in depth. Her mere capitulation was the high point. It was enough. Her partners could not dream of her hidden dimension. All in all, Harriet's last year and a half in high school was a period still cherished in her memory. Only one enigma had puzzled her at the time. Despite her nocturnal popularity, her bal-cony and back-seat and in-the-bushes popularity, she sat home alone the nights of the Junior Prom and the Senior Graduation Dance. On the eve of each public occasion, her vast following of energetic males had abandoned her completely.

The mass abandonment became clear only two years later, in New York, when Harriet was in training at Bellevue Hospital to become a registered nurse. The decision to become a nurse had been as natural as a choice between living or dying. She wanted an outlet for her warm, sympathetic nature, a respectable profession where the offer of kindness was welcomed and applauded, a way of life where The Mask would no longer hide her real inner beauty.

While most of her five hundred fellow students in the nurses' residence at Bellevue groaned and grumbled under the relentless pressures of class work, Harriet flourished with the joy of it. She was proud of her striped blue and white uniform, and black stockings and shoes, and pleased that she was actually being paid 240 dollars a year to learn a profession. She quickly felt possessive about the dining room overlooking the East River, and the snack kitchen which she often frequented, and the bowling alley which she attended with other female trainees. She looked forward to the traditional capping ceremony, with its ritual of candle-lighting, that would climax her first year. And she envied the seniors, who were allowed to wear white stockings and shoes, and who had stepped up from the grind of textbooks to instruction in surgery and the wards.

The only sad times were the weekends, when the other trainees dated, and Harriet had not only her private room but the whole dormitory almost to herself. Her solitude ended midway in her first year. A husky senior student, a future male nurse, who was myopic and made passes at any skirt that moved (it was said), found her alone in a vacant classroom. He absently kissed the back of her neck, and then found her in his arms responding fervently. So passionate was her response, that the male nurse, for whom her face was little more than a blur, was inspired to invite her to a friend's nearby walk-up apartment to learn if she was merely one more tease. He learned, even before the lights were turned down, that she was not. Soon, he learned more. In the evening and night and dawn hours that followed, he was transported to a new and hitherto unknown dimension in lust. He did not know if Harriet was the repository of all history's love techniques. He knew only that never, in his numerous and erratic seductions, had he found a partner who mated with such unreserved giving. His instinct, after the first night, was to broadcast the news of his incredible find to all of Bellevue and the wide world. But, difficult as it was, he held his tongue. He wanted this prodigy to himself. The affair, rarely vertical, lasted four months. Toward the end, Harriet began to believe that she had found her life's mate. As his graduation approached, she spoke to him of "their future." Thereafter, he called upon her less and less often, and after graduation he disappeared altogether.

The legacy that the male nurse left her was twofold: first, before departure, he spread the lurid story of his virility and her remarkable skill to half the male population of Bellevue; second, he told a friend, who told a friend, who repeated it to her in a moment of pique after she had pushed his hands away, that "she's a great kid, the most sensational piece alive on earth, she starts where all other dames stop, but what the hell, what the hell, how can you marry and drag around a girl who you'd have to show with a sack over her head unless maybe you only took her out on Halloween."

Realistic enough to accept his appraisal, Harriet was not shattered, but she was hurt. Thereafter, almost all of the male nurses, interns, male clerks, even several faculty members and physicians competed for Harriet's companionship. She was suspicious of all, and withdrawn, and only five more times in her three years at Bellevue did she make believe that her suitors wanted her for her essential self and accept them wholly—hoping, hoping, as she submitted to them. Except for the suitor struck down fatally in a car accident (she would never know if he might have proposed), the rest behaved as one. They would offer Harriet sweet words and copulation, and she would enjoy the pleasure of their bodies and their compliments. They would escort her to dark and crowded places, Radio City and Madison Square Garden, and they would take her to out-of-the way restaurants and dungeon nightclubs, but they would never escort her to dress affairs, house parties, relative gatherings, important dinners. And when Harriet challenged them, so tentatively, so nicely, they evaporated into thin air. My Judge Craters, she called them, to herself, wryly and unsurprised.

When Harriet graduated from Bellevue as a registered nurse, she took away with her besides her round, ruffled, starched Van Rensselaer cap, a devotion to her new career, an unfailing good nature, and a practical but resigned knowledge of the attitude men would always have toward her (until, poor bruised dream, the one in a million came along).

She obtained her first employment in a Nashville infirmary, her next at better money in a Seattle clinic, and finally, six months before, she had been hired by this huge San Francisco hospital. In Nashville and Seattle she had dwelt in a manless world. The Mask terrified all, and her reputation had not preceded her. In San Francisco, almost immediately, her social life had taken a turn for the better.

She had been late at night on a complex emergency cardiac case, and when she left surgery, exhausted, the young anesthetist, also exhausted, left beside her. After they had washed and dressed, he had suggested coffee. Both needed it, but, at the late hour, no small cafés were open. They were near her apartment, and she invited the anesthetist to her room for the coffee. As they drank it, and relaxed, she heard out the gawky, introverted young man's life— parents lost early, horrible relative guardians, scratching years of working through schools, an immature marriage that produced a mentally defective child and a wife who ran off with her employer. San Francisco was a new beginning for him, as it was for her, and her heart went out to the shy young man. She would not let him go home so tired, so late, and there was but one bed, the day cot, and they shared it.

The experience of that evening revealed to him a world he had not known existed. After two more such experiences, he realized that he was not for Harriet and she was not for him. He was one of those who mistrusted good fortune, and he worried that he did not deserve such carnal delights. Furthermore, her ability gave him not confidence but a sense of inadequacy, and he brooded secretly over it. Nevertheless, he might have gone on—the weekly treat was irresistible and almost overwhelmed introspection—had not he seen an opportunity to use Harriet to further his security, which was after all, the important thing.

As a newcomer to the hospital, the anesthetist needed physicians who wanted him, and would hire him for their most profitable patients. He had met Dr. Walter Zegner, but so far had not been recommended by him. If Zegner would begin to speak of him, he reasoned that his future at the hospital was made. What had brought Zegner to his mind was not only Zegner's reputation as a physician, but also his reputation as a ladies' man. Thus, the young man bided his time, and when the moment came, he casually pointed out Harriet going by in her crisp white uniform, and told what he was able to articulate of her talents. During the recital, Zegner's eyes had followed Harriet's homely person with a doubtful frown and he had not reacted otherwise to the provocateur's tale.

One week later, the anesthetist got the first in a series of well-paying cases, the result of Dr. Zegner's recommendation. It was then that he knew he had scored, and Zegner had scored. The anesthetist did not bother to visit Harriet again.

Harriet had learned much of this from Walter Zegner himself, one night late, as both of them lay depleted on her living room bed. Somehow, she had not minded at all. It was fair trade for all parties, and now she was on to her best hope yet.

During an afternoon, ten weeks before, Harriet had been having coffee and toasted muffins in the staff's cafeteria of the hospital. The stools on either side of her were vacant. Suddenly, one was filled, and the worshipful figure who occupied it was that of Dr. Zegner. Conversation came easily. He was interested, even charming. And he was childishly pleased when, in discussing his research in geriatrics, she was sufficiently well read in the subject to pose intelligent questions. He had to rush off, he said, but he was eager to continue their conversation. When was she free? Was she free that night? Almost tongue-tied, she said that she was. He agreed to wait for her in the physicians' parking lot.

When she appeared, trembling with excitement, he helped her into his Cadillac. He drove her to dinner at a Bohemian restaurant outside the city. They drank, ate lightly, talked and talked, and then drank more. When he took her to her apartment, she was too embarrassed by its shabbiness to invite him up. He invited himself, pleading the need of a nightcap. Once in her room, and both of them drinking, his conversation became less academic, more personal, more teasingly sex-centered. When at last he moved to kiss her good night, she felt that she was being kissed by Dr. Martin Arrowsmith or Dr. Philip Carey, the god images of her fantasies, and she melted into him, unable to release him. He did not want to go, it turned out, and he remained the night with her, on the unmade day bed. In all her unions with men, she had never abandoned herself so entirely, and from his choked utterances and indistinct, extravagant whisperings, she knew that he had never before in his life been so totally satisfied.

When he left at dawn, she guessed that he would be back, and she was not wrong. Three and four and five times a week he called for her, and they went to their obscure places, drinking, eating, dancing, and always returning to her room to revel in each other for hours. She was thrilled and she was proud. At the hospital, she wanted to shout her conquest to every nurse and every physician, and to every patient, too. But she kept her wonderful secret to herself. His standing must not be threatened. What agitated her the most was to overhear the nurses and interns include, when gossiping about the doctors, tales of Walter's peccadillos with society women and heiresses and all the high and the mighty of Nob Hill. Always, listening, she wanted to cry out: you fools, those idiotic false rumors, do you know where he is all those nights? With me! Yes, with me, unclothed with me, caressing me, loving me as I love him, yes me, Harriet Bleaska.

All the while, remembering old painful burns, she refused to entertain the one-in-a-million hope. That is, she had refused to entertain it until yesterday noon. Then, for the first time, she felt that her hold on Walter had gone beyond the possibility of betrayal. For the first time, a man had peered behind The Mask and understood her beauty whole.

What had occurred yesterday noon had followed, by three hours, the stunning announcement that Dr. Walter Zegner had been appointed the head of the hospital medical staff. Her head spun, as she listened to the buzzing talk. The Fleischer family influence, the old dowager, the youngest daughter, and so on and on. But the fact was a fact. Walter was an executive of the hospital and, overnight, officially proclaimed one of the most important physicians in the West. She would not allow herself to think of what this meant to their relationship. This was a test, and she waited.

At noon, she had her answer. He had arrived, was in the corridor, surrounded, accepting congratulations. She passed, pretending an errand, and she heard his voice. "Nurse—Miss Bleaska—aren't you going to congratulate me? I'm your new boss." Her heart leaped. Solemnly, before the others, she took his hand, and pumped it, the words caught in her throat. Then, he had her arm. "Now to business—I want to ask you about the patient in room—" He had guided her away from the others, and then had smiled and whispered, "Do we still have the date for tomorrow night?" She had nodded dumbly. He had said, "Good, I want to celebrate. We'll eat, and go on the town, and—well, see you later—here comes Dr. Delgado."

That was yesterday noon, her finest hour, and here it was tonight at three minutes to eight, and in one hundred and eighty seconds she would be in Walter's arms. The thought, the possibilities of the future, made her giddy.

She realized, with a start, that she was no longer pacing and smoking, but seated on the arm of her one big chair, seated uncomfortably so that the small of her back was stiff. She stood up, stretched, patted her cocktail dress here and there, and then decided to make two double Scotches on the rocks, one to steady herself and one to have ready for Walter (to show what a good wife she would make, what a wonderful, wonderful wife).

She took down two old-fashioned glasses, freed several ice cubes from the tray in her tiny refrigerator, then poured the Scotch slowly, generously over the ice in the glasses. After placing Walter's drink on the end table beside the big chair, she stood drinking and enjoying her own whiskey.

At one minute to eight the rapping came on the door, and she went gayly to it to admit Walter.

When she flung open the door, she was startled to find that the caller was not Walter at all. The male figure in the doorway, Latin, medium height, wiry, she recognized as that of Dr. Herb Delgado, an internist friend of Walter's who often substituted for him when he went off night calls. Harriet's first reaction, after bewilderment, was distaste. The nurses at the hospital did not like Dr. Delgado. He was disdainful of them, disrespectful, as if they were members of a lower caste.

"Good evening, Miss Bleaska," he was saying, as easily as if he had been expected. "Are you surprised?"

"I—I thought it was Wal——Dr. Zegner——"

"Yes, I know. But as they used to say at the doors of speakeasies —Walter sent me."

"He sent you?"

"That's right. May I come in a moment?" He did not wait for her invitation, but strode past her, into the room, unbuttoning his topcoat.

She closed the door, puzzled. "Where is he? He was supposed to be here at——"

"He no can do," said Delgado lightly. " 'Unavoidably detained' is the expression." He smiled, and added, "He got tied up at the last minute, and wanted me to come over and tell you——"

"He could have telephoned."

"—and sort of stand in for him, for the evening."

"Oh." Harriet was still confused, but somehow felt that this was thoughtful of Walter. "Will he meet us somewhere later?"

"I'm afraid not, Harriet." She wondered how Miss Bleaska had become Harriet and when Harriet would become Nurse. Dr. Delgado pursed his lips, and went on. "The Fleischers decided to throw an impromptu celebration—last-minute sort of thing—and Walter had to go—"

"Had to go?"

"They're his sponsors."

"Yes. I heard."

"Of course you have. So you understand." He noticed the drink on the end table. "Is that for me?"

"It's for Walter."

"Well, I'm his proxy." He lifted the drink, held it toward her. "Cheers."

He swallowed the whiskey, but she did not bring her drink to her lips. "I don't think I'd better go out tonight," she said.

"Of course you've got to go out. Doctor's orders."

"It's kind of Walter, and of you, but I prefer not. When Walter's free he'll call me himself."

Dr. Delgado studied her seriously. "Look, baby, I wouldn't exactly count on that any more. I'm leveling with you, as a member of the club. I wouldn't count on that."

For the first time, what had been the faintest apprehension took the form of inner pain. She felt the nameless fear clutch her stomach, and she winced. "I'm not counting on anything," she said weakly. "I know he's busy, and has new obligations. I also know how he feels about us. Yesterday noon—"

"Yesterday noon was the Dark Ages," said Delgado almost brutally. "Today's another era in his life. He's moved ahead, maybe even ahead of me, too. Anyway, his situation is different. He can't play around any more."

"Play around?" she echoed, wildly offended inside. "What kind of language is that? What do you mean by that?"

"Aw, cut it out," said Delgado, impatiently. She observed that he had at last made the transition from Harriet to Baby to Nurse. He had not even the pity of a bedside manner. "Look," he was saying, "he's told me all about you."

"What does that mean?" She tried to control her voice.

"It means I'm his close friend and he tells me everything."

"I don't like the implication in your voice. You make it sound like something—something dirty's been—"

"Baby, you said that, I didn't. I meant no such thing. Walter is fond of you, and to get me out on a night like this, he had to tell me why. On the contrary, I'm quite impressed by you. Anyway, I know Walter's been seeing a good deal of you. That's all I was saying when I said he can't play around any more. Tonight, he's being welcomed at the Fleischers, in their home, not as a doctor but as a social equal. Also, I happen to know, one of their daughters has planted a flag on him, or intends to, and she's damn pretty."

Harriet felt the unintentional stab of his words, and then she felt something else. The Mask, recently discarded, had slipped into place.

"Did—did he send you to say all this?" she found herself asking.

"He told me to play it by ear. The language is mine. The sentiments are his own."

"I—I can't believe it," she said. "He—only yesterday, he—" Her voice broke, and she could not continue.

Dr. Delgado was beside her instantly, an arm paternally about her, comforting her. "Look, baby, I'm sorry, I really am. It didn't occur to me you'd—what I mean is—I can't imagine what you had in mind. Men like Walter—"

"Men like men," she said almost to herself.

"You know, baby, if you'll put on your thinking cap, you'll remember a basic little test they used to run off in Psychology One. They'd take a male rat and starve him two ways—keep him from food—and keep him from sex. Then they'd let him loose in a box with food on one end and a female on the other. The question was —would he go for food, which is self-preservation, or would he go for sex and love. You know the answer. Self-preservation wins every time."

"What are you saying?" She had only half heard him.

"I'm saying it's won again."

"Goddammit, no—no—" She felt faint and groped for the arm of the chair.

Dr. Delgado kept her from collapsing. "Hey now, hey, don't take it so big. It's not the end of the world." He helped ease her into the chair, and handed her what was left of his drink. "Finish this. You look like you need it. I'll make a fresh one for myself."

She accepted the glass. Delgado removed his topcoat, and disappeared behind her. She heard him preparing his drink, and she heard, in the house of her mind, a distant wail. It had come from Mary Shelley, as she sat upstairs in Casa Magni, staring up at Trelawny, who had just returned from the beach near Viareggio where he had identified the body. Trelawny had stood in the eloquent silence of grief and bad tidings, and Mary Shelley had cried out, "Is there no hope?" and known there was none.

Harriet had read that in some old biography, and had never thought of it or Mary Shelley in all the years since, until now.

"Do you feel better?" It was Dr. Delgado standing over her.

She took one gulp of the whiskey and put the glass down. She had digested everything, and recognized her fate. "At least," she said, "he could have told me himself." All that was left to her were petty complaints.

"He couldn't. You know how sensitive he is. He hates scenes. Besides, he couldn't bear hurting you."

"He doesn't think this will hurt me?"

"Well, coming from an outsider—"

"Yes, I know."

He settled on the arm of the chair, his hand patting her hair.

"It's not just that I'm a nurse," she said straight ahead, to no one in particular, "it's that I am the way I am. Important doctors marry nurses. Lots of them do. But they don't marry ones who aren't pretty or rich or at least something special. I won't blame Walter. I'm just unlucky in what men put most value upon. I'm not a man's exterior image of a wife. For a man, a wife represents his good taste, his prestige and station, his judgment, his ego—she is his ambassador making introductions at the cocktail party, or presiding over his dinner table, or on his arm at someone's house, and I'm no good for anything except bed."

"Baby, don't be silly. Walter had only praise for you."

"For me in bed, nothing else. But he kept seeing me in spite of me. The bed part of me blinded him for—for a while."

Dr. Delgado gripped her shoulder cheerfully. "I won't deny he spoke of that, too. If I didn't know him, I'd think him a liar. I don't see how a woman can have what he says you have."

She hardly heard him. She gazed mournfully ahead.

He jostled her slightly. "Look, baby, be sensible. It's done and over. The King is dead, long live the King. Walter's gone, and old Herb is here. Why not take advantage of the situation? You look the sensible type. Why not laugh your troubles away? Lots of ladies think I'm mighty eligible. Well, they can't have me, but you can."

She had become attentive, and was looking up at him with bewilderment.

"Let's go to dinner just like you'd planned all along," Delgado was saying. "Then we can come back here and live it up, and—"

"Come here and do what?"

He stopped. "Live it up, I said."

"You mean you want to sleep with me?"

"Is that a crime?"

"You want to sleep with me tonight?"

"And every night. Don't look so insulted. After all, you're not exactly—"

"Get out."

He was taken aback. "What?"

Harriet stood up. "Get out, right now."

Dr. Delgado came slowly off the arm of the chair. "You're not— Are you serious?"

"You heard me twice."

"Young lady, get off your high horse. Who are you anyway? I'm trying to give you a break. You've had good press notices, so I'm here. You've got a great act, it says, but that's all you've got. Retire it and you'll die for lack of company."

"For the third and last time, beat it, or I'll have the landlord throw you out."

Dr. Delgado's face took on a disdainful smile. With insolent deliberation, he finished his drink, picked up his topcoat, and walked to the door. He held the knob. "Your funeral," he said.

He had opened the door, when suddenly he turned again. "I almost forgot," he said. He reached inside his suit coat and withdrew a long manila envelope. "Walter said to be sure to give you this. It's a letter he wants you to read."

He held it out, but she did not take it. Annoyed, he tossed it on the maple lamp table.

"See you at the hospital, Nurse," he said, and was gone.

Harriet remained immobilized in the center of the room, looking fixedly at Walter's letter. She was not interested in what he had to say to her now. It was like kissing someone after they were dead, like that Hemingway scene in Lausanne when what's-his-name kissed Catherine Barkley, the nurse, after she was dead, cold and dead.

After a minute or two, Harriet went back to the chipped sideboard near the kitchenette and poured herself a fresh Scotch. With glass in hand, she kicked off her pumps and wandered aimlessly about the room, sipping whiskey all the while. At her wardrobe, she halted, put aside the glass, and undressed down to her nylon panties. She lifted her terry-cloth robe off the hook and drew it on. For a moment she was undecided about making herself some dinner, a sandwich anyway, and then she thought she would drink a little longer.

She began to meander around the room once more, pausing finally at the window. It pleased her that the fog below had thickened. At least she would not have to go out in that damp sinus weather. Turning from the window, she became aware of the manila envelope lying on the maple table. Abruptly, she finished her whiskey, and crossed to the envelope and ripped it open. As she did so, she speculated on whether he had dared to send her money. If that was it, she would slap him the next time she saw him. Then she realized this scene could not happen because she would not see him, for now it would be impossible to continue at the hospital.

What she found inside the envelope was a long letter, on the stationery of Raynor College, addressed to "Dear Walter" and signed "Maud." Attached to this letter was a small white piece of memorandum paper with the imprint across the top, "From the desk of Walter Zegner, M.D." On this a feminine hand had scrawled, "Dear Miss Bleaska. The doctor has asked me to forward this enclosure to you. He thinks it might interest you very much. He is writing to Dr. Hayden on your behalf." The note was signed, "Miss Snyder for Dr. Zegner."

Mystified, Harriet carried both the letter and her empty glass to the big chair, and there she sat down, and for the next fifteen minutes she allowed herself to be transported to the unreal world of The Three Sirens.

When she was done, she understood Walter's generosity. He wanted her out of town. For one rebellious second, she was tempted not to leave, but rather to stay on at the hospital and be there as his guilty conscience. Then she knew that even if that would make him unhappy, it would not make her happier.

She glanced at Maud Hayden's letter again, and all at once she wanted to leave San Francisco forever. The Three Sirens was a perfect transition to such a change. It would divorce her from the present, now her past, forever. She wanted a new start, an absolutely new start.

Twenty minutes later, after one more drink, and with a melted cheese sandwich on a plate and a cup of coffee at her elbow, she uncapped her blue ball-point pen, brought her stationery before her, and wrote, "Dear Dr. Hayden . . ."

* * *

Maud Hayden had finished reading the carbon of the letter to Dr. Orville Pence, in Denver, Colorado.

"Well," said Maud, "this should make Marc happy."

"I'll never know what Marc sees in him," said Claire.

"Oh—you've met Pence. I quite forgot."

"Last year when we went through Denver," said Claire.

"Of course, of course. I suppose he's one of those people you have to get to know well—"

Claire would not agree. "Maybe," she said. Then she added, "Marc's more reasonable about people than I am. I react out of immediate instinct. I make up my mind about someone right away, and I'm not able to change. Dr. Pence revolted me the way some of those squishy, bloodless sea creatures do."

Maud was amused. "How fanciful, Claire—"

"I mean it. He has the fussy quality of a spinster, someone who won't let you smoke in the parlor. And his talk. Sex, sex, sex, and when he's through you think it is some epidemic that is gradually being quarantined for study. He takes all the idea of pleasure out of it."

"I've never concerned myself with his attitudes toward it," said Maud, gently, "but you know, it *is* his subject, his entire career. The Social Science Research Council and the National Science Foundation don't support him without good reason. The University of Denver wouldn't have him on its faculty if he wasn't highly regarded. Believe me, his studies of comparative sexual behavior have given him a solid reputation."

"I just have the feeling he's setting sex back a century."

Maud laughed. Then, sobering, she said, "No, really, Claire, don't be prejudiced after only one meeting . . . Anyway, it was Marc who thought Orville Pence might be interested in the Sirens

—it's right up his alley—and his findings could be valuable for my paper."

"I still can't get over that one dreary night. You should have met his mother."

"Claire, we're not inviting her."

"You're inviting him," said Claire. "It's exactly the same thing."

* * *

The spacious, drafty classroom of the University of Denver was chilly this hour of the morning, and as Orville Pence fingered his notes on the lectern, he realized that the cold reminded him of high places in his childhood. He remembered being led up the steps of the state capitol, and being shown the fourteenth step, which bore a plaque reading, "One Mile Above Sea Level"; he remembered the cog railway that took him, with his mother, to the summit of Pike's Peak; he remembered going, with his mother and the Cub Scouts, up Lookout Mountain to Buffalo Bill's grave. He remembered the numbing cold of it and his mother's favorite edict on such occasions—"It is good to be high, Orville, so people must always look up to you"—and now, this morning, it seemed that he had always been so high up that he had never come down to earth.

Yet, the chill of the classroom was not what disturbed him most this morning. What disturbed him most was the girl on the aisle, in the front row of seats, who had the disconcerting habit of constantly crossing her long legs, first the right leg over the left, then the shift and the uncrossing, and then the left leg over the right.

Orville Pence tried to keep his attention away from her legs as he lectured, but it was a feat of restraint he found impossible. He tried to rationalize the distraction. The act of leg-crossing, by the human female, was universal and natural. In itself, it was not wrong. The only part of it that was wrong was the employment of a faulty (i.e., morally loose or deliberately provocative) technique. If a young lady crossed her legs swiftly, tightly, while shielding the movement by holding down the hem of her skirt, it was decent. If she performed otherwise, it was suspect. He had observed, within the confines of his field, that when certain women crossed their legs, they automatically lifted their skirts or dresses rather high to do so. If, as was the case with the young female student before him, the dress was short, the legs long, the movements slow, an observer could often plainly glimpse the flesh of the inner thigh which began where the sheath of nylon hosiery left off. What kind of person could behave in so unseemly a manner? His eyes moved up the girl, and down again. She was a tall, shapely girl with disheveled rust hair, a soft face of innocence, a lemon-colored cashmere sweater, and a plaid wool skirt that would not fall below her knees when she rose.

Suddenly, she shifted in the wooden chair, and there was the skirt up and the legs apart and the flash of inner flesh exposed and then blocked out by the crossing. She was deliberately trying to unsettle him, Orville decided. It was a game too many women played. He was above it, in a high cold place, and he would show her and all of them. He lifted his sight to encompass the other young students in the room. Almost forty of them sat there, pens and pencils poised over notebooks, waiting for him to go on.

He cleared his throat, picked up the glass on the lectern, brought it to his lips, and sucked some water slowly. Next, to recover complete composure, he took out his handkerchief and mopped his brow, and this gave him a twinge, for there was so much brow. His hairline had receded considerably in recent years. One-third of his pinkish pate was prematurely bald. Stuffing the handkerchief back into his pocket, he peered over the shell-rimmed spectacles slipped low on his ferret nose, inspected his class, then, hunched over his notes, his eyes went to the lemon-sweatered, long-legged young girl again.

She could be no more than nineteen, he judged, and he was an old bachelor of thirty-four, and if he had married at fifteen she could be his oldest child. The distraction was ridiculous and time-consuming. His mind rode a coaster to Beverly Moore, of Boulder, with regret, and to his mother, Crystal, with guilt, and to his sister, Dora, with resentment, and to Marc Hayden and Maud Hayden and Professor Easterday and Chief Paoti, with interest, and finally —she had just uncrossed her legs, lifted her skirt, crossed them —to this, with regret.

The class was becoming restless, he realized, and this rarely happened. Usually they were intent and hung on his every word, since his subject recently had been the evolution of sexual morality in the last three hundred years. Then he grasped the fact that they were restless only because he had become bemused, as sometimes he did, and had forgotten to resume his lecture. He coughed into his fist, and began to speak.

"Let me summarize our last few minutes," he said, "before we continue our discussion of the beginnings of the family unit."

As he recapitulated the problems of monogamous marriage from primeval times to ancient Greece, Orville was pleased to observe that he again had their attention. Even the young girl in the lemon sweater was too occupied taking notes to cross her legs. With confidence he continued, but even as he did, his active mind disengaged itself from his vocal communication and careened upon its own way. This ability to speak on one subject, and think about another, was not uniquely Orville's but was one at which he was uniquely expert. This morning it was easier because the lecture he was delivering was part of the same series he had delivered the summer before, at the University of Colorado, in Boulder, where he had first met Miss Beverly Moore.

Even now, as he spoke, he could distinctly picture Beverly Moore in his mind. She was a young lady in her middle twenties, with shingled dark hair, a patrician face, and a graceful figure. He had not seen her in a month, but she was as clear in his mind as if she were before him this moment—indeed, right before him, in the front row, seated on the aisle, with those fantastically long legs.

When he had gone to Boulder to deliver those summer lectures, Beverly, an executive secretary in the Administration Building, had been assigned to guide him and look after his academic needs. Although he had painstakingly, through the years, constructed a fortress of ambition and activity around himself, as a protection against the assaults of aggressive and dangerous young women, somehow he had always managed to leave one bridge down over the moat. Occasionally, he had invited a young lady to cross the bridge. But whenever she had become an unwanted distraction, he saw to it that she was ousted from his fortress. In Boulder, he had encouraged—or permitted, for he was no longer sure which it had been—Beverly to cross this bridge. He had been impressed, from the start, by her seriousness, intellectuality, common sense. Above all, she had seemed to understand him and the importance of his work.

Their relationship, entirely cerebral, had ripened through the summer, so that finally he had not wanted to face the summer's end. By the time he had returned to Denver, he realized that Beverly had become as much, or almost as much, a part of him, a habit of his, as his mother, Crystal, or his sister, Dora. When he had missed her, he found himself doing what he had never done before—disrupting his routine to continue seeing her. Every week he had traveled the thirty miles northwest, into the Rocky Mountains to Boulder, commuting to Beverly. More and more, he had begun to entertain thoughts of what had once seemed impossible—thoughts of marriage to a young lady who would not change his life or upset his program or disturb his work, but rather improve his daily existence.

Yet, insensibly, three months ago he had begun to see less and less of her, and one month ago he had ceased seeing her altogether. She had telephoned, and accepted his excuse of an overload of work, and once more, she had called, and heard out his circumlocutions with less cordiality, and since that time, she had not called again.

Reviving all of this now, he tried to remember what had happened between them. The fact was, nothing had happened between them. They had not quarreled and their affection for one another had not lessened. But then, Orville did remember one thing. It had occurred to him a week ago, before falling asleep, and again the night before, but on both occasions he had shoved it aside as something he did not wish to believe. The thought was back, and this time, with some courage, he examined it.

Vaguely, until now, he believed he had decided to see less of Beverly, not become further involved emotionally, because of a defect in her personality. The defect was her superiority as a human being. She was uncomplicated, entirely integrated, self-assured, educated, attractive to men. If he married her, she would gain the ascendency. At present, she needed him, because she was a single woman who wanted to achieve social conformity through a good marriage. Thus, at present, he was the superior person. Once married to him, the close-up view, the intimacy, might bare his weaknesses—everyone had weaknesses. At the same time, her own qualities of independence, made stronger by the confidence that marriage gave a woman and reinforced by the inevitable knowledge of his shortcomings, would develop and make him uneasy and disrupt his life. She would be superior; he would be inferior. In marriage, their positions would change to his disadvantage. In short, she was not right for him. He wanted a mate who was less than he was, and would remain so, forever looking up to him, depending upon him, pinching herself for her luck in having him. Beverly was not such a girl. So, discreetly, he had ousted her and pulled up the last bridge to his fortress.

This, he had believed, was the reason for the rupture in their relationship. Now he believed something else, even though the new perception did not entirely invalidate his earlier feeling about her. What he saw now was that he had begun withdrawing from Beverly a week after he had introduced her to his mother, sister, and brother-in-law, three months ago.

He had wanted to make up his mind, and so he had put her to the final test, the obstacle course, as he liked to think of it. Only twice before in his life had he invited young ladies to the test. Beverly had responded with enthusiasm. She had come down from Boulder on the train, and he had been waiting at the Union Station, proud of her bearing and grooming. He had driven her to his mother's apartment, where Dora and her husband, Vernon Reid, in from Colorado Springs, and his mother, croaking from an arthritic attack and wheezing from her hay fever, had been heroically in attendance. Despite the pressure of the occasion, Beverly had acquitted herself with honors. She had been dignified yet friendly. Perhaps nervousness had made her talk more than usual, but her talk was interesting. The evening had gone smoothly. Later, driving Beverly back to Boulder, Orville felt a greater warmth and possessiveness for her than he had ever felt before.

The initial response of his relatives at breakfast the next morning had been favorable, as best he could judge. Actually, they had not discussed her much, simply referring to her as "a nice pleasant child" and "rather intelligent." However, in the week that followed —Orville could see this now as he had not seen it before—they had begun to chip away at Beverly. His mother had discussed not Beverly in particular, but "certain intellectual-type girls" who "lead a man around by the nose." Dora had referred to Beverly by name as someone "who has a mind of her own, you bet," the last somewhat darkly. Vernon had spoken of her irreverently as "a looker" and wagered that she'd "been around," and had been reminded by her of a tall coed he had known who had satisfied an entire fraternity. "I mean, don't get me wrong, Orville, I'm not inferring anything, only the physical resemblance reminded me of Lydia."

Unaccountably, in the days following, Orville had begun to brood about Beverly, wondering about her past, projecting her

strength into his future. Somehow, in some subtle way, her perfection had been tarnished. It was as if on instinct, on immediate
love rather than investigation, you bought an original sculptured
piece, and enjoyed it until friends began to make casual remarks
about the dubious quality of its originality, its beauty, its value, so
that in the end you were unsure and pure joy was modified and
finally dissipated by too much reflection.

With the sudden clarity born of honesty, a luxury that Orville
rarely permitted himself, he saw that he had come to avoid Beverly
not for her own defects but for suspicions of defects implanted in
his mind by his family. As always, they had successfully brain-
washed him. Long ago, he had known the truth about them, but
dependence on them had conditioned him to close his eyes to the
truth. Never would he allow himself to relate their tactics to his
state of bachelorhood.

His mother had been married four years, and had been delivered
first of Dora and then himself, when his father had abandoned her
for a younger, a less demanding, a more feminine woman. His
mother had blamed the catastrophe on sex, the evil in his father's
nature, the ugly, unclean, warped urge known as lust. Dora, the
moment that she was of age, had revolted against excessive maternity, left home, married Vernon, moved to Colorado Springs, and
raised children of her own to harass. Orville, without his older sister's anger to protect him, had been kept close to his mother, a hos-
tage for his erring father. It had taken him a decade after he had
come of age to dare to find an apartment that would give him some
privacy—but even now, with his own quarters, he spoke to his
mother on the telephone twice a day, dined with her three times a
week, and drove her to her multitude of physicians and club socials.

Through the Roentgen rays of this self-examination, Orville
could link these people of his blood with his bachelorhood. He
could see, plainly, their stake in keeping him single. Had he married Beverly, or any of the others before, his mother would have
been deserted by a second husband, left lonely and bereft. Had he
married, and undertaken a life of his own, his sister and brother-in-
law would have been forced to do their share for his mother. As
matters stood, they tolerated his mother for one week each year
under their roof in Colorado Springs, and contributed a small
monthly sum toward her Denver apartment. They spent money,
he thought bitterly, while he spent emotion. They gave up cash,

while he gave up freedom. Alone in Denver, he was forced to carry the real burden alone. Dora went her aloof and selfish way. If he were married, Orville realized, he might have an ally in independence, and Dora would have to do her fair part.

In the brightness of this beam of truth, Orville hated his sister. He dared not entertain so strong an emotion toward his mother, but he told himself that if he could not hate her, at least he would not love her. Knowing all of this, feeling as he did, why did he not rush off to Boulder and kneel before Beverly and ask for her hand? Why was he thus immobilized? Why did he not act? He knew the answers, and finally despised himself, too. He knew that an unnamed fear kept him in bondage. He tried to name and define the fear: he was afraid of loneliness, afraid to leave and possibly lose what was safe and dependable, the two wombs, for an untried and foreign womb that one day might be too superior to need him. That was the crux of his indecision. What to do? He would see, he would make up his mind.

He brought his attention back to the lectern, to his notes, to his class, to the one in the lemon sweater who was this instant uncrossing her legs, opening them—the pink inner thigh—and crossing them. Consulting the large wall clock, Orville could see that in seconds the period would be ended. He finished what he had been saying, straightened his notes, and then he said, "Next week, I will take up, in detail, the numerous threats to the institution of marriage, and show their role in the evolution of sex through the ages. To begin with, I will take up the role of the so-called Other Woman. During the past centuries, the illicit 'wife' of a married, or sometimes unmarried, man has had many names and faces—adulteress, common-law wife, concubine, demirep, courtesan, prostitute, cocotte, harlot, hetaera, strumpet, demimondaine, paramour, doxy, fille de joie, tart, kept woman, bawd, femme entretenue, lady of easy virtue. These, with but slight variations in implied function and performance, have described the same woman—the mistress. Next week, I shall discuss the mistress in the evolution of sex. . . . Thank you. Class dismissed."

Gathering his notes, hearing the bedlam of the students rising, moving, conversing, he wondered if the one in the lemon sweater was staring at him, still flirting. Although Orville's shining head was bent, he was able to lift his gaze slightly to bring her into view. She was standing, books and pad under one arm, her back to him, waiting for two girl friends to join her. Together, they began to leave the room. The one in the lemon sweater, whom he knew so intimately, passed before him without so much as a glance. It was as if he were no more than a neuter gramophone that had been shut off. He felt foolish and cheated and, finally, embarrassed.

After the room had emptied, and he had closed his brief case, he did not linger. Usually, he liked to join a few of the more intelligent members of the faculty at coffee, to exchange professional talk and departmental gossip. This morning, he had no time. He had promised the Censorship Committee of the C.S.W.A., the Colorado Senior Women's Association, that he would meet them at the theater at eleven-fifteen for the preview of the newly imported French film, *Monsieur Bel-Ami.* There was no time to waste.

He left the campus hastily, was briefly delayed in maneuvering his new Dodge out of the faculty parking lot, but at last he was on his way. Driving on Broadway, toward Civic Center, he remembered the letter from Dr. Maud Hayden. Most of the time, he did not read his mail in the morning. The personal mail sent to his apartment, he left for the leisure of evening; the business mail delivered at the office, he read after lunch. This morning's mail had contained the envelope with Dr. Hayden's name and return address on it, and he had not been able to resist opening it. The information on The Three Sirens had so absorbed him that, for almost the only time in a decade, he had come close to forgetting to telephone his mother. Because the letter had made him late, he had given his mother only five minutes' conversation. He had promised himself that he would give her more time when she telephoned him at the office after lunch. Now, going past Civic Center, he was less sure he would give her more time.

As he continued along Broadway, he analyzed the contents of Dr. Hayden's letter. His studies in comparative sexual behavior had been largely secondhand, based for the most part on the writings and memories of observers and fellow ethnologists. He, himself, had made only two minor trips in the field: the first trip, to gather material for his Ph.D. dissertation, had involved six months on a Hopi reservation (with his mother boarding in a hotel nearby); the second, backed by the Polar Institute at the University of Alaska, had been for three months among the Aleuts on the islands off the Alaskan mainland (cut short by his mother's illness in Denver). In neither case had he adapted well to life in the field. He had no affection for primitives or for discomfort, and he had, in truth, been grateful to be able to leave the Aleuts for his mother's bedside. He had vowed never to live like a savage again. He had told himself that active participation and observation were not necessary. Had not Da Vinci painted "The Last Supper" without attending it? Had not his guiding star, Sir James Frazer, written his immortal *The Golden Bough* without once seeing or visiting a primitive society? (An old anecdote supported him. William James had asked Frazer, "You must tell me about some of the aborigines you have met." And Frazer had replied, "But God forbid!")

Yet, despite his reluctance to travel, Orville had to admit to himself that the prospect of a visit to The Three Sirens titillated him, as did the sexual customs on all South Seas islands. Somehow, it was more glamorous, less rigorous and revolting, than the Hopis and the Aleuts. He had always been fascinated by orgy as practiced by the Arioi group of Tahiti, by *coitus interruptus* as practiced on Tikopia, by disapproval of breast petting but approval of scratching during intercourse as practiced on Pukapuka, by enlargement of the female clitoris through dangling a weight from it as practiced on Easter Island, by acceptance of mass rape as practiced on Ra'iva-vae.

Judging from Dr. Hayden's letter, the customs of the tribe on The Three Sirens promised far more, and Orville saw that it could be useful to his work. Furthermore, although he knew Dr. Hayden only slightly, he knew her son, Marc, quite well, and had found he had much in common with him. To work beside Marc in the field might be pleasant. Yet, now, as he wheeled his Dodge into Welton Street, he knew that he was only daydreaming. To participate in such an adventure was impossible. His mother would not permit it. His sister, Dora, would make scenes. And besides, if he just went off, he would alienate himself from Beverly completely, if he had not already done so. He would have to decline, and tender his thanks to Dr. Hayden this evening, and ask her to give his best regards to Marc and to the new Mrs. Hayden.

With this settled, Orville left his car in the parking lot on Welton, and walked the half-block to Sixteenth Street, where the motion picture theater stood. Entering the lobby of the empty theater, he wondered how long this French film ran and if it would be worth his time. Over one year ago, the C.S.W.A., inspired by editorials in the Denver *Post*, had created its Censorship Committee, and invited him to serve as its expert. He had served with no remuneration—a community service, he told himself—other than favorable personal publicity in the *Post*. Generally, he enjoyed the assignment. He was able to see foreign films, and some Hollywood ones, in a raw form that the public would not see. This forbidden knowledge made him an object of interest at parties. Also, he liked to think, he was saving the city from corrupting influences and uplifting its moral tone. He took a certain satisfaction in the statistics: of thirty films examined in the past twelve months, he had been responsible for having four of them banned, fifteen of them sharply expurgated, and six of them moderately edited. His neighbors were the better for his intelligent vigilance.

Inside the cavern of the theater, he found the three committee members waiting in the loges. With a smile, and courteous greetings, he shook hands with each—first with Mrs. Abrams, a small, darting woman who looked like something that had escaped from a broken thermometer; next with Mrs. Brinkerhof, who resembled a basketball player wearing a gray female wig; and finally with Mrs. Van Horne, who reminded him always of an entree that was ample, stuffed, jellied, and he was always surprised there was not an apple in her mouth.

Immediately, Mrs. Brinkerhof had signaled the projectionist. The lights dimmed, and the main titles flashed on the screen. Orville sank into his leather seat, lifted his spectacles higher on his nose, and squinted at the main title—*Versailles Productions present Guy de Maupassant's Monsieur Bel-Ami*.

Orville was well prepared for what would follow. The night before, he had read a synopsis of de Maupassant's original novel, published in 1885 and set in that period. Also, he had read the press book of the motion picture releasing company, and learned that the film was bringing the old novel up to date and setting it in the year 1960. As for all the rest, the characters—the newspaperman and scoundrel, Georges Duroy; the women he seduced, Madeleine Forestier, Clotilde de Marelle, Basile Walter; the benefactors he betrayed, Charles Forestier, M. Walter—and the plot—the story of Duroy's climb from impoverished journalist to winner of the Legion of Honor to candidate for the Chamber of Deputies—and the setting—Paris and Cannes—all were unchanged and faithful to the novel.

Orville concentrated on the screen. There was the long shot of the army transport plane from Algeria. Next came the landing at Orly Field. The occupants of the plane, discharged veterans of the French fighting forces in Algeria, emerged into the arms of relatives and friends, with only one remaining alone and unmet. This was the tall, handsome George Duroy, who watched the others and then limped to the waiting bus. The scene dissolved to the Champs Élysées in midafternoon. There was a trucking shot of Duroy walking, studying a card in his hand, searching for an address. Next, there was a dissolve to the office of *La Vie française*, where the editor, Forestier, heartily welcomed his former brother officer, Duroy. An interminable dialogue scene between the old buddies followed, and Duroy had a job on the newspaper, and suddenly the editor's wife, Madeleine, appeared, and the editor introduced his wife to his old friend.

Along with Duroy, Orville studied Madeleine. Whoever the actress was, her bust and buttocks were formidable, and her eyes an aphrodisiac. A veteran of French films, Orville knew the time was near, and he reached into his pocket for his notebook and flashlight pen. He was not to be disappointed. Forestier had invited Duroy to his country house near Chartres. When Duroy arrived, he learned his editor was ill from a bronchial ailment and confined to his bed. There was only Madeleine to welcome Duroy. Then came the expected dissolve, and another dissolve, and one more, and suddenly Orville's pen was busy. Madeleine, wearing brief lace panties and nothing else, lay on the bed of the lodge in the forest, a kilometer from the main house. Her eyes were closed, her full lips parted, her wide breasts bared, and Duroy, seen only from the waist up, naked, moved into the scene, and sat beside her. She writhed, murmured in French, and he caressed her, whispered back, and bent closer and closer.

Thereafter, for almost an hour and a half, Orville's pen scratched across his notebook . . . the indecency of Madeleine's undisguised enjoyment of her carnal appointments with Duroy . . . the disgusting scene between the newspaper's wealthy proprietor, M. Walter, and his wife Basile, in which his impotency was made a matter of humor . . . the shocking, cold-blooded seduction of Basile by Duroy in a wagon-lit compartment en route to Cannes . . . the degenerate shots of the French hussies in bikinis on the Riviera, the angles! the anatomical close-ups! . . . Duroy's meeting with Basile Walter's daughter Suzanne, and their passionate acrobatics in the close, damp confines of a cabaña . . . Duroy's blackmailing his women to attain power, with no retribution at the fade-out.

The lights had gone on. Orville considered what he had seen. In his own judgment, the entire picture should be banned. However, he did not want to go out on a limb. If the committee liked it, he would not oppose them. He did not want to be made to seem a puritan.

He turned around in his seat. "Well, ladies, what do you think?"

He could see, from their expressions, glazed and faraway, that they had enjoyed it very much. No one replied, and then Mrs. Abrams dared. "It's a little strong here and there, and I don't think the hero is a good example of a man to look up to, but—" She hesitated, and then said it. "It—I think it has artistic merit."

"Yes," echoed Mrs. Brinkerhof, "artistic merit."

"It'll have to have a 'For Adults Only' restriction," said Mrs. Van Horne.

They had passed their judgment, and Orville knew what was expected of him. After all, he reminded himself, their husbands were important. "I'm glad you feel as I do," he said briskly. "I think we can insist upon one major cut—the impotency scene, which is ugly and does nothing for the picture—and perhaps five or six lesser cuts. Shall I read them to you?"

The women, suffering group guilt, wanting to expiate this guilt, were eager to hear the cuts. Orville, in the professional monotone that he always assumed on such occasions, read aloud his suggestions. The committee's agreement was unanimous, and made with relief. Now that it was over with, they seemed gay, romantically enriched, and freed of inner shames.

When Orville bade them farewell, and left the theater, one more sensible compromise behind him, he carried a single riddle with him. The riddle was the ancient worn one, and it was posed in a single word: women. He had a Ph.D. in anthropology. How many years would pass before he could have a Ph.D. in women? When would he, or any man, ever understand them?

Once inside his car, and driving to his private office, he reviewed the film, what had been enjoyable and what had been distasteful, and he recollected the few women he had known, and he thought about his mother and his sister and Beverly. When he had parked in his regular niche in the lot on Arapahoe Street, and walked toward his suite of offices in the building at Arapahoe and Fourteenth, he discerned what in his reflections was disturbing him. He did not want to be Sir James Frazer, after all. He wanted to be Georges Duroy. His mother and Dora would not like it, of course, but that was what he wanted at this moment. Well, they need not worry, his mood would change.

His mood changed the moment that he entered the blue-carpeted reception room of his office suite. He heard his secretary say into the telephone, "One moment, please, he may be coming in."

He looked at her inquiringly.

She cupped her hand over the mouthpiece. "It's your mother, Dr. Pence."

Without glancing at his watch, he knew that the time must be exactly two o'clock. He glanced. It was exactly two o'clock.

"All right, tell her to hold on a second." Starting for his office, he realized that he had missed lunch. "Gale," he called back, "soon as you switch it over to me, send down for some sandwiches. Beef— no gravy. And skimmed milk."

After closing the door, he removed hat and coat, then settled on the swivel chair behind his large oak desk and picked up the receiver.

"Hello," he said and paused so that Gale, knowing he was on, would leave the line. As he heard the click that meant he was alone with his mother, his voice shed its professional dignity. "Hello, Mom," he said, "how are you?"

It seemed to him that Crystal's voice was becoming shriller with every new year. "You know how it is with me, nothing ever changes," she was saying. "The question is, how is my boy?" He winced at the "my boy," but he never had the courage to remind her that she had christened him with a name. She rambled on. "You sounded tired this morning. Did you work all night?" He tried to acknowledge that he had worked late, but she was not listening, so he desisted and settled back.

"You can sleep like a baby," she was saying. "I wish I could tell you how I envy the lucky people who put their heads on the pillow and—poof—asleep. I suppose I am cursed. The older you get, the harder it is to sleep. Maybe I have lived too long." He assured her that she had not lived too long. She had listened to this reply, for she said, "You are sweet when you want to be, always stay that way, my boy. Too many sons grow away, become too big, forget the people who are important to them in the end. Friends fall away.

You can't trust them. Only a mother—what is in her heart—can be trusted. You always read in the papers where mothers are giving up their lives for their children, jumping into a fire, anything. Ah, my boy, someday you will understand. But what I was saying—all night I couldn't sleep—the pills are no good—and dreams, I am cursed with dreams—people can't understand until it happens to them. When they are old and it happens to them they understand. The pills are no good, my boy, everything is different, you can't trust your own doctor. When I was young, you knew your doctor was like a member of the family. He would not lie any more than you would lie—he would not gouge and take advantage of you, and give you sugar pills and talk about everything being in the mind. In the mind—nonsense! What I feel in the bones is not in the mind. My boy, if only you knew how crippled I am today, my arms are like burning embers, and my feet, the ankles, it is torture . . ."

She's off and running, Orville thought, and he would not be called upon for an interjection for at least three minutes. Wedging the telephone receiver between his ear and shoulder, coughing softly from time to time to make her think that he was attentive, but only half-listening to her summation of medical ailments that would have enriched Burton's *Anatomy of Melancholy*, Orville began to sort his business mail. Setting aside Dr. Maud Hayden's letter for attention later, he opened the other envelopes one by one, marking some for reply and others for filing and others to be thrown away. The last letter, from his rare-book dealer in Paris, jubilantly announced that a fine copy of the 1750 edition of Freydier's *A Plea Against the Introduction of Chastity Belts* had been located. Pleased that the quoted price was so reasonable, Orville wrote on the letter, "Reply and instruct to purchase at once." There remained the stack of magazines. Since Orville preferred to give them his undivided attention, he shoved them to one side until he was free.

For another minute he allowed his mother to go on, and then he interrupted. "Mom—listen, Mom—look—there's a long-distance call from Pennsylvania—I've got to—yes, Mom, you should go to this new doctor, if that's what everyone says—yes, absolutely, I'll take you there, I'll pick you up at a quarter to three tomorrow—no, I won't forget—yes, I promise. Okay, Mom, okay. 'By."

He hung up, and sat unmoving, surprised, as ever, by his exhaustion at the end of these calls. After a minute, having gained his second wind, he rolled his swivel chair closer to the desk, and began to unwrap the magazines. As part of his study on comparative sexual behavior, Orville subscribed to every pornographic or racy magazine known in the world. Some years before, he had visited the late Dr. Alfred Kinsey's Institute for Sex Research at Bloomington, Indiana, and had been impressed by its valuable collection of erotica. In the interests of research, he had begun his own collection, and every week since had annotated and filed various articles, stories, and, most important, drawings and photographs.

Orville unfailingly found this portion of his day the most rewarding and enjoyable. Gale had instructions that he was to be undisturbed by phone calls or visitors in the half-hour after he had finished conversation with his mother. In this half-hour, he leafed through his magazines, not yet annotating them, but mainly to get the feeling of what was useful and what was not. On the weekend, he would take them to his apartment and go through them with greater deliberation, and then he would make his notes.

Gently, he took the first glossy magazine from the stack of seven. This was one of his favorites, *Female Classics*, a handsome seventy-five-cent quarterly published in New York, and a priceless contribution to any study of American sexual mores. Slowly, he turned the pages—here a redhead wearing white slacks, her arms crossed beneath her naked breasts—here a platinum blonde leaning against a doorway, entirely disrobed except for a black patch covering her vaginal area—here a brunette wading in the water to her knees, with her nude back and backside to the camera—here a magnificent gatefold, opening to a full-length beauty posing before a canopy bed, the girl wearing a hip-length purple sweater, unbuttoned to reveal her enormous nipples but secured at the very bottom button to shield her private parts.

Orville's eyes held on the provocative girl in the gatefold, and incredulity surfaced as always it did. This one's face was soft and chaste as a Madonna. Her complexion, skin, breast, belly, and thighs were young and flawless. She could be no more than eighteen. Yet, here she was, all but the final secret exposed to thousands and thousands of hot eyes. How could she do it, and why? Did she not have a mother, a father, a brother? Did she not have church instruction? Didn't she wish to save a vestige of decency for binding love? Such deliberate nudity and posture forever shocked Orville. This pretty young thing had come into a studio or home, and shed every item of her apparel, and slipped on a ridiculous sweater, no more, and received instruction from some strange man, or men, on how much of her bosom was to be revealed and how the last button must conceal her—her—Lord in heaven, how could she do it? Surely when she stretched her arms or walked or assumed varied poses, *all* was revealed to strangers? What was her pleasure in this? Compliment and adulation? The perverted pleasure of exhibitionism? The small photographer's fee? The hope that some film producer would see her picture and send for her? What was it?

Still studying the gatefold, Orville wondered where you found all these beautiful young girls who stripped off their garments so quickly. What if he should want to examine some of them—oh, the one in the gatefold, for example—for clinical purposes? Would she pose for one of America's leading sex authorities? And after she posed, and answered his inquiries, would she—well, *would she?*

Suddenly, staring down at the shameful crimson nipples, Orville glowered. Sinful young bitch, he thought. Flamboyant hussy, he thought, standing so wantonly to incite a multitude of helpless men, posing so indecently to mock all that was sacred and holy of procreation and love. No punishment would be too great for these scarlet women. A stray sentence, and still another, slipped into Orville's mind: "A great mercy has been vouchsafed me. Last night I was privileged to bring a lost soul to the loving arms of Jesus." Now what was that? Where had he heard it, read it? Then he remembered. The Reverend Davidson speaking of Miss Thompson.

With a sigh, Orville closed the gatefold and resumed turning the pages. When the first magazine was finished, Orville took up the others, one by one, permitting no further wonder or philosophizing. Almost a half-hour later, the scientific task was accomplished. He placed the magazines, neatly, with others, atop his bookcase, to await the weekend, and returned to his chair and desk to skim the Denver *Post*, before plunging into dictation.

After the magazines, Orville's favorite newspaper seemed dull. His eyes went fleetingly over the columns of type, from sounds of war to sounds of politics, from the mourning of accidents to the mourning of divorces. Not until he arrived at page seven did a headline over a minor news story arrest him and make him sit up. The headline read: VISITING ENGLISH PROF WEDS BOULDER GIRL.

A faint warning bell sounded in some recess of Orville's brain. He bent to the two-inch story and read it hastily, and then reread it slowly. The phrases came at him like clubs . . . "Dr. Harvey Smythe, Professor of Archeology from Oxford, on a year's exchange at . . . Miss Beverly Moore, attached to the Administration Office of the University of Colorado . . . surprised friends . . . elopement to Las Vegas yesterday . . . returned last night . . . second marriage for the groom . . . will next year make their home in England where Dr. Smythe . . . be feted this evening by the University faculty."

Orville allowed the newspaper to fall from his hands to the desk. He sat in silent grief, staring dry-eyed at the news story, his casket.

Beverly Pence was now Beverly Smythe, for now and for all eternity, forever, irrevocably, and let no man tear asunder.

Even in his sorrow, Orville was not unreasonable. He did not blame Beverly Moore. He was not her victim. He blamed his mother and his sister. He was their victim, the prey of two blood tyrants, the martyr of them and of his pale chromosomes and genes.

After many dumb minutes, he folded the newspaper before him and dropped it in the wooden wastebasket. What was left on the desk was the debris from his opened mail and, off to one side, the letter from Dr. Maud Hayden.

Orville reached for his telephone and brought it directly before him. His first thought was that he would call his mother and tell her that she would have to take a goddam taxi to the goddam new doctor tomorrow. But he decided that the call to his mother could wait. Instead, he ordered Gale to get him the number in Colorado Springs.

He waited, in complete control and relishing the wait.

When her voice came in, he was pleased to note that it was as shrill as their mother's voice.

"Dora? Orville here."

"What is it, calling in the middle of the day? What's the big occasion? Is Mom all right?"

He ignored the last. "The big occasion is this, Dora—I'm taking the summer off—I'm going to the South Pacific to work on a study with Dr. Maud Hayden. I wanted you to be the first to know —so that you wouldn't complain that you didn't have enough time to prepare—when you have to take Mom in."

"Orville! Are you out—"

"Way out, Dora, I'm way out, and you and Vernon are in. Bon voyage, Dora, and a happy Mother's Day."

He lowered the receiver to the cradle, and her tinny scream died in the telephone's throat.

His heart ached, but at last he could smile.

* * *

After Claire Hayden had filed the carbon copies of the letters to Dr. Orville Pence, Dr. Walter Zegner, Dr. Sam Karpowicz, and Dr. Rachel DeJong, and made copies of the new research that had come in, she and Maud had gone downstairs to have a light lunch with Marc in the kitchen. Afterwards, Marc had returned to his classes, and Claire and Maud had gone up to the study once more.

Now, at five minutes before two o'clock in the afternoon, Claire sat at the typewriter table beside her small desk. She pecked away steadily, transcribing from her shorthand notes a letter to Professor Easterday on practical problems that Maud had dictated earlier. At a paragraph break, she halted, unbuttoned her cashmere sweater, kicked off her flat shoes, and swung to the desk for a cigarette. As she lighted one, she could see Maud on the sofa, absorbed in reading and jotting notes from Radiguet's *Les Derniers Sauvages*.

Marveling at Maud's ability to concentrate, Claire turned back to her typing. She had just touched the space bar, when the telephone behind the typewriter rang out. She pulled the receiver to her ear, and answered. It was the long-distance operator.

She listened, and then said, "One moment, please, I'll get her. . . . Maud, it's Los Angeles calling, person to person. Cyrus Hackfeld."

Maud bolted from the sofa. "Oh, dear, I hope nothing's gone wrong about tonight."

Claire relinquished the receiver and her chair to Maud, and walked across the room, smoking, listening.

"Mr. Hackfeld? How are you?" There was the slightest edge of anxiety in Maud's tone. "I hope nothing's—"

Her voice drifted off and she listened at length.

"Well, I'm so glad you're coming. Eight will be just fine."

Again, she listened.

"Did you say Rex Garrity? No, I've never had the pleasure, but of course I know about him, everyone knows about him—all those books—"

With the mention of Garrity's name, Claire, near the sofa, was more attentive. Now both she and Maud were listening hard.

Maud was speaking. "Is that all that's bothering you? Why, you needn't have called about that. Of course, he can come. We'd be honored to have him. It only means finding another plate. Tell him it's all absolutely informal—Polynesian style." She laughed, and waited, and then she inquired, "Of course, Mrs. Hackfeld will be with you? I so look forward to seeing her again. Be sure to tell her the Loomises will be here. I think she enjoys him. . . . Until this evening, Mr. Hackfeld. We all look forward to it. Good-by."

After she had hung up, Maud sat rocking in the swivel chair for a meditative interval. Then she became aware of Claire's curiosity, and she stood up.

"He wanted to know if he can bring a guest. Rex Garrity is in his office, and Hackfeld happened to mention The Three Sirens, and Garrity begged to come along." She paused. "Do you know who Rex Garrity—?"

"To read him is to hate him," said Claire cheerfully. "I spent one summer vacation, when I was in high school, reading all of him. I thought he was the most romantic figure alive. When I got to college, I had to reread some of him for a paper I was doing and half-way through I sent out for Dramamine."

"What does that mean?"

"Nausea induced by motion sickness. Those dreadful, phony, patently staged heroics. Watered-down Richard Halliburton, if one can imagine such a thing. *My Adventure Trail*—swimming the Suez Canal, climbing Ixtacchihuatl—the Sleeping Woman—to tell her he loved her, a night in King Tut's Tomb—and what were the others? I remember—*On the Heels of Hannibal, In the Footsteps of Marco Polo, Following the Shadow of Ponce de Leon, In Flight with Lord Byron*—what fakery—and with that fan-magazine style surrounded by a forest of exclamation marks."

Maud shrugged. "I suppose he has his place—"

"In the garbage pail."

"—after all, they sold by the thousands."

"You're too objective about people," said Claire. "He and all the rest of those play-acting romantics corrupted a generation with lies. He hid truth about the realities of the world we live in. And I speak as a romantic, you know that."

Maud hesitated. "I haven't read much of him, I admit, but what I did read—I'm inclined to agree with you. Still, he may be a perfectly agreeable dinner companion."

"All right, Maud, I'll give him a chance, too."

Maud came thoughtfully to the sofa. "What's really bothering me is that I might have a hard time speaking to Cyrus Hackfeld alone with this Garrity here—and Lisa Hackfeld, too. I can't depend on the Loomises to divert them."

"You can depend on Marc and me," said Claire. "You keep Hackfeld behind after dinner, and I'll do my best with our travel author and Mrs. Hackfeld. In fact, I'm not too worried about Garrity. I'm sure he loves nothing more than to talk about old triumphs. All that worries me—" She looked at Maud. "Lisa Hackfeld is the one I'm concerned about. I don't know if I'll be able to connect with her. The only reference I ever heard you make to her was that you considered her frivolous."

"Frivolous? Did I say that?"

"I thought—"

"Perhaps I did. Well, that was the impression I had. It was unfair of me. Actually, I don't know her at all." She shook her head, troubled. "I wish I did now."

Until this moment, Claire had not realized the importance Maud was giving to the evening. Claire had somehow believed that if the higher budget Maud wanted was so crucial to the trip, Maud would have gone down to see Hackfeld in his business office. Now Claire perceived that her mother-in-law did not wish to argue the budget in a business arena, where Hackfeld was master and was used to saying no. Maud had wanted the matter served up after dinner, pleasantly as a smooth cognac, in an atmosphere that was mellow and easy, and where the harsh word "no" might be out of place. Understanding this now, and the significance of the larger budget, Claire determined to allay her mother-in-law's fretfulness.

"I'm simply not going to worry about tonight any further," Claire said firmly. "Rich people don't have to do what they don't want to do. If Mrs. Hackfeld wasn't interested in you, and in the project, she wouldn't be coming all the way up here tonight. That's a plus, as far as I'm concerned. Maud, I'm confident you can leave her—and Garrity, too—to Marc, with a feeble assist from me.

127

Maybe, by the time dinner's done, we'll have a line on Lisa Hackfeld—and then we'll divert like mad."

* * *

At five minutes after five o'clock in the afternoon, Lisa Hackfeld turned her white Continental into the driveway of the vast two-story mansion on Bellagio Road in Bel-Air, and parked inside the carport.

She hit the horn twice, for Bretta, her personal maid, to come and get several packages from I. Magnin's that were lying on the leather seat beside her, and then left the car and wearily entered the house. In the vestibule, she removed the silk scarf that had protected her blond hair, dropped it on the French Directoire bench, squirmed out of her full-length leopard coat, and half carried it, half dragged it into the spacious, expensive living room, where she threw it across the arm of the closest chair. Listlessly, she peeled through the mail on the mantelpiece, then wandered to the magazines on the coffee table, and poked at the new *Harper's Bazaar* with disinterest. And finally she moved to the sofa, collapsing on the downy cushions, impatiently waiting for Averil, the butler, to appear.

In half a minute, Averil appeared with the customary double Martini dry on the small lacquered tray.

"Good afternoon, ma'am. No calls."

"Thanks, Averil." She accepted the drink. "Just what the doctor ordered." He began to leave, as she sipped the cool tart drink, and she called after him, "Make it one more in about fifteen minutes. And tell Bretta to draw my bath."

"Yes, ma'am."

After he had gone, she drank half of the Martini, recoiling at the first sting of it—so like smelling salts—and then welcoming the liquid invasion through her limbs. It was too soon to make her feel better. She must give the potion time. She revolved the glass between her fingers, hypnotized by the shimmer of the olive, and then she put the glass on the table before her.

Leaning forward, elbows propped on her knees, she silently rebuked the Martini for lacking the magic to cure her.

There was no such magic on earth, she knew, and between her temples where it could not be seen, she wept. Oh Lord, she wept, Oh Deceiver, you did not tell me it would be like this, you did not tell me it would happen. Yet here it is, she wept. Today, is the last day of Life, and tomorrow begins the long slow torturous descent into Oblivion. Tomorrow, at three minutes after nine o'clock in the morning, the Old One would revise and enter her latest holdings in the Doomsday Book and tomorrow the entry would read: owner of Forty Years.

Where was the magic to stay tomorrow's entry? Once you owned forty years of life, the holdings accrued more swiftly, to fifty, to sixty, to too much, so that in the end He took it all away, and you had nothing because you were nothing, and the eraser moved across your name in the Doomsday Book.

Today had been wasted, Lisa knew, because no matter where she tried to hide, to protect the last, last day of thirty-nine years, she found that the Old One was there, jostling her, toothlessly smiling and waiting at each Samarra.

She had known, from the moment the filtered sun had touched her eyelids at ten this morning, that the day was doomed and that she was doomed and that she would never be young again. She had known because, after her full awakening, and going into the shower, she had begun to think not of the present day but of all days past, from the earliest memory of her beginnings.

She had thought of growing up in Omaha, where she had been Lisa Johnson and where her father had owned the hardware store near the Union Stock Yards. She had enjoyed being the prettiest little girl in grammar school, and the most popular young lady in high school, and the youngest actress ever to play a lead in the Omaha Community Playhouse. She had, with little instruction, been the best female singer and dancer, and the most attractive, in the city. Quite naturally, she had gravitated to Hollywood—going with a friend who was also in her early twenties—ready to accept immediate stardom.

It had surprised her that being the best female singer and dancer, and the most attractive, in Omaha, had not made her the best and the most in Hollywood, for in Hollywood there were so many. She had been gregarious, making many friends, and one, an agent, had got her chorus-line work in four gaudy musical comedies produced by major studios. These had led to nothing more, and after that she had made her way by doing singing commercials on radio and a solo in a few of the less select nightclubs. She had spent a portion of her earnings trying to learn to act in a little theater on La Brea Avenue, and it was to this little theater, after the war and his honorable discharge as a supply officer, that Cyrus Hackfeld had come as a spectator. He had seen her, and fallen in love with her, and adroitly managed to arrange an introduction. Although fifteen years her senior, Cyrus was younger than the young men she dated. He was more alive, more dynamic, more prosperous. After one year of going steady, she had happily married him and felt safe and snug about it.

She had recalled all of this in the shower, and had been surprised at how quickly the seventeen years of her married life had sped by. During those years, the only holdover from her early career had been an interest in dancing. She had continued with lessons sporadically, more and more irregularly as their son, Merrill, who had her easy ways and not his father's driving energy, had entered prep school in Arizona. And here she was, incredibly, with one last day between herself and forty.

All through the morning, she had tried to be philosophical and think deeply, a disconcerting process that she usually left to the lecturers appearing at her monthly meeting of the Great Books Forum. This morning, she had ventured into the perilous stratosphere on her own. She had thought that calendars were, after all, man-made, and therefore arbitrary frauds. If calendars and clocks had not been invented, and you did not count the comings and goings of the moon, you would know no special age and you would always be young. How, in one day, could you pass from young to old? It was such deceptive foolishness.

But the deep thinking gave her no relief. First of all, she had been remembering the past, which everyone said was a sure sign of advancing years. Second, she had been thinking of Merrill, and had known that you could not have a boy so old and still be no older yourself. Then, third, she had been thinking of Cyrus, and remembered that he had once been merely stocky and was now pachydermous, that he had once had only the small factory and now had twenty or thirty factories (and his Foundation, and Foundations were created by rich old men, not ambitious young men, and even if the Foundation was a tax thing and avocation, it represented a passage of many years). Finally, she had been thinking of herself.

Once her hair had been a flaxen, natural blond, but now she had no idea of what it really was, after a decade of shampoos, and rinses, and coloring. And all the rest of her, if she would be honest about it this once, had gradually changed, so that the countenance of the prettiest girl in Omaha was now the countenance of an older, faded woman, exposed to the sun of too many years, the face rounder, fleshier, with lines on the brow, and lines under the big eyes, and nicks here and there that she would not name wrinkles. The throat and the hands were the worst, because they had not remained taut and smooth. And her figure, not properly a figure any longer, unless O was a figure, had thickened and obscured the curves, had become more and more shapeless, although not fat, never fat. Yet, despite Nature's ambush, the essence of her that dwelt inside had not succumbed to years. An accurate wisp of wisdom, carried over from those monthly lectures, summarized her feelings. It was from one of those English playwrights who disguised truth in comedy. Probably, almost certainly, Oscar Wilde. What was the wisdom? Yes: The tragedy of old age is not that one is old, but that one is young. Yes!

That was the hateful morning.

Here it was late afternoon, and she slowly drank her Martini while considering the debacle of the hours between waking and this moment. She had tried to escape memories of the past, and the mirrors of the house, by driving into Beverly Hills and occupying herself, by generating too much activity to think deeply.

Savoring her Martini, she relived the early afternoon as if she were participating in each action and event right now, as if each moment of it were the present, so that it, too, would no longer represent the past.

She set her mind at twelve-thirty.

She had a one o'clock date with Lucy and Vivian for lunch at the newest Scandinavian restaurant in Beverly Hills, The Great Dane, but at twelve-thirty she thought that she might cancel the engagement if she could seduce Cyrus into dining with her. She was wearing her latest acquisition, a softly draped jade-green dress that subtracted both pounds and years, and it was too nice to waste upon her own sex.

She dialed and was put right through to her husband.

"Lisa?"

"Hello, darling. I just had an impulse to call."

"You caught me in the nick of time. I was rushing out to meet Rex Garrity at the Club."

"Oh. You mean, you're tied up for lunch?"

"I made the appointment some time ago. He was flying in for a lecture and wanted to see me on some Foundation business. We're having a quick lunch and then we'll come back here and—" He paused. "Why did you ask? Would you like to join us?"

"No, no. I only wanted to say hello."

"You might enjoy him. He's quite a talker."

"You're kind, dear, but no. In fact, I have a date with Lucy and Vi."

"Too bad. What are you doing today?"

"Well, this lunch. Afterwards, the hairdresser. Some shopping. You know."

"Fine. I'd better run. See you later."

"Yes, later. Good-by, dear."

After that, she drove into Beverly Hills. It was nice of Cyrus to invite her, she thought, especially in the middle of his always busy day. But she had no patience for the travel writer, whom she had neither read nor met, and had no desire to meet or read. She had wanted to be alone with Cyrus, to sit and chat, about anything, about themselves maybe. They had talked so little these last years, perhaps because he talked all day at his work, perhaps because she was so separated from his work (or anything interesting) that now they had almost nothing to discuss, nothing that is, beyond Merrill and friends and the news.

Lucy and Vivian were already in the reserved booth when she arrived at The Great Dane. They admired her dress. She admired theirs. Drinks and ordering took up some time. There was gossip about a mutual friend who had separated from her husband, and speculation as to whether there was another man involved. They discussed the road-company performance of a play they had all seen at the Biltmore. They discussed the latest best-seller and wondered how much of it was autobiographical and whether or not the fictional heroine was really based on a scandalous movie actress. They discussed the First Lady's new hair-do. With the entree, Lucy and Vivian began to speak of their daughters, and they discussed them interminably, and Lisa stayed out of it and was bored. Talk about growing children depressed her, like making out a will. The only subject she wanted to talk about was her birthday, but they would not understand this urgency, not yet, for Lucy was thirty-six and Vivian was thirty-one, and they possessed the luxury of time.

When it was ten minutes before her two-thirty hair appointment, she was glad to leave her share of the bill and escape. She could have walked, but instead she took her Continental the five blocks to Rodeo Drive, and parked in the special area beside Bertrand's Beauty Salon.

Once inside, she left her coat with the receptionist, accepted the salon smock, and entered the private dressing room. After removing her dress, and covering herself with the smock, she emerged and went to the sink farthest back, where her regular girl was waiting. On the way, she acknowledged Bertrand's lovely compliment in French, and Tina Guilford's hand-wave of welcome from under a dryer.

At the sink, she sat back in the tilted chair for a quick shampoo. The soap and water felt soothing, and she relaxed. What she liked most about the Salon was the ritual involved in preserving and enhancing beauty. It produced a pleasant euphoria that drained all anxiety from the mind. You became a subject that need make no decisions. Your only duty was to be there, a presence, existing, while practiced hands attended you. You were made to feel like —like Madame de Pompadour.

Automatically, Lisa moved to the private cubicle, accepted the perforated skullcap, felt the strands of her hair pulled nimbly through the holes. As her hair was being tipped, each strand colored, and then bound, she stretched her legs and lifted her slip to her girdle, while the second girl, who had brought in the metal tub of wax, efficiently undid her nylons, rolled them down her legs, removed her pumps, and then the stockings. She gazed at her shapely calves, pleased that they had not deserted her as youth had. Lazily, she watched the kneeling girl pat the wax strips on her legs with the wooden instrument, and then rapidly pull them off, removing any unsightly hairs by the roots.

When the tipping of her hair was done, and her legs were sleek as marble, she moved along the assembly line, her mind a vacuum. There was the second and more thorough shampoo, with the massage, and the rinse, and the stiff brush, and the fluffy towel. Then came the fifteen minutes with Bertrand, when he combed and swept and brushed, manipulating the metal rollers, at last clipping her hair in place.

After the net was on, she settled beneath a dryer for the next hour. She had begun to shake off her depression of the morning, when she saw Tina Guilford, dressed to leave, approaching her. She did not mind speaking to Tina, for Tina must be fifty if she was a day, and Lisa could feel some superiority. She reached up and shut off her dryer.

"Lisa, darling," Tina was saying excitedly, "I won't take up a minute of your time, but I've just heard of the most astounding miracle in Pasadena. A Swiss doctor, a plastic surgeon, has opened shop, and the girls are all raving, absolutely raving. He's expensive, very expensive, but they all say it's worth it. A new method discovered in Zurich. It's fast and absolutely unnoticeable. One session and no more sagging chin and neck, no more bags under the eyes, and if you want to go as far as your bust, my dear—"

"What makes you think I'd want to go as far as my eyes?" Lisa demanded icily.

"Why, my dear, I just thought—why, everyone's talking about him and—why, I thought when you get to be our age—"

Lisa was about to say: our age, in a pig's eye our age, your age you mean, you bitch. Instead, she said, "Thanks, Tina. If I ever decide I need it, I'll ask you for more details. Excuse me now, I've got to get out of here."

She reached up and started the dryer, and Tina's last words were lost in the whine and hum of the dryer.

As Tina left, Lisa's good mood vanished with her. She seethed at her friend's impudence. That old lady of fifty-something daring to draw a thirty-nine-year-old young woman down to her level. Almost instantly, her rage flattened and crawled into gloom. Tina was simply trying to be helpful, she could see, helpful and truthful. It must show already, Lisa thought, forty must show already and to everyone. She was miserable now and determined to flee from this gossip trap.

Once her hair had dried, and Bertrand had taken out the curlers and deftly combed her hair, all the while discussing his tiresome triumphs in Paris, she could not dress fast enough. She charged her visit, passed out three lavish tips, and walked to the car, wondering what method that Swiss facial surgeon had invented.

Maybe he had the ultimate secret. Maybe he had found the means to make you young inside, too. That inner surgery, despite Oscar Wilde, would be worth her entire portfolio of stocks and bonds.

When she reached the car, she realized that she was only a block and a half from Jill's shop. She had not visited the elegant slacks and sportswear store in over a year. She needed some young slender toreador pants or capris for the spring and summer, for the patio and their place in Costa Mesa. With rising optimism about the future, she started for Jill's.

She had forgotten what she always resented about the shop, until she had reached it and gone inside. The moment that she crossed the heavy carpeting to the center of the huge, square, mirrored room, she wanted to turn around and run. Jill Clark, who owned the shop but was never there, made a fetish of callow girlishness in her decor, her furnishings, the damn mirrors, the cut of the shorts and slacks and swimsuits, the clerks, most of all the clerks. Lisa could see them now, gathered before a pillar, chattering. They were all unblemished female children, the clerks, ranging from seventeen to twenty-one. Their complexions needed no make-up and shone, their small breasts were high and straight, their stomachs flat, hips narrow, and all were slat-assed. They smoked, wore outlandish blouses, capris, and open gold sandals, and they waited upon you with the insolence and arrogance of youth. They were disgusting.

Before Lisa could turn back to the door, one limber, light-footed adolescent approached her. This one wore a badge which identified her as "Mavis." Her hair was platinum, her face narrow and perfect, and her body lithe. Confronting Lisa, her condescending charitable look was that of one who must deal with some old baggage of a woman, in a shawl, seeking haven from the snow.

"May I help you, madam?"

"Yes. Those violet capris in the window. I'd like to see a pair."

"Your size?"

"You have all my statistics on file, sideways and up and down. Just look up Mrs. Cyrus Hackfeld."

She announced her name, rather than spoke it, but Mavis was a blank. No recognition registered. She drifted toward the cashier's counter, while Lisa wandered toward the rack of slacks, boiling.

Leisurely, after a long interval, Mavis returned carrying a card.

"Your last measurements were taken three years ago," she said meaningfully.

Lisa's anger surfaced. "Then that's my size."

"Very well."

Mavis searched the rack, and finally jerked free a pair of violet capris.

"Do you want to try them on, Mrs. Hackworth?"

"Yes. And the name is Hackfeld."

"Hackfeld. I'll remember. Right this way."

Trembling, and alone at last behind the curtain, Lisa hastily divested herself of the leopard coat, her dress, and her half-slip, and then pulled on the tight capris. She tried to zip them and they would not zip. She tried to button the waist but two inches separated button from hole. She wheeled and observed herself in the mirror and saw that the pants were too tight, impossibly tight, with ugly bulges at her hips and thighs. Filled with self-pity, Lisa rolled the capris down and struggled out of them.

She stood in her brassière and girdle, and called the young girl.

After a few seconds, Mavis strolled in, smoking. "How were they, Mrs. Hack—— Hackfeld?"

"You gave me a size too small."

"I gave you your size," Mavis, the picador, said relentlessly. "It's the size on your card."

Lisa was consumed by fury at the baiting. "Well, dammit, they don't fit, so get me the next larger size."

Mavis smiled sympathetically at the old girl. "I'm terribly sorry, Mrs. Hackfeld. That is the largest size we carry in the store. Miss Jill won't carry a larger one. It's her policy. I'm afraid you'll have to go elsewhere to find something that fits."

Lisa's fury had melted down into humiliation and grief. She knew her cheeks were hot and she hated their surrender. "All right," she said, "thank you."

The girl had gone and again Lisa was alone. Dressing, she was perplexed. It was the first time that she could find nothing to fit at Jill's. But then, she thought, finally adjusting her coat, it was also the first time she was going to be forty.

She left the shop swiftly, eyes pointed ahead, but warmly aware that the group of silly slat-asses were watching her with amusement. Going through the door, she knew one thing wealth could not fortify you against—and that was age. Those silly slat-asses were richer than she. Good-by, Jill, good-by forever. And damn you, *you'll* know one day.

Blindly, she made for her white Continental, and drove to Magnin's, where she belonged. Sweeping through the store, she shopped compulsively, but with constant disinterest, for toiletries and evening accessories. When she had what she did not need, she went out the rear exit, waited for her car, overtipped the attendant, and steered the vehicle to Wilshire Boulevard.

As she halted at a signal, her watch reminded her that there still remained an empty stretch between four-fifteen and six o'clock, and she wondered how she could best fill it. Briefly, she considered driving east on Wilshire to the Hackfeld Building and surprising Cyrus. Quickly, she vetoed the idea. She did not have the spirit to face his employees, his receptionist, his secretaries, more bubbling slat-asses, the children who had inherited her good years. They would nudge and whisper, after her entrance, there goes *the* Mrs. Hackfeld, the old man's old lady—how did she ever hook him?

Instead of turning east, she wheeled the car west. She would look in at the Coast Tennis Club—it was on the way home—she and Cyrus were charter members—and maybe she would have a drink and join in a casino or bridge game for a short spell. Ten minutes later, oppressed by the slate sky, she was relieved to arrive at the Tennis Club, relinquish her car, and enter into the fireplace-and-mountain-lodge atmosphere of the exclusive refuge. Carried upward in the gleaming self-service elevator, she half-listened to the strains of *Cocktails for Two* being piped in and played by a predominantly string orchestra, and she dreaded to think how long it had been since she had danced to that number.

Upstairs, the enclosed terrace was only partially filled, two tables of older men engrossed in gin rummy, one table with a pair of attractive young advertising-company types talking seriously and drinking, and a table of women, all familiar faces, playing bridge.

Lisa waved the uniformed waiter aside, and stood next to the window peering down at the reddish clay courts. All were empty in the cold save one, and on this court two hearties, a young man and his young girl, both in white shorts, hit and ran and scrambled vigorously, laughing and clowning. With a sigh, Lisa turned away and headed for the bridge game. The familiar faces greeted her effusively, as one of their own, and one of them suddenly volunteered her place to Lisa. As suddenly, Lisa had no heart for the foolish numbered pasteboards. She declined politely, explaining that she had stopped by to see if Cyrus was here, and she could just stay a minute. The waiter had drawn up a spectator's chair for her, and she accepted it and ordered a lemonade.

During the next fifteen minutes, chewing at the colored straws in the lemonade, she tried to concentrate on the bridge game, tried to match the pleasure and disgust of the players over an unexpected small slam, but was conscious only of someone's eyes upon her. Casting a sidelong glance toward the wall, she thought she could see the more attractive of the two advertising men staring at her. She enjoyed a chill of excitement, and, without being too obvious about it, she lifted her head higher to improve her neckline, and straightened in the chair to define her bust, and crossed her legs (her best points) to show off a slim calf. She felt like the girl in Omaha, and the feeling was very good, indeed. She became gayer, making comments, small jokes, to the other women about their play. She still felt his eyes upon her, and risked another sidelong glance. Yes, he was staring at her with his deep-set dark eyes and amused mouth and square jaw. She felt a flush of daring, and decided, recklessly, to stare back and see what would happen. She looked at him, and frankly stared, but there was no reaction from him. In that instant, she perceived their stares were not meeting. With sinking heart, she pivoted, trying to follow the line of his gaze, knowing that it missed her by an inch or two, and then she saw the bar. On a stool at the bar, where she had not been before, sat the young girl, twenty-five, no more, who had been on the tennis court. She appeared ruddy and Swedish, and the thin material of her white blouse strained against her breasts, and the tight white shorts set off her muscular limbs. She drank from her highball, then met the stare of the man across the room with a teasing smile, and bent again to her drink.

Lisa felt shame along with the squeeze of hurt in her chest: she was a fool, a young-old fool, barred from participation, henceforth spectator as well as intruder. Her stupid misunderstanding made her blush, and, in this day of flight, she once more desired only escape. Moments later, she left the Tennis Club, as whipped as any one of Napoleon's grenadiers in retreat from Moscow.

At the discreet cough, she sat up, and realized with bewilderment that she was on the yellow sofa of her own living room, emerging from recent past into present, and that the impeccable Averil was before her with a second double Martini dry.

The cocktail glass in her hand was empty. Morosely, she exchanged it for the filled one. "Thank you, Averil. That'll be all for now."

After Averil had gone, she drank, but without result. There was no floating euphoria. Instead, the Martini made her feel pulpy, soggy, sodden, like a soaked, crumpled newspaper.

She was distracted by the sound of a key working into the front-door keyhole. The door opened, and seconds later, yanking off his overcoat, Cyrus materialized in the living room. He was still business-brisk and alive with the day he had beaten, and he propelled his huge bulk toward her with vigor, stooped and kissed her forehead.

"How are you, dear?" he was asking. "Surprised to find you still down here. Expected you'd be dressing by now."

Dressing, she thought, sure, dressing in my pleated shroud. "Dressing? What for?"

"What for?" Cyrus looked stern. "For Santa Barbara. We're driving up to have dinner with Maud Hayden."

"We are?" she said stupidly. "I don't remember—"

"What the devil, Lisa, you've known for two weeks. I've mentioned it several times the last couple of days."

"I guess I forgot. My mind's been on other things."

"Well, let's hustle. Rex Garrity insisted on coming along, and I saw no harm in it. He'll keep us entertained in the few hours on the road. He'll be here in thirty or forty minutes. And we're expected for dinner at eight."

"Cyrus, must we? I don't feel much like it. I'm beginning to have a headache."

"It'll go away, your headache. Take something for it. What you need is to get out a little more. Being antisocial isn't going to make you feel better. This is a very special evening."

"What's so damn special about it?"

"Look, honey, I can't stand up Maud Hayden. She's one of the top anthropologists in the world. She's made a big fuss about having us to her home. It's sort of a celebration. She's discovered some tropical islands—remember, I told you a few weeks ago? The Three Sirens, they're called—down in the South Pacific. She's taking an all-star team there, and our foundation is backing her with a grant. It'll be a feather in my cap when she gives the paper before the American Anthropological League. Make those Ford and Carnegie people sit up and take notice of Hackfeld. And the book she does is a cinch best-seller and that, too—"

"Cyrus, please, I'm still not up to—"

Averil had come in with a bourbon and soda, and Cyrus was gulping it like water, swallowing, choking, coughing, and trying to speak between coughs. "Besides, I've been looking forward to this evening more than anything in recent weeks. Maud's a great wordsmith. Makes Scheherazade look like a shy, stuttering bore. I thought you'd be as interested as I am in The Three Sirens tribe, with all that crazy sex stuff—like the Social Aid Hut, that's supposed to have some trick way of solving all sex problems for married people—and the wide-open annual festival week in late June when—"

Lisa found herself sitting up. "What?" she said. "What are you talking about? Did you make all this up?"

"Lisa, for Chrissakes, I gave you Maud's prospectus, her outline of that culture down there and their customs, I gave it to you to read, those typed pages. Didn't you even look at them?"

"I—I don't know. I guess I didn't. I didn't think it was anything, only one of those dull sociological tracts."

"Dull? Wow. What those half-white, half-Polynesian natives are probably doing down there makes the House of All Nations look as staid as Buckingham Palace."

"Is it true—what you are saying—about that Social Aid———?"

"Maud thinks it is true. Her source is a good one. Now she's taking a team down there for six weeks in June and July to see for herself. We're going to talk about the whole thing tonight. That's the idea of the dinner." He rubbed his small florid face. "I'd better shave and get ready." He started to maneuver his dirigible of a body around, to leave, when suddenly he swung back to his wife. "Honey, if you've really got a lousy headache, then, hell, I'm not going to insist—"

But Lisa was standing, quite as energetic as her husband. "No—don't worry—I'm beginning to feel better. It would be a crime to miss an evening with Maud Hayden. You're so right. I'll go up and bathe, and be dressed in a jiffy."

Cyrus Hackfeld grinned. "Swell. Good girl."

Lisa crooked her arm in his, to thank him for the "good girl," and then she wondered how old forty was on The Three Sirens, and with her husband she went upstairs to prepare for her last young evening. . . .

* * *

Dinner at the Haydens had been served at nine-fifteen, and now Claire noted, as Suzu doled out individual cherry tart desserts, it was almost twenty to eleven.

The meal had gone wonderfully well, Claire felt. The Chinese egg drop soup had been consumed to the last spoonful. The Chicken Teriyaki surrounded by rice, Chinese peas with water chestnuts, and melon balls, and supplemented by warm sake in miniature white cups, had been well received, and everyone but the Loomises had accepted second helpings. Even Rex Garrity, who regarded himself as an international gourmet, had complimented Maud on the dishes, admitting he had not enjoyed a blending of Chinese and Japanese food so much since he had visited Shanghai in 1940, when nationals of both nations occupied the city.

The conversation, too, had been admirable in every way, friendly and amazingly stimulating, and Claire had enjoyed all of it as if it were new. Early in the evening, during the predinner drinking and hors d'oeuvres—Suzu had made Rumaki, cheese puffs, and laid out a hot crabmeat dip—there had been a brief, sharp skirmish, a verbal jousting, between Garrity and Maud. The two were the most widely traveled in the group, both full of experience and facts, both used to being listened to, and they had vied for dominance of the evening, sparring, hitting out, defending, countering. It had been a fascinating bout. Garrity had seemed eager to impress both Hackfeld and Maud with his worldliness and importance. Maud had been determined to make this a Hayden evening and make Hackfeld proud that he was supporting the expedition to The Three Sirens. By the time Suzu had announced dinner, Garrity, filled with liquor, muddled by Maud's anthropological terminology, sensing that the guests were more interested in her than in himself, had dropped his lance and pulled back from combat.

Through the dinner, Maud had the field to herself, and her handling of this victory and her presentation of her new exhibit had been engrossing. Except for salvaging his pride by confirming, one authority to another, some of Maud's digressive travel observations,

Garrity had devoted himself to his food. Two or three times, in an undertone, he had engaged Marc, privately, and Marc had seemed absorbed by him.

It pleased Claire that Garrity was exactly what she had expected, except for being even more pathetic and foolish, and there was no surprise in him. For Claire, the real surprise of the evening had been Lisa Hackfeld. Except for her attire, there had been nothing frivolous about Lisa. She had been easy, nice, unassuming, and curious. She had come prepared to sit at Maud's feet, and so she had come to Maud without any guard of pretense. She knew little about anthropology, about field work, about Polynesia, and she admitted it, but she wanted to know more, know everything all at once, consume gobs of information. Throughout the dinner she had questioned Maud steadily, especially about The Three Sirens, to Maud's utter delight and Hackfeld's relaxed pleasure.

Now, picking at her dessert—she had been too nervous all the evening to eat properly—Claire covertly studied the guests. When she had made out the place cards in the afternoon, Claire had wondered whether or not the arrangement should be female-male-female, but Maud would have none of it. She had wanted the guests seated to the best political advantage. Maud sat at the head of the table, with Cyrus Hackfeld at her right, and Lisa Hackfeld at her left, and at this moment she was prophesying what living conditions would be like in the field when the team settled on The Three Sirens.

Next to Lisa, cutting his cherry tart, sat President Loomis of Raynor, resembling somewhat the ailing President Woodrow Wilson, and across from him, cutting her cherry tart, sat Mrs. Loomis, resembling no one. Once, during the time of the second drink, and again, during the soup, Loomis had tried to set forth his views on the contrast between higher education in America and the U.S.S.R., this apropos of nothing, and he had found that no one except Claire was attentive and had retired into the attitude of wise listener, as did his mate. Now they remained silent, masticating their desserts, two distinguished pillars of salt. Across the table from Garrity, Claire was seated beside President Loomis, and on her other side, at the foot of the table, Marc leaned toward the travel writer, nodding as he heard him out, the words an indistinct hum to Claire.

With everyone occupied, Claire examined Rex Garrity more closely. She had guessed a little about him before this evening, but now she felt that she knew considerably more, perhaps all that there was to know. Watching him, intently bent toward Marc, she could see that he must have once been a beautiful man, like an ancient Greek poet who was also a hero of the Olympics. In his prime, a quarter of a century before, he must have been a graceful, slender young man, with wavy blond hair, a thin and angular face, a curiously effeminate manner overlaid on a strong, wiry body. Time had been his worst enemy, and in more ways than one, Claire suspected. His hair was still blond, still wavy, but it appeared stiff as straw and artificial as a toupee. The face had fought a thousand dietary battles, so that it had probably been fatter and thinner many times, and now it was so ravaged by vanities and drink that the flesh hung loosely and the skin was red-blotched and veiny. As to the body, it was a desperate remnant of the old Yale slenderness, the old best-seller and on-the-heels-of-Hannibal and in-the-foot-steps-of-Marco-Polo slenderness, the shoulders wide and hips narrow but the belly oddly protruding, as if it were the only anatomical part of him to surrender to time.

Claire examined him ruthlessly, and estimated to herself that he was between forty-eight and fifty-two. And she understood, as positively as she knew about herself, that these were his bad years. Shortly after his arrival, she had overheard a light bantering between Garrity and Cyrus Hackfeld. It had told her that Garrity had gone to Hackfeld this day to request a grant from the Foundation for some kind of travel stunt, and Hackfeld had turned him down, explaining that the Board would spare no funds for unscientific, carnival endeavors. Claire suspected that the worst of it, for Garrity, was that the world had gone on past him, and he had stood still with his same old repertory, and the world was no longer interested in the performer it had left behind.

During the decade of the thirties, there had been an audience for Garrity. It was a time between big wars, and there was still some hangover from the crazy twenties, and there was the Great Depression from which men wanted to escape by assuming other identities. Garrity had provided them with a romantic identity for just such an escape. He had embodied, in his person, all dreams and yearnings for faraway places and exotic adventures. He followed the trails of legendary heroes, avoiding death, saving damsels in distress, discovering hidden ruins, scaling lofty mountains, musing in the shadows and moonlight of the earth's Taj Mahals, and he wrote about these juvenile escapades and he lectured about them. and millions paid to leave their skulls and skins and vicariously get away from it all with him.

It was the forties that had damaged Garrity, and the fifties that had destroyed him. In the forties, the sons of his audience had been forced to leave their insular existence and go out into the world, to the aged cities of France and Italy and Germany, to the sands of Africa, to the jungles of the Pacific, and they had seen these places with the hard cynical eyes of reality. They had been where Garrity had been, and they knew his romantic adventures were lies. They knew more than he did about the faraway places and the truth of them, and they had no patience with Garrity, despite the permanent credulity of their parents who did not know better. By the fifties, the old audience was slipping away and the new audience was not his own. The new audience, and its heirs, had no inclination to read about adventures, presuming there were any left, when in the time it took to read a Garrity book they could visit, in person, via jet transportation, the ruins of Angkor and the Isle of Rhodes and the Leaning Tower of Pisa. The world was suddenly too small, all of it too accessible, for interest in secondhand travel romance. When you could see for yourself inside the magician's box, as he sawed the girl in half, there was no more wonder in seeing the magician. An international war and the turbo jet were Garrity's graveyard.

Claire's musings gave her almost a sense of pity for this relic. He still published, but almost no one bought. He continued to lecture, but too few came to hear. He still traded on his name, but not many under fifty remembered or cared. The matinee idol had been forsaken, but would not believe it. He carried his past with him every waking minute, and kept it alive with liquor and fanciful projects. He was gesturing now, as he whispered to Marc, and these gestures were even more effeminate than earlier. In a sudden revelation, Claire saw what had been concealed so long but was now, from uncontrollable anxiety over failure, exposed often. He was a homosexual, had always been one, but before this, his virile paper romances had provided camouflage. Tonight, without this camouflage, the truth could be seen nakedly.

Promptly, Claire sorted her own judgments of Garrity-as-homosexual. Claire had no negative feelings about deviates. The few that she had encountered, in her short life, she had found wittier, more clever and sensitive, than normal males. Also, she supposed, she felt easier with them because they were nonthreatening. No, definitely, it was not Garrity's obvious deviation that was making Claire relinquish distaste for him and replace it with pity. It was his *pretense* that made her want to commiserate with him.

Observing him across the table once more, she abandoned understanding for her original emotion of disapproval. She sat back, touching her napkin to her lips, wondering again how Marc could be so absorbed in this bluff half-man, held erect by no more than yellowed press notices and remembered compliments.

She turned her head and looked up the table as the dessert plates were being removed, and she caught Maud's eye. Almost imperceptibly, Maud nodded to her, and Claire dipped her head in acknowledgment.

"Well," Maud called out, "I think we'd all be much more comfortable in the living room. Claire, would—"

Claire, with a fumbling gesture of assistance from President Loomis, had already risen. "Yes, I think that's a good idea. Mrs. Hackfeld—Mrs. Loomis—and Marc, forgive me, Marc, I hate to interrupt, but if you'd get the liqueurs . . . ?"

There had been a general rising of all guests. Like a social director in the Adirondacks, Claire was at the archway, herding the Loomises into the living room, and then Garrity and Marc. As she took Lisa Hackfeld's arm, she saw, over her shoulder, that Cyrus Hackfeld was about to start for the living room, too. But Maud, who had been addressing him, added something more, and Hackfeld eyed her questioningly, nodded, and moved with her to the far dining room window. The moment of truth, Claire thought, and she crossed mental fingers, and went with Lisa Hackfeld into the living room to play diversion.

While Marc doled out slivers of apricot liqueur and of Cointreau, and droplets of Armagnac and of Benedictine and Brandy, the guests aligned themselves uncertainly around the broad living room. It was, Claire told herself, so much like the opening of a play before the main actors appear, when the telephone rings and the maid answers it, and the supporting players, marking time, cross the stage with their banalities. Desperately, one wanted the stars to generate excitement. Nevertheless, Claire had her duty and was determined to perform.

She sat across from Lisa Hackfeld. "Mrs. Hackfeld, did I overhear you ask my mother-in-law about the festival on The Three Sirens?"

"Yes," said Lisa. "It sounds absolutely fascinating, like a celebration we should have over here."

Marc paused in his serving of drinks. "We have holidays, we have the Fourth of July," he said wryly. And then, because Lisa Hackfeld appeared bewildered, Marc hastily explained with a forced grin, "I'm only kidding, of course. But seriously, within the confines of our civilized state, we have countless means of celebration. For better or worse, we have places to—to relax with a drink, places to buy happy pills, places to seek diversion of every sort—"

"It's not the same, Marc," Claire said. "It's all sort of artificial and unnatural. You were joking about our holidays, like the Fourth of July, but that's a great example of what separates us from the Sirens. We celebrate with firecrackers—on the Sirens they become firecrackers."

Lisa Hackfeld beamed at Claire. "Exactly, Mrs. Hayden! We have nothing like that at all—"

"Because, as Dr. Hayden indicated, we're civilized," interrupted Garrity. His blotched face had assumed the solemnity of a cardinal reading a papal decree. "I've been around those islands, and they all have festivals as an excuse to revert to their old animal ways. It is their way of getting around the missionaries and governors, to indulge themselves in base passions. I have no patience with the egg-heads and ethnologists who give all those holiday games and dances, those lewd pelvic displays, high and fancy esthetic interpretations. Civilization has put a stopper on their indecent behavior, and they use any excuse to pull the stopper."

Claire felt annoyed. "Is that bad?"

Quickly, Marc intervened. "Really, Claire, you sound—"

Claire beat him to it. "Uncivilized? Sometimes I wish I were, but I'm not." She turned to Lisa Hackfeld, who had been listening, wide-eyed. "I think you'll understand me, Mrs. Hackfeld. We're all so kind of stepped on, squashed, pushed down, emotionally. It's not natural. I think laws and rules and inhibitions are fine, but once in a while there should be license to shout and romp and let go. We'd all be better off."

"You took the words right out of my mouth," said Lisa Hackfeld, happily. "I couldn't agree with you more."

"Well, it's all in the point of view," Marc said, studiously. His manner had become all deliberation. "Mr. Garrity may not be far from the mark. Recent studies have indicated that the islanders most often use custom to disguise eroticism. Take the Fijians. They have this holiday game called *veisolo*. The idea is that young women invade the homes of young men to steal and hoard their food. But both sexes know the real object of the game. It is, unquestionably, an excuse to—to have intercourse. Basil Thomson wrote about such a game in 1908. A strapping Fiji girl entered a male hut to steal food, and found herself outnumbered by the male occupants. 'Then followed a scene,' said Thomson, 'which suggests that there is a sexual significance in the custom, for the girl was stripped and cruelly assaulted in a manner not to be described.' Now, as an anthropologist I find this very interesting. And I have no judgment to pass on it, except one—" He had turned fully toward his wife and Mrs. Hackfeld. "Surely, Claire, you would not suggest this is fun or a practice desirable for—for all of us in this country?"

Claire knew him now, knew he was repressing irritation, from the slight tipping edge to his voice, from the bunching between his eyes that did not match the half-smile on his lips, and she realized that she must handle this. "Marc, you should understand me better than that—I was joking—I wouldn't seriously suggest such a thing." She could hear Lisa Hackfeld's exhalation, a disappointment, as if Lisa felt she had lost an ally. While mollifying her husband, Claire fought to hold Lisa's faith in her. "But to go back to that festival on The Three Sirens, it must be good for them since they've practiced it for so long. Of course, we can't truly judge, because no one knows much about them." She smiled at Lisa Hackfeld, and winked at her. "I promise you a full report next August."

After that, the conversation was less spirited, more contrived and sluggish. Lisa Hackfeld made a few tentative inquiries about Polynesian customs in music and dancing, and Marc replied pedantically by quoting from published studies. President Loomis brought up the subject of Kabuki, but Garrity overrode him to relate an adventure he had once had with a harem of hula dancers at Waikiki.

During this last, there was the sound of footsteps. Cyrus Hackfeld came into the room cheerily, and made for the brandy tray, and behind him came Maud. Claire could tell by her mother-in-law's lips, which were set in a forced public smile, that she was not happy. For an instant, she had stood between Marc and Claire and

her guests, had physically blocked out these others and had her son
and daughter-in-law alone, and in that instant she made a flash of a
gesture, her fist turning in front of her body with her thumb down,
this accompanied by the briefest grimace.

Claire's heart sank. Maud was telling them that Hackfeld had
rejected her appeal for a more reasonable budget. Claire wondered
what would happen. It did not mean the field study would be canceled, but it did mean that the trip would be skimpy, limited, pres-
sured. Did it also mean that some of the letters that had gone out,
inviting experts to join the team, would now have to be recalled?
Claire wondered. She also wondered why Maud had risked announcing her failure to them. Did she still hope to appeal the decision, did she expect Claire or Marc to succeed somehow, socially,
in getting what she had failed to obtain?

Thereafter, bemused by the failure, Claire withdrew more into
herself. She had lost her joyful party manners. She slumped, and
she listened.

She heard Garrity's voice, extraordinarily loud and high-pitched,
directed toward Maud.

"Dr. Hayden," he was saying, "I must tell you why I came to
Los Angeles. My lecture agents, Busch Artist and Lyceum Bureau,
have worked up a fabulous series of bookings for me for next year
—but, quite frankly, on the condition that I find a new subject. As
a matter of fact, I want one, too. I've rather tired of the old things.
Well, now, I hit upon an idea, and I did some research on it. I
thought it a marvelous idea. You know, in times like these, say what
you will, people want to escape, put their heads in the sand. There
is much to be said for ostriches, indeed there is. So it came to me
that to get away from all this horrible nuclear-war-and-fallout talk,
my people would like to escape with me for an evening to the City
of Gold in the unexplored sections of Brazil's Matto Grosso jungles. There was said to be such a place, you know. I decided to outfit a small, a modest expedition, guides, motion picture crew, and
go up the Amazon, follow the old Fawcett trail, and make a rare
adventure of it. Now a thing like this takes financing, and I
thought of Cyrus, who is an old friend, and laid it in his lap, but
Cyrus felt that it wasn't scientific enough—"

Hackfeld squirmed uncomfortably. "Not I, Rex, but the Board,
the Board of the Foundation," he said.

"Well, be that as it may, I still think they're wrong," said Garrity, his tongue loosened by drink. "No matter, no matter, that's neither here nor there now." He was pointed toward Maud again. "Tonight you've convinced me, Dr. Hayden, that the City of Gold is a passé thing compared to your Sirens."

"It's not my Sirens, but thank you," said Maud.

"You've got a good thing there, Dr. Hayden. It's an adventure, it's a titillation, and at the same time—forgive me—it can pass as scientific inquiry—you know—it is science with built-in box office."

Claire shuddered for her mother-in-law, but knew that Maud could manage by herself. "I can't subscribe to your description of our anthropological study, Mr. Garrity," said Maud tightly.

"No offense," Garrity replied. "Only meant a compliment. Say, aren't we both dealing with the public? Anyway, I'll come straight to the point—you'll find I always come to the point. I'd like to go to The Three Sirens with you. I was discussing it with Marc at dinner. You've got me sold. This is a brand-new subject. It could be a sensation. Think of it—an unknown island laboratory for new modes of sex and marriage. Why, I'd double, triple my bookings—and get a best-seller that wouldn't conflict with your own. I have a lot to offer in helping you, and, in fact, I'd pay you a royalty on all my—"

"No," said Maud.

Garrity teetered on a phrase, and fell back, mouth slack. "But—"

Marc swerved toward his mother. "Matty, maybe this is something we can take up later with Mr. Garrity."

"Absolutely not," said Maud.

All eyes were on the pair, and immediately Marc tried to defend his position as scientist. "What I'm trying to say, Matty, is—well, I agree with you completely that we can't get mixed up in any sort of undignified popularization—but it occurred to me that there might be some other areas—I don't know—small areas, where Mr. Garrity could be beneficial to us, and where we could be—" He paused, lifted his palms outward, and shrugged. "I was only suggesting this is something we might explore at another time."

"I appreciate your trying to help, Marc," said Maud, "but there is simply nothing to explore." She had spoken the last with the slightest smile, but now, turning to address Garrity, the smile disappeared. "I respect your position and needs, Mr. Garrity, and you must understand my own. We are going to visit a unique people on a hitherto unknown island *on the condition* that their locale is never exposed to the public—"

"But I wouldn't!" said Garrity with fervor.

"—and that any account of their life and customs is not distorted by sensationalism," Maud went on. "By the very nature of your calling, that of a successful popularizer, you might exploit the Sirens in a way that could ultimately be damaging. I am determined to keep this on a purely scientific level. When I speak about it later, write about it, or members of my team do, it will be strictly in anthropological terms, and the interpretations will be sociological. This, I hope, will cast the proper light on the tribe and make the study useful. I am bound by my word not to incur any risks beyond that. Heavens forbid, I am not rebuking you, Mr. Garrity—there is a place for your—your findings—and another for ours, but I cannot see a partnership between the two . . . Marc, I think Mr. Hackfeld might like another brandy."

Thereafter, Garrity ceased contributing to the general conversation. He lapsed into sullen silence, moving only to refill his brandy glass with Armagnac. Lisa Hackfeld had become lively again, crowding Maud with more questions about what she expected to find on The Three Sirens and with still more questions about life in Polynesia, and Hackfeld seemed pleased to see his wife so entertained.

Sometime before midnight, Claire heard Garrity hoarsely ask Marc to lead him to a telephone where he might make a business call. Obligingly, Marc rose and guided the travel writer down the hall to the phone in the room where the television set was kept. They had been gone five minutes when Hackfeld came heavily to his feet. "Honey," he was saying to his wife, "we've got a long drive back."

"Must you go?" said Maud.

"I certainly hate to, believe me," said Lisa, rising. "I haven't been so stimulated by conversation in years."

The Loomises were on their feet, too, and Claire hurried into the hall for the coats. From the closet, she could see Marc and Garrity standing inside the door of the small television room, engaged in an intense whispered exchange. Odd, Claire thought. Garrity had not wanted the telephone, he had wanted Marc's ear.

She paused, holding the heavy coats on her arm. "Mr. Garrity," she called, "Mr. and Mrs. Hackfeld are leaving."

Garrity came out of the room nodding, tendered Claire a false smile, and went back through the hall to the living room. Marc was following behind him, thoughtful, when Claire stepped between her husband and Garrity. "Marc, help me with the coats."

As he did so, they were by themselves.

"What goes on between you two?" Claire wanted to know.

Marc's eyes were bright. "He was briefing me on the lecture business. He was saying with a subject like The Three Sirens he could make over a million dollars—a million, imagine—as a starter, for all of us."

"All of us?"

"I mean, if Maud let him in on this."

"He'd wreck the whole project. He's horrible."

"Don't make your snap judgments, Claire. He's likable, if you get to know him. And he's very successful. In fact, I have a hunch he's more conservative and restrained than he sounds. I think it's his public manner that throws you and Matty."

"He's a leech," said Claire. "There's a whole breed of bloodsuckers, without talent, who live off people like you and Maud, who have talent. They bait you with reckless talk of big money, like this Garrity is doing, and—"

"Easy, Claire." Nervously, Marc looked off. "He might hear you."

"Let him."

She started to go, but Marc restrained her. "Look, I stand by what I said before. We're not interested in making a circus of our findings. It's just that—well, you know as well as I do how much innocuous data winds up in dead files. I thought maybe we could dump the excess on Garrity, and still not compromise ourselves. I mean, if there's all that loot floating around, why not get some of it? I'd like to get you your own car, and some new clothes—"

"Lovely," said Claire, "only there must be easier ways. Like holding up a bank . . . Stick to what you believe, Marc. Let Mephistopheles find himself another Faust."

"Oh, hell, honey, I was just talking."

"And so was Garrity." She tugged his sleeve. "Come on, they'll miss us."

Five minutes later, Maud Hayden stood in the open door, watching her guests leave. Claire came beside her, shivering at contact with the chilled night air. Outside, she observed a strange tableau.

The Loomises had driven off, but the Hackfelds' Cadillac limousine still was parked before the walk. Garrity had already dropped into the front seat, and the chauffeur remained at attention next to the open rear door. But Lisa Hackfeld had drawn her husband aside some distance from the car, and they appeared to be arguing, as they stood there below the house.

"I wonder what's going on?" asked Claire.

"I don't know," said Maud. "All I know, worse luck, is that he turned me down. He said not enough was known about the Sirens to warrant the granting of extra funds."

"What will that mean?"

"Well, I suppose—"

She stopped. The ponderous figure of Cyrus Hackfeld was approaching slowly up the path, as his wife ducked into the car. Hackfeld halted some yards away. "Dr. Hayden," he called out, "can I speak to you for a moment?"

Quickly, Maud pushed open the screen door.

"Wait," said Claire, "I'll get you a sweater."

"No, never mind—"

She went down the walk. Claire watched her a moment, saw Hackfeld engage her in conversation, saw Maud nodding, and then Claire left the door so that she would not be eaves—— well, eaveslooking, she supposed you might call it. She assisted Marc, who was removing the bottles and glasses, and emptying the ashtrays, until at last her mother-in-law returned.

Maud shut the front door, and leaned back against it, while the limousine outside started, warmed up, and crunched away, the sound of it receding. Both Claire and Marc tried to read Maud's face as she came slowly to the coffee table. Her face showed relief, but no joy.

"Well, children," she said, "we're getting the extra money, after all—and we're also getting Mrs. Lisa Hackfeld."

Marc reacted first. "What the devil does that mean, Matty?"

"It means that Lisa Hackfeld had the time of her life tonight. She's a bored rich woman, and the talk about the Sirens was the first thing that has interested her in an age. Tomorrow is her birthday, and she asked her husband to give her the trip with us as her present. She wants to come along. She insists upon it. She needs a vacation, but she also thinks she can be helpful. He says she knows something about dancing, studied it. Hackfeld will do anything to please her. As a matter of fact, I had no time to object. He said to me, 'Of course, Dr. Hayden, if you have to take another person along, it would mean more expense, and I'd have to raise your budget anyway, wouldn't I? Okay, let's raise it the amount you requested after dinner, and I think I'll personally throw in, out of my own pocket, an added five thousand. Will that do?' " Maud snorted. "Will that do? I'll say it'll do. We'll be traveling with a big and strange company, but by God, children, we're on our way, and that's all that counts!"

* * *

Even though it was after two o'clock in the morning, and she was physically tired, Claire was not really too tired for *that*. She knew that he wanted her, as he always did those infrequent times when he made sly innuendos and stared at her bust.

They had undressed, and Claire was already in the double bed, wearing the flimsy white nylon nightgown with the thin straps and full pleated skirt. He was still in the bathroom, and she lay on her back and waited. Except for the dim lamp on the table beside his end of the bed, the room was intimately darkened, and comfortably warm, yet her waiting was in her mind and not in her lower limbs, and she wondered why. Actually, she knew the answer but hated to face it. She disliked always blaming herself. The truth was, she did not enjoy the act, but enjoyed only the romantic idea that justified the act. Its accomplishment was a symbol. This participation in sex made her feel married and normal and at one with all the women on earth. The participation itself gave her no body pleasure. In recent months, she had feared that he suspected her true feelings. Otherwise, why would he come to her so infrequently?

He had emerged from the bathroom, in his striped pajamas, and as she turned her head on the pillow, toward him, she could see from his expression, his movements, that he was ready. She lay waiting without tension, or expectation, for the steps were familiar. He would sit on the edge of the bed, kick off his slippers, slide under the blanket, put out the lamp, stretch out. His hand would reach for her, and suddenly he would edge over to kiss her mouth, tearing down the thin straps, and then kiss her breasts, and then grab for the bottom of her nightgown, and that would be it, and in minutes she would be normal. It was worth anything to be normal and married, she told herself, and she waited.

He sat on the edge of the bed and kicked off his slippers.

"It was a good evening, darling," she said. "I'm glad it went so well."

"Yes," he said, except that something disapproving had crossed his features. "Just one thing—"

He slipped under the blanket, but was still propped on an elbow. She showed that she was puzzled.

"—just one thing that bothers me, Claire," he said. "What gets into you, compels you to speak so loosely in front of utter strangers? All that silly stuff about approving of sex festivals, and wishing we had that sort of abandonment here. What can people think? It gives them a bad impression. They don't know you, they don't know you're joking."

He reached up and turned out the lamp.

"I wasn't joking, Marc," she said in the sudden darkness. "There *is* something to say for the way primitive people enjoy themselves. I only retracted because I saw you were getting angry."

Seconds before, his voice, although critical of her, had still been thick with desire for her. Now, suddenly, it changed, desire thinned out to displeasure. "What do you mean—I was getting angry? What is that supposed to mean?"

"Oh, nothing, Marc, please—"

"No, I'm calling you on it—what does that mean?"

"It means, whenever I happen to talk about sex—which is rare enough—you become annoyed with me. It always turns out this way—for some reason."

"For some reason, huh?"

"Please, Marc, don't make a federal case of it. I don't know what I'm saying—I'm tired—"

"You're darn right you don't know what you're saying. I'd like to know what really goes on in that head of yours, but one thing I'll tell you, sooner or later you'd better grow up, become a responsible married woman, not—not—"

She felt weak with helplessness. "Not what, Marc?"

"Look, let's knock it off. I'm tired, too."

The bed shook as he sat up and shoved off the edge. He found his slippers, and once shod, he stood up in the darkness.

"Marc, what's the matter—where are you going?"

"I'm going downstairs to have a drink," he said gruffly. "I can't sleep."

He stomped across the room, bumping into a chair, and then he was out of the door and down the stairs.

Claire lay on her back, in the wasted white nightgown, unmoving. She was sorry, but it was not the first time this had happened, either. Strangely, these occasional flare-ups had a pattern, she could see. Whenever she repeated a story she had overheard, a joke or a bit of gossip, that involved sex, whenever she was frank, he would become annoyed with her. The last time had been two weeks ago, at just such a moment of intimacy as this. They had gone to the theater to see a film in which the hero was a prize fighter. Later, when she had commented on the brawny good looks and physique of the male star, and tried to analyze his appeal to women, Marc had chosen this remark as a reason for being disagreeable to her. Yes, somehow it seemed that each time Claire made some favorable reference to sex or any aspect of sexuality, Marc took this as a personal affront, a subversion of his virility. At such times, almost in a flash, his kindness, his good humor, his solid adultness seemed to evaporate, leaving only tense and defensive petulance. Thank God, it did not happen often, but it happened. And then she was confused, as she was confused now. How ridiculous of him, she thought, and she worried. What can bother him at times like this? And then she wondered. Are such flare-ups common among all men?

Sleepily, she reviewed her earliest dreams of love and marriage, when she was eleven and twelve in Chicago, when she was fifteen and sixteen in Berkeley, when she was eighteen and nineteen in Westwood, and when she was twenty-two and had met Marc. In some ways, she could correlate her dreams with the current reality. There was a certain coziness and security in marriage, especially during the day. At night, well, like tonight, the chasm between dream and reality was bottomless.

He was downstairs drinking brandy, she knew. He would remain there, waiting for her to fall asleep before returning to bed.

For an hour, she tried to sleep, and could not.

When he returned to the bedroom at last, she pretended to be asleep. She wanted him to be happy . . .

III

Lɪᴋᴇ ᴛʜᴇ colossal brown bird of Polynesian legend, the amphibian flying boat soared through the void of dark, preparing to give birth to the Beginning.

There were many myths of the Creation in Oceania, but the one that Claire Hayden believed in tonight was this: in the boundless universe existed only the warm primeval sea, and above it flew a gigantic bird, and into the sea the bird dropped a mammoth egg, and when its shell broke there appeared the god, Taaroa, and he produced heaven and earth above and below the sea, and he produced the first breath of life.

For Claire, drowsily caught between sleep and waking, it was not difficult to fancy Captain Ollie Rasmussen's seaplane as the brown bird of Polynesian legend, soon to give birth on the Southern Sea to the Eden of The Three Sirens, which would be their only world.

They had left Papeete in the night, and it was night still, Claire knew, but since she had slept fitfully, she had no idea where they were or how far they had flown. This mystery, she knew, had been Rasmussen's intent from the start.

Uncomfortable in the worn bucket seat, one of the ten that the copilot, Richard Hapai, had reinstalled—the main cabin had been used for cargo before their coming—Claire sat up, stretched her legs, and tried to accustom her eyes to the dim light of the battery-powered lamp. Trying not to disturb Maud, dozing in the seat to her right, or Marc, snoring softly across the way on her left, she groped below and then into the aisle for her spacious carry-all handbag with its shoulder strap, located it, and extracted cigarette and lighter.

Once smoking, and fully awake, Claire twisted to survey the interior of the crowded main cabin. Besides the three of them, and excepting Rasmussen and Hapai in the pilots' compartment, there were seven other members of the team present. In the unnatural light, she counted heads, unconsciously seeking another who was aroused and inwardly as filled with expectancy as herself.

Slumped low beside Marc was Orville Pence, his ridiculous gray tropical helmet pulled down to cover his bald spot and his beady eyes. She could see that he had removed his shell-rimmed spectacles, and now he snored faintly, in duet with Marc. Despite the fact that she had found Pence more friendly, less sex-obsessed, than the time they had met in Denver, she could find no common bond with him, although evidently Marc had done so. Without the hovering specter of his mother, and away from his own surroundings, Pence was less repulsive, but physically no less ludicrous.

Behind Pence and Marc sat Sam Karpowicz and his Mary, the father sleeping soundly, like one who had been through this wrenching transportation before, the daughter sleeping restlessly, like one (like Claire herself) apprehensive of the unknown. Observing the Karpowiczes now, including the mother, Estelle, sideways and asleep in the seat behind, Claire remembered feeling instant affection for them upon first meeting them. She had liked Sam, a skinny high pole of a person, a scholarly Ichabod Crane, with his fervent liberal views and his enthusiasm for his cameras and plant presses. She had liked Estelle, doughy and complacent, because she seemed dependable, the Earth Mother. The sixteen-year-old Mary was temperamentally her father's child, straightforward, bright, partisan, and keyed up. Her black Rebecca eyes, setting off her dawn-tinted faultless complexion, combined with her spring burgeoning figure to make her a decorative addition to the team.

Next to Estelle Karpowicz, upright and wide-awake, slowly chewing on a gumdrop, sat Lisa Hackfeld. Like Orville Pence, who wore a necktie and starched shirt collar with his washable charcoal business suit, Lisa Hackfeld was incongruously attired. Her expensive, impractical Saks suit was of snowy white linen, fashionably correct at the Racquet Club in Palm Springs, but an impossibility on an anthropology field trip whose destination was a rugged Polynesian island. Already, one lapel of the white suit bore a grease smudge, and at the waist it had wrinkled in many places. Claire tried to catch Lisa's eye, but failed, for Lisa was lost within herself, deep in some subterranean introspection.

At the rear sat Rachel DeJong and Harriet Bleaska. With difficulty, Claire caught glimpses of them. They were either napping, or trying to rest. From their first meeting, Claire had been unsure of her feelings toward Rachel DeJong. Coupling Rachel's profession of psychoanalyst with her cool, precise, formal bearing, Claire had found conversation with her laborious. What surprised Claire was that Rachel DeJong was both young and handsome. Yet the stiff, unyielding air about her made her seem considerably more than thirty-one, and hardened her chestnut-colored hair, quick eyes, classically regular features, long figure.

Claire turned her attention to the nurse. Harriet Bleaska, she decided, was quite another matter. Once one recovered from the initial shock caused by her homeliness, it became possible to discern her excellent qualities. Harriet Bleaska was an extrovert, easygoing, kind, warm. She wanted to please, a trait that was in some persons strained and oppressive, but in Harriet natural and sincere. Somehow, you felt comfortable and glad to know her. In fact, these inner virtues were so dominant that, after a short time, they seemed to rise above and obscure their owner's ill-favored countenance.

Claire felt better about Harriet Bleaska now, and was pleased that Maud had been forced into taking her on the expedition. After the addition of Lisa Hackfeld to the team, and the necessity of taking along Sam Karpowicz' family, Maud had been prepared to reject Harriet, nurse, as a substitute for Dr. Walter Zegner, physician and researcher. There had been one last familiar protest to Marc and herself. Maud had said, on that occasion, that the perfect field team was a team composed of one person, or at the most two or three, and that her original plan to take seven had been a concession to Hackfeld's grandness, but seven was the absolute limit. With the presence of the Karpowicz women, Lisa Hackfeld, and Harriet Bleaska, the investigation might become a comic opera, its scientific approach dangerously impaired. If the Karpowiczes and Lisa were unavoidable expediencies, at least Harriet, a nurse unknown to her, could be left off the roster. Nine was more feasible than ten.

"I know I've said it before, and I'll say it again," Maud had protested, "but a big group of anthropologists dropped into a small culture might alter that culture and ruin it. There's a classical example in recent years. There's a known case where a team of twelve field workers, in two motor cars, arrived to study a native tribe, and they were stoned out of the village. They represented an invasion, not a few participants who might integrate. If we take ten of us to the Sirens, we'll wind up an American colony in the middle of a bunch of natives, unable to melt into tribal life, become part of it, and we'll end up studying each other."

Maud had gone to Cyrus Hackfeld with her roster of nine, and immediately Hackfeld had missed Zegner. Maud had pointed out that Dr. DeJong had completed medical training many years before, but Hackfeld had remained adamant, insisting upon Harriet Bleaska as a replacement for Zegner. He demanded a professional person who was familiar with the most recent medical techniques as a safeguard for his wife, since she had never before been to a primitive place or a tropical isle. Maud, not used to Waterloos and Appomattoxes, known for her willingness to fight beyond her means, had known when to surrender. And so here was Harriet, and here they were ten.

The seaplane, lurching in and out of an air pocket, bounced and trembled, and then the twin engines whined higher, and it leveled again. Claire had been shaken in her seat, and quickly she looked across at Marc, to see if the jolt had awakened him. It had not. He slept on, no longer snoring, but his breath a low rasp. Claire watched her husband in slumber. The tense face seemed more reposeful. In fact, except for his noisy exhaling and inhaling, he seemed as attractive as in the time before she had known him well, and he seemed—the crewcut did it—like a clean, healthy, aggressive young collegian. His garb added a dash to this picture. He wore a light denim jacket with six pockets, a washable thin plaid shirt, khaki trousers, and ungainly paratrooper boots.

Trying to admire him, to be proud, she recollected several of their last conversations at home. Since Dr. Walter Scott Macintosh had assigned Maud a prominent place to deliver her Sirens paper at the autumn meeting of the American Anthropological League (and felt positive that she would overcome Rogerson for the post of executive editor of *Culture*), Marc had become absolutely ebullient about his own future. Once his mother left Raynor College, he would inherit her exalted chair in anthropology. Although he would have the position because of her, because of the family name, he would be freed of Maud and Adley, and be on his own, with his own identity and his own sycophants. It was his one objective, to be on his own, to be Somebody. He had not put it to Claire exactly that way, but it was what she understood him to feel and mean when he spoke of the immediate future and the necessity for making the Sirens field trip a success.

The heat of Claire's cigarette had touched her nicotine-stained fingers, and she leaned forward, dropped it, and ground the butt out with the sole of one flat shoe. She sought a fresh cigarette, and after it was lighted, she lay back in the bucket seat, legs out-stretched and crossed at the ankles, and considered the unreality of these moments. Until now, despite the background research, the end-goal of Polynesia and the place known as The Three Sirens had been a chimera, a holiday oasis that might resemble one of the fake Hawaiian restaurants that she and Marc occasionally visited in Los Angeles or San Francisco. Now that this ancient amphibian flying boat and the morning and the atoll destination were converg-ing, she was mildly confused about what awaited her and what her life would be for six weeks. For reasons that she had not examined in depth, this trip and the place soon to be their temporary home had assumed some kind of milestone importance to her. It was as if she were readying to exchange the dulled knives of routine and habit and a certain unfulfillment for something razor-sharp, that would, in a stroke, cleave her from the past, and allow Marc and herself to enter on a new and happier level of life.

Folded in her hard seat, she felt the tightness across her chest, which extended even to her arms beneath the pale blue sweater. Was it concern over what was unfamiliar, not before known, as she suspected it was with young Mary Karpowicz and Lisa Hack-field? Or was it simply a fatigue after the drive of building toward the climactic arrival these last days? She compromised. It was both, a little of each.

Only five days before they had all gathered as a team, for the first time, at the Hayden house in Santa Barbara, and President Loomis had graciously provided living accommodations on campus for the visitors. The ten of them had met and mingled, feeling one another out, trying out each other's personalities, and there had been a series of briefings by Maud, as field director, and after that a series of informal question-and-answer sessions. There had also been a last-minute scurrying for supplies that had been forgotten, and much repacking, and then a luncheon tendered by Loomis and the senior faculty members.

Late in the afternoon, in three limousines supplied by Cyrus Hackfeld (two for themselves, one for the luggage) they had been taken down to the Beverly Hilton Hotel at the edge of Beverly Hills. Hackfeld had reserved rooms for them—his own wife had refused to return with him to their Bel-Air mansion, and in spite of his opposition had stayed with the rest—and then there had been a press conference, expertly handled by Maud, followed by an early farewell dinner, planned by Hackfeld and several of the Board members of the Foundation.

At eleven o'clock in the evening, they had been driven in the private limousines through waning traffic the long distance to the International Airport on Sepulveda Boulevard. In the vast modern terminal, where Maud had checked passports, visas, smallpox certificates, the list of luggage, they had all been pervaded by a sense of loneliness, as if standing huddled in a hospital corridor after bedtime. There had been no one but Cyrus Hackfeld to see them off. A telegram from Colorado Springs had arrived for Orville Pence, and Rachel DeJong had been paged for a telephone call from someone named Mr. Joseph Morgen. Otherwise, the strands of old ties were lying loose. It was as if they had been abandoned by the known world.

At last, Flight Number 89 of TAI had been announced, and, with a cluster of other night-weary passengers, they had filed out of the terminal, and presently into the metal capsule of the DC8 jet aircraft of the Compagnie de Transports Aériens Intercontinentaux, which was scheduled to speed nonstop from Los Angeles to Papeete, Tahiti. Their accommodations had been economy class instead of first class—Maud had fought Hackfeld on this, and with Lisa's support had won out—and this meant but little deprivation to realize a savings, round trip, of 2,500 dollars on tickets. In economy class, the soft fabric chairs had been three on one side of the aisle, and three on the other, so that they sat six in a row, and took up most of two rows. The rest of the second row had been filled in by an amiable Pomona dentist, off on a vacation, and a beefy, well-dressed, bearded youth, celebrating his graduation from college.

At precisely one hour after midnight, their jet had begun to move, lumbering slowly, then picking up speed, finally roaring down the concrete runway, and soon they were airborne. Too quickly, the multitude of yellow dots of the metropolis below, and another patch of shimmering habitation, and yet one more, were left behind, and they were catapulted high above the Pacific Ocean into the inky blackness.

This portion of the journey had been restful. Sitting between her husband and her mother-in-law, Claire had begun to read a compact guidebook to Oceania, while Maud and Marc leafed through the free magazines in three languages furnished by TAI. Later, at reduced rates, they had ordered glasses of Mumm champagne, served by a raven-haired Tahitian stewardess wearing a blue cotton *pareu.*

The champagne had given Maud a feeling of well-being, and her pudgy person relaxed and her tongue loosened. In her festive mood she had, finally, reconciled herself to the size of the team, and had even thought that the variety of experts might prove advantageous to the study. "Ten persons isn't a record number, you know," she had said. "Once, a wealthy young man—I think his family was in the banking business—took a team of twenty—twenty, mind you—to Africa, and I believe it worked out. This wealthy young man dressed himself as fastidiously as our Dr. Pence. In the field, he wore a dressy shirt and tie, and a Brooks Brothers suit. According to the story, one day the natives of the African tribe invited this wealthy young man to dine with them. Their *pièce de résistance* was a fried patty-cake made up of various greens, vegetables, and mud. When the young man told the experience later, someone asked him, 'Well, did you eat it?' He threw up his hands. 'Don't be silly,' he said, 'I can barely eat the food at the Yale Club!' "

Claire and Marc, and Lisa Hackfeld across the aisle, had laughed, and Maud had gone on reminiscing for another half-hour. Eventually, she had tired, and turned upon her side to doze off. Gradually, because there was nothing to do or see, lulled by the even monotony of the flight, by the champagne, by sedatives, most of the team had gone to sleep.

At six-thirty in the morning, one by one, they had been awakened. The remnants of the night still hid Polynesia from sight, and so they had occupied themselves with the bathrooms and with packing their loose effects and having breakfast. Through all of this, the night had fled, the sun curved over the horizon, and the broad glassy ocean was to be seen far below. The loudspeaker had crackled instructions: secure safety belts, put out cigarettes, in several minutes Tahiti.

For Claire, the legendary island had meant a jumble of all her readings, had meant Cook and Sieur de Bougainville, Bligh and Christian, Melville and Stevenson, Gauguin and Loti, Rupert Brooke and Maugham, and she had strained against her window for sight of the enchanted place. At first there was only the cloudless pale sky merging with the cerulean sea, and then, like a faint and distant color slide of an exquisite and fragile Hiroshige—in Oriental emerald-green projected on a curtain of air—there was Tahiti.

Claire had gasped audibly at seeing the lovely print take dimension and grow in her vision. Briefly, she had felt an ache that this had been on the earth so long, and she on the earth so long, before their meeting. But she had appreciated her good fortune in possessing this for a memory at last, and she had remembered exactly, as a caption for the scene, the words of Robert Louis Stevenson: "The first love, the first sunrise, the first South Sea island, are memories apart, and touched a virginity of sense." Silently, she had thanked him for his perception of her feelings.

What had next dominated the view had been the velvety green of towering Mont Diademe, and suddenly they were dropping. Maud had leaned over, partially blocking the window, and Marc had engaged Claire with some instructions, and after snatching one final flash of the red-brown roofs of Papeete, she could see no more.

There had been the rush and noise of their landing, the gradual slowing on the runway, and the final stopping. They had all come to their feet with their hand kits, and descended into the misty, tepid, early-morning air. What awaited them was an indescribable confusion of brown people and scented flowers and airport music. The chortling pretty native girls, so graceful and supple, in their vivid pareus and thong sandals, wearing white tiara blossoms on their ears like jewelry, were everywhere. One had thrown a wreath of flowers around Claire's neck, and another had laughingly kissed Marc and called out "Iaorana," the Tahitian welcome.

Claire had singled out Alexander Easterday immediately, before their introduction, and once more had marveled at Maud's accuracy of memory and description. Observing Easterday, as he pumped Maud's hand, Claire saw a squat and waddling Germanic type in pith helmet and neatly pressed but worn beige tropical suit. It had made her nervous to watch his precarious pince-nez and graying mustache jiggling on either end of his tomato nose. It had also seemed incredible to her that this caricature of a Herr Professor, so unlikely amid the swarm of flowers and bosoms and pareus, had been responsible for the ten of them standing here on the island of Tahiti.

There was a bump that shook Claire loose from the memory of their arrival in Tahiti, and set her firmly into the bucket seat of Rasmussen's seaplane heading for The Three Sirens. Shifting her position, Claire could see that Maud had been rocked into slight wakefulness, but with determined eyelids still hooded over tired eyes she continued to sleep. Across the aisle, Marc remained undisturbed in his slumber, but Pence had awakened and was trying to get his bearings.

Claire's cigarette was but one-third burned. She shook off the ash, brought the cigarette to her lips and inhaled, determined to enjoy the rest of it in Tahiti. She tried to fasten her mind on the fantasy of the day past that had gone so swiftly. It had been a kaleidoscope of a day, and in her mind she turned it and turned it, sorting the fragments of colored glass, trying to fix on the actual pattern of what she had witnessed.

The variegated pattern would not take form, but changed in memory, so that she could see only one piece here and one piece there. They had gone through customs easily, she recalled. They had been taken, in rented Peugeots, outside the city to a cluster of thatched huts and coconut palm trees, near a lagoon, opening on the ocean, and this had been the Hotel Les Tropiques, with several huts reserved for those of them who wished to change or rest.

The early lunch in the patio had included steamed fish, fried chicken, Martinique rum, and hot poi, consisting of taro with pineapple, banana, and papaya in coconut cream. There had been a remarkable view of Moorea, ten miles across the way, and Easterday had said that Captain Ollie Rasmussen lived on Moorea and would be coming over on the launch after dinner.

Easterday had given Maud the schedule for her group. He had taken the liberty of arranging for everyone an auto tour of the island of Tahiti, over one hundred miles around the perimeter. This, and sightseeing and shopping in Papeete, would use up their afternoon. He had hoped that the Haydens would be his guests for dinner. The others would eat at the hotel, of course. He had left the evening open, suggesting they rest, since they would need their strength for the trip to the Sirens. At midnight, he would escort Maud, alone, to the Vaima Café on the waterfront to meet Rasmussen, while the others of the team, together with their baggage, would be driven to the quay and put aboard Rasmussen's seaplane. Easterday had thought that they would take off for the Sirens an hour or two after midnight, and arrive at their destination by dawn. He had made all arrangements, through Rasmussen, with Courtney and Paoti on the Sirens. The team would be accommodated for the six-week period that had been agreed upon. There was one more thing, Easterday had added, just one thing—the pledge of secrecy about the location of the Sirens must begin this minute. There must be no loose talk. He had begged Maud to impress the need for this self-control upon every member of the team, and she had promised to do so.

For Claire, the rest of the seventeen hours in Tahiti had been a dizzying experience. She had been given no leisure or meditative period during which to adjust to the change-over. In a single night she had gone over from the world of Raynor, Suzu, Loomis, Beverly Hilton to the world of Polynesia, Easterday, Rasmussen, Les Tropiques.

There had been the tour, the rented autos heading northward in the heat: the tomb of Tahiti's last King, Pomare V, such a lover of liqueur that a coral replica of a Benedictine bottle crowned the tomb amid the aito trees; the sights from Venus Point, where Captain Cook had stood in 1796 to observe the moon's path across the sun; the far-off waterfall of Faaru, like so many white threads swaying in the breeze; the late lunch in the bamboo dining room of the Faratea Restaurant, with the smell of pink acacias all about; the coolness of the Grotto of Maraa, with its pool inside the deep cave; the walls of black lava at the Temple of Ashes, where priests recited pagan rites; the cluster of huts representing the island's second-largest city, Taravao, with the nearby blowholes of spray.

When they had made the full circle, and entered Papeete, the colored-glass fragments of Claire's mental kaleidoscope reflected an odd assortment of remembrances: the foam on the coral reefs; the wayside café with its Algerian wine; the colonial house encircled by breadfruit trees thick with green leaves; the white churches with rust-colored steeples; the boxes, like mailboxes, along the highway, for the delivery of long French breads and pasteurized milk; the rickety native bus, packed with schoolgirls in navy blue, with blocks of ice on its roof; and everywhere, the green gorges and sparkling streams and red bougainvillaea.

Of Papeete, the city, she remembered only the sturdy laughing girls in their colored pareus, walking along in pairs; the buzzing motor scooters weaving in and out of wide baked streets; the copra schooners, yachts, fishing boats, and one gray liner in the water along the quay; the bamboo lettering that spelled "Quinn's" over a raucous nightclub; the French and Chinese stores, and the jumble of exotic artifacts inside Easterday's shop in the Rue Jeanne d'Arc.

She had been weary at dinner, eye-weary, leg-weary, senses fatigued, and through dinner with Easterday at Chez Chapiteau, she had eaten her filet mignon and fried potatoes and hardly listened as Maud and Marc discussed Rasmussen and The Three Sirens with their host. Back at Les Tropiques, she had flung herself on her bed and slept hard and motionless the hours before midnight. When Marc had shaken her awake, he told her that Maud had already gone off to meet Rasmussen at the Vaima Café, and that a young Polynesian named Hapai was waiting outside to drive them to the seaplane.

It had been after one o'clock in the morning when the flying boat had churned through the water, leaving behind the lights and music and shouts of Papeete, and lifted them into the sky once more toward The Three Sirens. She had met Rasmussen briefly, after the take-off. While Hapai was at the controls, Rasmussen had entered the main cabin, and Maud had made the introductions. Claire had been pleased by his appearance: a waterfront character wearing a venerable marine cap, open-collared, short-sleeved white shirt, blue jeans, and dirty tennis shoes. His bloodshot eyes had been rheumy, and his scarred, unshaved Scandinavian face a battleground of dissipation. His speech had been raspy, grammatically unpolished, but direct, serious, humorless. After the introductions, he had disappeared whence he came, into the seaplane's nose, and had not been seen again.

Claire's cigarette had burned out, and she dropped it beside her feet.

She heard the creak of a seat, caused by Maud's plentiful per-

son beside her, and she turned to find her mother-in-law seated
erect, arms up, stretching, wagging her head to shake off drowsi-
ness.

"I must have been sound asleep," said Maud, yawning. "Have
you been up all this time?"

"Yes. I'm wide awake. I had all that rest after dinner."

"What's been happening? Has Rasmussen come back in here?"

"No. Everything's very quiet. Only Mrs. Hackfeld and I have
been awake."

Maud was peering down at her large stainless-steel wrist watch.
"It's after six. Rasmussen said we'd be there by daybreak. We
should be very near."

"I hope so."

Maud studied Claire. "Are you all right?"

"Of course. Shouldn't I be?"

Maud smiled. "A young person's first field trip is like her first
date. Something new and important. She has a right to be uncertain. What is ahead? How will she react and perform?"

"I'm all right, Maud." She hesitated. "It's just—" She halted.

"Go on. You were about to say . . . ?"

"My only concern is that I might be useless on this trip. I mean
—what is my specialty? Wife?"

"Heavens, Claire, sometimes the wife of an anthropologist can be
ten times more important on a field trip than her husband. Countless reasons. A man-and-wife team seems less intrusive, less outsiders, more acceptable in many cultures. Furthermore, a wife can
find out more about wifely things, and understand them better,
than her husband. You know—household care, child rearing, nu-
trition—it is easier for her to recognize differences in these areas
and absorb them. Perhaps more important is the fact that—well,
countless societies have tabus against men, foreign men, observing
and interviewing their females. I don't know how it will be on the
Sirens, but Marc might be barred from learning about—oh, men-
struation, sexual intercourse, pregnancy, how these women feel
about being women, their pleasures, dislikes, longings—simply because he is a male. But his wife could be acceptable, even welcomed. You know—she's one of the girls, et cetera, just as I am,
except I'll have other tasks to keep me occupied. So you'll have
plenty to do, Claire, and real value."

"Pretty speech and thank you," said Claire, drawing her sweater about her blouse and buttoning it.

"Besides, I hope you'll continue to give me a hand with notes and—"

"Of course I will, Maud." She was amused by her mother-in-law's anxiety for her. "In fact, I already feel overworked."

"Good." Maud lifted herself from the bucket seat. "Come on, Claire, let's find out where we are."

Claire rose and preceded Maud into the aisle. Slowly, in the semi-darkness of the plane's interior, they progressed up the passageway, past the landing-gear compartment, past the mail and baggage sections and lavatory, past the main entrance hatch, and suddenly they came upon Rasmussen and Hapai in the smoke-filled cockpit of the flying boat.

At the sound of their approach, Rasmussen quickly turned from the controls and, like a naughty boy caught with a coffin nail behind the barn, he lowered his cigar. He brushed away a bluish cloud of smoke with his free hand, and ducked his head in a greeting.

"Hiya, there," he said, and leaned sideways to squash his cigar stub in a metal tray on the floor.

"I hope you don't mind our curiosity—" Maud had begun to say.

"Not at all, ma'am, nope. You're payin', so you're entitled to a free look."

Claire squeezed herself beside Maud, behind the pilot chairs. Her eyes lifted from the complex instrument panel to the windshield, and sought what lay beyond the twin engines. It was still night, no longer black night but gray night, as if a dense fog were lifting and lighting. The ocean below was not yet visible.

"It's getting light," Claire said to Maud.

"Yes, but I can't see—"

"Give her another fifteen minutes, ma'am," Rasmussen interrupted, "an' you'll have the first piece of sun and have yourself a look at the ol' Pacific."

"Uh—Captain—" Even Maud found it difficult to give him rank. "Do we have very far to go?"

"I said fifteen minutes to see the day—an' give it five minutes after to see your first look of the Sirens."

Conversation with Rasmussen was as easy as sludging through

a quagmire, but nevertheless Maud went on. "How did The Three Sirens get its name?"

Rasmussen covered his mouth and belched, and mumbled an apology. "That's the sort of thing to ask Tom Courtney, but, matter of fact, I know pretty well from him. Back in 1796, when old Wright—the first one—was sailin' up from Down Under, lookin' for some place to roost, he was doin' lots of readin' in between times, readin' the old books. An' when the lookout yelled that he spotted some new islands—these ones you're goin' to—old Wright was below in his bunk, readin' away at the writer with one name— Homer—you know Homer—?"

Maud and Claire nodded gravely.

"—he was readin' the book, never can remember the name, where the fellow is wanderin' all around, in an' outa trouble, tryin' to get home to the old lady—"

"*The Odyssey*," said Maud tolerantly.

"Well, whatever the name, anyways, old Wright is down there an' he's readin' about where this fellow is sailin' past the islands where *vahines* are singin', tryin' to seduce—beg your pardon—so as he's got to put wax in his ears not to listen and gotta get hisself tied up to the mast—forgot how it goes—"

He fell to ruminating about the passage, and Claire summoned up her courage. "Circe said to Ulysses, 'First you will come to the Sirens, who bewitch everyone who comes near them. If any man draws near in his innocence and listens to their voice, he never sees home again—' "

"Yup, that's it!" Rasmussen shouted. He squinted at Claire as if she were an admirable discovery. "You're mighty smart, ma'am, just as smart as Courtney."

She was pleased to be as smart as Courtney. "Thank you, Captain."

"Anyways," Rasmussen went on, "there's old man Wright up on deck an' he's sayin' those three islands look beautiful an' if they're the ones, why he's goin' to name them what he's readin' which is like you said—the Sirens—an' since there was three he always called them The Three Sirens, so that explains it."

For Claire, the utter incongruity of the discussion, considering both the backgrounds of the participants and their position of animated suspension somewhere between six and ten thousand feet above sea level, amused her and made her happy.

"Captain Rasmussen," Maud was saying, "do you mind a personal question?"

His rough, worn face closed suspiciously, so that he appeared toothless. "Depends what," he said.

"Professor Easterday, everyone, has imposed such a curtain of secrecy over the Sirens," Maud said, "that I keep wondering how anyone, outside those islands, knows about it. For example, this Courtney. And yourself, too. How do you know about it?"

Rasmussen contracted his brow, as if examining the reply he must make. Obviously, thinking was a slow and painful process for him. He needed time for his reply. At last, he made it. "Won't speak for Tom Courtney. It's his business an' he might not wanna tell how he come there, an' you ask him. You'll have time enough. He's a good easy talker, like all of us down these parts, but he's not given much to talkin' about hisself. So you ask him."

"But what about you?" Maud persisted.

"Me? I got no secret about that from you, specially since you're goin' in there. Me? Well now, haven't remembered it for a century, maybe. Was like thirty years ago, when I was more a kid than grown, an' shovin' my nose in everywhere, an' sometimes even gettin' it bent out of joint, you bet. Well, I'd been workin' for them big copra outfits—the ones that took over from J. C. Godeffroy an' Son, an' those British, the Lever Brothers—an' I got me a little stake roll, an' I was pretty feisty. I bought me a schooner—a beaut—an' went off on my own. Well, on one of my tradin' voyages, I got off the regular path, kind of lookin' around—an' one mornin' we sighted this young Polynesian fellow adrift in an outrigger canoe—had a ripped pandanus sail—an' was kinda wheelin' around in the water. Well, we picked him up, sorta got him revived, an' what happened was he was goin' somewhere, then got sick in the gut—beggin' your pardon, ma'am—an' he went out like a light an' then just layin' there he got sunstroke. Anyways, I don't know much what to do with him. He says he'll die unless we take him to his home, which he says is near. He says they can fix him. He tells where his place is an' I thought he was sick an' off his rocker at first, 'cause I never heard of no such place, an' I knew most of them. Anyways, we take him there—in the direction—an' sure enough—we find the Sirens an' drop anchor off. By the time I got the kid on shore—he's feelin' better by then—he's scared stiff, because he give me the directions when he was delirious an' no one up to then knew about this place an' strangers are strict tabu. But bein' a feisty kid myself, I don't give no damn about that native nonsense, an' I see the kid's in no condition to even get off the shore. So I kinda get whichway outa him an' half lug him to the village. Well, I tell you, instead of takin' off my head, those villagers make me practically a hero, because the kid I saved, he's a blood relative of the Chief. He's also—well, he's dead now—but he was Dick Hapai's father."

Maud and Claire followed Rasmussen's finger to the dark-haired, light-brown young man bent over the controls. He turned slightly, briefly meeting their eyes, and he bobbed his head. "Yes, true," he said.

"To make a long story short," said Rasmussen, "the medical guy in the tribe, he saved Hapai's father. He only died a few years ago. Me—they wouldn't leave me go—wined an' dined me till I couldn't hardly move—an' to overcome the tabu, they had rites an' made me an honorary member of the tribe. How do you like that?"

"Yes, it is sometimes done," said Maud.

"It was done for me an' they couldn't do enough. I could have whatever I wanted. Well, after a year or two I got to the habit of droppin' in for a visit, just for the sport—it's a great rompin' place, full of high jinks, wait'll you see—an' I keep learnin' about the place an' them. Then, one day I find out they gotta special product which I can see is better than copra or pearls or Trochus shell an' I ask permission to exclusively export an' trade it, in return payin' them with outside goods they need from other islands. An' I been doin' this ever since. In the olden days, I used to come here in my schooner maybe four times a year, but after the second war I could see everything was turnin' to speed an' flyin'. So when there was a chance to grab this old flyin' boat, I bought it. I miss the lazy olden days of the schooners—"

"What about your crews?" asked Maud. "Why didn't they go out and tell everybody about the Sirens?"

Rasmussen snorted. "Crews? What crews? I used to take along two drinkin' Chinks, see? They couldn't read a compass even, never knew where we were, an' I kept them boozed up whenever we got near here. They never even once went ashore. Later on, when the Chinks was dead, Paoti started tellin' me I should use his own people to keep it safer, so that's how I got Hapai here, an'

I had his cousin before him. Good boys. So there's how the place is still secret. I never had cause to snitch to anybody about it, 'cept once, an' that's my business. I always kept it secret because it give me the exclusive rights on the produce I export, but that's not the real reason either, ma'am. You see, I'm part of these people now, honorary kin, an' I'd die before betrayin' them—or havin' the place spoiled by outsiders. That's what was drivin' me nuts about that professor, old Easterday, his hittin' on this by accident an' forcin' my hand."

"Captain Rasmussen," said Maud, "you need have no fear about us. We are all, every member of the team, pledged to protect the privacy of the Sirens. And even if one of us were indiscreet, not one of us knows, has the slightest knowledge, of where we are."

"You still gotta be careful," said Rasmussen, "because now you know the general area. If someone had a clue, and searched long enough, they'd find it sure one year or another."

"When I do my paper," said Maud, "I intend to locate it in Polynesia, saying no more, no less."

"Captain," Claire said, "I'm surprised someone didn't find it during the Second World War. The Pacific was buzzing with Japanese and American aircraft and ships. And since then—"

"I'm sure loads of flyers and ship lookouts seen it," said Rasmussen. "But from the sea, it looks uninhabited, and the ones who seen it, they also seen it don't look like much an' it got no bay, an' is too shallow, and often there's a hard surf runnin'. As to the airplanes, sure they passed over, but they seen nothin' either—that's the great thing about the Sirens—it's so set up that the one village is practically all hidden from sight, from the sky or the sea—there's nothin', looks like nothin'. As to these days, all the same holds true, an' besides it's off the main trade routes an' everyone wants to go to the known islands anyways. They figure everythin' good is known and everythin' else is nothin'. That's what's saved us."

Maud was about to say something more, when Hapai's hand touched Rasmussen's arm.

"Cap'n," said Hapai. "Siren Islands ahead."

They all looked off. The night had disappeared, and it was sunrise. The ocean below, gray-blue and gold-flecked by the early rim of sun, stretched before them for seemingly endless liquid acres. Claire's eyes swept the sea, and there, somewhere before infinity, exactly as Easterday had described it in his letter of months ago, she saw the vague sketch against the horizon of an arc of land. She savored the announcement: Siren Islands ahead.

Maud's sighting of it came seconds later. She exhaled pleasurably. "I can see it, Captain. What would you call it—a moist atoll or a weathered volcanic island?"

"I'd call it both and be right," said Rasmussen, who had turned his back to them. "Actually, callin' it a high island would be correcter, because it's got that small empty volcano—you see, where the thick white clouds are bunched above—but it's not as rugged and jungly as most of the high islands out here, an' while it's got a ring of coral, it's also got some salt swamps, an' better vegetation than the atolls. The good thing about it, you'll see—from the Sirens' point of view—is that it's craggy and steep-to an' hard to get into like Aguigan and Pitcairn." He paused. "You'll be seein' for yourself in a few minutes."

Claire and Maud stood rooted in awe as they sped over the tight pongee sheen of the Pacific, and the top of the yellow disc of sun expanded and enlarged, circularly framing the main island, a torn and unpolished piece of jade immobile in the tropical calm.

They were almost upon it, sliding across it and bending around it, and Claire could distinctly see what Easterday had seen: steep terraced black cliffs sculptured by erosion, rain, time; a luxuriant verdigris carpet of plateau; a broken mountain rising high and proud as the ruin of an ancient castle; splashes of purple lagoons; ravines scooped out by Loti's "patient hand of ages"; slopes of trees and crystal brooks and creases of green valleys. Yet, Claire thought, all delicately detailed in miniature as if from a Polynesian Breughel's brush.

They had dipped past the two adjoining atolls and were heading back toward a gash in the rocky perimeter. Claire could make out the strings of coconut palms, their fronds tiny bursts of celebration in the sky. Beyond lay the cobalt ocean, greening brightly as it neared a strip of sea beach, where the narrow run of sand sparkled back to the sun. All lay inanimate, except for the bubbling white foam against the cliffs gathered about the small extent of beach, all still except for these tentative breakers and signs of movement far below on the sand.

Claire's heart leaped. "Aren't those people down there on the beach?"

Rasmussen grunted. "Yeh, probably Courtney to make you welcome an' some of the villagers to carry your baggage." But now Rasmussen was busy at the controls. "We're goin' in. Better wake up your people an' then sit down. Sometimes the water's a cushion an' sometimes it's like a rutted road."

Maud was the first to turn away, and Claire was reluctant to follow her. One more moment, her eyes feasted on the primitive place, the rainbow of color beneath the wing, and then she murmured, to herself alone, "*Iaorana*." She tore her gaze free from what was deflowering her senses, and went back to the reasonable security of mate and companions.

When Claire reached her seat, she saw that Marc and the others were awake, and she waved vaguely, still seduced, and sat just as the seaplane slumped forward. She held tightly, staring at the boarded portholes, and descended with the fat, brown Polynesian bird, felt it contact the water, bouncing and slithering, until the engines coughed their last spasms and were still, and they roosted wonderingly on the calm waters off the sand beach of The Three Sirens.

The egg of Creation has been dropped, Claire thought. She waited for the shell to break and free her, so that life could begin, at last . . .

* * *

It was still early morning, although they had waited on the sand of the beach for over an hour while Rasmussen and Hapai assisted nine young males of the Sirens in moving the crated supplies, and now their baggage, from the rolling seaplane to the shore.

The sun was a full blazing orb by this time, and the rays of heat it sent toward them could almost be seen. The air about was still and incandescent, faintly moist with the consistency of steam, boiling ever so slowly. It was a heat unusual to find in this part of Oceania.

Claire stood, sweater over her arm, enjoying the heat on her face and neck, and the warmth of the grains of sand covering her sandals. Beside her, Rachel DeJong and Lisa Hackfeld were less comfortable. Rachel appeared wretched in her black wool suit, and she began to remove her jacket. Inspired by this informality, Lisa Hackfeld also started to shed her white jacket.

"It must be the humidity," Lisa said apologetically. "It's smothering."

174

"We'll have to learn to dress properly," said Rachel DeJong. Claire watched a tall young native, the color of maple wood, darker than his friends, as he bent forward, hands on his knees, ready to receive the oncoming long canoe. From behind, the native appeared naked. His sloping shoulders, ridge of spine, long flanks and thin buttocks were entirely exposed. Only his waist held the string which supported the pubic bag.

When first she had been helped down into the canoe, and met these natives, their masculinity accented rather than hidden by the bags, Claire had averted her eyes with embarrassment. She had dreaded reaching the beach, where she knew that the white man, Tom Courtney, would be waiting with Maud, who had gone earlier in the first canoe crossing. On the natives, the brevity of attire, if embarrassing, was at least acceptable. They were, after all, of another race, another people and place. You did not equate them with yourself, did not identify or imagine. But for one of her own to be similarly revealed would be unsettling.

With dread, Claire had endured the gliding passage to the beach, no longer aware of either the scenery or her oarsman. She had stood on the sand as Maud introduced her to Mr. Thomas Courtney, and to her wild relief he was not flesh and codpiece but civilized decency itself.

"Welcome to the Sirens, Mrs. Hayden," he had said.

As she had taken his hand, avoiding looking up at his face, she could see that he wore a thin cotton gym shirt already blotched with perspiration, wrinkled light-blue dungarees rolled up at the ankles, and his bare feet were caught in leather thonged sandals. Only later, when he was occupied elsewhere, had she matched his face with the image her mind had created from Easterday's letter. She had expected him to have sandy hair, but it was a darker brown, as were his eyes, and it was thick and tangled. His face was longer, more sensitive and amused than Easterday had reported, and it was wonderfully seamed at the smile lines by the outdoors, the weather, the years of early middle-age. He was rangy, probably strong, but he moved about them on the beach in long strides that were awkward, as if he were too tall and too shy. He possessed when he was still, Claire had noted, the gift of repose, of letting go, of seeming deceptively indolent—a contrast to her own Marc, who was always coiled tight and taut.

Now, beside Rachel DeJong and Lisa Hackfeld, as she watched

the rear of the native at the water's edge, Claire had a feeling that he and the other natives were sensible about their attire and that she and the team were not. She had a momentary feeling that, as much as she enjoyed the morning heat, she wanted to rid herself of her blouse and skirt and fling them away and know the entire pleasure of the sun and air and water.

Lisa had complained of smothering, and Rachel of having to learn to dress properly, and now Claire said lightly, "Well, Dr. DeJong, maybe we'll have to learn to undress—imitate the natives."

Rachel offered only her lips in a smile. "I doubt it, Mrs. Hayden. I'm afraid we're in the position of the Malayan Englishman, in Empire days, who dressed for dinner in the jungle."

"Thank God for people like him," said Lisa Hackfeld. "How can they run around like that?"

"They don't usually have company," said Claire.

Rachel DeJong nodded off. "This should be our personal luggage now. I hope they're careful."

They all looked at the sharp pointed prow of the oncoming canoe being steadily paddled by eight of the husky young natives. The canoe was piled high, in the center, with the luggage of the team.

"I can't get over how they look," said Lisa. "I expected them to be darker, more native."

"They're both English and Polynesian," Claire reminded her.

"I know, but anyway . . ." Lisa said. "Why, the American— Mr. Courtney over there—he's more darkly colored than they are. I hope I can get a tan like his. I'll be the envy of everyone back home."

Rachel DeJong had been concentrating on the approaching canoe. "Their complexions may be fair," she observed, "but I believe their features have a definite Polynesian cast. They are all big and muscular, black hair, broad noses, rather full lips, yet there is some kind of effeminate air about them, I suppose their grace of movement."

"I think they're definitely masculine," said Claire, and for a second glanced about to be sure Marc had not overheard her.

"They leave no doubt," said Rachel dryly.

The thirty-foot canoe hit the shore, and the paddlers spilled out into the shallow water to push it up on the sand as their waiting tribesman, at the prow, pulled with all his strength.

"I want to see if my things are there," Lisa said. She started through the sand toward the canoe.

"I'd better check, too," said Rachel DeJong, and she went after Lisa.

Claire had no interest in her luggage for the moment. Her eyes followed Rachel and Lisa to the canoe, and then she wheeled about to see what everyone else was doing. In the shade of a boulder, Maud, Marc, and Orville Pence were absorbed in a discussion. Nearby, Courtney crouched with Hapai, going over a list of some kind, while Rasmussen stood listening, mopping his forehead. Some distance off, at the water line, Mary Karpowicz was wading, while her father and mother observed her with parental pride.

Briefly, Claire considered joining her husband, but decided that she wanted this time to herself. Turning her back on the others, she lifted her shoulder purse from the sand, and, lazily swinging it, she strolled past the canoe which was being unloaded. She made her way toward a group of curving coconut trees, and when she reached the first, she lowered herself to the sand, plucked a cigarette from her package and lighted it, and then leaned back against the base of the tree and dreamily soaked in the landscape before and above her. It was easy to depopulate the scene, to return it to its virginal state, for it had a magnificent grandeur that overwhelmed all its temporary habitation.

Closed in as she was by the reaching cliffs, the raw and uncontained vegetation, she felt for the first time that she was severed from civilization, from all that was familiar and controlled. It was as if she had stepped off the safe world into outer space, and been the first to land on a hot unknown planet. Gone was the pasteurized, sanitary, antibiotic, aluminum, plastic, electrical, automatic, Constitutional world of her entire life past. Here was the primeval first world, unregimented, unchecked, undefeated, uncultivated, untamed, untaught, uncultured, uninhibited. Gone was the way of gentility, sophistication, progress, and here, instead, the way of nature, crude, primordial, pagan.

For the first time since infancy, she was at the mercy of others. How would she exist? Her mind fled to the cocoons of her recent life, their easy silken safeties, the downy soft bed from which she rose, the bathroom with its gadget splendors, the kitchen with its mechanical gluttonies, the living room and study with their fabric and leather and wooden furniture, and records and books and art. At home she was visited by civilized friends who could be understood and who were reassuringly garmented and who were as conscious of the amenities and obedient to the rules as was the Victorian gentry.

The past had been forsaken, and now what did she have in its stead? A volcanic isle, a patch of land and jungle, so lost in a mighty sea that it was not on any map. A people, a culture, so strange that it knew nothing of a policeman, a ballot, an electric lamp, a Ford, a motion picture, a washing machine, an evening gown, a Martini, a supermarket, a Literary Guild, a fire hydrant, a caged zoo, a Christmas carol, an uplift brassière, a polio shot, a football, a corsage, a hi-fi set, a *New York Times,* a telephone, an elevator, a Kleenex, a social security card, a Phi Beta Kappa key, a TV dinner, a corn plaster, a Diner's Club membership, a deodorant, a nuclear bomb, a crayon, a Caesarian section. All these, all this, had vanished from her life, and there was left on the desolate sand, on a speck of Oceania, only the five feet four inches and 112 pounds and twenty-five years of her own oversheltered, overcivilized, underprotected, unprepared self. Not more than thirty-two hours stood between the comfortable gadget paradise of her United States and the rude primitive islands of The Three Sirens. She had bridged the time and distance in body. Could she bridge them in her mind and heart?

Despite the glare of the sun beating upon her head, she shivered. After one more lengthy puff of the cigarette, she buried it in the sand, and pushed herself to her feet. She stared across the beach. The entire group was gathering near the piles of luggage beside the canoe, and she knew that Maud would need her as well as the inventory in her purse. More energetically than before, she waded through the sand, remembering the Chicago lake front of her childhood, and soon she was once more part of the company formed by her mother-in-law, husband, and the members of the team.

While each of the group had been permitted to retain his personal effects, to the limit of forty pounds, in his own suitcase, the scientific supplies had been pooled and packed in wooden crates. After Maud assisted each member in identifying his lightweight luggage, she summoned Claire and asked for the inventory of the supplies.

Claire, list in hand, stood behind Maud, while she examined the outside of the crates. "They seem in good shape," announced Maud. "Let's see if they're all here. You read the list aloud, just enough for me to identify each one."

"One carton of sleeping bags, lamps, batteries for lamps, and portable tape recorder," Claire read. "Also—"

"I have it," said Maud.

"One carton with Dr. Karpowicz' drying cabinet, plant presses—"

"Check."

"One carton of Dr. Karpowicz' photographic equipment—motion picture camera, two still cameras, tripods, portable developing equipment, film—"

"Check."

"One carton—no, two cartons—of Miss Bleaska's first-aid kits, other medications, insect repellents—"

"Yes, here they are, Claire."

"Then six cartons of assorted foods—canned goods, powdered milk—"

"Wait, Claire, I've located only two—three of them—hold on—"

Watching Maud kneel and search the crates, Claire remembered how odd she had thought it was to bring their own food along. Maud had explained that, for the most, they would share what the natives on the Sirens ate, but a limited larder of their own food might be useful. For one thing, Maud had said, sometimes you came upon people when they were in the midst of a famine or shortage, and by eating out of your own cans, you did not deprive them. Another reason for importing American staples was that some members of the team might not take well to bizarre native dishes, and prefer to starve rather than eat what revolted them or disagreed with them. Maud had a scarred memory of one field trip with Adley when she had been forced to eat boiled wood rat rather than insult her hosts or, indeed, starve.

"All right, Claire, go on," Maud called.

Claire consulted her list. "Let me see. Here, I have it. One carton of office supplies—portable typewriter, reams of paper, Dr. Pence's projective tests, your own notebooks and pencils—"

Maud nodded as she hunted through the crates. "Yes, Adley always liked to say, 'All I really need on a field trip are pencils and shaving cream.' . . . Check, I've found it."

"Books," said Claire, "one carton of books."

She had personally assembled and packed the several dozen volumes of basic works—*The Outline of Cultural Materials*, Kennedy's *Field Notes*, the British Museum's *Notes and Queries for Anthropologists*, Merck's *Manual* (owned by Miss Bleaska), Malinowski's *Argonauts of the Western Pacific*, Lowie's *Primitive Society*, Mead's *Male and Female* (owned by Dr. Pence), were the ones that came immediately to mind—but team members had carried their own recreational reading. Orville Pence had brought along some pornographic novels, explaining that he was making a study of them. Harriet Bleaska had packed half a dozen paperback mysteries. Claire, herself, had taken with her Melville's *Typee*, Gauguin's *Noa Noa*, Hakluyt's *Voyages*, Frederick O'Brien's *White Shadows in the South Seas*, each chosen as being appropriate reading for the journey.

"Found the books," said Maud.

Hastily, Claire went on with the inventory. The remaining crates contained such a diversity of goods as surveying equipment, soap, water purifiers, steel tape measures, color charts, photographic albums of natives in other cultures, maps, fishing tackle, children's toys, all items earmarked for use in specific studies.

Maud had finally straightened, and was massaging the small of her back, and Claire was tucking the inventory into her purse, when Tom Courtney loomed between them.

"Everything in order?" he inquired.

"It's all here and we're all here," said Maud cheerfully. "What's the next step, Mr. Courtney?"

"The next step, Dr. Hayden, is dogged ambulation." He smiled. "It's really not too forbidding. The distance is short, but in some spots the going is treacherous. There's one gradual climb to the plateau, then a descent, another climb, rather steep, and a last descent to the village. About five hours, I'd say, allowing for three or four breaks along the way." He indicated the crates and luggage. "Don't worry about any of that. There'll be a dozen more young men coming from the village to help these nine. They'll carry the stuff by another route, a short cut, but a little too rugged for many of you, unless you're in shape."

"We'll take the slow, less taxing route," decided Maud.

By this time, Marc had appeared alongside Claire and his mother, and the majority of the team had banded themselves behind Courtney to listen. They were like so many new infantrymen, gathered around their sergeant, eager for any tidbit of information that would dispel the unknown and give them reassurance about their near futures.

Lisa Hackfeld had held up her hand, and when Courtney noticed it, she inquired tremulously, "The route we're now taking—is there any danger from wild animals?"

"None whatsoever," Courtney promised her. "Like many of these small Pacific islands, the fauna is limited, and most of it is marine life concentrated about the shores. You know, turtles, crabs, some harmless lizards. As we go inland, you may see a few goats, short-haired dogs, chickens and roosters, descendants of domesticated animals brought here by Daniel Wright in 1796. They're allowed to roam freely. The sheep are now extinct. Then the island itself has some wild hogs and skinny pigs, fairly docile. It is tabu to kill any of them, except for the Chief's feasts and during festival week."

As Courtney spoke, a beautiful, long-legged bird had swooped down from a cliff to a sodden tree trunk, and peered at them. "What kind of bird is that?" inquired Claire.

"The golden plover," said Courtney. "You'll also see, from time to time, a variety of terns, Noah's doves, crowned pigeons, and that's about it." His gaze went back to Lisa Hackfeld. "No, there's nothing to be concerned about, except sunstroke."

"It sounds safe as a picnic outing," said Maud, cheerfully.

"I guarantee you, it is," said Courtney. Yet, scanning his audience, he perceived a lingering anxiety. He seemed to consider what more to say, and then he added, "Well, now that the supplies are in order, and you know the route we're taking, and you know something of the fauna, there's not much else to add at this time. I can guess this is all strange to you, and there's a good deal more you'd like to know, but I don't think the open beach is the place for it. The sun is becoming hotter every minute, and there's little shelter. I don't want you roasted before we begin. I'll answer, through Dr. Maud Hayden, or directly, any other questions once we're in the comfort of the village."

"Comfort of the village?" said Marc mockingly.

Courtney was startled. "Why, yes, Dr. Hayden. I meant relative comfort, of course. It's not an American community, no hot and cold running water or electric light bulbs or drugstore, but it's not this lonely beach, either. You'll find huts prepared for you, places to sit and to lie down and to eat, and good company, too."

Maud, who had been frowning at her son, faced Courtney with a forced smile. "I am sure it will be agreeable, Mr. Courtney. A number of us have been in the field before. We know it's not home. If that's what we wanted, we wouldn't have come here. And, as I told you, we're honored—feel privileged—to be permitted to come here and to be accepted by Chief Paoti."

"Good," said Courtney with a perfunctory bob of his head. He surveyed the faces of the others, his eyes coming to rest on Claire's intent features. "Some of you may feel bewilderment, a sense of isolation from the world. I wouldn't be surprised. It was exactly how I felt when I first set foot on the Sirens four years ago. From experience, I can assure you that the feeling will disappear by tomorrow. What I really want to say is this—you are not quite so isolated as you may think. Captain Rasmussen has agreed to step up his contact with us, to come here once a week. I believe Professor Easterday will be holding your incoming mail. Well, the Captain will bring it weekly, and take out any mail you wish sent from Papeete. Also, if you find a lack of certain supplies, portable facilities, the Captain will buy anything for you that you need and can be acquired in Tahiti, and he will deliver that weekly, too. I believe that should—"

"Hey, Tom!" Rasmussen's unmistakable grating bellow came from down on the beach.

Courtney whirled around, and all of the others looked behind them. Rasmussen and Hapai were pointing at Sam Karpowicz. The botanist was wide-legged, in the wet sand at the water's edge, with a diminutive silver camera aimed at the seaplane in the water.

"The joker's takin' pictures!" Rasmussen shouted.

Immediately, Courtney broke free of the group, pushed past Pence and Lisa Hackfeld, and ran toward Sam Karpowicz, who was not many yards away. Rasmussen's last outburst had penetrated the botanist, and he lowered his camera, confused by the disturbance and the approach of Courtney. Quickly, Maud, followed by Marc and Claire, and then the others, crowded after Courtney.

"What in the devil do you think you're doing?" Courtney demanded.

"Why—why—I—" Befuddled, Sam could not find words without an effort. "I'm only taking a few pictures. I carry this Minox in my pocket. It's just for—"

"How many have you taken?"

"What do you mean? You mean here?"

"Yes, here."

Observing this prosecution, Courtney's stern, accusing expression, the sudden harshness of his voice, Claire was disturbed. She had thought him gentle, only gentle and amusing, too good-natured for temper, and this scene frightened her. She wondered what had got into him.

"I—I—" Sam Karpowicz had fallen into stuttering again. "I was only trying to get a complete record. I took two or three shots of the beach—and one of the plane now—and—"

Courtney held out his hand. "Give me the film."

Sam hesitated. "But—you'll—it'll expose the—"

"Give it to me."

Sam dug a nail into the back of the Minox and jerked it wide-open. He shook the tiny roll of negative into his palm, and gave it to Courtney.

"What are you going to do with it?" Sam asked.

"I'm going to throw it away."

Sam's myopic eyes, behind the rimless square spectacles, were those of a wounded doe. "You can't, Mr. Courtney—those—there are fifty frames on those rolls—and I've got twenty shots of Papeete."

"I'm sorry." Courtney swung away, reared back, and pitched the tiny metal roll in the great arc across the water. It fell, hit, with a miniscule splash, and sank from sight.

Sam stared at the water, shaking his head. "But—but why—?"

Courtney came around, glancing at the botanist, then at the others. His face no longer held stern anger, but it was serious. "I convinced Paoti, the entire tribe, to allow you to come here. I gave my pledge that you would do nothing, nothing whatsoever, to give away their location or endanger their security."

Marc protested. "Really, Mr. Courtney, I hardly think a few harmless scenic stills of a primitive beach—it looks like hundreds of others—"

"It doesn't," said Courtney firmly. "Not to a South Seas hand. Every inch of every atoll has its characteristics, its individuality, to experienced eyes. Each is distinctive. These shots of the beach, the area around, once shown and published, might give some old pro a clue—a definite clue—"

Sam had Maud by the arm, appealing to her as if she were the higher court. "They agreed we could take pictures—"

"Of course, you can," Courtney interrupted. He, too, was addressing Maud. "Dr. Hayden, I have some understanding of your —your work—what you require—the importance of photographic evidence. I have a blanket agreement from Chief Paoti that you may shoot what you wish inland—anything and everything— scenery—the inhabitants—all flora, fauna, dances, daily activities— everything except what might give them away. I'm sure you understand. There is risk for them if you record film of the outer perimeter of the island. There is risk if you shoot identifiable landmarks—the remains of the volcanic peak, for example, or long-shots of the two small atolls nearby—but as for the rest—this is your studio, do as you wish."

Maud had nodded through the last, and she looked up at Sam Karpowicz. "He's perfectly right, Sam," she said. "They've laid down certain rules, and we must abide by them." She returned to Courtney. "You'll find no one more cooperative than Dr. Karpowicz. His mistake—I'm sure we'll all make ours in turn—was one of ignorance of the limitations. As soon as possible, Mr. Courtney, you will have to inform me of the tabus, and I will pass them on to every member of the team."

As he listened, Courtney's countenance had entirely lost its severity, and once again Claire, studying him, liked him.

"Fair enough, Dr. Hayden," Courtney was saying. He yanked a handkerchief from the hip of his dungarees and wiped his forehead. "Now I think we'd better get off the beach and head inland."

He called an order in Polynesian to the natives at the canoe, and one of them responded in a gesture that was a salute of assent. Then, detaching himself from the team, Courtney took several steps toward Rasmussen and Hapai.

"Captain, thanks," Courtney said. "You, too, Dick. See you here the usual time next week."

"Yeh, next week," said Rasmussen. He looked past Courtney at Maud and Claire, grinned, and winked. "Here's hopin' they got your fit in grass skirts."

Maud ignored this. "On behalf of all of us, Captain, we appreciate your cooperation."

Courtney clapped his hands for attention. "All right, everyone! Off we go to the village!"

He waited for Maud to reach him, and then turned his back to the others and to the sea, and started through the sand, toward a cleft in the giant boulders. Raggedly, the other nine fell in behind the pair, and soon they had reached the narrow footpath that led upward between the rock walls to the interior of the island.

With Marc beside her, Claire brought up the rear. She felt her husband's hand on her elbow.

"What do you think, Claire?"

She halted, and shifted the strap of her purse so that it was more secure on her shoulder. "About what?"

"This whole setup—the place—that fellow Courtney?"

"I don't know. It's all so different. I've never seen anything like it before—beautiful but so away from everything."

"It's isolated all right," Marc agreed. His gaze went to the path the others were slowly ascending. "So's our new friend there."

"Who? Mr. Courtney?"

"Yes. He baffles me completely. I hope he'll make a dependable informant."

"He seems educated and sensible."

"No doubt about his being educated," said Marc. "As to being sensible, it depends on what you mean. He's practical and efficient, that's evident, so why this self-imposed exile? If he were a leper, or a cripple, or an obvious fugitive from the law, or even a shirtless bum, I could understand it. But he appears normal—"

"I don't know, Marc, but I'm sure there are some very real personal reasons for his being here."

"Maybe . . . maybe not," said Marc, meditatively. "I thought I should establish an open, forthright relationship with him right off, so I asked him what he was doing in a place like this. You know what he said? He said, 'Staying alive.' I must admit that threw me. What kind of person would hole up a thousand miles from nowhere among naked primitives, and just sit and vegetate?"

Claire did not answer. But she wondered, too. Then, as Marc entered the footpath, she turned for one last look at the beach and the ocean. And then she wondered something else. The next time she saw this scene, would anything or any one of them be different?

Resolutely, she pulled away and began to climb the trail that would soon bring her to what had so long eluded her in her dreams.

* * *

They had been walking, tramping, trudging, dragging in the stifling heat for almost four and a half hours.

During the first part of the hike, when she had her full strength and was not yet tired, when her senses were fresh and alive and able to absorb every new sight and sensation, Claire had enjoyed the journey. The first climb through the weathered and lofty lava boulders, with its gradually increasing vegetation, dense scrub, and twisting vines, all sunless and lightless and constricted, had been easy, even invigorating as she felt the stretch of unused muscles.

The magnificent green of the flat plateau eventually giving way to great gullies and gaping ravines, heavily and moistly thicketed all through, had been agreeable, too. Before her eyes danced the parades of breadfruit trees, the scraggly vines indicating wild yam, the sugar cane, the pandanus leaves, the coconut palms, the banana trees, the bamboo groves, the mangoes, the yellow and white acacia, the taro swamps, so much of the exotic, so much of the colorful, that vision was gradually dulled, and reaction to vision jaded and limp. Soon, all that had remained had been the smells, the faintest whiff of the salt sea behind, overpowered by the odors of tropical flowers, fruits, plants, and coconut husks.

Now she was tired of the island's excesses, tired of beauty and movement and sun. Her muscles and her senses ached.

After the last break an hour earlier, she had found a place beside Harriet Bleaska, and a few feet behind Courtney and Maud, who led the way and were hatefully tireless. Like a dray horse following another in a team, she tried to keep in step with Maud's military strides—what had happened to her arthritis?—and Courtney's monotonous, jerky, swinging gait. They were going upward on a rounded ribbon of earth, ascending a hill, the furry slope rich with pandanus and scaevola (or so Sam Karpowicz said), and they had attained a level summit. There they approached an arbor of thick-leafed breadfruit, shady and fronting a small rushing stream that cascaded off somewhere down the hill.

Courtney slowed, lifting an arm, then revolved to face them all. "All right, we can rest here in the shade—last break before the village—it's no more than twenty or thirty minutes away, and that's downhill, so it won't be hard. If you're thirsty, the stream is fine, it's fresh."

Without delay, Mary Karpowicz broke out of the line and made for the water, followed quickly by her panting mother, and then Orville Pence and Lisa Hackfeld.

Claire, who had been watching them, suddenly realized that Courtney was above her, watching her. His face was concerned. "You're tired, aren't you?"

"Do I look that bad?"

"No, but—"

"Yes, I am," she said. "I don't understand it, either. I'm no girl athlete, but I do keep in shape back home—you know, tennis and swimming—"

He shook his head. "No, it's not a physical tiredness—it's the other kind—too much hitting you at once. Like going to Paris or Florence the first time for one day, and trying to do it in a single gulp. Your head becomes disconnected and indifferent, your eyes smart, and you feel it in your back and calves."

"Are you clairvoyant or something? How did you know?"

"It happened to me when I came here, the very first day. After I rested I was fine, and by evening, all in one piece and receptive again. You'll be okay tonight."

"I'm sure I will," said Claire. "Anyway, I hate it showing on me."

"I swear it doesn't. Your mirror will testify to my honesty. I was just guessing . . . Better sit down there in the shade with the others. The ten minutes will refresh you, and in no time we'll be there and you'll have your own place to lie down."

She liked him, and wondered if this attention was personal, or simply a kindness that he would have tendered Rachel DeJong or Lisa Hackfeld, had they been the nearest to him. He turned away to walk to the stream. She decided his attention had been impersonal, and she went to the breadfruit grove and dropped to the grass a few yards from Maud.

The relief of sitting, as well as hiding from the sun, revived her somewhat. She was able, almost for the first time since the beach, to become interested in the others lolling on the grass. All but Courtney had returned from the stream. Claire found a lemon drop, and after she had it in her parched mouth, she began to study the others, speculating on the ones who were silent, tuning in on those who were conversing.

Maud, she noticed, was silent. She sat cross-legged, like a stunted female Buddha, her broad face mottled from exertion and heat, rocking her corpulent body, eyes vacant to the present, reversed inward to the past. Claire guessed: she is daydreaming about Adley, of their field trip to Fiji nearly a decade ago, of what it had been like then, with a beloved one, and what it was like now, again in Polynesia, but emotionally alone.

Claire moved her attention to the three Karpowiczes. Estelle and Sam were sprawled on the grass. Mary was on her knees irritated by some question. Claire tuned in.

"Well, how do I know, *Pa?*" Mary said impatiently. "I haven't seen anything yet—just a bunch of trees and some natives in jock straps."

"Mary—your language." It was Estelle. "Where do you pick up such things?"

"Quit treating me like a baby, Mother."

Estelle turned imploringly to her husband. "Sam—"

Sam stared at his daughter. "Mary, this will do ten times more for you than a summer at home. I promised you it would and it will."

"Oh, sure," said Mary with thick sarcasm.

"Leona Brophy and the rest will envy you."

"Sure—sure—"

"And that Neal Schaffer, he's no bargain. He's not running anywhere. He'll be interested in you for yourself when you get back."

"Sure, he's going to sit around and wait." She waved her hand at the scenery. "This is just great for a summer vacation. Real sharp. I'll come back home with a ring in my nose and tattoos. I don't care what you say, it wasn't fair to drag me all the way—"

Claire tuned out, and regarded Lisa Hackfeld with pity. Lisa appeared haggard and disheveled. Her white outfit was soiled and crumpled. Her face, under the blond hair, was puffy, streaked, and she was desperately trying to repair it from her compact. Claire observed Lisa staring into the glass of the compact. What was on her mind? Claire guessed: she is thinking that, for the first time, she looks her age, feels her age (the long flight, the long march), for earlier she had spoken to Claire, wryly, of her fortieth birthday.

She is thinking, guessed Claire, that her years weigh on her like a knapsack with forty stones, and it is heavier now that she is weaker. She is thinking, guessed Claire (as Claire herself had thought on the beach), that this is a mistake, that now the initial excitement and gaiety of planning and take-off are gone, and the beauty shop and the Continental and the servants and Saks and the Racquet Club are gone, too, and what in the hell was she left with but perspiration and palm trees and no air-conditioned tearooms.

Claire's eyes caught Rachel DeJong and Harriet Bleaska talking together, Harriet with her head thrown back, eyes closed, soaking in the fresh air, and Rachel, cheeks drawn in some vise of unhappiness. Claire tuned in.

"—just love it," Harriet was saying. "I've never felt more energetic. I can't tell you what it's done for me, these few days, to have gotten away, away from hospitals and—and the people there—what goes on—to be free, on my own."

"I certainly envy you," Rachel said. "I'm afraid I don't have your nature. It is really quite a gift—to cut away from cares, I mean. I—I left so much behind, unfinished. I refer to patients and —oh, personal affairs. Quite irresponsible of me."

"Stop worrying, start living, Doctor, or you'll wind up on a couch!" Harriet laughed with delight at her joke, and squeezed Rachel's arm to prove that it was only fun.

Claire tuned out, and twisted to observe Courtney, returned from the stream, crouching beside Marc and Orville Pence. Quickly, Claire tuned in.

"I was just saying to Marc here," said Orville, "that the beauty of Polynesian women is highly overrated. I mean, as far as I could judge from my first visit to Tahiti. I know it was only a day, but I've read quite broadly on this subject. The outside world has been propagandized, bamboozled by published fairy tales and plays and movies. I found those Tahitian girls thoroughly unattractive."

"In what way?" asked Courtney.

"Oh, broad Negroid noses," said Orville, "and gold teeth, full waists, thick ankles, bunions and blisters and calluses all over their feet—there's your South Sea beauties."

"I'm inclined to agree with Orville," said Marc, pedantically. "My research convinces me that the whole legend was created by those early explorers and sailors who had been at sea for many months. They were starved for femininity. Naturally, the first females they laid eyes upon, and especially permissive ones, were beautiful to them. I trust, Mr. Courtney, your Sirens women have more to offer."

"I'm no expert on the opposite sex," said Courtney with the faintest smile. "However, the females in the village are not pure Polynesian—they are half-English—and so they reflect the best—or the worst, also—of physiques in both societies. I will say this—I disagree with both of you. I think Polynesian females are the most beautiful in the world."

"Those heavyset creatures?" said Orville Pence. "You must be joking."

Marc nudged Orville. "Our Mr. Courtney has been at sea too long."

Courtney conceded no humor, but said, "I've learned a woman's real beauty is not in her outer appearance. It's inside—and inside, the Polynesian women, the Sirens women, are incomparably beautiful."

"Beautiful inside?" said Marc, uneasily. "What is that supposed to mean?"

Courtney's mouth was mischievous. "You're the anthropologists," he said, as he stood up. "See for yourselves."

Belatedly, Marc was abashed. He said lamely, "We'll do our best, if we have cooperation."

Claire tuned out, and once again she wondered about Thomas Courtney. She patted her black hair absently, and tried to imagine how she, and the other women in the group, appeared in Courtney's eyes, and how he judged them, judged her, alongside the Sirens women. Suddenly, she felt unsure of her own femininity, and what lay immediately ahead seemed hostile. They, ahead, were beautiful inside. What was she inside?

Courtney was approaching. "Rise and shine, my friends," he called out. "The last lap, and you'll be home."

With the others, Claire came to her feet. The question occupied her entirely, and then the answer, and she was tempted to cry out: Mr. Courtney, I know the answer—I am beautiful inside—only, because it is locked inside, no one can see it—not Marc—not you—not me—but I can feel it—that is, that is if you mean what I mean.

But she was not exactly sure what she meant. She closed her mind to the enigma, for the time, and fell into motion behind Maud and Courtney.

* * *

The walk of the next twenty minutes, for Claire and the others, was less taxing than the earlier portions of the march. It was single file, gradually down and gradually up, like treading a roller coaster for children. They were single file on a deeply worn trail, through dense bright greenery, once passing several grazing goats, and it was pleasant, like a morning's stroll in an English countryside, like a sweet English phrase, *o'er hill and dale* . . . how comforting it must have been for the first Daniel Wright, Daniel Wright, Esq., of Skinner Street.

The immense yellow platter of sun above seemed to fill the blue sky, and its fierce heat followed them relentlessly. Claire could see that Courtney's white cotton shirt was now a spreading blotch that clung to his muscular back. Her own neck and the flesh above her breasts and the cleft between were wet. Yet, somehow, it was better than before, and the hotness made one's skin glow with health.

They had been mounting slowly, higher and higher, through the vegetation, which was also higher and higher, she realized. They were inside the shade of rows of acacia and mulberry trees, and other trees Karpowicz identified as kukui, and their movement through the fragrant tunnel scared half a dozen brightly feathered birds and sent them winging into the sky. Soon, they emerged into the sunlight, and found themselves on a broad, flat precipice. Courtney had stopped, shaded his eyes, peering beyond the brink, and then he turned, as the members of the team continued to emerge from the path, and he said, "If you'll gather around, you'll see the village below."

Claire, with Harriet Bleaska and Rachel DeJong at her heels, hastened to the edge of the elevation, and looking down, she saw it.

The one community of The Three Sirens stretched out before them on the grass floor and setbacks of the long valley. The village had been planned in a perfect rectangle. The center was a grass and dirt compound, bisected through by a shallow running thread of a stream crisscrossed by perhaps a dozen minute wooden bridges. On both sides of the compound, running in parallel lines, were the shaggy, woven huts of the village, like so many square baskets turned upside down. There was not a single row of huts on each side, but several, one row set behind the other, but spaced far enough apart so that every hut had its own private border of grass on all sides. Between the huts were footpaths and a scattering of trees that appeared to be eucalyptus.

All of the dwellings, on either side of the long compound, had been built under vast stretching overhangs from the hills, which provided natural roofing and shade. It occurred to Claire that these mammoth projections had probably been the main reason why the tribe had settled here centuries ago. For, except from the point where they stood, the village would be hidden from prying eyes searching down from other heights, hidden from the sight of explorers who had ventured inland, and hidden, in modern times, from the crews of airplanes above. Yes, Claire decided, it was this, as well as the stream and the flat area for a compound, that had located the people of the Sirens here instead of on higher land.

Claire pulled her sunglasses from her purse and slipped them on, since the glare had hidden the far end of the village in a haze. The dark lenses made the distant portion of the village clearly visible, and Claire could make out what she had not seen before, three mighty huts, one actually as enormous as a small college field house, but all were one-story and elongated as caterpillars, and set in groves of trees.

Claire removed her sunglasses. For these moments, the scene below had been oddly lifeless, like a tropical ghost town, but now she could make out two tiny bronzed figures, probably males, entering the compound, followed by a dog. The pair traversed a short bridge, and, going to the other side, disappeared into a hut.

She turned to inquire where the natives were, when she saw that Courtney and Maud, who had been discussing something in undertones, separated and acknowledged the curiosity of the company.

"There you have it, my friends," Courtney said aloud. "If you're wondering where the people are, they are inside, eating their noon meals or resting, as any sensible human being should at this hour. Those who aren't in their huts are out in the hills doing their quota of work. Normally, at this hour, you would see more people coming and going across the compound, but today is a special occasion for them—the occasion being your arrival. I told them you would be here about noon, and you are, and out of respect for you—Chief Paoti has endowed you with special mana to over-come the old tabu against strangers—they are indoors. I know that in the States everyone turns out to celebrate an important arrival —parades, confetti, keys to the city—but here the mark of respect and welcome is to give you, for your arrival at least, the freedom of the village without being inspected and observed. I hope you will understand that."

"All of us understand their hospitality, I am sure," said Maud.

"As a matter of fact," said Courtney, "many of them will be wearing ceremonial dress tonight, in your honor. I know that Professor Easterday told you that the Sirens males generally attire themselves in pubic bags, the females in grass skirts, and that youngsters run around naked. That is correct, as far as it goes. You will find some exceptions, however. In the infirmary, in the school, in several other places, males wear breechclouts, loincloths, kilts, whatever you wish to call them, and in these places the women wear breast binders along with their grass or tapa skirts. The young and very old have a choice of garmenting themselves as they please. During feasts, and special occasions, such as your welcome tonight, the more formal attire is worn."

Orville Pence waved his hand for attention. "Mr. Courtney, besides Professor Easterday and the Captain and yourself—are we the first outsiders—whites—ever to come here?"

Courtney's forehead furrowed. He weighed his reply, "No," he said at last, "besides the three exceptions you made, you are not the first they have seen since the time Daniel Wright settled here and his descendants intermarried. According to their legend, a Spanish party landed here about five years after Wright—I'd say about 1801—and they were cruel, and tried to remove some of the girls forcibly. They were ambushed returning to the beach and slaugh-tered to a man, and those remaining on the ship were overcome in the night and killed. In more recent times—early in this century—an elderly, bearded seafarer, going around the world alone, sailed his sloop to the beach. He came upon the village, and when he wanted to leave, they would not let him leave. He resigned himself to staying here, but died of natural causes before a year had passed."

"Captain Joshua Slocum and the *Spray?*" asked Claire.

Courtney shrugged. "There's no record of his name. They don't write here, and history is passed down by word of mouth from generation to generation. I thought of Slocum, too. But when I looked him up, it turned out he disappeared in the Atlantic during 1909. Could he have got this far without anyone knowing it? Possible, but not probable."

"There must be some evidence, a grave, a tombstone, something?" persisted Claire.

"No," said Courtney. "As you will learn, their funeral rites require absolute and total cremation of a corpse and the burning of all his possessions." Courtney turned, and addressed himself to Orville Pence. "During the Second World War, a Japanese bomber made a forced landing on the plateau, but it exploded and burned. There were no survivors. Late in the war, an American transport, lost in the night, hit the side of the peak. Again, no survivors. Aside from those instances, your group is, as far as I know, the first—and I hope the last—from the outside to visit The Three Sirens."

Maud had been studying the village beneath them. "Mr. Courtney, do all the tribesmen live in that one village?"

"They all live there," said Courtney. "There are several huts scattered about the island, overnight shelters for those who are away farming, hunting, fishing, and near the peak there are some stone colonnades, the remains of an ancient sacred *marae*, but this is the only actual community. It is a small island, and all the advantages are centered in this one hamlet. At last count, there were two hundred and twenty natives. There are about fifty or sixty huts down there. In the last month, four new huts have been built, and two vacated, to accommodate the ten of you."

Mary Karpowicz, who had been absorbed in the village, suddenly called out, "What are they made of—the huts? They look like a breeze could blow them down."

"You'll find them much sturdier than that," said Courtney, with a smile. "There are no walls as you would think of them, but the framework of each hut is solid timber, influenced by eighteenth-century English architecture, and the roofs are of native thatch, pandanus leaf over cane or bamboo, and the walls are similar, but more heavily reinforced with cane. Most of the huts have two rooms, some have three."

"Mr. Courtney." Maud was pointing toward the groves at the end of the village. "Those larger buildings—"

"Ah, yes. One might say the municipal part of the community. In fact, you can't see all of them from here. Among those trees you'll find the Sacred Hut—a sort of museum, really, and for some a place of worship—and there are several connected larger huts that represent the school. The food storehouse is near there, also. Two important buildings are in the very center of the village. One is the medical dispensary. The other is Chief Paoti's hut, rather grand and spacious, many rooms for his kin, for meetings, for feasts. You can't see it well from here."

"But the biggest and longest at the end, the one with the thatched-dome top?" asked Maud.

Courtney studied it a moment, and then said gravely, "That is the Social Aid Hut that Professor Easterday wrote you about."

"The brothel," said Marc with a grin.

His mother turned upon him angrily, and snapped, "For heaven's sake, Marc, you know better than that."

"I'm just kidding," said Marc, but his smile had become uncertain, and finally apologetic.

"You'll only confuse the others," said Maud. She turned to Courtney. "As anthropologists, we've a broad knowledge of the pleasure houses of Polynesia. On Mangareva, it is called *are popi*, and on Easter Island it was known as *hare nui*. I assume this hut may have a similar function?"

"Only somewhat," said Courtney, hesitantly. "To my knowledge, there's nothing quite like it anywhere in the world. In fact, there are many other things down there utterly unknown to the outside world. To me, for the most, they represent a—an ideal way of life —in the matters of love, at least—that we of the West should one day hope to achieve." He glanced down at the village with an expression that was, in itself, an act of love. "You'll see and learn soon enough. Until then, it's useless for me to prattle on. Let me take you to your assigned huts. There's a steep path over there, but it's safe. We'll be down in ten minutes."

He descended the slope of the ridge, and disappeared around a stone ledge. One by one the others followed. Claire turned to go, and saw her husband passing Orville Pence. Marc snickered at Orville, the way men do at a stag, Claire supposed, and he said, "I still say brothel."

He was gone, and Orville with him, and at that second Claire did not want to walk with either of them.

She was furious with Marc, and his unfortunate attempt at levity, and in her heart she knew that Dr. Adley R. Hayden would have been furious, too, and would have liked her more.

She waited until they had gone around the bend, and then she followed. She wanted to enter the village of The Three Sirens alone.

* * *

It was midafternoon in the village.

Claire Hayden, cooler now in a fresh sleeveless gray Dacron dress, leaned in the open doorway of the hut assigned to Marc and herself and absently observed the men of their party—Marc, Orville, Sam, employing tools they had brought along—assist two of the young natives from the beach in opening the last of the wooden crates.

She found her gaze directed at the two young natives, so strapping and graceful, because there was a certain suspenseful fascination in this. As the native youths moved, bending and rising, she was certain that any moment the single strands about their waists, holding in place the pubic bags, would break and expose them. It was impossible to understand why this did not happen, but so far it had not.

Suddenly, she was ashamed of the diversion, and she looked off beyond the men and crates toward the heart of the village. Some inhabitants were in the compound now. There were children and women, at last. The younger children, running, jumping, playing, were stark naked. The women were, as Easterday had promised, nude from the waist up and their short skirts precariously concealed their private parts. Only a few of the older women had pendulous breasts, while the younger ones, and even the middle-aged ones, had high, firm, extremely pointed breasts. When they walked—in short, mincing, peculiarly feminine steps, obviously an attempt to keep their grass skirts properly down—their conical breasts jiggled and their grass skirts undulated, occasionally revealing a portion of buttocks. It puzzled Claire how the women could go about this way, so revealed, and, indeed, how their men could pass them constantly without at least being provoked, if not violating them.

Observing them from afar—they were still too shy, too polite, too correct to come nearer—Claire felt uneasy. Automatically, her hand touched her dress, and for all its thinness, it covered her so completely, just as her brassière and half-slip and panties covered her, that she felt outlandishly unfeminine. She continued to watch the women of the Sirens, their lustrous raven hair, their tipped bobbing breasts, their seductive hips, their long bare legs, and she was ashamed to be so chastely garmented, like a missionary's wife.

She began to turn away from all living reproach, determined to resume her unpacking, when she heard Marc.

"Well, Claire."

He came up to the doorway, wiping the back of his hand across his forehead. "What have you been up to?"

"I was emptying suitcases. I took a break for a few minutes. I was watching the—the people."

"So was I," Marc said. He stared off toward the center of the compound. "Courtney may be off base in a lot of ways, but he was certainly right about these women."

"What does that mean?"

"They make the Tahitian girls look like boys. They're really something. Ten times better than a Miss America contest. I've never seen anything like that at home." Then, observing her face, he added lightly, "Present company excepted."

She still had a residue of the old resentment, and this became overlaid with a new resentment. She wanted to retaliate in kind, to wound him where he was most vulnerable. "That goes for the men, too," she said. "Have you ever seen any others so athletic and virile-looking?"

His face darkened, as she knew it would. "What kind of talk is that, anyway?"

"Your kind of talk," she said, and she pivoted and started inside with her hateful victory.

"Hey, Claire, for God's sake," he called after her, contritely, "I was only speaking as an anthropologist."

"All right," she said. "You're forgiven." But she did not rejoin him.

For a few minutes, blindly, she carried their clothes and toilet articles from the front room to the rear one, until she had simmered down, regained her equilibrium, and was able to push Marc's insensitivity from her mind. Pausing to rest, she surveyed her quarters. The front room was sizable, at least fifteen by twenty feet, and although warm it was much cooler than outdoors. The cane walls were cozy, and the pandanus mats that covered most of the sanded, gravel floor were springy and soft. There were no large furnishings of any kind, no tables, no chairs, no decorations, but Sam Karpowicz had hung two battery-powered lamps from the ceiling. There was one window facing Maud's hut, and it was shielded from the sun and heat by a dark-cloth flap that could be fastened.

Earlier, an adolescent native boy, attired in a short loincloth, had brought in two clay bowls of fresh water, and had explained in halting English that one was for drinking, the other for washing. Next, he had delivered a bundle of strong wide leaves, replying to Claire's question that they were to be used for plates. This room, Claire decided, was supposed to be their living room, dining room, study.

Arms crossed over her chest, Claire walked slowly to the rear, through the opening into a six-foot corridor. Here, a slit in the roof was visible to serve as an outlet for smoke, and beneath it, next to a strip of matting, was the earth oven, a round hole in the ground ready to be filled with hot stones, and huge leaves nearby to cover it. The end of this passage opened into a smaller room, resembling the front room, with but one window. Here, atop the pandanus mats, she had opened their two sleeping bags, but they appeared cumbersome and thick, and if the evenings were as now, she thought that she would sleep on her bag instead of inside it, or even sleep on the native mats themselves, which were several layers thick in this room and probably meant to serve as beds.

Home, sweet home, she thought, and felt adventurous about the primitive hut. Marc had complained instantly, upon entering it, of the crudity and barrenness, and even she had worried briefly at the inevitable discomfort, but now she adored it and wanted nothing else.

She knelt and sorted the clothing, Marc's in several piles to one side, her own to the other side. Then, tired once more, she fell back from her kneeling position to sit on the mats, legs under her, and extracted the cigarette pack and matches from her dress pocket.

Once smoking, and at ease—how wonderful to have no telephone, no market lists, no social appointments, no car to drive anywhere—she listened to the rustle of a breeze waltzing with the thatch above. Harmonizing, from a distance, too faint and feminine to be from those outside the door, were tinkles of laughter. These gentle sounds, the outdoorish plant smell that pervaded the room, comforted Claire thoroughly, giving her a feeling of feline languor.

Presently, she was able to measure her inner emotions against what they had been upon first entering the compound three hours before. Except for Maud, revived by the challenge of the field, and the indefatigable Harriet Bleaska, the group mood had been a mixture of disappointment leavened by interest. Claire's own mood had been attuned to the group. She understood it better now. No actuality of paradise can be the replica of the dream of paradise. Dreams of paradise are flawless. To leave a dream, you have to come down and down—in fact, down to earth—and the earth had fumbling and knobby fingers and marred what it built from the design of delicate dreams.

For Claire, it was better now because the most useful, oiled part of the mechanism that was she, was moving all that was around her, to adjust it to her own needs, to make all compatible to her. It was her strength—or perhaps her weakness—this, the talent to abandon so automatically details of a cherished dream and to rearrange cold reality to match what was left of a dream. In others, she would have named it flexibility or compromise or called it meeting life halfway. She was a veteran of many romantic dreams, of endless high hopes, expectations, anticipations, and she was a veteran of countless disappointments, and so, long, long ago, she had armed herself with the machinery of reconciliation. It worked, too— else how could she still smile in the mornings of her marriage?— but recently, ever so often, the machinery responded less noise-lessly, creaked and protested. Today it worked, was operating nicely. Paradise somewhat resembled the recurring dream of all the spring.

Lighting a new cigarette off the old, snuffing out the old in a broken coconut husk she had brought in for an ashtray, she wondered if the others on the team had made an adjustment similar to her own. Recollecting fragments of their initial re-actions to the village, as they had come through it behind Court-ney, and their words upon entering their lodgings, she had her serious doubts.

Courtney had pointed out the six huts that were to be their own for the six weeks of their visit. The huts were in a line, under the hoary overhang, directly on the grass compound, rather closer to the entry of the village than to the center where stood Paoti's impressive hut. The Karpowiczes had been assigned the first quarters, exactly the same exterior and interior as the hut that Claire and Marc had been loaned, except that off the rear room there was a third small room for Mary Karpowicz. Claire and Maud had accompanied Courtney and the Karpowiczes in their first examination of their temporary home. While Sam had been dismayed only by the lack of a darkroom—Courtney had immediately promised to see that he had the materials and help to build one—he and Estelle found the conditions, if not quite up to Saltillo the year before, at least acceptable for so short a stay. Mary, on the other hand, was dismayed by the lack of privacy and the gaping emptiness. "What am I supposed to do here all summer, twiddle my thumbs?" she had asked.

Lisa Hackfeld had been deposited in the next hut, which, out of deference to her husband's financial support, she was being permitted to have to herself. She had taken one quick look through it, and then had overtaken Maud in the compound. "I can't find the bathroom," she had gasped, "there's no bathroom." Courtney had overheard this, and had tried to mollify her. "There is a public lavatory some distance behind every ten huts," he had explained. The nearest one to you is about thirty yards away, behind the hut where Dr. DeJong will be. You can't miss it. It is standing by itself. It looks like a circular grass hut more than a privy." Lisa had been horrified at the idea of a public lavatory, but Courtney had told her that she was lucky to have even this. In the decades before Daniel Wright's coming—the public water closets had been his innovation—the natives had none at all, but merely went out to the bush in the rear. Miserably, Lisa had retreated to her toiletless castle to brood until her luggage came.

Orville Pence, never having been in Polynesia before, had confessed, upon entering his hut, that somehow he had expected accommodations with real windows—in Denver, being addicted to bronchial congestion, he had always slept with his windows tightly shut—and some office furniture and shelves for his books. They had left him, in the middle of his room, forlorn and immobilized.

The next hut had been reserved for Rachel DeJong and Harriet Bleaska, who were to share it. Harriet had loved their dwelling, so much more picturesque than the lonely apartments she had known in Nashville, Seattle, and San Francisco. Rachel DeJong had been less impressed. While registering no vocal complaint, and indifferent to the actual living conditions, she had worried about the lack of privacy for her work. "One doesn't need a couch," she had said wryly, "but one does need seclusion with a patient—or, in this case, subject." Eager to oblige, Courtney had promised to find a vacant hut, elsewhere, that she might use for a full-time consulting room.

After that, Claire and Marc had been shown their residence, and Maud had departed, with Courtney, to her office and living quarters next door. A half-hour later, the supplies had arrived, and since lunch had been overlooked by their hosts, Marc had cracked open the crate containing Spam, and had passed out cans of it with openers at each hut.

Recalling some of the complaint and irritation now, a stray phrase, a marvelous cliché, crossed Claire's mind: the natives are restless. Foolishly, it delighted her. She was here, among them, and the natives weren't restless at all, not at all. The eggheads are restless, she thought, the poor scrambled eggheads, out of their frying pans into this.

Maud, she thought, the mighty Maud, alone, would be unruffled, would be as resolute as a granite profile on Mount Rushmore. She had a sudden pointless desire to see Maud, to draw enthusiasm from her. Tiredness had vanished. Claire uncurled and hoisted herself erect. She could hear the men still toiling outside. She went through the hut and into the compound, expecting to find Marc, but while Orville Pence and Sam Karpowicz labored with the young natives, Marc was nowhere to be seen. Where had he gone? She meant to inquire, and then she did not, for she guessed that she knew. He had gone deeper into the village. He had gone to the naked breasts. Goddam them all, she thought; not the breasts but men; not men, either, but men like Marc.

She had reached her mother-in-law's hut when the cane door swung open, almost hitting her. She backed off, as Courtney emerged. It surprised her that he had been with Maud all this while.

"Hello, Mrs. Hayden," he said. "Did you get some rest?"

She was suddenly shy and tongue-tied. "Yes, I did."

"If there's anything I can do—?"

"No."

"Well then—"

They had just been standing there, awkwardly faced toward each other like unwound dolls, both helpless to move toward one another or away.

"I—I was going in—" she started to say.

"Yes, I—"

A voice was shouting from afar, and now more distinctly, "Oh, Claire—Claire Hayden!" The summons wound them, and they moved apart and spun toward the female clamor behind them. It was Lisa Hackfeld, hobbling toward them in hot disarray.

She came to them breathless and spilling over with some minor horror and incredulity. So intent was she upon Claire, that she hardly recognized Courtney.

"Claire," she gasped, too caught in urgency to remember they were not yet on a first-name basis. "Claire, have you been to the bathroom?"

The inquiry was so unexpected that Claire did not know how to reply.

Lisa Hackfeld was too feverish with distress to wait. "It's—it's coeducational!" she blurted. "I mean—it's cocommunity—one plank of wood with holes in it and when I walked in—there were three men and one woman sitting—talking—*together*."

Bewildered, Claire turned to Courtney, who was fighting to conceal his amusement. Succeeding, he nodded at Claire and then at Lisa Hackfeld. "Yes, it's true," he said, "the lavatories are communal, shared by men and women at the same time."

"But how *can* you—?" Lisa Hackfeld implored.

"It's the custom," said Courtney simply, "and, as a matter of fact, it's a good one."

Lisa Hackfeld seemed about to dissolve. "A *good* one?" she cried out.

"Yes," said Courtney. "When Daniel Wright came here in 1796, he found the natives uninhibited and natural in such matters, and he saw no reason, once he'd got the privies up, to change their attitudes. There's simply nothing wrong, in this society, in going to the bathroom and mingling with the opposite sex. For an outsider, it takes getting used to, but once you do, once you break down your modesty, it'll be easy and commonplace. Nobody gives a darn about you, and you don't have to give a thought to them."

"Some things should be private," insisted Lisa Hackfeld. "This would be a scandal at home."

"It depends where your home is, Mrs. Hackfeld. This is a familiar practice in parts of Europe and Latin America. And not so long ago, in sophisticated France, in the time of Marie Antoinette, great ladies would order their carriages to stop at the roadside, and step down and perform this same act in full view of their fellow passengers and retinue."

"I can't believe it."

"It's true. Mrs. Hackfeld. I understand how you feel. This is all strange and there will be some shocks, small shocks. I remember when I first came here, I was startled—I admit it—the first occasion I visited the bathroom. But as time went on, I saw the value of the custom in brushing aside one more singled-out, hidden area of false modesty. Since then, I have discovered another value to communal privies. They are nature's great leveler. When I came here, I was in awe of a very attractive and haughty young native girl. I wanted to speak to her, but her family was the best, she was important, and I was hesitant. A short time later I found myself beside her in the common privy. It broke down every one of my fears and restraints. If the institution were made universal—it would be the one democracy extant. Today, there is no equality. We have the elite, the wealthy, the talented, the strong, the intelligent, and we have everyone else inferior. But here we would have the only leveler, as I said, the one place where royalty and peasants, actresses and housewives, saints and sinners, would appear as absolute equals."

"You're not serious, Mr. Courtney."

"I'm perfectly serious, Mrs. Hackfeld." He paused, cast a sidelong glance at Claire, and then he smiled at her. "I hope I haven't offended you, Mrs. Hayden."

As disturbed about the sanitation as Lisa Hackfeld, Claire's only anxiety was not to be considered Lisa's ally in prudery. "No," she lied to Courtney, "quite the contrary, you may have a good point there."

Doubtfully, Courtney acknowledged her independence, and hitched his dungarees higher. He said to Lisa, "Unless you have incredible kidneys, I suggest you avail yourself of what we have to offer." He started to leave, turned, and, in a mock conspiratorial whisper to Lisa, he added, "But, as one ex-timorous person to a timorous one, let me suggest that if you visit the communal lavatories after the sound of the breakfast, lunch, and dinner-hour gongs—seven, twelve, and seven—you'll most likely find complete privacy, at least from the natives."

"What about privacy from our own men?" Lisa demanded, tearfully.

Courtney cupped his chin with his hand. "Yes," he said, "that would be a problem, wouldn't it? Well, I'll tell you what, Mrs. Hackfeld. Out of deference to backward ways, I'll see that the concession is made. Before the end of the day tomorrow, somewhere behind your huts, you'll find two brand new outhouses, one marked *His* and one marked *Hers*. How's that?"

Lisa Hackfeld exhaled with relief. "Oh, thank you, Mr. Courtney."

"Anything at all, Mrs. Hackfeld. Good afternoon, and—good afternoon to you, Mrs. Hayden."

He left them, striding down the compound in his bobbing gait, heading toward the great hut of Chief Paoti.

"Isn't he an odd one?" muttered Lisa. "Of course, he was teasing me with all that talk, wasn't he?"

Claire nodded slowly, eyes still upon his retreating figure. "I suppose he was," she said. "But I wouldn't bet on it."

"Well," said Lisa, "anyway, he was helpful. We'll have our privacy tomorrow . . . I've made up my mind to write Cyrus once a day, a sort of diary of the trip, to mail every week with Captain Rasmussen. This little experience will certainly give me something to start off with."

Claire had brought her attention back to Lisa. "It certainly will," she agreed.

Lisa shook her head, to herself, as if having made discovery of some profound observation. "I can just see his face," she said. "It's amazing, no matter how sophisticated we think we are, how much prudery there is in all of us."

"Yes," said Claire.

Lisa fanned her face with her hand. "I hope it's not this hot every day. I think I'd better get out of the sun. See you later."

Claire watched her as she went to her hut, and sympathized with her for what she might yet have to endure. Then, realizing what she had meant to do for herself, Claire opened the cane door and stepped inside to visit her mother-in-law.

When Claire had made the visual transition from the outer glare to the inner shade, she could see that there was no one in Maud's front room. In Maud's structure, the front room resembled her own, except that it was considerably larger and already bore the accouterments of an office. Beneath the covered window stood a crude wooden table, the top surface planed smooth, but the roughly hewed hazel-colored legs looked as if they had been recently cut and quickly added. Upon the table rested the silver metal portable tape recorder and the flat pancaked portable dictating machine. Behind these were a calendar and a battery-powered lamp, and at one end of the table two coconut trays, one filled with new pencils and small cheap sharpeners, and one empty and apparently for ashes. An unfinished chair, extremely sturdy and with a high plank backing, obviously constructed by unpracticed hands, held together by thongs rather than nails, completed the desk set. Off to the right were two long, low benches, with crude plank tops that could not have been cut by a saw.

Claire was about to call out for her mother-in-law when Maud materialized, briskly, through the rear passageway, her arms laden with large bound notebooks.

"Oh, Claire, I was about to look in on you."

"I've been loafing. All this unpacking—you make me feel guilty."

"Nonsense." She dumped the notebooks on her table. "My own neurotic sense of orderliness. You're behaving correctly. One should take it easy, at least during the day, on a tropical island." She waved a plump hand at the desk, and continued the gesture to include the entire room. "What do you think? Mr. Courtney tells me this is real luxury on The Three Sirens. Chief Paoti insisted, weeks ago, that since I am a Chief like himself, I must be pampered as one. According to Mr. Courtney, the Chief has the only Western furnishings on the island—a chair like this one, for his throne, and a huge feast table. Now I have a chair, a more practical table for a desk, thanks to Mr. Courtney, and benches for my subjects." She grimaced. "Maybe I should not have accepted all of this. Not only might it create jealousy among the team, but it removes me, a trifle, from living as a native, from being a participant. But, I must confess, it *will* make my work easier."

"I'm for a wealthy class," said Claire. "It gives the rest of us something more to strive for."

"I told Mr. Courtney we'd want a little table for your typewriter. He's having one built tomorrow."

"Will you put it in here, Maud? I'd prefer that. I want to keep our two rooms as they are, absolutely authentic native. I've become positively enchanted with our hut, and I like it open, airy, with nothing in it but ourselves. Incidentally, Maud, speaking of Mr. Courtney—"

Then Claire spoke of him, of the incident outside the door between Lisa Hackfeld and Courtney, and of Courtney's digression on the value of coeducational lavatories specifically and of the public water closet as the great human leveler in general.

Maud was amused. "Poor Mrs. Hackfeld. Well, she—and not only she but all of us—have bigger surprises in store, I would expect. Yes, I remember years ago, in the field, when Adley and I first encountered the mixed public lavatory. Our Mr. Courtney is right, you know. There's much to be said for the custom. He's also right, only slightly inaccurate, about his memory of history. It was in seventeenth-century England that a lady might leave her carriage, guests, and retainers, to perform her needs at the wayside in full view of everyone. It was in seventeenth-century France that an aristocratic lady would sit side by side in a lavatory with male friends, conversing. This was in the Restoration period, after Richard Cromwell had been removed from power. It was a period that rebelled against false modesty. Women wore provocative artificial breasts of wax over their real breasts, and they wore no drawers. I never forget the story of Casanova's meeting with Madame Fel, the singer. It is so representative of the upper-class morals. Casanova saw three young boys playing about Madame Fel's skirts. He was surprised that there was no resemblance among them. 'Of course not,' said Madame Fel. 'The eldest is the son of the Duc d'Annecy, the second of Comte Egmont, and the third is the son of Comte Maisonrouge.' Casanova apologized. 'Forgive me, Madame,' he said, 'I had thought they were all your children.' Madame smiled. 'So they are,' she said."

Claire did not hide her delight. "Wonderful!" she exclaimed.

"What is wonderful, Claire, is the two of us standing here beneath a thatched roof, in the middle of the Pacific, recollecting the easy morals of civilized France and England more than three hundred years ago—and finding they nearly correspond with some of the morals of a half-Polynesian tribe. At least, in the matter of privies."

Somewhere in Claire's mind the lank figure of Courtney lounged. Casually, she brought him forth. "Anyway, Thomas Courtney started this way-out—or, I should say, way-back—discussion. I was surprised to see him leaving here so late. Was he with you all the while?"

"Yes, before the furniture came in, we sat on the pandanus mats and talked. He's an engaging fellow, widely read, widely lived, extremely liberated in all matters. He gave me an immediate briefing on the tabus, what is and isn't, on what is mana or prestige-making and holy in the community. He explained a little of the routine and behavior we would have to understand. Very enlightening. I'm going to make some notes and have a meeting for all of us early tomorrow. I think everyone should know what he can do and cannot do and what, in a general way, he must expect. Mr. Courtney was exceedingly articulate. He will be of inestimable help to us here."

"Did he—did he tell you anything about himself?"

"Not a word. He ventured nothing and skirted around the personal. He did ask me about you and Marc. You seem to have made a favorable impression upon him."

Claire was instantly alert. "About me and Marc? Like what?"

"How long you two had been married—if you had children—where and how you lived—what Marc did—what you did—that sort of thing."

"And you told him?"

"Only a very little to be polite. I didn't think it was for me to reveal anything of you."

"Thank you, Maud. You were right. Did—did he inquire about the others, also?"

"A little. He had to know about each of our specialties, what we're after, so that he can make arrangements for our investigation. But nothing personal about the others, only you and Marc."

Claire nibbled her lower lip thoughtfully. "How extraordinary he is—his being here—and he's—I don't know, unusual in so many ways. I wish I could find out more about him."

Maud moved the chair to her table. "You'll have a chance tonight," she said, and sat down and began to arrange her notebooks. "Chief Paoti is giving us a big feast of welcome in his hut. Highly ceremonious and important. The Chief will be there with his wife, Hutia, and his son, Moreturi, and daughter-in-law, Atetou, and a niece who is now in his family—uh—Tehura, her name is Tehura. Then I am invited with my immediate family, namely you and

Marc. Mr. Courtney will be the—the intermediary—to bring us together."

"What's a feast like?" Claire wanted to know. "What do we wear and—?"

"You'll wear your best and simplest dress. It'll be warm there. As for the feast, Mr. Courtney spoke of a speech or two, and music and endless eating—native food, also native drinks—and entertainment and a rite of friendship. After that, we will possess official mana and be able to circulate freely in the village and be considered a part of the tribe. The dinner begins at nightfall. Be sure to tell Marc to be ready on time. You, too. We can expect Mr. Courtney to call for us about eight. It'll be fun, Claire, and a new experience, I promise you."

* * *

At some time between ten and eleven o'clock in the evening—in her present condition she could not make out the exact hour on the diminutive dial of her gold wrist watch—Claire remembered Maud's earlier prediction and acknowledged (to herself) its accuracy. Every exotic second at Chief Paoti's festive board had been fun; every singular minute beneath the thatched dome of his immense yellow bamboo hut had been a new experience.

She was not herself, she knew, that is, not her recent self, and the latest arrangement of herself, which was surprising, added to her pleasure.

After failing to make out the exact hour, her neck seemed to shoot upwards—"Now I'm opening out like the largest telescope that ever was!" Alice had cried out in Wonderland long ago, when she had become more than nine feet tall—and like Alice's head, Claire's own almost touched the ceiling, but then floated free, high, high above, an almost independent planet with signs of human life. From above, her elongated person looked down upon the receding contours of her evening world. There was the rubbed stone floor and the smoking earth oven and in the center, between the oven and platform, the low-slung rectangle of the royal table still heaped with the remnants of the roasted suckling pig, the marinated pahua, the hot taro dumplings and coconut cream, the cooked breadfruit, the yams, the red bananas. Around the table, seated cross-legged on mats (except for Chief Paoti Wright at the head of the table, on his squat chair, its four legs each one foot high), were the nine of them, including the one which was the body that belonged to this soaring head.

Her head was the all-seeing eye, but her body was the flesh sponge that soaked in the rise and fall of spoken words in English and Polynesian, the chants and clapping of the male singers, the erotic rhythm of the flutes and bamboo percussion instruments from an adjacent room, the fragrance of the multicolored flower petals dancing on the large wooden basins of water, the rustling of the native servants and diners in their tapa-cloth raiment.

It was the combination of the two drinks, Claire knew, that had sent her head kiting off above the table. First, there had been the elaborate ceremony of the kava preparation and serving. The green kava, roots of pepper shrubs, had been brought to the Chief in a huge container. At a signal, five young men, toothy, barechested, had entered, kneeled about the container, and quickly brandished bone knives to scrape the rind off the kava and slice the roots into small pieces. Then, to music, they had all taken pieces of kava in their mouths, chewed industriously, and placed the masticated lumps in a clay bowl. Afterwards, water had been added to the bowl, and someone had mixed and stirred the concoction, and finally, through a strainer made of the fiber of hibiscus bark, the green fluid had been pressed free. The milky kava had been presented to each of them in an ornamented coconut cup.

Claire had found the drink easy to swallow and deceptively bland. She had listened to Courtney explain that kava was not a fermented beverage, it did not make its user drunk. Rather, it was a drug, a mild narcotic that usually stimulated, enlivened the senses, did not affect the head but frequently deadened the limbs. After the kava, Claire had been served a fermented drink—"palm juice," Moreturi, beside her, had named it—an alcoholic beverage made of the sap of a palm tree, and this liquid had the sting of whiskey or gin. The palm juice, and the serving had been considerable, affected in Claire what the kava had not—her head, her sight, her hearing, her balance. Blended, the effect, for Claire, was that of a cocktail of drugs. Her senses scrambled and separated, some high up, some down low, and she felt irresponsible, pleased, mildly gay. Her sensory faculties had all been heightened. She had completely lost focus—her inability to make out the time, for instance—but she had retained a narrower focus, as if an aperture had been partially closed, so that she saw, heard, smelled, felt less, but what came through to her seemed sharper, deeper, truer.

Attempting, once more, to locate herself in the time of the evening, Claire tried to assemble the sequence of events recently behind her. This was difficult, too, but there was some success. With darkness, Courtney, in a white sport shirt open at the throat and white ducks and white tennis shoes, accompanied by Maud, had called for them, for Marc and herself. Marc was wearing a blue shirt and tie and navy slacks, and she was in her favorite sleeveless low-cut yellow shantung dress and the small diamond pendant, set in fourteen-karat white gold, that Marc had given her on their first wedding anniversary. They had gone together along the compound, their way lighted by the torch stumps beside the stream and the strings of burning candlenuts winking through the cane walls of the dwellings. After a short walk, they had entered into the Chief's big hut, their hosts waiting, then Courtney's formal introductions, next all seated, and the Chief's entrance and head inclined to each as each was announced.

A surprise, but then no surprise, for Courtney had explained earlier. Instead of the pubic bags, the two native men, the Chief and his son, Moreturi, wore ample matted kilts, as did the retainers. And here the women were not bare-breasted, not grass-skirted, but bound around the bosoms and waists in colorful tapa cloth, although shoulders, midriffs, legs, feet were bare. Then, speeches from the Chief and his son. Then music. Then kava, served differently than she had read about, served both men and women, and as part of the feast. Then palm juice. Then endless courses, the roasted pig taken from the earth oven filled with heated stones, and then the rest, the relays of alien foods. Then, eating with fingers, with a leaf to wipe them, and talk and talk, mostly the Chief and Maud, sometimes Courtney, sometimes Marc, the women silent, Moreturi restrained but friendly, amused. And now, more serving. Poi with coconut sauce.

It must now be ten-thirty, Claire decided.

Slowly, her neck contracted and her head came down and settled, and she squeezed her eyes and sobered and looked around the table. They were eating their food, absorbed, enjoying. At the head of the table, to her right, above them on his ridiculous chair, being fed by a kneeling child-girl, was Chief Paoti Wright. In the reflected light of the flickering candlenuts, his wrinkled parchment skin was browner than any other in the room. His face was skeletal, sunken, sunken eyes, sunken cheeks, almost toothless. Yet, the cropped hair, banker-gray, the alertness of the eyes, with white bushy eyebrows, the clipped but unnatural preciseness of his English, sometimes archaic, often colloquial, the importance of him—the scurrying and ducking about him—gave him the dignity of any monarch, an Indian ruler, an English chairman of the board, a Greek billionaire. She judged him to be in his late sixties, and she judged that the benign aspect hid cunning and severity.

To his left sat Maud Hayden, and then Marc, and then herself. And beside her, the boundary for her side of the table, sat Moreturi, the heir. Upon meeting him, Claire had brought forth Easterday's memory of him: black, wavy hair, broad face with slanted eyes and full lips and tan complexion, powerful and muscular to the hips, and slender. Easterday had said: about thirty, about six feet. Since meeting Moreturi, Claire had tried to revise the portrait she had held of him. There was no single detail that she could correct, except that he was less lean, somewhat stockier than she had expected. Yet, he appeared different from what she had imagined, and now she knew why. She had, in her mind, categorized him as strong and silent. This would be the type. To her surprise, he was neither. Despite the bulge of his muscles, he resembled no athlete that she had ever seen. Because his skin was devoid of hair, without fat or wrinkle, there was a natural smoothness, grace, beauty to his form. As to being the silent partner of strong and silent, she detected from his occasional utterances, above all from his reactions to the talk of others, the air of the amused extrovert. She guessed that, removed from the presence of his father and the solemnity of the feast, he might be foolish fun.

Automatically, as Easterday had done, Claire sought to compare Moreturi to Courtney, his white counterpart and friend. In making the visual transition from Moreturi to Courtney, Claire's eyes had to pass across the woman who sat opposite Moreturi. Of the party, Claire knew her least. She had been introduced as Atetou, wife of Moreturi. Alone, of them all, she had not spoken a word since the meal had begun. Avoiding her husband's eyes and any reply to Courtney's asides, she devoted herself to food, drink, secret soliloquies.

Atetou was handsome, Claire decided, but not attractive. Her features, small, regular, unyielding, were carved from a beige ivory complexion. There was something sullen and disappointed about her, too old for her hardened face, which could not have known more than twenty-seven or twenty-eight years. She seemed the embodiment of all women who had married young, with high hopes and great expectations, and had been soured by the economic or romantic failure of their mates. Claire squeezed her eyes: poor Atetou, she can no longer laugh at her husband's jokes.

At last, Claire had reached Thomas Courtney. She had meant to compare him to Moreturi, as Easterday had done, but she saw that there was no comparison, for there was hardly any similarity, except that both were male, both good-natured. Courtney was the more mature, Claire's instinct told her. It had nothing to do with more education or more years of life. It had nothing to do with a seamier, hawkish, wiser face. It had entirely to do with the quality of Courtney's sense of humor versus Moreturi's sense of humor. Moreturi's drollery was boy merriment. Courtney's amused air was grown-up, its roots deep and fanned out in layers of experience, self-probing, understanding, philosophic adjustment. He may be cynical, she thought, but he is not entirely bitter. He may be sardonic, but he would not be cruel. Guessing, guessing. Kava, palm juice.

Suddenly, Claire realized that she was gazing at two persons, for the one on the other side of Courtney, the youngest and most beautiful female at the table, the niece of the Chief, was leaning close to Courtney, whispering into his ear. Listening to her, he smiled and smiled, nodding, and then Claire detected something else. The niece, Tehura, as she whispered, absently had placed her hand nearest Courtney on Courtney's thigh, and she rubbed the hand gently, possessively, intimately across his thigh. Claire felt a pang of envy and regret, envy of Tehura, for the naturalness of that hand, regret for herself, for herself and Marc and their self-conscious condition.

As if to acquire information, a lesson in the art of artlessness, Claire inspected Tehura more carefully. Paoti's niece was exquisite. Melville would have known her at once as the daughter of Fayaway, yet the crossing of two races had made her more. Her perfection, Claire knew, could be measured by Marc's stunned dumbness upon being introduced to her. In the morning, both Marc and Orville Pence had chided Courtney about Polynesian young women, had referred disparagingly to their heaviness of nose, jaw, waist, ankles. Courtney had replied by calling these women beautiful inside. If the loveliness and grace of the young women in the village, seen from afar in the afternoon, had already supported Courtney's refutation, the presence of Tehura, now, in the evening, as his prime exhibit, made his case secure. Claire still could not perceive Tehura's inner beauty, but her magnificent physique was enough. Certainly it had been enough to reduce Marc to mute. Eating the poi, Claire was aware that Marc constantly watched Paoti's niece. Yet, Claire was not jealous, any more than she would have been jealous had her husband been entranced by some classical work of artistic genius.

Tehura had straightened away from Courtney, to finish her meal, and Claire tried to locate the sources of her beauty. She was, for one thing, a shining girl: her jet-colored hair, tumbling down her back, was lustrous; her large round eyes were liquid and capering bright; her sheath of taut flesh had the glow of burnished light copper. Her facial features, dainty as those of a Romney portrait, were contradicted only by the sensuous line of her neck and sloping shoulders. The bosom, tightly constricted by the tapa cloth, appeared small, but the exposed belly and navel above the skirt line, and the outline of hips beneath the knot, were fuller. No more than twenty-two, Claire judged. There were other factors that were anomalous. When inattentive, there was a languor about Tehura's person. When speaking or spoken to, she was filled with vivacity. The delicacy of her countenance gave an impression of unapproachable virginity, yet conflicting with this was her bold, almost flirtatious, almost wanton, manner toward Courtney.

Tehura, having finished her poi, leaned away from Courtney to listen to something her aunt, Chief Paoti's wife, was saying to her. The Chief's wife, Hutia Wright, was a squat and considerable person. Her face was round and serious, unwrinkled although she must be almost sixty, and in her profile there were traces still of youthful fairness. She spoke English as precisely as her husband, took her rank seriously (for she measured the content of her every remark), and served, Claire had overheard, as her husband's delegate on one of the village's most important ruling or policy committees.

Hutia Wright had finished speaking to Tehura, and had turned her attention back to her husband and to Maud. Tehura, freed of conversation and food, glanced about aimlessly, and her eyes intercepted Claire's concentrated study of her. Almost appreciatively, Tehura's gleaming teeth were revealed in a smile. Embarrassed to be caught, Claire strained to return the smile, then, flushing, she bowed her head over the untouched poi, automatically sought a spoon and found none, and awkwardly began to take what she could of it with her fingers.

With her eyes cast downward, distractions removed, Claire could hear again. She heard the beat of the percussion instruments from the next room. She heard the scrape of the coconut shells on the table. She heard, at last, the voices around her. She listened.

"—but ours is an insular society—insular—sheltered by good favor from the outside world." It was the voice of Paoti Wright that she heard. The voice, reedy, singsong, went on. "The system works so well for us—so well—that we have always challenged any —any—Mr. Courtney, that legal phrase you are fond of employing—?"

"Invasion of privacy, sir," said Courtney.

"Yes, yes, our life is so smooth that we have always resisted any invasion of our privacy. I am certain this insularity has its infirmities, yes. Perhaps we are too ingrown. Perhaps we are too complacent. An excess of happiness can weaken the fiber of a people. To be strong, contentious, a society must have its ups and downs, unhappiness as well as happiness, conflict. This is the combustion of progress, survival in war, but you see, Dr. Maud Hayden, we need no such strength, for we require no further progress, we have no wars to survive, and we compete with no one outside our little community."

"Are you not curious as to exactly what is on the outside?" Maud inquired.

"Not very," said Paoti.

"Sir." It was Marc, and Claire lifted her head to support her husband. "I'd like to enlarge upon my mother's question," said Marc. "As satisfied as you are with what you have, hasn't it ever occurred to you that a knowledge of the more civi—— more sophisticated islands of Polynesia might improve your own village? Or furthermore, that you might gain by adopting progressive ideas from America or Europe? We've advanced fast and far since the eighteenth century, you know."

The faintest paternal smile touched the old Chief's lips. "I know," he said. "You have advanced so fast and so far, that before

your time, you are at the brink of the grave. All that remains is one
more step . . . Do not think me arrogant and vain about our own
ways. We have our lacks—yes, lacks, and there is much, I understand, we can gain from you. However, these benefits might bring
with them—might bring—certain nuisances, penalties that would
outweigh them. So we keep to the old ways." He cleared his
throat. "I might add, the outside is not a complete mystery to us on
the Sirens. For a century, our young men have been permitted to
sail their long canoes and outriggers on the sea, and have frequently
touched on the nearest islands, never revealing from whence they
came. Occasionally, they do this today, as a feat of strength. They
have always returned to this place, been pleased to return, and have
always brought thither extensive data concerning the more progressive islands of Polynesia. On a few occasions, in the past, people of your race have come to us, and what they have revealed
has told us more of the outside. Then, Captain Rasmussen, although
often not the most profound observer, has educated us further,
and Mr. Courtney here has been generous with information on
your own country. We have much admired the technology in your
place called America. We have held less admiration for the manner
of life brought on by that technology, and by your customs."

Claire could see that Marc had been restless throughout Paoti's
recital. Now Marc spoke, controlling the pitch of his voice. "I
don't know what Mr. Courtney has told you of our culture, sir.
Each of us has our personal prejudices and viewpoint, and it may
be that the America he has described would not be the same America my mother and I might show you."

Paoti ruminated on this, bobbing his gray head slowly. "True,
true, yet—yet, I wonder." He turned his head from Marc to Maud.
"As you know, Dr. Maud Hayden, we have pride in the enduring
success of our mating system. We all partake of its emoluments. It
is the core of our happiness." Maud nodded, but did not interrupt.
Paoti continued. "From Mr. Courtney, I have been brought up to
date on your own mating system. Perhaps Mr. Courtney has colored
the facts with his own personality, as your son suggests. On the
other hand, if what I have heard is approximately true, I am astonished. Is it true that your children receive no practical education in
the art of love at any time before maturity? Is it true that virginity
is much admired in women? Is it true that a married man is supposed never to enjoy the pleasures of another woman, and that if

215

he does it is usually done in secrecy and is called 'adultery' and is regarded with a tincture of disapproval by the law and society? Is it true that there is no organized method for sexually pleasing a man or a woman left unsatisfied by the act of love? Is this approximately true?"

"It is true," said Maud.

"Then, I believe, your son would have little to add to what Mr. Courtney has told us."

Marc leaned forward. "Wait, now, what I—"

Maud ignored her son, and overrode him. "There is more to say, Chief Paoti, but all that of which you speak is true."

Paoti nodded. "Then there is little that we would wish to adopt from your society. On the other hand, it is your way, and I respect it. It is your way, and so perhaps you wish it that way and prefer it to all else. However, Dr. Maud Hayden, as you discover our way, I will be interested in your opinions of how it compares, in every detail, to the customs in your own homeland. I said that I am not greatly curious about the outside. I am not. Nevertheless, I have pride in my people, our system, and I will have interest in your comments."

"I look forward to these conversations," said Maud.

Claire, made more lightheaded than ever by the drink and the implications of Paoti's words, suddenly leaned forward and called out, "Mr. Courtney—"

Courtney turned toward her, surprised.

"Tell us," Claire said, "tell us what you really told them about our mating habits." She settled back, waiting, unsure what had impelled her to speak, yet smiling so that he would know she was not allied with Marc here, not challenging.

Courtney shrugged. "There's so much, nothing that we, all of us from the United States, don't know."

"Like what?" Claire persisted. "Name one big thing about our sex lives that's different from here. Name one. I'm interested."

Courtney stared at the table a moment. He looked up. "All right," he said. "We live in a sexual pressure cooker in America, and they don't here."

"Meaning what?" asked Claire.

"Meaning there's pressure on sex at home, all kinds of stupidity and ignorance and foolishness, all kinds of inhibitions, leering, four-letter words, puritanism, secrecy, the cult of the breast, all that."

"For women, maybe," said Claire, "but not for men so much, it's easy for men." She found Tehura and Hutia Wright listening to her with interest, and she said to them, "Men have fewer problems than women in our society, because—"

She felt Marc's hand on her arm. "Claire, this is no place for a sociological—"

"Marc, I'm fascinated by the subject." She faced Courtney once more. "I'm absolutely fascinated. Don't you think I'm right?"

"Well," said Courtney, "I had really been telling Chief Paoti about our morality as a whole, our whole society—"

"Did you tell him that men have less pressure?"

"Not exactly, Mrs. Hayden," said Courtney, "because I'm not sure it is true."

"You aren't?" said Claire, not dismayed but eager to know what he thought. "All through Western history, men have forced chastity on their women while they chased around, still do. They've enjoyed themselves, whereas women—" She opened her hands in cheerful despair.

. "If you really want my views—" said Courtney. He glanced about, somewhat apologetically, and saw that all were intent upon him.

"Please go on, Mr. Courtney," said Maud.

"You asked for it," he said with a grin. At once, he was solemn. "I think that Mrs. Hayden is right about one thing. From the time of the cave man through the Victorian era, men had it fairly much their way. It was, indeed, a man's world. Women were merely the vassals of men, in all matters including love. The ultimate goal of a coupling was that the man be satisfied. The woman was there to give pleasure, not to share it. If she enjoyed herself too, that was incidental. That's the way it was in other times."

Listening, Claire's giddiness had subsided and she tried to examine what Courtney was saying. A noiseless servant behind her crept closer, unobtrusively offering a fresh drink of palm juice in a coconut shell. Automatically, Claire accepted it. "Do you think anything has changed?" she asked Courtney. She was conscious of Marc's annoyance with her questions, and now with her accepting the coconut shell. In deliberate defiance of him, she drank and waited for Courtney's reply.

"I believe a good deal has changed, Mrs. Hayden," said Courtney. "Somewhere between Freud and Woodrow Wilson, the age of emancipation, liberalism, confession came into being. Men conceded equality to women, privately as well as publicly. This filtered down from the ballot box and the office to the bedroom. Women won not only the vote, but also the right to the orgasm. They enjoyed their discovery and dinned it into all ears and used it as one measurement of happiness. Overnight, it seemed, the tables were turned. Men, who'd had it their own way for so long, had to give as well as take, had to satisfy as well as be satisfied. Men had to restrain their natural animal love-making, inhibit it while devoting themselves to being considerate. Overnight, their primitive pleasure became conditional on their other halves. This is what I mean by pressure on the male in our own society today."

Claire had nodded throughout this recital, but then she was diverted by Chief Paoti addressing her mother-in-law.

"Dr. Maud Hayden," the Chief was saying, "do you agree with Mr. Courtney's observation?"

"More or less," said Maud. "Mr. Courtney's observation has validity, but it is oversimplified. For example, he equates male virility entirely with his ability to bring a woman to orgasm. I don't think this is a valid criteria in America or England or Europe. Our women have varying definitions of virility. If a man is a good provider, dependable, safe, rather than a great lover, he may be considered a real man. On a different level, a man who has wealth or power or prestige will find these effective substitutes for the virility conferred by orgasm-giving."

Paoti had turned to Courtney. "An interesting qualification to your point, yes?"

Courtney accepted the qualification. "Absolutely, Dr. Hayden," he said. "Rich or famous men are exempt from this modern pressure. If they fail to provide sexual pleasure, they are still capable of providing other pleasures even more valuable in our society. I'd go this far—I'd say that the upper and lower classes of men suffer less pressure than the middle class. The upper classes have other means of satisfying their women. The lower classes are generally too poor and uninformed to care about mutual orgasms. In women suffering from poverty, the desire for basic security supersedes the desire for orgasm, and a mate who can give this security is man enough. These women want to be satisfied economically first. The other, they regard as a refinement of leisure."

"But the middle classes?" asked Paoti.

"There the pressure on men is unremitting," said Courtney. "The broad, so-called average, in-between economic class, literate enough to know of the new equality, secure enough to get along on payments, without wealth or prestige or the obsession for bread as substitutes for virility, these are the male members of our society under the greatest tension. They go along now, in their mating, aware that they must be what the books call thoughtful and considerate, succeeding sometimes, failing more often, aware constantly that this whole thing isn't as pleasant as it used to be for their grandfathers. This nostalgia for the past, I sometimes think, is what accounts for the prostitutes, call girls, party girls who accommodate the middle and upper-middle classes. These girls are a throwback to the vassal girls of old. They give pleasure, but demand none, and for this fun they ask only an impersonal commodity, a little gift or a little cash."

For a few moments, except for the distant music, the great cane and bamboo room was still. Claire sipped her palm sap, and she wondered what the native hosts made of this talk, which she was now convinced was mostly true. Of course, she told herself, Courtney had omitted discussing women, the universal ennui and dissatisfaction of most married women, and the causes of this and the problems involved. Who had said that the final tragedy of love is indifference? Mr. Maugham had said that. Final tragedy of love, indifference. Claire considered bringing it up, but then refrained because of Marc, so restless beside her. Instead, lowering her coconut-shell cup, she determined to find out what Courtney had yet left unsaid about the pressures on men.

"Mr. Courtney, I—you—you seemed to be speaking only of the condition of men in America, in the West—"

"Yes."

"Don't men have exactly the same pressures everywhere on earth, even here, even on the Sirens?"

"No. Not men, not women either."

"Why not?"

Courtney hesitated and glanced at Paoti, who sat hunched above them all. "Perhaps Chief Paoti is better qualified—"

Paoti waved his frail hand negatively. "No, no, I defer to you, Mr. Courtney. You are more eloquent at speechifying, better able to represent our way to your countrymen."

"All right," said Courtney simply. His serious eyes went from

Maud to Marc to Claire. "I speak from the experience of four years among these people. These pressures don't exist on The Three Sirens because of their upbringing, their education, their traditional customs, all of which contribute to a healthier, more realistic attitude toward love and marriage. In the United States or England, for example, our prohibitions about sex have created a warped and magnified interest in it. Here on the Sirens the prohibitions are so few and minor, the consideration of the subject so natural, that it becomes a normal, acceptable part of day-to-day living. Here, when a woman hungers for food, she takes it and sees nothing wrong or special about eating. In the same way, when she hungers for love, she has it, and there's no more to it. And the point is, she has it in the best way, without guilt or shame. On the Sirens, children learn about love in their school, not only in theory but in practice, so that they know as much about it as they know about their history and language. Growing young people are not avidly curious about sex, for nothing has been concealed from them. Nor are they repressed. If a young man wants a woman, or a girl wants a man, neither is frustrated. And the act of premarital coitus is gay, passionate but gay, great sport, because there are no tabus to create guilt or worry, no need to be furtive or afraid. In marriage, both partners are always fulfilled, if they wish to be fulfilled; the community guarantees this. Provisions are even made to satisfy widows and widowers, spinsters and bachelors. There is no homosexuality here, no violence, no rape, no abortion, no dirty words on walls of latrines, no adultery, no secret longings and unfulfilled erotic dreams. Because the old carefree Polynesian ways have been preserved, and interwoven with and improved by Daniel Wright's liberal social ideas, the practices of sex, love, marriage are all synonymous with contentment on The Three Sirens."

"Those practices can be satisfactory in the United States, too," said Marc coldly.

"I'm sure they can be and sometimes are," replied Courtney. "However, from my experience as an attorney handling civil cases, and from my reading, I think they are less enjoyable than they should be in America. As I look back, now that I have lived in these two contrasting societies, I believe what I find most incredible is this—that we in the so-called civilized nations, with all our overpowering teaching, learning, education, with our communications and know-how in all fields, with our machines to wash and dry,

220

and machines to hurtle across the country, and machines to X-ray our insides, and machines to toss a human being beyond the reach of gravity—with all that, we have not invented the simple machine, or improved the human machine, to raise children sensibly, to make marriages happy, to make life relaxed. Yet here, on this remote island, where they have not a single machine, not a suit or dress, hardly a book, where *orbit* and *gravity* and *X-ray* and *jet* have no meaning, these people have been able to create and perpetuate a society where children and parents are wonderfully happy.

"And one last point. While humans are the most emotionally complicated of all mammals, yet like the rest, in the matter of coupling, they are most simple. One is concave, the other convex. You join them, and there should be automatic pleasure and sometimes procreation. Yet, in the West, we have not mastered nature's set of directions. Somehow we join the concave and the convex, and while the result is often procreation, it is too rarely pleasure. With all our expertise, our progress, our genius, we have not solved this first problem of all peoples on earth. Yet here, on this bump of land in the Pacific, a couple of hundred white-brown, nearly naked, semiliterate people have solved it. I think, in six weeks, you will agree with me. I hope so . . . In any event—" He had turned from Paoti and Maud back to Claire. "—I apologize for my overlong discourse, Mrs. Hayden. This will teach you not to ask me questions about my favorite subject. I've talked more tonight than in the last four years. I blame it on the kava, the kava and the juice, and a growing desire to become a missionary."

Claire's bleary eyes went wide. "A missionary?"

"Yes. I want to lead a set of holy fathers, from the Sirens, to New York and London and Rome and convert the heathen to nature's way."

Claire faced her husband, squinting him into focus. "Let's be converted, Marc."

"Not so fast, dear," Marc said. "I'm not buying a pig in a poke. Mr. Courtney may be exaggerating, may be taking a certain poetic license in his praise of this place."

Marc is angry, Claire thought, that is why he is speaking too loudly. But Marc's face was contained, as he went on to his wife, but speaking for all ears. "After all, would Mr. Courtney leave his own country for so long if he were not discontented? And staying here so long, may he not have lost his perspective?"

Marc looked at Courtney, whose expression was bland and uncombative. "Mr. Courtney, do not misunderstand me," Marc continued. "I am only saying what I said this morning—sailors, long at sea, came upon these islands when they were edgy and disgruntled, and therefore they found them more pleasurable than they really were. I'm not calling you a romancer. I'm not trying to be argumentative. But, you see, I am a social scientist, most of us on the team are scientists, and we like to judge all phenomena against impartial, unemotional, scientific standards. I only say I would like to reserve my judgment until I have seen and studied, seen for myself."

"Fair enough," said Courtney.

Throughout this exchange the native women had not uttered a word, had sat phlegmatic as graven images. Now Tehura, with a toss of her long black hair, had lifted herself to her knees and taken Courtney's arm. "It is not fair enough, Tom!" she exclaimed. She stared directly at Marc across from her. "It does not need the scientific study you speak about. It is all true—about America I do not know—but about here on the Sirens I know, and it is true. Everything Tom says is exactly the way it is with our people. I am one of our people, so I know."

Marc was suddenly all gallantry. "I wouldn't dream of disagreeing with a beautiful young lady."

"Then you must listen, for a little, to this young lady. I will tell you a lovely nice story about Thomas Courtney and Tehura Wright."

Marc folded his arms impassively, an artificial smile pressed into his face. Maud's head was cocked in the devoted attitude of anthropologist to informant. Only Claire's expression reflected her inner excitement, like that of waiting for a curtain to rise and disclose a drama that would reveal the truth about the enigmatic Courtney.

Tehura had slipped her arm inside Courtney's arm, and she resumed earnestly. "When Tom first came here, so long ago, he was not the one you see today. He was like a different soul. He was—I do not know every word to describe it—sad, he was sad, and—Tom, how would you say it?"

Courtney considered her with affectionate indulgence. Revealing some inner amusement, he said, "He was Odysseus in a wash-

and-wear shirt and seersucker suit, with the battle ribbons of Ogygia, Ilium, Aeolia, and other Madison Avenues, on his patch pocket, who decided that since he had no Penelope awaiting him, he had no reason to return to Ithaca. So he managed to untie himself from his ship's mast, and listen to the Sirens, and succumb to them. Some evil god, even like Odysseus' Poseidon, had infected him with weariness, lack of spirit, apathy, cynicism, and a distrust of life. He offered himself to the Sirens because he was tired of his journey, and prayed they could give him the strength to go on—or remain."

Tehura squeezed Courtney's arm. "Exactly." Some private look passed between them, and then Tehura turned her attention to the others once more. "When he was taken into the village and made one of us, his bad spirit fell away. He lived with us, and he became alive with being curious. He wanted to know everything we did and why we did it. Like music, our life was an ancient rhythm, and after many months Tom took off his old ideas the way he finally took off his foolish hot clothes, and he became more sympathetic. I desired him from the first day, and when he understood us, was more sympathetic, I was able to tell him my love. It was then I learned that he had much passion for me. At once we were lovers. It was beautiful, was it not, Tom?"

Courtney touched her hand. "Yes, Tehura, very."

"But not immediately," Tehura said to the others. "At first he was not good—he had much goodness, but in sex embrace he was not good. He was too formal, too worried, too hard—"

Courtney, staring down at the table, interrupted. "They may understand, Tehura. We have spoken of the pressures on love in my homeland—for both sexes—so much of it a mixture of alcohol and drugs, hostility and guilt, so much of it anxiety and fear and stress."

"But I was different, I had not suffered such things, and I knew the happiness of it," said Tehura to the Haydens. "And so I taught Tom, with what I had been taught, to enjoy the sport, the game, without a heavy mind, without a heavy body, to be so natural as the waves rising and falling and so free as the breeze blowing through the forest. Many months passed, and we had the tenderness, the passion, the life we lived together, in our own hut—"

Marc was staring at her strangely. "Then you're married?"

Tehura's face was transformed. "Married?" she whooped with

glee. "Oh, never! We are not to be married, we are not for each other in too many ways. We loved each other only that body way, until last year when it ended. I had enough of Tom's body. He had enough of mine. We no longer needed each other's love. Besides, I had deeper feeling for another—for Huatoro—but that is the future. Now, Tom and I are not the lovers, but we are the friends. When I have a trouble, I go to his hut and I speak and speak, and he counsels me. When he has to have more understanding of my people, he comes to me in my house, and we sit and eat taro and speak of my people and his people. I tell you of Tom and myself because I am proud of our once love. When I told the village, the first time, Tom was surprised. He said in his country a woman would not reveal to all of her body love when unmarried, but you see, as he has learned, we do not think it wrong, and we are happy, and I am proud."

"I am proud, too, Tehura," Courtney said quietly.

Paoti coughed. "We have spoken enough for our first meeting. The hour grows late. It is time for the ceremony of the rite of friendship to begin." He fumbled for the gnarled wooden walking stick against his chair, and reached over and hit the table twice. He pointed his stick to the platform beyond Moreturi and Atetou.

Everyone turned to watch the platform. Claire, her gaze on Tehura and Courtney, saw Maud and Marc twist toward her and she tried to read their familiar faces. Obviously, Maud had enjoyed Tehura's frank, simple, unembarrassed recital, and seen rich material for her paper. Marc's face was clenched, and Claire guessed at his growing dislike for these open, simple people. Shifting herself toward the stage, Claire tried to define her own reaction to Tehura's confession. What she felt was uneasiness and inferiority. It was an emotion sometimes engendered at parties in Santa Barbara or Los Angeles, when another couple made some veiled references to their sex life that made it appear that their mating was superior to all others. Claire suffered this emotion now. They had the magic. She had none. They were healthy. She was crippled. She suffered even more for Marc, who was more vulnerable than she, and then she put Tehura out of her mind.

A tall, lithe, statuesque girl, no more than nineteen, had materialized on the center of the platform. She stood motionless, arms outstretched, legs wide apart. Two brilliant garlands of hibiscus dangled from her neck and partially covered her young, small breasts. From her waist hung two short strips of white tapa cloth, one in front between her legs, and one behind, with her naked hips and thighs exposed entirely.

The percussion and wind instruments filled the room, the sounds slithering and insinuating themselves among those around the table. As the swell and beat of the music grew and grew, the tall, tan girl on the platform began to move, never leaving her place, letting all but her bare feet become animated. Her snaking hands caressed the air, and the parts of her face and body began to dance, first one, then another, until all were alive in sensuous motion. Her eyes danced in her head, and her mouth opened and closed, and her tiny breasts shimmied in and out of the flowers, and her belly shook, and her seductive hips revolved. At first the undulations were slow, but gradually they picked up tempo, and her face was transported and her figure shaken with fleshly tremors, until she exploded into the air, and slowly sank down to a crouch on the platform.

Enrapt, Claire understood what was being performed, the wild ecstasy of love fulfilled, and what was following now was the procreation, the labor pangs that would bring forth the birth of friendship.

The dancer lay on the stage, on her back, drawing up her legs and lifting only her torso into the air. The almost naked pelvic muscles pressed, and strained, and heaved to the music, and Claire held her arms tightly and felt the dryness in her mouth and the terrible throb in her throat and the want in her own body. The taunting scene became filmed over for her by her drunkenness and moist eyes, and she envied this symbol on the stage, and wanted some man, a man, a man who wanted her, to come into her and leave the seed of a new life. And suddenly, as the music abruptly stopped, and the dancer swayed erect and frozen, Claire caught the sob in her chest and maintained her poise.

The tall dancer on the platform was immobile once more. Two young males, carrying a large steaming wooden bowl, had lifted it to the platform before the dancer. There was a rapping on the dinner table, and it was from Paoti's stick.

"Dr. Maud Hayden," he was saying, "we reach the final step of our traditional rite of friendship, a rite infrequently used in recent centuries. One female of our blood and one female of your blood amongst you will ascend the platform. They will stand on either side of the dancer. They will remove their upper garments, and hold ready their naked breasts for the holy anointment which joins our peoples in friendship and removes the tabu against strangers. To represent our blood line, I designate the female who is my dead brother's daughter, I appoint the one known as Tehura."

Tehura bowed her head to Paoti, uncrossed her legs, leaped gracefully to her feet, and ascended the stage to stand on one side of the dancer.

Paoti was addressing Maud again. "And which female of your blood family do you designate to represent your party?"

Maud pursed her lips, thoughtfully, and then she said, "I believe it best that I represent my family and our party."

"Matty, for Chrissakes—" It was Marc.

"Don't be foolish, Marc," said Maud, crisply. "When your father and I were in the field, I engaged in similar rites on several occasions." She addressed Paoti. "We are familiar with the rites of acceptance in all cultures. I once did a paper on the Mylitta, whose custom it is to receive a visitor by offering him one of their young women. When she gives of her love, she receives a coin, and after this exchange there is friendship."

Clumsily, Maud began to rise, when Marc restrained her. "Dammit, Matty, I won't have you getting up there—we'll get one of the others—"

Maud showed her annoyance. "Marc, I don't know what's got into you. This is a tribal custom."

Dizzily witnessing the disagreement, Claire suddenly felt shame for her husband and for herself before the natives. She knew that she could not allow Maud to go up there and uncover her aged, pendulous bosom. She knew that she, Claire, Tehura's counterpart, should enact the rite. The idea gripped her, and the kava and palm drinks swam beneath her, lifting her to her feet.

"I'll do it, Maud," she heard herself say.

Swaying, she had started for the platform, when Marc had grabbed for her, and missed, and fallen foolishly to the matting. "Claire, cut it out!"

"I *want* to do it," she called back, "I want us to be friends with them."

On the platform, she stumbled, finally taking her position on the other side of the motionless dancer. Briefly, she noted the ring of faces below, Moreturi approving, Marc fuming, Maud worried, Paoti and Courtney revealing no emotion.

The tall dancer had moved to Tehura, and was slowly unwinding the tapa-cloth binder that covered her chest. The cloth ran out, was released, and fell to the floor. With the removal of the upper garment, Tehura's breasts seemed to burst free. Claire tried not to look, but curiosity consumed her. She must know what Tehura, who knew of love, had offered to Courtney. From the corner of an eye, Claire inspected her opposite number, and she could see that the sloping, shining shoulders had kept their promise, as they blended without a break or crease into the two curved rises of high rigid breasts with their distinct red nipples.

The dancer was facing Claire, and the moment had come, and to her relief Claire found that she was unafraid. And then she knew why, but before she could think about it, she realized that her attendant required help. The brown-skinned dancer had never been introduced to the mysteries of a Western dress. Claire nodded, understandingly, and reached behind her, unhooked the top of the yellow shantung, zipped it downward, and wriggled free of the upper half of the garment, which collapsed to her waist. She was wearing her new transparent lace brassière, and she was glad of that. Quickly, she reached behind once more and opened it, and then she dropped her arms to her sides and waited. The attendant understood, immediately taking the loose straps of the brassière and drawing them down Claire's arms, so that the large webbed cups were pulled free of her flesh and she stood in nudity to the waist.

When her white brassière had been dropped away, Claire straightened to her full height. She could see Tehura, whom she had envied, staring at her with admiration, and then Claire knew why she was unafraid. In a world where protuberant mammary glands, their capacity, their contour, were marks of womanly beauty, she would seem highly favored. The size and arch and firmness of her breasts, the circumference of the brown nipples now soft, accentuated by the sparkle of the diamond pendant that had fallen into the deep cleft between, were her femininity, her advertisement of love. Thus revealed, she was no longer Tehura's inferior, but her equal, and perhaps in the eyes of those below, her superior.

The attending young girl had knelt, dipped her hands into the bowl, and brought up a warm oil. She poured some into Tehura's open hands, and some into Claire's, and then she signaled them to come forward, to meet over the friendship bowl. Tehura reached out, and lightly she applied the oil over the tops of Claire's breasts, and Claire, realizing this was expected of her, in turn smoothed the oil over the top portions of Tehura's bosom. Tehura smiled and stepped back. Imitating her, Claire stepped back, too.

The attending girl sang out a single word in Polynesian.

Chief Paoti rapped his stick on the table, and trembled to a standing position.

"It is done," he announced. "We welcome you to the village of The Three Sirens. Henceforth, our life is your life, and we are as of one blood."

*　*　*

Fifteen minutes later—it was almost midnight—Claire walked beside Marc through the village, darkened and asleep, the only illumination coming from the few torch stumps flickering on either side of the stream.

Since she had dressed, and said her farewells, and since they had come into the compound together—Maud having lingered behind with Courtney—Marc had not looked at her or spoken one word to her.

They went on in silence.

When they reached their hut, she stopped and saw the ridges of anger in her husband's face.

"You hate me tonight, don't you?" she said suddenly.

His lips moved but no words came, and then they came in a shaking abrasive rush. "I hate anyone—I hate anyone who gets stinking drunk—and provokes a lot of filthy sex talk—and who behaves like a goddam whore."

Even in the cushioning softness of the night, the slap of his words stung and pained her through. She stood, weaving, ashamed of him, so ashamed of him. He had never, in almost two years of marriage, spoken to her with such unrestrained fury. Always, his criticisms had been controlled, and when they had been made, she had taken them with little contention. But now, in this terrible moment of the night, all that had happened, all that she had seen and heard and drunk, gave her support, an odd safe freedom to be herself for once, to speak her true feelings at last.

"And I," she said low and unafraid, "I hate anyone who is a shameful, dirty-minded prig."

She waited, breathless, expecting him to strike her. Then she knew that he was too weak for that. Instead, he shot her a look of loathing, turned his back on her, and slammed into the hut.

She remained where she was, shivering. Finally, she fished a cigarette out of her dress pocket, and lighted it, and slowly she walked toward the stream and then back to the hut, and then back and forth, smoking, remembering her life before Marc, remembering her life since, picturing Tehura with Courtney, reliving the rite of acceptance, then reviving old dreams and fond hopes. After a half-hour, she had calmed down, and when she saw that the lamps in their hut were all out, she started for the door.

He had been as drunk as she had been, and he would be asleep. She felt kindlier toward him, and better about everything, and when she went inside she felt certain that they would both be sober and forgiving in the morning.

IV

CLAIRE HAD SLEPT as if in a deep pit, enveloped in black and deadened air, slumbering without the twisting or turning of partial wakefulness. What had brought her back up, at last, had been the thin stretching fingers of the new morning's sun, groping through the cane walls, finding her, baking and warming her with their tips, until she had opened her eyes. Her left arm and hip felt stiff and bruised from the first night on the matted floor. Her lips felt cracked, and her tongue parched and swollen, and so finally she remembered the events of the evening before. She picked up her wrist watch. It was twenty minutes after eight in the morning.

Hearing footsteps, she rolled over, pulling down the nylon pajama top that had crept up on her—she remembered that, too—to the undercurve of her public breasts, and she saw Marc beside the back window, holding up an oval mirror, meticulously combing his close-cropped hair. He was already dressed, sport shirt, denims, sneakers, and if he was aware that she was awake, he did not acknowledge it. For Claire, the invasion of the sun, the freshness of the day, the crispness of her husband, made the activities and talk of nine hours before seem distant, remote, improbable.

"Hi, Marc," she said. "Good morning."

He hardly took his eyes from the mirror. "You slept like a log."

"Yes."

"Did you hear Karpowicz? He came around with a message from Matty. She wants us all in her office by ten."

"I'll be ready." She sat up, and was relieved that she had no hangover. "Marc—"

This time he turned and acknowledged her, but about his lips there was no yielding.

She swallowed and wanted it over with. "Marc, I guess I *was* drunk last night. I'm sorry."

His lips let go slightly. "It's all right."

"I don't want to hate myself all morning. I—I'm also sorry about the things we said to each other."

He bent, and dropped the mirror and comb into the pile of his personal effects. "Okay, honey, let's forget it, let's just forget it. I didn't say what I said. You didn't say what you said. Clean slate. Only let's—let's both remember who we are, and not lower ourselves before anyone's eyes. Let's keep our dignity."

She said nothing, wishing that he would at least come to her and lift her up, and kiss her, only kiss her. He was at the door to the living room, and leaving her with no more than a pinned note of reminder.

"Try to be on time, Claire. The weekend is over. We're back at work."

"I'll be on time."

After he had gone, she straightened her sleeping bag and his, observed that he had tidily set aside the clothes that he had worn and which were to be washed, and then, listlessly, she unbuttoned her tepid pajama top. She had no interest in her public breasts, but then she noticed that the diamond pendant still hung between them. She removed it, and knelt to put it in her leather jewel box. In this posture, she could not be unconscious of her breasts, and she looked at their white mounds and conjured up the male eyes—Moreturi, Paoti, Courtney (an American!)—that had seen them like this, and now, in the embarrassment of daylight, she felt truant and shameless. This moment, she did not blame Marc for his anger. She was a wife, an American wife—she had almost added "and mother," but had not—and she had behaved, her first night out, like a nymphomaniac, well practically. Until now, she had trapped such outrageous behavioral fancies in her head, properly classified in the cabinet of shibboleths marked Strictly Brought-Up and Men Respect A Decent Woman, and Love, Honor, and Obey. Her restraining wall had been built up of Modesty, Decency, Chastity and one more brick—yes, Timidity. How and why had she brought it all down last night? She had been wanton, and now, as she reconstructed the restraining wall, brick upon brick, she did not see how she could bear to have Courtney or the others see her again. What must they think?

She decided that she must make her shame clear to Marc, she owed him that. Then, as she rummaged through her clothes for the white blouse and white tennis shorts, she realized that she was always apologizing to Marc for something, for lesser stupidities, indiscretions of speech, memory lapses, omissions of behavior, and it was not pleasant, it simply was not pleasant, and not fair either, always to be on the defensive. But last night was no small thing, a special failure, and she would apologize more strongly the second that she saw him.

She dressed quickly, and then, somewhat dragging, she made her way to the communal privy. She entered cautiously, and thanked the Lord only Mary Karpowicz, moody and monosyllabic, was there. After that, Claire walked slowly through the hot, marvelous sun to their hut. In the front room she did her toilet, and after making up her lips, she realized that someone, Marc or a native servant, had delivered a great bowl of fruit and cold cooked meat for breakfast, and near the bowl, piled high, their ration of canned foods and drinks. She ate sparingly, leisurely, from the native bowl, and when it was near ten o'clock, she went out into the bright village compound to seek Marc, tender her apology, and join the others in Maud's office.

Except for children at the stream, the immediate thoroughfare was deserted. There appeared to be some human activity, comings and goings, at the far end of the village, before the Social Aid Hut and school. Then, she saw the two figures before Maud's hut, and one was Marc. He was deep in conversation with Orville Pence.

Approaching, she wanted Marc to herself briefly, to tender the apology.

"Marc—"

He looked up, and suddenly his face clouded. He touched Orville's arm, and he came to her.

"Marc," she said, "I was just thinking about—"

His hand cut her off, sweeping downward before her, indicating her entire person. "My God, Claire, where the devil do you think you're going?"

Taken aback, her knuckles went to her throat. "What—what's the matter?"

He stood, hands on his hips, surveying her, shaking his head with exaggerated disgust. "Those damn tennis shorts," he said, "look at them, right up to your crotch. What's wrong with you? You know better than to wear shorts on a field trip."

She was too stunned by his criticism to fight back. "But—but Marc, I didn't know—"

"Of course you knew. I heard Matty warn you and all the women in Santa Barbara. She's always quoting old Kroeber—be delicate about the subject of sex, don't wear shorts, don't tempt the natives. You don't listen to anyone, or if you do, you want to defy them. You seem set on breaking all the rules. Yesterday, you took care of sex, today you're flaunting the shorts—what's left? Sleeping with a native?"

"Oh, Marc—" she said brokenly, tears welling. "I didn't—I didn't know. It seemed sensible in this heat. They cover me. They're a hundred times more chaste than those grass skirts—"

"You're not a primitive, you're a civilized American. That getup not only shows disrespect—the natives expect more of you—but it's deliberately provocative. Now change, and better make it fast. Everyone's in the office, waiting."

She had already turned her back on him, not wanting him to have the satisfaction of seeing her hurt. Without another word, she left for the hut. She walked on legs that felt wooden, despising herself for having intended to apologize and despising him for making every day impossible. Either he was getting worse, she told herself, or she was performing more poorly as his wife. It was one or the other or—no, there was a third possibility that seemed more accurate: the influence of The Three Sirens, from the morning it had entered their lives with the Easterday letter, to this moment in the compound of the village—it was to blame. The sorcery of the islands had acted upon him and upon her, brought out the meanest side of him, every weakness and defect, and brought sharper, ruthless vision to her, so that she saw him, his essential self, unretouched by her own guilts, and she saw herself more clearly, too, and their life, their little life together as it had been, as it was, and as it would be.

Not until she arrived at the door of their hut did she fully defy him. Her shoulders went back, her breasts thrust against her blouse, and she was proud of last night. She hoped the men had looked hard and long. She hoped they had appreciated her. She was tired, tired,

tired of being not enough, when she was so much, if only someone on earth would understand . . .

When Claire returned to Maud's thatched office fifteen minutes later, in the acceptable anthropological uniform of blouse and cotton plaid skirt, she found all but Maud on hand for the morning's meeting. They were gathered about the room in clusters, Marc still with Orville Pence near the table desk, and around the benches and seated on them, the rest of the team. Animated conversations were going on.

Ignoring Marc and Orville, Claire crossed the mat-covered floor to the group formed by the Karpowiczes and Harriet Bleaska. They were discussing the feast they had attended the night before, given by the native woman, Oviri, a close kin of Paoti, who was in charge of the forthcoming festival week. They were engrossed in re-creating a historical pantomime they had witnessed, and Claire slid away and sat down beside Rachel DeJong and Lisa Hackfeld on the far bench.

So distraught was Lisa that she hardly greeted Claire, although Rachel winked at her pleasantly. Claire tried to pick up the thread of Lisa's aggravation.

"—know how upset I am, how much it really bothers me," Lisa was saying. "I had personally packed the full six-week supply of those precious bottles, wound them round with cotton batting—"

"What bottles?" inquired Claire. "Scotch?"

"Much more important," said Rachel DeJong, making a good-natured grimace at Claire. "Poor Mrs. Hackfeld brought along a supply of peroxide and blond rinse, and when she went through the crate this morning, she found every bottle smashed."

"Gone, all of it gone," groaned Lisa. "And no one has anything suitable to loan me. I could weep. I don't know, Claire—may I call you Claire?—maybe you have something—"

"I wish I did, Lisa," said Claire, "but I haven't a dram of anything."

Lisa Hackfeld wrung her hands. "Ever since I've—since I've grown up—I've used hair coloring. I've never been a week without it. Now what's going to happen to me? In a couple of weeks, it'll all be natural. I've never seen myself that way—Jesus, suppose I have some gray hairs?"

"Mrs. Hackfeld, there are worse fates," said Rachel with reassurance. "Many women think it smart to prematurely gray their hair."

"You can do it when you don't have to," said Lisa, "but when maybe you have to, that's another thing." She caught her breath. "I'm not an ingénue any more," she said. "I'm forty."

"I can't believe it," said Claire.

Lisa stared at her with startled gratefulness. "You can't?" Then she remembered, and said bitterly, "You'll believe it in a week or two."

"Mrs. Hackfeld," said Rachel, "in a week or two you'll be too occupied to think about it. You'll—" She halted abruptly, and pointed off. "There's Dr. Hayden coming in now. She should have a good deal of news. I'm sure we all can't wait to get started."

* * *

Everyone was seated, either on the benches or on the floor matting, except Maud Hayden, who stood beside her desk waiting for the last private conversation to cease. Despite her ludicrous attire— she wore a wide-brimmed straw hat, locks of her gray hair straggling out from under it, no make-up on her puffy sunburned face, several strands of colored beads around her neck, a sleeveless print dress from which her jelly arms protruded, khaki scout stockings that came to below her knees, square contour shoes that seemed Martian—she appeared more professional and zestful than any other person in the room.

When her colleagues were quiet, Maud Hayden began to address them in a manner that vacillated from the brisk scientific to the conversational maternal.

"I imagine most of you have been wondering what is going to happen next," she said, "and I've called this first meeting to tell you. I've spent the morning since daybreak with Chief Paoti Wright and his wife Hutia Wright, both charming and friendly human beings. While Hutia has some fear of us, and consequently some reservations about what we should be allowed to see and do, Chief Paoti has overruled her on every count. Since we are here, he is determined that we shall see and do everything that we wish. He depends much—he was clear about this—on Mr. Courtney's word that we will respect their customs, their way of life, their dignity, their tabus, and report what we shall observe and learn honestly and scientifically, while maintaining our pledged secrecy about the general location of their islands.

"Now, everything is not being offered us on a silver platter, so to speak. We shall be guided by others at the outset, offered every bit of information, introduction, cooperation that we require. After that, it is understood, we will largely be on our own. Every effort will be made to integrate us with the village and its daily life. I pleaded for this. I don't want any special considerations. I don't want concessions and changes made for us. I don't want them to consider us as visitors to a zoo. And I don't want any of you to regard them as a zoo. The understanding is that, as much as possible, we are here as fellow tribesmen from the other side of the island. Being realistic, I know it can never work that ideal way, but Paoti has promised to do his best for us, and I have, on behalf of all of you, promised that this will be our own attitude. In short, we are not here as mere outside observers, but as participant observers, trying, when we can, to eat, labor, fish, farm, frolic with them, and take part in their rites, such as their games, sports, festival. This is, to my mind, the only approach to take in finding their real cultural pattern. The degree to which we succeed will determine, for each of us, what contribution we make to anthropology, and our respective fields, with this study of The Three Sirens.

"Few of you have been in the field before. The Karpowiczes—Sam, Estelle, Mary—have been in the field several times, Marc made one trip some years ago, and Orville—I think, from this moment on, we should get on a first-name basis with one another—Orville has made a number of these field trips. However, Claire is new to this, and so are Rachel, Harriet, and Mrs.—and Lisa. And so, though I may be covering old ground for the experienced ones, I want them to bear with me while I address mainly the ones to whom this is unfamiliar. In certain specifics, of course, there will be some valuable information for the veterans among you, too. So, I repeat, bear with me briefly, all of you, and when I am done, I think you will understand better your role here, what is expected of you, preliminarily what you can and cannot do, and what lies ahead for all of us.

"Now, social anthropology and study in the field may be older than you think. Among the first to leave his home—in his case Oneida, New York—and go out and scientifically observe another society was a young scholar named Henry Schoolcraft. He went among the Chippewa Indians, he made notes—good notes, recording numerous fascinating customs—for example, that when a Chippewa woman touched an object, it was automatically tainted and thereafter shunned by males of the tribe.

"However, many regard Edward Tyler, an English Quaker, as the man who made social anthropology into a science. In his long life, he went on many trips into the field, one of the most notable to Mexico. He gave us two important doctrines—that of recurrence, meaning you go out and find a similar custom or bit of folklore in Canada and Peru and Egypt and Samoa, and this gives you a lead to reconstructing prehistory—and the doctrine of survival, meaning that certain seemingly pointless behaviors that have survived the past probably had real purpose at one time. These pioneers gave greater motive to future work in the field.

"I can see from some of your faces that you fear old Maud might be winding up for a long lecture. You need not worry. This is not the time or the place for teaching anthropology. I'm just trying to make you understand the historic impetus that sent you catapulting across a great ocean to this strange place. One or two more references to history and then I promise you, no more, and we'll delve into practical matters. The first team, a team like our own, to go out into the field and make a scientific study of a culture was one led by Alfred C. Haddon around 1898. Years before, Haddon had visited volcanic Murray Island, off New Guinea, and lived among the Papuans. The second time, he went back with a team of experts—two psychologists, a photographer, a musicologist, a linguist, a doctor, and himself, as anthropologist. The psychologists gave the natives tests in drawing and sense perception—they pioneered what Rachel and Orville will be doing here—and Haddon and the others, since the island had been somewhat corrupted by missionaries and white magistrates, toiled at reviving the rites and ceremonies of the past, when the Papuan men went naked and the women wore no more than split-leaf skirts. The team worked eight months in the field, and when they brought their findings back to Cambridge, they had proved the value of using a team of experts and had opened a new approach for future anthropologists.

"I could go on for hours speaking to you of the great anthropologists and field workers who are indirectly responsible for our being here this morning. I wish I had the time to tell you about that German genius, Franz Boas, who taught me—who taught Ruth Benedict, Margaret Mead, Alfred Kroeber, as well—so much about collecting, tirelessly collecting, raw data. Do you know, once Boas became interested in the graying of human hair, and he went about the barber shops of New York until he had collected and classified more than one million strands of hair. I suspect that he disliked living in the field, but he was determined to verify every theory through firsthand inquiry. He was constantly in the field, from the time of his initial trip to the Arctic to live among Eskimos when he was twenty-five to his last trip among Indians when he was seventy. How much you might learn from knowing Boas, and of the other giants in anthropology—Durkheim, Crawley, Malinowski, Lowie, Benedict, Linton, Mead, and my own beloved husband, Adley Hayden—but it is enough to know that we are their heirs, and that because of what we have learned from them, we can study the Sirens' society here with some effort at scientific precision.

"Of course, you may wonder how scientifically valid our findings can be. Anthropology, I readily admit, is caught in the middle of the unending controversy between the sciences and the humanities. Scientists like to criticize us for being too slipshod in our field methods, and say we try to measure qualities that cannot be subjected to statistical analysis. Humanists, on the other hand, like to criticize us for usurping the province of the poet by our reducing the infinite complexity of human life to flat descriptive categories. I have always contended that we must remind both sides that we, and we alone, stand as the bridge that can join the sciences and humanities. It is true that our native informants are rarely completely reliable. It is true that while we can measure the width of a hut or a skull, we cannot measure a tribesman's deepest feelings about love and hate. It is true that while we try to communicate our findings, while we sometimes absorb and move our audience, we perform poorly as troubadours because we are limited to passing on facts. Such are our limitations, yes, and yet, despite them, we must continue to hunt and seek scientifically, and to translate humanistically what we have discovered for the waiting world.

"Now, here we are—and you are asking yourselves, what is next? I will tell you. The investigators whom I have mentioned have taught us—and this is my own experience, too—that it is a bad policy to be aggressive or businesslike in a field study. Generally, it is less effective to call natives in by appointment, sit them down for three or four hours, and try to pump them dry. It is equally undesirable to go barging in on them blindly. If you do this, you might make an alliance with the wrong faction in the village and earn hostility and cut yourself off from the majority. The wisest approach is to learn the power structure of the community, and carefully select the most reliable informants. The best way to establish rapport is not to press. You kind of settle down in the middle of a society and wait, play a waiting game, rely on their natural curiosity and on your own instinct to tell you when it is right to make a move. The major problem is always finding the key informant, the one person who links past and present, who is articulate, who is honest, who will speak freely of his own world and wants to know what things are like in your world.

"In the matter of rapport, we are extremely lucky. We have our entree. Technically, we have been invited here. Last night, we were made a part of the society. We have not one key informant, but two to start with. We have Chief Paoti Wright, the head man, and a wise one, and we have Thomas Courtney, who has been here a fairly long time and knows their ways and our own. I will work with Paoti. I believe we will have an excellent interpersonal relationship. As for Mr. Courtney, he has agreed to be available to all of you, to guide and assist you in your respective fields.

"Certain short cuts have been arranged for you, but most of the time you will be on your own. When there is a problem you cannot overcome alone, I would suggest you come to me with it or arrange to discuss it with Mr. Courtney. In a half-hour, Mr. Courtney will be here to start you off. He will introduce you to the village, to the places you want to see, to the activities you want to observe or participate in, to potential informants who know of you and may help you. Once you are introduced this way, you are independent and expected to make your own progress.

"Now to take you up one by one, starting with you, Harriet. Nurses are not standard personnel on a field team, but they have been known to come along, and have often proved very useful. I recall that when Robert Redfield went to the Yucatan to study the Mayan village of Chan Kom, he took a nurse along. The Mayans were unfriendly, but the nurse made friends through healing some of their sick, and the introduction of modern hygiene, and then the tribe was impressed and cooperative. You'll find the Sirens has a good-sized but crude clinic or dispensary supervised by a young man named Vaiuri. You will be taken by Mr. Courtney to meet him today. There is an understanding that you will be permitted to assist this Vaiuri. While one of your functions here, Harriet, is to take care of us, your more important function will be to learn what you can of native illnesses and medical remedies and make copious notes of your findings. Also, if Vaiuri proves amenable, you can introduce new methods of treatment and sanitation, so long as you don't jostle any of their beloved customs or step on any tabus.

"As for you, Rachel, I had a devil of a time trying to explain psychoanalysis to Paoti and Hutia. It made no sense to them. They thought it childish. But I think I convinced them that it was a special kind of magic that worked wonders with disturbed people. Anyway, while they don't seem to have any true-blue psychopaths on this island, they do have their small minority of unhappy persons, of maladjusted ones. Hutia heads a board of five elder men and women called the Marriage Hierarchy. All marital complaints, pending applications for divorce, come to them. So she has the case histories that are acted upon every month. She agreed to let you select three patients from among a half-dozen or more current cases, and go ahead and do what you can for them with your own brand of cure. You will meet with Hutia today, interrogate some of the cases, make your choices, and proceed. Incidentally, Mr. Courtney will have a private hut for your consultations—it'll be available this afternoon.

"Now you, Lisa, I made it known that you wished to study the primitive dance. I must say, Paoti was delighted, and you couldn't have come at a better time. They are just beginning to rehearse their program for the annual festival. Dancing dominates the entertainment, so you'll have a chance to witness, even participate in, the best they have to offer. The woman named Oviri is in charge, a sort of director, and you shall meet her shortly, and see what is possible.

"Orville, your situation is a little different, since your study of comparative sexual behavior enters all our areas. I imagine you'll be doing fairly much what Cora DuBois did on the island of Alor in 1937—apply psychodynamic techniques to these villagers—I know DuBois employed the Rorschach successfully, and I suppose you will, too. We discussed your possible schedule, and it was decided that for the first day you would be oriented to the sexual customs of the community—I think you'll see the Social Aid Hut today—and be introduced to a variety of the natives of both sexes. After that, you can attempt to establish some kind of rapport, and pick the informants most suitable, and question or test them, as you see fit.

"Next, the family Karpowicz. Well, it would be gratuitous of me, Sam, to tell an old hand like you anything. Mr. Courtney says you will have your darkroom, behind your hut, by the day after tomorrow. You may shoot your movies and stills, in and around the village, as you wish, no restrictions. When you go further afield—remember the incident at the beach—you must be accompanied by Mr. Courtney or Moreturi or someone they designate. As to your botanical work, you are free to roam anywhere.

"I've arranged nothing specific yet for you, Estelle. I assume you'll be helping Sam out, as usual. If you want to go into other things, the workaday female life here, the cleaning, cooking, laundering, weaving, all that, it would be helpful to me. I think we can discuss that privately, and see how far you want to go. I did follow the suggestion you and Sam made about your young lady, and we have the green light . . . Don't look so apprehensive, Mary. It's a refreshing project; it'll give you a great conversation piece when you return to Albuquerque. They have a rather primitive schoolhouse—or school hut, series of huts—at the far part of the village, and there is one group of students from fourteen to sixteen. You may attend this class, if you care to—no pencils, no books, no blackboards, no homework, if that relieves you—all word of mouth and demonstration by an intelligent male instructor named Mr. Manao. I think you might find it a lark meeting Sirens youngsters of your own age, and, for six weeks, learning what they learn. The instructor will be expecting you to look in on them today, and, of course, I'd like a full report on your experiences. I promise to give you credit in my paper—and a lovely gift at Christmas.

"That brings me to my own family. Marc, I expect you'll want to devote yourself largely to one informant, as I myself intend to do. Chief Paoti is expecting you this morning, and he may have some suggestions. You may start with one of his family or one of the marginal people in the village. And you, Claire, I'm hoping that you'll assist me—in fact, I'm rather counting on it—and also act as sort of a liaison between me and Chief Paoti and Mr. Courtney.

"As I have told all of you, your participation will be unrestricted and freewheeling, within the boundaries of certain deep-rooted tabus. From my conversation with Chief Paoti, I know that the Social Aid Hut and the Sacred Hut are tabu and may be entered only with the express permission of Paoti himself. Visiting the two adjacent atolls—the ancient gods, still worshiped by the conservative, are supposed to dwell there—is tabu, unless you are accompanied by a villager. In some of the huts you will find dark-gray or black basalt idols, and touching or tampering with these is tabu. The kinship system—children belong to a broad kinship group consisting of parents, uncles, aunts, and so forth—this system prevails, and incest is a strong tabu. So is physical violence. You may be provoked beyond endurance, or ill-treated, but you never strike another or do him bodily harm. Instead, you take your grievance to the Chief. Killing, even in retribution or for punishment of a major crime, is considered barbaric. An ailing person is considered to be invaded by higher spirits who are judging him, and such a person is tabu to mortal hands, except those with mana, with high official privilege. All the ocean surrounding this place is held tabu to strangers. Therefore, entering or leaving the main island is not permitted, except with the consent of the Chief. There are probably a few minor tabus Paoti overlooked. When I learn them, I shall pass them on to all of you.

"While on the subject, I might add that anthropology has a few tabus of its own—restrictions, that is—on certain practices or behavior. These are not hard, fast rules, but represent a code gained from long experience. First off, never, never lie to them, about yourself or your own customs. If they find out you've lied, you will be rejected. When you realize you've made a misstatement, admit your error at once and clarify what you really meant. Don't become angry if they tease or mock you, or laugh at you, for they may be testing you. Ride out such situations, and you will build rapport. If you find yourself blocked by one of their superstitions, don't bully them or try to argue with them about their beliefs. Let the superstition stand, and skip that phase of your work. I recollect that on one field trip among the Andamanese, Adley tried to take pictures, and the natives were horrified, positive that the camera stole their souls. Well, Adley had to put aside his camera and forget photography. In dealing with these Sirens people, try not to be eccentric or stuffy or pompous. Condescension will get you nowhere. After all, who is to say if our way is superior to their own?

"As a general rule, I would advise sobriety. I don't know your personal habits, but if you are fond of narcotics or drink, I would suggest you avoid it as much as possible in these next weeks. Of course, it is expected that you drink, if you can, with them, when they drink. But even then, you should not become intoxicated. Loss of control may make you appear ridiculous or offensive.

"Since we have seven females—myself included—in our group of ten, I think a brief digression on the role of the female in the field might be pertinent. You should all dress as you dress at home, comfortably and conservatively, If it becomes hotter, you need not wear undergarments—slips, brassières, briefs—since the men on the Sirens have no avid curiosity about your private parts. As you have already seen, concealment hardly exists here and all are natural about their appearance. Most communities of this sort dislike pugnacious women, overwhelming women, humorless women. I would keep this in mind at all times.

"Now we come to a delicate subject, one which frequently concerns women in the field. I refer to cohabiting with the natives. We've been set down in a society where sexual activity is casual and fluid. There is a minority school of anthropology that believes you should welcome rather than avoid romantic entanglements. Certainly, cohabitation with a native can be easy, simple, unobjectionable. The native population may not look down on you for it, in fact may be rather pleased. Despite the possibility that such an affair may give you knowledge as well as pleasure, I must point out the drawbacks. If your affair is secret, then the fact of it will inhibit your scientific writings. You will be unable to report the truth. If your affair puts you in competition with a native woman, you may cut yourself off from the rest of the community. There is yet another problem. I will illustrate it with an example. Years ago, when Adley and I were in Africa, we had with us three graduate students, two males and one female. The female became quite attracted to one young colored native, and she cohabited with him. She did so openly. The other colored tribesmen were delighted. She was behaving as their women did, and moreover, because she was a white visitor with power and prestige, they regarded her affair as the height of democratic practice. The problem here was not that she upset the natives—she was conforming with their way—but that she upset the male members of our team. They were disturbed by her action, and resented her, and innumerable political difficulties in our own group resulted.

"So let me say this final word about cohabitation—and I address all but Mary. You know the profits, you know the pitfalls. I cannot guide you further. I am not one, you will find, who would call any such conduct scandalous—that is for laymen—for, to me labeling anything like this as scandalous is a value judgment, and I cannot and will not make one. You look into your hearts, into your consciences, and perform as you think right.

"While I am discussing our behavior, there is an area where I wish my moral judgment to prevail. I want each of you to pledge, to yourself, to me, that you will not plot to alter any aspect of this society for selfish purposes. In the pioneer days of anthropology, there were certain individuals—the German ethnologist, Otto Finsch, who was in the South Seas off and on between 1879 and 1884, was one of these—who disrupted tribes with their offensive, unwanted Don Juanism. There were similar individuals, in times past, who made natives drunk on Western whiskey to goad them into re-creating old orgiastic and erotic practices. I will not permit friendly natives to be seduced by offensive love-making or alcohol to satisfy our needs for research. A few years ago, Harvard University sent a team into the Baliem Valley of Dutch New Guinea to study primitive activity. According to missionaries, this team, eager to obtain motion pictures of every phase of native life, fomented a local war in which lives were lost in the interests of research. I have no idea if this really happened, if it is true, but it was widely publicized, and I want no such accusations made of a team led by Dr. Maud Hayden.

"In fact, I will not even permit minor provocation. I know that so respectable an investigator as Edward Westermarck—whom Adley and I met before his death in 1939—employed elementary magic tricks in Morocco to awe the Arabs and acquire information from them on their morals. I simply won't condone tricks of any kind. Childish firecrackers become dangerous explosives in the wrong hands.

"Above all, I won't have any Leo Frobeniuses on this study. He did brilliant anthropological work on Africa, but his methods and prejudices left much to be desired. He talked down to the priests at Ibadan, exploited the poor people in acquiring their religious possessions, wormed his way into a secret murder society and then exposed it, and treated African natives as an inferior race, especially the partially civilized ones whom he contemptuously spoke of as 'trouser niggers.' I absolutely won't have that here. I won't permit exploitation, emotional or material, of these fine people, and I won't allow, as far as I can control it, a feeling of superiority among any of us toward them.

"If you cannot respect these people, you should not remain here. As Evans-Pritchard has said, you must make an intellectual and emotional transference to the natives you study, try to think and feel as they do, until their society is inside you and not merely in your notebooks. I remember a few lines from Evans-Pritchard that I once memorized. 'An anthropologist has failed unless, when he says good-by to the natives, there is on both sides the sorrow of parting. It is evident that he can only establish this intimacy if he makes himself in some degree a member of their society . . .'

"Concerning participation, Malinowski felt that there was some information no amount of questioning could ferret out. You must research—he used a wonderful phrase—'the imponderabilia of actual life'—that is, make yourself a part of daily living on the Sirens, know the feel of a native's toil in the brush, know his vanities and dislikes, know how he cares for his body, know what his mind fears, know what goes on between his spouse and himself, and his offspring and himself. To attain this transference, we owe it to ourselves not to become ingrown, groupy, a special isolated club from faraway. The danger in coming here as a large team is that, after the day's work, we may tend to retreat to one another's company exclusively, seek one another's companionship, instead of devoting this time to the community.

"Someone—I think it was you, Rachel—wondered how we could repay the people of the Sirens for their time and trouble. We owe them something. What do we give them in return? We cannot pay them. If their help is put on a wage basis, we destroy much of the reciprocal interpersonal relationship. Gifts, given excessively, can be as harmful as money. I should suggest that an occasional inexpensive present, a gadget, some of our food, toys for the children, offered spontaneously, would be all right. More than that, I think helping them, in any way that we can, might be more acceptable— oh, if Marc or Sam assisted them in constructing a hut or gathering food, or Harriet treated the ailing, or Rachel gave advice where it was wanted, or Mary taught games—all of that would be a form of repayment. Too, I would suggest we reciprocate all specific hospitality tendered us. Last night, my family and I were the guests of

Chief Paoti. Presently, we shall find the occasion to have him and his family as our guests, to be treated to our American foods.

"A few last tips. Orville asked me how we handle a situation where someone on the Sirens offers us something we cannot accept. This often comes up in the field. When Westermarck was among the Arabs, they offered him several wives. He did not want to reject them outright, so he cleverly told them that he already had a half-dozen wives at home and simply could not afford to support more. Out of hospitality, a family may try to give you a child to adopt or a grown daughter to take as mistress or wife. The easiest way to handle this is to tell that family that in your own society, taking someone else's child for your own, or a mistress, or another wife, is strictly a tabu. You invent you own tabu as you need it, and it is hardly a lie. This will be understood, and you will have offended no one.

"One final word, and then I promise you, I am through. Most of us are social scientists, and we ask ourselves why are we here, suffering anxiety in this unknown atmosphere, enduring physical discomforts, and fighting exhaustion from gathering data all day and recording it until the dawn hours? You may be in the sciences, and here in the field, for material reasons, of course. It is one way to make a living. Because of what you see here, you will advance in your profession, make money in business or government or by publishing. But advancement is the smallest motive. There are bigger ones. There are scientific, humanitarian, and philosophical motives that drive you. You want to acquire knowledge, and pass it on. All the breadth of human behavior is your discipline. You want to refresh yourself, obtain a different world view, in a new culture. And yet, there is even more. There is a kind of romanticism in us that goes very deep. We are romantics with restless intelligence. We are not armchair people. We are not what Malinowski called hearsay anthropologists. We like the glamour and stimulation of other environments. We cast aside routine to explore exciting new worlds, to enter briefly into the lives of, and become part of, exotic peoples.

"Above all, above everything, whatever the diverse routes that brought all of us together and to this morning, we are here for the very reason that brought Bronislaw Malinowski, so alone, to Boyawa, an island of the Trobriands, near New Guinea, one August morning in 1914. His motive, I suspect, was not different from your motive or mine. 'Perhaps,' he said, 'through realizing human nature in a shape very distant and foreign to us, we shall have some light shed on our own.'

"To this, I say—Amen. To you, I say—let us begin."

* * *

Marc Hayden stood uncertainly in the middle of the reception chamber of Chief Paoti's hut, where Courtney had left him while he went into another room. Marc could not remember the chamber from the night before. The floor was composed of slabs of stone that had been made slippery by exposure to the sea, and here and there, representing chairs he supposed, were thick palm mats for sitting. Except for the charcoal-gray stone idol in one corner, the room was barren.

Marc moved closer to the idol to inspect it. The head and body were distortions of a male, probably a god, and one had the impression that this had been a drunken collaboration between Modigliani and Picasso. Backing off from the grotesque idol with its elongated head, Marc could see why it repelled him. The representation, despite the weird features, was that of a phallus four feet high.

Filled with disgust by this reminder of the obsession of the village, Marc turned away. Impatiently, he circled the room, snubbing the idol. His mood was still dark. From the arrival of Easterday's letter, so long ago, it seemed that things, small things in small ways, had gone from bad to worse. He was sick of the heavy chains that held him to anthropology—had always hated the dull slavery of it —and he envied one like Rex Garrity, a free soul, big with life, running the world up and down at his command as if it were a yo-yo. An adventurer like Garrity, Marc knew, had no chains. He was not one of the herd. He had identity. Moreover, he was in a popular business where one could become not only known but wealthy overnight. Garrity himself, the evening of the Hackfeld dinner, had given Marc this vision of what was possible, had hinted at a partnership, and for a moment had allowed Marc to soar with him above the earth-rutted, bound-in academic world of anthropology, a world where Marc could never be as much as his mother or father and would always be less than himself.

Once again, he resented Matty for brushing off Garrity, separating him from Garrity's potential, keeping him manacled to her as a pseudo-Adley. The resentments multiplied: Matty holding him for her slavey boy, Matty continuing her spiritual marriage to the mediocre and pretentious man he had had to call father, Matty forever lecturing him. She had been lecturing him, not the others, but him, a half-hour ago in her silly office. Who was all that lofty talk for—about Leo Frobenius and his superiority toward natives—if not for him? Reviewing it, Marc damned Matty for her tiresome objectivity and liberalism—the trick she had of putting everyone on the defensive and making herself, alone, the pure person and pure scientist. Damn her.

And while he was about it, Marc, in his mind, damned his wife, too. Claire was a growing disappointment. In the last year, she had become too demanding—in her eyes, those goddam cow eyes—in her silences, those goddam condemning silences—too demanding, and too cloying, and too sticky, and too female. Like Matty, like so many females, she was a guilt-giver—exactly—an automatic guilt-giver, so you felt always off balance, always as if you had not done enough, always unsure and unsettled and anxious. Most of all, Marc resented her recent behavior. She was displaying a side of her that he had long been suspicious of, but had not seen in the open. Her preoccupation with sex talk at home had been disquieting enough, but the sluttish display of last night was unforgivable. Parading those big tits, actually sticking them out to get a rise out of that young ape Moreturi and that phony bum Courtney, had been nauseating. She was only acting out her hostility to her husband. And this was the whore who wanted to be a mother. Thank God, he told himself, he had not let her browbeat him into that further self-imprisonment.

Marc revived the incident of this morning, and became more furious. First the bare tits, then the shorts and bare ass. What next? Next, one of those grass skirts so that all the men could see all there was left to see. The bitch, the unwholesome, goddam bitch. And now she had Matty on her side, all those bitches did, with license to fornicate. He mimicked his mother's voice in his head: "Certainly, cohabitation with a native can be easy, simple, unobjectionable." Christ.

Marc realized that he was no longer alone. Courtney had returned. Quickly, Marc hid his anger, and quickly, he slipped on his professional smile.

248

"He'll see you now," Courtney was saying. "He'll be right out. No ceremony necessary with Paoti. Just straight talk. I've told him your needs. He'll tell you what is possible."

"Thanks. I certainly do appreciate what you've—"

Courtney, at the door, curtly interrupted. "Nothing at all. Forget it. I've got to get back to your mother's hut and give the others a hand."

He was gone, and Marc, relieved, could hate again.

But immediately, Chief Paoti was in the room. "Good morning, good morning, Dr. Hayden." Paoti, bare-chested and barefooted, wore a plain white breechclout. Although frail to the eye, he advanced with bony vigor.

"Good morning, sir," said Marc. "It's awfully kind of you to help me."

"I find one always helps others—others—to help one's self. It is in my own interest to make certain that you receive the best impression of my people." He sank down upon the thickest palm mat, and crossed his matchstick legs. "Sit, please, sit," he commanded.

Marc settled uncomfortably on the mat across from the Chief.

"Mr. Courtney tells me you wish to spend some time interviewing one of my people."

"Yes, I need an informant, an articulate person who is highly conversant in your history, legends, customs, someone who will speak with honesty and enjoy discussing your life here."

Paoti chewed his gums. "Male or female?"

Inexplicably, Paoti's use of the word *female* plucked a fresh chord of memory in Marc. He heard again the primitive music of the night before, and it enkindled the image of the native girl on the platform, the one with the distended red nipples, slash of a navel, shimmering flesh, and shapely calves. Her figure hovered behind his eyes, wriggling sensuously. Tehura, that was her name, Tehura, of the round heels.

Paoti, wrinkled hands folded in his lap, had been waiting patiently, and Marc blurted, "Female."

"Very well."

"Preferably a young person," Marc added. "Since you will be my mother's informant, I am sure that she will have a complete picture of your society from the point of view of a senior male member. As a matter of contrast, I feel I should have the point of view of someone younger, perhaps a girl in her twenties."

"Married or unmarried?"

"Unmarried would be better."

Paoti considered this. "There are so many—"

Marc had made his decision, based on the fantasies in his head, and it was now or never. "Sir, what I have in mind is someone like —like your niece."

Paoti showed a glimmer of surprise. "Tehura?"

"She seemed to me exceedingly articulate and intelligent."

"That she is, yes," said Paoti. He was still thinking.

"Of course, if you have any objections—or you feel she might be uncooperative or shy—why, then, any other would—"

"No, I do not have any objections. As for Tehura, she is decidedly outgoing, one of our young who is as headstrong as a brave young man, ready for anything that is new . . ." His voice had trailed off, as if he had been speaking to himself. Then he fixed his eyes on Marc. "Exactly what do you have in mind for Tehura? What will be your procedure?"

"Informal talks, nothing more," said Marc. "An hour or two at the most each day, every day she is free. We will sit as we sit here, and I will ask questions, and she will answer them. I will take extensive notes. That's all there is to it."

Paoti appeared satisfied. "If that is all—very well, she will be capable. Of course, the decision to cooperate must come from her. However, if she knows I sanction it, she will no doubt be agreeable . . . When would you begin?"

"Today, if possible. Right now. We'll need a few short sessions to break her into this, put her at ease."

Paoti turned from Marc, cupped one hand at his lips, and shouted, "Vata!"

Like a jack-in-the-box, a skinny boy of fourteen popped out of the next room. He came on the run, bent in a half-bow to Paoti, and went to one knee before him. Paoti spoke in Polynesian, in a cadence that made Marc think that he was reciting a long poem. After a full minute, the boy Vata, who had been inclining his head all the while, murmured one word of assent, straightened, and retreated to the wall.

Paoti turned back to Marc. "A clever boy, the son of a cousin. He will remember. He will explain everything to Tehura, and she will decide for herself. Now he will take you to her. She is of this house, but finds it crowded, and has wheedled her own place out of me. I am weak with my brother's daughter. She has always had her way with me." He waved his veiny hand in dismissal. "You may go to her. The boy will lead you."

Marc pushed himself to his feet. "I'm most grateful—"

"If she is uncooperative today or in the future, return to me. I will find you another."

"Thank you, sir."

The boy was holding the door open, and Marc went through it into the sunlight. With a leap, the boy was ahead of him, showing the way. For the first time, Marc entered the far end of the village. As it had been yesterday morning before the midday meal, the compound was virtually deserted. A group of naked children cavorted in and around the stream. Two old women, carrying fruit heaped in bowls, waddled along in the shade. Three men, weighted under cane shafts, trudged over a wooden bridge.

Approaching the enormous Social Aid Hut, the boy suddenly veered to his left, crossed a bridge, and beckoned Marc to follow. He scampered ahead to the row of large huts, and up a grade to the second row of dwellings set more deeply beneath the stone overhang.

At the door of a narrow hut, he waited. When Marc reached him, he said, "Tehura is here. You stay. I go speak Paoti's words."

"All right."

He rapped on the cane door, put his ear to it, heard a muffled female voice, nodded happily to Marc, and ducked inside.

Marc waited in the sun, wondering what the boy had been ordered to tell her, wondering what she would say to it. The idea of using Tehura as an informant had come to him on the spur of the moment, a decision born of impulse. As an anthropologist, he had acted hastily. She might prove too young, too shallow, to contribute information of any value. Logically, he should have felt his way around, taken more time, met more potential informants, waited until he found that marginal person—perhaps one at odds with the tribe—who had ideas and liked to talk. Logically, too, he should have sought out a man, preferably one close to his own age. With a man, rapport might more easily be established. With a woman, and so young a one, rapport might be harder to achieve, for women did not often speak frankly to men. Yet, Tehura had been frank enough last night, too frank. Recollecting her little speech, he was now sure that she had exaggerated for effect. In short, she had an excess of vanity and a streak of dishonesty, and these made her even more unlikely to be a reliable informant. Then why had he requested her? Without hesitation, he knew. He did not give a damn about his role as anthropologist. All he cared about was his role as man. This was his revolt, the first overturning. This was anti-Adley, anti-Matty, anti-Claire.

He saw the boy emerge wearing a broad smile.

"She says yes, she is happy very to help," said Vata.

"Good. Thank you."

"She says to wait. She comes soon. I will tell the Chief."

The boy departed in a trot and was soon out of sight among the huts below. Marc continued to stare at the route the boy had taken. He felt the good feeling of elation. He was having it his way, and it pleased him that he did not even have his notebook and pencil along. He wondered what he could ask of this girl, but then there were so many things. He was inquisitive about her morals, her handling of men, the prowess she had boasted of last night. Would she be so candid in the day, unsupported by kava and palm juice?

Behind him the reedy door shook open and banged shut, and he spun around. She was coming toward him, and he was astounded. He had completely forgotten her beauty. He had also forgotten how the native women dressed. She wore nothing, no cover, no ornament, nothing except the unnerving short grass skirt, rising and falling against the tops of her thighs. Seeing her like this was like seeing a ballerina appear on the stage in the tutu or high puff skirt, without a brassière above or tights below. Desperately, he tried to ignore her breasts, shimmying gently as she walked, but he could not ignore them.

"Hello," she said. "I did not know which one of you waited for me. Now I see. It is the one who does not believe in our love."

"That's not exactly what I was saying last night—"

"It makes no difference," she said. "My uncle wishes me to answer your questions."

"Only if you want to," Marc said stiffly.

She shrugged her shoulders, indifferently. "I have no feeling about this. I have a feeling to make my uncle pleased." Her eyes met Marc's, and she asked, "What will you do with my words? Will you tell many people in America what Tehura tells you?"

"Thousands of people. They'll read about you in my—in Dr. Hayden's book. When it is published, I'll send one to Captain Rasmussen to give to you."

"Do not bother," she said. "I cannot read. Only a few can read —Paoti, Manao, who is the teacher, some students—and Tom, who has a high hill of books. It is a waste. I think to learn to read is a wasted time."

Marc tried to judge if she was teasing him, but her expression was intent. He prepared to defend literacy and National Book Week. "I can't say I—"

"If you read to yourself it is like making love to yourself," she went on. "It keeps you away from talking and listening with another. That is more pleasure . . . You want to talk and listen with me?"

"That's why I'm here."

"I have not so much time today. In the next days, if I am interested, I will make more time." She peered up at the sky visible between the openings in the ledge, shading her eyes. "It is too hot in the sun. You look like a cooked fish in the fire."

"I feel like one."

"Take your clothes off, then. You will feel better."

"Well—"

"Never mind," she said. "I know you cannot. Tom told me about Americans."

Marc felt a surge of anger at her, at them. "What did he tell you?"

Again, she shrugged her shoulders. "It is not important . . . Come, we will go where it is cooler."

She had turned to the left, preceding him on a sunken path between the huts, going parallel to the compound, until they were some distance beyond the end of the ledge and behind the Social Aid Hut. Here the path swung into the hills. Tehura bounded ahead, climbing, and Marc stayed doggedly at her heels. Twice, as she went over impeding rocks, her grass skirt flapped high, and Marc plainly saw the twin curves of her exposed rump. Although she had irritated him minutes before, he again began to find her a desirable object.

They had come to the summit of the rise, and just off the path was a rich green dell, the thick grass floor encircled by breadfruit sentries whose broad leaves made up a sheltering canopy.

"Here," said Tehura.

She went toward the trunk of the most substantial tree, and sat on the grass, legs folded sideways under her skirt. Marc had followed her, and he dropped down across from her, persistently conscious of her semi-nudity.

"Ask me your questions," she said regally.

"To be honest with you, I have no—no formal questions yet. As I learn more, I'll have many things to ask of you. Today, I intended only to become acquainted, just casually talk."

"You talk. I will listen." She gazed up at the wide fan of breadfruit leaves.

Marc was taken aback. She was not the gay and open person of the feast in Paoti's hut. He was puzzled by the transformation in her personality. Marc knew that if he did not solve it without delay, their relationship would be a brief one. "Tehura," he said, "I find it difficult to speak to you. You seem to be deliberately unfriendly. Why are you so antagonistic?"

This brought her gaze down abruptly. She regarded him with more respect. "I feel you are not sympathetic to us," she said. "I feel you disapprove of everything."

His perception had won her respect, and now her perception of an inner attitude that he had not yet defined won his respect. Until this moment, in his eyes, she had been an empty-headed, naked chippy, a promiscuous sex vessel and nothing more. But there evidently was more, much more, and she would be a worthy opponent.

"You're wrong about that," he said carefully. "I'm sorry if I gave that impression. I've been overtired, and last night I was drunk and combative. Of course, your culture is odd to me, as mine must be to you. However, I'm not here to change it or you, or pass any judgment. I'm here to learn—that's all—learn. If you give me half a chance, you'll find me agreeable."

She was smiling for the first time. "I like you better."

Marc felt the coiled springs of tension released inside his chest, and his distress was mitigated. He sought in his pocket for the thin cigar, made soggy by perspiration. He thought: "Words, words, words," so Hamlet had spoken to Polonius, Act II, Scene II. He thought: no male weapon, not physique, not skill, not anything, can seduce a female so easily, so thoroughly as words. He had just proved it. He must remember it from this moment on.

"I'm pleased," he said, "because I want you to like me. Not

alone to help my work. Simply, because I want to be liked by you."

"You will be liked if you are sympathetic."

"I am and will be," he promised. He was uncertain what he should say next. He held aloft the soggy cigar. "Do you mind if I smoke?"

"Go ahead. We are used to it. The old Wright brought the habit here. Our men grow black tobacco and roll it in banana leaves to smoke. I like most the pipe. Tom Courtney has a pipe."

He had his best cue yet, and he responded to it. "This Courtney," he said, "he's still a mystery to me. What made him come here?"

"You ask him," she said. "Tom speaks for himself. Tehura speaks for herself."

"But you spoke freely of him last night—"

"Not of him, but of us. That is different."

"I was impressed the way you spoke of your—your—"

"Our love?"

"Yes, that's right. If you don't mind my asking, was it of long—?"

"Two years," said Tehura promptly. "It was my life for two years."

He considered what was in his mind, and determined to test her candor. "I remember something else you said last night. You said Courtney had goodness, but was not good at love. What did you mean?"

"I meant it was not enjoyment for me at first. He had strength but no—no—" She pinched her brow, seeking the correct description, and then found it. "Strength but no finesse. You understand? Here love flows from the first gift of the tiara flowers to the dance to the touch to the full naked embrace. It is natural, so natural, so simple. Then, because the embrace has been taught and practiced and become an art, it is good—it is one with the dance—the man sways within you, and you, the woman, freely join his dance with your waist, hips, legs—many positions in the one embrace, not one, but many—"

As she went on, Marc felt suffocated with heat, and he knew that it could not be the sun. There was a trembling beneath his skin, a passion for what he had never known. He had ceased meeting her eyes, and had pretended—assuming the all-knowing, nodding pedagogue's mien of impersonal attentiveness—to be staring past her, past her shoulders. Yet, in the rim of focus were her moving breasts aimed at him, and he did not know how long he could endure not reaching out. He chewed the cigar, and lifted his mind to her speech.

"—but Tom was so different," she was saying. "He made the love embrace so important, like it was something outside of living. He made me feel he owed me something for having given me the love. And always, he tried too hard. He had strength, yes, but more is wanted. Americans are not taught sex love, he told me, they learn as they go along, they follow their instincts. It was wrong, I told him, it was something that must be learned, an art, and instincts are not enough. He would do it only one way, maybe two, and that was wrong. He would do foolish things like press his lips on mine and touch my breasts and other wasted things we do not do. To desire is enough preparation, and once the embrace, the dance is enough." She paused, lingering over some memory, and then she said, "He has learned our way of love, and it has helped him with all other parts of his life, too."

Down deep, Marc detested Courtney for his learning and experiences. He tried to keep his voice even. "What you're saying is that eventually he learned to satisfy you—physically, I mean."

Tehura shook her head vigorously. "No, no, no. That was not the main thing. On The Three Sirens, all women come to such giving and release very easily. That is because certain body preparations are made during childhood. The main thing is not this physical satisfying, but that Tom learned to be more spontaneous and more relaxed, like most of us. He learned when you love a woman, you owe her nothing, you have done nothing wrong or forbidden, but only performed the way the High Spirit prepared you."

Now that he had her talking, Marc speculated on how far he dared draw her out. He chanced it. "Tehura, you seem to have implied there were some men before Courtney. Were there many?"

"I have not counted them. Does one count the breadfruit eaten or the times one has swum or danced?"

Marc blinked, and he thought to himself: Dr. Kinsey would have come away from here with his pencil points intact, and Dr. Chapman would have had no report at all. Clearly, the Sirens Islands offered nothing for the statisticians of repressed love. But then, Marc told himself, he was no statistician, and he would do better. Observing Tehura, he saw her youth and freshness, and sensed some unused quality about her that contradicted her implication that she had known countless men. He had to be sure that he had not misunderstood her.

"Tehura, when did you first have sexual intercourse with a man?"

"Body love?"

"Yes, I guess that's what you call it."

She did not hesitate. "We all have it the first time at the same age. It is the age of sixteen. Those who wish can continue to visit the school for other subjects until the age eighteen, but by sixteen they have been taught all about the love-making. Up to then, it is explaining and showing. The last step before growing up is to do."

"To do? I see. In other words, after sixteen there are no virgins."

"Virgins?" Tehura was genuinely horrified. "To be a virgin after sixteen would be a disgrace. It would be a sickness below as some have above, in the head. A girl cannot grow, become a woman, if she is a virgin. She would always be a girl. Men would despise her."

Marc thought of his friends on the staff at Raynor College, and his friends down in Los Angeles, and how they would enjoy this information. His mind leaped beyond California, to New York, to the nation between the two, and how vast audiences would enjoy every word he repeated. Overnight, he might become—and then, coldly, he pricked the bubble of his fantasy, knowing he would become nothing with this information. For Matty would have it, too, from other sources, and Matty would be the first to reveal it to the nation, and she would be the center. He would remain what he had always been, her assistant, echo, the one in her shadow.

Then this was all hopeless. Yet, aside from its audience value, there were elements that intrigued him personally. "Tehura, what happened to you at sixteen?"

"The usual ceremony," she said. "I was taken to the Sacred Hut. A special physical examination was performed on me by an elder woman of the Marriage Hierarchy. I was pronounced ready to enter the Social Aid Hut, and I was asked to select my first partner from among the older, experienced, unmarried men. I had always been attracted to one, a handsome athlete of twenty-five, and I pointed to him. We were led to the Sacred Hut and left together for a day and a night. We came out only to visit the lavatory and take in our food and drink. I had been taught all about love, and had no fears to practice it. We made body love six or seven times, I do not remember, but I was limp, and the next day I was a grown woman."

"And you were free to make love with anyone after that?"

"No, no—not anyone. The unwed girl can only have pleasure with the unwed man—the married man is tabu, except one week in the year or when he has need of the Social Aid Hut—I do not have the time to tell you all of that today—another time I will. But I answer your question. I was free to make love with anyone I desired who was not married. Do not have the wrong idea about this. Tom had the wrong idea in the beginning, but then learned the truth. Tom taught me the word *promiscuous*, and later the word *selective*. We are not promiscuous. We are selective. I have never lay down with a man I did not want."

"Have you ever been married?"

"No. It will happen. One day I will wish it, and it will happen. Now it is better this way. I am happy."

She smoothed out the wide grass of her skirt, and drew her long hair back over her shoulders, preparatory to rising and returning to the village.

Marc cast aside his cigar butt. "I wish we had more time. I have so many questions—"

"You will ask them next time." She came to her feet lightly, then, legs apart, arms lifted high, so that her breasts flattened and widened, she stretched like a cat. Dropping her arms to her sides, she considered Marc a moment. "I have one question to make to you."

Marc was standing, dusting his trousers. He looked up with surprise. "A question? Go ahead."

"Last night you were angry with your wife when she came with me and showed her breasts. Why were you angry?"

"Well . . ." Tehura's breasts were before his eyes, and Claire's behind his eyes, and he must be careful to explain one without insulting the other. "You know by now, Tehura, that customs in my country are much different than those in your village. In my country, for many reasons—historical religious strictures, morals, the climate—women almost always, except when they are dancers or such, almost always cover their bosoms in public."

"That is so? Then something else is strange. Tom once showed me American book magazines with pictures—the way your women wear so much on their bodies except in the front the garments are cut down to show some of their breasts—"

"Yes, low-cut gowns—décolletage, it is called. Our women know this attracts men, so they expose a little here, a little there, a trifle, but they do not show everything. It is simply not done, except in private."

"That is why you were angry with your wife? She broke the tabu?"

"Exactly."

Tehura smiled sweetly. "I do not believe you."

Marc felt the jab of fear in his chest. He stiffened to counter the threat. "What in the devil is that supposed to mean?"

"Simply, I do not believe you. Come, let us—"

He moved to intercept her. "No, wait—I want to know—Why do you think I became angry with my wife?"

"I cannot explain to you. It is a feeling I have that there are other reasons. It is also some things Tom has told me about the American men. Maybe someday I can speak of this. Not now. Come, I will be late."

Sullen at her superiority, Marc walked beside her.

Her eyes, on his features, were amused. "You should not always be so angry at everyone, at yourself. You have so much, have you not? You are a handsome man—"

"Well, thanks for that."

"—with a beautiful wife. I am beautiful, too, and proud of it, but when I was beside her last night, I felt less beautiful."

"Don't tell me you envy a poor American."

"Oh, no. I have more than Mrs. Hayden in other ways. I am jealous of no woman. What is there to want?" She started toward the path, stopped, and slowly turned, "The bright ornament she wore from her neck. I have never seen such—"

"You mean, the diamond pendant?"

"Is it rare?"

"It is costly, but not rare. Countless American women receive them as gifts from their husbands and lovers."

Tehura nodded, thoughtfully. "For a female, such things are nice, very nice."

She turned and went down the path. Marc's heart swelled. Until this second, her self-satisfaction, her supremacy, had been impregnable. In the prism of Claire's diamond, he could see the crack in Tehura's armor. She was vulnerable, after all, this too-perfect, too-assured child of nature. She was a female like any other, to be lured, to be enticed, to be finally bought and brought down.

Almost jauntily, hands thrust in his pockets, Marc entered the path behind her. For the first time, he looked forward to what lay ahead.

* * *

A half-hour after lunch, Dr. Rachel DeJong stood in the front room of the vacant hut that Courtney had located for her work, and ruefully she considered its shortcomings.

Missing from the room were couch and chairs, desk and lamps, bookcase and file cabinets, telephone and message pads. While the primitive office was hers alone, tabu to all but patients, any atmosphere of seclusion, so necessary, was shattered by the village noises —squealing youngsters, chattering women, shouting men, cawing birds—that ambushed her through the thin cane walls.

So very far from the hushed slickness of Beverly Hills, California, U.S.A., Rachel thought. If only her learned colleagues, with their endless social weekends in Ojai and sports cars and decorators, could see her now. The idea of this diverted Rachel, and she could not repress a smile. With a practical eye, she studied the room, trying to figure out what might be done to improve it for her consultations.

Since there were only the pandanus mats, she set about rearranging those. She brought all the extra mats from the edges of the room, and by piling one on the other, she created a legless couch and headrest that would elevate the patient several inches from the floor. For herself, next to the headrest but slightly behind it, she built her legless chair with added mats. This done, all furnishing possibilities had been exhausted.

Rachel's watch told her that in ten minutes the first of her three patients would arrive.

As frugal about time as she was with her income and her emotions, Rachel prepared to use her ten minutes gainfully. She found the pen and shorthand pad in her purse, and with these she sat on her mat chair and resumed the diary, the supplement to her clinical notes, that she had begun writing yesterday afternoon.

"Morning began with orientation lecture by Maud Hayden. Enjoy her, but find her platform manner cross between Mary Baker Eddy and Sophie Tucker. Most of it elementary tenderfoot Baden-Powell handy hints. Got kick out of her advice we emotionally transfer to natives. Doesn't she know they must transfer to me?

Actually, she was very good on necessity of establishing rapport and being participant observer. I shall be firm with myself on this, overcome that in my nature which makes me stand off, watch from arm's length, regard everyone as specimen. That, I suppose, was the barrier between Joe and me. (I had better make this diary less personal or there will be nothing of The Three Sirens in it.)

"After lecture, Courtney escorted Marc H to Chief's place. Marc not unattractive, but one feels strain held behind amiability—suspect potential paranoid schiz—battered superego—possibly paranoid defense against latent homosexuality—can't be sure yet.

"Afterwards, Courtney took Orville Pence and self across village to the Social Aid Hut. I find Pence a dictionary of repressed tends. I can almost see him writing the letter John Bishop wrote to Increase Mather: 'The Lord rebuke that worldly, earthly, profane & loose spirit up & down in the country . . .' To know his fantasies! I had double curiosity about the Social Aid Hut—for myself, to know what it was really like, and for Orville, to see how he would react. His shield of professionalism hides everything. Except his eyes. They sparkle. The voyeur, no question.

"The Social Aid Hut looks like a huge hill made of woven bamboos. I did not know what to expect inside. Revels? Orgies? It turned out to be quite as proper and orderly as Brigham Young's Lion House, except in one respect. The unclad young men and women everywhere, the excessive amount of vigorous flesh, gave the center its sensual character. How can I describe the pleasure house? Inside it was comparable to a huge sport field house with many locker rooms. Actually, there were private rooms and open compartments and several big social rooms. We saw healthy young men, and some older ones, squatting or lolling about, smoking, gossiping. Could not find out why they were not working. Also, here and there, six or seven women napping or having their meals. Women ranged from—a guess—nineteen to one of fifty years.

"According to Courtney, the Social Aid Hut is a central meeting place, a club forbidden to all others, for the diversion of unmarried natives, meaning bachelors, single women, the divorced, the widowed. Here they consort, and have social as well as sexual intercourse. It serves another function, at which Easterday hinted, some unique method of giving the villagers full sexual satisfaction, but what this method is our Courtney would not reveal. He preferred that the information come to us directly from a native. The

Social Aid has for its overseers not chaperones but administrative heads, decision-makers—one woman of forty-five, Ana, and one man of fifty-two, Honu. The woman was not present, but the man was, a straight, spare, kindly man whom I liked instantly. Honu offered to show us around more carefully, but Courtney had made an appointment for me with the Marriage Hierarchy, and since this concerned my immediate work, I left with Courtney. Orville Pence stayed behind with Honu, and I shall have to find out what he learned."

Rachel's fingers felt cramped on the pen, and she ceased recording the events of her day momentarily to knead her hand. Doing so, she read what she had written, and then she idly considered whether Joe Morgen would or would not have the opportunity to one day read her diary. What would he make of it, of her apparent ability to write about love and discuss it frankly and with detachment, and her inability to face it in her own life?

When she had sent him the long, personal letter informing him —if he was still interested—of her six-week sabbatical to the South Seas, and alluding to certain problems of her own that were at the root of their separation, he had responded speedily. He had met with her in a neutral area, the quiet booth of a cocktail lounge, and he had been amusingly concerned and formal, poor bewildered bear. He had assured her that he was interested in no woman (she made no mention of the Italian starlet) except Rachel. His marriage proposal stood as before. He hoped to spend his life with her.

Relieved by this, grateful for it, Rachel had told him more of her secret self than ever before, of her fears of having a real relationship with a man and of facing the consequences this relationship might produce in marriage. She had come to the feeling, she had told him, that she might solve her problem on this trip. If she succeeded in doing so, she would become his wife upon her return. If she was unable to solve it, she would tell him so, and that would be the end of their association. The getting away, the time to think in a new environment for six weeks, might give her a rational view of herself, and of Joe and herself, and if he would wait, she would do her best. He would wait, he promised. She would write, she promised.

She had the urge to write him this very minute, merely to have contact with him, to know he was there and she was here, and that she was thinking of him. But she knew the diary came first. The mail pickup was still five days off and there would be plenty of time to tell him of her adventure, one that she was not yet sure would profit them.

For a short interval, she stared unseeing at the ledger in her lap, then she recalled what she wanted to make note of, and she resumed her diary.

"In a room of the Chief's hut, I met the five members of the Marriage Hierarchy, three women and two men, all in their late fifties or early sixties. Their spokesman, a plump lady, dignified (a real triumph, for she wore naught but the grass skirt, and was drooping and bulging), was one named Hutia, wife of the Chief. After Courtney had effected the introductions, and gone off, Hutia explained to me in most general terms the function of her board or panel or whatever it is, the function being largely to supervise marriages and divorces on the Sirens, and to investigate and arbitrate marital disputes. I imagine this is somewhat like a marriage counseling service, but I am not sure.

"Hutia requested that I clarify my own requirements and wizardry. Since Maud had prepared me for this, I was ready. Obviously, not one of them had heard of Dr. Freud or the psychoanalytic process, and trying to explain this, relate this to their everyday life, was not easy. I think we came to an understanding that I had a means of helping the troubled exorcise demons from their souls. Hutia said that they had six applications for divorce, and that she and the Hierarchy would defer investigating any three that I chose to subject to my own techniques.

"Applicants were led in one by one, to sit with me while the Hierarchy remained in background. As each came in, Hutia merely announced a terse biographical summary of the person. For example a short man in his middle forties entered. Hutia said, 'This is Marama, woodcutter, whose first spouse of twenty years died five years ago. Recently, he took, by mutual consent, a second wife considerably his junior, and now he requests a divorce.' I was given a minute or two for interrogation of applicant.

"Of the six natives I met so briefly, there were four I could make judgments upon at once. The man Marama was good. Also, a thirty-ish woman named Teupa. Two other women were less promising, and I rejected them. That left two, and I was undecided which I should take. One was a placid young man, probably not too imaginative, whom I might have handled with ease. The other young man was named Moreturi, and Hutia announced that he was the Chief's son, which would make him her own son, too. This made Moreturi a personage, but I could not tell if the Hierarchy wanted me to accept him or reject him.

"Moreturi proved of powerful stature, but I thought his manner and personality less than attractive. He smiled condescendingly the entire period I questioned him, and turned back my inquiries with teasing quips. Veiled hostility, I believe, toward the idea that a female could have magic and authority to solve his problem or advise him. Before we had finished, I had decided that he would be uncooperative and disruptive and that I had better select the more compliant man. After Moreturi rose, smirking, and left the room, I turned to the panel to tell them I would choose the other and not Moreturi. Somehow, it came out that I wanted Moreturi. It was as involuntary as the speech blunder I committed several months ago in Beverly Hills.

"Sitting here, I try to analyze why, once having made the mistake, I did not retract it before the Hierarchy and present them with the correct name. I suppose, unconsciously, I preferred the Chief's son for a patient. I do not think it is because of his high station, which would give me prestige in the village. Nor do I believe it is because his position will enhance my paper. I think I was compelled to choose him because his insolence had challenged me to do so. Also, to prove to him that I am not merely an inferior female. It always irritates me when I run into the kind of man who thinks women are good for one thing and nothing else. (In fact, this may be a part of his problem.) At any rate—"

There was a heavy knocking. Startled, Rachel looked up and saw the cane door shudder under someone's fist.

"Come in—come in," she called out.

The door flung open, and Moreturi filled it, squinting down at her with a grin, inspecting her from his manly height. He nodded a slow greeting, stepped inside, closed the door softly, and waited, rocking on the balls of his bare feet.

"They say you chose me to come," he drawled. "I am here."

The unexpectedness of his appearance—somehow, she had thought that Marama or Teupa would be first—and the fact that he had come upon her just as she had been confiding his name to her notebook, both disconcerted and embarrassed her. It was as if she had been caught *flagrante delicto*. She could not restrain the redness on her cheeks.

"Yes," she said, "I—I thought we should get started."

Momentarily, she was dumb. All of the familiar routine and patter was impossible in this situation. No couch. No person who respected her. No person who desperately sought her help. No person like any person she had ever known, no neat tie and shirt and narrow-shouldered suit, but instead, Rousseau's noble savage, unappareled except for the conspicuous white bag between his legs. Her worried eyes lifted to meet his slanted mocking ones.

"What do you want me to do, Miss Doctor?" He had given her title a special emphasis, to show that his regard for her was still qualified by cynicism.

Quickly, she shut the diary, and shoved it into her purse. She patted her hair, and sat more erect on her heightened mattings, recovering some vestige of composure.

"Let me explain, Moreturi," she said, attempting a schoolteacher approach. "In my country, when one is troubled, has a problem, and seeks psychiatric care, he comes to my office. I have a couch —like a cot, a bed—and the patient lies down, and I sit on a chair next to him or behind him . . . that—that is the way we do it."

"What should I do now?" he asked stubbornly.

She indicated the thick strips of matting beside her. "Lie down here, please."

He seemed to shrug, not with his shoulders, but with his eyes. As if to indulge a child, he carried his muscular body past her, knelt, and stretched out at full length on his back.

"Make yourself as comfortable as possible," she said, not looking at him.

"It is not easy, Miss Doctor. Here we do not lie this way except to sleep or make love."

She was too conscious of his presence, and she knew that she could not avoid it. Deliberately, she half-turned to face him, and then, having done so, she regretted it. She had meant to hold on his face, the taunt in it, but almost by uncontrolled reflex her eyes went to his sleek, block chest, and narrow hips, and intrusive codpiece.

Hastily, she averted her eyes, and studied the floor. "It is not necessary to lie down, but it is better," she said. "It is more comfortable. This is a method of treatment we have to relieve you, to make you happier, better integrated, to free you of guilts and doubts, to help you correct poor judgments and—and impulses. You are called the analysand. I am your analyst. I cannot cure you. I can only advise you, help you cure yourself."

"What must I do, Miss Doctor?"

"You must talk, just talk and talk, whatever comes to your mind, good, bad, no matter what. We call this free association. You must not think of me. You must allow nothing to interrupt or hinder your flow of memories, feelings, ideas. Do not worry about being polite. Be as rude or frank as you wish. Speak out the very things you would usually not mention aloud, even to your wife or family or male friends. Speak of everything, no matter how trivial, how secretly important. And when you hesitate to repeat some idea, image, memory, know that I want to hear that, too, and want you to hear it aloud, for it may have significance."

"I talk," said Moreturi. "What do you do when I talk, Miss Doctor?"

"I listen," she said, her eyes finding his face at last. "I listen, sometimes discussing certain points, commenting, advising, but most of the time merely being attentive to what you are saying."

"That will help me?"

"It probably will. To what degree it can help in six weeks, I cannot say. But out of all of your confused, unrelated, mixed-up, seemingly meaningless thoughts there will eventually appear—first to me, later to you—a meaning. Things will add up, things will connect, things will fall in place. Central threads will become visible, and we can draw them out, and find their sources, and eventually we will find out what is wrong."

His supercilious demeanor had vanished. "Nothing is wrong," he said.

"Why are you here?"

"Because I was told to be hospitable and—" He stopped abruptly.

"And what? What other reason, Moreturi?"

"You," he said. "I am curious about an American woman."

She suddenly felt uneasy and incompetent. "What is so curious about an American woman?"

"I look at all of you and I think—I think—" He halted. "Miss

Doctor, did you mean I should speak everything in my mind?"
She was sorry for her professional invitation, but she nodded her
permission.
"I think, they are only half-women," he said. "They have jobs
like men. They speak words like men. They cover all parts of their
beauty. They are not full women."
"I see."
"So I am curious."
"Then you intend to examine me while I try to help you?" said
Rachel.
"I intend to help you while you help me," he corrected her
nicely.
Good-by old Seventeenth Amendment, she thought. When in
Rome, she thought. "Good," she said. "Maybe we can help one an-
other."
"You do not believe it," he said.
Be honest with them, Maud had cautioned, do not tell a lie. "I
believe it," she lied. "Perhaps you will help me. Right now, I'm
concerned with you. If you are concerned with yourself, we can
go on."
"Go on," he said, suddenly sullen.
"You say there is nothing wrong with you. You say you are here
for other reasons. Very well; yet, you have appealed to the Hier-
archy for assistance?"
"To divorce my wife."
"Then there *is* a problem."
"Not mine," he said. "Her problem."
"Well, let's find out. Why do you want a divorce?"
He studied her suspiciously. "I have reasons."
"Tell me your reasons. That is why I am here."
He fell to brooding, eyes fixed on the ceiling. Rachel waited and
waited. She surmised that almost a minute had passed before he
turned his head toward her.
"You are a woman," he said. "You will not understand man's
reasons."
"You yourself told me that I am not like your women, I am a
half-woman, more like a man. Regard me as a man, a man doctor."
The absurdity of this appealed to him, and for the first time in a
while, he smiled. The smile, she could see, was not born of the
previous mockery but of genuine merriment. "It is impossible," he

said. "I take your garments off with my eyes and I see a woman."

It was the second time his impertinence had made her blush, and this reaction left Rachel perplexed. Then she knew that it was not impertinence that got through to her, but rather a sexual arrogance that he possessed. "I'll tell you what, Moreturi," she said, "let's go at this another way. Tell me a little about your marriage. What is your wife's name? What is she like? When did you marry her?"

The specific questions reached him, and he responded directly. "My wife is Atetou. She is twenty-eight. I am thirty-one. She is not like most village girls. She is more serious. I am not that way. We have been married six years."

"Why did you marry her?" Rachel wanted to know.

"Because she was different," Moreturi said instantly.

"You married her because she was different, and now you want to divorce her because she is different?"

A shrewd expression crossed Moreturi's countenance. "You mix the words up," he said.

"But it's true, what I said."

"Yes, maybe true," he conceded.

"Was Atetou your first love when you married her?"

"First?" Moreturi was astonished. "I was an old man when I married her. I had twenty girls before her."

"That's not an answer to my question. I did not inquire how many girls you'd had. I inquired if Atetou was your first love."

"I did answer your question," Moreturi insisted, combatively. "Atetou was not my first love because I had twenty girls before her and I loved them all. I do not make sex with a woman unless I love her with my whole inside and outside."

He was earnest, she could see, and devoid of sexual arrogance now. "Yes, I understand," she said.

"I love even the first one, who was fifteen years older than me."

"How old were you with the first one?"

"Sixteen. It was after the manhood ceremony."

"What kind of ceremony?"

"In the Sacred Hut. They took my—my—"

"Genital," she said hastily.

"Yes. They took it and quick slit the top foreskin."

"Like circumcision in America?"

"Tom Courtney told me no, you do it different, you take off the whole foreskin, we open only the upper part. Then it heals and there is a scab. Before the scab falls off, we are taken to the Social Aid place to find an older, experienced woman." He smiled, relishing some memory. "I took a widow of thirty-one. Even though I was a boy, I was strong as a tree. She was stronger. I lost the scab quickly. I was fond of her. For a year after, in the Social Aid place, when I could have anyone, I would have her."

The room was humid, and Rachel hoped that she was not obviously perspiring. "I see," she said. Then, to say anything, "What do you use for contraceptives here?" He did not understand. She elaborated. "To retard—to stop conception of children?"

"The first one taught me to rub the prevention salve on the genital."

"A salve?"

"To make feeble the male sperm. It retards the procreation more than not, though Tom says you have better means in America."

"Very interesting. I'll have to look into it." She hesitated, and then said, "We started out discussing your wife—"

"Not my first love," he said with a smile.

"That's clear," she said dryly. "And now you don't like her because she is different."

He rose on an elbow, and instinctively she recoiled. "We have talked of love matters and so I can speak more frankly of Atetou," he said. "She does not like to do the—the—I cannot think of Tom's word—the word for embrace—"

"Intercourse? Coitus?"

"Yes, yes—she does not like it, and for me it is a joy all the time. I am not angry with Atetou. The High Spirit makes each person not the same, but it is not good they be put together. When I wish the joy of it, my wife does not. It is difficult. More and more, I must go to the Social Aid. More and more, my night dreams are filled with the women I have seen in the day. Too much, I wait every year for the festival."

Rachel had a hundred questions now, but she locked them securely inside. Moreturi's lustiness repelled her. She wanted no more of it dinned into her ears. Worse, for the first time, Atetou had become a living person in her mind, because Atetou had a face, and it was Rachel's own. Her mind slipped back to the glacial Miss Mitchell on the couch in Beverly Hills. And then to others. And then back to Atetou. And finally to herself. The half-women.

She consulted her watch. "I have taken too much of your time,

Moreturi—" She was conscious of him sitting up, the bulk of him. She swallowed. "I—I have a better picture of your immediate problem."

"You do not blame me for needing the divorce?"

"Not at all. You are what you are. There is nothing wrong with your—your requirements."

His features reflected the slightest admiration. "You are more than I thought. You are a woman."

"Thank you."

"We will talk again? Hutia says you wish to see me every day at this time. Is it true?"

"Yes, you and the others. We'll continue to—to go into all this, arrive at a better understanding of your conscious and unconscious conflicts, and your wife's as well."

He had pushed himself fully erect. "You will see Atetou?"

Rachel had no need of another Miss Mitchell, but she knew her duty. "I haven't decided yet. I'll want more time with you. Later, I suppose—well, since it is a divorce matter I may have her in for a consultation."

"When you meet her, you will understand me better."

"I'm sure she has her side of the story, too, Moreturi. After all, the problem may arise from your own neurotic—" But she broke off, because the psychiatric patois would mean little to him here on The Three Sirens, and because she knew that she was defending Atetou on behalf of herself. "At any rate," she said, "I want to concentrate on your side of it for the next few weeks. Try to remember everything you can about your past. And dreams, you mentioned dreams, they give valuable insight into your unconscious. Dreams may be symbols for—for unconscious fears."

He was above her, hands on his hips. "I only dream of other women," he said.

"I'm sure you'll find there is more—"

"No, only other women."

She rose, and extended her hand. "We'll see soon enough. Thank you for cooperating with me today."

He enclosed her hand in his large one, shook once, and released her hand. Reluctantly, she thought, he went to the door, opened it, and then turned, his wide face serious. "I had a dream last night," he said. "It was about you."

"Don't tease me, Moreturi. You'd never seen me before today."

"I saw you come into the village with the others," he said, gravely. "Last night, I dreamt." His smile began. "You are a woman—yes, very much."

He was gone.

Slowly, Rachel sat down, hating the perspiration on her brow and upper lip, and dreading the night that would soon be upon her. She did not want to dream.

* * *

Mary Karpowicz, arms wound around her knees, rocked in her place on the floor in the last row of the main classroom and wished that she were twenty-one and could do as she pleased.

While she resented her father for bringing her to this idiotic island, she could not, in all filial fairness, blame him for forcing her to attend the school. She had only herself to blame. It had been the sheer boredom, and finally convincing herself the experience might give her an ascendancy over the other girls back home (providing her with a daring background that would make up for her virginity), that had driven Mary to enroll.

Without moving her head, merely by shifting her eyes from one side to the other, she took in half of the thatched circular room before her. There were the bare backs of the two dozen students, the girls in pareus, the boys in loincloths, mostly attentive, but occasionally engaging in horseplay and giggling. There was the caricature of an instructor addressing them in English. And there was herself, dulled down and wearied by the routine.

Three hours before there had at least been hope of something different. Three hours before, she had parted company with her father, who was wearing cameras like so many dangling medals, and nervously followed Mr. Courtney into the building that from afar had resembled a mossy three-leafed clover. They had entered a cool, shaded room, much like the ones in her own hut, except here round instead of square. She had expected furniture, but there were only open chests along the walls, all the chests heaped with the instructor's books and other teaching paraphernalia.

Mr. Manao, the instructor, having heard them, had come swiftly into the room, accepting Mr. Courtney's introduction to her with a courtly bobbing. Mr. Manao had proved to be an almost bald, stringy man—you could see all his ribs in front, and when he turned, his vertebrae in back—who was not quite as tall as her father. He wore old-fashioned steel-rimmed spectacles, pinched low on his nose, and below he wore a floppy loincloth (like Ghandi) and thonged sandals. The incongruous spectacles had made him seem like a nineteenth-century deacon out for a chaste swim. His English, she had supposed, was textbook perfect, although his inflection gave one the feeling that he was conjugating as he spoke.

Mr. Courtney, whom she admired for being enigmatic and casual, and for not talking down to her (as if she were merely somebody's kid and not a grown woman), had tried to put her at her ease with a really funny anti-school joke. She and Mr. Courtney had enjoyed it the more for enjoying it together, since Mr. Manao had been only bewildered. After that, Mr. Courtney had left her, and the very Dickensian—her classical semesters back home were paying off—Mr. Manao had escorted her on a guided tour.

Mr. Manao had explained that the room they were in was his study as well as living quarters for his wife and himself. A hall had led to the next circular room where Mrs. Manao and two student teachers were suffering with the eight-to-thirteen-year-old group. Another hall had led them to the last and largest room, where the fourteen-to-sixteen group was already assembling. Mr. Manao had introduced Mary to native girls her own age, and she had felt awkward in their presence. They had been shy but friendly with her, and tried not to be obvious about staring at her blue Dacron dress and ankle socks and sneakers.

She had been directed to sit in the rear between a native girl and a nice native boy, who, she was soon to learn, was named Nihau and was her own age. There had been three monotonous classes. The first was devoted to the history and legends of the Sirens tribe, filled with long head-swimming names of old chiefs and their deeds, and deferential references to Daniel Wright of London. The second was devoted to manual arts; the sexes were separated, and the boys were taught practical skills like hunting, fishing, building, and agriculture, while the girls were taught weaving, cooking, household ceremonies, and personal hygiene. The third, and last, was devoted for a portion of the year to oral instruction in English and Polynesian, another portion of the year to flora and fauna, and one more portion of the year to *faa hina'aro*, which Mary had not bothered to have interpreted.

The best parts of the three hours had been the two social breaks or recesses between classes, when most of them had gone outside, some to attend the lavatory, some to sprawl beneath the trees, and some to converse or flirt. During the latter of the two breaks, Mary had found herself with the boy who had been at her left in the classroom, the boy named Nihau, and he had timorously invited her to try a fruit drink. When he brought her the drink in a half shell, and haltingly revealed the pleasure all the villagers had in the fact that she and her parents would be on hand for the annual festival, Mary became aware of him as a person, and her contemporary, for the first time. He was a few inches taller than she, with a sunburned rather than brown complexion, eyes slitted, nose a bit flattened, chin determined, neck and chest sturdy like the football players back in Albuquerque. Mary, sensitively attuned to every degree of male interest, had decided that Nihau was interested in her. She remained reserved, noncommunicative, because she was not certain if his interest was in her as Mary Karpowicz, a she-individual, or as Mary Karpowicz, a mammalian species from across the sea.

Thinking of Nihau now, she brought her attention to his profile —Paleolithic man, but with sensitive mouth and alert eyes directed toward Mr. Manao up front teaching the class—and Mary decided that she owed it to him, and the swell Mr. Courtney, to display the courtesy of attention, too. She peered between the bare backs ahead, found Mr. Manao, and tried to understand what subject he was discussing. Quickly, she realized that he had finished his instruction for the afternoon and was speaking of a new subject that would be undertaken in this same period tomorrow but only for the sixteen-year-olds.

"The study of faa hina'aro," Mr. Manao was saying, "will commence tomorrow and go on for three months. It is, as you all know, the culmination of what you have studied on this subject before. It is the final teaching, the practical supplanting the theoretical, before those of you in your sixteenth year undergo the long-anticipated ceremonies that bring you to manhood and womanhood. The subject of faa hina'aro—"

The references to manhood and womanhood piqued Mary's interest. She leaned toward Nihau and whispered. "What do those words mean?"

Nihau continued to look ahead, but from the corner of his mouth he replied in an undertone, "It is Polynesian for physical love. The translation to English-American is—I think—sex."

"Oh."

Immediately, and for the first time, Mary was entirely attentive to Mr. Manao.

"In the ancient times, before our ancestors Tefaunni and Daniel Wright modified and improved our education," Mr. Manao was saying, "the young Polynesians of the tribe here learned faa hina-'aro by custom. No one was ignorant then just as no one is ignorant now. In those times, all the family lived in one room, and the young ones could observe their parents in the love embrace. Also, in the ancient times, there was often spontaneous coupling in the public places of the village—especially during festival periods—and the young ones could learn from observation. There were also the ceremonial dances where all the processes of love, from coupling to birth, were re-enacted, and this, too, was instructive. In those days, when a boy had reached manhood or a girl arrived at womanhood, their last instruction came from an older neighbor of the opposite sex. When Daniel Wright settled here, he arrived with many proposals he had learned from the writings of the Western philosophers—Plato and Sir Thomas More, among others—these proposals including one that mating be eugenically supervised, another that bride and groom see each other naked before marriage, another that there be a free-love period of living together before formal wedding ceremonies. While Daniel Wright's proposals were not entirely acceptable, the one proposal that he got incorporated into custom was that education on matters of love become part of the formal curriculum in a school. Tefaunni agreed to this without reservation. In all the generations since, as you well know, we have taught the art of love in this school. Upon your completion of the study of faa hina'aro, three months from tomorrow, those of you who are sixteen will be taken to the Social Aid Hut and the Sacred Hut to begin a lifelong practice of what you have learned. Knowledge of love, skill at the game, are necessary to your future health and pleasure. In the weeks to follow, the last phase will be taught you through description, observation, demonstration, and when you leave here, there will be no mysteries, there will be wide knowledge, and you will be prepared to encounter the truth of life."

Mary had listened with almost breathless expectation, waiting for every new sentence, and slowly digesting it. Within her there swirled sensations similar to those that she had known at the beginning of the year, when Leona Brophy had slipped her a copy of

Lady Chatterley's Lover marked with pencil. A door to adulthood had opened that afternoon, in the secrecy of her bedroom, and now, in this weird classroom, a larger door was beginning to open, and tomorrow it would be wide open and the last mysteries of maturity would be revealed to her.

What had concerned her most, as she hung on every word of Mr. Manao's, was his unexpected candor and the lack of reaction to it by the native students. Back at her high school, the subject was never in the open. It was one of those hidden things, as if outlawed. In the corridors, when she saw Neal Schaffer and his friends, all huddled and talking in low voices, she suspected that coarse and lewd references were being made to *it* and to the girls who were the recipients of *it*. As to Leona Brophy and several other female friends, they were furtive and winking about *it*, about each new morsel of knowledge, as if *it* were a forbidden vice. All of these attitudes had crystallized, inside Mary, the feeling that *it* was wrong but smart, that *it* was an enormous surrender to be endured to achieve peace and worldliness.

Somehow, Mary had always regarded *it* as an unpleasant experience that must be undertaken, sooner or later. The offer was the price youth paid to enter the grown-up world. It was a giving-up. But Mr. Manao's extraordinary promise that this was something to look forward to, something good and desirable, and necessary to "future health and pleasure," had confused Mary entirely. Equally remarkable had been the instructor's statements that there was an "art," a "skill," to *it*, to be taught like—well, like cooking or elocution. In Albuquerque, if you were a young girl, you just did *it* or did not do *it*, and if you did *it*, what happened and what was done was up to the boy and, in fact, for the boy.

Mary realized that someone was touching her arm. It was Nihau. "School is over for today," he said.

She looked around, and all the others were standing, chattering, or leaving. She and Nihau were almost the last still seated. She jumped to her feet, and made for the door. When she was outside, she saw that Nihau was a step behind her.

Instinctively she slowed, and automatically he accepted the invitation.

As they crossed the grass to the village compound, he inquired anxiously, "Do you like our school?"

"Oh, yes," she replied politely.

"Mr. Manao is a devoted teacher."

"I liked him," said Mary.

Her approval pleased the native boy, and he became more voluble. "Few can read here. He reads the most. He reads all the time. He is the only person among those on The Three Sirens who wears Western spectacles."

"Now that you mention them, I thought his wearing glasses was unusual."

"Mr. Courtney bought them for him in Papeete. Mr. Manao's eyes were hurting because he read so much, and Mr. Courtney said that he needed spectacles. Mr. Manao could not go from here, so Mr. Courtney made measurements how far and how close he could read well, and two years ago went with the Captain to Tahiti and returned with the spectacles. They do not fit exactly, but Mr. Manao can read again."

They had reached the first hump of wooden bridge, and Nihau waited for Mary to cross it, then followed her to the other side.

"You are going to your hut?" he asked.

She nodded. "My mother will want to know all about the first day of school."

"I should enjoy walking with you."

She was flattered, although still uncertain whether he was interested in her personally or in her foreignness. "Of course," she said.

They went slowly through the village, under the hot sun, with an adolescent shyness and ten inches separating them. She hoped to ask him about Mr. Manao's last speech. She wanted to know, in more detail, what the class in faa hina'aro would really be about. Yet, embarrassment held her hundred questions down, pressed them inside her, like a big red cork.

She thought that she heard a gurgling, and turned her head to see that he was trying to address her. "Uh—Miss Karpa—— Karpo——"

"My name is Mary," she said.

"Miss Mary."

"No. Mary."

"Ah—Mary—" The effort to bring himself to informality had been so exerting, he seemed to have no strength left for his question.

"Were you going to ask me something, Nihau?"

"Your school in America, it is like this?"

"No. It's completely different in Albuquerque. Our high school is tremendous, made of—of bricks and stones—with a first floor and a second above it—and hundreds of students. And many teachers. We have a different teacher for every subject."

"How good. The subjects are the same as ours?"

She considered this. "Yes and no, I guess. We have history the way you do, except we learn about our country—the famous Americans—Washington, Franklin, Lincoln—and about the history of other countries, too—their kings and—"

"Kings?"

"Like your chiefs . . . We have handicrafts, too, the practical things, the way you have, and also languages of other countries. The main difference is that we cover more subjects."

"Yes, you are in a bigger world."

Trying to recall the other subjects that she had been studying in high school, she knew there was one that was not included. Here was an opportunity to gently remove the red cork of embarrassment and let several questions go out to him. The moment was appropriate. There was no shame in this. "One subject we don't have, though. We don't have real classes in sex education."

His face expanded with incredulity. "Is that possible? It is the most important of all."

A flag of patriotism flew above her, and she hastily qualified her original statement. "Maybe I'm exaggerating a little. We have some education, of course. We learn about lower animals—and about people, too—about planting a seed in a woman—"

"But *how* to make love—do they not teach you *how?*"

"N-no, not exactly," she said. "No, they don't. Of course, everybody learns sooner or later. I mean—"

Nihau was adamant. "It must be taught in the school. It must be shown. There is so much. It is the only way." He glanced at her, as they strolled past the Chief's ornate hut. "How—how do you learn in your country, Mary?"

"Oh, that's easy enough. Sometimes your parents, or your friends, they tell you. Then, well, almost everybody in America can read, and there are millions of books that describe—"

"That is not real," said Nihau.

Mary thought of the night before she had learned she was to come to the Sirens, the night she had gone to Leona's birthday party. She had got drunk, instead of flirtatious, to show that she was daring, too, and afterwards, in the car, when they were off and alone together, Neal had wanted to do *it*, said everyone did, and she had not wanted to do *it* (because she was not truly in love with him and did not want a baby, and did not want it to get around, and was afraid). But so as not to be different, foolish, a child, she had let him put his hand under her skirt, briefly, briefly, hoping that would hold him. Thereafter, the boys had treated her better. Apparently, Neal had talked, had half-scored, and she was a possibility, more acceptable, and it would only be a matter of time. The time would be the summer, but it was summer and she was out of reach, and relieved.

She brought her mind to her new friend. "There are other ways we learn," she found herself saying. "What I mean is—well, sooner or later, everyone wants to, and it happens naturally."

"No good," said Nihau. "Does a woman one day decide all at once to cook naturally or sew naturally? Never. She must learn first. Here love comes naturally—but only after learning—so it will not be clumsy and disappointing and all—all mixed up."

They had come to the Karpowicz hut, which was the last on that side of the compound. They left the heat of the sun for the relief under the ledge, and stopped before her door.

She did not know what more to say. When she spoke, her voice was small. "Will—will all that be in the new class that starts tomorrow?"

"Yes. I have heard of it from my brothers and my older friends. It is good. Much is taught."

"Then, I look forward to it, Nihau."

He beamed. "I am glad," he said. "I am honored to know you. I hope we will be friends."

Leaving him, and the sun, she went into the dark interior of the front room, so filled with wonder that she was hardly conscious of her surroundings.

In the passageway, near the earth oven, she found her mother kneeling over a bowl, slicing vegetables. Her mother looked up. "School is done already? How was it, Mary?"

"Oh, all right. The same as home."

"What did you do?"

"Nothing, Mom, absolutely zero. It was a drag, real dullsville."

She could not wait to be alone in her room. She had deep thoughts, and she wanted to explore them before tomorrow.

* * *

The moan of a patient behind one of the reedy walls had made Vaiuri, the medical practitioner on the Sirens, excuse himself and scurry off, and Harriet Bleaska had what she supposed was the combination reception room and examination room of the infirmary to herself.

She had been brought here a half-hour before by Mr. Courtney. On the way to the infirmary, Mr. Courtney had given her an idea of what to expect. A young man of thirty, Vaiuri by name, was in charge of the ramshackle clinic. He had inherited the post from his father, who in turn had inherited it from his father. As far as Mr. Courtney could ascertain, the health of the Sirens had always been in the hands of the Vaiuri line. Once, before the advent of the first Wright, there had been shadowy ancestors who were nothing more than witch doctors, naked Merlins, whose mana and incantations drove off the evil spirits. For medicine, those ancestors used the island herbs, sorting out the most effective through trial and error. Some practiced minor surgery with a shark's tooth for a scalpel. It was Daniel Wright, bringing a medical manual that discussed "Small Pocks or Measels" as well as "Treatment of Wounds and Fractures," a copy of Albrecht von Haller's *Elements of the Physiology of the Human Body* (1766 edition), and a kit of medical instruments and supplies suggested by an assistant of John Hunter, who gave The Three Sirens an elemental representation of modern medicine.

Actually, Mr. Courtney had told Harriet, Vaiuri was the first of his line to receive formal medical training. As a boy, he had accompanied Rasmussen to Tahiti for one month. Through Rasmussen's wife, Vaiuri had met a native medical practitioner who had been to school in Suva. In return for a few artifacts, the medical practitioner had taught Vaiuri what he could, in his spare time those few weeks, of first aid, dressings, simple surgery, and something of personal hygiene and general sanitation. Vaiuri had come away with this skimpy knowledge, several hypodermic needles and drugs, and a practical pamphlet on medicine. Since he could not read easily, the teacher, Manao, had read the pamphlet aloud to him several times.

Vaiuri had assisted his father in the infirmary, and upon the old man's death had supplanted him, taking on two boy assistants as his own apprentices. In return for bartered goods, Rasmussen kept Vaiuri's infirmary stocked with malaria medication, aspirins, sulfa, antibiotics, dressings, instruments. Much of the stock was wasted because neither Vaiuri nor anyone else on the Sirens had diagnostic knowledge or sufficient training to use medication properly. Mr. Courtney had admitted to Harriet that, on a number of occasions, he had tried to lend support to Vaiuri, based on what memories he had of forensic medicine in legal cases and on what he had learned of first aid in the army. Fortunately, Mr. Courtney had added, little trained help was required on the Sirens, because the natives were healthy and durable. Moreover, there had been no epidemics or plagues in their history, since they had not been sullied by germ-carrying outsiders.

"Nevertheless, you can perform a great service here," Harriet remembered Mr. Courtney telling her. "You can give Vaiuri a refresher, pass on to him what new knowledge you have, show him how to use his supplies. In return, you'll be learning a good deal about their own methods of healing, their herbs and salves, and that should be useful to both Dr. Hayden and Cyrus Hackfeld."

Harriet had been in the best of spirits since her arrival—the hurt of Walter Zegner's rejection had lessened with distance—but then, passing through the village with Mr. Courtney, nearing the infirmary, she had been fleetingly disturbed by the natives coming and going. They were all, at least the ones near her age, so attractive. She was sure human façades were admired here as much as at home. She would be recognized for what she was, the homely one, and again none would see behind The Mask. She had failed to escape, after all.

This faintly dampening mood had hung over her for a portion of her half-hour with Vaiuri. He had turned out to be a fair-skinned, thin but solid young man, an inch shorter than herself, with muscles like steel cables in his arms and legs. His face had a hooked eagle look, but with no fierceness in it. Rather, he was a businesslike, benevolent eagle who was serious, dedicated, objective. Harriet had regarded his appearance as decidedly unmedical, mainly because she could not imagine a real healer dressed in a sarong (or whatever it was called) and sandals.

With unhurried politeness, Vaiuri had discussed his work and problems. She felt his remoteness. She worried over his refusal to look at her as he spoke (blaming it, as she always did, on The

Mask). Because she became insecure when those whom she was with were not responsive, she worked harder to draw him out. She tried, as best she could, to make it clear that she was prepared to surrender a degree of autonomy, offering friendship for consideration. Except for the occasional flicker of his steady eyes, and once a crinkle at the corners, Vaiuri's demeanor remained aloof. However, he had shown real concern when one of his patients had made a cry of suffering, and he had hastened to the rescue, which she liked.

Temporarily left to her own devices, Harriet rose and tried to smooth out her spotless white nurse's uniform. She wondered if the uniform made her appear too formidable or if, in any way, it was impractical. Actually, she decided, what with the short sleeves and puckered seersucker texture, it hardly resembled a uniform at all. And the fact that she was barelegged and in sandals added to her informality. At home, the attire promised care and kindness. Here, the white costume was strange, and she could not imagine what it promised. Yet, while it was strange, it could be no more unusual to the villagers than Claire Hayden's equally unfamiliar bright cottons. As to being practical, it was Dacron and drip-dry, so she could rinse it in the stream every evening. The important thing was that it made her *feel* like a nurse.

She longed for a cigarette, but decided that would be improper on duty. Also, she wanted to show no disrespect for Vaiuri. She would have to find out if women were considered mannish if they smoked. Maud had warned them of slacks, and maybe cigarettes were the same.

She noticed the large open square boxes across the room, and went to see what was inside them. They were filled with bottles and cartons of basic medicines, the labels on each container bearing the name of a Tahiti pharmacy. Crouching, she poked through the bottles, taking an inventory, and she was still doing this five minutes later when Vaiuri returned.

Ashamed to be caught prying, Harriet leaped upright, a half-formed apology on her lips.

"You are interested in my little collection?" Vaiuri asked with a trace of concern.

"Forgive me. I shouldn't have been—"

"No, no. I am pleased by your interest. It is good to have someone—someone else—" His voice drifted off.

"You've got a wonderful assortment," Harriet said, hopeful that she had finally made some connection with him. "I see you have antibiotics, penicillin, disinfectants—"

"But instead I still use herb leaves," he said.

She perceived an implied self-depreciation in his statement, the glimpse of a weakness that was the first gesture toward friendship, and she was grateful. "Well, of course, certain herb leaves have their—"

"Most are useless," he interrupted. "I do not employ the modern medicines often because I do not know enough about them. I am afraid to misuse them. Mr. Courtney has sought to help me, but it is not enough. I do not have sufficient training. I am merely one step ahead of my patients."

Her instinct was to reach out, with words or hand, and give him the assurance that she was here to help him. She did not do so. Reason restrained instinct: If American males resented knowledgeable females as threats to masculinity, the males of the Sirens might feel equally resentful. She held her tongue. Yet, how could she make her offer? He solved her dilemma for her.

"I was thinking—" he began. He wavered briefly, and made the decision to go on. "I have no right to make a requisition on your time, Miss Bleaska, but I was thinking how much you could do for me, for the villagers, if you could find the energy to instruct me in modern—"

All her warmth went out to Vaiuri for being more than so many American men she had known. "I want to," she said fervently. "I'm not a physician, of course—I don't know everything—but, as a registered nurse, I've been in hospitals for some years, in many wards, and I've read a good deal, to keep up. Besides, I can always get Dr. DeJong to advise us in a real emergency. So if you forgive my limitations—yes, I'd love to do what I can."

"You are good," he said simply.

She wanted to make a curtsy to his maleness. "And you can do a lot for me," she said. "I want to make notes on all your diseases, case histories of your patients, learn what I can of your—well, you mentioned herb leaves—I want to know everything about your native—local—medicines."

He inclined his head. "My time, apart from my patients, is entirely yours. My infirmary is your home. You must come and go as you please. For your stay, I will consider you my partner in this work." He indicated a passage to the interior of the infirmary. "Shall we start now?"

Vaiuri, walking softly, preceded Harriet into a spacious community room which held seven patients, six of them adults: two women, four men, and one little girl. The child and one woman were dozing, and the other patients were lying about listlessly. The appearance of a foreign woman in white brought them to reclining attention.

Vaiuri led Harriet among them, pointing out several suffering from ulcerous sores, another with an infected coral cut, one with an arm fracture, two recovering from intestinal hookworm. The atmosphere of the humid room was that of a cellblock filled by torpid prisoners. As they left it, Harriet, who missed the sounds of radio or television, inquired, "What do they do with themselves all day?"

"They sleep, they dream of past and future, they speak amongst themselves, they complain to me—most of our people are not used to such restraint on their activity—and they amuse themselves playing our traditional games. Now, Miss Bleaska, I will show you our private rooms where I keep only seriously ill patients or contagious ones or those who—well, who are incurable. We have six small rooms here. I am happy to say only two are occupied. It is cooler back here, is it not?"

Vaiuri pushed open the first cane door to disclose a narrow confined room, with a window, occupied by an emaciated older man stretched on a mat, snoring. "Tuberculosis, I believe," said Vaiuri. "Once, he visited another island, and was exposed to it there."

They continued down the corridor to the door at the very end.

"This case saddens me personally," Vaiuri said, before entering. "Here is Uata, formerly one of our leading swimmers, a young man my age. We were once in the school together, had our manhood ceremonies in the same week, many years ago. Despite his physique, he suffered a severe weakness two months ago, and I took him here. From my reading, and my ability to read is very poor, I believe it to be a heart disease. Each time he rests, regains his strength, another attack puts him down. I do not think he will leave here alive."

"I'm sorry," said Harriet, and her healthy heart went out to the other's frail one, although she had not yet seen him. "Maybe it would be unwise to disturb him?"

Vaiuri shook his head. "Not in the least. He will welcome company. You see, on The Three Sirens, the ailing are isolated from all visitors, an ancient tabu. Only those males of the Chief's blood may visit one of their own. Uata's father is a cousin to Chief Paoti, so some members of the family are permitted to come here. Yes, Uata will be pleased to have a visitor—" His eyes enjoyed some secret amusement. "—especially one of the other sex." He added quickly, "In due time, I would appreciate your diagnosis."

He opened the door and went inside the tiny cubicle, and she followed him. Near the window, his back to them, a massive hulk, like a great piece of light mahogany, lay on a mat. At the sound of their entry, the patient, resembling a print of Milo of Crotona, rolled over and smiled up at his medical friend, then showed perplexity and interest at the sight of Harriet.

"Uata," said Vaiuri, "you have heard of the coming of the Americans to visit us? They are here. One of them is a medical practitioner more trained than I am. She will be with me the next month and a half. I want you to meet her." Vaiuri stepped aside. "Uata, this is Miss Bleaska, from America."

She smiled. "I prefer to be Harriet, my given name, to both of you—" She saw the Goliath, shorn, yet struggling to sit up, determined to rise, despite his incapacity, and, almost as a reflex, she rushed to him, went to her knees, thrusting her hands against his shoulders. "No, you mustn't! I want you as still as can be until I've had a chance to examine you. Lie down." He tried to protest, then gave up with a sickly smile and a shrug. Harriet, her left arm around his broad shoulders, eased him to the mat. "There. That's better."

"I am not so weak," said Uata, from the floor.

"I'm sure you're not," agreed Harriet, "but save the strength you have." From her kneeling position, she had twisted toward Vaiuri. "I'd like to check him over right now, unless you have something else—?"

"Excellent," said Vaiuri. "I will bring the stethoscope and whatever else I can find."

When he had gone, Harriet turned to her patient. His liquid oval eyes had not left her, and feasted upon her still, and she felt unaccountably elated. His chest heaved several times, and she was concerned.

"Are you having trouble breathing?" she wanted to know.

"I am well," he said.

"I don't know—" She placed the flat of her hand on his chest, and moved it down to the tight waist of his short breechclout, and sliding her hand under the band, lifted it from his stomach. "Does that make it easier."

"I am well," he repeated. "Your coming gave me—" He searched for the word, then said, "*Hiti ma'ue*, which means—excitement."

She withdrew her hand. "Why should it?"

"I have not been visited by a female in two months." There was a fine point to make. "It is not that alone. You have sympathy. It is rare in the female. Yours came out and entered my soul."

"Thank you, Uata." Her hand had already encircled his wrist. "Let me take your pulse."

After she had done so, trying not to frown, she lowered his hand, and realized that he was still staring at her.

"Do I appear different to you?" she inquired.

"Yes."

"Because of my dress—because I come from far away?"

"No."

"Then why?"

"You are not like other women I have seen and admired. You are not as fair in the bones and flesh, but your beauty is deep inside and so you will possess it forever."

As she listened, it was as if her breathing had been suspended. It had taken thousands of miles to find a man, so unlikely a man, so brutish of body, with the vision to dissolve The Mask and search beneath.

She meant to tell him that he was a poet, to say something, but before she could speak, the door opened and Vaiuri returned with a tortoise-shell bowl of medical instruments.

While Vaiuri stood aside, Harriet began a minute examination of Uata, pressing and probing as she questioned him about his spells of shortness of breath, and vertigo, and occasional double vision. She noted that his ankles were swollen, and learned how long they had been this way. She took up the stethoscope and put it first to his chest, and then to his spine, listening carefully.

When she was done, she stood up and glanced at Vaiuri. "I have blood-pressure apparatus in my hut," she said. "I also have Heparin —an anticoagulant—if we need it. And some diuretic drugs, if their use is indicated. I'd like to examine him again tomorrow."

"Absolutely," said Vaiuri.

He had placed the stethoscope in the bowl as he went out of the room, and Harriet was about to follow him, when Uata summoned her back from the door. Vaiuri had disappeared, and Harriet was once again alone with the patient.

"You must never deceive me," he said quietly. "I have lived my full life."

"One never knows until—"

"You will not deceive me?"

"No, Uata."

"I do not mind my condition," he said. "What I mind is that the last of a good life should be wasted in isolation. You cannot know how much your coming here has given me joy. I was too lonely for the company of a woman. For me, women have been the whole pleasure of my life."

She wanted to reach out and comfort him, as he comforted her, but she checked herself. She wondered if she should tell him that she would try to get Maud to prevail upon the Chief to remove the tabu, so that he could receive his women and his last days would be spent with them. As she tried to form her plan, she heard someone enter, and her attention was diverted to the door.

An attractive, dark-haired young native had come into the room, easily, familiarly, and Uata introduced her to his visitor and best friend, Moreturi, the Chief's son. Briefly, the two men teased each other in English, and then suddenly Uata blurted a sentence in Polynesian to Moreturi. In response, Moreturi's eyes shifted from his friend to Harriet, and she felt uncomfortable under the scrutiny of the two men. Uata had said something about her. She wondered what it was, but instead of inquiring, she hastily excused herself.

In the large examination room, she found the intense medical practitioner pacing. To her surprise, he was smoking some kind of native cheroot.

"Mr. Courtney tells me women in America smoke," he said. "Will you have one of ours?"

"Thank you, but if you don't mind, I'll have one of my own."

After she had the cigarette lighted, she saw that Vaiuri was waiting for her to speak.

"It's serious with him," she said.

"I was in fear of that," Vaiuri said.

"I'm not positive," she added quickly. "I'm only a nurse, not a cardiac specialist. However, the symptoms of cardiovascular trouble are so evident, that I'm surprised he is alive today. I may know more after my next visit. I'm sure I'll never be able to say specifically what kind of heart disease he is suffering from—it may be rheumatic heart disease or a degenerative disease or some congenital defect that's caught up with him. I doubt if anything can be done, but I'll try my best, I'll try everything. I expect he will just go suddenly. Perhaps you should prepare his family."

"They await the worst. Already, they mourn."

She shook her head. "It's too bad. He seems such a wonderful person." She dropped her cigarette butt into a shell filled with water that already held discarded cigarette stubs. "Well, I'm glad you've made me welcome, Vaiuri, and I'm truly pleased to be here . . . Until tomorrow then."

He hurried to see her to the door, and bowed his head as she went outside. For some seconds, Harriet stood motionless in the shade beyond the infirmary, thinking of the patient and sorrowing for him. She started at the rattle of the door behind, heard footsteps, and Moreturi was beside her.

"I thank you for helping my friend," he said.

On impulse, she retorted, "Maybe you will help me? Uata said something to you in your language, just before I left, and you both stared at me."

"Forgive us."

"Did he say something about me?"

"Yes, but I do not know if—"

"Please tell me."

Moreturi nodded. "Very well. He said in our tongue, 'I would gladly die if once, before I go, I could tell a beautiful woman such as she, *Here vau ia oe.*' "

Harriet squinted at the Chief's son. "*Here vau ia oe?*"

"It means, 'I love you.' It has more meaning here than in your tongue."

"I understand."

"Are you offended?"

"On the contrary, I—"

Behind them, the door creaked. Vaiuri had put his head out inquisitively. "Is everything all right?"

"Everything is fine," Harriet called back. Then she had a second impulse. "Vaiuri—"

"Yes?"

"Instead of tomorrow, I'd like to come back tonight and complete the examination. I'm deeply concerned about Uata. I want to see what can be done."

"Please come," said Vaiuri. "I am away tonight to a kin feast, but a boy will be here and expect you."

After Vaiuri had withdrawn, Moreturi regarded Harriet thoughtfully. "You think you can save my friend?"

Harriet felt a brush of breeze on her cheeks, and with it came Maud's words of the morning, to adhere to the truth, to "never, never lie to them."

"Save him?" Harriet heard herself say. "No, I don't think I can. All I can do—anyone can do—well, it's simply this—no human being should die alone."

With that, Harriet left Moreturi, and the shade, and went down the slope into the sun of the village compound. Lost in thought, ignoring the surreptitious interest her white uniform was generating, she passed over the stream. Then, coming to the decision that she must discuss Uata with Dr. Maud Hayden, and find out if Maud could intercede on her behalf and have the tabu against female visitors to the infirmary set aside, she quickened her step.

She had not gone far when she heard her name. Stopping, she looked over her shoulder and saw Lisa Hackfeld, arm aloft, flagging her. As Harriet waited until the older woman had caught up, she realized that she had not seen the sponsor's wife looking this way before.

Lisa Hackfeld was, indeed, transformed. Gone was her spruce, immaculate, expensive, coiffured, manicured, girdled Beverly Hills bearing. Gone, too, her pudgy dolefulness. The Lisa linking her arm in Harriet's was one who appeared to have survived a hurricane and exulted in the victory. Her blond hair was a torn bird's nest, her face had lost its caked make-up and yet been made younger by the flushed excitement that hid the few furrows, her silk blouse was untidy, with two buttons missing in front and part of the garment tail dangling free.

"Harriet," she cried, "I'm bursting to tell someone—"

Halting, comprehending that the nurse's eyes had gone over her and widened, she paused to free her arm, and rapidly, with both hands, cupping her hair, fumbling at her blouse, she tried to bring some order to herself. "I must be a sight," she mumbled. Then, in exasperation, she let go of herself. "What the hell, who gives a damn? I feel great, that's all that counts."

"What happened?" Harriet wanted to know.

"I've just had a ball, darling." As they began to walk, Lisa continued to bubble over. "It's unbelievable. I haven't had as many kicks since I was Lisa Johnson in Omaha and going to my first dances. And the funny part is, I was depressed as the devil this morning. You probably couldn't see it on me, but all the while I sat on that bench in that stuffy room listening to Maud, I kept thinking—what am I doing here? No privacy. No toilets. No lights. Not a single comfort. What a way to spend the summer. Who needs it? I could be down in our Costa Mesa place, having drinks with Lucy and Vivian—they're friends of mine—and living it up, and here I am in this dreary hole. You know, after her little speech, I was on the verge of going up to Maud and telling her I was quitting and that I was going back with the Captain the next time he came and catch a plane from Tahiti for good old California."

The outpouring had made Lisa breathless, and as she tried to recover, Harriet asked, "What made you change your mind?"

"The dancing, darling—wow!" She dug into her pockets, and then said, "I even lost my cigarettes. Can I borrow one?"

As she accepted one, and the light, Lisa resumed her recital. "Even when that Courtney took me out to where they're rehearsing for the festival, I didn't want to go. I kept saying to myself, What am I letting myself in for at my age? And who gives a hoot about a bunch of undressed natives wriggling around in the sun? Anyway, our beachcomber friend kept saying it would be sport, so I pretended that it might be, and dragged along with him. We got to a clearing, fifteen minutes from the village, and there were about twenty of them, young men and women, getting together. Courtney turned me over to a snappy young woman, sort of the Katherine Dunham type, her name was Oviri. She runs the show. Well, she sat down on the grass with me, real friendly, I must say. She explained a little about festival week. That got me interested, I'll tell you. Have you heard about it?"

"Not much," said Harriet. "Only what Maud told us about a

big dance, and sporting events, and a nude beauty contest. Also, something about giving license to married couples—"

"To everyone, that's just it," interrupted Lisa. "You know how it is back home. Before you're married, you see a man who interests you, maybe in the street or in a store or across the room of a bar, but usually you never meet him. I mean, you simply don't. You meet only the people you're introduced to and get to know. And after you're married and become older—well, you wouldn't know that yet, Harriet, but take my word—it gets worse, it just does, it's gruesome, sad as hell. Lots of people have their cake and eat it. All kinds of furtive ratty cheating and infidelity goes on. I'm sure Cyrus has been unfaithful to me more than once, though I've never done that to him, I wouldn't consider it. I mean it's improper and dangerous and simply wrong. So you become older and older, a woman does, until you haven't got a chance, and you sort of die bit by bit on the vine."

She was lost in reflection a moment, and Harriet waited. Walking, Lisa stared at the turf, and then she looked up.

"I was just thinking—no, it's not like dying on the vine—it's like —well, you have only one life to live—and it lets out of you so gradually, like the air leaking out of a poorly tied balloon. There is nothing left. Do you understand, Harriet? All the while this is happening, you sometimes meet another man at a party or someplace and he thinks you're still something and you think he is charming and sweet. And you wonder, you wish—well, you think —maybe here is someone who could tie the balloon, stop life escaping. You would be new to him. He would be new to you. Everything would be taut and fresh again, not doughy and old. When you've been married as long as I have, Harriet, you collect a lot of bruises and bumps along the way. Every time you go to bed with your husband, you take beneath the blanket the scars of every disagreement, every unreasonableness, every lousy day. You also take all you know of his weaknesses, his failures as a person, his attitudes toward his mother, his father, his brother, his ineptness with his first business partner, his stupidity about his son, the way he couldn't hold liquor that night at the beach party, his childishness about getting into that club, his fears about colds and heights, his lack of grace at dancing and the way he can't swim and his awful taste in pattern neckties. And you take under the blanket yourself, your oldness and being taken for granted and neglected, and you know he thinks about you, if he thinks about you at all, the way you do about him, all the scars. You forget the good parts. So sometimes you long for someone else—not variety or sex alone —but only to be new to someone and be with someone new. You can't see their scars. They can't see yours. But what happens when you find a candidate? Nothing happens. At least not with women like myself. We're too conventional."

She seemed almost to have forgotten her companion, when suddenly she looked at Harriet. "I guess I got off the track a little," Lisa said, "but maybe not. Anyway, what I started to say is that right here on this island they've got it licked. The yearly festival is their safety valve. That's where you're recharged. According to this dance woman, in that one week any man or woman, married or unmarried, can approach any other person. For example, take a native married woman, maybe married ten or fifteen years. She is fascinated by someone else's husband. She simply hands him some kind of token—I think a shell necklace—and if he wears it, it means he reciprocates her feeling. They can meet openly. If they want to sleep together, they do. If they only want each other's company, fine, that's it. After the festival is over, the wife goes back to her husband and life goes on. No recriminations. It's tradition, perfectly healthy, acceptable to all. I think it's great."

"Are you sure about no recriminations?" asked Harriet. "I mean people are possessive, they get jealous."

"Not here," said Lisa. "They've grown up with this custom and it's with them all their lives. The dance woman, Oviri, said there were some adjustments sometimes, an appeal to the Hierarchy to shed one mate and take a new one, because of the festival, but rarely. I still think it's great. Imagine, doing whatever you want for a week with no one watching you or caring, and yourself not feeling guilty."

"It's fantastic. I've never heard anything like it."

"Well, we'll be here, we'll see it. Anyway, this Oviri said the whole festival kicks off with the ceremonial dance exhibition the first night. It is supposed to create an atmosphere of—of celebration and freedom. That's what I saw them rehearsing an hour ago. After Oviri left me to go and work with her troupe—there were some new ones who had to be taught to perform with the group— I sat there alone, kind of apart, a little wound up by what I'd heard, but still sort of lonely and by myself. Once they started dancing, I couldn't take my eyes off them. I know something about the dance, but, honey, I've never seen anything like this. Speak about our bumps and grinds. Kindergarten play. They had a fertility dance going, a line of men and a line of women, facing each other, everything synchronized and planned—a couple of musicians started with the flutes and wooden drums—and those women started clapping and chanting, throwing their heads way back, pushing their breasts and pelvises way out, all their muscles going, going in a frenzy, and the men, hips rotating, it was wild. I'm surprised it didn't end up in an orgy. I guess I was impressed and showed it, eyes bugging, palms slapping on my hips, because Oviri skipped over and offered me her hand. Well, I had no more thought of joining them—at my age—and I haven't really danced for years—but I got caught up in it, and there I was in that pack of strangers, swinging away. After a few minutes they took a break, thank the Lord, because my mouth was dry and my arms and legs ached and I thought I'd collapse. Drinks were passed around, some kind of milky something made of herbs, and Oviri explained the next number, and I hadn't intended to go on, but all at once I was eager and ready. They formed a circle, and I was in it, and we began stamping, and twirling, and going in and out, and I picked up the rhythm and went crazy. I'm glad Cyrus and the old crowd couldn't see me. What a spectacle. It got so frenzied—I was wet through and through—that I wanted to be like those Sirens women with nothing on but some grass around the middle. I still had enough sense not to be foolish, but I kicked off my ballet slippers, and as we were wheeling and grinding, I yanked out my blouse and tried to unbutton it and finally ripped it off—that's why no buttons—and there I was in bra and skirt, a maniac. I'm a quick study and I learned the motions fast. Well, it's been years since I felt so free, not giving a damn about anyone, even about myself, only having a ball. And when it was over, I wasn't even tired or sore. Isn't that something? Anyway, they liked me, I liked them, and I promised Oviri I'd come there every day. I'll have to make notes on it for Maud . . . One funny thing. That kind of crazy dancing is for young people. At least, at home it is. Married women my age, and with a son in prep school, they don't do the young Zelda Fitzgerald or Isadora bit. But you know, when I was leaving, I got up the courage to ask Oviri her age. She's older than I am—forty-two

—can you imagine that? I guess the letting-go agrees with her. I know it does with me. I can't wait for tomorrow."

Listening to Lisa Hackfeld's enthusiasm, Harriet was delighted for her. As always, she wanted everyone to be happy. She had almost forgotten her own recent sorrow, but now, visualizing the festival dance, she conjured up an image of Uata as part of it. How abandoned and alive he must have been.

She was reminded of her duty, and halted, aware that they had gone several huts past Maud's dwelling. "It sounds sensational, Lisa," she said. "You'll have to show me how it goes one day . . . Listen, I almost forgot, but I have to see Maud on some business. Will you excuse me?"

"You go along. Forgive my running off at the mouth like this."

They had started to separate, when Lisa remembered an amenity. "Oh, Harriet, I meant to ask, what kind of a day did you have?"

"Like you, a ball, a great big wonderful ball." She knew that Lisa would not detect, and not understand if she did detect, the irony in her tone.

* * *

It was a little after four in the afternoon—at home always the purgatory part of the day, when you regretted what you had or had not done up to that moment, when you suffered the approach of night with its disappointments—and Claire Hayden was glad, at this time, to be occupied.

Since her own table would not be ready until tomorrow, she sat at Maud's desk, finished the last of the typing on the third letter, pulled it from the machine, and fixed paper, carbon, paper for the fourth letter. Before leaving to see Paoti, Maud had dictated seven letters to colleagues in the United States and England, each short but provocative, each hinting at an amazing forthcoming study.

Maud's casual letters were carefully calculated to spread favorable gossip by word of mouth in anthropological circles. A Dr. So-and-So would open his letter in Dallas, flattered to hear from the legendary Maud, curious about "the secret island" from which she was writing, and he would remark to others in the field, "Sa-ay, Jim, guess who I heard from last week—Maud—Maud Hayden— the old battle-axe is out in the South Pacific on some hush-hush field trip, a big one this time—can't count her out—she's off and running. Got to give credit to those Boas-Kroeber gals." Thus, artificially seeding the atmosphere, Maud would create the right climate for a dramatic appearance and paper at the American Anthropological League this fall. Thus, she would reinforce Dr. Walter Scott Macintosh's support. Thus, she would brush aside the threat from Dr. David Rogerson. And thus, she would be en-shrined as executive editor of *Culture*. Her daughter-in-law knew that from this day on the typewriter keys would not be still.

Satisfied to collaborate in this promotion, to help win Maud her high post, thereby winning Marc a better position and their own privacy for the first time in their marriage—although, today, she was less sure she wanted that—Claire slipped the blank pages into her machine and rolled them through.

She had bent to read her shorthand ciphers, when suddenly the door swung open and the bright sunlight enveloped and blinded her. She covered her eyes, heard the door close, dropped her hand, and saw that the caller looming above her was Tom Courtney, appearing congenial and attractive in a T-shirt and blue dungarees.

He showed surprise at finding Claire behind the desk. "Hello . . ." he said.

"Hello yourself."

"I-I guess I expected to find Maud."

"She's with the Chief." Her mind swiftly reversed itself, and she found she had no patience for work. She wanted company. "She should be back any minute," Claire said quickly. "Why don't you sit down?"

"If you don't mind? Because if you're busy—"

"I'm through for the day."

"All right." He made for the bench, pulling pipe and pouch from his hip pocket, then sat down and packed his pipe bowl. "I should apologize for bursting in without knocking. Everything is so informal here. You gradually forget your—your American manners."

She watched him put the flaming lighter to his pipe. She wondered what was in his mind about her, if anything. Aside from her husband and doctor, no other white man, except this stranger, had ever seen her unclad to the waist. What had he thought?

She slid around in the chair to face him, drawing her skirt down. He had his pipe billowing smoke, and he looked up at her, smiled crookedly, crossed his long legs.

"Well, Mrs. Hayden—" he said.

"I'll trade you Claire for Tom," she said. "It might as well be Claire. You know me practically as—as intimately as my husband."

"What does that mean?"

"I'm afraid I made a spectacle of myself last night. 'Ladies and gentlemen, come and see the new strip queen of The Three Sirens.'"

Some concern touched his features. "You're not really worried about that, are you?"

"I'm not. My husband is." She did not mind being disloyal to Marc today. "He thinks the place is making me dissolute."

She had spoken the last lightly, but Courtney's reply was devoid of humor. "It had to be done, and you were right to do it," he said. "I thought you handled yourself with dignity. You made a wonderful impression on Paoti and the others."

"Well, hurrah for that," she said. "I'll have to bring you as an affidavit for my husband."

"Husbands are a special breed," he said. "They are often possessive and resentful."

"How do you know? Were you one of the breed?"

"Almost. Not quite." He worried his pipe. "My knowledge of the breed is secondhand," he said carefully, speaking to the pipe. He looked up. "I was a divorce lawyer."

"Sellers, Woolf and Courtney, Attorneys-at-Law, Chicago, Illinois. Northwestern and Chicago Universities. Army Air Force, Korea, 1952. En route to the Sirens, 1957."

He blinked steadily, and made no effort to hide his surprise. "Where did you say you were from—221B Baker Street?"

"It was all very simple," said Claire. "Maud is extremely thorough, and she researched what she could, including Daniel Wright, Esquire, including Thomas Courtney, Esquire."

He nodded. "Yes, I see. I suppose nothing can be secret any more. There must be a file somewhere on the most non-nonentity. You know, Mrs.—are you sure I can call you Claire?—all right, Claire, you know, sometimes when I was with the firm, preparing divorce settlements, it astonished me how much I could know of a person without meeting him or her. A man would come to us, instigating divorce, and I might never see his wife, yet I would know all about her—and probably accurately—from papers, documents—things like income tax returns, leases, financial statements, clippings, just things like that, let alone what the husband would tell me. So I shouldn't be too surprised that my life is an open book, too."

Claire liked him. She liked his courtesy and his intelligence. She liked his amiability. She wanted to know more, much more. "You're not quite an open book," she said. "Our dossier on you reveals when you left Chicago. It doesn't tell why—or why you came here—and how—or why you've stayed so long. I suppose it's none of my business—"

"I have no real secrets," he said. "Not any more. I have a shy streak. I'm not certain anyone is interested in—well, in motives."

"Very well. I am interested. I adopt you as my key informant. I'm doing an anthropological paper on divorce lawyers and their society."

Courtney laughed. "It's not as dramatic as you might expect."

"Let me be the judge. One day you're shooting at MIGs over Korea. The next you are back as junior partner in a big, stuffy law firm. The next you are an—an expatriate on an unknown South Seas island. Is that par for divorce lawyers?"

"For ones who have come to distrust their fellow man, yes."

"Fellow man? Does that mean everyone?"

"It means specifically women. Out of context, that sounds juvenile. Nevertheless, it is what I mean."

"Based on the evidence at hand—I quote Tehura, as of last night —you hardly seem misogynous to me."

"I'm talking past tense. Toward the last of Chicago, I was a confirmed misogynist. The Three Sirens reformed me, gave me a proper perspective on myself."

"Well, you've been to the spa. You're healed. Why don't you go home, American?"

He hesitated. "I've become used to it here, I guess. I like it here. It's an easy life, no demands, a man can have as much solitude or companionship as he desires. I have my work here, my books—"

"Your women."

"Yes, that, too." He shrugged. "And so I stay."

She stared at him. "And that is all of it?"

"There may be other reasons," he said slowly. He smiled. "Let's save something so I have an excuse to talk to you again."

"As you wish."

He sat straighter. "Why did I leave Chicago? I don't mind telling you. In fact, I'd like to. I think our attitudes harden early. I know my own, toward women, toward marriage did. My parents were hellishly married. There was one roof, but it was like two separate houses. If they met in one room, it was the same as throwing two cocks into a pit. Well, when it's that way, you grow up with the notion that marriage is not exactly Elysium. And when your mother is the dominant shrew, that colors your attitudes, too. You get to think Disraeli was right. You know: 'Every woman should marry—and no man.' I spent a lot of time with girls, through school, and after, too, but always very cautiously. Then, late in '51, I met the one, I was smitten, and my defenses went down. We were formally engaged. Before we could be married, I was off to Korea. We swore to be true, to be chaste, to wait for one another. Sure enough, she was there waiting for me when I returned. I married her. It was only after the ceremony that I found out she had been pregnant before I came home and before we were married. She didn't give a damn about me any more. She needed a fall guy, a sucker, someone to give her and her kid legitimacy and a name. The minute it came out, and I saw how I had been taken, I left her and had the marriage annulled. That's why I could say to you before that my knowledge of the husband breed is secondhand. I stand by that. I don't feel that I've ever been married."

"I'm sorry that happened, Tom. It shouldn't have." She felt comfortable with him, more familiar, now that he had revealed a personal failure.

"No, I shouldn't have let it happen, but I did."

"So it's the crippled old cliché—one woman spoiled all women for you, soured you on everything?"

"Not quite. There's more to it. After that experience, after all not uncommon, which only reinforced what I had known of my parents, and which made me suspicious of close relationships with people, I concentrated more than I ever had on my legal work. In a short time, I was promoted to junior partner, and it was Sellers, Woolf and Courtney. But a curious drift was occurring in my work. I had been doing a good deal of tax law, advising corporations, that sort of thing. Then bit by bit, I began usurping, from others in the firm, more of the court cases, much of it divorce work. I became an expert on divorce law, handled hundreds of litigations, and soon was giving this field my entire energy. Looking back, I can see what drove me into this. It was as if I wanted firsthand evidence to buttress my own thinking about women and marriage. I didn't want to see the best side of it—healthy, relatively happy couples in solved marriages. That would have made me the outsider, the unsuccessful one. By burying myself in the world of marital strife—and I can't tell you how women and men look in a divorce office, the hostility, hatred, petty meanness, sheer misery—by making myself a part of this, pretending this was the norm, I justified my determined bachelorhood. I was warped to begin with. You have no idea how much more warped you can become if you live in the world of separate maintenance, property settlement, child custody, suit and countersuit, and bitter divorce. You come to say to yourself, All women are untrustworthy or sick, and all men are the same, and the devil with both. You understand?"

"Do you still feel that way?" Claire asked.

Courtney was thoughtful a moment. "No," he said. "I don't think so." He considered the entire matter once more, a kind of communing with himself, as he absently lighted his cold pipe. "Anyway," he said, lifting his head toward Claire, "I became so tired of the people I was in contact with daily—everything was so expected and boring—and I was so revolted by the chicanery of the life around me, that one day I studied my bank account, saw that I had enough, and quit. My partners made it a leave of absence. But for me, I quit. I hear from one of them about every six months, or did, asking if I've got this nonsense out of my system, if I'm ready to come back to those dark green walls and detailed briefs, from wherever I am. I write back no. Lately, the letters have been fewer."

"Did you come straight here after you quit?"

"First I went to Carmel, California. I thought I would rest, think, and occupy myself with an attorney's biography of Rufus Choate —I became interested in the wonderful historical coot when I was going to school, had loads of notes—but I didn't feel like working. And Carmel was full of the same kind of people I had known in Chicago—well, like the set in Woodstock, Illinois—so I knew I had not run far enough. Finally, I went up to San Francisco, joined a Pacific cruise, and took the S. S. *Mariposa* for Sydney. When we stopped over in Tahiti, and went ashore, I was the only one with enthusiasm for the island. Almost all the passengers expected too much, and I expected nothing, and we were both fooled. They were disappointed at the tawdriness and commercialism. I was elated to find the first place on earth where one was infused with—with languor—all bad poisons drained out of you. You could lie in the sun and say to hell with the world. So, when the S. S. *Mariposa* went on, I stayed behind . . . There you have it, the whole Courtney saga. Do we stand adjourned?"

Claire, who had hardly moved in her chair, protested mildly. "Objection," she said. "I don't have the whole saga. We last left the hero indolent on Tahiti. But the past three or four years he has been on The Three Sirens, not Tahiti. Do you want to skip the transition?"

"Objection sustained, but really nothing to skip. I hung around Papeete several months. I drank a lot. When you hit the bottle, you make friends, and sometimes they become good friends. Captain Ollie Rasmussen was one. We drank together. We became quite close. I liked the cynical old boozer, and he liked me. I came to know about him, most everything except his work, which didn't interest me much anyway. All I knew was that at intervals of two weeks, he was off to acquire imports. Anyway, one such interval came, and I understood him to be away, and waited for his return in a couple of days. When he didn't show up, and when a week passed, I became concerned. Just as I began making inquiries, I received a message from his wife on Moorea. She said that Ollie was ill, and had to see me right away. I hurried over there on the launch. I found the Captain in bed, gaunt and weak. I learned he had been down with pneumonia for a couple of weeks. At the same time, his copilot, Dick Hapai, had cut a foot, suffered a bad infection, and was still in the hospital. As a result, the Captain had missed his last two trips out, and it meant that for at least a month the people he usually visited had been missing him. All the while he spoke, he kept appraising me, and suddenly he took my wrist and said, 'Tom, I wanna ask you somethin'—"

Courtney halted, apparently reliving what had followed, and shook the ash from his pipe into a coconut tray. He considered Claire's intent features, then resumed his narrative.

"What Captain Rasmussen wanted to ask me was if I could still fly. He knew I'd had a fighter over the Yalu. I told him I hadn't forgotten a thing. Then he had another question. Did I think I could manage his Vought-Sikorsky? I said I thought so, provided I had someone to brief me first. The Captain said that would be no problem. He was too unsteady to handle the plane, but he would be able to prop himself up and come along, showing me what to do, if I would execute his directions. I said fine, but I wondered why the necessity to get the amphibian up. Couldn't he wait until he was well, and able to handle the controls himself? That was the crucial moment in our relationship. He wanted to know if he could trust me with a secret. The secret involved not only his honor, but his livelihood. He hardly waited for my reply. He knew very well that he could trust me with anything. 'Okay, Tom,' he said, 'I'm gonna spin you a yarn about a place you never heard of—even the old lady don't know about it—a place called The Three Sirens.' For two hours he confided the whole story to me. I sat through the recital dazzled, like a boy at the feet of Strabo or Marco Polo. Wasn't that the way you felt when you read Professor Easterday's letter?"

"I'm not sure how I felt," said Claire. "It seemed too much of a marvel in a mundane world. Our distance from Polynesia, I suppose. It seemed unreal."

"Well, I was closer, and it was real enough filtered through Ollie Rasmussen's down-to-earth language," said Courtney. "After he told me of the Sirens, he went on to say that when he had last left Paoti, there was some fear of their having the first epidemic in the islands' history. The Captain had promised to return with needed medications. Now, he was a month overdue. He was afraid to risk a longer delay. Someone had to fly his plane to the Sirens. The upshot of this was that two days later I was at the controls, and a weak Ollie Rasmussen beside me. I managed the flight and the landing with no difficulties. My unexpected appearance on the Sirens was greeted with some hostility. When Ollie explained who I was, and what I had done, Paoti was satisfied. I was treated to a feast and welcomed as a benefactor. In the next few months, in Hapai's place, I accompanied Ollie on every trip to the Sirens. Soon I was entirely accepted by the villagers, as much as the Captain himself. These visits began to have a peculiar effect on me. I found the very antithesis of what I despised at home. And while Tahiti, along with liquor and women, had been an escape, I had not entirely thrown off my old bitterness and feeling of strain. The Three Sirens had the effect of making me feel content and peaceful. On one visit, I asked Ollie to leave me behind until he called again. When he returned, I had shed my clothes and other inhibitions. I had no desire to return to Papeete even for my belongings. In fact, I didn't. The Captain got them for me. Presently, I was initiated into the tribe. I had my own hut. Because of my learning, I had mana. Except for occasional forays into Tahiti, to buy reading material and tobacco, I've been here ever since." He paused, and offered Claire an apologetic smile. "You're very effective, Claire. I haven't been so totally autobiographical in years."

"I'm pleased," said Claire simply. "However, I don't think you've been totally autobiographical. I think you've told me what you wanted to tell me, and no more."

"I've told you what I know of myself. The rest is being processed and inventoried."

"But you're perfectly satisfied here?" She had put it as the slightest question, without challenge.

"As much as a man can be—yes. Waking every morning is now something I look forward to."

"In other words, you don't plan to return to Chicago?"

"Chicago?" Courtney repeated the word as if reading from a scrawl on a lavatory wall.

Claire saw the grimace he had made, and at once she had to be loyal to her childhood, the most treasured of her possessions. "It's not that bad," she said. "It was always enjoyable on the Outer Drive and swimming in Lake Michigan and going to the Loop on Saturdays. I can even remember the pony rides in Lincoln Park. Why, I—"

"You mean you come from Chicago, too?" he said, incredulity on his face.

"What's so unusual about that?"

"I don't know. You don't look it, whatever that means. You look more California."

"Because I've been longer in California. I was in Chicago only until I was twelve, when my dad was—when he died in an accident. He used to cart me around with him everywhere. He was wonderful. I was a fixture in the press box at Wrigley Field and Soldier's Field—"

"Was he a sports writer?"

"Yes. His name was Emerson. I don't know if you—"

Courtney slapped his knee. "Sportorials by Alex Emerson! Your father?"

"That's right."

"Claire—I'll be damned—how incredible to be sitting in this tropical hut speaking of Alex Emerson. I owe my literacy to him. When other kids were being raised on Tom Swift and Huck Finn and Elmer Zilch, I was loose among the great philosophers—Grantland Rice, Warren Brown, and Alex Emerson. I'll never forget his account—in 1937, I think—when Joe Louis knocked out James J. Braddock in the eighth." Courtney looked at her. "How old were you then?"

"Three weeks old," said Claire.

"And he died when you were twelve?"

Claire nodded. "I've never stopped missing him—his lackadaisical manner—his laugh—"

"What happened after that?"

"We had relatives in California, in Oakland and down in Los Angeles. My mother took me to the Oakland branch, and we lived with them. When I was fourteen, my mother married again, an army career man, a colonel at the Presidio. His standard for family life was military life. I was guarded like a vestal virgin. The cloistering went on until I was graduated from high school. My stepfather wanted me to go to the University of California in Berkeley, so I could remain under his vigilant eye. I rebelled, and wheedled a compromise. I could live with my relatives in Los Angeles, and attend the University of California in Westwood. I can't tell you the exhilaration in being half-free of the Colonel. It wasn't easy, though. My entire experience had been lived through books. It was a jolt learning life and books don't always match."

"When did you and your husband meet?"

"I was out of school, and I wanted to be my father's daughter. I wanted to be a reporter. I finally obtained a job as a stenographer on a Santa Monica newspaper. I kept writing and submitting features, and a few found their way into print. I began getting assignments. Mostly human-interest interviews. Then, the redoubtable Dr. Maud Hayden came down to lecture, and I was sent to interview her. She was too busy, but her son suggested that he could speak on her behalf. That's how Marc and I met. I was terribly impressed. First of all, he was Maud Hayden's son. Then, an anthropologist. He was over ten years my senior, and he seemed very worldly, yet settled and nice. I think he found me very naïve and —well, the opposite of worldly—and apparently he liked that. Anyway, a short time later he was in Los Angeles again, and he telephoned me for a date. And that was the start of it. We went steady for a long time. Marc had to grow used to the idea of marriage. He finally took the step. In two weeks, I'll have two years of being Mrs. Hayden behind me." She opened her palms. "There. Now you know all about me."

"All?" He doubted her, teasingly, as she had doubted the depth of his own story of himself.

"No more, no less, than I know about you."

"Yes, I suppose that is so," he said. "I bet you never dreamt you'd be spending a wedding anniversary on a tropical island. It'll be strange, won't it?"

"I rather like the idea. When I first married Marc, I thought there would be a lot of exotic places in our lives. After all, he was an anthropologist. But he doesn't like to travel outside the United States, really. It throws him off. I'd about given up, when suddenly this came along. I find it all marvelous. There is so much I want to see and know about the village. Somehow, I keep feeling I can relate everything to myself, my own life. I type Maud's letters, and they stimulate me. I catch myself saying, If only I could visit a place like that, and then I realize I am here."

"What would you like to see the most?"

"Why, everything. Whatever Baedeker gave two stars, as he gave two stars to the Louvre, the Kremlin, Niagara Falls."

Courtney was amused. "We have no Louvre on The Three Sirens, but we have their own version of what might deserve two stars. I should say that you must visit the Sacred Hut. Everything in this society begins there. Manhood begins there, and womanhood, and the customs of the tribe itself. When would you like to see it?"

"Whenever you're free."

"I'm free right now." Courtney uncrossed his legs, and stood up. "I really don't have to wait for Maud Hayden. I'd rather do this. What about you?"

"Wouldn't miss it." Claire had already removed the blank, curled sheets from the typewriter, and was neatly stacking them.

In a few minutes, she accompanied Courtney into the compound. The rectangle of the day's heat, almost solid, still filled the center of the village. But with the waning afternoon, the sun was setting, and the blaze from the sky overhead had been removed. More comfortable than earlier, Claire walked with Courtney through the village.

"One thing has puzzled me," Claire said. "The captain and able seamen on the brig that left Daniel Wright and his colony on the Sirens and sailed off, they must have had charts and maps of their landing. How come they never revealed the location of the Sirens to the outside world?"

"They would have, of course, had they lived," said Courtney. "In fact, Mrs. Wright had requested the brig's captain to come back in two years, to take them off if Utopia had soured. But the brig was fated never to return. One day some planks and barrels— one with its name—were washed up on the beach of the Sirens. Apparently, not long after dropping off the Wright party, the brig ran into a tropical hurricane. It disintegrated in the storm and all hands perished. With this, the only knowledge of where Daniel Wright had landed was lost to the outside world. That hurricane preserved the Sirens society from 1796 until today." Courtney pointed. "The Sacred Hut is right through those trees."

They entered a path winding past a dense, cooling grove of trees, and suddenly, with almost no preparation, came upon a circular, oddly peaked hut that looked as if it had been constructed after the design of a wizard's hat.

"This is the original Sacred Hut built under the direction of Daniel Wright and Tefaunni in 1799," said Courtney. "Actually, I believe only the timber of the frame is original. All the thatching and cane has undoubtedly been replaced many times, after rains and winds. Let's go inside."

There was a wooden catch on the high entry door. Courtney unhooked it, pulled the door out, then signaled for Claire to follow him.

She was startled by the smallness and darkness of the round room. Then, she realized that there were no windows, only long ventilation slits high on the sides, where the curved walls bent inward as they reached toward the conical ceiling.

"The tallest structure in the village," said Courtney. "To bring it closer to the High Spirit."

"The High Spirit? Is that their God?"

"Yes, except they don't worship one deity. The High Spirit— there are no altars to him, no images of him—is a sort of director of all other divinities who are assigned specific powers." He pointed to three gray idols, several feet tall, huddled in a dark curve of the room. "There you have the gods of sexual pleasure, fertility, matrimony." To Claire, the three stone carvings vaguely reminded her of representations of Quetzalcoatl, Siva, and Isis.

"The religion here," Courtney went on, "a rather loose code, incorporates sex and advocates it. This is important to know, since in the West, generally, religion is against sex, except for procreation. When Daniel Wright appeared, he was clever enough not to oppose this loose religion or to insist upon imposing any beliefs of his own. Such opposition would only have made Polynesian worship stronger, and would have divided the natives from the English colonists. Instead, Wright proclaimed that all forms of worship should be permitted, each kin group to believe what it wished, with no proselytizing permitted. And so it stands today. This Sacred Hut is the closest thing to a church on the island, but, except for the coming-of-age rites, it is only a symbol of the higher powers. On special occasions, the villagers have religious ceremonies, very simple ones for birth, for death, for marriage, but these are performed under their own roofs, before their own idols."

Claire's gaze had strayed from the sculptures to a large glass display case, similar to those used in jewelry shops. It was so incongruous, the modernity of it against the primitive background, that she barely muffled an exclamation.

"What is it?" Courtney asked quickly.

Claire indicated the showcase. "How did *that* get here?"

"Ollie Rasmussen and I bought it in Tahiti and flew it in," said Courtney. "Let me show you—"

She started with him across the room, but her forward foot sank so deeply into the matting on the floor that she lost her balance and tripped. Courtney caught her by the arm before she fell.

She surveyed the floor. "I've never seen such thickness of coverings. It's like walking on a mattress."

"Exactly," said Courtney. "The idea is luxurious comfort. Don't forget, here is where adolescents are first initiated, introduced to the act of love."

Claire swallowed. "Oh," she said. She tried not to look at the floor as Courtney took her elbow and guided her to the glass counter. Beneath the panes, laid out on blue velvet-lined trays, were the Daniel Wright treasures. There were a faded brown book which was *Eden Resurrected* by D. Wright, Esq., a light green leather-covered bookkeeper's ledger with inked lettering that read "Daily Journal—1795-96," and a ream of old manuscript with foxed pages.

"When I arrived here, I found these rare items piled in a big scooped-out log on the floor here," said Courtney. "Time and the elements had already made their inroads. I suggested to Paoti that something should be done to preserve these rarities for future generations. He was agreeable. The next time I was in Papeete, I bought the glass counter, secondhand, from a jeweler. I also ordered a gelatin solution to help preservation. Actually, Wright's papers are in fine condition, considering their brittleness and age. They are in a dry place, removed from excessive heat and humidity, and he wrote on strong handmade rag paper—not the rotten wood-pulp we use these days—and the paper has survived. Consequently, most of Wright's unique ideas have survived, not only in the villagers, but on the pages in this case. I occupied myself the first year making a copy of all the manuscripts here. I keep my copy in a bank vault in Tahiti. I've long ago given up the biography of Rufus Choate. But I have the notion that one day I'd like to do the definitive— well, really, the only full-length work on Daniel Wright of Skinner Street. I don't think your mother-in-law's paper will conflict much with what I plan. She's doing the whole society that resulted. I want to do Daniel Wright himself, the idealistic Londoner who sets his family down among primitives."

"Did he have much of a family?"

Courtney moved behind the case and pulled out the velvet tray. Gently, he took up the worn ledger and opened it. He showed Claire the first page. "Here, you can see, Claire: 'Third of March, 1795 . . . I, Daniel Wright, Esquire, philosopher of London, am aboard the vessel in the port of Kinsale, from whence we sail, within the hour, to New Holland in the Southern Sea. Because of government disapprobation of my principles, I seek a clime of compleat liberty. With me are my dear ones, my spouse Priscilla, my son John, my daughters Katherine and Joanna. With me, also, are three disciples, namely: Samuel Sparling, carpenter, Sheila Sparling, spouse, George Cover, merchant.' "

Courtney closed the ledger, and returned it to the tray. "The colonists were prolific with offspring. Wright's three children all intermarried with eligibles on the Sirens, and Wright had—there's no written record, only a tradition—twenty grandchildren. The

Sparlings had four girls of their own who, in several decades, gave them twenty-three grandchildren. As for the bachelor, George Cover, he successively married three Polynesian wives, taking the family name of each in turn, and they gave him fourteen children. That's what I call integration."

"Who's their fertility god?" said Claire. "Send him over some time."

She saw that Courtney had shot her a look, but she ignored him to bend over the glass and examine the ream of manuscript.

"What's this?" she asked.

"The manuscript? All of Wright's notes suggesting ideas and practices for his ideal society. Perhaps one-third of them were applied to The Three Sirens. The rest were discarded by him in favor of the tribe's own ways or were rejected by Tefaunni." With care, Courtney lifted out an upper portion of the manuscript and laid it atop the glass. He turned several of the pages. "Wonderful archaisms, eighteenth-century words, phrases," he murmured. "Listen—'for those subject to ebullitions of ill-temper . . . render him a coxcomb . . . one suffering mortifications . . . scurvy tricks . . . speechifying . . . do so whilst we can . . . partake of its emoluments.' " He looked up. "Wonderful to be reading that in the original here and now."

"Yes, it is," agreed Claire. "What sort of practices does he advocate in those pages?"

"He touches on everything that involves human society. For example, my own interest was in law. Well, old Wright was for trials and judges, but against lawyers. He got that from Sir Thomas More's *Utopia*. Here, let me find it . . ." Courtney was turning the pages, and then his finger ran down one page. "Yes, here it is. Wright says he concurs with what Thomas More advocated in 1516. He quotes More on the Utopians: 'They have no lawyers among them, for they consider them as a sort of people whose profession it is to disguise matters and to wrest the laws; and therefore they think it is much better that every man should plead his own cause, and trust it to the judge.' "

"Surely, as an attorney, you don't subscribe to that?"

"That's the practice today on the Sirens," said Courtney. "Members of the village plead their own causes, not before a judge but before the Chief. Of course, this wouldn't work in highly sophisticated societies, where laws have become so complex that it requires experts to understand them, and the experts are the members of the legal profession. If I were to play Daniel Wright back home, I would not dispense with lawyers but with juries, as we know them. Mind you, I believe in the jury system, but not as it is now constituted. What do you get on the average jury? Amateurs at law, doing their duty, trying to spare time from their work for a pittance, or loafers who have no work. You get ordinary untrained men and women steeped in the same amount of neuroses and prejudices that we all possess. In short, panels filled with some intelligence and good intentions, but dominated by inexperience and instability."

"At least it is democratic," said Claire.

"Not good enough. I'll tell you what should be done. Just as men and women are trained to be lawyers, men and women should be trained to be jurors. Yes, being a juror should be made a profession in the United States, like law, medicine, accountancy, journalism, mathematics. A youngster should say he wants his life work to be that of juror, and go to a university to study and prepare for it, learn law, psychiatry, philosophy, learn objectivity, and when he has his diploma, he should be assigned to a federal or state pool of jurors, with graduated annual salary depending on the court or cases he is assigned to hear. Then we'd have a better judicial system. Certainly as good a system as they have on the Sirens." Courtney paused, and smiled. "One thing I'll say for old Wright, he makes one think."

"He certainly does."

Courtney assembled the portion of manuscript before him, laid it on the tray, and closed the case. "Of course, sixty percent of Daniel Wright's writing pertains to courtship and marriage, every conceivable aspect of both. Wright favored sex education, disapproved of relatives marrying, favored monogamy, felt children should be taken from parents and raised in a common nursery. The Polynesians had most of these ideas already, but in less drastic form. Parents kept their children, but there were so many included in the extended kinship groups that it was almost as if each child belonged to the entire village. Wright wanted eugenic mating, but it was impossible here and he compromised, using a sort of selective mating that brought equally good results. He believed a couple that desired to marry should live together for an entire month first. Trial marriage, you know. This was a radical concept inspired only by

Anglo-Saxon needs. In Polynesia, it was not necessary. There was enough sexual permissiveness and free choice and experiment without making a law to achieve the same ends. Have you heard of Wright's marriage code?"

"No. Whatever is that?"

"He was hoping to make sex life happier by finding rational grounds either to improve marriage or justify obtaining a divorce. He tried to reduce sex to formula. I don't recall the figures now— they're in the manuscript—but he drew up performance charts, minimum requirements. All couples who marry between the ages of sixteen and twenty-five were expected to make love together at least three times a week, unless, by mutual agreement, they preferred less activity. In this age group, the minimum time for intercourse was given as five minutes, and it could be less only if both partners agreed. If either partner was dissatisfied because the love-making fell below three times a week or less than five minutes in duration, that partner could apply for and obtain a separation while the other partner went back for a probationary period of sex instruction. There was another schedule for couples between the ages of twenty-six and forty, and so on. Wright was very intent about introducing this system, but Tefaunni and his Hierarchy ridiculed it out of existence. They argued that numbers could not be applied to love, that numbers did not guarantee pleasure and happiness. Tefaunni showed that his married subjects were relatively happy all the time, and the unmarried ones had the Communal Hut. Well, Wright got interested in the Communal Hut, and saw how he could apply his sex ideas to improve that. So he convinced Tefaunni that they should add new functions to the Communal Hut and rename it the Social Aid Hut. Pretty radical stuff, too. If Maud Hayden lets out these functions in the United States, England, Europe, she'll have a greater response than she ever bargained for."

"Meaning what?" said Claire. "By now, I have a notion of what the Social Aid Hut is for, but what are the extra functions or services everyone is always mysteriously alluding to? What goes on?"

"It's in the manuscript. I'll let you read it one day."

"Can't you tell me about it now?"

Courtney's reluctance to continue was evident. "I don't know—"

"Is it some wild sex thing? I'm shockproof. You don't think I'm a prude, do you?"

"No, I don't believe you are, but—well, after last night—I just wouldn't want your husband to think you're being corrupted."

Claire had stiffened. "You have *me* on tour, not Marc," she said.

"Okay," Courtney conceded quickly. "Wright had seen too much sexual maladjustment in Great Britain. While he found matters improved on the Sirens, he wanted perfection. He wanted no one dissatisfied, ever. He has some eloquent passages on this point in his manuscript. He knew that his suggested innovations would not solve all marital problems, but he felt they laid a better foundation for happiness. So he introduced the idea of a second love partner, when a second one was required."

Courtney waited to see if Claire understood. She did not. "I may be slow," she said. "I still don't grasp what you mean."

Courtney sighed, and went on. "Wright found that, too often, after coitus, one partner was satisfied and the other was not. Usually, the man had enjoyed his orgasm, but his mate remained unfulfilled. Sometimes, it was the other way around. Under the new custom, if this occurred, the unfulfilled mate, let us say a married woman, could tell her husband she was going to the Social Aid Hut to finish her love. If he felt that she was not justified, was just being promiscuous, he had the right to challenge her and protest to the Hierarchy for a trial. If he felt that she was justified, and this was usually the case, he would let her go, and turn over and himself go to sleep. As for the unfulfilled one, she would make her way to the Social Aid Hut. Outside there were two bamboo shoots, each with a bell on the end, each tied down. If the visitor was a man, he would untie and release one bamboo, which jumped upwards and rang the bell. If the visitor was a woman, she would release both bamboos. These would be heard inside. Having released two bells, she would proceed into a darkened room, unseen by anyone, and there would be a single man of sexual prowess waiting. What her husband had begun would now be finished by another. There you have it."

Claire had heard out the last with growing disbelief. "Incredible," she said. "Does it still go on?"

"Yes, but the practice has been modified since the turn of the century. The bells were torn down, thrown away. They were found to be too noisy—in fact, because of their sound, inhibiting. Today, the unfulfilled mate merely goes to the Social Aid Hut, quite openly selects a single man, bachelor or widower for her partner, and retires with him to a private room."

310

"And there is no embarrassment or humiliation in this?"

"None whatsoever. Don't forget, it is a revered and accepted practice. Everyone is told of it from childhood. Everyone participates, at one time or another."

"What of tenderness and love?" Claire demanded abruptly.

Courtney shrugged. "I agree with you, Claire. It seems cold and mechanical, even revolting, to someone from another culture who hasn't lived with it for generations. I felt the same way. I can only say it works for these people. You know, old Wright was no fool. He knew about the tenderness and love of which you speak—well, they were almost abstract requirements—you couldn't touch them, measure them. His mind, materialistically oriented, wanted to solve everything in a practical way. So he came up with this custom. It never eliminated basic problems, or fully solved love needs, but it was an effort. Actually, today, mismating is not permitted to continue for long. The Hierarchy steps in fast to investigate and grant divorce, and neither partner has much trouble finding a new mate who is more suitable. There's always someone right for every person."

Claire pursed her lips. "Is there?"

Courtney nodded gravely. "I believe so." Then he added, "The only problem is, at home, convention sometimes keeps us from meeting the right person. Here, it is easier."

Claire looked about the room vaguely. It seemed to have darkened. "It must be late," she said. "I'd better get back and start dinner." She saw Courtney watching her. "All right," she said, "I am a little confused—all those weird practices—they make the head spin. You don't know what is right and what is wrong. What I do know, Tom, is—this has been an absorbing afternoon. I'm glad you brought me here. And I'm glad—well—that we're friends now."

He had come around the glass case, and now he led her to the door. "I, too, am glad we're friends." At the door, he stopped, and so she did, wondering. "Claire," he said, "I may have stated the case for the Sirens poorly, today, last night. This is not an erotic brothel, not a place of depravity. It's a progressive experiment, the collaboration of the best and most advanced ideas of two cultures, and it has worked for a long time and it is working still."

Her face, so recently tightened by tension, loosened. She touched

Courtney's hand with her own with impulsive reassurance. "I know, Tom," she said. "Just give me time."

After he had secured the door, they went through the trees and into the compound of the village. No disc of sun could be seen, but daylight lingered. The women and the children were gone—preparing the evening meal, Claire thought—and groups of big, almost naked men, were entering the village from the fields. Claire could hear the running of the stream ahead, and she was tempted to sit on the bank, kick off her shoes, and immerse her feet in the fresh water. But then her wrist watch reminded her of responsibility. Marc would be in the hut, famished, waiting with highball in hand. She would have to prepare her first meal in the crude earth oven.

She turned toward their hut, and Courtney kept step alongside her. "I'll walk with you up to Maud Hayden's," he said. "I should look in on her."

They went ahead without a further word. Although she and Courtney had bridged the gulf of unknowing between them, she still felt too conscious of his presence, too judged, and consequently awkward because of this. The worried emotion was not unfamiliar, and then she remembered when she had last felt it. One afternoon in Oakland, in the high school year when she had been a sophomore, the football captain, a senior with mana, had walked her home from school. It had been an inexplicable minor test, as was this.

When they reached Maud's hut, Claire said suddenly, "I think I'll say hello, too."

Courtney held the door open for her, and she went inside. Her step faltered. Marc was seated behind the desk, in an attitude of distaste, listening to prim Orville Pence, who had pulled up a bench and had been addressing Marc. The unexpectedness of meeting them disconcerted her. Then she knew it was something else that made her feel ill at ease. It was the fact that Courtney had held the door open for her, a subtle intimacy, and that she had entered with Courtney unaware that her husband would be inside with a friend. She had perpetrated a small act of disloyalty, for it had been clear to her even before coming to this island that Marc had aligned himself with Pence against native debauchery, and now he considered Courtney a traitor to civilized decency.

"Well, look who's here," Marc said to her, ignoring Courtney.

"I just came by to see if Maud—" she began.

"She's been in and out twice," said Marc. "I've been looking everywhere for you. I wanted to tell you that you won't have to worry about dinner. The Chief's son and his wife have invited Maud and ourselves to join his family at seven."

"Good," said Claire nervously. "I—I was out with Mr. Courtney. He was kind enough to take me on a tour."

"Very considerate of him." Marc stared past Claire. "Thank you, Mr. Courtney. Where did you go?"

Courtney advanced amiably, until he stood beside Claire. "I took your wife through the village. Then I showed her the Sacred Hut."

"Yes, I've heard about *that*," Marc said. "I gather it's pretty much on a par with the Social Aid Hut. Orville has spent the entire day in the Social Aid—"

"Quite an eye-opener," Orville said to Courtney.

"—and he's been explaining its purpose," Marc continued. "Do sit down, both of you. Of course, you know more of this than we do, Mr. Courtney."

"No, I'm interested in Dr. Pence's reaction." Courtney leaned against the wall, and busied himself filling and lighting his pipe, while Claire sat gingerly on the bench some feet from Orville Pence.

"I was just telling Marc that I examined a couple of the old bamboo shoots with bells on the end that visitors to the Social Aid once used," Orville said to Courtney. "I must say, fascinating relics."

Marc shifted in his chair, a thin smile on his lips. "Only these days, if I understood you correctly, Orville, it's all done more efficiently. No bells. They just walk straight in for service and repair."

"That is correct," agreed Orville.

Ignoring his wife and Courtney, Marc continued to stare at Orville, and he began to shake his head slowly. "I don't know, Orville. I—" He hesitated, but quickly resumed. "Why not be frank? I keep remembering that I am a social scientist, virtually shockproof, and I must retain some vestige of my objectivity, but I feel I can pass an early judgment that may sound unduly harsh to you. I've never known of another place on earth as sex-obsessed as this island. Think of the kind of mentality that could conceive of the Social Aid. I tell you—"

"Not so fast, Marc," Orville interrupted. "I'm not disagreeing with you in general, but in this specific instance you are on shaky grounds. After all, pleasure huts are—"

"I know very well what they are," said Marc, impatiently. "I also know what they are not. The usual Polynesian pleasure huts are letting-off-steam chambers for the young, the growing, the unattached. But this one here—" He stopped. His eyes took in Courtney and Claire. As if to bring an end to a distasteful conversation, he gripped the edge of the table and scraped his chair noisily backwards. "Well, what the devil, each to his own, and to his own opinion, and I happen to have mine. Forget the Social Aid Hut. Call it a curiosity. File it away as more grist for Matty's mill. It's not any single thing but the whole atmosphere of this place that I find repugnant."

"Marc." It was Claire who had addressed him. "As an anthropologist—"

"My dear, I'm perfectly aware of my outlook as an anthropologist. I also happen to be a human being, a normal and civilized human being, and as such—I repeat—I find the environment of this island repugnant. It's all very well to be scientific about each institution and individual here, to go among subjects with calipers and pigmentation box, and treat them as guinea pigs supplying data. Well and good, but these are supposed to be people, at least they look and move like people, yet when I try to find some link between them and us, I simply cannot. The over-all behavior patterns of this society are deplorable. They are simply not desirable by any ethnic standard." He paused, determined to defend himself to his wife. "Yes, I know that's a judgment, and Matty's hair would curl, but I'm making it. I tell you, Claire, if you really knew some of the degrading practices that emanate from the Social Aid—"

Claire had suffered this, before Courtney, but she could stand no more. "Marc, I know all about it. Mr. Courtney has been kind enough to brief me."

Marc's jaw went slack, and his head swung slowly from Claire to Courtney. He considered the enemy a brief moment, his jaw closing and stiffening, and then he said with a tremor, "And I suppose you also tried to convince my wife all of this is civilization."

Courtney remained uncoiled against the wall. "Yes, I did," he said quietly.

"We're a team of experts in many sciences," said Marc, "and we have experience in studying many societies. I assure you this one is low down on the scale of progress. I've seen—"

Claire's hand half-reached toward her husband. "Marc, please, let's not—"

"If you don't mind, Claire, I'd like to finish my statement," said Marc firmly. He returned to Courtney. "I was trying to say, I've been here two days, and I doubt that I will learn more in forty-two days. What do we have on this piece of backward real estate? A handful of illiterate half-castes going about in grass skirts and athletic supporters, worshiping stone idols, their minds filled only with superstitions and fornication. And you have the nerve to call that civilization?"

"Yes," said Courtney.

Marc regarded him with exaggerated pity. "Mister, I've said it before and I'll say it again—you've been away from the United States too long."

"Have I?" said Courtney. "You consider the United States a utopia?"

"Compared to this island, yes, you're damn right I do. Whatever our minor faults, we've progressed, become enlightened, refined, whereas here—"

"One minute, Dr. Hayden." Courtney had straightened to his full height.

"I just don't like you confusing my wife's values—" Marc went on, trying to contain the momentum of his anger.

"One minute," Courtney insisted. "Let me have my day in court. You've come here with an anthropology team and denounced this society in the strongest terms and proclaimed that it is backward and uncivilized compared to the progressive society you've left behind."

"That's right, Mr. Courtney. It's my privilege as a man, if not as an anthropologist."

"All right," said Courtney evenly. "Let's play turnabout. Let's suppose something. Let's suppose the Sirens society was in your shoes, and you in theirs. Let's suppose a team of experts from The Three Sirens got into a sailboat and went off across the Pacific to make a study of an unusual society they had heard about, the tribe composed of a native known as *homo Americanus*. What would their final paper be?"

Marc sat rigid, drumming his fingers on the table top. Orville Pence showed interest. Claire, miserable and ashamed of her husband's outbursts, clasping and unclasping her hands, fixed her eyes on the floor matting.

"The Polynesian anthropologists would report the American tribe as one that lived in many cities and villages, the cities suffocating mausoleums of concrete, steel, glass, the air of the cities putrid with smoke, gas vapors, food smells, body sweat. In these airless, sunless, clanging, pushing cities, the American tribesmen worked long hours in confined, artificially lighted rooms, toiling in constant dread of those above them and in fear of the ones below them.

"Occasionally, these tribesmen were diverted from their routines by senseless wars. The men, who had been taught on Sundays to love their neighbors and turn the other cheek, would go forth with explosive weapons to annihilate, mutilate, enslave their brothers. If a man slaughtered many men, he was honored with a piece of metal hung from the chest of an outer garment.

"Life proved difficult for *homo Americanus*, so difficult that to survive it he drugged himself a portion of every day, either with bitter alcohols taken internally that made him take leave of his senses or with medical capsules that calmed him unnaturally or gave him temporary oblivion.

The tribe was composed of a great variety of males and females. There were females, in black garb, pledged to eternal chastity and wedded to a deity of another age, and there were young women devoted to giving their bodies for various sums of money to any man who telephoned, and there were older women who belonged to special bands called clubs who spent their time helping others to the neglect of their own families and huts. There were men, also pledged to chastity, who sat unseen as their fellows poured out confessions of sin to them, and others, not pledged to chastity, who sat quite visible, listening to suffering patients rattle forth chaotic memories and feelings. There were men with years of education that taught them how to gain a murderer freedom or how to swindle money from their governing body. There were men who painted pictures similar to those children painted naturally, and became millionaires, and men who wrote down words in books that could not be understood, and became living idols. There were men selected to rule all others, not for their wisdom, but for their ability to speak or a talent for connivery or a resemblance to a universal father image.

"A curious society, this, that rested only every seventh day, that celebrated a holiday for all mothers, a holiday for Cupid, a holiday for labor. A society, this, in which were worshiped a thug named Robin Hood and another named Jesse James and another named Billy the Kid, and which also worshiped women for the size of their mammary development.

"In this medieval tribe, superstitions abounded. Great structures were raised without a floor numbered thirteen. People preferred not to walk under ladders, or see black cats, or knock over salt, or whistle in certain rooms. At a wedding, the groom usually did not see the bride all of the day preceding the ceremony.

"The tribesmen would not permit the killing of a bull in public. But they applauded a sport wherein one man, with leather on his fists, beat down, and maimed or sometimes murdered, another man, and they equally enjoyed a sport wherein twenty-two full-sized males bullied each other over a pigskin ball and knocked each other down, often to their serious physical detriment.

"It was a society of plenty where some went hungry, a society that consumed snails and cows but held a tabu against eating cats and dogs. It was a society which feared and discriminated against those of its members who had black skins, yet whose fairer members considered it reflections of wealth and leisure to lie in the sun and blacken their own skins. It was a society where intelligent leaders were held suspect and named after eggs, where men wanted education but would not give money to support education, where fortunes were spent on medicines to keep men alive and other fortunes were spent to kill men by electricity.

"The sexual mores of the tribe proved the most difficult to understand. In marriage, men swore fidelity, yet concentrated most of their waking hours on thoughts and acts of infidelity, usually committed in secrecy and against the laws of the tribe. It was a society in which men whispered about sex, gossiped about sex, joked about sex, read about sex, but regarded open, public discussions and writings on sex as unclean and revolting. It was a society that did everything possible, in the advertising of its goods and celebrities, to incite passion in males and compliance in females, especially the young, but sternly forbade them the resultant pleasures.

"Despite so much evidence of hypocrisy, so many contradictions and evils, so many barbaric customs, the Polynesian team, if it were objective, would see that this society had produced many marvels. Out of the dungheap had risen and soared Lincoln, Einstein, Santayana, Garrison, Pulitzer, Burbank, Whistler, Fulton, Gershwin, Whitman, Peary, Hawthorne, Thoreau. If the study were a comparative one, the Polynesian team would admit that not one of their own brown people had ever won a Nobel Prize or created a symphony or thrown a human being into orbit. In creative and material terms, Polynesia and the Sirens had given history nothing—except two things, if Western man would only take the time to look. The Sirens had invented and sustained a way of existence that provided peace of mind and joy of life. In his long time on earth, Western man, for all his brilliance and industry, had achieved neither. In that sense, the Polynesian team would decide that their civilization was higher than and superior to the one they had visited."

Courtney paused. The corners of his mouth went up, an offer of armistice at the end of a battle, and he concluded, "You call the Sirens a brothel. I call it Eden . . . Yet, that is honestly not the point. I am only trying to say what you insist you already know— that one society is not worse than another simply because it is different. Certainly, your mother's writings have shown this to be her belief. I know it is mine. I suspect it is your own, behind your antagonism toward what is foreign and bizarre . . . Forgive me the allegory and editorial, and good day."

With a fleeting smile toward Claire, he turned and went swiftly out the door.

Claire's eyes stayed on the door. She could not bear to look at Marc, so humiliated was she. But then, she had to hear him.

"That goddam snotty sonofabitch, with all his big talk," she heard Marc say. "Who does he think he is, lecturing us?" And then she heard his follow-up plea for allies. "Imagine that know-nothing trying to tell *us* what's good or bad about our lives." And then she heard his rage balled into a grunt. "Maybe we're the ones who should be doing some missionary work here—eh, Orville?"

* * *

Night had come to The Three Sirens.

The compound was empty, shrouded in stillness, made hospitable only by the erratic lighting of the torches on both sides of the stream. The dinner hour, and the sociability following it, had long passed, and except for the occasional lights of a candlenut burning on its bamboo holder, most of the village had retired.

Only in one cubicle of the infirmary was there any human activity. There, within the circle of illumination given off by her lamps, Harriet Bleaska concluded her thorough examination of Uata.

During the afternoon, Harriet had met briefly with Dr. DeJong to discuss her patient. Later, she had tried to win Maud's consent to break the tabu which kept Uata isolated from female visitors. Harriet had spoken of Uata's condition, and his need, his last desire, and her own instinctive wish to find someone to please him. Maud had told Harriet, firmly, that she must not take it upon herself to break the tabu. "I know you wish to act only out of charity, Harriet," the older woman had said, "but you would be subverting the custom here. It might bring our entire project to grief."

Some time after, Harriet had dined over simple fare with Rachel DeJong and Orville Pence. While they had devoted their conversation to the rituals of the Social Aid Hut, Harriet, half-listening, had continued to think of poor Uata in the infirmary. Once, knowing full well the answer, she had inquired if the Social Aid Hut extended its services to the infirmary. Orville had replied, as Maud had done before him, that such contact with the ailing was strictly tabu. But, having brought them around to her subject, Harriet had proceeded to review several of the case histories in the infirmary, saving Uata for the last. Casually, she had inquired if a cardiac patient could indulge in coitus. Rachel, who seemed well informed on the subject, had said that it depended upon the nature of the infirmity. She thought that many cardiac patients were permitted to enjoy limited coitus, as long as there was not extended preliminary play and as long as the sideways coital position was maintained. Satisfied, Harriet had allowed the subject to be dropped.

When dinner was finished, she had changed to a multicolored cotton dress, washed her uniform in the stream, and then, a medical bag gripped in one hand, she had made her way at a slow pace to the infirmary. All the way, she had brooded about the problem, and as she arrived at the infirmary door, she arrived at her decision. Humanitarianism outweighed superstition, she had told herself, and she would provide Uata with the woman he wanted the most.

She would conspire with him, in defiance of all tabu, and draw the woman who was to please him into the secret conspiracy.

All that had been more than an hour ago, and now, completing her examination, returning the sphygmomanometer to her bag, her findings made her resolution the stronger. Uata suffered, she believed, a congenital heart defect that had manifested itself only recently. Although outwardly powerful, his inner condition had deteriorated. His cardiovascular-caused death should have taken place weeks ago. There was no doubt that it would occur soon. He was incurable, and for this, and the mortality of all on earth, Harriet mourned.

Throughout the examination, Uata had remained unprotestingly on his back, permitting Harriet to do what she wished, observing her constantly with his liquid eyes. He watched her still, as she put away her instrument and brought forth rubbing alcohol and gauze.

"This will cool you," she said. "You will sleep in comfort."

As she applied the alcohol to his chest, he said, "How am I? As before?" Then he added quickly, "No, it is not necessary to answer."

"I will answer," said Harriet, stroking the gauze down to his abdomen. "You are ill. To what degree, I cannot say. Tomorrow I will begin a series of injections."

Kneeling over him, rubbing him with a practiced hand, she had reached his waist. Automatically, she undid his breechclout and removed it, and seeing the state of his excitation, she felt that she could not go on. But then, she reminded herself, she was a nurse, and he was her patient, and so she went on. Quickly, she applied the alcohol to his naked torso and loins, and quickly, she began to speak. "I know you need a woman, Uata. I have decided to find one for you. I will bring her in. Tell me a name."

"No," he said, the word emerging from deep in his throat. "No, I can have none. It is tabu."

"I don't care—"

"I do not want them," he said fiercely. "I want you."

Harriet felt suddenly calm and relieved. A few more strokes and she was done with his thighs. She capped the bottle of alcohol, pushed it into the bag, and shut the bag. She stood up.

His dark eyes were more liquid than ever. "I have offended you," he said.

"Be still," she said.

She went to the door, partially opened it, and scanned the corridor. Through the quiet darkness, in the dim light of the wick burning in coconut oil at the far end, she could make out the sleeping figure of the adolescent boy who was Vaiuri's assistant. All the patients, she guessed, were also asleep.

Withdrawing into the private cubicle, she closed the door. She turned to the weakened giant on the mat beneath the window, his breechclout still open as she had left it. With deliberation, she advanced toward him, unzipping her cotton dress, so that the straps fell down her shoulders. Slowly, she stepped out of the dress, then freed the brassière from her flat breasts, and finally she took the elastic band of her blue nylon panties and, bending, pulled them off.

Nude before him, she could permit herself the truth: what she had done, what she was about to do, she had planned all the afternoon and evening.

She went down on her knees, and then into his reaching brawny arms, enjoying the crushing grip of his hands on her ribs. With his help, she stretched full-length on her side, one hand caressing his face, the other caressing his body. He groaned with passion, and she brought him over on his side, facing her, feeling his enormity from head to toe and desiring all of him.

"I want you, Uata," she gasped, drawing him closer, and then she pressed her fingers into his back, sobbing, "Ah—ah—ah—"

After that, all through their early love, she wondered if she was breaking a tabu. And when she had banished consideration of that, she worried that he might think less of her, for her unrestrained performance. But then, in the ecstasy of his face, in the rhythm of his giving, she saw and she felt that he thought more of her, more than even before, and that he was being fulfilled. Relieved, she could at last close her eyes and cease thinking thoughts. Except one . . . It was good to be beautiful again.

V

IT WAS during the early morning of their thirteenth day on The Three Sirens, immediately after finishing her solitary breakfast of hot taro dumplings and coffee, that Maud Hayden decided she had better start thinking of the letter she wanted to send off to Dr. Walter Scott Macintosh.

From her place behind the desk, she could see the small canvas mailbag, half-filled, propped against the wall near the door. Tomorrow, Captain Rasmussen would be in for the second time since they had been here. He would arrive with supplies and gossip, and visit Maud to leave incoming letters from the States in exchange for the bag of outgoing mail. Maud knew that something for Macintosh should be in that bag.

Not that she had neglected her sponsor at the American Anthropological League entirely. In the past week, she had dictated a colorful outline of her first findings on the Sirens. Claire's neatly typed original and two carbons—original for Macintosh, first carbon for Cyrus Hackfeld, second carbon for file—were stacked to one side of her desk. What was wanted now was a short, discursive, personal letter, a sort of covering letter, to go along with the outline.

How much time did she have? Through a portion of open window she could see that the gray new morning was beginning to yellow, which meant the sun was creeping into the sky. Her desk clock read ten minutes after seven. Paoti had agreed to see her at seven-thirty. It would be a busy day. She planned to spend the entire morning questioning the Chief. Then, the afternoon, except for the visit to the community nursery, would be given over to elaborating upon and bringing up to date her scraps of jottings, that is, entering them in more detail, and in sequence, in her notebook.

She picked up the perforated silver microphone of the portable tape recorder, pressed the button on the machine marked "Record," briefly watched the thin brown ribbon run from one spool to the other, and then she began to speak.

"Claire, this is a letter to go out with the original of the outline," she began. "Send it to Dr. Macintosh. When you type this, don't let it look dictated. If you make a mistake, don't redo the page. Just X it out. All right, the letter—" She paused, eyes on the unwinding tape, and, in a more confidential tone of voice, she spoke to the microphone:

"Dear Walter. By now you have my letter from Papeete and the one I dashed off the second day we were on the Sirens. Almost two weeks have passed, one-third of the time we are permitted to remain, and I can honestly state that what we have found here has exceeded my highest expectations . . . Claire, new paragraph . . . The enclosed outline, too premature to be more than sketchy, represents a summary of our combined findings to date. As you will see, the cultural pattern of this society offers several customs hitherto unknown to anthropology. Over-all, I believe the presentation of this data will attract as much attention as did *Coming of Age in Samoa* and *The Heritage of the Bounty* when they first appeared so long ago . . . New paragraph . . . In any event, Walter, I do not think you will regret scheduling me for the three morning sessions at the annual meeting. I am pleased you will be chairman of the first 'Culture and Personality' session, and I am grateful you are giving me an hour. I expect to unload my big guns in that session. The two symposiums the following days will be perfect for the mop-up. I am absolutely as confident as you that we will run our Dr. Rogerson right off the map, especially if you go through with that mass press conference for me that you are considering. I'm eager to have your reaction to the enclosure. I want to hear from you that your faith in this little excursion, and in my immediate future, is not misplaced . . . New paragraph . . . Subordinating business for a moment, I will confess that this field trip, about which I was so apprehensive, has gone even more smoothly than I could have wished. Being in the field again, for the first time alone, that is, without Adley, has revitalized me . . .

Claire, cut the last sentence, revise as follows . . . Being in the field again, after all those sedentary mourning years, has revitalized me. Adley would be so pleased. I will not lie to an old friend like you, Walter. I do miss Adley not being here. You will understand that. When I'm alone at night, and all are asleep, and I'm making my notes, I often find myself automatically looking up to discuss a point of information with Adley, and I am surprised that he is not sitting across from me. This is a hard reality of life. I do not know if more and more years will change it. There is simply no one to replace him. I doubt that there will ever be. But I am grateful for the gifts he has left me, a generous share of his wisdom, a strength derived from him . . . New paragraph . . . Do not misunderstand, Walter. I have no deep complaints. I am wealthier than most, in that I have a work I love, and a family I love. My daughter-in-law, Claire, whom you have not yet met, has adapted marvelously to the field. She has my own lively thirst for knowledge, and many abilities. She has been of inestimable value to me. In the past weeks, she has carried the burden of my stenographic work. She has served as my lieutenant with other members of our group. She has spent considerable time in the company of Mr. Courtney, interrogating him, and reported information to me that I might not otherwise have learned. As to Marc, he has been . . ."

Her mind wandered. He has been—what? Maud watched the tape continuing to unwind, and she was not sure what she should tell it and Walter Scott Macintosh. Quickly, she pressed the button marked "Stop." Abruptly, the tape was still, poised, waiting.

Marc disconcerted her. He had always been a docile child, and as a grown man he had been submissive, only sometimes sulky. But since Adley's death—no, since his marriage, really—or, more accurately, in the past year—he had proved openly willful. More and more often, Maud had found him sarcastic and rebellious in public. And his private moods were blacker and his depressions more protracted. For all her efforts to keep out of the way, to pretend she did not see what she saw, Maud could not help but be aware that her son's marriage was not the happiest. Often, she wondered what was wrong with it, and often, she thought it might be her own presence. An opportunity to separate herself from Marc and Claire, she had come to believe, would solve their marital problems. Since arriving on the Sirens, she was less certain this separation would solve anything. Marc's behavior, from the time the project had been considered to the present time, especially during the two weeks on the Sirens, had been a cause for increasing alarm. Something about this field trip, possibly the impact of this society upon him, had heightened an imbalance in his personality. From statements Marc made to her, delivered with unaccountable hostility, from his pronouncements to Claire and several others on the team, Marc's growing lack of objectivity was only too apparent, and it was deplorable. He was neither anthropologist nor gentleman guest, but rather an adversary of the Sirens.

Should she speak to him? What would Adley have done? As anthropologist, Maud was confident and decisive. As mother, she was confused and reticent. The moment that she had to communicate with this product of her flesh and blood on an emotional level, deeper than their work, she was held dumb. Still, something must be done to curb his public displays of disapproval. Perhaps, if the right opening came, she would find a way of drawing Marc out, and advising him. Perhaps, first, she might consult with Rachel DeJong, who was, after all, experienced in these matters. Then, Maud realized that she could not consult a psychoanalyst. If it got out, Marc would be furious at being made to seem yet more inadequate. No, there was no avoiding a face-to-face, mother-to-son confrontation. She would wait for the opportunity. She would see.

Maud reached for the lever beneath "Rewind," swung it left, saw the tape whir into reverse, immediately stopped it. She punched the "Play" button. She listened.

Her voice, with a rasp unfamiliar to her, came through the speaker. "—reported information to me that I might not otherwise have learned. As to Marc, he has been . . ."

She stopped the tape, pecked at "Record" again, and lifted the microphone closer to her mouth. "—extremely helpful," she dictated, feeling, in this attempt to further Marc's career, motherly, protective, and therefore justified. "He spends several hours each day interviewing a valuable informant who is the Chief's niece. I have not seen Marc's notes, but from what he passes on to me in conversation, the young lady is articulate. The result will be a penetrating contribution to our study on the mores of the unwed young people of this society. What Marc is learning from Tehura, and Claire is learning from Mr. Courtney, wonderfully supplements the information I am acquiring from Chief Paoti. I have had the Chief recount to me the history of his people and their traditions. Yesterday, I encouraged him to speak of his own life, and he told me of his early years. I hope to bring him along in this vein for another week or more . . . New paragraph . . . As to the others on the team . . ."

She paused to recollect what they had accomplished these weeks, and what they were doing now. The tape was running blank. Absently, she reached out and pressed down on the "Stop" button.

She took a hasty mental census of her team, and tried to organize their activities for the benefit of Dr. Walter Scott Macintosh. Of them all, Lisa Hackfeld had been, to Maud, the greatest surprise. Maud had accepted her membership under silent protest, written her off from the start as spoiled and vapid, pegged her as the team's albatross. Yet, after an unpromising beginning, Lisa Hackfeld had adjusted completely to the rigors of the field. More than that, she was enthusiastic about her role of participant observer. No longer did she complain of the lack of hair dye, although gray was showing at the roots of her hair. No longer did she object to the crude new lavatory, or the lack of furniture, or the omission of dinner service. She had rediscovered the Dance, not for money, fame, health, but for the pleasures it gave her body. From morning until night, every day, she was absorbed in rehearsing with Oviri's group. She had not found the time, she had cheerfully told Maud yesterday, to write Cyrus her weekly letter.

From Lisa, Maud's mind jumped to the professionals of her team. Rachel DeJong was carrying on her lengthy psychoanalytical consultations with Moreturi, Marama, and Teupa. Except for two brief meetings with Maud—to discuss the role of *morais* and other venerated relics in the present society—Rachel had been, not unexpectedly, close-mouthed about her patients and her findings. Rachel moved about in a perpetual state of preoccupation. If anything, her familiar phlegmatic air had intensified in the thirteen days. Maud could not know if she was satisfied or dissatisfied, but she was apparently absorbed.

Harriet Bleaska, on the other hand, was an easier personality to read. Before coming here, she had displayed the practiced extroversion and bounce of so many unwed ugly women. In this society, basically outgoing, she appeared to flourish. Except for the one occasion when she had shown concern over a dying patient and had wished to break a tabu to make him more comfortable,

Maud had not seen her solemn. Harriet worked regular hours at the infirmary in collaboration with Vaiuri, a formal young native who was its head man. When she had time to spare, she spent it trying to learn the traditions behind the plants used for drugs that Sam Karpowicz brought her, mindful that one of the reasons she was on this trip was to find, if she could, something of value for Cyrus Hackfeld's pharmaceutical network. Harriet kept meticulous, if uninspired, notes, and every Friday she submitted them, written on ruled paper in a stilted hand, to Maud, her mentor. Mostly, they were a nurse's histories of patients in the infirmary. A small percentage of the material was beneficial, in that it revealed the diseases found on the Sirens. Yesterday, Harriet had reported, quite calmly, that she had lost a patient under her care. She alone, of the entire team, had been invited to attend the funeral services today. Maud was pleased at how well this young lady had been accepted by the natives.

The Karpowiczes had blended into their surroundings as casually as three chameleons. Maud had seen and heard little of them. Sam Karpowicz had decided to defer the major part of his botanical searchings to the last three weeks of the field trip. So far, he had concentrated his energies almost entirely on photography, taking both stills and motion pictures. He had spent entire days preparing a pictorial record of the Social Aid Hut, the Sacred Hut, the Chief's hut, daily life in the village compound, an afternoon meeting of the Hierarchy. The contact prints that he had shown Maud, not all professionally slick and glossy, were less concerned with artistic niceties of composition and light than they were with bringing the little-known community alive in the flesh. The natives of the Sirens seemed to leap from Sam's prints. Ahead of him still lay a busy photographic schedule. He had told Maud that he planned to cover the infirmary, the school, the various festival activities, spend a day with the village craftsmen, at labor, another with the fishermen, another (under Courtney's supervision) in the hills and the islets across the way, one more showing the life of a typical young female like Tehura, and an afternoon of candid shots of Maud herself at work in the field.

In her own unobtrusive way, Estelle Karpowicz too was making a contribution, though more culinary than scientific. When she was not reading or keeping house, she was collecting native recipes, her investigation motivated by nothing more than a personal interest in unusual dishes. Yet Maud saw that her findings might have some footnote value in the published study.

Originally, Maud had thought that the only person other than Lisa who might not integrate with the group would be young Mary Karpowicz. She had, so to speak, pouted her way across the Pacific. She did not hide her mammoth disinterest in this entire adult balderdash. Maud had feared that her chafing might infect others. Yet, like Lisa, young Mary had done a complete about-face after her second day on the island. While uncommunicative—or rather, given to monosyllabic replies—and possessed of adolescent intensity, she was now a tractable and cooperative child. She attended her school classes willingly, and could often be seen sitting under a tree lost in conversation with a male schoolmate named Nihau. Estelle was delighted, and Maud was satisfied.

The last member of the team, Orville Pence, had spent the first ten days making a careful study of the Social Aid Hut, its origins, history, regulations, and current operation. Half of his time was given over to recording what he had learned. Only two or three days ago, he had undertaken a new phase of his work. He had begun to test a mixed group of the natives, using not only the standard Rorschach inkblot tests and the Thematic Apperception Test, but several of his own devising. One of these, he had explained to Maud in his sniffing, pedantic manner, was to be the presentation of a portfolio of Western pictorial erotica, to obtain and gauge native reactions. The method was not unfamiliar to Maud, who, with Adley, had frequently in the past showed natives of one culture various picture books of another culture or of life in the United States, in order to stimulate discussion. Orville's idea of exhibiting Western erotica to a sexually free South Sea society was an inspiration. Maud told herself that she must remember to remark on this in her letter to Macintosh. Aside from his work, Orville Pence, the social being, was less at ease than the others in the group. Except for a nightly highball with Marc, he mingled little with his colleagues. His spinster character, the fussiness and superiority that Claire always mentioned, made it impossible for him to become a participant observer. Although he worked efficiently with the villagers, he was apart from them, and Maud sensed that he did not like the villagers and they had no special affection for him.

But at least, Maud told herself, Orville had the good sense, the control, to represent himself as a pure scientist. If he felt displeasure, or distaste, he did not reveal it publicly. He tried to perform according to the rules. In this way, he was above criticism and better adjusted than Marc.

Maud offered the lonely room an involuntary unhappy sigh. Her own Marc, of all people, her Marc, who was trained, experienced, cognizant of what was expected of him, he alone, of the entire team, was proving destructive. She *must* admonish him.

Another sigh escaped her, as she leaned forward, pressed the "Record" button, and brought the silver microphone before her to conclude her spontaneous, informal letter to Dr. Walter Scott Macintosh . . .

* * *

For Marc Hayden, the moment with Tehura that he had been fantasying much of every day and all of every night was almost upon him. His breath quickened at the provocation of her words, and he waited for them to end, so that he might make the decisive move.

They were high above the village, in an isolated grove shielded from the path by shrubbery and trees. The midday heat encompassed them. He could almost smell the desire of his flesh, and the sensuality of her body. He sat cross-legged on the grass, listening to her, and she lay a few feet from him, stretched on her back, one leg straight and limp and the other bent at the knee, so that the short grass skirt was lifted and tantalized him. He wondered if this posture was deliberate, if she knew her power as a female and his desperate hunger for her, or if this was simply her ingenuousness. He could not believe that she did not know what she was doing to him now, did to him every day. If she knew, then the ultimate result was possible.

Hypnotized, he watched her bosom. One arm was behind her head, cushioning it against the grass. The other was free for the fluid gestures she made when she spoke of the social attitudes of girls like herself on The Three Sirens. When she moved her free arm and shoulder to underline something she said, her breasts swayed with the arm.

Exhausted by anticipation, Marc shaded his eyes and nodded

slowly, thoughtfully, steadily, a pose of deep scholarly meditation. He did not want her to see his eyes, not yet.

He tried to shake free of her words and remember the road that had brought him so close to the climactic moment. Familiarity breeds attempt, he thought, and congratulated himself for wit. He had seen her regularly, every day, in the two weeks. Most often they came up to the grove for two or three hours. He would begin with a few prepared questions, and she would reply, going on and on, with amazing candor. Sometimes they would hike through the woods, and talk, and one of these strolls took an entire afternoon. Twice she had invited him to light lunches that she had prepared in the earth oven. Once, he had accompanied her to the communal storehouse for food, and, like a schoolboy carrying his girl's books, had carried her ration of yams and breadfruit back to her hut.

Before her, he had played a character he had invented to replace himself, performed the role with the unwavering passion of a great actor impersonating Hamlet on opening night. Whenever he was not listening, he played this character of Marc Hayden. And whenever he had a chance, he inserted this character into her attentive mind.

Fortunately, while he felt obligated to ask about her and her life on the Sirens, she was more interested in his life in the quaint, distant land of California. In that land, he projected himself as a mythological figure of national importance and immense power. Since Tehura had never been there, she could not contradict him. Of course, some portions of her vision of the American male had been corrupted by that sonofabitch Courtney, but in two weeks Marc had sought to correct Courtney's picture of their milieu. Marc felt that he had succeeded, or was succeeding, because Tehura was young, imaginative, and wanted to believe in marvels— and because, subtly, he had undermined Courtney's authority.

Marc had tried to point out, without being obvious, that Courtney's opinions were not typical, for Courtney was not typical. Else, why had Courtney fled a land where millions remained? And why had he stayed in exile from his own people? And why did he admit so many sicknesses of the mind? Courtney had been a failure, a small person, affable, attractive but defeated, and had run away. Ergo, his words reflected personal bitterness, not the clarity of truth. Marc had never spoken of Courtney exactly thus—indeed, he represented himself as having affection and pity for Courtney, his countryman—but this was the impression that he had tried to implant in Tehura.

More affirmatively, he had built up the invention of himself. He had explained that scientists were among the nobility of the West, and that he was a scientist with considerable stature. Because Tehura had once revealed to him a weakness for the material things of life, Marc painted himself and his position in American society in terms of the material. He spoke of the great university under his thumb, and of students and supplicants who hung on each gem of his wisdom and scurried at his command. He spoke of the mansion on the sea where he dwelled with his kin, with servants and magical gadgetry at his command. He spoke of his automobiles, his airplanes, his ships. He spoke of the women who had sought him, and sought him still, and how from among them he had airily crowned Claire. His wand had brought her a life of regal luxury. He spoke of her furniture, her bed, her staffed kitchen, her clothes, her jewelry, her rights. He had made her, as he had the mana to unmake her. He could command any woman, any woman on earth, to this high throne.

At such times, as he spoke of these autobiographical magnificences, Tehura listened quietly. Except for her eyes, so alert, her countenance conceded no interest, ambition, or wanting. Sometimes, speaking without inflection, which was unnatural for her, she would pose a question, and another, but that was the total sum of her reaction. To someone else, she might have appeared faintly bored or mildly disbelieving, yet held by rhetoric. To Marc, who felt that he knew her inner workings, she seemed impressed with his world and his life, but too proud to reveal it. Only sometimes did he doubt his subversion of her. These were the times when she challenged an American custom as being inferior to her own way of life, but she voiced such objections less frequently now.

What Marc did not speak of to her, biding his time, waiting until she was entirely disarmed, was his all-consuming desire for her. His instincts told him that if he moved too soon, he would repel or frighten her. The right moment was that moment when she was so in awe of him, or what he represented, that succumbing to him would enhance her pride. Awaiting that moment, through the past

331

two weeks, Marc had lived out an entire imaginary life with her that she knew nothing about. He had no time for the tedium of note-making—it would have stunned Matty to know he had made not a single note since his arrival—and he had no patience with his mother or interest in his wife. His mind was filled entirely by his seduction of Tehura.

Among the twisting nerve cords of his gray brain matter he had slept with the naked Tehura on the mats of her hut, in the grass of their grove, on the sand of the beach; he had slept with her in Papeete, in Santa Barbara, in New York; he had slept with her in this position, in that, in the other one, too; he had slept with her an hour, ten hours, one hundred hours, and she had clung to him, always transported, and he had let her cling, enjoying less her art than her begging need of him. His brain had swarmed with the erogenous parts of her stripped anatomy, and when he brought the parts together, the public parts and the private parts, she was always reclining, her face the face of love, and this first seduction was the moment he fantasied the most and doggedly worked toward in each day's reality.

Now the moment was nearing. He sat, cross-legged on the grass, shading his eyes, and impatiently waited.

"—and so, when we grow up with such freedom, we must feel as I do," she was saying. "Our life of love is simple, like everything else we do."

He dropped his hand from his eyes. "I understand everything you've said, Tehura. Only one thing puzzles me. You, and everyone here, keep referring to love as an art. You did so a few minutes ago. Yet, you admit you—I mean all of you—do not believe in preliminaries, what we in America call foreplay. You do not believe in kissing or permit a partner to pet you above the waist—"

She came off her back and around, toward him, on her side, so that he could watch her breasts become full again. "I did not say that, Marc. Of course we have what you call preliminaries. They are different than yours, that is all. In your country, women wear garments and take them off to excite the man. You do not see breasts, so when you see them uncovered, you are excited. Here we all wear the same, there is little to take off, and breasts are always exposed, so they do not excite. Here a man will show his ardor by bringing gifts—"

"Gifts?"

"Tiara flowers arranged very beautiful. Or necklaces. Or food he has hunted. If I am interested, I will meet with him. We will dance together. Do you know our dance? It excites more than your foolish custom of touching mouth to mouth. After the dance, a woman will lie down to catch her breath, and a man will stroke her hair and shoulders and thighs. With that, a woman is ready."

"And no more? No kiss, no caressing?"

She shook her head. "Marc, Marc—when will you understand? If only we could educate you."

Marc stirred. "I wish you would."

"It is for your wife. She must be taught, and you must be taught, if you will understand our way."

"I want to understand you. I want to be like you. Teach me, Tehura."

She lay still on her side, began to speak, did not speak, then averted her eyes.

The moment, thought Marc. An old maxim played through his head: silence gives consent. Now, he thought. His entire body was filled with his craving. Slowly, he changed his position, lowering himself full-length beside her, eyes on her face, as she avoided his gaze.

"Or let me teach you," he said in an undertone.

She remained silent and motionless.

His hand reached for her arm above the swelling breast. "Tehura, if I—if I touched your breasts, are you sure you know how you'd feel?"

"Yes. I would feel nothing."

"You are positive?"

"It would be the same as if you touched my elbow or toe—or put your mouth on mine—nothing."

"Let me prove you are wrong," he said with intensity.

Her eyes, meeting his, showed confusion. "What?" she asked. "What do you mean?"

"This," he said. He had clutched her arm, and fiercely, pulled himself over her. His mouth found her open, startled lips, and as he kissed her hard, the palm of his hand was at last upon one breast, moving over it.

It surprised him that she did not struggle, and he pressed his conquest, grinding his lips against her lips, dropping his hand to her grass skirt, then lower to her thigh. As his hand began to inch upward, she suddenly shoved hard against his chest, pushing him away.

"No," she said, in the tone one used to rebuke a child, and then she sat up, drawing down her skirt.

Dismayed, Marc straightened. "But, Tehura, I thought—"

"What did you think?" she said, flatly, without anger. "That your advances brought me to the time of love? No, I have told you, I am not given desire by such silly touches. I let you go on to see if I would be, but I was not. When you went further, I had to stop you."

"Why did you have to stop me? You can tell I need you, want you—"

"For you that is good. For me it is not enough. I have not yet a want of you."

"I thought you cared for me. These last days—"

"I am interested. You are a different one. You have mana. But to offer myself without the desire—no."

Words had brought him this far, and he was determined that they should win the day. He gripped her arm. "Tehura, listen to me—I've told you—in America I'm very—I—a hundred, a thousand young girls would be thrilled by my attention."

"Good for them. Good for you. I am not in America."

"Tehura, I want to prove my love. How can I convince you this is not merely a sport? How can I show my seriousness?"

She considered him shrewdly. "You have a wife. On The Three Sirens married men are tabu."

"So I have a wife. I did not know one like you existed, or I would have waited, I would not have a wife. I'll do anything. I'll treat you as well as I do her."

"Yes? How?"

"You can have whatever she has. I'll buy you expensive clothes, all the things—"

"Clothes?" She regarded him as she would a madman. "What would I do with that foolishness here?"

"Other things, then. You said your men give a girl they love all kinds of gifts—beads—I'll get you beads—anything you want." He remembered. "The diamond necklace—pendant—my wife wore. You admired it. I'll order you one just like it. I'll have it flown in. It'll cost a fortune, but I don't care. Would you like that?"

She hesitated, frowning, before replying, too lightly, "Do not bother."

His anxiety had made him frantic. "Dammit, then you name it. What can I do to impress you?"

"Nothing."

"You told me yourself—you gave your love to Courtney—all those other men. You are even thinking of taking up with that new one—whatever the hell his name is—"

"Huatoro. Yes, he is good."

"Well, what's so good about him? Who the devil is he? Why should you regard him more highly than me?"

"He is free, for one thing. He loves me—"

"So do I," he interrupted.

"You are prominent in America, but here Huatoro has more mana. He will be our first athlete in the festival. He will win the swim, and all my friends will want him. I will have him."

"That's ridiculous. You'll give yourself to a man because he wins some lousy swimming race?"

She bridled. "It is important to us," she said. "It is as important to win the race here as to make much money for the bank or own a building and big house in America."

"All right, I grant you the importance of your damn race," he said hastily. "But who says he's going to win? Hell, I probably can outswim him by a country mile. Back home, I was on the team in college—we had more candidates for that team than you have people in this entire village—and I still swim all the time. I can beat any man on our college faculty, and most of the students, too." He abhorred reducing himself to her juvenile level. "Will your uncle allow me to enter the race?"

"Everyone on the island can race. There will be maybe ten or twenty. Tom was in it a few times and always losing."

"Okay," said Marc churlishly. "Count me in. And if I beat your friend, Huatoro—and I will, you can count on that—if I beat him, what then?" He paused. "Will you treat me as you would him?"

She laughed, and jumped to her feet. "Beat him first," she said, "and then we will see."

With that, she ran through the trees and was gone, and he was left fuming over his immediate frustration and grateful only that the moment he fancied was not yet hopelessly lost.

* * *

Mary Karpowicz held her breath and prayed that no one, not Nihau beside her in the last row of the classroom, or anyone, would detect her apprehension.

The instructor, Mr. Manao, had seconds before removed his steel-rimmed spectacles, twirled them, set them low on his nose again, and announced, "The introductory phase in our study of faa hina'aro is completed. For twelve days I have discussed the evolution of mating in animals, from the lower species to the higher. Today we reach the highest order of life—the human being. As with the animals, our method will emphasize the practical rather than the theoretical. I have two volunteers in my room from the Social Aid Hut. I will bring them forth, and we shall begin."

Hitching his loincloth up the sharp side of his frame, Mr. Manao had left the room.

The students in front of her were whispering, and Mary Karpowicz forced her shoulders, involuntarily raised high around her head like a tortoise shell, to drop, and she exhaled. She wanted to turn to Nihau, who had been so friendly, and inquire what would happen next. Yet, she was afraid to betray herself. Above all, she did not want to reveal unsophistication.

She kept her eyes straight ahead. She reviewed Mr. Manao's teachings of the last days. What he had to say of animals had been, well, interesting, but somehow disappointing and unrelated to herself. There were oddities. But nothing you could not learn, if you read between the lines, from your *Reader's Digest* or biology textbooks. Certainly there had been no acquisition that would be useful in Albuquerque. Knowledge of the gestation period of the wild boar would give her no equality with Leona Brophy. She had wanted to learn about herself, about the mysteries of *it*, and filled with great expectations she had dutifully attended classes every day, fully reporting to her parents the news of each subject but this one (which she had decided not to mention). Now, what she had anticipated so long, the key to self-assurance, was about to be offered her. And she was scared and longed for the wild boar.

The whispering in front of her had ceased, and necks stretched and strained for the best view. Mr. Manao had returned, followed by the pair from the Social Aid Hut. Mary's back stiffened, and she pretended that she wore protective blinkers. The pair were uncommonly handsome. The young man, in his late twenties, was of medium height and darkly tanned. His face was wide and good-natured, his shoulders broad, and his entire naked body above the white supporter laid over with muscles like the bony plates of an armadillo's armor. The young lady, also in her twenties, was entirely of Polynesian caste, with black hair streaming to her shoulders, perfectly round cantaloupe breasts, and flaring hips that precariously held the band of her grass skirt.

Mary heard Nihau's breathing, close to her ear. "The two of them are well known to the village," Nihau said in an undertone. "He is Huatoro, one of our best athletes at every festival. He is twenty-eight. She is Poma, only twenty-two but a widow, and much loved by many men for her manner."

Mary nodded her thanks without looking at Nihau. Her eyes remained on the living exhibits.

Mr. Manao had taken the young lady named Poma by the elbow and led her to within three or four feet of the first row of seated students. Her partner, Huatoro, the athlete, had remained behind, settling on the matted floor to await his turn.

Still holding Poma's elbow, the instructor addressed the class. "We will begin with the female," he said. "While every part of the body is concerned with sexual pleasure and procreation, especially several sensitive areas, we will devote outselves in the beginning to only the genitals, externally and internally." He released her elbow, stepped back and sideways, facing her. "Please, Poma."

Watching from the last row, Mary could not believe it would happen. Her hands, locked together in the lap of her cotton summer dress, tightened, as she saw it happening. Poma had reached both hands behind her, and suddenly the grass skirt was untied and held before her like a screen. She flung it to the floor, and stood revealed in the nude, her ample figure erect, her arms loose at her sides, her eyes staring over the heads of the class. Because the grass skirt had protected her pelvic region from the sun, her skin was light from the waist to the upper thighs.

This brazen exposure overwhelmed Mary with mortification. Back home, she and her girl friends went about nude in the gym locker room and sometimes at pajama parties, with complete equanimity. Never before had Mary seen a young woman stand unclothed before mixed company. Her shame was less for Poma than for herself and her own femaleness, reflected so openly before the males of the class, especially the one beside her. What would he see the next time he looked at her?

The back of Mary's neck ached, and her hand went behind her head to massage it.

Distantly, she heard the instructor addressing the class. She realized that her hearing had registered none of his opening description, and her sight had been directed at the floor. With effort, she lifted her sight. She recorded no more than a glimpse of what was taking place: Poma, standing there, as unconcerned as an artist's model; Mr. Manao, his hand a pointer, designating and explaining *that* part of woman's anatomy. Mary felt dizzy. It was not to be believed.

Once more her eyes were averted, but her eardrums resounded at the impact of clinical words and phrases for the female organs, terms she had read but rarely heard spoken aloud. Worse, far worse, there were Mr. Manao's sentences, elucidating precisely, in excruciating detail, the reason for, the purpose of, the workings, the uses, which each part—oh, to be temporarily deaf!

Stubbornly, she tried to will herself, her hearing, into becoming impervious to the instruction. For a while, she succeeded, but the effort was too much for her, and she allowed the voice to enter. She guessed that Mr. Manao was, fortunately, almost finished with his exposition on Poma.

She could hear him droning, "In other parts of the world, this tiny organ above the main organ remains throughout the life of a female very small on the surface. I know this is unbelievable to most of you, since it makes excitation of the area most difficult. It is our practice, as the girls in the class know, to develop and elongate the surface in childhood, in order to guarantee fulfillment in adulthood. I would say that what you observe of Poma's development in this respect is typical of all our young ladies on the island. Now then, let us go further, so that everything will be clear, so that you young men will know what to expect and you young women will understand your own pleasure systems—"

Mary had kept her eyes downcast, but her ears open, through the last crude revelation. With determination, she had posed herself in an attitude of appearing undisturbed and attentive. Especially had she tried to maintain her poise during Mr. Manao's remarks about women "in other parts of the world" as compared to women on The Three Sirens. She had imagined all eyes upon her, or felt they should be upon her, for she was the one who had something "unbelievable," she was the outsider, the freak. The passage had been her Calvary. She dreaded the time when she must stand before their eyes at recess.

She looked up to observe her neighbors. All eyes were concentrated on the spectacle before them. She had the privacy to close her eyes and her ears. No one would notice. She did not dare actually close her eyes, but she again dropped her gaze to the bare back of the boy in front of her. Then, through some resource of strength unknown, she lowered the register of Mr. Manao's voice, so that his discourse was indistinct. Thus, she sat in a somnolent state.

Once, relieved to find that the instructor's voice had ceased, wondering if it was over and time for recess, she had raised her eyes over the shoulder ahead. Indeed, the nude female exhibit was no longer there, only the instructor in an attitude of waiting, and suddenly the athlete, Huatoro, strode into focus, casting aside some shred of white cloth. He turned toward her. She sucked in her breath at the sight of what she had never seen before. Against all the censors of her brain, her gaze stayed fixed. It was only when Mr. Manao pointed to Huatoro, and calmly resumed his lecture, that she ducked her head. She tried to defend herself against the running of the words, but they sped at her, the clinical male words. She wanted to rise and flee, even intended to, but did not, because she would then be the spectacle instead of what was being demonstrated.

When she heard the recess call, she blindly scrambled to her feet. She wanted to see no one, and wanted no one to see her. She was naked, and they were naked, and it was wrong in public. Her one wish was to hide.

Emerging into the glare of the outdoors, she had intended to run. She desired as much distance between her and this bawdy house as possible. The students who had preceded her, and filled the school lawn in clusters, made running impossible. Swiftly as she could, ignoring all eyes, Mary wove in and on, and hastened toward the compound.

Departing thus, she realized that Nihau would miss her. In the last two weeks it had been their unspoken agreement to meet during the two recesses. If she came out of the class ahead of him, she would wait beneath a tree, and in seconds he would inevitably appear, shyly smiling, his strong face more tentative than ever, his hands holding forth two half-shells of fruit juice. They would sit beneath the tree, frequently joined by one or another of his friends, and review what had gone on in the classroom or in the years of their lives. Today, for the first time, she would not be under the tree. What would Nihau think?

She really did not care what anyone would think. The startling ugliness of what had passed before her eyes, in the school, had suffocated all reason. She just wanted to be away from it, where she could breathe.

She came fast down the decline, out of sight of the grassy schoolyard, and running at last. Reaching the rim of the village compound, she halted, stood panting, not knowing which way to turn. If she went to their hut, her mother or father or both would be there. They would see that she was agitated. They would know she was supposed to be in school. There would be questions. She would be cajoled into describing the one class she had omitted telling them about. She wanted none of that, not right now.

"Mary!"

Hearing her name, she responded, and saw Nihau jogging down the grass toward her. When he was beside her, she saw that his sensitive face was drawn tight with concern.

"I was not far behind when we came out of the room," he said. "I could see how you left. Something is bothering you?"

"I don't want to talk now."

"I am sorry—sorry—I do not wish to disturb you—offend—"

His manner was so supplicating, that she could not bear it. "I guess it's nothing so terrible, Nihau. I just—" She looked about. "Where can we sit?"

He gestured to the left. "There, near the Sacred Hut."

They went in that direction, along the edge of the compound, without another word. After they had entered the small woods, he indicated the semicircle of the first shaded clearing.

"Is this all right?" he inquired.

"I mustn't keep you," she said. "You'll be late for the next class."

"Never mind."

They sat on the cool grass, but then Mary did not know what to say. She laced her fingers, and rocked, her clear young features pained.

"I hate to tell anyone," she said. "It makes me a child."

"What is the matter, Mary?"

"All we just saw in the class—I've never seen anything like it before."

Comprehension seemed to come to him slowly. "You mean Poma and Huatoro?"

"Yes."

"But you have seen other people unclothed. Children. Your friends. Your parents."

"That's different. This was so—so—raw."

"It must begin some way, Mary. You must learn, as we all learn."

"I don't know, I just can't explain," she said. "Maybe I've been too sheltered, and—and too romantic. Somehow, the way it was done, taking their things off in front of a mixed group, in the daytime, pointing to their—to each—I don't know. It suddenly made everything about that seem so sort of unattractive. Like it was being forced on you in the wrong way. It's like I told you about my gang—my friends—the ones I know in Albuquerque. I'm one of the outsiders in a way because—well—I don't think you should see or do certain things just because you're supposed to or have to, instead of wanting to. You should do things when you want to, at the right time. Do you understand me, Nihau? No. I'm mixed up right now. I mean, suddenly, at the wrong time you see and learn things and it sort of spoils love."

She was relieved to have said this much. She tried to see if he understood. He was quiet, staring down at his hands, examining this important emotion.

After an interval, he raised his head. "I understand what you feel," he said. "It is difficult to come from one place where things are hidden to another place where they are open, and not be confused. We are prepared for the teaching, and you are not. I have been brought up, all of us in the class, to know everything. I have always seen many women, men, all ages, unclothed. I have often seen love-making. For all of us, the seeing Poma and Huatora was not the first. They were not new to us. Manao unclothed them as in your school the instructor would pull down a chart from the wall or display a skeleton. He wanted to show exactly, as it will be for us in life, and explain exactly." He paused to consider what he would say next. "If it is new to you, I can see it must be frightening. I am sorry to think you believe it will spoil love. That is not so, Mary. What will spoil love is shame, is fear, is ignorance. Seeing what you did see, and learning what you will learn, will not spoil anything when your heart is truly in love. Then the man you are with will be like the first man you have ever seen or known. If you are wise, not afraid, you will enjoy him more and please him more, and be happy for the good beginning."

He had given her such a different view of it, that she felt comforted. In her mind, the photographs of Poma and Huatoro, unclad, and Mr. Manao's vivid descriptions of their anatomies, were diffused, retouched, less harsh. Finally, the photographs were even attractive.

Nihau seemed suspended, as if awaiting a momentous decision.

Finally, her smile was as bashful as his own. "Thank you, Nihau," she said. "You'd better get back to school."

He hesitated. "And you?"

For her, she felt a sudden wave of rightness—the mysteries were going, going, soon to be gone—and she would be grown and sensible, confident, superior to anyone in Albuquerque, and healthier. Fear and shame had vanished. It was as if she could not wait to become adult. She wanted to spurt, to be there all at once. She wanted the many days of learning to be one day, to bring her up overnight.

"Not today, Nihau," she said. "I'll just sit here and—and think. But tomorrow—yes, I'll see you in school tomorrow."

* * *

For more than one hour in the torrid sun of early afternoon, Harriet Bleaska, wearing her nurse's white Dacron, had stood in tearless mourning, watching the funeral of Uata.

Before coming to the funeral, Harriet had been tremulous about her invitation. Maud had reassured her that rites of separation, on most Polynesian islands, were simple. The rites on The Three Sirens, Maud had explained, consisted primarily of separating Uata's soul from his fleshy being and purifying it for its rise to the Valhalla of the High Spirit.

Of the American visitors, Harriet alone had been requested to attend. Somehow, she had expected several of her companions to be present, but they were not there before Uata's hut on the rise, a half-block from the infirmary. Harriet had found herself standing near twenty or more of the villagers, all of whom proved to be Uata's kin. She recognized, and acknowledged, the brief bows of Chief Paoti and his wife, Moreturi, Tehura, and several others.

The beefy old gentleman and withered woman in the foreground she assumed to be Uata's parents.

Harriet's appearance created no inquisitive ripple of attention. For this she was grateful, but still she puzzled as to why Moreturi had personally singled her out to appear. The attention of the group was directed to Uata's hut. After several minutes, a half-dozen young men, of Uata's years, came into view, and made their way with their burden through the respectful mourners. They carried a long, high wicker basket in which reposed the corpse of Uata. They had brought him directly from his cubicle in the infirmary to his dwelling. With dispatch, they deposited his remains in the center of the front room of his home. Immediately upon leaving him, and locking his door, the pallbearers efficiently set about destroying his hut. Using sharpened bamboo knives, they cut the strands holding the pandanus-leaf roof and walls, allowing the branches to fall inward. A mass of pandanus leaves and broken cane lay in a heap over the deceased and his possessions. Then it was that Paoti applied a torch, and the funeral pyre became a roaring fire. The blaze was surprisingly brief, but long afterwards spiraling columns of smoke and dust climbed toward the sky. It was presumed, Harriet guessed, that Uata's soul, burnt free and pure, had soared upwards astride the smoke columns to his final haven.

Throughout the cremation, Harriet had suffered the pangs of sorrow, yet no grief. Uata's doom had been so absolute to her, after she had examined him, that his passing two nights before gave no surprise. She had cohabited with Uata not once but three times, gloriously, before his death, and she was proud of his last joy and without self-reproach.

When the flames had died, and the embers cooled, leaving only irregular piles of ashes, Harriet wondered what was expected of her. Should she console the parents and other kin? Should she quietly leave? However, before her decision had to be made, Moreturi stood beside her. She realized that he had been passing out drinks, and he handed her a brimming shell.

"To celebrate his arrival above," said Moreturi. "You need but taste it." He began to wander away, then stopped. "I thank you, Harriet."

Perplexed, she sipped the sticky sap, and set the unfinished drink on the turf. When she straightened, she found that a line of natives, led by Uata's parents, had formed before her. Each, in turn, paid respect to her with a gravely muttered, "Thank you," and trudged away. Chief Paoti was next, followed by Hutia Wright, and then there were several more elders, and finally at least a dozen young men and women, all giving their verbal thanks to Harriet.

When this ceremony was done, Harriet observed that the mourners were departing. Quickly, she took her leave, too, going down into the village, confining herself to the strip of shade until she arrived at the infirmary.

Inside, she discovered Vaiuri rummaging among his medicines. At her entry, he leaped to his feet, his bearing grave and formal.

She extracted a handkerchief from her purse and patted her face. "Hot," she said.

"Ah, the burning and the sun," said Vaiuri. "I will fetch you water."

"No, no—I had something to drink. I'm fine. All I need is a cigarette." She took one from her purse, and Vaiuri was beside her to light it. She exhaled a billow of smoke. "Whew," she said.

"How was it?"

"Sad. Very dignified."

"Yes. Usually, there are no tears. We live. We die. Perhaps we live again."

She drew on her cigarette, and decided to ask him. "Vaiuri, do you mind if I ask you something about the ceremony?"

"Of course, please."

"After the cremation, almost everyone came up to me—to *me*— and thanked me. For what?"

Vaiuri showed his astonishment. "You do not know?"

"Haven't the faintest idea."

"You are famous on this island."

"Famous?"

Vaiuri nodded. "Yes, you have mana. You were kind to Uata in his last days of life. You were good to him. You pleased him. Everyone is in your debt."

Was he saying what she thought he was saying? "Do you mean —did Uata tell of our love-making?"

"He was proud. It was no disgrace here. He was one of those who live by the body. He was in need of only this to end his stay happily. The custom would not permit it. Only you, as an outsider, could transcend the custom, and you did. His family, those near him, hold you as a deity. Also—" He stopped suddenly. "Anyway, that is why they thanked you."

"Also what, Vaiuri? You were going to say more."

"I do not wish to offend you, though it is not something that should give offense. It is something that should give you pride."

"There needn't be any secrets, Vaiuri. We work together. Now even you know that I—I've made—I've had love with one of your patients. That's why I was invited to the funeral, wasn't it?"

"You were considered to be a kin of Uata."

"Please tell me the rest."

"From the first night, and the other nights after, Uata confessed to me, to Moreturi, to all his male visitors of his affair. He could not contain himself, he was so happy. He had known many women, many—women of passion and experience—but he said none he had ever known were your equal. He told one and all of your magnificence. He said no female possessed your ability to give pleasure. He meant not so much your skill as your warmth, your outgoing warmth. The word went to all the kin, and to all the village. You do not know it, but today you are a legend. You are regarded by all of us as the most beautiful woman, the most desirable and beautiful, on the island."

Her mind raced through time, to the high school in Cleveland, the men at Bellevue in New York, the anesthetist and Walter Zegner in San Francisco. All the men in her history had thought her desirable and beautiful in bed, but only in bed and nowhere else. Not one had penetrated beyond The Mask to know that the beauty of her love was also the beauty of her person. Yet here— her heart pounded—perhaps here, perhaps here—The Mask had dissolved forever. Still, she could trust no one, not after Zegner. She must be cautious.

"I—I don't know what to say, Vaiuri. Believe me, poor Uata, God rest his soul, he exaggerated. I'm not all that."

"You need not be modest. It is true. It is proved. You are the most desirable and the most beautiful of women to everyone here."

Unblinking, she studied the serious, artless, oddly Roman face of the practitioner. "To everyone here, Vaiuri? That's a sweeping—"

"To *everyone*," he said fiercely, and she knew that he meant it, and her heart sang.

*   *   *

Never, in all the years devoted to his study of comparative sexual behavior, had Orville Pence been more frustrated than he was this moment.

The sweat, like a bevy of transparent ants, crawled down his receding forehead, and into his eyes, so that he had to remove his shell-rimmed spectacles and wipe his eyes. His necktie, which he persisted in wearing despite Sam Karpowicz' teasing and Marc's entreaties that he discard it, clamped his collar to his wet neck and made breathing laborious.

At times like this, he wished that he had it all to do over again. Instead of the matrimonial bliss that had been within his grasp— damn Crystal, damn Dora, and damn Beverly whateverhernamewasnow—he had gone on this dreadful trip, and now he sat miserably on the floor of the front room of his hut surrounded by a semicircle of stone-faced, idiot semiprimitives who would not cooperate.

There were six of them, three men, three women, between twenty and fifty years of age. They had volunteered to present themselves for Orville's projective tests. The initial test, which he had invented and developed and experimented with successfully, was his own beloved P.P.R.I.—Pence Pictorial Response Inquiry— and for the first time, it seemed inadequate.

Orville was proud of his P.P.R.I., and he hoped to write a remarkable paper on its application to a remote society, such as the one on the Sirens, a society highly preoccupied with sex. He did not deny, even in his conference last night with Rachel DeJong and Maud Hayden, that his P.P.R.I. was derivative.

"Of course, it grew out of my work with the Thematic Apperception Test, the Szondi Test, the Rosenzwig Picture Frustration Test," he had admitted freely to Maud. "But each of them had shortcomings, at least for me. Consider the Thematic Apperception Test. I take the twenty pictures—human beings in different provocative action situations—and I ask these natives to tell me what they see. The situations are too strange for them to comment upon. I show them a man about to commit a murder with a dagger, and I ask them what has happened and will happen. When I showed it in the islands off Alaska, it was too foreign to bring response. The situation was incomprehensible. So how could I expect any revelation of their attitudes and conflicts? I showed the Szondi, those forty-eight photos of abnormal human types, and it was just as fruitless. The subjects don't identify. They don't know the types. Or those cartoons in the Rosenzwig—have you seen them, Maud?—always presenting two persons, one annoying the other in some way, and the subject is asked to tell what the party of the second part, the one being annoyed, would do or say. Primitive subjects don't identify. So that's why I conceived the Pence Pictorial Response Inquiry. There was a lot of trial and error, but I finally narrowed it down to thirty mounted photographs of classical and modern-day paintings or sculpture showing love-making. Now everyone knows what *that* is all about in any language or society. You stimulate real response, whether your subject is permissive or prudish. You show those pictures, and before he knows it, the subject is projecting all his wishes and anxieties, spilling out his attitudes toward himself and others. It should work perfectly here. They'll *understand*."

After conceding to Rachel DeJong sole dominion over Dr. Hermann R. Rorschach's Swiss inkblots, all intelligence quotient tests, and the use of word association, Orville Pence had left the meeting of the night before as sole proprietor of his own P.P.R.I., with the Thematic Apperception Test to be held in reserve, if there was time for its use.

With considerable anticipation, Orville had awaited the arrival of his volunteers. After a short, lucid briefing, he had, minutes before, unveiled his invention. From the stack of pictures, lying face down beside him, he had removed the topmost, and offered it to the curious scrutiny of his six subjects.

Snapping on his portable tape recorder, he had said to his subjects, who were passing around the reproduction without comment, "That is a picture of one of many wall frescoes, in the Casa del Ristorante, in Pompeii, an ancient city of the country of Italy. These famous frescoes show all methods of sexual mating. The one you see has the nude woman on her knees on the bed, with the man behind—"

The picture had returned to him.

"Well," he had asked, "how do you feel about it?"

He had waited for the expected babble of comment, but not one of the six spoke or moved.

"Let's take you each in turn," he had said, to help them overcome what was undoubtedly nervousness. He pointed to the first person in the semicircle, a middle-aged native woman. "What comes to your mind?"

He had held up the reproduction of the fresco.

"Very beautiful," she had said.

Orville had nodded to the second, an older man. "And you?"

"Good," he had said, "much good."

"And you?"

"Beautiful."

"And—?"

"Beautiful."

Orville had halted, bewildered. "Have you no more to say? Aren't you surprised? Aren't you shocked? Aren't you stimulated?"

Orville had waited. The members of the group had looked at one another and shrugged, until on their behalf, the first middle-aged woman had spoken.

"It is ordinary," she had said.

"You mean it is familiar to all of you?" Orville had demanded.

"Familiar," she had said, and all the heads had bobbed.

Nonplused, Orville had tried to go on. Unless he could extract some real reaction, he could not examine their stimulus-response pattern. "Does any one of you want to discuss this picture? What would you guess happened before this moment, during it, and can you imagine what will happen next?"

The semicircle had consulted silently, with arched eyebrows and lifted shoulders, as if in agreement that their visitor was a lunatic. One had raised his hand. He was a thin young man of twenty. "I will discuss," he had announced. "He wants the love, she wants the love, they make the love in the picture. Soon, he is happy, she is happy, they rest. Then they love again if they do not sleep. They are strong. They love many times, I think."

"Yes, yes," Orville had said impatiently. "But isn't there anything else you feel like saying? Does anything about this make you think of yourselves—or bother you—or make you hope—I mean—"

"There is nothing to think," the young man had said, stolidly. "It is too common. We all do. We all enjoy. Nothing more to say."

Orville had glanced inquiringly at the other five. Their heads curtsied in unison, agreeing with their neighbor.

Crushed, Orville had held the impotent Pompeii fresco in his lap, staring down at it. The picture evoked an immediate response in *him*. For one thing, he had never employed the averse position with a female, and the possibility made him wonder. For another, he had never engaged in any position but one, and that with no more females than a few, which made him remorseful. For another, he had never enjoyed the pleasure so evident in the picture, which made him sad. For another, his mind went to Beverly Moore, which made him lonely.

These thoughts, overlaid on the failure of his invincible P.P.R.I. to affect his six subjects, brought him to this moment of utter frustration.

Grimly, he determined to persist, until his subjects capitulated. Tossing the Pompeii fresco aside, he yanked the next picture from the pile. It was the Jean François Millet called *Lovers*. It depicted in modern times exactly what the Pompeii fresco had depicted in ancient times. Orville had always regarded the Millet as a find because it startled his friends. Most knew Millet only for the traditional *Angelus*, and could not believe that the same artist had concerned himself with blatant sexuality. Orville passed the reproduction of the painting around. Once again, the stone faces were impassive, and once again, when asked for their reaction, they had nothing to say except that the performance was familiar.

The third and fourth pictures were Rembrandt's *The Bed* and Picasso's *Embrace*, both realistically revealing men and women in familiar face to face copulation. To these, the reactions were those of utter boredom and the six subjects were mute. In desperation, Orville reached deep into his pile to extract the reproduction of Pascin's *The Girl Friends*. The response to the fleshly painting of two nude French lesbians was immediate, loud, unanimous. The six natives laughed with undisguised delight. At once, Orville was hopeful.

"What's so funny?" Orville wanted to know.

The thin young man of twenty spoke. "We laugh because we all say—what a waste of time!"

"Is this not done here?"

"Never."

"How do you feel about it?"

"We feel nothing except the waste."

Orville pushed on, trying to provoke something more. He got nothing more. Pascin had drawn a blank.

With mounting dejection, Orville passed out the sixteenth-century print by Giulio Romano. This represented an unclothed couple with the female in ascendancy. For the first time, the group showed interest. They huddled over the print, discussing it in Polynesian.

Orville's spirits lifted. "Is that familiar to you?"

The middle-aged woman at the end nodded. "Familiar."

"Is it popular on the Sirens?"

"Yes."

"Most interesting," said Orville. "You see, it is practiced less in my homeland, among my people, than—"

"Your people practice it often," said the middle-aged woman. She had made a flat statement.

"Not exactly," said Orville. "According to statistics I have—"

"Uata says your women wonderful this way."

"Who is Uata?"

"The one who died."

"Ah, yes," said Orville. "I'm sorry about him. But with all due respect, he would not have known how we—"

The thin young man interrupted. "He knows. He has loved one of yours."

Orville hesitated. His ears had deceived him. The constant problem of communication. "How could Uata have known one of our people?"

"You are here among us."

"You mean—one of *us*—our women?"

"Of course."

Orville tried to contain himself. He must not over-react, lest he frighten them into conspiratorial silence. Careful, careful, he told himself. He must handle it casually.

"Interesting, interesting," he began. "You are being helpful. You can be more so. I'm curious to know the details of Uata and the member of our team—"

In five minutes he had every detail, every horrifying detail, and in six minutes he had dismissed them, vaguely requesting a future meeting, when he would resume with the Thematic Apperception Test.

After his hut was emptied, Orville remained shaken, actually found himself trembling, at the perfidy, the unpatriotic and shameful behavior of their weakest link. There was only one thing to do, to reveal the scandal to Dr. Maud Hayden and have the offender drummed from the island.

Bursting out of his dwelling, Orville went on a gallop past the residence of their Hester Prynne, past the residence of Marc Hayden, and, too distraught to knock, pushed his way unannounced into Maud Hayden's office.

She was at her desk, writing, and he was before her, face abashed and necktie awry.

"Orville, what is it? You look terribly upset."

"I am, I am," he said, trying to control his breathing. "Maud, I hate to be the one to bring this to you—it is too terrible—"

Maud had laid her pen down. "Please, Orville, what is it?"

"Through one of my tests, I just learned from the natives that one of your team, one of the women, has been—has been—has—" He could not bring the word out.

"Fornicating?" said Maud gently. "Yes. I assume you are referring to Harriet Bleaska."

"You *know?*"

"Of course, Orville. I've known all along. It's my business to know. Anyway, these things get around very fast in this kind of confined society."

Orville advanced, crouching lower, until his posture was that of an outraged Quasimodo, searching Maud's face. "You sound like you approve of this degrading—"

"I don't disapprove," said Maud firmly. "I'm neither Harriet's mother nor her guardian. And she is well past her twenty-first birthday."

"Maud, where's your sense of propriety? This can work against all of us, lower us in their eyes. Besides—"

"Quite the contrary, Orville. Harriet's performance was so superior, in an area where sexual prowess is admired, that she is regarded as royalty, and so are we. She will receive more cooperation, and so will we. In short, Orville, in their eyes we are no longer a strange company of prudes."

Orville had straightened at this unexpected defense of a bawd, and he almost jigged with anger. "No, no, Maud, you're all wrong —you're too scientific—too objective—you can't see how this looks. For all our sakes, you've got to intervene, restrain this nurse from stooping so low— Send her back, that's what you should do, send her back. Will you speak to her?"

"No."

"You won't?"

"No."

"All right, then, all right," he sputtered. "If you won't, I will— for her own sake."

With outraged dignity, he pulled his tie knot down from where it had worked up onto his shoulder, and stalked out.

Maud sighed audibly. She had thought the Reverend Davidson long dead of a self-inflicted razor wound on the beach of Pago-Pago. She was mistaken. She wondered what Orville would do, if anything. She promised herself to keep her eye on him. One missionary, Adley used to say, can destroy in a single minute the work of ten anthropologists in ten years. Satisfied that Adley was on her side in this, she picked up her pen and resumed her notes.

* * *

Rachel DeJong had not known what to expect when her door opened, ten minutes before, to admit Atetou, wife of Moreturi, to her primitive consultation room.

It was surprising that, in a village so small, where the female population circulated in a limited area, she had never set eyes upon Moreturi's wife during a period when she had seen so much and met so many. She had not realized this when the appointment had been made. Only when she had awaited Atetou, and tried to remember something of her, did Rachel DeJong become aware of the omission. She pondered, then, as to whether the fact that she had not set eyes upon Moreturi's wife had been an accident or a deliberate avoidance, either on Atetou's part or on her own.

Now, serving cold sweetened tea in tin cups that the Karpowiczes had brought along, Rachel was able to fix upon a certain knowledge or expectation that she had of Moreturi's wife. While she had not met her before in person, she had met her daily in Moreturi's highly colored free associations. She had expected— what? Certainly, an older woman and a woman less physically attractive. She had expected a shrew and a witch, a canker sore festering on Moreturi's extrovert, lusty person. She had expected Xantippe. An old school memorization from *Taming of the Shrew* floated through her mind: "Be she as foul as was Florentius' love,/ As old as Sibyl, and as curst and shrewd/ As Socrates' Xantippe, or a worse,/ She moves me not."

Yet, here, on first meeting, there was none of this evident, although Rachel suspected there must be some of it beneath. From their opening handshake, Atetou had been composed and an equal. She had come to this appointment with deep reluctance—Moreturi had made that clear—but her presence did not betray this. Rachel guessed that she could not be more than thirty: her diminutive features were smooth, too smooth; her neck was young; her small breasts were high and rigid. She had a disconcerting habit of looking past one, and you were not sure that she was really addressing you or listening to you. Her voice was hushed, so that it was necessary to lean forward to catch what she was saying, thus putting you to a strain and at a disadvantage.

"Here you are," said Rachel, setting the cold tea in front of her. "I hope you find it refreshing. Have you ever had tea before?"

"Several times. On occasions when Captain Rasmussen brought it in."

Atetou took up the tin cup and drank impassively. Rachel settled on the matting across from her, and drank her own tea. Rachel felt the chill of her visitor's hostility. Moreturi had confessed telling his wife of the details of his psychoanalysis. Atetou would naturally resent the meddling by an outsider, would put the outsider in a league with her husband against herself. Atetou was here merely to prove that she was not the misfit her husband claimed her to be to this outsider.

If there was to be an honest exchange between them, Rachel knew the initiative must come from herself. Atetou would initiate nothing, and it was understandable. To make her speak up at all, Rachel would have to taunt her with Moreturi's disapproval of his domestic state. Rachel deplored the tactic, but it would be necessary. There could be no hope of putting Atetou on the couch, so to speak, of casting her in the role of patient. Atetou would not permit it for a second. She was here as one lady to another, as a maligned neighbor prepared to straighten out one who had been misinformed. She was here for tea and careful talk.

For Rachel, in the last days, Moreturi had proved easier as an analysand. Once the barrier between them had dropped, he had cooperated within his limitations. He treated the sessions as a lark. Stretched out on his back, hands behind his head, he chided his "Miss Doctor," and spoke wildly and freely. He enjoyed discomfiting Rachel with his amorous experiences. He liked to report his dreams elaborately. He took pleasure in trying to shock. Rachel saw through him at once and steadily. He was not seriously interested in his unconscious motivations. When his domestic crisis boiled over, there would always be the traditional Hierarchy to look after him. His sole interest, his game, Rachel perceived, was to reduce his analyst to female. He was not unintelligent, but he was not interested in intelligence. To investigate his own mind, to ride introspection into the unexplored jungle of his brain, lured him not at all. His concern, like that of his late friend Uata, was in physical sensation. The compleat hedonist: food, drink, sport, dance, copulation. For a free soul, a born bachelor, the responsibility of a wife was a burden. He did not necessarily want to divorce himself of Atetou, but rather of the unnatural prison of matrimony.

Perhaps, Rachel had thought in this past week, Atetou is not so frigid as Moreturi had made out. Perhaps, in the eyes of one like Moreturi, any wife would be frigid. Unconsciously, Rachel supposed, she was always defending Atetou, because this was a defense of her sex. Men like Moreturi were a threat to the dependence women must have upon monogamy. At the same time, although Rachel did not examine this ambivalence in herself too deeply, she was secretly with Moreturi against his wife. Somehow, Atetou stood between Rachel and her patient. There was no direct line between analyst and analysand, because Atetou made it a triangle. Rachel squirmed under the restriction of guilt, whenever caught up in Moreturi's crazy babble, and the guilt that held back further communication was the warden eye of Atetou.

But Rachel knew that she was deceiving herself. Atetou did not stand between Moreturi and herself at all. The major inhibition was Rachel's insistence upon continuing to communicate with Moreturi through psychoanalysis. With each day, it was proving more impossible. She would speak to him of a young female's penis envy or a young male's castration fear, and Moreturi would roar with laughter. She would speak to him of Oedipal guilts and displacement of unacceptable desires, and Moreturi would ridicule her until she was brought to the verge of tears.

Gradually, Rachel was coming to this conclusion: a system of mental help, originated before the turn of the century in sophisticated Vienna by a brilliant Jew with a beard, did not work well, if it worked at all, in a civilization not oriented to the tensions of the West. It was arduous for Rachel to relate her knowledge of neurotics and psychopaths who developed out of a highly literate, clothed, repressed, material, competitive society to a relatively indolent, unpersevering, hedonistic, isolated semi-Polynesian society, where so many values were reversed. Yes, Rachel could see that if Freud, Jung, Adler had taken over the Hierarchy on The Three Sirens, they would have been driven by despair into analyzing one another.

But then, Rachel saw, this was a second subterfuge. It was not Atetou and it was not Western psychoanalysis that were the obstacles between her and a success with Moreturi. It was, finally, herself. Her patient's assurance, lack of inhibition, maleness, these frightened her, and shackled her. She would pursue no relevant point with him, pursue him down no path, because he was strong and she was weak, and she dared not let him know it. Superior knowledge was fine. It gave you control in an air-conditioned office in Beverly Hills. It gave you dominance over a person who was ill in the judgment of an orderly society. On the other hand, it gave you no strength in the primitive brush when it was your only armament. Coming upon a large animal, a free roaming animal that survived by instinct and appetite, you did not curb him by applying the wisdom of the Id, the Ego, and the Superego. What you did was to avoid close contact. You ran like hell.

Now, here was the mate of the King of the Beasts before her. The mate represented one-half of a real problem that Rachel had undertaken to resolve. Something must be done. Rachel saw that her visitor had put down the cup and was waiting, the fingers of one hand fidgeting across the waistband of her grass skirt. Rachel finished her own cup, set it aside, and, with effort, assumed her professional mien.

"I repeat again, Atetou, how pleased I am that you have come here," said Rachel. "Do you understand anything of my work?"

"My husband and mother-in-law have told me."

"Good. Then you appreciate I want to help you and your husband with your problem."

"I have no problem."

Rachel had predicted that she would be unyielding, and Rachel was not surprised. "Be that as it may, your husband appealed to the Hierarchy for a divorce on the grounds that you were having marital troubles. The matter was turned over to me. I am merely trying to serve in the place of the Hierarchy."

"I have no problem," she repeated. "He has the problem. He made the appeal."

"That is true," Rachel conceded, recalling that Moreturi had made a similar denial and accusation in his first visit. "Nevertheless, if one member of a marriage is unhappy, that would indicate the other member may be, too." Then she added, "In certain cases, anyway."

"I did not say I was happy. I could be happy. The problem is his."

"Well, would you be willing to let things go on as they are between you two?"

"I do not know . . . It is possible."

Rachel could not allow this to continue. She would have to bring Atetou into the open. "You know I have been seeing your husband daily, do you not?"

"Yes."

"You know he speaks of his own life and his life with you?"

"Yes."

"Do you know of what he speaks?"

"Yes."

"Atetou, I have his side of it. To be fair to both of you, I want your side. When he tells me, day after day, you are not friendly, not sociable, not performing as a wife, I must believe that he should have a divorce—that is, if I listen only to him. But it would not be right to listen only to him. I must listen to you. Truth has two voices."

For the first time, features on Atetou's face shifted. Her composure was disintegrating. "He lies," she said.

"Are you sure? How does he lie?"

"He says I do not perform as a wife. I perform as well as any wife in the village. When he says I am not a friendly wife, a sociable wife, a wife at all, he means one thing. He has no more sense than a child. He does not know a wife means not one thing but many things. I cook for him. I make his home clean. I am interested in him. I take care of him. All this is meaningless to him. Only one thing matters."

Rachel waited for her to say more, but she did not. "You said only one thing matters. What is that?"

"Body love. That means wife, nothing else."

"Do you object to body love—sexual intercourse, we call it— do you resist it?"

Atetou's face showed indignation for the first time. "Object, I do not. Resist, I must. Is there no more to marriage than this? Three, four times a week, I am ready, I have the feeling, I join. But morning to night, every day, every day? It is a madness. One wife cannot satisfy this. A hundred wives cannot. That is not marriage."

A thrill of incredulity shot through Rachel, followed by bewilderment over the fact that Atetou's version differed so much from her husband's version. "What you are saying is not what Moreturi has told me," said Rachel.

"He tells you what is not true."

"He tells me you are an excellent wife in all ways except what to him is the most important. He says you are cold, and turn him away always. He says he demands only what is normal here, but you will not sleep with him more than once or twice a month."

"That is a lie."

"He speaks of constantly calling upon the Social Aid Hut to satisfy him. Does he?"

"Of course. What one woman can satisfy him?"

"Let me ask something else, Atetou. When you do sleep with him, are you pleased?"

"Sometimes, I am pleased."

"Most of the time you are not."

"There is too much pain in his love."

"Can you clarify that?"

"He is not himself when he loves. He is crazy. He gives hurt. We are not made the same and he gives hurt."

"Was it always this way?"

"Maybe yes, but I did not care. Pleasure overcomes the pain. Now it is worse, no pleasure, only pain. He wants to be rid of me."

"Why not be rid of him? Why endure this?"

"He is my husband."

A thought came to Rachel. "And he is the Chief's son."

Atetou's reaction was immediate. Her expression was irate. "Why do you say that? What is the meaning?"

"I'm trying to find out if there might be other motives you don't understand that influence—"

"Do not speak to me that way!" She had sprung to her feet, infuriated, and stood over Rachel. "You are with him as one. I try all the time to have patience with you. Maybe you are fair. But he has won you, like all the women. You think he does not lie. You think I lie. You think I am cold. You think I do not please. You think I try to hold him only for the mana. You want him to divorce me."

Rachel came quickly to her feet. "Atetou, no, why would I want to do that? Be reasonable—"

"I am reasonable. I see you plain. You want him to divorce so he will be free for you. That is the truth. You think of you and not of me, and you are against me."

"Oh, Atetou, no—no—"

"I see your face and I know the truth. Do what you will but do not bother me."

Hastily, Rachel followed her to the door, took her arm to restrain her. Atetou shook free. She opened the door, and hurried away.

Rachel intended to call after her, but she did not. Closing the door, she remembered that it had been this way at the Hierarchy. She had meant to reject Moreturi's name, and had not. Then she knew why, and she shivered. Through some gift of instinct, Atetou had caught a glimpse of Rachel's subconscious, and had seen what Rachel had refused to see—that Rachel was competing with her for her husband—that Rachel was trying to help herself but neither of them.

Rachel remained beside the door, ill with self-loathing.

Long minutes later, when her emotions had been flogged back into place, and reason reigned, she was able to make her decision. She must wipe her hands of those two, forever. She would go to Hutia and the other women and men of the Hierarchy and turn the case back to them.

As a field investigator, she would be a failure. As a woman, she would not be a fool.

* * *

For more than a half-hour, in the waning afternoon, Tom Courtney had been taking Maud and Claire on a tour of the communal
nursery.

The nursery consisted of four rooms—actually, one airy hall
seventy feet in length divided by three partitions—and these were
sparsely furnished except for rods of bamboo, blocks of wood,
carved representations in miniature of adults and of canoes, cheap
toys Rasmussen had brought in from Tahiti, refreshment bowls of
fruit, all intended to occupy the youngsters.

Several children between the ages of two and seven bounced in
and out of the rooms, active and noisy, supervised by two young
women (mothers who volunteered to serve a week at a time). According to Courtney, attendance was not compulsory. Youngsters
were deposited here or came here as they desired it or as their
mothers wished it. There was no rigid program. Sometimes the
youngsters undertook a project or sang or danced in a group, with
instruction, but for the most they did as they pleased. Juvenile
anarchy reigned.

Courtney had explained that originally old Daniel Wright hoped
to introduce a radical system, rooted in Plato, whereby the newly
born were taken from their parents and raised with other newly
born. Since identities would be merged, parents would be required
to love all children as their own. However, this dream broke down
when it came up against the Sirens' strict incest tabu. Wright's plan,
if put in effect, might have been responsible for brother and sister
marrying one another, in later years, without knowing their blood
relationship. The very thought was abhorrent to the Polynesians.
Courtney had quoted Briffault as saying that it was not a moral
sense that made incest unacceptable to the natives. Rather, the tabu
existed for ancient mystical reasons, and because, subconsciously,
mothers loved their sons and wanted to stave off the competition
of their daughters.

In the end, old Daniel Wright had given the Polynesians their
way, and had never been sorry, since their system attained his own
ideal by less drastic means. Wright's only major contribution to the
raising of children on the Sirens had been the communal nursery,
which had survived to the present day.

While the three of them observed the children playing in the last
of the rooms, Maud and Courtney discussed the merits of the
Spock and Gesell disciplines as compared to those on the Sirens.

Claire, half listening to the two, half observing the recreational activity in the room, had retreated into herself, her mind reviving recent resentments against Marc for keeping her childless.

She became aware of Courtney, so gangling, moving toward the door. "Let's have a look outside," he was saying. "The kids usually play in here when it's too hot outside, or during rainy spells. Most of the time they're out in the back, romping around like little savages."

Claire and Maud followed him through the open door into the unkempt grassy court. Neither fence nor wall guarded the area. Instead, the three open sides were bounded in a haphazard pattern by trees and bushes. Except for a few strays skipping and throwing, most of the children outside were gathered about the first rising of what would soon be their own playhouse, each contributing to the construction of the dwarfed hut of bamboo stalks and leaves. Claire watched for a while, then found herself alone. Courtney had brought Maud to the wide shaded arc beneath the leafy umbrella of an ancient tree. Maud settled to the turf slowly, like a dirigible. Courtney flopped down beside her. In a moment, Claire had joined them on the turf, stretching luxuriously.

Claire knew that Courtney was scrutinizing her, not the children, but she pretended that she did not notice. Yet, conscious of him, she tried to arrange herself as gracefully as possible, like Canova's reclining Paulina Bonaparte in the Villa Borghese. Continuing contact with the self-exiled Chicago attorney had not dulled Claire's interest in him. Despite his one revelation to her of his past, twelve days earlier, he still remained an enigma in Claire's eyes. Not once since that time had he spoken at such length about himself. Occasionally, like a player at the end of a stud poker game, he would turn up information one card at a time, exasperatingly, so that she would receive a single autobiographical fact, the clue to only a small insight into him. He had settled into the role of combination guide and mentor, and when his audience came too close, he held its members off with banter or cynicism.

Suddenly, she decided to let him know that she knew she was being observed. She met his eyes frankly, without a smile. But he smiled. "I was just watching you," he said. He spoke past Maud, as if Maud were not there, which in a sense she was not, for she was concentrating on the play of the youngsters. "You have the same kind of curling-cat grace as the little girls out here," he said.

Claire was disappointed. She had tried to project Canova and represented only Marie Laurencin. "It's the air here," she said, "playful air, good for little girls." She glanced at the youngsters building their hut, and then back at Courtney. "Do you like children, Tom?"

"Generally, yes." Then he added, "My own, more than others."

She was surprised. "Your own? I didn't know—"

"I'm making believe," he said. "I mean, I'd like my own, lots of them, lots of little me's around."

"I see," she said, and she laughed.

He had become solemn. "Of course, ideally, if I had my own, I'd hope to have them brought up in an atmosphere like this."

Maud had become attentive to the last. "That might not work, unless they stayed on here," Maud said. "Otherwise, they might be incapable of coping with the outside world. Child-rearing on the Sirens seems perfect only when compared to the kind of stresses we put on our children back home. But who can really say that the kind of stresses we put on our young are wrong—I mean, in terms of what they have to contend with later in our rather difficult American society."

"True," Courtney agreed.

Claire was still not satisfied that she understood why child-rearing on The Three Sirens might be superior to child-rearing in Los Angeles or Chicago. "Tom, what's so especially good about this atmosphere for children? I can see how the adults here differ from us, but mere children? There they are—playing just as they do in California."

"Yes, but it is not the same," Courtney said. "The pressures are fewer here; though, of course, the later adult demands are fewer, too. These youngsters enjoy extremely carefree lives. Up to the age of six or seven, they run around naked. There are hardly any restrictions, and consequently hardly any fears. They have no concern about sex. Almost nothing is concealed, as you both know. They don't have to worry about crossing a street or dirtying the house. There are no streets, no vehicles, and there is nothing in their huts to soil. They don't have to worry about how to fill their time—I mean, their parents don't have to hustle around carting them to or from friends or camps or regulated play. They are simply turned loose. Alone, or with others, they roam. They can't get lost. They are independent. By trial and error, or imitation, they learn to build, hunt, fish, plant. They can't starve. If they are hungry, they pick fruit or vegetables. If they are hot, they wade in a stream. If they are cold, anyone will give them shelter, for they are children of the entire community."

"I'm beginning to see your point," Claire said. "Complete independence."

"Almost complete independence," Courtney said. "Of course, the key to the whole thing is the foundation of security these kids possess, from the word go. These children know they are loved. A father or mother here would cut off his or her hands before striking a child. More important, children don't have two parents—they have two birth parents—parents who conceived them—but they have a great array of mothers and fathers, all aunts are mothers, and uncles are fathers, so each child has a large kin group doting over him. He gets a feeling of family safety and solidarity. He always has someone to show him affection, give him advice, support or teach him, always someone to confide in. These children have no chance to be lonely or afraid, and yet they do not sacrifice individuality or privacy. I was discussing it with Dr. DeJong, and she agrees —Sigmund Freud would have become an idler here. How could a son on The Three Sirens suffer the guilt of an Oedipus complex when he has, in effect, ten mothers and seven fathers? You'd have to look a long time among these children to find a tantrum, a wet bed, a stutterer . . . I'm sure the Sirens has its weaknesses. I'm not wearing Chamber of Commerce blinders. But I'm convinced that they do two things better on the Sirens than we do in the United States. They manage their marriages better. They raise their children better. Of course, I'm not an expert. That's simply my personal legal opinion." He had turned from Claire to Maud Hayden. "You are the expert, Dr. Hayden. Do you concur or disagree?"

Maud's face, a sunburned pumpkin, was thoughtful, as her thick fingers absently counted the beads of the Lolos necklace draped from her neck. "I hate to make a value judgment about anything like this," she said, more to herself than to Courtney or Claire. "However, from what I have seen of the Sirens, already learned here, and what I know of Polynesia in general, I'm inclined to agree with you, at least about child-raising." She appeared to weigh what she would say next, and then went on. "I believe that in Polynesian societies, youngsters pass from childhood into adulthood without the confusion our youngsters go through in America. Certainly, adolescence is a period of less strife here than at home. It isn't hedged around with all sorts of sexual frustrations, other shames and fears, and the whole terrible business of finding one's place in the adult world. Somehow, here, as on other South Sea islands, the transition to adulthood is gradual and happy, which is often not true in the West. There are many reasons, of course, but—well, I don't think this is the time to go into all that—"

"Please," said Claire. "What are the reasons?"

"All right. To be as honest as possible, I think children are more desired in this kind of society than in our own. Here it is all very simple. No one worries about the economics that unnaturally enforce birth control. There is no fear of a population explosion. They want children because children bring pleasure, not problems. And because they lack our scientific advances, the infant mortality rate is higher, and so each child that survives is held more precious. In our American society, while there are certain satisfactions in parenthood, there are not enough. Parenthood is a negative value, in that every new child means a financial sacrifice. So, while children are so desirable here, they are somewhat less so in the West, and these attitudes transmit to the growing youngster and create the differences in their personalities. But Mr. Courtney cited the basic strength behind child-rearing in Polynesia. It is the kin system, the clan, the so-called extended family. That absolutely beats anything we have."

"We have loyal families at home, too," insisted Claire. "Most American children are born into American families."

"Not the same as here," said Maud. "Our families are small: mother, father, a sibling or two. Relatives are usually not part of the basic families. In fact, there is much hostility and brawling, and little deep love, in our loose relationships with relatives. Otherwise, why all the in-law jokes at home? Present company excepted, in-laws are outlawed in our society. On the Sirens, as in most of Polynesia, the widespread, extended family is the basic family. Marriages may not always be permanent here—we know they are not —but the big families are permanent. An infant is born into an immovable institution, a secure haven. If the parents die, or if they divorce, it does not affect the child, for he is still secure with a family. If the same thing happens to an American or European child— the parents dying, let us say—what is he left with? An insurance policy. Do you think an insurance policy represents real security?

If you think so, try to seek advice from a double-indemnity clause, try to get love from an annuity provision."

"I'd never thought of it that way," said Claire.

"Well, it is so," said Maud. "No premiums on earth can buy the benefits of the kinship system. Mr. Courtney mentioned many mothers and fathers, and sisters and brothers, but a family here also consists of grandparents, uncles, aunts, cousins, and these are all in the child's real family, not merely distant relations. These people are all responsible for the child. They owe him certain rights and support, and he, in turn, owes them the same. No child is ever orphaned here, any more than an aged person is neglected. The Sirens is a patrilineal society, and if the parents die, the child goes physically to his father's family, but not as an adopted orphan, for they were always his blood family. This is the marvel of these societies —no one, not child, not adult, is ever *alone*, unless he chooses to be."

Courtney hunched forward. "And as for marriage here as opposed to the West? Are you less sure of that?"

"I want to learn more," said Maud, "before stating that marriage here is more admirable than at home. I suspect it is in certain areas. I want more information before I make up my mind. Certainly, I think the absence of sexual restraint tends to eliminate aggression and hostility, so prevalent at home. Certainly, there is more of a communal feeling in this place—as in the Israeli kibbutz. Everyone knows he won't go hungry or without shelter or without care—and the rewards of competition are limited—so that takes considerable stress off marriages. Too, I have reason to believe that they solve their marital problems here much better than at home. There is simply not as much confusion in the relationship. In the American marriage, it is not clear what a man should do and what a woman should do. On the Sirens, there's no misunderstanding about this. The man is the head of the family. He makes the decisions. His wife defers to him in all social situations. Her identity and power exist in the home. She knows her place. He knows his. Much easier all around."

Maud's discourse had somehow drained and weakened Claire. She had hung on each succeeding sentence as if it were a life raft. She wanted to be saved, to grasp something that would rescue Marc and herself, and she found it had slipped away. Yet she was impelled to speak of the thought that had surfaced first.

"Maud, what would happen in a marriage here if—if the wife wanted children and the husband didn't, or vice versa?"

"I'm afraid you are imposing an alien Western problem on a culture where such a problem does not exist," said Maud. She turned to Courtney. "Correct me if I'm wrong."

"You're right," said Courtney. He looked at Claire. "What your mother-in-law said of marriage and children in Polynesia applies to this island. Children are desired by all. It would be unthinkable that one mate would want a child and the other not. If it happened —why, I suppose the Marriage Hierarchy would intervene. The pair would be divorced promptly, and the one who wanted children would have no trouble finding someone of a like mind."

Claire felt stifled and unhappy. An old California thought darted at her, posed a question: if you are married to a child, how can you have one? And then a sub-question: how can a child properly mate to give you a child, and create his own rival? Damn men, she thought, all child-men of America.

Maud and Courtney were speaking to one another, but Claire did not hear them. She saw them rise, to get a closer view of the native children at their construction play. She did not follow.

She hoisted herself to an elbow, body still outstretched, reflecting on men, on Marc as a man. How incredible, she thought, that American men, men like Marc, think of themselves as manly. She wanted to cry out to them all, for they all had the face of Marc. She wanted to cry out: You men, you read your sport pages and hit a golf ball a mile and swear in the locker room or over the poker table and belt your whiskey without falling down and talk about girls you've laid and would like to lay, you great big men, you gamble and booze and kid waitresses and drive seventy miles an hour, and you think that's masculine and that makes you a man. You fools, she thought, you child fools to think those false trappings are manhood and virility. What has real manliness got to do with strength or speed or stag habits? Do you want to know what manliness is, what real virility is—to know what it is with a mature woman, a woman who is your wife? Manliness is the giving of love as well as the taking of it, manliness is the offering of respect and the taking of responsibility, manliness is kindness, thoughtfulness, affection, friendship, reciprocated passion. Will you listen, all of you? Kindness needs no boudoir conquests. Thoughtfulness does not have hair on its chest. Friendship is not muscular. Passion requires no bawdy words. Virility is not a penis or a cigarette or a bottle of booze or a bluff at table stakes. Oh, all of you, when will you learn? Marc, oh Marc, when will you not be afraid to be truly tender and a man and to give me our child?

Claire's eyes had moistened, but her tears were inside. She must banish these inner soliloquies before she made a scene. She must stop thinking. How does anyone stop thinking? For one thing, you move, you don't stand still. Especially when it is the day of your second wedding anniversary.

She came to her feet like an old person trying in vain to show the last strengths of youth, and she walked hastily to Maud and Courtney. She flourished her wrist watch. "It's nearly five," she said. "The cook they're sending will be over soon. I'd better be on hand."

"The cook?" said Maud vaguely.

"Anniversary tonight," said Claire with artificial gaity pitched high for Courtney. "Second wedding party, remember?"

Maud hit her palm on her forehead. "I entirely forgot—"

Claire confronted Courtney. "I hope you haven't forgotten. I asked Paoti and his wife to bring you along. There'll only be the six of us."

"I haven't forgotten," said Courtney. "I've been looking forward to it."

"Strictly the American food we have with us, but it won't make you homesick," said Claire, linking her arm in her mother-in-law's arm. "Let's go."

After they had passed through the nursery once more, and emerged into the village compound, they parted company with Courtney. For a moment, Claire's gaze held on Courtney as he proceeded toward his quarters near the Sacred Hut in his ambling, loose-limbed walk. Then she and her mother-in-law started off in the opposite direction.

"I found the last hour most enlightening," Maud said.

"I found it depressing," Claire said.

Claire was aware that Maud had glanced sharply at her. Usually, Claire perceived, Maud did not investigate the pain or disturbance of those around her, or, in fact, of anyone. It was as if she reserved her feelings for her work. Everything else was an indulgence that sapped energy. If Maud was concerned about Marc and Claire, she had apparently tried never to give a sign of it, lest she be drafted from noble peace into lowly battle. But now, Claire had deliber-

366

ately tried to provoke her mother-in-law. If Maud refused to take note of it, her attitude would indicate disinterest in a close one, which would mar her kinship role. Claire waited, wondering how her mother-in-law would handle the obvious cue line thrown at her.

"Depressing?" Maud repeated with reluctance. "In what way, Claire?" She made an effort to guide the complaint to an impersonal plateau. "Because their child-rearing system is so good or so bad?"

Claire would not be misdirected. "Because there are children at all, and they like having them," said Claire bitterly. "I have none. That's depressing."

The faintest frown pinched Maud's warm forehead. "Yes, I see, I see." She stared at the ground as she walked. "You and Marc will work it out, I'm sure. Those things always work out."

Before Claire could challenge her mother-in-law's statement, her hands-off policy, they were intercepted by Lisa Hackfeld. It irked Claire to see her mother-in-law's exhalation of relief, her quick beaming and insincere pretense of interest in Lisa, whom she must have regarded as the Marines to the rescue.

Resentfully, Claire listened to Lisa and Maud chattering, as they went along the compound. Lisa had lost at least a dozen pounds since coming to the Sirens, and while this created some sagging of the skin on her face and neck, it made her younger and more vital. The controlled and cultured accent Lisa had acquired somewhere between Omaha and Beverly Hills was forgotten in her bubbling enthusiasm. She was pure Midwest, and almost as energetic as she had been in that Midwest, as she spoke of her day's triumph. She had been selected to lead one of the ceremonial dances that would start off the annual festival which was beginning at noon tomorrow. Maud treated the news with as much importance as if she were Victoria Regina listening to Disraeli report that India was now her bauble. Claire knew that her mother-in-law's fervent interest, so feigned, was less an effort to butter up the sponsor's wife than to cut herself free from a discomforting domestic quarrel.

Going along the compound, Claire kept her eyes steadily on Maud's features. Claire could now see some of the reasons why Marc had become Marc. Maud was the prototype. She had been above family, and the joys and heartaches of domesticity. How had she conceived Marc? But she had done so, perhaps as a social experiment, a field experience, a preparation for wider knowledge. She had borne Marc, and neatly filed him away with the rest of her work. She was an awesome, unfeeling machine. No heartbeat, only cogs and wheels turning, turning.

Yet, Claire could not hate her mother-in-law. Before things had worsened, Maud had seemed a superior relative—friendly, interesting, unobtrusive, and famous enough to be a feather in the hat of a young bride. Maud had liked Claire for Claire's brightness, prettiness, curiosity, respect, and Claire understood that she was liked and for this liked Maud even more. Maud was the perfect relative, Claire saw, as long as your demands were intellectual and not emotional. It grieved Claire now, when she needed a human being to confide in, a close maternal being, that she had only a highly advertised machine. The anthropology machine named Maud, Claire thought, who understands all peoples but no person. How happy to be a Hayden on anniversary number two!

Suddenly, a gesture of Maud's, a fluttering of her hand to someone off to the left, broke across Claire's introspection. Beyond the stream, before Paoti's hut, Claire could make out three people in a group. One was Rachel DeJong. Another was Hutia Wright. The third, a scrawny old native woman, was unknown to Claire. They had been engrossed in conversation, and it was Rachel DeJong who had waved, and who beckoned as she called out, "Can we see you for a moment, Maud?"

Maud halted, and backed away from Lisa and Claire. "Rachel seems to need me," she said. She added one more brief congratulation to Lisa, then half-turned to Claire. She forced a smile at Claire, impulsively, awkwardly, reaching out and touching her daughter-in-law's arm. "I'm looking forward to tonight," she said, and with that she pivoted and marched toward the nearest bridge.

"What's tonight?" asked Lisa.

"A celebration," said Claire, and she resumed walking, with Lisa a half-step behind.

*　　*　　*

Relieved to be free of her daughter-in-law, of whatever untidy mess Marc and Claire were making of their lives, of the time waste and energy waste her own intervention might mean, of worry about Marc and guilt about Marc, Maud Hayden was glad to be absorbed once more in a field problem. In practical discussions like this, she felt, you grew and gained, whereas arbitration of family squabbles only subtracted from you and reduced you.

Maud stood solidly before Rachel DeJong, Hutia Wright, and the member of the Marriage Hierarchy named Nanu, an elderly widow with stringy hair, quick eyes, gummy smile, and infinite knowledge of matrimony. Maud listened to Rachel explain her reasons for giving up her study of Moreturi and his wife, Atetou. The imposing bamboo entry to the Paoti residence, which Maud faced, lent dignity to the conclave. However, its architecture diverted her attention, and she dismissed it from her vision to concentrate on Rachel's earnest explanation.

"—and so for all of those reasons, while I'm managing to make headway with the other two patients, I'm afraid I'm failing with Moreturi and his wife," Rachel was explaining. "Their versions are so different, that it would take more time than I have to learn the truth. Moreover, there is such antagonism between them, that the case takes on an aspect of emergency. I really don't feel I can make a sound judgment soon enough, and one should be made, either to find a means of helping their marriage survive or of granting Moreturi the divorce he has applied for. I've advised Hutia I am dropping the case, or rather, turning it back to the Marriage Hierarchy to make the final judgment. I'm sorry about this."

"Well, I'm sorry, too," said Maud, "but I wouldn't regard this as any serious failure. I'm sure you've gained some valuable insights into the lives of—"

"Oh yes, I have," said Rachel.

Maud addressed herself to Hutia. "Then it is back in your hands. The loss of two weeks won't disrupt your investigation?"

Hutia Wright, who seemed a well-done native replica of Maud, albeit shorter, rounder, smoother of complexion, remained placid. "The Marriage Hierarchy has undertaken these matters since the time of the first Wright. We shall proceed with our investigation immediately. There must be one change. Since I am a parent of the one who had complained, and could be accused of blood prejudice, I will disqualify myself from the investigation." She indicated the elderly woman beside her. "Nanu will lead this investigation. I would make one suggestion, Dr. Hayden. I think you should replace me on the Hierarchy for this single case. I value your judgment as highly as my own. Also, it will give you an opportunity, such as you might not have again, to observe precisely how our Hierarchy performs. You had spoken to my husband of the desire to participate, had you not?"

"Indeed I have," said Maud, enthusiastically. "This is a great honor. I accept your invitation. When does our work begin?"

"Tonight," said Hutia.

"Tonight? Excellent. Then I'll—" Abruptly, Maud stopped and snapped her fingers. "Almost forgot again. Hutia, I'm terribly sorry, but I can't do it tonight. Why, you know the reason. We're all having dinner together—my son's wedding anniversary."

Hutia nodded. "Of course. But you will be available the rest of the week?"

"I wouldn't miss it," said Maud. "About tonight though, I have another idea." She turned toward Rachel DeJong. "Look, Rachel, why not be my substitute for tonight, spell me? I want us to be in on this investigation from the beginning. I need it for my paper, and you may touch on it in your own. The divorce mechanism here is one thing we know nothing about—"

"Because it is difficult to explain," Hutia interrupted. "We have always planned you would follow such a case in person. It will be clearer that way. There is no mystery, but words will not make it so clear as seeing the many steps."

"Yes, I understand, Hutia," Maud said, and resumed rapidly with Rachel. "Please, Rachel, only for tonight."

Rachel hesitated. She had promised herself that she was through with Moreturi and his wife. Still, she owed Maud Hayden a debt for inviting her on this field trip. She could not deny so small a favor. One more participation, and she would be done with it. She gave her assent. "Very well, Maud, this once." She looked at Hutia. "What am I expected to do?"

"You will meet at nine o'clock this evening," said Hutia, "in the Hierarchy hut. Nanu and one other she will select will await you. Shortly after, your investigation will begin."

Bewildered, Rachel's eyes strayed to the old crone. "What is this investigation? What do we do?"

Nanu's upper lip massaged her upper gum. "You will see soon enough, young lady. It is best you see for yourself."

* * *

Throughout dinner, in the hut that she shared with Harriet Bleaska, a persistent feeling of uneasiness oppressed Rachel De-Jong. It was as if she must soon undertake an unpleasant task that promised no reward of pleasure or feeling of duty accomplished. It was, Rachel thought, like having to attend the funeral of one who had been a mere acquaintance, or having to do business with one who (you had heard) had spoken ill of you, or being backed into extending an invitation to out-of-town visitors who had once been schoolmates but whom you hardly knew, or agreeing to take a series of hypodermic shots that might or might not help. Or, worse, it was like being forced to become a member of a cabal, whose designs were mysterious, suspect, and indefinably threatening. For Rachel, the Marriage Hierarchy investigating group was such a cabal, and she wanted no part of it.

The knowledge, or lack of knowledge, of what lay ahead in twenty minutes, fashioned her mood, which was thinly unhappy.

Thus troubled, she continued to eat listlessly, knowing that she was being uncivil, or just barely civil, to Harriet, who had cooked the dinner, and to Orville Pence, who had invited himself over, grumpily insisting that he was tired of bachelor fare. Rachel hoped that the two of them did not misunderstand her despairing mood, since she liked the homely nurse enormously for her good humor and good heart, and she found Orville, despite his fussy ways, intellectually refreshing. Nevertheless, tonight Rachel could not abide company, and so despite their presence, she ate alone.

She really had no appetite. It was the first time, on the island, that her roommate's culinary talent did not interest her. Wearily, Rachel picked at the food in her bowl and made an effort to listen to Harriet's praise of the infirmary and the native practitioner who supervised it. She could see that Orville, also listening with effort, was in an even worse mood than herself. His interruptions of Harriet, his sarcastic comments on the loose behavior of the villagers, were constant and vehement. It surprised Rachel that, being a guest, Orville could be so disagreeable to his hostess, and it surprised Rachel that his contentiousness did not get through to Harriet. Fleetingly, Rachel had the impression, once, twice, that Orville was spoiling for a fight with Harriet. Rachel speculated on the accuracy of her impression. How could anyone on earth find anything on earth to fight with Harriet about?

Suddenly, Rachel realized that it was ten minutes before nine, and that she must hurry to the meeting with the Hierarchy. She pushed aside her unfinished bowl, and started to rise. "Hate to eat and run, Harriet, but tonight I'm substituting for Maud on a project. I'll barely be on time. The food was divine. I'll take over the cooking next week."

She went to the small mirror she had hung beside the window, and combed her hair.

"I'd better run, too," Harriet said. "I'm expected at the infirmary."

Orville sniffed loudly. "I wanted to talk to you, Harriet."

"How sweet," said Harriet, absently. "Any time, Orville, except tonight. I've got to change into my uniform. Would you be a dear and dispose of the debris? See you both tomorrow." She ran into the back room.

In the mirror, Rachel DeJong caught the reflection of Orville's face. It was prim and pursed, yet welted with rage, as it glared at the door through which Harriet had disappeared. Inquisitively, Rachel turned around and studied Orville.

"Anything wrong, Orville?"

He hesitated. Then he said, "Nothing wrong. I was just thinking about nurses. They were regarded as nothing more than streetwalkers in Florence Nightingale's time."

To Rachel, the remark would have seemed like an idle comment except for the venom with which it was spoken. "What is that supposed to mean?" asked Rachel.

"Just that nothing's changed to this day."

"Oh, really, Orville—" she had begun to say, but before she could finish, he had gone stiffly through the door and outside, carrying the dinner bowls.

Puzzled, Rachel wondered what had provoked Orville's mystifying behavior, his antagonism toward Harriet, his childish remark about nurses. Rachel would have liked to find out, but there was no time to talk to her roommate. It was three minutes to nine, and she would be late.

Scooping up her notebook and pencil, she went swiftly into the compound. Orville was not in sight. Across the stream, three men were on their haunches, beneath a torch, playing some kind of game in the dirt. In the distance, a woman, cradling a piece of pottery, was crossing the bridge. Except for the modulated sounds of a tape recording of Gershwin's *Rhapsody in Blue* (how incongruous in this place!) coming through the window of the hut where Marc and Claire Hayden were giving their party, the village was quiet and most of its inhabitants abed.

Going briskly, Rachel DeJong reached the hut of the Marriage Hierarchy only two and a half minutes late. The wise crone, Nanu, was seated with an elderly man in mid-room. She greeted Rachel with a toothless smile and introduced the slight, gray-haired man, all ribs and knobby knees, as Narmone.

Before Rachel could sit with them, Nanu tried to rise, wheezing, grunting, complaining, joints creaking, and Rachel rushed to join the man Narmone in assisting her to her feet.

"The three of us will go," said Nanu.

Rachel's earlier apprehension returned and anchored her to where she stood. "Go where?"

"To the dwelling of Moreturi and Atetou, of course," said Nanu.

"Why?" Rachel wanted to know. "Do they expect us?"

"Expect us?" Nanu cackled with delight. "No, they will not know we are there. That is the essential."

In a tone of protest, Rachel said, "I simply don't understand what this is all about."

Narmone bent down toward the old woman, and spoke rapidly, voice low, in Polynesian. "*Eaha? . . . Eaha? . . . Eaha?*" she kept muttering, and, as her wrinkled features lighted with comprehension, her head went mechanically up and down.

When he was through, Nanu said to Rachel, "*Ua pe'a pe'a vau.*" Seeing Rachel's bewildered expression, Nanu realized that she was still speaking Polynesian. With a grunt, she returned to English. "What I started to say to you is, 'I'm sorry.' My friend reminds me to tell you—but I am so forgetful each year—that Hutia wanted us to explain our procedure before we leave. The request had gone from my poor mind. I will explain our function. It is simple. It will take not a minute. Then we must hurry, before they sleep. Where to begin? First, the theory . . ."

The theory that governed all Marriage Hierarchy activities, the old woman recited, was that actions always spoke louder than words, louder and more accurately. Words of the complainants could deceive; their performance, witnessed firsthand, could not. When one member of a married couple on The Three Sirens filed for a divorce, the member made no statement of cause or condition.

The Hierarchy was not interested in what either party had to say, since each would be prejudiced and would present a different version of the truth. Once protest was filed, the Hierarchy set out to see for itself. Irregularly, without set pattern, the wise ones of the Hierarchy posted themselves in such a way as to keep the combative couple under close observation. Sometimes, the subjects of the investigation were studied in the morning, less frequently in the afternoon, most often in the evening. This kind of people-watching went on relentlessly over many weeks or months, in some cases as long as half a year. In the end, the five members of the Hierarchy had as true a picture as could be obtained of the couple's daily life, its favorable aspects and its failures. With this information, the Hierarchy could decide if the couple should be given teaching and counseling and remain united, or if the pair should be divorced. Furthermore, the long period of firsthand observation enabled the Hierarchy to arbitrate, in the event of granting divorce, conflicting claims of the two parties, particularly those claims concerning their offspring. Beginning tonight, Moreturi and Atetou would be made the objects of this kind of investigation.

Rachel DeJong had heard out Nanu's explanation with a throbbing sensation of disbelief. "But how do you observe them?" she wanted to know. "If a man and wife know you are there, they will be inhibited, they will not behave naturally, and you will learn no truth."

Narmone replied in a hoarse voice, "The man and wife do not know we are there."

"What?" said Rachel. "They do not know? How is that possible?"

"We see them, they do not see us," said Nanu.

For Rachel, these two were Lewis Carroll and Charles Dodgson, about to lead her down the rabbit hole. "They must see you," Rachel said uncertainly.

"They cannot. Since the time of the first Wright, every hut for the married couples in the village is built with an extra, false wall on one side. The Hierarchy enters into this—it is like a corridor, a passage—and stands posted, not seen from inside or outside, looking through the leaves into the room. We see, we hear, we are not seen, not heard."

This unabashed voyeurism shocked Rachel. It was the first time, in this visit to the Sirens, that she had been shocked. "But, Nanu—

it is morally—it is—I don't know—it's wrong to—" She paused. "All human beings have the right to the dignity of privacy."

The old woman's eyes narrowed at Rachel. The eyes were suddenly shrewd slits. "Do you give people privacy?" she croaked.

"Me? Do I?"

"Yes, Dr. DeJong. I have heard of your work. I cannot remember the name of your work—"

"Psychoanalysis."

Nanu nodded. "Yes. Do you give your patients privacy? You peek into their heads where no one has ever looked before."

"My patients are ill. They've come for help."

"Our patients are ill," said Nanu, agreeably, "and they, too, have come for help. It is no different. I think our way is even more decent. We only look at their outsides. You try to penetrate their insides."

Rachel's shock had subsided. She could see, for different reasons than those voiced, that the Marriage Hierarchy's practice might be justified. Maud would tell her that what was revolting to one society was perfectly acceptable to another. Live and let live. Each to his own. What is good? What is bad? Indeed, what is absolute? Her attitude was friendlier now. "You are quite right, Nanu," she conceded. A question came to her. "Are those extra observation posts ever misused?"

"Never. They are tabu to all but the Hierarchy."

Another question came to her. "How can you hope to observe the married couple behaving normally, when they know they are being watched?"

"A good question," said Nanu. "I remind you, they never know exactly when they are being watched, what day, what time of day, what week. We have found they cannot be self-conscious and perform for possible other eyes all of the time. Over a long period, it is as if they have forgotten we may be there. Their pose slips off, their guard falls, they cease being alert. They revert to their everyday behavior. Especially this is so when they have serious problems. The conflict comes out quickly."

Rachel realized that soon these conditions would apply to Moreturi and Atetou. Fortunately, in the beginning, they would be on guard, restrained, and tonight she would not have to suffer observing them as they really were. Yet, she wanted to be certain of this. "About Moreturi and his wife," she said, "I imagine at this point they will expect to be under your study."

"No, to our good fortune," Nanu said. "We have not yet advised Moreturi you have given him up and turned his case over to the Hierarchy. He has no idea we are acting. We will see him—his wife —as they are." Nanu masticated her gums. "In fact, Dr. DeJong, Hutia is going to request a favor of you. She will ask you, tomorrow, to continue treating her son, no matter how superficially, in order to keep from him the knowledge of our investigation. It will make our work easier, save us much time. It will be beneficial to Moreturi and Atetou."

Any good feeling that had been resuscitated in Rachel disappeared. Once more, she felt uneasy. She did not want Moreturi as a patient again. More intensely, she did not want to see him tonight —she did not want to peek, did not want to play Peeping Tom, odious tailor of Coventry.

The old lady had started for the door. "It is time to begin," she said.

Narmone gestured to the exit, and Rachel went out on unwilling legs, followed by the old man.

The village was entirely deserted. They turned right, and walked in silence for several minutes, until Nanu halted and held a finger to her lips. She stabbed the finger at the thatched hut beside them. It stood hidden in the shadows, except for the faint yellow illumination behind the covered window.

Nanu whispered to Rachel. "Follow us. Do as we do."

Nervously, Rachel picked at strands of her chestnut hair that had fallen into her eyes, and nervously, she tracked after the Hierarchy pair. They went quietly around the hut, and then stopped midway along the side of the structure. Narmone prowled near the cane wall, knelt, and lifted the bamboo swinging door.

Bending low, Nanu ducked through it, quickly followed by Rachel. Narmone was through the opening, too, noiselessly lowering the broad flap, and then rising next to the other two. Rachel stood between them in what seemed pitch darkness. Presently, her eyes accustomed themselves to the condition. She found that the moonlight from behind, and the candlenut from inside, mingled to lighten the area on either side. She was in a corridor, about four feet wide, that ran the length of the residence. Before her was the true wall of the hut, and while the hidden framework was of sturdy timber and cane, the upper surface of the wall consisted of tropical leaves laid over one another like shingles.

Nanu had gone silently down the dirt corridor of the false wall to the far end of the hut. Rachel could make out only her silhouette. In a moment, she returned, shading her shriveled mouth and whispering to her companion voyeurs, "We are late. Atetou has removed her skirt and fastened on her *ahu* for sleep."

Nanu's hand went forward to the shingled leaves, slid under several of them, lifted them slightly with a practiced motion. She peered into the slit opening that she had made. Rachel could see that the arrangement, while primitive, was as ingenious as the one-way glass in use back home. Because of the overlap of leaves, Nanu was able to observe what went on inside the hut while herself remaining undetected. To Rachel's right, Narmone was also engaged in this questionable business of prying.

Rachel held back, dreading the necessity of playing her own role. Her mind sought escape hatches, but before one could be discovered, the old woman was crooking a finger at her. Woodenly, Rachel made a step toward the shingled leaves. "Do as we do," Nanu whispered. "The observation is underway. We continue until both sleep."

Rachel tried to imitate her mentor, lifting a row of leaves. A yellow line of light became visible. Awkwardly, messing her hair, she placed her head beneath the leaves, her eyes to the opening, and squinted to see what was inside. She saw Moreturi, followed him as he slowly paced the mats of the front room. He seemed bigger than she remembered him. Smoking a native cigarette, he circled the room with the powerful grace of a caged oceloid leopard, his muscles swelling and falling. All of his person seemed at ease except his broad Polynesian face, which was contorted by some inner concern.

Suddenly, as he reached the middle of the room near the candle, he came to a halt. His gaze went to the corridor leading into the bedroom.

"Atetou," he called out.

There was no reply.

He moved several steps closer to the corridor. "Atetou, have you lain down?"

Atetou's voice came back faintly. "I sleep. Good night."

Moreturi muttered something, half to himself, some phrase in Polynesian, Rachel thought, and he went swiftly to a clay jar in the far corner and discarded the butt of his cigarette. Absorbed in his own thoughts, he advanced toward the wall behind which Rachel, Nanu, and Narmone crouched. His eyes were fixed on the wall—on herself, Rachel feared—in a moment he would find her, mock her. Arms folded across his expanse of naked chest, he came closer and closer. Although the wall stood between them, Rachel felt that she would be trampled down. She wanted to withdraw, let the leaves drop between them, flee, but she remained frozen, fearful that any movement would give her away.

Several feet from the wall, Moreturi stopped, and looked over his shoulder into the bedroom. To Rachel's confined vision, a light brown giant hung over her, visible from his mouth to his knees. As ever, he wore nothing but the white pubic bag. Rachel tried to swallow, to stifle her breathing. It was inevitable what would happen next, she knew, and then it happened. His hands went down to the string holding the codpiece. In a quick gesture, he loosened the string, drew down the codpiece, and let it drop to the floor out of sight.

Rachel emitted a gasp of horror, positive she was giving herself away, but the exposed naked frame was revealed before her for only an instant. He had turned away, and was purposefully striding toward the bedroom. The front room was empty. Shaken, relieved her ordeal was ended, Rachel pulled her head from under the leaves, and gratefully let them obscure the room.

But then she felt the encirclement of Nanu's bony grip upon her forearm. Nanu was hastily dragging her up their secret passage toward the bedroom. Rachel attempted to resist, to no avail. Narmone was immediately behind her, almost bumping into her, fully blocking flight. Rachel's mouth was open, intending to protest this mad spectator sport, but words did not come. She found herself stumbling after Nanu, still tugged by the repulsive old woman, as Narmone pressed from behind.

In a moment, the three of them were in place behind the bedroom wall. Nanu kept pointing at the shingled leaves, until Rachel did her duty. Rachel wanted to resign, but there was the rising murmur of voices from the bedroom, and she was afraid to speak. She bent to the old woman's will. She lifted the row of leaves, and peered into the room.

Except for the moonlight, the bedroom was darkened. Rachel wanted to make the sign of the cross and thank the Lord. Then, dimly, she made out the two figures in the foreground. Apparently, the one on his knees was Moreturi, and beneath him, twisting away, was Atetou. The words exchanged were indistinct, but which was male and which was female was clear, and the intonations were clear, too. Moreturi was pleading for physical love, and his wife was resisting him. Moreturi bent lower, and Atetou began to rise, pushing him away.

Moreturi backed off, and leaped to his feet. "All right!" he bellowed in distinct English. "I go to the Social Aid!"

"Go—go—go—" Atetou chanted at him. "That is your way to show love—go."

Moreturi whirled, and stamped through the darkness to the front room.

Having witnessed this, Rachel closed her eyes, unable to control the chattering of her teeth. She pulled back from the sheaf of leaves, feeling totally unstrung, then became aware that Nanu's hands were on her, pushing. Rachel opened her eyes. Narmone was already on his way toward the post that looked into the front room. Propelled by the old woman's rough hands, Rachel tripped, regained her balance, and made her way to a spot beside Narmone. Again, Nanu was at her elbow, lifting the leaves, both the leaves that confronted Rachel and her own. Unable to protest, Rachel submitted, lowered her head beneath the leaves, and looked into the hut.

The lighted room blinded her momentarily, but soon she could see. Moreturi's great brown naked frame, back, buttocks, legs stiff, was at the door. In one hand he held his supporter. Only his rear could be seen, and Rachel prayed that he would not turn around. At the door, Moreturi hesitated. For a suspended interval, it appeared that he would pull on his brief garment, but he did not. Coming to some decision, his shoulders heaved, straightened, and he flung the supporter aside. As he began to turn around, Rachel shut her eyes, shut them so tightly that sparkling pinwheels sped round and round behind her lids. She heard his step approaching, then receding, but she would not look. A minute passed, perhaps two. Rachel's eyes hurt, and she relaxed the lids, and finally she opened them.

Again, she had cause for gratefulness. He was seated on the mat ting, in the center of the room, his long curved back toward her. His arms encircled his knees, and his head hung low. He remained in this posture for what seemed an eternity—five minutes, perhaps —and gradually, uncontrollably, Rachel felt pity for him. She wanted to reach out, touch him, comfort him. She wanted to be beside him, speaking soothingly to him. As an analyst, she had heard much of the animal desire in men, and understood it, and understood the iron bands of repression and frustration. Then her position as onlooker, espionage agent, overwhelmed her, and she was suffused in shame.

She intended to whisper to Nanu that they must leave, but before she could do so, there was a sound of footsteps inside the hut.

She heard Atetou's small voice, although Atetou could not be seen. "You did not go, Moreturi?"

His head came around, and whatever he saw made his black eyes dilate. "No—no—I did not go."

"You still want your Atetou?"

"I must love," he said fiercely.

"Then come to me." Her voice was fading, as she returned to the bedroom. "I wait."

Before Rachel could close him from sight, Moreturi had come to his feet and turned toward her. Rachel felt the tremor in her arms and across her chest, watched hypnotically as the huge naked aroused animal crossed the room, left her vision and the room.

Rachel's gaze remained fixed on the vacated room, and she hated Atetou and swore she would not be a witness to Atetou's triumph. Then, Rachel started at the first sound from the bedroom. It came from Atetou's throat, and it was not restrained. It was a female cry of pain, comingled with pleasure, and the cry melted into a drawn-out groan.

Rachel felt her stomach rise into her throat, and she began to choke. She tore herself from the wall, batted down the old crone's grasping hand that was trying to bring her to the bedroom. Rachel whirled toward Narmone, plunged past him, almost bowling him over, fell down to her knees, groping for the exit that would liberate her. Something gave, the door swung high, and Rachel, intending to rise but still crawling, was out of the false wall, free of the Hierarchy, free of the copulating beasts.

She staggered to her feet, and ran into the compound, and not until she reached the stream did she halt. She stood over the water, between the torches, disheveled and panting.

After a while, her heart ceased pounding, and her trembling disappeared. Atetou's outcry no longer resounded against her eardrums, and she was able to sit down on the slight embankment, relatively calm. She located a cigarette, and smoked, and tried to erase from mind the memory of the recent experience. What had driven her to this, and this place? How she longed to be home, a housewife drab, in a cottage without false walls, in a community without a Hierarchy, in the security of the title that could be Mrs. Joseph Morgen. But that was impossible, too. She was too smart to expect to find such a refuge. She could not escape her skin. She was she.

It was ten minutes later when the pair came across the compound to stand over her.

"They sleep," the old woman said. "Our work for the first night is ended." Nanu cocked her head at Rachel. "Why did you leave in such a way?"

Rachel rose, brushing the dust from her skirt. "I began to get a coughing spell," she said. "I had to leave before I gave us all away. It would have been awful. So I ran out, where I could cough and have fresh air."

Nanu contemplated her, apparently unconvinced. "I understand," she said. "I hope the evening was instructive."

"Yes—yes, it was," said Rachel. "Actually, it is more in Dr. Maud Hayden's line. She will be taking over tomorrow."

"You had better have some sleep," Nanu said. "We all need sleep now."

Rachel nodded, and walked with them a short distance, and then parted from them and went on alone. There were still lights and music and the sounds of voices in the Marc Hayden hut, but she hardly noticed. She was very tired, too tired to enter the experience either in her journal or in her clinical notes. By tomorrow, she would have probably forgotten the details, so she would not bother to enter them then, either. At least, she hoped she would not. She wanted total recall in her patients. She wanted none of it in herself.

* * *

It was after midnight. The second anniversary party of the Haydens had ended a half-hour before, with the departure of Paoti,

Hutia, Courtney, and finally Matty. The cook and servant, Aimata, a tall sinewy, unsmiling native woman in her late thirties, had cleaned the earth oven and the front room and left ten minutes ago.

Marc Hayden was alone, at last, in the front room of his hut. Claire had gone into the back, with their presents, to undress for bed. Marc was grateful for a respite of solitude, but he was uncomfortable. The room was clammy, humid, foul with the lingering smoke of the oven, the cigarettes, the candlenuts Claire had used in place of the lamp. There was a faint odor of whiskey in the air. He had drunk too much, everyone had drunk too much. Instead of feeling light and cheerful, he felt sodden and dispirited. He felt waterlogged, whiskey-logged.

He shuffled aimlessly about the dank room. His clothes were sticky. He tore off his necktie, unbuttoned his shirt and pulled it off and dropped it on the floor. This was better. He loosened the belt of his gray slacks one notch, went to the front door, opened it, and sat on the stoop, trying to revive himself with fresh air. He scanned the empty, dark compound, automatically bringing out his last bent cigar, biting off the end, and lighting it. He puffed and puffed, and still felt wretched. He tried to review the events of the eventless evening, but found trouble concentrating. The whiskey had numbed his brain. Nevertheless, he was able to resurrect a few of the better or worse moments.

Everyone appeared to have an enjoyable time, except Marc. It was to be, Claire had decided, a thoroughly American evening, an oddity for Paoti and Hutia, a nostalgia for Courtney, a good digestive interlude for Matty, a bit of auld lang syne for the young married celebrants. There were Scotch and bourbon highballs from the team's imported stock, and there were Vivaldi, Gershwin, Stravinsky from the portable tape. Claire cooked the canned vegetable soup, canned chicken, canned fruit dessert, and Aimata served each course. There were toasts from Courtney and Matty, which Marc accepted with forced smiles. There were elaborate recollections by Claire of her first meetings and courting period with Marc, all over-romantic (for she was high with drink), which irritated Marc. There were grave questions about American marriage from Paoti, which Marc intended to answer but which Matty and Claire answered before him.

The anniversary presents were opened after dinner by Claire. There was a piece of native sculpture—it resembled something pre-Colombian—from the Paoti Wrights. There was an ancient Sirens feasting bowl from that bastard Courtney. There was a Polaroid camera, brought along for this occasion, from Matty. There was from Claire to Marc, with love, all old sins and omissions forgiven this anniversary night, so with love, a tooled-leather cigar case, expensive, attractive. There was from Marc to Claire, there was nothing, absolutely nothing.

He had forgotten to shop before leaving home. He had forgotten to dig up something here on the Sirens, because his mind was not on Claire or on their damn anniversary. He pulled it off well, though, he thought, and the crestfallen look on Claire's face was fleeting. He had ordered something for her from Los Angeles, a secret, a surprise, and it had not come in time. It would be waiting for her when they returned home. He preferred not to identify it tonight. That would spoil the fun of it. Claire had displayed her pleasure with a quick, Scotch-scented kiss, but beyond Claire's puckered lips Marc caught a glimpse of his mother's bland face. He knew that *she* knew the truth. Well, damn her, he thought, damn her and all X-ray machines that gave no approval, only trouble.

After that, there survived in his mind but three fragments of the conversation. The rest had floated away on whiskey. Three fragments of no consequence.

Fragment one.

He was making another drink, another drink, and Claire was beside him, complaining in an undertone. Probably about the drink. "What are you, Carrie Nation or somethin'?" he said to her, yes, it was about the another drink, and he said exactly that.

She said, "We're all drinking, but I don't want you passing out on our anniversary, darling."

"Yes, *wife*," he said, and finished making the drink. He had taken a swallow, when Courtney joined them.

Courtney said, "Well, Dr. Hayden, I hear you're participating in our festival, entering the swimming contest."

Marc said, "Who told you?"

Courtney said, "Tehura told me. If it's true, I feel I should caution you, one red-blooded American to another, it's a rugged go. You may be out of your league."

Marc said, "Don't you worry about me. I'm a fish in the water. I can beat those monkeys with one arm tied behind me." His eyes narrowed at Courtney. "I heard you entered a couple of times."

Courtney said, "Twice, to my regret. Never again. It's a big dive and long haul, and unless you're built the way they are, there's no chance. I ached for weeks after."

Marc said, "You're you and I'm me. I'll be there tomorrow."

Claire said, "Where tomorrow, Marc? What are you two talking about?"

Marc said, "The big sports event that kicks off the festival. A swimming contest tomorrow. I'm in it."

Claire said, "Oh no, Marc—but why?—you're not a schoolboy any more—contests, my God—why are you in it, Marc?"

Marc wanted to say, said it only in his head, "Because I'm after a real piece of tail, honey, not a castration artist like you." Marc said aloud, "Participant observation, wife, the key to field anthropology. You know all about that, don't you, wife? Isn't that why you showed the natives your tits the night of Paoti's feast?"

Claire flushed crimson, and Marc felt better as he lurched away to ask the others if they needed refills.

Fragment two.

Doctor Matty, good ol' Whistler's Mother Matty, with her usual oral diarrhea, bending ears, noisily talking and talking, still talking to Paoti and Hutia when he served her a fresh drink.

"Matty," he interrupted maliciously, "here's your drink, getting cold."

Matty shot him a skewer look, half turned her back to him, to ignore his rude tone, and went on, while Marc, reduced to inferior sonhood, stood lamely listening.

"For years," Matty said to Paoti, "the big problem with science —I include social science—in our countries was that it could not communicate itself to the masses below, who had no preparation, no understanding, yet whose support was needed. It was not enough to come up with a Theory of Evolution or a Theory of Relativity. One was required to explain it, filter it down to the broad base of the uninformed for their approval, because without approval there would be no interest in and financing of basic research. Today, in America, Great Britain, France, Germany, Italy, Russia, everywhere, science is understanding this, and finding a way to communicate itself popularly, and therefore receiving more support."

Marc watched Matty-Maud-Mother sip her drink, and heard her go on. "We in the field of anthropology have been especially successful in getting across our findings. We are learning to speak the language of our people. I, personally, have always been fanatically interested in writing to be read by everyone, to be read widely and understood. I believe in having a commercial publisher bring out my work; even when it is technical, I always prefer a commercial publisher to a university press. Now, some anthropologists resent those of us who publish for popular consumption. I have been called a self-publicist and a drum-beater. I have been castigated for running pieces in nonprofessional magazines. The hard core who believe only in their own journals and in university presses feel that money and reputation are external to anthropology. They feel an anthropologist should be a scientist, and not a writer or popularizer. Some are sincere. But most of the resentment is motivated by sheer envy. And also by intellectual arrogance and snobbery. My own position, Chief Paoti, is that I don't want to limit my study of the Sirens only to my friends and enemies down the hall. I want *everyone* to know about it, and to be wiser for it."

Woozily, Marc continued to watch her and listen with wonder. His mother was not a puddly mom at all, he told himself, she was a Force of Nature, with the grandeur of a Juggernaut. Paoti had spoken something to her, which Marc had missed, and then he saw that Matty was nodding, smiling, and resuming.

"Yes, that too," she said. "We are what we are. What drew me into anthropology was that it was a field that I understood, a science that encompassed all mankind, and one that I could popularize. You see, the obscurities of science, which I might understand but others would not, interest me less than the living drama of science. I'll tell you what interests my mentality. It interests me that the gill arches of ancient fish are still part of the human ear apparatus —how dramatic, this carry-over from the past. It interests me that fossilized sea shells and sea creatures are now found impressed in the strata of inland mountains, hundreds of miles from open water —another living link. It interests me that there still swims in the ocean off South Africa a fish known as the Coelacanth, a fossil fish that was swimming there fifty million years ago when dinosaurs roamed the shores—the dinosaurs are extinct but the Coelacanth is alive. It interests me that the bright star we see shining outside this window is sending light to us that began traveling toward us a thousand years ago, so that message of light there, the one we see now, first began shining and traveling toward us when the Saracens were destroying the Venetian fleet and Constantine was an emperor. It interests me that you, Chief Paoti, hidden from the world, enforce a set of standards first created almost two centuries ago. That is the science I value—understand—the science that makes my blood tingle—and in those terms I try to enlighten the world around me, no matter what some of my colleagues may think of me."

Wondrous, wondrous Matty, Marc thought, and he felt puny, disabled, and felt incredulous that a mountain had loins that had produced a molehill.

Fragment three.

The last drink had been served. The guests prepared to leave. Claire thanked both Paoti and Hutia for the use of their servant, Aimata, the most efficient housekeeper she had ever known, even counting Suzu back in long-ago Santa Barbara.

"Oh, she is not our servant," Hutia Wright said. "She is the slave of another family. We borrowed her for you."

"Did I hear you correctly?" asked Claire. "Aimata is a slave?"

"But yes—for her crime . . ."

The perplexity on Claire's face made Maud quickly intercede. "It is something that Easterday touched on in his letter, but which has not yet been fully explained to you or the others," she said. "There is, at least we would consider it so, a unique system of punishment of crime on The Three Sirens. There is no capital punishment here. In fact, there is much to be said for the system. It is both humane and practical. In the United States if a person commits wilful murder, we most often deliberately execute him by rope, electric chair, poison gas, firing squad. While this eliminates the possibility of his killing again, such vengeful retribution by society neither gainfully serves the community nor recompenses the bereft family of the victim. Here on the Sirens, if a person commits murder, he is sentenced to slavery, to serve the family of his victim for the number of years of life the victim has probably lost." She gestured to Paoti. "Perhaps you can relate this principle or law to the person of Aimata."

"Yes," said Paoti to Claire. "It is simple. Aimata was thirty-two, her husband thirty-five, when she decided to murder him. She pushed him off a cliff. He was killed instantly. There was no trial before me, for Aimata confessed. Our criminal custom states that the average person should live seventy years on this island. Therefore, Aimata had deprived her husband of thirty-five years of life. By murdering him, she had also deprived his other kin of help, support, and attention. Therefore, Aimata was sentenced to replace the one she had murdered, for those thirty-five years. She is the slave of the victim's blood kin for that period, without privileges; she cannot marry, enjoy love, enjoy recreation, and must eat only the scraps of their meals and wear the garments they discard."

Claire's hand had gone to her mouth. "I've never heard anything like that. It's terrifying—"

Paoti smiled sympathetically. "It is effective, Mrs. Hayden. We have had only three murders in the village in thirty years."

"There are systems and systems in this world," Maud added to Claire. "There is a tribe in West Africa, the Habe they are called, who also never hang a murderer. They consider that a waste, as here. They send a murderer into exile for two years. Then they bring him back from exile, and make him live and copulate with a relative of the murdered person until a child is born to replace the victim. Odd, but it has a justice of its own, like this system here. I'm not so certain we in the West have better ways of dealing with crime." She turned. "Mr. Courtney, you are the lawyer—what do you say?"

"I say aye," said Courtney, "and now I say thank you and good night."

The fragments had dissolved.

Marc found himself seated still on the stoop, his shoulders and chest somewhat cooled, but his mouth and tongue hot and raw from all the whiskey and the half-finished cigar in his fingers.

It was then that he heard Claire's muffled voice from the rear room. "Marc—it's so late—"

He did not reply.

Claire's voice again. "Marc, aren't you coming to bed? I have a surprise for you."

Surprise, surprise. He knew the surprise for their anniversary, and he knew that he had been sitting here, alone, avoiding it. She was going to offer her tiresome body. It was a gift he did not desire. Two years of her had wearied him of that body. But then, assessing the two years, a vague computing, he realized that he had not possessed that body intimately as many times as he imagined. It was just that the body was there, always there, always around, always irritatingly available, and what went with it, the rebuke of her person, that made her seem so used.

He realized that he had not slept with her in a month or two. Now he was being drafted for an Occasion. He hated the duty. He did not want her. He wanted the brown one, with her arrogance about sex, and bare breasts, and beautiful thighs hidden by nothing but grass. He remembered the incident earlier in the day, how he had almost possessed Tehura, and was certain he would possess her yet. The imagined passion of fulfillment with Tehura coursed through his frame and awakened him. He wanted her now, but he could not have her, and so he decided to waste the passion on duty.

He rose, throwing his cigar into the compound. "Be right with you," he called to Claire. He shoved the door closed and fastened it.

He crossed to the corridor, went through it, and entered the dimly lighted bedroom. The room seemed empty. He could not find Claire on the sleeping bag or in the shadows. He heard a movement parallel to him, to his right, and then she emerged from the shadowed wall toward the candle and wheeled in its circle of yellow to show herself to him.

He blinked dumbly.

"Surprise on our second, darling," she said.

In his amazement at her appearance, he thought for an instant that by some trick this was Tehura, but his sobering sensibilities told him it was Claire. She was garmented exactly as Tehura was garmented, as all the women of The Three Sirens were dressed. There was an outrageous flower in her hair. The diamond pendant hung between her bold white breasts with their indecent brown nipples. The slash of her navel contracted and expanded above the band of the too-short grass skirt. The thighs, legs, feet were bare.

Rage bolted through him. He wanted to crush her, brand her with a shout, brand her as a harlot, strumpet, doxy, bawd. That she would dare to mock him with the wanton undress of this tropical whorehouse! That she would insult him with this evidence that she was one of these village animals, a sex animal, and he was less!

"Well, Marc," she said happily. "Say something."

Say something! "Where in the hell did you get that goddam getup anyway?"

Her smile fell away. "Why, I thought I'd surprise you—I asked Tehura to loan me one of her—"

Tehura! "Take that goddam idiotic costume off and burn it, dammit."

"Marc, what's got into you—I thought you'd—"

"I said get rid of it. What in the devil do you think you're doing? What are you turning into? I've seen it from the first day—first night—when you couldn't show them your tits fast enough—and going around with that Courtney—talking sex, seeing sex, thinking sex—wiggling your ass at him and all the rest of them—asking for it—trying to behave like—"

"Shut up!" she screamed. "Shut up, shut up, and damn you—I'm sick to the bones of you—of your prissiness, your prudery—sick of keeping it to myself—sick of being alone, untouched by human hands—sick of being unloved by my great big genius, my big athlete—I tell you—I—I—"

She was breathless like someone struck. She stared at him, panting, hands turned into claws, wanting to tear at the humiliation of him, wanting to kill him and kill herself, wanting to cry and cry like an orphan child.

She covered her eyes, and fought the sob. "Get away—go away from me—go away and grow up," she said brokenly.

He was shaking uncontrollably from her unexpected retaliation. "Damn right I'll go away," he said in a floundering voice. "I'll come back when you're yourself again, when you remember who you are and behave that way . . . Christ, I wish you could see yourself in that costume. If that's your idea how to hold a husband—"

"Get out!"

Instantly, he left her, chased by her wrenching sobs all the way to the door. He stumbled into the compound, and, striding as fast as he could, he fled the shame of her.

He did not know how long he walked in the semidarkness. Presently, he found himself near the Social Aid Hut, which was unlighted, and he coughed and expectorated in its direction, and then retraced his steps.

Long later he sat by a waning torch, across the stream from his hut, satisfied that he was too exhausted to be angry any longer. He sat and wondered what this hell-hole was doing to her and to him, and what would happen to them, and, more important, what would happen to him. He thought of the authentic Tehura, and he thought of his future, and as he so often had lately, he thought of the admirable Rex Garrity.

Finally, he reached into the hip pocket of his slacks and drew out the soiled one-page letter he'd received two weeks ago. Garrity had sent it to him, care of General Delivery, Papeete. In a flamboyant hand, Garrity had reminded him that the visit to The Three Sirens could be the one chance of a lifetime. If Marc would consider selling some of the material that his mother did not need, Garrity would pay a large sum of money for it. Or, if Marc could think of something else, suggest some other arrangement, Garrity would cooperate in any way and be receptive to any proposition. "Marc, old boy, this is an opportunity to grab the gold ring, to join the celebrity circle, to escape the role of scholar peasant with frayed cuffs," Garrity had written. "Keep in touch, and tell me what you think or ask me anything you like." Within an hour of reading the letter in Papeete, Marc had replied to it in haste, but at length, with Matty-imposed restraint, but with many questions.

He returned Garrity's letter, the one magic scroll on earth that could obliterate Adley, Matty, Claire, and Nonentity, to his hip pocket.

He stood up and inhaled the night air, and felt stronger. Claire would be drugged asleep by now. He would go to the front room, and begin a letter to Rex Garrity. Tomorrow was mail day. If Rasmussen brought in some further word from Garrity, the answers to the questions, then Marc would finish what he would begin writing tonight. He would finish it, and mail it, and do what he must do, and nothing would ever be the same again.

He stared up at the vast sky above. Shake your goddam head, Adley, he thought, but I can't see you, can't hear you, don't need you any more, because you're dead forever and I'll soon be alive.

He started for the hut, already writing the savior letter in his mind.

VI

RESTLESSLY, Marc Hayden moved about the lofty, flat precipice that hung, like an observation point, over the village of The Three Sirens far below.

Not since their arrival at this place, exactly two weeks ago, had he visited this rise, from which descended the path around the stone ledge to the rectangular community set deep in the long valley. Marching around the precipice, Marc had occasional glimpses of the shaggy miniature huts beneath the overhangs, of the gleaming ribbon of stream in the compound. By now, late morning, the compound was lightly populated, the usual animated brown dots of children, some women, no one else, for the men were off to their work, the adolescents in their school, the members of Matty's team (not his team) sheltered with their pencils, tapes, and boasting informants.

If the view from the high and isolated vantage point was beautiful, Marc was unaware of it. The village was there, but it was no part of him. Since the night, he had separated his identity from it almost completely. It was as remote and unreal as a color photograph in the *National Geographic Magazine*.

For Marc, the village and its inhabitants were merely Things, accessories to aid him in his escape from an ancient and hated way of life. What was real, what was animate, what was even beautiful, was that Magna Carta of the soul—his private Declaration of Independence—enclosed in the right-hand pocket of his gray Dacron trousers.

The letter in the right-hand pocket was only three pages long, and the pages and envelope were thin, yet they filled his pocket and body and mind with the displacement of—he tried to think of an accurate simile—of an Aladdin's Lamp, ready to fulfill his Wish.

He had stayed up most of the night, in the front room of the hut, composing those three pages to Rex Garrity in New York City. Most of his time had been consumed not with writing, but with plotting what he must tell Garrity of his intentions. When he had finished, he had gone to sleep easily and slept well for the first time in months, with the feeling of one who has done a day's work in a day and done it properly, and has no remorse and infinite high hopes, and so can accept good sleep as a reward. He had ignored Claire's lumpy outline on the sleeping bag, set his alarm, and closed his eyes and slept.

When his alarm had awakened him, he had slept only three hours, and yet he was not tired at all. During breakfast, Claire had appeared, still wearing her night-before face. Her face was drawn and rigid, and her good morning curt and combative, while his own good morning was so slight and slurred as to hardly exist as a greeting. She moved about noisily, bumping, tramping, all obtrusive, demanding without speech but with an oppressive presence his attention and apology for his behavior of the night before. She had wanted to have it out and done with, the domestic band-aid of talk and more talk, to patch her wounds. She wanted him to mitigate his cursing and his rejection during the night hours, to save face by invoking the plea of drunkenness but yet to apologize, so that she could save face by agreeing it best be forgotten and their life together could hobble on.

Through this silent sparring, and waiting out, he had given no ground. He had eaten in silence, and avoided her, simply because this morning she no longer had existence for him. His disinterest was total. In the night, he had grown, become the man he had always known he would be (and therefore a stranger to this woman), and he wanted no part of an old contract that he no longer need honor.

He had fled his hut in haste—a great show of finding notebook and pen, to throw her off the scent, make her believe he was off to work—and with the letter to Garrity in his right-hand pocket, he had gone swiftly to the path that climbed out of the village and above it. He knew that he must not be late. His purpose had been to intercept Captain Rasmussen—it was Rasmussen day, mail day, supply day—before the old pirate got down into the village and to

Matty. If there was a letter from Garrity, in reply to his own from Papeete, he did not want Matty to see it or know about it. He wanted the letter alone, early, for himself. Its contents would determine his final decision—to mail or not to mail to Garrity the statement of intentions in his pocket.

He had sat for over an hour in the shade of the dense acacia, mulberry and kukui trees, a few feet from the path Rasmussen must take, nervously awaiting the bearer of his fate. Rasmussen had not appeared in that time, and Marc had restlessly left the cool rows of trees to rove the baking cliff nearby.

Now, he had been moving about the precipice for twenty minutes, wondering if there would be a letter, if it would fulfill what he daydreamed, if he would have the nerve to reply with the letter in his pocket, until he realized that this exposure to the rising sun was unbearable.

Slowly, wiping his face and neck with his handkerchief, he retraced his steps up the trail to the trees. The sloping path that led to the sea was still devoid of Rasmussen's figure. Momentarily, Marc worried whether he had miscalculated the day or, if he had not, whether Rasmussen had been delayed or had postponed his mercy flight. Then he decided that he was being unduly anxious. Of course, Rasmussen would appear.

Standing beside the path, Marc felt the bulk in his right trouser pocket. He extracted the unsealed envelope addressed to Garrity, and his spirits revived, and he slid the envelope back into its place. He squinted off once more—the path was still empty of life, except for two scrawny goats in the distance—and finally he walked back to the coolest cubicle of shade he could find and dropped to the grass. He took out a cigar, and was hardly aware of preparing it and lighting it, as his mind returned to Tehura and what he had written Garrity of her and of her possible role in the decisive days to come.

When next he looked at his wrist watch, it was nearly noon and he had been on his lookout for three hours. He lapsed back into his thoughts, and then into flabbier daydreaming, and had no idea how much more time had elapsed before he was aroused by the harsh, off-key sounds of someone whistling a seaman's chanty.

Marc scrambled to his feet—his watch told him it was past twelve-fifteen—and ran into the path. Twenty yards away, approaching him, was the glorious visitation of Captain Ollie Rasmussen, marine hat tilted back from his warped, stubbled Göteborg face, attire consisting of open worn blue shirt, filthy denims, tennis shoes as shabby as ever, and the mail pouch slung over his left shoulder.

Drawing closer, Rasmussen recognized Marc, and waved his free hand. "Hiya, Doc. You the reception committee?"

"How are you, Captain?" Marc waited nervously until Rasmussen had come abreast, and then he added, "I was up here hiking, and I remembered you'd be along today, so I thought I'd hang around and get a quick peek at my mail. I'm expecting something important to my work."

Rasmussen threw the pouch off his shoulder and dropped it to the path. "Sure somethin's so important it can't wait? Mail ain't sorted."

"Well, I just thought—"

"Never mind, there ain't much to sort through anyways." He dragged the pouch through the dirt to the grass, sat wide-legged on a coconut log, straightening the pouch between his knees. "Guess I could use a second's breather." He opened the pouch, as Marc hovered over it. Rasmussen sniffed and looked up. "You got another of them stogies, Doc?"

"Sure thing, absolutely." Quickly, Marc extracted a fresh cigar from his shirt pocket, and handed it to Rasmussen, who accepted it with a belch, and placed it beside him on the log. While Marc watched fretfully, Rasmussen dug his horny hand into the pouch, and produced a packet of letters bound tightly by a leather strap. He unbuckled the strap, then, muttering Marc's full name, he went through the mail.

At last, he proffered three envelopes. "That's all there is, there ain't no more for you, Doc—'cept maybe some of the bigger pieces —but you don't want them now."

"No, this'll do," said Marc quickly, accepting the envelopes.

While Marc fanned open the envelopes, like a gin rummy hand, to note the return addresses, Rasmussen dropped his packet into the mail pouch, and concentrated on unwrapping and lighting the cigar. The first letter, Marc saw, was from a faculty colleague at Raynor College; the second, addressed to Claire and himself, was from married friends in San Diego; and the third was from "R.G., Busch Artist and Lyceum Bureau, Rockefeller Center, New York City." The last was Rex Garrity writing from his lecture agency offices, and Marc tightened with anticipation. Yet, he was reluctant to open the envelope before Rasmussen. The Captain still remained seated, sucking the cigar, bleary, alcoholic eyes observing Marc.

"Get what you want, Doc?"

"Dammit, no," Marc lied. "Only some personal letters. Maybe it'll come your next mail day."

"Hope so." Rasmussen took a grip on the pouch, and came to his feet. "I better get crackin'. Wanna clean up an' fill my belly an' be sharp for the festival. Starts today for the comin' week, you know."

"What? Oh, yes, the festival, I'd forgotten—I guess it does start today."

Rasmussen eyed Marc meditatively a moment. "Matter of fact, I'm rememberin'—Huatoro an' some of the native lads met us down the beach when we come in—they're cartin' the supplies the short route—he said somethin' about you—guess you're the one—you enterin' the swim competition today. Is that bull or the truth?"

The festival swimming match, scheduled for three o'clock, had been the farthest thought from Marc's mind. He was surprised by this reminder of it.

"Yes, Captain, it's true. I've promised to enter it."

"Why?"

"Why? For the exercise, I guess," said Marc lightly.

Rasmussen pulled the pouch over his shoulder. "Want an old-timer's advice? You can get better exercise bangin' some of those Sirens broads, Doc—meanin' no disrespect to the Mrs., understand —but that's the real fireworks of the festival. I'm givin' you the advice in the interests of scientific research. Jus' keep it in mind if one of the maidens hands you a festival shell."

"What's that?"

"That's what unties the grass skirt, Doc." He laughed in a hoarse bark, coughed, removed the cigar, choking, and stuffed the cigar back between his discolored teeth. "Yeh, that's what does it."

"I'll keep that in mind, Captain," Marc said weakly.

"You bet your life, that's what does it," said Rasmussen. He started into the path. "You comin' down with me?"

"I—no, thanks, I think I'll walk a little more."

Rasmussen had started moving away. "Well, jus' don't wear yourself out before the swim an' you know what." He barked his laugh again, and went trudging off toward the precipice.

Briefly disconcerted by the Captain's reference to the festival, Marc remained standing, looking after him. By the time Rasmussen had gone through the rows of acacia and kukui trees and reached the precipice, and then disappeared around the stone bend that led down into the village, Marc's mind had returned to Garrity's long, flimsy envelope.

Hurrying off the path, into the shade across the way, Marc folded two of the envelopes and stuffed them into his hip pocket. Uneasily, he turned the Garrity envelope around, picked at the glued flap, and almost reluctantly tore at it, slitting it open with his forefinger.

Carefully, he unfolded the four typewritten onionskin pages. With restraint, like a gourmet who would disdain bolting a long-awaited delicacy, he read the letter, word by word.

There was the informal salutation, "My dear Marc." There was the pleased acknowledgement of Marc's hasty inquiry from Papeete. Then, there was the business at hand. Before reading it, and learning what his future could or could not be, Marc closed his eyes and tried to fix in his mind a portrait of the letter's author. Time and distance and wish diffused memory's picture: Garrity, blond, tall, lean, with his refined patrician Phillips Exeter-Yale features, the youngest juvenile of fifty on earth, the doer, the idol, the succeeder, the glamorous man of action, the on-the-heels-of-Hannibal adventurer—he—the one—in some lofty tower of Rockefeller Center, at a golden typewriter, writing, "My dear Marc"!

Marc opened his eyes, and read Garrity's definitive statement of the business at hand:

I want to remark straight off that I doubly appreciate hearing from you so promptly because I think I, alone, am attuned to your sensitivity, personality, and position. I know you are hobbled by innumerable restrictions. For one thing, your renowned mother, God bless her, who, for all her genius, has a narrow and pedantic view of the living, commercial world. Her rejection of me, her undoubted aversion to those of us in public communications and entertainment, is based on an outdated code of ethics. For another thing, you have been handicapped by being imprisoned so long in your mother's world, the so-called "scientific" world of pedants. But you are of a new, more sophisticated generation, and, forgive me, Marc, but for such as you there is hope, nay not hope alone but vistas of glory. From my one private conversation with you at your home in Santa Barbara, for your championing of me before your mother and wife and the nearsighted Hackfeld, and, indeed, for your letter from Papeete that revives my faith in you and our relationship and future, for all of these reasons I see in you a New Hayden, a strong individual with his own ideas and ambitions, ready to go before the world and conquer it at last.

As best I can interpret your few careful paragraphs, you speculate on the propriety of putting before the vast, general public the information you are garnering on The Three Sirens. You wonder if the material might not be misused and oversensationalized in the wrong hands. You wonder if any scientists, or anthropologists, have ever presented their findings to the nation in "the Rex Garrity manner." You wonder about the true economics of the lecture circuit today, and you say, somewhat skeptically, you are certain I was jesting at your house when I remarked that proper presentation of The Three Sirens investigation and adventure could earn both of us "a million dollars."

After careful consideration of your letter, I have decided to take your interest seriously, absolutely seriously. I was doing a lecture in Pittsburgh when your letter was forwarded to me, and immediately I canceled an engagement in Scranton to hurry to New York and visit with my agents in Rockefeller Center. In confidence, I told them what little I knew of your current field trip, of the Sirens itself, and I asked them what all of this could add up to in practical terms, "the true economics" of it, as you put it, and after two days here, I have all the real answers. It is, believe me, Marc, with a sense of high excitement that I write you now. I hope my excitement will transmit itself to you in that incredible faraway place where now you work, wherever it is, exactly.

At the outset, let me allay any fears you may possess as to the propriety of communicating The Three Sirens adventure to the public. Also, any fears you may have that the material would be misused. I know your mother accused me of being a successful popularizer who might exploit the Sirens material in a way that would be damaging both to anthropology and the hidden islanders. Marc, your mother is wrong. Forgive me again, but she reflects the outmoded thinking of prewar social scientists, a closed group or cult who kept what was valuable to themselves. In fact, the reputation your mother and father built was based on their breaking out of this eggshell, somewhat, and presenting their books in a more popular way. But, I contend, they did not go far enough. Their findings, those of others in the field, have not really gone out to the masses, have not been valuable or beneficial to the millions who could profit most. If what you are seeing on The Three Sirens is useful to America, why should it not be disseminated widely to help Americans? If what you are seeing is of no value to anyone, only curious or different, what harm in showing your fellow countrymen how foolishly others live and how happy your countrymen should be with their own lots? Remember, the great movers of our time, Darwin, Marx, Freud, shook no worlds until their findings came into hands like yours and mine and were popularized. When you question me about propriety, I question you about the right of any group to withhold or censor information that will enrich minds. No, Marc, fear not, only good can come from putting this material into the hands of men who understand the masses of people.

And how could your material be misused or sensationalized? If we went ahead, it would be together, as collaborators. You would have control of editing and presenting the material with me. You know my work, my reputation of long standing which is based on good taste. Members of both sexes, of all ages, of varied social strata, have been my devoted followers for years. The sales of my books, the cities that have turned out to applaud me, the endless fan mail that flows across my desk, the huge sums I annually pay Internal Revenue, all are testaments to my conservatism, universality of judgment, and taste. Finally, we would serve under the auspices of the Busch Artist and Lyceum Bureau, founded in 1888, a firm of highest distinction that has had, variously, on its roster, such names as Dr. Sun Yat-sen, Henry George, Maxim Gorki, Carveth Wells, Sarah Bernhardt, Lily Langtry, Richard Halliburton, Gertrude Stein, Dr. Arthur Eddington, Dylan Thomas, Dr. William Bates, Count Alfred Korzybski, Wilson Mizner, Queen Marie of Rumania, Jim Thorpe—and, forgive me a third time, yours truly, Rex Garrity.

As to your concern about anthropologists going out before the lay public, put it aside. I have documentary evidence that dozens of your colleagues, from Robert Briffault to Margaret Mead, have done this, and have enhanced rather than harmed their professional standing.

So at last we come to my talks with the Busch people, and the "true economics" of what insiders call "the chicken à la king circuit." I have analyzed the most successful platform artists, and the most successful were those who were Big Names (Winston Churchill, Eleanor Roosevelt, etc.) or those who had something timely or unusual to say (Henry M. Stanley, General Chennault, etc.). The Busch people assure me that we could not fail, for between us we possess both elements of potential success. I have the reputation. You have at your fingertips the material that is both timely and unusual. Between us, we could make The Three Sirens a household name like Shangri-La—yes, the Shangri-La of love and marriage.

In return for arranging our bookings, transportation, hotels, meals, guidance, the Busch agency would take 33 percent of our gross earnings. That would leave each of us 33½ percent free and clear of expenses. If your findings are as electric as I promised them they would be, they believe it possible that in a ten-month period (lecturing combined with radio and television, exclusive of writings) our gross could be $750,000 minimum! Think of it, Marc, in ten months you could have a quarter of a million dollars free and clear, and a national reputation to boot!

The Busch people would require only one thing from you, besides your presence. They would need a single piece of corroborating evidence, that is, evidence that The Three Sirens exists and is what you say it is. In short, they want to suffer no Joan Lowells or Trader Horns. What could this evidence be? A color film showing the unique side of life on The Three Sirens, or color slides or a large collection of stills that could be projected, to accompany our appearances. Or even—as Captain Cook did on his return from his first visit to Tahiti—a native man or woman from the Sirens to appear side by side with us.

Perhaps I have gone too far in trying to perceive your thoughts and ambitions. I hope not. If you can find a way of joining me in this endeavor, you will not regret it. You will become, overnight, independently wealthy, and as famous, even more famous, than your mother.

Think of that, think of all I have related to you, not fancies but facts, and make your decision to strike out on your own. If you do, riches and glory await you. There is nothing more for me to add, except that the Busch people and I eagerly await your reply. If it is favorable, as I trust it will be, we will make any arrangement suitable to you. If you wish, I will fly posthaste to Tahiti to await your emergence, and we can return triumphantly to New York together to undertake Project Fame.

The close of the letter, signed with a Hancockian flourish, read, "Your friend and, I pray, future collaborator, Rex Garrity."

When Marc had finished, he did not reread the letter. It was as if every word of it was chiseled deeply into his consciousness. He held it in one hand, sitting there on the grass, surrounded by the color and fragrance of the acacia grove, and stared off at the path.

He realized that, despite the heat of midday, there was a thin pimpled chill on his shoulders, arms, forearms. He was frightened by the prize, and the enormity of the step that he must make to reach and hold it.

But then, coming to his feet, he knew that his decision had been made. What lay ahead, Garrity's way, was unknown and terrifying, for he did not know his strength, yet it was satisfying beyond any ambition he had ever held. What lay ahead, Matty's way, Claire's way, was known and horrific, for he knew his weakness, and it was more dismaying than any nightmare of being buried alive for eternity. So, the choice was clear.

He tried to think. The first step was to seal and mail the letter written to Garrity last night. It needed no amendment, no elaboration. It anticipated and responded to everything in the pages that he had just read. Yes, he would drop it into Rasmussen's outgoing mail pouch. That was the first step. The second step was to learn if his plan was practical. Everything hinged upon that, and thus, everything hinged upon Tehura. He would see her after the swimming match, when her primitive heart would welcome him as conquering hero. As to Claire, to hell with Claire, she was now the small-town first wife who was out of place and would never belong. Well, not quite that, either, for maybe she could be made to belong later by being brought to her knees, no longer a reproach but a beggar for his touch and glance. Claire, well, he would see, he would see. She was the least of it now. Momentous events were in the offing, and they were all that mattered.

Marc folded Garrity's letter, slipped it into his hip pocket, put a match to his cold cigar, and started for the path and the village. He felt like a quarter of a million dollars.

* * *

The classes in the school had been shortened this day, and had run straight through the lunch period. It was because of the festival, Mr. Manao had announced at the outset. School would be dismissed at two o'clock, and they would have an hour before the festival began with the annual swimming contest. "We will follow this schedule all of this week," Mr. Manao had added, and this edict had imparted to the students an air of frolic and merrymaking.

Surrounding Mary Karpowicz, the others in the classroom, usually so attentive and restrained, punctuated Mr. Manao's lectures with hushed but exhilarated whispering, poking, giggling, teasing, and tugging. Even Nihau, so solemn always, was less studious this day. He smiled more, and constantly met Mary's gaze with a reassuring nod and grin. Part of his good cheer, she knew, was his pleasure in having convinced her to return to the classroom after yesterday's upset. In fact, her sudden disappearance, during the recess that followed the study of faa hina'aro and the live anatomy lesson involving the buxom girl Poma and the manly Huatoro, had not gone unnoticed by the all-seeing Mr. Manao. When Mary had come into the room, determinedly early, the instructor had approached her and, out of hearing of the others, inquired if she was well. He had missed her, he said, for the last of the classes. Mary had spoken vaguely of a headache, of having to lie down, and the instructor had been satisfied.

Now, listening to the last of Mr. Manao's lecture on the island's history, Mary felt a hollowness in her stomach pit. She tried to attribute it to the missing of lunch—but knew it was not that at all, for there had been an extra recess with refreshments of fruit—and then she admitted to herself it was the apprehension of seeing the naked Poma and Huatoro again, soon, any minute, and her worry over what would be shown next.

Thinking about it, the hollowness in her stomach pit filled, and she was less conscious of it, as her confidence returned. She had seen the most of it, she reminded herself, and there would be nothing really new today. She was aware of Nihau shifting his position beside her—the history lecture was done—and she recollected his words yesterday in the cool clearing near the Sacred Hut. "What will spoil love is shame, is fear, is ignorance," he had said. "Seeing what you did see, and learning what you will learn, will not spoil anything when your heart is truly in love." This, Nihau had said, would make her ready for the One, when he came, and she would never know displeasure. The evident superiority she would wear, when again she faced the old gang in Albuquerque, suffused her, lifted her heart. She felt calm, and almost eager for the hour that lay ahead.

While Mr. Manao prepared for the last class, cleaning his spectacles with a portion of his loincloth, attaching them on his ears, then studying a single sheet of paper, and while the students in the room buzzed, Mary's eyes wandered to the open windows to her right. She could see her father, still beside the Rolleiflex set on a tripod. Oddly, he was doing what Mr. Manao had just done, wiping his rimless glasses.

Mary had not seen her father at breakfast. He was, she learned, at an early meeting with Maud Hayden. Later, when she had arrived at the schoolyard, she was surprised to see him, loaded under equipment, crouching, jumping, circling, squatting, squaring his fingers like a frame before his eyes, trying to find sights to shoot.

She had sneaked up behind him, and tickled the back of his warm, moist neck. He had gasped, almost lost his balance while crouched, tipping sideways, holding himself up with one hand, as he turned. "Oh, it's you, Mary—"

"Who did you think it was? Some sexy Siren?" Then, as he opened vertically, like an accordion, to his full height, she had asked, "What are you doing here anyway?"

"Maud wants a complete layout on the school, black and white, color, color slides."

"What's there to shoot here? It's just like any old school anywhere."

Sam Karpowicz had unslung his Rolleiflex. "You're becoming jaded, Mary. It's the one affliction every photographer has to watch out for. I mean, that the camera eye doesn't get too old, too used to everything it sees. The camera eye must always remain young, fresh, aware of contrasts and curiosities, never taking anything for granted. Look at Steichen's art. Always young." He half-turned, and nodded toward the thatched bowl of the building. "No, there isn't a school like that one in America or Europe, certainly no students dressed like those in your class, no teacher on earth like Mr. Manao. Maybe what you mean is that what you are learning is old hat, parallels your subjects at home." He had halted, thoughtfully considering his daughter. "At least, from what you've been telling us every day, the subjects here, history, handicraft, all that, do seem similar to those in your high school." He hesitated. "They are, aren't they?"

The question had alarmed Mary, probing so near her omission, and her mind conjured up Poma and Huatoro as she had seen them in front of the class yesterday. Hastily, she had concealed them. She had swallowed. "Yes, Dad, I suppose that's what I meant." She had not wanted the conversation to go on, for there might be traps, and so she affected disinterest. "Well, I'd better get going," she had said. "Happy time exposures."

That had been several hours ago, and from time to time, she had caught glimpses of her father and his cameras through the various open windows. Looking again, she saw that the window no longer framed his presence, his Rolleiflex, his tripod. She supposed that he had finished his series of pictures. Mr. Manao was speaking once more, and her concentration was again on the instructor.

There would be no further discussion of the human organs today, she learned. She was relieved, but she wondered what would be discussed. In a few minutes, she knew, and her back arched alertly, and inquisitiveness overcame embarrassment.

Mr. Manao had promised that his discourse on arousal of a partner would be detailed, require several days, and be undertaken only after he had covered broad basic points. This afternoon, he would discuss, and have demonstrated, the major positions assumed in love-making. There were, he said, six basic ones, and the variations of these were perhaps thirty more.

"First, the major ones," he announced, and hit his hands together in the manner of a magician saying "presto." From the back room, Huatoro and Poma emerged, their expressions phlegmatic. While the muscular athlete retained his brief garment, the twenty-two-year-old widow, Poma, quickly undid her grass skirt and threw it aside.

Although Mary was in the rear of the class, she could see the demonstration clearly between the rows of students. To her surprise, there was no contact between the actors, only a kind of posturing. They performed with the grace and fluidity of a pair of disinterested tumblers, brought together by their spindly director's narration.

Although mildly disappointed, Mary's attention remained riveted on the players, following them as she might two trained amoebae under a microscope. In fact, so absorbed had she become, that she did not, even in the silence of the room, hear the angry shuffle and stir directly behind her.

Suddenly, Mary felt a hard hand on her shoulder, squeezing and pulling, so that she winced with pain.

"Mary, I want you to leave the room!"

The voice was her father's voice, high-pitched in anger, and the sound of it pierced her eardrums and slashed through the room.

The demonstration before the class halted, Mr. Manao's sentence hung suspended, all heads turned to the rear as one head, and, in shock, Mary twisted around. Sam Karpowicz was standing over her. She had never seen his face so contorted and livid before. All kindliness, all fatherliness, had succumbed to the outline of outrage.

"Mary," he repeated loudly, "get up and get out of here at once!"

Paralyzed on the matting, mouth open in the confusion that precedes humilation, she remained as she had been. Her father's hand left her shoulder, hooked under her armpit, and roughly hauled her from the floor.

Gasping, as she scrambled to her feet, full humiliation fell upon her. All eyes, she knew, were on her back and this disruptive, rude old man who was breaking up the class. And Nihau, Nihau, he was seeing this, and thinking what—what was he thinking?

She tried to speak, working her mouth, but her lips quivered and her teeth chattered and her lungs were dry and strangling.

Sam Karpowicz was glaring at her. "You've been coming here every day, indulging in this filthy—filthy—this sporting house—and not telling us—"

Her words came out, at last, broken fragments tearing from her throat. "Pa—no—don't—it's not—it's—don't, please—" Her eyes had filled, and control became impossible.

Mr. Manao materialized between them, a perplexed spider. "Sir—sir—what is it—what is wrong?"

"Goddammit, dammit man," Sam was sputtering, "if I hadn't just come in here to shoot pictures of this goddam class—I was so busy these last five minutes setting up equipment I didn't even look to see what was going on up front—but goddammit, how dare you expose a sixteen-year-old girl to a low-down sex circus? I've heard of this going on in Paris and Singapore, but you people are supposed to be advanced—"

Mr. Manao kept lifting a hand, to interrupt, to explain, the imploring hand shuddering as if attached to an epileptic. "Mr.—Dr.—Karpowicz—you do not understand—"

"I understand one thing, dammit—what my eyes see! I'm as progressive and liberal as anyone on earth, but when an immature child is made—when her head is stuck in the mud—when she's forced to look at the two of them up there—look at them—that half-naked big lover up there, trying to excite these young people—and look at her, just look at her—with her—her—her ass flying in the breeze!"

It was then that Mary screamed. "Paaa! Stop it—shut up, will you —shut up—shut up—shut your mouth—"

He stared at her as if slapped, and she wheeled and faced the class, all of them, Nihau, his face wrenched by despair and anguish for her, and all the others, half-understanding, understanding, and the two up front, and she tried to say something to them all, some apology, but there was no voice. She stood before them, mute, tears pouring down her cheeks, until she could not see them, and then she stumbled, tripping once, toward the exit, and plunged outside.

She went blindly across the recess area, seeing nothing, wanting only a grave and to pull the earth over her blazing face and dying heart.

No one was following her, but she began to run. She ran all the way home, sobbing and sobbing and wildly hoping God would strike him dead, and her other parent, too, and make the hut an orphanage.

*　　*　　*

It was not yet three o'clock when Claire and Maud completed their climb to the point overlooking the sea where spectators were gathering to watch the opening event of the annual festival.

The throng was the largest and noisiest that Claire had seen since coming to The Three Sirens. One hundred, maybe closer to two hundred, brown torsos were gathered, as closely packed as the crowds on the Champs Élysées the morning of Bastille Day, all settled here along the curved rim of the ridge that dropped sharply down to the water. The members of the American group were almost all present, and had attached themselves to Chief Paoti and his wife, who sat cross-legged at the farthest brow of land in the choicest sightseeing area.

During the short hike from the village, Claire had been oblivious both to the direction they took and the new scenery along the way, so intent was she on the inward film, passing through her mind, running in reverse, of her life with Marc. His insensitive, even brutal behavior of the night before, so loveless, even worse, so patently hateful and sick; that, and his horrid avoidance of her, of offering any softening, compromising apology or explanation this morning, these had generated the backwards unreeling of her past. What she saw, in the private projection room of her head, frightened her. For, while the past year, especially the past months, had been unsatisfying, somehow she had clung to the remembrance that the year before that, the first year, and the courting period before that, had been beautiful, or at least not unattractive, and she had clung to the belief that what had been enacted once could be lived again. That had been her hope.

In her walk behind Maud, as the film ran backwards, the images that were brought to mind, instead of being prettified by their distance in time, had remained as enlarged and candid as pictures of the present time. Perhaps, she had told herself, the present was discoloring the images of the past. But then she was not so sure of that, either. Her married past was as marred with daily life's acne as the present, so that none of it was fresh or handsome. The picture of her honeymoon night in Laguna, even. After the first union of their nude bodies in bed, right afterwards, he had wept, unaccountably wept. It had seemed to her then an emotional reaction of such goodness and sweetness, that she had held him, cradled him with after-love, until he slept like a child in her arms. But now, now, the rerun of the old scene was less romantic, was not romantic at all, only ill and suspect and the entire connotation somewhat ugly.

However, the moment that Claire had reached their destination, joined the hubbub of the gallery, the film had run blank. What filled her sight and mind was the activities and drama of the moment, sans Marc, and she was distracted from her misery. She greeted Harriet Bleaska and Rachel DeJong, and waved to Lisa Hackfeld and Orville Pence.

When Sam Karpowicz, a heavy sixteen-millimeter motion-picture camera in hand, came by, Claire spoke a hello to him, too. He saw her, yet did not see her, rudely ignored her, his features oddly twisted as if by some partial paralysis. He did not seem the gentle botanist and amateur photographer she had known these weeks. With wonder, she cast about for Estelle and Mary Karpowicz, but they were nowhere to be seen.

Maud had come away from Paoti's side, and Claire said to her, "What's eating Sam Karpowicz?"

"What do you mean?"

"He simply went past me when I said hello. Look at him shoving over there. Something must be wrong."

Maud dismissed it. "Nothing's wrong. Sam's never in a bad mood. He's busy. He's going to shoot the entire swimming race, and he's always absent-minded when he has things to do."

Claire rejected this explanation, knowing it came from the usual blind spot in Maud's sensitivity about individuals. Then, as if to confirm her own suspicions, Claire watched Sam's surprising bullying continue and knew that she was right. Bad, bad mood. But, she asked herself, why not? It was a democratic prerogative—every human being's inalienable right under God, Country, and Freud— the privilege to be moody. Wasn't her mood bad? Damn right. Except at least she was trying to observe the civilities.

"Come here, Claire," she heard Maud calling. "Isn't this a sight?"

Maud stood at the edge of the drop—"like stout Cortez . . . with eagle eyes"—a proprietary arm flung toward the Pacific. Claire went to her and looked off. The midafternoon view, the hot yellow of the sunrays softened and greened by the placid velvety carpet of water, was awesome. Her eyes roamed from the infinite expanse of ocean to what was directly below. She stood on the elevated center of a horseshoe of land, and this horseshoe cupped the ocean, a particle of it, into an enclosed pool of water beneath her. This pool, apparently, would be the arena for the race. To her right, the water seemed to graduate into a steep incline of rock that resembled, with its rising indented ridges, a natural stone stepladder. Past the stone stepladder could be seen a corner of one of the two small, uninhabited coral atolls that adjoined the main island of the Sirens. If one sailed on between that atoll and the shore, almost the full length of the main island, Claire guessed, one would arrive at the far beach where Rasmussen's seaplane rested.

Claire half-turned toward the opposite cliff enclosing the pool below, and this was sheer perpendicular. Her eyes moved along it, and at the very top she saw the contestants bunched. They were perhaps one hundred yards off, not distinct, yet clear enough so that she was immediately able to separate the blocky frame of her husband. This was easy because he, alone, was pinkish white and hairy and wearing navy blue trunks in contrast to the two dozen men of the Sirens around him who were light tan to dark brown and hairless and attired in supporters. Seeing her husband thus, in an athletic contest, she thought not of participant observer but of second childhood. Anger entered her chest again like a terrible heartburn. Consciousness of the pain spoiled the beauty of the scene. Claire turned away.

Maud, she saw, had gone to Harriet Bleaska and Rachel DeJong, and then she saw that they were being joined by a rather short young-old native man with an intent face rather curiously Latin in profile. She recognized him as Vaiuri, the one who was the head of the hospital or clinic and Nurse Harriet's collaborator.

Keeping her back to Marc's afternoon idiocy, Claire wandered from the cliff, until she came to the fringe of the group that she had been observing. With little interest in what they might be discussing, she pretended interest and social absorption.

Vaiuri was addressing Harriet. Even in his loincloth, he seemed to have the solemn and wise manner of all the world's physicians. He was saying, "—and because of our work together, Miss Bleaska, I was assigned to bring to you the word of the final voting. I am honored to inform you that you will be queen of the festival."

He waited, like a practiced public speaker who pauses for the expected burst of applause, and he was not disappointed. Harriet's hands clapped together, and then held together at her wide mouth in a pose of prayer fulfilled, and her eyes appeared to bulge. "Oh!" she had exclaimed, and then she said, "Me? I'm going to be queen—?"

"Yes—yes," Vaiuri was assuring her, "it is voted in the morning by the adult males of our village. It is one of our great honors of the festival week."

Harriet stared uncertainly at the others. "I'm overwhelmed. Can you imagine—me a queen?"

"It's wonderful, wonderful," Maud was saying.

"Congratulations," said Rachel.

Harriet had faced Vaiuri again. "But why—why me?"

"It was inevitable," he replied seriously. "The honor every year is for the most beautiful young woman in the village—"

"You're embarrassing me," Harriet interrupted with a nervous giggle. "Really, Vaiuri, I'm no—I know my assets and defects— there are a hundred really beautiful women—Claire here—the Chief's niece—"

Claire realized that Vaiuri had nodded respectfully toward her, but addressed Harriet with gravity. "No disrespect to the many others, also deserving. I repeat. The men have voted you the most beautiful."

Claire tried to see Harriet as these men saw her. Had she heard of such a thing when she had first met Harriet, Claire might have thought the award a mean mockery. Harriet's plainness—no, truth —absolute homeliness, had often intruded upon Claire's attentiveness to her. Since then, Claire realized, more and more the friendliness and gaiety of the nurse's personality had married themselves to her features and made her features acceptable. In this crowning moment, Claire could see that the nurse's joy in it, pride in it, had indeed made her almost physically fair.

"I'm still practically speechless," Harriet was saying. "What am I supposed to do, I mean as queen?"

"You will open and close tonight's dance," said Vaiuri. "I shall teach you the words. There will be several other similar ceremonies in the week that you will preside over."

Harriet turned to Maud. "Isn't this something? Queen—" A feminine concern passed across her face. "Vaiuri, what does the queen wear, a robe and diamonds or what?"

Vaiuri seemed suddenly uncomfortable. He cleared his throat. "No, no robe. You—you will sit on a bench on a platform above the others. Yes."

Harriet bent toward him. "You haven't answered me. What does your festival queen wear?"

"Well—in times past, in accordance with tradition—"

"Not times past. Last year, what did she wear?"

Vaiuri cleared his throat again. "Nothing," he said.

"Nothing? You mean nothing?"

"As I attempted to explain, it is the tradition that since the queen is the reigning beauty of the village in the men's hearts, her beauty must reign. On the special occasions she appears in disrobe—that is —divested of all garments." He hastened to the next. "But I must say quickly, Miss Bleaska, in your case, since you are a foreigner, it was agreed that this old tradition may be modified. You may appear as you wish."

Harriet had already assumed a monarch's concern for her subjects. "What would *you* wish? What would please the village men most? I mean—honestly, now."

The medical practitioner hesitated. All interest was concentrated upon him. He massaged his jaw with one hand. "I believe it would please everyone if you made your appearance in the—the day-by-day costume of our women."

"You mean grass skirt and nothing else, period?"

"Well, as I said—"

"Is that what you mean?"

"Yes."

Harriet grinned at Claire, then Maud and Rachel. "I'm not much in the balcony department, but anything once." She winked at Vaiuri. "Tell the boys the Queen is grateful, and will be on hand in grass skirt and total décolletage. What a sight—but really, Vaiuri, I'm thrilled, I'm so thrilled."

The medical practitioner, relieved and more composed, had turned to Rachel DeJong beside him. "Dr. DeJong, I have been entrusted with a gift for you."

Rachel showed her surprise. "A gift? How very nice."

Vaiuri dug into a fold of his loincloth, unknotted it, and handed a gold-colored object to Rachel. She examined the object with bewilderment, then held it up. It was a highly polished, porcelainlike shell that hung from a strand. "A necklace," she said, half to herself.

"The festival necklace," explained Vaiuri. "Most often they are mother-of-pearl, but sometimes they are cowries or terebras. This one is a golden cowrie."

Rachel remained puzzled, but Maud had quickly reached out, touched the brilliant shell, and asked the practitioner, "Is this the famous shell that solicits a meeting?" Vaiuri inclined his head in assent, and Maud seemed delighted. "Rachel, you've made it," she said. "Don't you remember? For festival week, the men prepare these and present them to women they have high esteem for all year. Like the Mabuiang tribe's grass bracelets, these are statements of admiration and invitations to—I suppose you might say invitations to secret rendezvous—and if, after receiving one, you wear it, you give consent. The next step is a meeting, and the next step is—well, you are on your own . . . Am I right, Vaiuri?"

"Absolutely, Dr. Hayden."

Rachel frowned down at the bulbous shell. "I'm still not sure I understand. Who is it from?"

"Moreturi," said the practitioner. "Now, if you will excuse me—"

Claire had watched the psychoanalyst through the last, and she could see that Rachel's face had paled. Rachel looked up, caught Claire's eye, and shook her head, her lips tight. "He's untractable," she said, with a trace of indignation. "Another act of hostility. He's determined to fight me, embarrass me."

"Aw, Rachel, cut it out." It was Harriet's happy voice. "They love us. What more can a woman ask for?"

Before Rachel DeJong could reply, Tom Courtney joined the group. "Hello, everyone—hello, Claire—better find your places. They'll be off and splashing in a few minutes."

Obediently, the group splintered in different directions, except for Claire, who remained where she had been. Prepared to leave, Courtney hung back, as if waiting for her. "Mind if we watch it together?" he asked.

"I'm not sure I want to watch it at all, but—oh, all right, yes, thank you."

They went to the right, toward the brink of the cliff, past Rasmussen, who was leaning over a native girl, whispering to her, and he wagged his hand at them without looking up. They found a vacant area apart from the members of the team and the villagers.

Before sitting, Claire glanced past Courtney at the spectators. "Tom," she said, "why all this?"

"What do you mean?"

"I mean the festival. The whole week. I've heard Maud lecture us on it a dozen times. But still, I'm not sure—"

"Have you ever read Frazer's *The Golden Bough?*"

"Much of it, yes, in college. And Maud's always having me type quotations from it."

"Maybe you'll recognize this quotation." He squinted up at the sky a moment, and recited it from memory, " 'We have seen that many peoples have been used to observe an annual period of license, when the customary restraints of law and morality are thrown aside, when the whole population give themselves up to extravagant mirth and jollity, and when the darker passions find a vent which would never be allowed them in the more staid and sober course of ordinary life. Of such periods of license the one which is best known and which in modern languages has given its name to the rest, is the Saturnalia.' " He paused. "There you are, Claire."

"Umm, I remember," she said. "I remember wondering, the very first time I heard about it, why we didn't have something similar at home. I wondered it aloud, at a party, and I'm afraid I committed social heresy." Then she added, "In Marc's eyes, I mean. He believes the Fourth of July, Christmas, Flag Day fill all our needs." She was unable to modify this with a smile. After a moment, she peered off and could see the brown bodies and the single white one, in the distance, beginning to line up on the cliff's edge. "The race starts it off, I'm told. How do they race?"

Courtney followed the line of her vision. "The starter will blow a bamboo whistle. They'll dive off into the water."

"That's a terrifying dive."

"Sixty feet. They swim free-style, no rules, across the lagoon. It's about one mile across, I think. I timed last year's swim at twenty-three minutes. When they reach the opposite terraced slope, over there, they go scrambling the fifty feet to the top. First man on top is the winner, king of the hill."

"What's in it for the winner?"

"Considerable mana before the young ladies. The whole event is an important symbol of virility and quite appropriate for starting off the festival."

"I see," she said. "Now it begins to make sense."

"What do you mean?"

"Just something private. I was thinking of my husband."

"I hope he can swim."

"Oh, he can swim, that's one thing he can do." Then, curtly, she said, "Let's get off our feet."

They sat down in the trampled grass, Courtney with his long legs folded high before him, encircled by his arms, and Claire with her arms hugging her bare knees.

She studied Courtney's broken bronze profile, as he looked off at the contestants readying for the event. She said, "Tom—after this—what goes on tonight, every night? That quotation from Frazer keeps sticking in my mind. It conjures up a mighty unruly week."

"Nothing like that at all. No need for a Saturnalia, Roman style. There is just more freedom, more license, no recriminations. It is the week of the year in which these people open the valve and let

412

off steam, sanctioned and legalized steam. Everyone gets double rations from the communal storehouse, including fowl and pig, double amounts of intoxicants if desired, there are dances, beauty contests, all sorts of Polynesian games to watch or participate in, and there is the giving and taking of the festival shell—"

Claire thought of Rachel DeJong's anger—real or feigned? probably real—at receiving a shell from Moreturi. Would she wear it? Participant observation, you know, unquote Maud Hayden. "Why that business of the shell?" she asked Courtney. "They have license all year with the Social Aid Hut."

"Not quite," said Courtney. "A native can use the Social Aid only if there is a real reason to use it. If challenged, he has to prove his need of it. During festival week, no one has to prove or explain anything. If a married woman has an eye on someone else's husband, or some single man, she need only send him a polished shell to arrange an assignation. She can send out as many as she wishes. And the same goes for the men."

"It sounds pretty dangerous to me."

"It isn't, Claire, not really, especially against the background of this culture. It is all discreet fun. If I've been married and had a secret crush on you all year, well, today or tomorrow I'd send you a shell. If you wore the necklace I'd made, we'd talk, arrange a meeting outside the village. This doesn't mean that automatically you'd sleep with me. It means let's meet and talk, drink and dance, and see what comes next."

"What happens next week?"

"Well, my fictional wife wouldn't be angry with me, and I'd have nothing against her. Life would resume its routine course. Sometimes, not frequently, after this week, there are readjustments. New love affairs burgeon, and then the Hierarchy steps in to mediate."

"What about nine months later?" asked Claire. "What if an extramarital child is produced by one of these affairs?"

"It rarely happens. Great care is taken. Their precautions are effective. When an offspring does result, the mother has the option of keeping the infant or turning it over to the Hierarchy to dispose of to some barren couple."

"They think of everything," said Claire. "Okay, I'm still for it."

"It wouldn't work back home," said Courtney. "I've thought about it often, but no. These people have had a couple of centuries of orientation to it. They are prepared by background and from birth. We're not ready at home. Too bad, too. I think it's so sad, at home, the way you grow up toward marriage not being able to meet many people you think you might love. I remember once, in Chicago, standing on the corner of State and Madison, and seeing a slender young brunette, so lovely, and for ten seconds I was in love, and I thought, if only I could speak to her, go out with her, see if she was for me, but then the green light changed and she disappeared in the crowd and I went my way and never saw her again. No shell necklace to pass, you see. Instead, I had to confine myself to artificially created and limited social groups and make my choice from these. I sometimes feel I was shortchanged. You know what I mean?"

"I know."

"And after marriage, well, the anthropologists know this, there's no extramarital freedom at home, both sexes chafe along on the same rails toward old age, scenery ignored, side trips not allowed. Church and State are kept happy. It is unrealistic, and if you stay on the rails, it's a strain, and if you don't, if you sneak in a few detours, it's also a strain. I've been there, Claire, I know. Remember, I was a divorce attorney."

"Yes," said Claire. "I guess a number of us have had the same feelings, brought on by the purpose behind the festival. We just haven't been able to articulate it, or maybe don't want to. Although, come to think of it, Harriet Bleaska did tell me that when we first came here, Lisa Hackfeld mentioned to her an awareness of some of the same shortcomings at home, the confinement of being single or married, that you've been talking about."

"I wouldn't be surprised," said Courtney. "My own years in the Midwest seem incredible to me since I've lived here—"

A piercing, reedy whistle sliced through Courtney's sentence, and an immediate powerful chorus of cheering from off to the left ended his reflections completely. Courtney and Claire swiveled their heads in unison and they saw the faraway line of contestants plunge free of the earth and plummet through space. Some arched gracefully and some spun crazily, flopping through the ozone like so many Raggedy Andys. The bodies all seemed brown, and then, near the water, Claire saw the one that was white and hairy, arms forward like an arrowhead, body rigid as a plank of wood.

Marc was among the vanguard of a half-dozen to hit the water.

Of them all, Marc alone did not actually hit the water, spatter it, but appeared to knife into it, cleanly, beautifully, and disappear from sight. Around him were splashes and geysers, and then heads bobbing afloat. And then, Marc slithered out of the water, five or ten yards ahead of his nearest competitor. Employing the Australian crawl, his white arms began to revolve, pulling at the water, head pillowed against the hospitable sea, legs opening and closing like scissors, leaving a trail of foam, as he sped ahead.

"Your husband's got the early lead," Courtney said, above the steady din of the spectators. "That's Moreturi behind him, and right behind him Huatoro."

Claire's eyes shifted from Marc to the two brown figures thrashing in pursuit of him. Their swimming was choppier than Marc's, more primitive and explosive. Both Moreturi and Huatoro were beating the water harder with their hands, rolling farther onto their sides to suck for air, kicking their legs more visibly. Minutes were passing, and yards behind the three leaders the other brown faces, brown shoulders, brown arms were beginning to string out.

Claire watched without emotion, quite detached here high and above, as if viewing the spectacle of small windup toys pitted against one another in a tub of water.

She became aware of Courtney's watch, his finger touching the crystal. "Fifteen minutes and they're at the half-mile," he was saying. "Very good time. You were right. Your man can swim."

My man, she thought, thinking at last, letting *my man my man my man* echo and reverberate in her brain chamber.

"Look at him open up that lead," Courtney was saying.

She had been looking, but had not seen, so now she put mind's sight into her eyes. It was true. There was open sea between Marc and the native pair, maybe a full twenty yards. She stared down at the white one, the great white lover, superior man, superior race, putting on his symbolic show of virility. Here again the persistently nagging questions: Do manly manners and manly feats make a manly man? Is Marc a man? Unless I know, how am I to know if I am a woman?

"You must be so very proud!" It was a thrilled young female voice addressing her, and Claire realized that the beautiful Tehura had come to kneel between Courtney and herself. The native girl's eyes glistened and her white teeth shone.

Claire gave some kind of dumb nodding assent, and Courtney said teasingly to the girl, "Your friend Huatoro is not used to looking at another's feet."

"I have no favorite," said Tehura primly. "Huatoro is my friend, but Moreturi is my cousin, and Marc Hayden is my—" She hesitated, groping in her limited word cupboard, and then concluding, "—he is my mentor from far away." She pointed below. "Look, Tom, Huatoro is passing poor Moreturi!"

Ignoring the race, Claire stared wonderingly at the native girl. She had always regarded her as just one more attractive female of the village, a special female since Tehura had stood beside her at the first night's rite of acceptance, but still one more member of a tribe being studied. Yet, for the first time, she realized that the girl had a closer relationship to Marc and herself. Marc was her "mentor." She was Marc's "informant." For a good part of two weeks, Marc had spent long hours of days with her. This girl had probably seen more of Marc, in this time, than had Claire. What did she think of Marc, that strange, sullen, almost middle-aged man from California? Did she think of him as a man at all? How could she, who knew so much, think so, if Claire, who knew so little, was not sure? But these questions were fruitless. Tehura did not know Marc at all. She knew an anthropologist asking questions and making notes. She knew a muscular white man swimming ahead of her fellow villagers. She did not know the Puritan Father who had insulted the grass skirt, Tehura's own, that Claire had worn in love last night.

Claire saw that Courtney and Tehura, and everyone behind them, were absorbed in the contest below. She sighed and leaned forward. Since she had last looked, the design on the green water, formed by the swimmers, had altered. Minutes before, she had thought that they resembled a long rope of foam, with knots strung out along the rope, the knots being the heads and shoulders of the competitors. The foam rope was gone. Instead, the design on the water was that of a tight triangle moving toward the stone shore beneath her. The front point of the triangle was still Marc, his wet, chalky arms moving out of the water and over and stroking down, like paddles of a Mississippi gambling boat. Diagonally behind, to his left, quite near Marc it seemed, was the broad-shouldered one called Huatoro. Diagonally, to the right, further back, was Moreturi. Then, closer than they had been before, the rest of the triangle formed by the other brown swimmers, with their relentless flaying arms, fluttering kicks, rollings, exhalings, inhalings.

She heard Courtney's voice announcing to Tehura, "They're closing in on him in the stretch. Look, there's Huatoro. I didn't think he'd have that much left—"

"He is strong," said Tehura.

Claire was conscious of the swelling clamor of the spectators, and then it burst into pandemonium. As if lifted by the detonation of two hundred throats crying out as one stentorian bellow, Courtney and Tehura leaped to their feet.

"Look at them—look at them!" Courtney shouted. He half-turned, "Claire, you must see the finish—"

Unwillingly, Claire responded. The contestants, a portion of the front ones, had been briefly out of her vision, but when she came up next to Courtney and Tehura, she could see them all.

Marc had just touched the foot of the great benched cliff, and he was hauling himself out of the ocean like a soggy albino seal. He was upright, the first on land, and as he shook free of the film of water, he glanced over his shoulder in time to see the broad, powerful frame of Huatoro hoisting itself ashore.

Spurred by the closeness of the other, Marc started up the incline, with a five-yard lead over his rival. The banks of the cliff were craggy and steep. There was no worn path. One did not merely walk up it or march up it. Rather, one snatched it, each indentation above, did a pull-up, and caught one's breath, climbing when the ladder rungs of stone were closer, but gripping and rising by force when they were separated. In this manner, Marc ascended the terraced slope, with Huatoro steadily behind him, as a swarm of others just touched the rocky shore.

Marc and Huatoro were halfway toward their summit finish, the judges on their knees above, waving, beckoning, encouraging, and then they were two-thirds toward the final height, and then Claire could see that Marc was faltering. As he reached each small bluff, and pulled himself erect, he took an increasingly longer time to propel himself to the next precipice above. Until these seconds, he had been as regular as a machine, but now it was as if the machine had become clogged and was slowing. Marc's ascent became slow-motion, painful to behold. His pauses were longer and longer, as if the last of his strength had seeped out of him.

Fifteen feet from the top, on a narrow ledge, he stopped, staggering on rubbery legs, whiter than before, almost deformed by fatigue. And here it was that Huatoro caught him, clambering onto a parallel ledge no more than three feet to one side. For the first time, Claire, who had been concentrating upon her husband, could plainly see his rival. Huatoro came up, side by side with Marc, with the vigor of a young, plunging bull. He hesitated only a split second to look across at his opponent, and then he reached one muscular arm upwards, and the other, and followed his arms with his rippling shoulders and torso.

Claire could see Marc shaking his head, hard, like a gladiator risen from the arena floor, trying to unscramble his senses and make them signal his unsteady calves into motion. The next high ledge was near, and Marc attained it with hardly any help from his hands. As he reached it, Huatoro was already a full stride ahead in the climb. Desperately, Marc tried to keep up with the other. Higher they went, nearer the finish, pull, jump, stop, climb, crawl, stop, another, another, and then they were on the same small promontory, but not long side by side, for Huatoro was still moving, scrambling upwards, while Marc was wavering near collapse, going down to one knee, the gladiator fallen again, not by a blow but by weakness and loss of will.

Then it was that Claire once more became conscious of the thunderous cheers of the spectators, and heard Tehura screaming, shaking Courtney's arm, screaming, "Look—look—oh, nooo— nooo—"

Claire turned back to see the finish, and found that Marc was upright, not climbing, but snatching for the ledge directly above which Huatoro had just scaled. But instead of grasping the ledge, Marc's hand closed on Huatoro's ankle. The native, starting to move, found himself one-legged, the other leg fastened down by his rival's grip. Bewildered no doubt, perhaps angered (his features could not be clearly seen), Huatoro shouted something at Marc, and he shook his captured leg once, twice, and a third time hard, kicking free of Marc, as if kicking free of some small troublesome terrier.

Liberated, Huatoro climbed swiftly upwards to the very summit and his victory, while Marc remained where he had been kicked down by the other, down on both hands and both knees, immobilized, by fatigue and public humiliation. And it worsened, for as he stayed on his hands and knees, prostrated, Moreturi came vaulting up, glanced down at him, and then continued to work his way to the finish. Then came the others, the tenacious and robust young men, the first passing Marc to reach the summit third, and then another and another. Finally, finally, Marc rose, and shakily and all palsied, so slowly, he went up the last few ledges, ignoring outstretched hands, to lift himself to the summit. Huatoro and Moreturi, and one or two others also, approached him, evidently trying to speak to him, but he turned from them and, shoulders and chest heaving, went off alone, to one side, to recover his strength and his pride.

The shouting had dropped to a low babble of voices in the air. Claire twisted away from the scene, firmly put her back to it, only to find Courtney observing her.

She did not attempt to smile or shrug off her reaction. Quietly, on a pitch of irony, she quoted, " 'When the Great Scorer comes to write against your name, He writes not that you won or lost but how you played the game.' "

Courtney frowned. "I don't think so, Claire, I don't think he really tried to hold Huatoro back. He was reaching for the ledge and by accident—he didn't know what he was doing—he grabbed Huatoro's ankle, just held on—instinct of self-preservation."

"I don't need that pill, Tom," she said, suddenly angry. "I know the patient. He was a fool to enter this, and he was a double fool in the end. If a man's got to prove himself, I know better means, and different means. No more sweeteners today, thank you, Tom."

Tehura had come forward, a strange questioning look in her face as she confronted Claire. "Is that what you see, Mrs. Hayden? I see different." She paused, and she said stiffly, "I think he did well." With a nod, she departed.

Claire's eyebrows shot up with puzzlement as she watched the native girl leave. Claire turned to Courtney, and she shrugged. "Well, when the Great Scorer comes, I guess he had better come to The Three Sirens first . . . Thanks for your company, Tom. I think I'd best get back to the hut, and put a bandage on my hero's virility." She blinked at his expressionless face, and she added, "We'll need our strength. It's going to be quite a festival."

* * *

At several minutes after eight o'clock in the evening, the fringes of the village were darkened, and this served to accentuate the great decorative ball of light in the very center of the compound.

The ball of light was actually a blending of three rising rings of blazing torches surrounding the mammoth platform constructed in the early morning. The torches went up from the ground like candles surmounting a three-decker birthday cake. There was the wide ring of torches, broken in half only by the stream, planted in the earth itself, among the clustered villagers. The fingers of flame went straight up, without flickering or bending in the windless calm of night, as if the High Spirit was not panting or breathing heavily upon his children, but sitting serenely with them for an interlude of pleasure uninterrupted by work. The second circle of lights came from the torches attached to the wooden step built around the platform, two feet above the turf, two feet below the stage, and which was used as stairs by the performers. Upon the platform itself was the topmost circle of illumination, where the stubbier, wider, brighter torches resembled footlights on four curving sides.

Courtney had told the Hayden team that the oval platform was almost forty feet in length and twenty feet in width, and the planks were used over and over again, for every annual festival, so that the surface was worn smooth as carpeting by innumerable dancing bare feet.

At the moment, except for the seven native males who were the musicians—young, enthusiastic brown men, two beating hollowed tree trunks made into slit drums, one with a flute, two with bamboo rods they struck together, two with big hands clapping loudly—the stage was empty.

The members of the Hayden team had been given the seats of honor, places in the first row which began fifteen feet back from the front of the platform. They sat on the grass, with villagers seated row upon row behind them, until lost in the outer darkness.

Claire was at the end of their row, looking relaxed in her sleeveless white Dacron blouse and navy blue linen skirt that covered her knees. Her sandaled feet were discreetly crossed beneath the skirt. She sat quietly, hands folded in her lap. She heard Orville Pence, kneeling beside Rachel DeJong and Maud, who were next to her, saying, "—and the musicians insisted that even their instruments are ancient sex symbols; the hollow drum up there represents the female, and over there the wooden flute, obviously the male. All one more part of the festival theme. Then, if you consider—"

Claire closed her ears to the rest. She was bored with the Freudian patter. There would be this, and there would be Boas and Kroeber and Benedict, and always Malinowski, and most certainly Cora DuBois and the island of Alors, and inevitably the subject of Psychodynamics. For Claire, these would be the intruders, the unwanted guests, who analyzed, who explained, who took apart and put together, who peeled off primitive beauty so that only the misshapen core was left in full disfigurement.

Tonight, Claire wanted none of this. The scene and setting were romantic, and Claire wanted the contentment of it to soak into her pores and not into her poor head. She wanted to escape from the technical talk of the team, from her own situation really, and this one night she was determined to make the flight, no matter how briefly.

She diverted her attention to the stage above, and to the activity around it.

A childhood carnival, she thought, a magical carnival for a time when you were too small, eyes too small, mind too small, to see the tawdry, the imperfections, the daily dyings. She remembered—she had not remembered it in years—the one on the Oak Street beach, in Chicago, on the magnificent lake shore, when she was little. Perhaps she had been five or six or seven. She remembered her father's firm hand covering her hand, as they went down to the lake front from Michigan Boulevard. She remembered that everyone seemed to know him—"Hi, Alex" . . . "See you got a date, Alex"—even a pair who whispered as they passed, one saying, "Yes, Alex Emerson, the sports writer."

Suddenly, she remembered, they were plowing through the warm sand, and there was the riot of sound and lights, and the rows of bazaar shops of wonderland. They had gone through the carousing people, stopping here and there, this booth and that, her father laughing and laughing, and lifting her up and putting her down. She remembered hot dogs, endless hot dogs, and gallons of lemonade, and a billion puffs of pink cotton candy, and she remembered popcorn as endless as grains of sand on the beach, and a zillion dolls and ceramic dogs and cats, and the wheelings of the merry-go-round and the ferris wheel and the whip, God, the whip, how she held him for dear life.

The imprint on memory faded, but clear still was the feeling of the night, the wondrous, immortal, hugging swell of the one emotion that she felt when she drowsed against his broad chest as he carried her up to the car—it was Being Loved she had felt, and she had not known it again, not once, in the heavy, slow, unpopulated, unfun years since.

She tried to evoke the old childhood carnival once more, overlay it upon the revelry here on the Sirens, but it was no use, for she was grown, and her veteran eyes saw behind booths, behind corners, behind masquerades. Feeling had given way to thinking. And besides, besides, where was Alex? Yet, objectively, all this before her, primitive and strange, had a grown-up attraction of its own. The trouble was, she was apart from it, interested and bystander, not of it.

Also, she was alone. Maud did not count. Nor did Rachel count, nor did the disagreeable Orville Pence. She was married two years and one day, she was one-half of two who (by matrimonial mathematics) were supposed to be One, yet here sat she like a spinster woman, a half-person, alone. Where had the equation gone wrong? With the chalk of memory, she redid it on mind's blackboard . . .

Marc was already there, in the rear room of the hut, when she had returned from the swimming contest. His trunks, still soggy, hung limply from a wall peg. He lay, shirtless and shoeless, but in washable slacks, upon the sleeping bag, soundly napping, breath exhaling in low honks as if from an exhausted canine. His excursion into juvenility—juve*senility* was the observation she coined—had sapped him entirely. She was embarrassed for staring at him, unbeknownst to him, as he slept. It was unfair, for he was defenseless against judgment.

She had left him to occupy herself with the dinner. In celebration of the festival, there was an added supply of native food and drink: lobster, red bananas, sea cucumbers, turtle eggs, yams, taro in palm-frond baskets, coconut milk in one earthenware pitcher, and palm toddy in another pitcher. Beside these lay a new foodpounder, fashioned from the ribs of coconut leaves. Claire carried the baskets, pitchers, and pounder to the earth oven, and began her cooking. Shortly afterwards, she had heard Marc shuffling about. She called out that dinner was served.

Somehow, she had expected him to appear sheepish. That would have helped. This tone established, she could have teased him, and there would have been banter between them, and there might even be laughter. Instead, he was petulant. She knew that he watched her closely as she served, as if he were on guard against an obligatory jab about his performance. She withheld comment.

Once she was seated across from him, he had said, "I should've had him. In fact, I did have him until the damn climb. I wasn't in shape for that. Hell, I entered a swimming meet, not a mountaineering contest. I beat him swimming."

The immaturity of this had sickened her, and she'd replied dully, "Yes, you beat him swimming."

"You know, I didn't realize it was his ankle—I thought I had hold of the ledge—it took me a few seconds before I—"

"Marc, who gives a damn about that nonsense? You did your very best. Now eat."

"I give a damn. Because I know you. I know what you're thinking. You're thinking I made a fool of myself."

"I didn't say that. Now, please, Marc—"

"I didn't say you said that. I said I know you well enough to know how your mind operates. I just wanted to straighten you out—"

"All right, Marc, all right." She had had a spasm of choking on some food, and after she had recovered, she'd said, "Went down the wrong way. Let's finish in peace."

When they were through, and she was clearing the dining mat, he had puffed on his cigar and his eyes followed her through the blue smoke.

"You going to the festival tonight?" he had asked, suddenly.

She stopped. "Of course. Everyone is. Aren't you?"

"No."

"What does that mean?" she had wanted to know. "You've been invited like all of us. It's one of the highlights, one of the reasons we were invited this time of the year. It's why you're here. You have your work—"

"My work," he had repeated with a grunt. And then he'd added with an edge of sarcasm, "After all, you and Matty will be there."

"Marc, you must—"

"I did my part for research this afternoon. I'm bushed, and I've got a splitting headache—"

She had examined him, and he had looked serene with his cigar. She doubted the headache.

"—and what'll I miss?" he went on. "A bunch of naked broads, and that idiot Lisa, shaking their fat behinds. I can do better at any two-bit burlesque back home. No, thanks."

"Well, I can't force you."

"That's right."

"Do as you please. I'm going to change." She had taken several steps to the rear, slowed, and swung around toward him. "Marc, I— I just wish we—"

He had waited, as she hesitated, and he said, "What do you wish, wife?"

She had not liked his tone, or the *wife*, and so it was no use exhuming their marriage and old hopes. "Nothing," she had said. "I've got to hurry."

It had gone like that, exactly like that, Claire remembered, and on mind's blackboard the equation was still incorrect, for one-half plus one-half added up tonight, every night, to one-half. Damn.

She shivered, and adjusted herself to her place in the first row of the festival audience. She was pleased to find Tom Courtney down on one knee to her right.

"Hello," she said. "How long have you been here?"

"A few minutes. And you?"

"Mentally, I just arrived," she said.

"I know. That's why I didn't want to break in. Mind if I stay here, or have you had about enough togetherness for one day?"

"Don't waste amenities on me, Tom. You know I'd be pleased." She indicated the platform. "When does the show begin?"

"Right after this Sirens version of the fanfare. Then Nurse Harriet, Queen of the Festival, appears to open the proceedings."

"Nurse Harriet Unsheathed," Claire stated, as if reading a headline. "Well, if she's not embarrassed, I'm not. In fact, I can't wait."

"She's not. I've seen her backstage, so to speak. The Sirens men are attached to her like barnacles."

Claire suddenly smiled. "I just remembered again—who am I to talk?—after my strip-tease that first night here, Tehura and I at Paoti's dinner."

There was a flicker on Courtney's face that was not pain so much as concern. He said resolutely, "As I told you before, the rite of friendship was natural, just as this will be."

She was going to say, Tell Marc. Instead, she swallowed the words, withdrew, and pretended to concentrate on the platform before them.

There was activity on the platform. The music had ceased, but left no void of silence, for the babble of voices all around hummed and sang in the warm night. Two native boys, carrying a bench that resembled a high square coffee table, were climbing onto the platform. With great care, they centered the bench on the stage. Then, like twins crouching, they accepted from outstretched hands below a gigantic bowl, which they handled gingerly, for it was filled to the brim with liquid, and they placed this bowl on the middle of the bench.

As they hopped off the huge dais, two more natives ascended it, grown men, sleekly handsome, and one Claire recognized as the swimmer who had humbled Marc. And as they came to their full height, Claire realized that they had helped a young woman up on the stage between them, and the young woman was Harriet Bleaska, Queen of the Festival.

Apparently, Harriet had been rehearsed, for she moved with practiced assurance. When she advanced toward the bench, away from the ring of flame, and sat down, Claire was able to make her out plainly.

"My God," murmured Claire.

Harriet's cinnamon mouse bangs and long hair were festooned with a garland of tiara blossoms. Hung low from her bumpy hips, covering her from an inch or two below her navel, was a flaring green grass skirt no more than eighteen inches in length. What held Claire's attention first was the unrelieved whiteness of her in this setting, and next, the oval of space between her thighs curving inward to knock-knees. Nothing on her body moved as she went in regally measured steps to the bench, and the reason that nothing moved was a preponderance of unfeminine flat planes in her figure and the lack of protuberant mammaries. If one strained, one could make out nipples that seemed pinned to her like brown clasps or broaches, and only when she half-turned to sit on the bench did one see the tentative swell of bosom. Nevertheless, such was the dignity of her bearing, the delight in her narrow gray eyes and wide mouth, that her unsightly features and physique seemed again to transmute into comeliness before the eye, and lo, Miss Hyde was Miss Jekyll.

Claire could hear the slit drums and the flute, and a kind of hur-rahing all about, as the ceremony opening the festival began. The swimming champion, the sturdy humbler of Marc, had dipped a coconut half-shell into the bowl, and handed the spilling drink to Harriet. She accepted it like a love potion, rising with it and toast-ing the members of her team and the natives behind them. Then she drank. Next, she moved to another side of the square bench, sat, stood up, toasted the villagers on that side, and drank again. And so she went around the bench, toasting and drinking, to the accompanying roar of the entire adult Sirens population.

By the time Harriet had returned to her original place on the bench, Claire became conscious of a new and nearer activity. Older women of the village, in pairs, were hurrying up and down the aisles, one partner passing out clay cups, the other filling the cups with palm juice from a tureen.

Presently, everyone had been served, and Harriet was standing once more, flanked by her native escorts, surrounded by the ani-mated musicians. Harriet held her coconut cup aloft, and revolved her long whiteness and brown broaches majestically to booming acclaim, and then she drank deeply.

Claire looked down to find Courtney touching his clay cup to her own. "With this drink," she thought she heard him say, "the Saturnalia begins."

Obediently, she did as he did, and drank. The liquid went down warmish and sweet, conjuring to mind the first night on the island when she had become inebriated on kava and this palm juice. Courtney winked at her and gulped again, and once more she did as he did, except this time the toddy was not warmish and sweet but smooth as an old whiskey. She continued to drink, until the clay cup was empty, and the effect upon her was incredibly swift. The effect of the liquid, as best she could comprehend, was to blot up and absorb from her head, especially behind the temples, and from her arms and chest, anxiety, apprehension, clotting memories of the past, be the past an hour ago or a year ago. What remained was the head-spinning present.

When she turned away from Courtney, she found the two older native women before her, one taking the cup from her hand, the other holding out the tureen. And then Claire had her cup back, again full to the top with the remarkable fluid.

Another drink, and she raised her head and pointed it to the stage. At first, she could not see clearly, and she realized that between her and the platform crouched Sam Karpowicz. His white shirt was pasted to his back by perspiration, his neck was pink, and his eye was fastened to a Leica.

She shifted her position closer to Courtney to see what Sam was shooting. What Sam saw through his view finder, she now saw: Harriet Bleaska, flower garland askew, grass skirt slipping precariously, waving her now unfilled coconut cup as she paraded, pranced really, before the alignment of male and female dancers, who beat their hands and stamped to her impromptu gyrations. Claire could make out Lisa Hackfeld, wearing bra and red pareu, among the dancers in the background. Lisa's gray-streaked blond hair was in Medusa disarray, and her fleshy arms and shapely legs in constant animation.

The entire unrestrained scene, Claire thought, had the curiously old-fashioned quality of an early talking motion picture about errant daughters and boozing young blades of the roaring twenties. Or better, it all seemed a moment out of Tully's *A Bird of Paradise*, *circa* 1911, with Laurette Taylor doing the hula dance. It is not to be believed, Claire thought. But there it was, it was, indeed.

A sudden altercation, almost lost in the noise, removed Claire's attention from the platform. Sam Karpowicz, who had been before her, had crawled to his left, crouched low, going crabwise, to stamp better the half-nude Harriet Bleaska for posterity on his Leica film. His position, shooting upwards, was directly before Maud, Rachel DeJong, and Orville Pence. Unexpectedly, Orville, his partially bald cranium yellow in the torchlight, his shell-rimmed spectacles jumping on his sniffing clerical nose, had come to his feet, bounded forward, and roughly taken Sam Karpowicz by the shoulder, throwing the photographer off balance.

Sam looked up, his long face unnaturally livid. "What the hell! You made me lose the best shot—"

"I want to know what you are taking pictures of—of what are you taking pictures?" Orville was demanding, his words dragging themselves through palm juice.

"Chrissakes, Pence, what do you think I'm taking pictures of? I'm shooting the festival, the dance—"

"You're shooting Miss Bleaska's bosom, that is what you are doing. I say it is highly improper."

Sam screamed incredulity. "What?"

"You are supposed to record the activities of the natives, not the shameful excesses of one of our own. What will people back home say when they see these pictures of an American girl exposing herself up there, without decency—"

"Chrissakes, now we got Anthony Comstock to deal with. Look, Pence, you attend to your knitting and let me do mine. Now, don't bother me."

He pulled away, determined to ignore Pence, and focused his Leica upon Harriet Bleaska once more. She loomed overhead, laughing and pounding her palms together, shaking her shoulders and brown broaches, grinding her hips, waving in response to the cheers breaking out of the semidarkness.

As Sam froze her to his film, Orville grasped the photographer's shoulder a second time, in another effort to censor this obscene outrage.

"Cut it out!" Sam roared, and he lay his free hand against Orville's profile and shoved him away. The push sent Orville reeling backwards and down, to land ludicrously on his haunches. He regained his feet, trembling, and might have started for the photographer again, had not Maud risen and planted her authoritative mass in his path.

"Orville, please, please, Sam is only doing his job."

For a moment, Orville tried to find words, found none, then gestured toward the stage, and the gesture was a fist. "It's her—that disgraceful performance up there—"

"Please, Orville, all the villagers are—"

"I will not endure another minute of this—this revolting spectacle. I'm shocked that you condone it, Maud. I had better not say more. I bid you good night."

With a snort, he yanked his tie into place, stuffed the tail of his shirt into his trousers, and marched off into the crowd. Maud was openly perturbed, when next Claire could see her face. Maud surveyed all of them, and, muttering "Some people should not drink," sat down beside Rachel to try to enjoy the remainder of the dance.

For fleeting seconds, the altercation dwelt in Claire's mind. Strange, strange, she thought, what our coming here seems to be doing to some of us. The island has a spell that accents our weakest and worst qualities: Orville, bloodless at home, heated with indignation here; Sam Karpowicz, amiable at home, furious here; Marc, serious and withdrawn at home, angry and cruel here. And me, Claire, so—well, whatever—at home, and so—well, dammit, enough of that, I'm going to drink—here.

She drank. She and Courtney drank. Everyone drank. Sometimes she saw the stage, and the undulating dancers, weaving and swaying, behind the torches. Sometimes Lisa Hackfeld dominated the stage, as gay, as abandoned as Nurse Harriet, who had disappeared with her entourage, Lisa of Omaha not Beverly Hills, Lisa of rediscovered youth exorcising the demons of matronage.

Claire knew not how much time had passed, nor how many pourings of palm juice had filled her cup, but faintly she was hearing Courtney's voice. She knew it beckoned her from above, for he was standing, and all around others were standing, yet she remained seated. Then he was bending down, and lifting her as easily as a feather pillow to her feet.

"Everyone's dancing," he was saying in her ear. "Want to dance?"

Her bleary eyes gave consent, and she had his hand, and then some native man's hand, and there was this circle of people, and in they went like red Indians whooping and kicking, and backwards they went shouting and laughing, and all around there were these circles. And now their circle broke into smaller ones, and Claire felt set free in the melee, throwing off her sandals, letting her hair fly loose, allowing her hips to swing-a-ring-a-ding.

Then there was no more circle at all, only Tom Courtney, and the torches were further away, and the music, too. She could not find Maud or Sam. Briefly she had a glimpse of Rachel DeJong walking with some native, and here and there she could see, as she clung to Courtney, spun round and round with him, she could see native couples dancing, everyone dancing everywhere.

Her legs were jelly, she knew, and even though Courtney held her, she stumbled, and lurched deeply into his arms. She was caught by his arms, and lay her head, panting and exhausted, against his chest . . . and then it was almost like that other time, coming up from the lake front in Chicago, in Alex's arms, drowsing against his chest . . . yet now it was different, hearing as she did the pounding of Courtney's heart, and listening to the pounding of her own, and not knowing about his, but knowing about hers,

knowing the hammering came not from the exertion of the dance
. . . yes, it was different, for Alex's chest meant Being Loved,
which was safety, and this strange tall man's chest meant . . .
something else, something unknown, and what was unknown was
dangerous.

She managed to extricate herself, tear herself away. She did not
look up at him. She said, "I've been overmatched, like my husband." Then she said, "Thanks for a good time, Tom. Please take
me home."

* * *

Only when they were in the narrow canoe, and he was thrusting
the paddle rhythmically into the silver sheen covering the black
water, sliding them through the hushed channel a world away
from the populated large island and closer to the nearer coral atoll,
did Rachel DeJong sober ever so slightly. She considered ordering
him to stop, to stop and turn around, to stop and turn around and
take her back to her civilized friends and civilization.

She had meant to verbalize her change of mind, but seeing
Moreturi's smiling face in the semidarkness, and the bulging and
easing of his biceps as he sank the paddle into the channel waters,
she knew that she could not speak what she felt. Her instinct told
her that her voice would be the sound of fear. She recalled: you
did not show fear to an animal; any weakness gave the beast ascendancy over you. She was still Rachel DeJong, M.D., trained
into superiority, master of human destiny, hers, his, and forever in
control of any situation. And so she maintained her silence in collaboration with that of the night.

Once more, she realized that she was deeply seated in the hollow
of a canoe, legs stretched before her. She had never in her life been
in a canoe before. She wondered why not. She reasoned that it was
because canoes were so fragile—what kept them afloat? what kept
an airplane aloft?—and she always imagined that they rolled over,
and you went to a watery grave like that poor thing in the Dreiser
book—yes, Roberta Alden—but that had been a rowboat, had it
not?—and Clyde had hit her with his camera. Well, this was a canoe
and she could see that Moreturi was born in one. His canoes would
never tip over.

She tried to relax in the sliver of hollowed log that held her between the sweet night air and the cool water. What did one do in a canoe? One played a guitar, banjo—heavens, how that dated her —so, what else? One trailed one's hand in the water. Rachel De-Jong lifted a limp hand and dropped it over the low side into the swiftly passing water. The water was sensuous, and seemed to enter her pores, course upwards through her arm and across her shoulders and around her heart cavity. She could see Moreturi peering at her, as he worked the paddle, and she feared that his observation of her well-being might give him another view of weakness, and so she closed her eyes, so that he could not read anything in them.

Thus cradled and lulled by the motion of the sliding canoe, she let her mind off its leash and permitted it to run its own way.

She must have been drunk, she decided, to have come along even this far. Rachel DeJong did not drink, never drank. Occasionally, at a party, she might have something candyish, like an Alexander maybe, that kind, and then lots of hors d'oeuvres. She did not drink because she saw how drink made people behave, and it was not proper and orderly, and she believed one should always be one's self. The Maker gave each person a self, and drink cut you off from that self. Or were there granted really two selves per person, one public, and one that floated up out of that recess of privacy on a drink? Of course this was so, and she knew it, for she was a psychoanalyst, and she avoided drink because one self was all that she could really cope with. When you kept one self, it was your good ship. Drink, on the other hand, was firewater that burned the ship behind you. Then you had no ship at all except the one that swam up with the drink, and the new craft was not dependable at all.

Lord, what crazy, incoherent fancies. She had consumed several of those palm-juice toddies because they tasted like Alexanders, rather pink and sugary and harmless like something at one of her niece's birthday parties. Yet their childish smile was deceptive. They paralyzed the senses, burned the ship, and you had to take any foreign craft offered, a canoe, for example. Which brought her to Moreturi.

When the dance on the stage had finished, she thought the evening ended. She had meant to leave with Maud, but Maud had gone off with Paoti and his wife. After that, she had searched for Claire, but Claire was having herself a barefooted whirl with a bunch of natives and Courtney. Rachel had started for her hut reluctantly— reluctantly because there was so much life and hilarity wheeling about her, and she hated to shut a door on it, and felt good, wanting to be with someone, not necessarily Joe Morgen, although that would have been good, but someone, anyone who was not a solemn one.

Feeling very apart from the merrymakers, she had squirmed through the writhing groups, noting that Claire appeared quite drunk, in fact everyone did, but not being critical of them, for her own feet seemed inches off the ground as if she were walking on a trampolin. When she emerged from the revel, almost out of reach of the torchlight, and was alone, she had sensed someone approaching her. She slowed down, turning, and was pleased and distressed that it was Moreturi who had found her.

"I was hunting everywhere for you," he had said, and he did not say "Miss Doctor," and his tone was without derision.

"I was in the front row," she replied.

"I know. I meant after—I went there—you were gone."

She had hoped for an accidental encounter with him tonight, and dreaded it, refusing to define for herself her dread. Except for her early-morning meeting with Maud, to report on her performance with the voyeurs of the Hierarchy the night before, she had forced out of her mind the occurrences of the night. With Moreturi's presence before her, everything returned. She had hated his nakedness. He wore his pubic bag, it was true, but he might have seemed less exposed without it. He was all tan muscle, the most naked male in the compound, and his proximity disconcerted her. While she willed herself to suffocate the memory of what she had seen of him last night, the sight of him when he had gone into his wife's bedroom, she could not. The exact pitch of Atetou's wail and moan still reverberated against her eardrums and stabbed against her heart. Instantly, she had wanted nothing but escape and isolation.

"I was tired," she had said. "I was just on my way to my hut to sleep."

He had studied her speculatively. "You have not the look of the tired."

"Well, I am."

He had stared at her throat, and her hand went to it. He said, "I sent you the festival necklace. I see you do not wear it."

"Of course not," she had said indignantly, remembering *that* and knowing it was in the pocket of her skirt.

"You speak as if I insulted you," he had said, troubled. "Such a gift is a compliment here."

"How many did you send out as gifts?" she had asked sharply.

"One."

The way that he had said *one*, simply, seriously, shamed her. She had been forcing unnatural anger into her voice and manner, against the drugging of the palm juice, because she was unnerved by him. She began to let the anger recede, but held to one more shaft of it.

"Maybe I should be grateful then," she had said, "but I wonder if your wife is grateful for your generosity with necklaces?"

His eyes showed that he was puzzled. "All wives know of this. They send necklaces, too. It is our custom, and this is the festival week."

Rachel had felt all wrong, and she wanted to soften herself for him. "I—I guess I keep forgetting the custom."

"Besides," he was saying, "I have been your patient, and Atetou, too, and you know how it is between us."

She had thought, Yes, damn you, I know how it is between you and Atetou, I saw some of it, heard some of it, through the open leaves of your side wall last night. She had said, "That has nothing to do with my wearing your necklace. It is your custom to give such things. It is not our custom to accept them."

"My father tells it that you are here to learn our ways, and live as we live."

"Of course, Moreturi, but there are restrictions. I am an analyst. You know all about that. You are my analysand. You know about that, too. I mean, we can't have clandestine meetings—"

He had appeared to comprehend some of this, for he interrupted, "If you could wear it, would you want to?"

Her arms, face, neck had felt prickly hot, and she cursed the drinks. She had the perfect reply, she knew, and the reply might put a stop to this uncomfortable talk. She could say that she was in love with another, one of her own people, back home. She could inform him of Joseph E. Morgen. That would raise the glass wall between them. She had meant to evoke Joe, and end Moreturi, and yet she had not. Unaccountably, the night was young, near midnight still young, and she had not wanted to be alone. "I—I really don't know if—under different circumstances—I'd wear it. Perhaps, if our relationship were different, if I knew you better, I might."

His face had turned on bright as an electric bulb. "Yes!" he had exclaimed. "That is it, we must become friends. I will go with you to your hut and we will talk—"

"No—no, I couldn't—"

"Then let us sit somewhere in the grass, and rest, and talk."

"I'd like to, Moreturi, but it's late."

His hands were on his hips. He had smiled down at her, and for the first time he was smiling that too-familiar cocky smile. "You are afraid of me, Miss Doctor."

She had been furious, but her voice was uncertain. "Don't be utterly ridiculous. Don't bait me."

"You are afraid," he had repeated. "I know the truth. This morning you spoke to your Dr. Hayden, and she spoke to my mother, and my mother has told me. You have made a special request to end our work, to have me no more in your hut."

"Yes, I thought we should terminate the analysis. I decided I was doing you no good, wasting your time, and so I asked that your case be returned to the Hierarchy."

"You have not wasted my time. I have looked forward to the meetings."

"Only so you can ridicule me."

"No, that is not true. I ridicule to hide my feelings. I have learned much from you."

She had hesitated. "Well, I—I've made my decision. You'll manage without me."

"If I cannot see you again, it is more reason to see you tonight."

"Another time."

"Tonight is the main night. There is no one I shall see but you. I want to explain myself."

"Please, Moreturi, you're wearing me out—"

Once more, he had smiled. "Maybe that is for the good. Maybe you will become more of a woman. You are used to commanding men, to advising them, to telling them this and that, to be above them. You are afraid to be with a man you cannot treat as a sick one. I am normal. I look at you not as Miss Doctor but as a female like Atetou, except you are more, far more. This is what makes you afraid."

It was really, she remembered, that little speech that had done it. It reached into the pit of her fears, and she would not have him know so much and possess this dominance over her. He had made it impossible for her to go to her hut alone, to try to sleep with his damn speech and Atetou's outcry of last night haunting her in this far reach of the Pacific. The palm juices inside her were fermenting, and they had soaked and washed away her last prop of superiority, so that she was ready to meet him and defy him by showing him she was unafraid, as a woman would, as a psychoanalyst would not.

She had not argued with him. She continued conversing, until they arrived at those words that made it possible for her to agree, without loss of face or any sign of surrender, that she was prepared to go with him where the others were not. She had agreed that, for a short time anyway, they would talk. When she strolled off with him, in the direction of the Sacred Hut, past it, but in that direction, she had been secretly pleased at her strength.

They had climbed a hill, and gone past the cliff where the swimming meet had been held, and she had gripped his hand tightly as he preceded her and guided her down a steep footpath to a small rocky harbor she had not seen before.

Once, she had asked, "Where are you taking me? I hope it is not too far. I told you, I can't stay out long."

He had replied, "There are three Sirens, and you have seen only one. I will take you to another."

"But where—?"

"Just minutes across the channel. We can sit in the sand, and talk with no disturbance. You will have a memory the others do not of the beauty of our place. I go there often when I want to be by myself. There is nothing but the sand and grass and coconut palm trees, and the water all around. When you wish to return, I will bring you back."

He had found the canoe in the darkness, and shoved it into the water, and then balanced himself in it and waited.

She must have held back, for he called out, "If you are still afraid of me—"

"Don't be silly."

She allowed him to help her into the canoe, and now in the canoe she still was, eyes closed, hand trailing in the water, his unseen, fluid presence somewhere before her, gracefully dipping the paddle.

She felt a bump beneath her, and heard him say, "Here we are, the little atoll that is the second Siren."

She opened her eyes and sat up.

"Take off your shoes," he said. "You can leave them in the canoe."

Obediently, she removed her sandals. He was already in the water. She tried to step out of the canoe by herself, but he reached out and lifted her as if he were lifting a palm frond, and lowered her into a foot of water.

He pointed off. "Go to the beach."

She waded through the water, across ridges of the sand bottom, until she was on the shore. When she turned, she saw that he was pulling the canoe out of the water, and wedging it between rocks.

After he joined her, he took her by the arm and led her through a vast cluster of palm trees, their mop heads lost in the high darkness, past a shallow lagoon, to a grass clearing, and then down a gradual slope to a tiny beach of thick sand that seemed to sparkle like starlight.

"The ocean side of the atoll," said Moreturi.

Where the water in the enclosed lagoon behind them had been level and still as glass, the surf on the ocean side was turbulent and alive. Here they stood before thousands of miles of winds and tides, and watched as the combers with their margins of whitecaps rolled in toward the islet, and broke, and tumbled down, and washed high onto the sand. The sea was lost in night, without horizon or end, it seemed, and the foamy heads of the waves came toward them like the charge of a white brigade, unhorsed and brought to earth by the beach.

"It's magnificent," Rachel whispered. "I am glad you brought me here."

Moreturi dropped to the sand of the sea beach, and stretched his tan body, and then lay flat with the back of his head in his locked hands. She sat beside him, knees up, skirt pulled down over them, but a mild breeze stole under it and moved gently over her legs and thighs.

For a long time neither one of them spoke, and there was no need to speak. But when she found his eyes upon her, she was prompted to shatter the intimacy of the quiet. She asked him to tell her something of his early life, and he conjured up remembrances of his early youth. She hardly listened to him, but rather heard the waves pouring out of the dark and lathering the sand, and she marveled at how the sound of them was keyed to the sound of Atetou's outcry of love last night. Insensibly, she was tempted to mention last night, what her eyes had witnessed. She fought the impulse, conceived by palm juice, and instead, recalling some fragment of their analytic sessions, she asked him about one festival week of several years ago, when he had possessed twelve married women in seven days and nights. He discussed his enjoyment of them, their differences, and all the while she was summoning up her own barren and shoddy love life, the bumbling college boy from Minnesota, the three times with the remote married professor on Catalina, the teasings with Joe.

Suddenly, she said, "Did you ever bring any of them here?"

Moreturi seemed surprised. "What?"

"Did you ever bring any of your women to this coral atoll and—and make love to them?"

He lifted himself to an elbow. "Yes, a few."

She felt curiously feverish, her forehead, the nape of her neck, her wrists. She fanned herself with one hand.

"Are you all right?" he wanted to know.

"I'm all right. I just feel a little warm."

"Let's swim then—"

"Swim?"

"Of course. The water is wonderful at night. It will make you feel better than you have ever felt." He came to his feet, and took her hand and pulled her upright.

"I—I don't have my swimming suit," she said, feeling embarrassed to have to say it.

"Go without your suit." He waited, then smiled nicely. "This is not America. Besides, I promise not to look."

She intended to say no, and to the devil with him and all this trouble, but standing there, knowing he was waiting, she remembered with an ache that time on the beach outside Carmel when she and Joe had walked along the water. He had wanted to swim, too, and they had no suits, and he had said it did not matter because they were practically married. She had hidden behind the rock to undress, had unbuttoned her blouse, had been unable to move her fingers further, had rushed out to tell him and found him disrobed, and had run away from him and their marriage. She had done that! Oh hell, hell, hell, but then, how many people had a second chance to be unsick?

"Very well," she found another voice saying for her aloud. "I have something on underneath. But don't look anyway. I—I'll join you in the water."

He waved happily, trotted down to the water's edge. She thought that he would go straight in, but instead he stopped, did something with his hands at his waist, and she saw the strap and white bag in his hand. He threw it over his shoulder, stood poised before the water, all one piece of beautiful statuary, and swiftly he was off, a released Dionysus, charging and splashing into the water and into the darkness.

Stolidly, a fraudulent Aphrodite, she unbuttoned her cotton blouse. This time no Carmel. She pulled it off and dropped it on the sand, and adjusted her deep-cupped brassière to cover every inch of her too-obvious breasts. Slowly, she unhooked her skirt, ran the zipper down, lowered the skirt, and stepped out of it. Her white nylon panties felt abnormally tight about her boyish hips. Briefly, she wondered if the panties were transparent, but then realized she was clothed by the lateness of the hour.

Standing there, more free than she had been in years, she enjoyed the curling breeze on her skin, and felt less feverish. Her chestnut hair was carefully set, and for no reason whatever, she suddenly ran one hand through it, tousling it, and she did not feel thirty-one and woman-with-a-career at all. She felt foolish-gay, and her mind thumbed its nose at Carmel and the old she, and with that private gesture, she ran through the heavy sand into the water.

The first impact of the water jolted her, for it was colder than she had expected, but she kept going deeper, because she wanted the water to cover her underthings. As soon as she was in water to her waist, she fell forward, and began to swim, first striking out strongly, then letting up, going easily.

In the self-indulgence of the water, the romp in it, she had almost forgotten that she had, somewhere in the darkness, a partner, sex opposite.

"Here I am!" she heard Moreturi call, and she came off floating on her back and immersed herself to her shoulders, treading the water, until she caught sight of him stroking toward her. In seconds, he was only yards away, his black hair plastered across his head and forehead.

A sea wave came unexpectedly, higher than those before, and she caught it in time, managing to rise above it, and sink down with it, but Moreturi was momentarily engulfed.

"Here!" he shouted.

She swung around in the water, and he was behind her, going up and down in the water like a happy idiot, and once when he shot up and revealed himself to his abdomen, she gasped, swallowing the salt water, praying that she would not see more. She turned away, swimming, wondering how she could get to the shore and dress without being observed, and how he would dress so that she would not have to see him naked.

But then, as she swam, the apprehension became minor in the soothing pleasure of the sea. She swam round and round experimenting, trying side stroke, overhand, breast stroke, feeling marvelous as a marine creature, a mermaid, and she gave thanks to the drinks and the one who had brought her here.

She would tell him she was pleased, she decided, he deserved that much for all of his trouble, and she began to turn in the water to tell him. As she did so, she heard a frantic shout, her name, from him, the first time he had called her by name, and then she met head-on the powering sheet of the great smashing comber. It hit her like a Gargantuan slap, and the liquid curve sent her reeling backwards and then down and down into the deep greenness of the sea. She was underwater interminably, no sensation of time, amid the shimmering formations beneath the ocean, where everything was an unfamiliar planet of slow motion.

Then, she was kicking upwards, upwards, surfacing, and when she came out of the water, lungs exploding, she was choking for air, fighting off, desperately trying to rip aside the curtain of blackness. And all the while, from afar, thinly in the wind, she heard her name, and as her strength ebbed, the oaken arm came around her and held her out of the water. She looked up into Moreturi's blurred film of face.

"Are you hurt?" he was demanding. "It hit you with great force."

"Fine, fine," she gasped, coughing.

"I'll help you."

"Yes, please, please—"

He took a fist full of her hair, and thus keeping her face above the water, he swam sideways, using one arm, toward the shore. In a minute he stood up, and braced her upright, but her knees began to buckle, and he held her with both his hands. He lifted her out of the water, cradled her in his arms, one arm under her legs, the other supporting her shoulders, and he carried her to the sand.

By the time he had come out of the sea with her, she had regained her senses. Her head was against his hard arm, and her left breast was under his hand. With surprise, she looked down at herself and saw that her breasts were entirely exposed. Dumbly, she tried to re-create what had happened, and then she knew that the violence of the breaker had slashed through the brassière and torn it from her.

"Oh, God," she moaned.

"What?"

"Have I still got something on—my pants—?"

"Yes, do not worry."

He would have been amazed, but she was not worried at all. She was pleased, since it was no act of her own, that her brassière was gone. She wished, in an irrational way, her nylon panties had gone, too, since that might have solved everything.

Gently, he was putting her down on her back on the warm sand, and she lay on her back, arms outstretched, knees partially drawn up, staring at the black ceiling of night above. She closed her eyes, wanting surrender to lassitude, but there was too much that was wound tightly beneath her skin. And the water had not cooled her, after all. She opened her eyes, to find him on his knees above her, and then, even in her daze, she was frightened, for she had forgotten that he would be entirely naked. He was entirely naked, and he was ready for love, and this was what frightened her the most.

Yet, she did not move. The flesh across her body frame was so taut that she wanted to cry out, as Atetou had cried out the night before. Then it was that Rachel groaned. She was conscious of the groan, and hated it, for it had been beyond her restraint, an involuntary whimper that hung in the air above her like desire, as real and articulate as his love apparatus. She feared that she would groan again, for the nipples of her breasts had swollen and were as painful as two bruises, but with effort she held the sound in check.

Lying there, she felt his large hands on the flanks of her legs, felt them on the wet, clinging nylon panties, felt the panties being drawn down her thighs, and then up and over her knees, and down the calves of her legs. Her defenses stirred, but she could not protest. Nor could she look at him. It had come this far, she told herself, and nothing more mattered. For once, for once, let what will happen—happen. This was the crossing, so long feared, and when you were there, it was nothing at all, really nothing at all. The worst death was in all the endless dyings that came before, but when you were there, at the crossing, it did not matter.

As she felt his movement, she wondered that he had not kissed her lips or kissed away the pain of the bruises, but then the pain was everywhere, fanning out everywhere, as his fingers played across her skin. She knew that she could not endure this a second longer, that every organ in her was near bursting, and that if he did not cease, she would scream something, do something foolish.

But then, an incredible thing happened, and it had never in her life happened this way before. She had hardly been aware that his bulk was between her legs, but now she was totally aware that his being was gradually entering into her being. The filling of herself with him was so continuous, so incessant, and so unexpected, that it petrified her brain and anesthetized all pain.

When his motion began, it was, for her, as if the pain was shocked to life, and all brought down from the red bruises, from her ribs, all brought up from her calves, from her thighs, to where he had invaded her. For the first time, she was jarred out of helpless inertia, throbbing with the feeling that she was not being relieved at all but being harmed.

In a surge of revulsion, she tried to escape. She placed the heels of her hands on his shoulders and attempted to push him off, to be divested of him. She failed, and these efforts only intensified his movement and the resultant pain. She dropped her arms to her sides, lips begging for freedom, but it was no use. She lay there, feeling like some marine thing that had flopped on the beach, out of its natural element, alien, afraid, gasping, but deeply speared and captured, no matter how much it tried to return to the old place and the old freedom.

Minutes and minutes had passed, an eternity of infinite pain and humiliation, and she marshaled inside her, secretly, to surprise him, what was left of pride and reserve. Suddenly, her forces gathered, aligned, for the break to freedom, she opened her eyes, and snatched at his perspiring shoulders, tearing her nails across them to retaliate, to give him equal pain, and heaved her torso to throw him off. Then she knew that her efforts were misunderstood, for his broad tan features mocked her with grim appreciation.

Wildly, she thrashed in the flying sand, but his thrusts sent her down and backwards, so that her shoulders, spine, buttocks made a deep groove in the white sand. And in this way, they squirmed out of the loose dry sand, until her flesh beneath felt the firmer wet sand of the water's edge, and she realized that if she withdrew again, they would be in the water.

Confused, emptied of strength, she ceased her resistance. She could feel the last of a receding wave of water slithering under her shoulder blades, and then more of the surf surrounding her backside and the soles of her naked feet. And then the gentle water was in her hair, sometimes washing over the red bruises, finally lapping over and enveloping their joining.

It was odd, for her, what the water did. Inexplicably, it gave this wanted-unwanted union a kind of pagan ritual blessing and grace. Inexplicably, too, it cleansed her of civilization's dirty wounds, cleansed her of shame, of guilt, of fear, and finally, finally, of restraint. The soft, cool water made this endless act of love natural and right, in this time and place, and gave her the crossing, and so she crossed.

What had been painful became pleasurable, sent barbaric and voluptuous joy careening through the veins of her head, and the arteries of her heart, and the vessel below.

Thus, in the unyielding, wet sand, applauded by the waves, she succumbed to a union hitherto unimagined in all that she had read, heard, dreamed. It is his life, she thought, his everything, and so no wonder, no wonder. Once, she thought of the other two she had had, and of what she had heard from the victims on the couch, poor things, poor us, with our rigidity, our clumsiness, our studiousness, our thinking—we, the barbarians, chaining and torturing this with our habitations, clothes, drinks, drugs, words, always words, destroying all that mattered, the primitive act of love itself.

such as here and now and now and now, undiluted by anything but desire and fulfillment.

All of her had quickened, with the miracle of the crossing. She gazed up blindly at him, as she might at some marvelous celestial creature seen in a shaft of heavenly light, and she had a vision that she had become one of the anointed few. The experience would set her life apart from all the other lives on earth. Instantly, she was sorry for every woman that she had ever known or ever treated in the faraway, dim, dim civilized world of long ago, the feeble mortals who would never know this extra dimension of pure happiness, those pitiful ones who would live and die and never know what she now knew, and it grieved her that she would not be able to impart this to them, to anyone, ever.

Suddenly, she gave not a damn about anyone on all the earth but herself and this man. She embraced him, she possessed him, she was insane with him, and finally she heard the cry in her throat, and at last she let it escape . . . to be certain that she had escaped, too.

*   *   *

In the village, it was quiet again, all muffled down under the quilt of late night. Even the last of the celebrants, strolling to their homes to sleep or into the hills to love, even these last stragglers spoke in whispers softer than the breeze.

Inside the thatched hut so familiar to him, slightly above the compound, he had been sitting in the faint light of a single wavering candlenut for a long time. He had been waiting for the footsteps of her coming. He wondered if there would be one pair of footsteps or two pair, and if there were two pair, what he would do to explain his presence in her room.

He had drunk more than his usual quota before coming here, four straight Scotches, no more, and they had not affected him in any way. Although perhaps it was only the drinks that had fortified him with the courage to come here at all, to risk what he must undertake, he would permit no liquor to dull him for the task to which he was dedicated.

It was near midnight, he knew, and the festival sounds had disappeared a half-hour ago. Since then, there had been the unnerving silence, but now he thought that the silence was being intruded upon. He cocked his head, distending his aquiline nose, pursing his thin lips, listening hard. The slight noise was that of human feet padding on the turf, certainly footsteps, not two pair but one, and he guessed, from the light tread of the bare feet, that it was she, and that she was alone.

He pushed himself up from his slouch against the wall, sat erect and intent, just as the cane door swung open. Tehura, covered only by the two strands of long black hair that fell down across her bosom and the short grass skirt, entered the room of her hut. She did not see him at first. She appeared lost in some thought, as she automatically closed the door. This done, she threw the strands of her hair back over her shoulders, and turned fully into the room. That was when she saw him.

Her features displayed no surprise, only interest. "Marc," she said. Then she said, "I wondered where you were tonight."

"I was here most of the evening," he said. "I wanted to see you alone. I was worried you might return with Huatoro."

"No."

"Please sit down with me," he said. "If—if you're not too tired, there is something I want to discuss with you."

"I am not tired at all," she said.

She crossed the room, and came to rest on the matting a few feet from him.

He did not look at her, but at the opposite wall, meditatively. "Yes, I was afraid you might bring Huatoro back with you. You had said you might favor the winner of the swim."

"I still might," she said.

"But not tonight. Why not?"

"I do not know . . . He gave me his festival necklace."

"You do not wear it."

"Not tonight."

"He must have been angry."

"It is no concern of mine," she said. "He will wait."

"Will you make love with him?"

"If I knew, I would not tell you," she said. "I do not know." She paused. "He wishes me to be his wife."

"And you?"

"I repeat, I am not in the mood for such decisions." She reflected on this a moment. "He is strong, much admired. I am told he loves well. With the winning of the race, he has much mana."

Marc shifted uncomfortably. "I'm sorry about the way I be-

444

haved in the race, Tehura. I've pretended to everyone it was an accident. You know better."

"Yes," she said.

"I couldn't help myself. I just wanted to win, no matter how, because I had told you that I could and would. That was all that counted." He hesitated, and he added, "Should I tell you a crazy thing?"

She waited, her expression impassive.

"Tehura, all through that race I kept thinking of you. As I was going along, I kept looking at the cliff ahead and telling myself it was you. As I got nearer, it even began to resemble you. I mean it. There was a rounded overhang above, and that became your breasts. There was an indentation in the cliff side, and it became your navel. And then below, there was in that cliff, there was a kind of—" He stopped. "I told you it was crazy."

"It is not crazy."

"All I could think as I swam was that I've got to get to her first, before anyone else does, and if I do, if I reach her, ascend her, she is mine." He caught his breath. "I almost made it."

"You swam well," she said. "You need not be ashamed. I admired you."

He moved again, to be closer to her. "Then you've got to tell me this—do you admire me as much as Huatoro?"

"I cannot speak of that. He is stronger than you. He is younger. You are weaker in our ways, and sometimes strange to me. But this I admire—you came to our ways because of me—you did everything, even the wrong, to show me you were worthy of us and me. This I admire. In your country, I know, you have great mana. Now, for me, you have it in my country, also."

"I can't tell you how wonderful that makes me feel, Tehura."

"It is true," she said simply. "You asked how I felt toward you beside Huatoro. To be honest, there is one more thing I must say." She considered it, and after a moment she said it. "Huatoro loves me seriously," she said. "This is important for a woman."

Impulsively, Marc took her hand. "For God's sake, Tehura, you know I love you, too—why, yesterday—"

"Yesterday," she repeated, and withdrew her hand. "Yes, I will speak of yesterday. You tried to remove my skirt, to own my body with your body. I do not speak against that. It was all right, even though, when it happened, I had not yet the feeling for your body. What I speak of now is not that alone. Huatoro's love is that, of course, but it is more, much more."

He had both hands on her arm now. "So is mine, Tehura, believe me, so is mine."

"How can it be?" she demanded. "We are—what is your word? —yes, I have it—we are an unusual two people together. Sometimes, I am the insect that you study. Other times, I am the female you want for your passing appetite. Never am I more. I have not complained. I do not know. I understand your feelings, because you are already wealthy with your work and your woman. You have love, the great love, you have your beautiful wife, who is everything—"

"She is nothing!" he cried out.

The savagery of his disavowal of Claire gave Tehura pause. She stared at him with new interest, mouth set, waiting.

"That is the real reason I waited here for you tonight," he went on in a rush. "To tell you that it is you I love, not Claire. Does that surprise you? Have you heard or seen any evidence of my love for her?"

"Men are different in their public ways."

"My public actions are the same as my private ones. I met that girl, I courted her, I found her agreeable, and because I knew that I must marry someone—it was expected, part of the conformity of our society—I married her. Now I can truly say there was no love between us. I had no desire for her, no burning inside such as I feel for you. When I am with Claire, I can think of a million other things. When I am with you, I can only think of you. Do you believe me?"

She had watched him, wide liquid eyes shining. She said, "Why have you not left her before? Tom has said this is possible in your America."

"I've always intended to, but—" He shrugged. "I was afraid. It would have been a social embarrassment. I worried what friends and family would say. So I went on, because it was easier to cause no eruption. Besides, there was nowhere else to go. I've gone on for two years, kept her satisfied physically, and in other ways, too, but myself have always been secretly dissatisfied. And then I came here. I met you. And now there is somewhere else to go, and I am no longer afraid."

"I do not understand you," Tehura said quietly.

"I'll make myself clearer," he said. He was up on his knees, fumbling one hand in the pocket of his sport shirt. "I know what ceremonial rites mean to you. I will now perform a rite, one of transferring my full love from the woman who was my wife to the woman who—" He had found what he wanted, and he held it out in the palm of his hand. "Here, Tehura, for you."

Puzzled, she reached for what was in his palm, and took it, and let it dangle from her fingers. It was the dazzling diamond pendant set in white gold that hung from a delicate chain, the very one that Claire had worn the first night and that Tehura had admired so constantly.

With satisfaction, Marc could see that the gift had made her speechless. Her eyes were wide, her lips parted in awe, and the brown hand that held the jewel shook. She looked up from it at Marc, eyes brimming with gratefulness. "Oh, Marc—" she gasped.

"It is yours," he said, "all yours, and there will be a thousand more evidences of my love in the days to come."

"Marc, put it on me!" she exclaimed with childish glee.

She twisted about, on the matting, her naked back to him. His hands went over her shoulders, as he took the diamond pendant from her, and looped it around her neck, and fastened the clasp behind. As she bent her head to enjoy it, her fingers fondling the gleaming diamond, Marc's hands caressed her shoulders, and glided down her arms. Shaken by the texture of her flesh, the imagined promise of it, his hands went to her pointed breasts. She did not seem to mind, as she concentrated on her bauble. Marc's hands enveloped her breasts, and every limb and organ of his person was inflamed. Releasing one breast, his hand went to her skirt, pulled high on her thighs, and he massaged the inside of her thigh. Never, in his entire life, had he wanted possession of any object as much as he wanted her sexually.

"Tehura," he said.

She glanced from the diamond to him, but did not touch either of his hands.

"Tehura, I want you forever. I am leaving Claire. I want you for my wife."

For the first time, this night, her face was mesmerized by his every word. She said, "You want Tehura for your wife?"

"Yes."

She spun around, to face him, pulling her breast and inner thigh from his caresses. "You want to marry me?" She saw his hands, and covered them with her own. "They will love me, Marc, but wait—I must know—"

"I want to marry you, as soon as possible."

"How?"

He came down from his knees, trying to let his ardor subside. He told himself what she had just told him, that there was time for love, their love, and they would have it, but first he must explain himself to her. The crucial moment had come, was upon him, he knew, and if he could put aside this towering need to consume her with his lust, he could be rational and persuasive.

He had planned to propose to her, as he had written Garrity. The first necessity would be to ally her with his ambition. She was the only one here whom he could trust, who could make his dream come true. Without her help, anything further would be impossible. The offer of marriage, coldly calculated, would bring down her defenses, and make her a partner to his scheme. Yet, oddly, the offer of marriage had not been as business-measured as he had planned. It had become warm moist with his surging want of her, his grinding desire to split her asunder, to wrench her away from her haughty untouchability, to have her beneath him, below him, his dependent beggar of love. Out of this had burst his proposal, the very proposal that he had intended to make anyway, but now for the wrong reason, and he saw that he must redirect his motivation and manner, or he would accomplish nothing. He had made a gain with his earnestness, with the stupid pendant, with his offer of marriage. He must exploit it immediately. If she would not acquiesce to all that he had in mind, everything was lost.

He exhaled, and attempted to consider her with a new, Garrity-oriented objectivity. "How?" she had asked. She wanted to know how he could marry her. He would tell her how, and make his plan *their* plan.

"Tehura, I want to take you away from the Sirens, first to Tahiti, and after that to California," he found himself saying. "The moment that we are in my country, I will divorce Claire, and the day the divorce is granted, I will marry you."

"Why not do it here?" she inquired, with a hook of shrewdness that he had often suspected she possessed.

"You know that's impossible, Tehura. You have no machinery for my divorce. Except the Hierarchy. They'd have to investigate Claire and myself. Suppose I allowed this—even if we extended our stay—then we would marry by your law, which would not be acceptable in my country. Whatever we do must be legal in the United States. For, there is where I want us to live our lives. From time to time we will come back to this island, so that you may see your own. But my life must become your life. This island is a lovely place, but so small, so inadequate, compared to what you will find and own in my great country. There you will be treated as an exotic beauty, worshiped by a million men, envied by a million women. You will possess not a hut but a house ten times the size of this hut, and servants, and the most expensive clothes, and a car—you know of these things from your learnings—and you will have precious stones like that diamond, as many as you wish."

She had listened, it seemed, as a girl child listens to a fairy tale, yet she was not fully carried away. There was something older and more careful about her, the shrewdness again. "Everyone is not so rich in your country," she said. "I have asked Tom. He says in your country you are not so rich."

This was the opening. Marc entered it. "He is right in a way. I am rich when put alongside one such as Huatoro or others of your village. I am not the richest in my own land. I have enough, of course, much mana, as you know. Yet, you also know the value of that pendant. But I will be richer, very, very wealthy, Tehura. To become so, I must have your confidence in what I say next."

She nodded. "It is between us."

"There is enormous interest about places like The Three Sirens in my homeland. You are aware of that. Otherwise, why would we be here studying your people? In a month or two, when my mother brings the news of you to America, it will be scientific and make no one rich—do not ask me to explain this tonight, there is too much to explain—but it is so. On the other hand, if I were to leave here with you as soon as possible, taking with me information on the existence of this place, and offer the news in a popular way to the American public and the world, they would reward us with infinite wealth. Believe me, we would be rich beyond our imagination. I have the proof. I can show you letters. I have a man who will meet us in Tahiti. He has organized it. The three of us will go to the United States by airplane, such as the one Rasmussen owns, and we will tell the world of your remarkable island—"

"And break the tabu? It would overthrow and put to an end the Sirens."

"No—no, Tehura, no more than my mother's writings and speeches will end the Sirens. I promise you that we will keep its location secret. We will have proof enough of its existence in information I will bring—in—in the fact of you, my wife—"

"Me?" she said, slowly. "Your people will want to see me?"

"They'll want to meet you, see you, hear you, love you. They will shower you with everything you wish. Do you know what is possible?"

"I have seen the pictures in Tom's books."

"Everything will be yours."

Absently, she fiddled with her pendant. "I will be so far from here—I will be alone—"

He edged toward her, and placed his arm around her. "You will be my wife."

"Yes, Marc."

"I have promised, I will give you everything."

She gazed at the matting, slowly lifted her head, sadness in her smile. "All right," she said, almost inaudibly.

His heart skipped and jumped. "You'll marry me? You'll go with me?"

She nodded.

He wanted to leap and shout with joy. He had accomplished it! Garrity! "Tehura—Tehura—I love you—"

She nodded blankly, still overwhelmed by the enormity of her decision.

He was alive now, and efficient. He removed his arm from her. "Here is what must be done—first off, this must be an absolute secret between us—even that pendant, don't wear it outside, Claire must not know—"

"Why must she not know?"

"She loves me. There would be terrible scenes. I just want to elope, go off with you, and afterwards I'll write her through Rasmussen. And my mother must not know yet, none of them, for they'd try to stop us. They are greedy to have the gains of this island, the discovery of it, for themselves. They would not want us to have the riches the news can bring. And your people must not know either, not Paoti or Moreturi or Huatoro, absolutely no one must know. They might try to stop you, as my people might try to stop me, out of fear or envy. You will keep it secret?"

"Yes."

"Good." His head reeled with visions of the potential booty of his victory, and he clambered to his feet, and walked the room. "Here is what we will do. I have thought it out. I am told that from time to time some of your braver young men take canoes or sailing vessels to other islands—"

She nodded. "They are good with the sea."

"We need one of them, Tehura, one we can trust. Are there any such?"

"Maybe."

"We can offer him anything he wants, anything I possess. We would have to slip out of here at night, both of us, and meet with the friend of yours who has a sailing vessel. He would take us to the nearest island where we can obtain a ship or flying boat to Tahiti or can find passage to another island where we can get transportation to Tahiti. After that we would be safe. Can this be done?"

"It would be bad for the one who helped us."

"When he returned, he could tell Paoti I forced him—I had a weapon—I forced him to do it. That would absolve him. Or maybe he would not have to return. I could give him enough to remain on the outside. Surely, there must be someone."

"There might be. I cannot be sure."

"Do you want to undertake finding someone?"

"Yes."

He stood over her, beaming down at her. "I knew you would. It is for both of us. How long will it take—to arrange everything?"

"I do not know."

"Can you guess?"

"A short time. A few days. A week. No more." She hesitated. "If it is possible at all."

"You will have to be careful, Tehura."

"I know."

He bent, and brought her up to her feet, so light, so pliable in his arms. "And you know I love you, Tehura."

She nodded against his shirt.

"I must teach you to kiss. It is part of our way. I want to seal this, Tehura—love you—kiss you—"

She brought her head up, full lips parted, and he put his mouth to them and his hands to her breasts. Throughout the last hour, his inner ego and outer being had grown, expanded, enlarged with his achievement, his first knowledge of independence and achievement, so that he felt almost full-grown into manhood. There was only this one unfinished thing left, to impart his new manhood to her, so that he might be certain he had it himself.

"Tehura—" he whispered.

She disengaged herself completely, and stepped back, arms at her side, entirely poised.

"There has been enough tonight, Marc," she said. "We will know each other the night we leave."

"You promise?"

"I do."

"I'll go then, Tehura." He went to the cane door. "We will continue our meetings every day, anthropologist and informant, pretend to work. There must be no hint of any change. When you have made the arrangement, you will tell me. I will need but a few hours' notice."

"I will tell you."

"Good night, darling."

"Good night, Marc."

Once outside, and making his way toward the village compound, he decided to write Rex Garrity a second brief airmail letter. The first one, dropped into Rasmussen's outgoing mail bag in the afternoon, had outlined his intentions. The second letter, the postscript, would announce his triumphant progress, and would request Garrity to meet them in Tahiti. He thanked God that Rasmussen had stayed over an extra day for the festival, and he could post the later news at daybreak.

By the time he had arrived at the stream, and traversed the bridge, his mind was again on Tehura. A speculation teased his mind. How ingenuous was she? How clever? Everything had gone exactly according to his plan, yet it made him uneasy to think that perhaps everything had also gone according to her plan. This was no reason to feel uneasy, since their goals were one and the same. Yet, a sudden suspicion that she might be as smart as he, not inferior but equal to him, even superior to him, was disconcerting. It was probably not true; still, it was possible. He felt less completely in control, and therefore less his own man. Damn these introverted speculations. Somehow, he felt a shade less happy than before . . . damn all women, damn everyone . . .

VII

🦋　　🦋　　🦋

Dr. Maud Hayden, smelling faintly of deodorant, sat behind her makeshift desk, squinting past Claire, trying to compose her thoughts. Already, even though it was only mid-morning, Maud's drip-dry khaki-colored blouse and skirt were beginning to wilt, so that she resembled an obese Girl Scout leader after a two-hour summer's hike.

As Claire waited, one leg crossed over the other, her stenographic pad on her knee, her pencil poised, she could feel the oppressiveness of the heat. The sun came through the hut windows like molten pig iron out of a blast furnace, and once inside the room, the sun had a compact thickness that lay against the skin and seared it. Drugged sleep was the one escape, and Claire wished that she was still asleep in her room. But she had been awakened early by Maud, who apologized and explained that the portable tape machine did not work, and was being repaired by Sam Karpowicz. Meanwhile, there were outgoing letters to be dictated and deposited with Captain Rasmussen when he arrived at noon.

To Claire, her mother-in-law, divested of the familiar portable tape recorder at her elbow, seemed as helpless as an admiral divested of his epaulets.

"Well, let me see . . ." Maud was saying. "Let's start with Dr. Macintosh. A brief note to keep him up to date."

Unconsciously, Claire winced. Until now, she had enjoyed typing the reports to Dr. Walter Scott Macintosh. Each titillating report, Claire had felt, more firmly secured Maud's chances to become lifetime executive editor of *Culture*. Claire had instinctively regarded this as good for her own future. For two years, two women had made demands on Marc's time. With one of the women, namely Maud, off to Washington, the other woman, namely Claire, might receive the attention she had long desired. With Maud out of the way, Marc would be freer to move alone and upwards in the academic world, and Claire would be mistress of her own home at last. This had been Claire's view of it until this week. Now, suddenly, everything was different and her emotions had been forced into a turnabout.

Until their arrival on The Three Sirens, Marc had been reserved, difficult, often cold, but he had been possible. He had sometimes been her husband. There was always the hope that he would be a better one. In these recent weeks, he had ceased being her husband altogether. He had become impossible. Hope had vanished. Despite their close quarters, Claire rarely saw him. It was as if he deliberately arranged to be gone in the morning when she awakened, to have always to eat out, to return long after she was asleep. When they were together, there seemed to be other people around them. In the rare times that they were alone, he did not even appear to be avoiding her. It was just that he treated her as if she were not there, as if she were a shade, an invisible woman.

Never in her life had Claire felt more hurt, more abandoned and lonely. Tom Courtney was kind, very kind, sometimes gallant, and this filled many hours, but Courtney was careful with her. He treated her too correctly, as Someone's Wife. So, that left Maud. Claire had always adored Maud, a strange contradiction since she had also been hopeful of being rid of her. Recently, Claire had held less regard for her mother-in-law, because Maud had refused to be her confidante in this trying period with Marc. Yet, now that Claire had been abandoned, Maud loomed before her as the last friend on earth, a sheltering Gibraltar. And consequently she hated to take down in shorthand, and to type and send off, another letter that would help separate Maud from her.

Claire realized that Maud had begun to dictate, and quickly she caught the words floating past, and bent to her pad, hooking in the Gregg symbols.

"Dear Walter," Maud was saying. "I wrote you one week ago, but here I am again with a hasty note that will go out with Captain Rasmussen tonight. This is simply to tell you that these last days have surpassed all that came before in providing us with meaty information on these Sirens people . . . Paragraph, Claire . . .

Today is the final day of the annual festival, and today represents the halfway mark of our field trip, for we have been here three weeks. I wrote you earlier of the festival schedule, as I learned about it from Chief Paoti Wright. However, to have been a participant observer in the events of the festival has given me a close-up view of it, an understanding of it, that could not be acquired at second hand . . . Paragraph . . . The festival began seven days ago with an afternoon athletic event, a strenuous one-mile swimming race, which Marc was courageous enough to enter. His notes will be invaluable. I might add with motherly pride, he almost defeated the natives at their own game, barely losing out at the very finish."

Maud's inflection at the end of the last sentence made it clear, to Claire, that she would report no more of that fiasco. Claire looked up sharply, determined to goad Maud with her glance, force her to mention Marc's foul, or at least chastise her with a visual reproach for omitting it, but Maud's back was to her. Maud was staring out the window.

"That evening," Maud went on, "a large platform was erected in the village compound, ringed with colorful torches, and our nurse here, Harriet Bleaska, opened the festival week. She had been elected to the honor by the young men of the village. After that, there was an intricate ceremonial dance and, believe it or not, one of the stars was Mrs. Lisa Hackfeld, the wife of our backer. Mrs. Hackfeld acquitted herself astonishingly well. The second afternoon there were new games, mainly wrestling, more in the Japanese than the American style, and in the evening we were treated to a pantomimic performance, a form of fertility rite, and once again Mrs. Hackfeld was the mainstay. For her, this place has been a veritable Fountain of Youth. The feature of the third evening was the nude beauty contest, most of the young single girls of the village participating. All the young men were on hand, cheering their favorites. It was similar, somewhat, to the nude beauty contests that Peter Buck witnessed on Manikihi, in the Cook islands. In those contests, as I recollect reading, the beauties were even studied from behind, to see if their legs were close together, for if they were, it was considered a sign of virtue and much esteemed. This kind of judgment was not made here, I assure you. Chief Paoti could not trace the origin of this beauty contest, but he did not disagree when I suggested that it might be a sort of display case for young girls who wanted to show off their wares to potential suitors and husbands. Also, I suspect, it is part of the stimulant of the entire heady festival week. On the fourth night—"

Suddenly, Maud came around on her chair, holding up one pudgy hand.

"Wait, Claire, before we get into the fourth night, I want to add something to my last sentence. Can you read it back?"

"One second." Claire found it. " 'Also, I suspect, it is part of the stimulant of the entire heady festival week.' "

"Yes. Umm, add this . . ." She considered what she would add, and then she dictated. "Dr. Orville Pence was one of the judges of the nude beauty contest, and his choices were well received and coincided with those of the other judges, two natives, save in one instance. The last of the female entries proved to be one of our own team, the indomitable Miss Bleaska, who had been convinced by her large village following to take part. She might have won, she is a great favorite here, except for Dr. Pence's dissenting vote. In any case, she received runner-up honors. As you can see, we are not merely observers here, but industrious participants, and have been from the very first night of our arrival, and Paoti's feast, when my daughter-in-law volunteered for the rites of friendship."

Claire's head came up. "Really, Maud, do you have to mention that? It's embarrassing enough to know I got looped and did that without—"

"Don't be silly, Claire. It is in all my reports. I'm mentioning it with maternal pride."

"Well, if you insist—"

"Since when have you gone Victorian on me?"

"Since my husband went Victorian on me," Claire shot back.

Maud's expression conceded nothing. "Oh, men, men are so possessive," she said. And then she said quickly, "Let's go on, we've a lot to do this morning. Let me see—ah, yes—" She was dictating again. "I do believe that our functionalist friend, Bronislaw Malinowski, would have been proud of the active participation of his disciples in the field . . . Paragraph . . . Each of these festival events, which we have observed and experienced, has been captured on film by Sam Karpowicz, whose darkroom here is filled to the ceiling with reels of movies, still photographs, and color slides. I am going to give our members at the American Anthropological League not only an earful, Walter, but an eyeful as well . . . Make that an exclamation mark, Claire . . . As you predicted, Walter, The Three Sirens was the shot in the arm I needed, and it will be the first fresh study to come out of Polynesia in many years . . . Paragraph . . . But, to resume with the highlights of the festival week behind us. On the fourth night—"

There was a rapping on the door, and Maud halted, disconcerted.

"Come in!" Claire called out.

The door opened partially, and more heat oozed into the hut, followed by Lisa Hackfeld, wearing a white nylon jersey dress and a broad wreath of smile. Before her, she held a small bowl filled with cut plants.

"Oh," she said, when she saw Claire with pad and pencil, "If I'm interrupting I can—"

"It's quite all right, Lisa," Maud said, briskly. "I'll be at this all morning with Claire. You seem bursting with some news—"

"I am, I am," replied Lisa in a kind of chant. With reverence, she placed the bowl of cut plants before Maud. "Do you know what this is?"

Maud leaned forward and peered into the bowl. "Looks like some kind of seed plant—" She picked up one of the yellow-green mossy stems and examined it. "It's a soft herb that—"

"The *puai* plant!" Lisa Hackfeld exclaimed.

"Yes, of course, that's right," Maud agreed.

Momentarily, Lisa was taken aback. "How do *you* know about it, Maud?"

"Why, it's indigenous to the islands here and quite famous. I suppose I first heard about it from Paoti Wright. It's the so-called drug that Captain Rasmussen takes out of here every week—in fact, I discussed it with him, too—"

"And no one told me," said Lisa, incredulously. "To think I might never have found out. Anyway, I did find out, but not through the Captain, although I've been talking to him about it for the last hour—"

"You mean Rasmussen is in the village already?" asked Maud. "He usually comes straight here."

"I abducted him, Maud," Lisa admitted, proudly. "I dragged him into my hut, and put some whiskey in front of him, and made him come clean. Right now, I've got him writing down everything he knows about it—for Cyrus, you know—"

"But why?" Maud asked.

"Why? Because there's a fortune in it, that's why." Lisa turned to Claire, who had been half-listening, doodling. "Claire, do you know what this puai plant does?"

Claire shrugged. "I'm afraid I haven't the vaguest—"

"It makes you feel young, act young, it rolls away the wrinkles and lubricates the creaks," Lisa announced, her voice as falsetto and fanatical as that of an evangelist. "I tell you, with this, life can really begin at forty. Forgive me, I'm higher than a kite about my discovery." She was addressing both Claire and Maud, and she had one of the pulpy herbs in her hand and waved it as she spoke. "It was an accident, how I found out. You know, I've been rehearsing with those native dancers for days, and you saw the two performances I put on this past week—"

"You've been remarkable, Lisa," said Maud.

"Well, I have been, kidding aside. I've exceeded myself. Look, I used to be a dancer, a real high-stepper, and I was limber and pretty good, but then I was young. Let's face it, I'm no spring chicken any more. Back home, when Cyrus took me to the club, I'd be winded after one waltz, and anything livelier laid me out for a week after. So I came here with you, and I got into this dance bit, and you know, from the first day practically, I was never tired. I just felt great, and could do anything, and I felt like a kid. I couldn't figure it out, this kind of second wind, this rejuvenation—and then, the other night, something struck me. Just before the fertility dance, they passed around cups of some kind of greenish drink. I remembered that we'd always had that during rehearsals, even before the first night of the festival, and it wasn't that palm juice or anything alcoholic. So I asked about it, and they told me it was an extract of the puai plant—'puai' means 'strength' in Polynesian—grows around here like a weed—and for centuries it has been given to dancers, to provide them with vigor. It's not an intoxicant—I mean, you don't take leave of your senses—but it's a sort of native narcotic or stimulant, a kind of liquid kick in the fanny, and no addiction and no side effects. I found out this is the magic herb Captain Rasmussen has been exporting from here for years, and exporting from Tahiti to Hong Kong, Singapore, Indochina, the East Indies. He buys cheap, sells high. He and his wife have only a small business going, but it's kept him in nice shape for years.

"Well, I got to thinking about it, and the more I thought,

the more excited I became. Of course, you know what I have in mind—"

"You want to import it into the United States," said Maud.

"Exactly! I could hardly contain myself until this morning, when I got my hands on the poor Captain, and I guess I overwhelmed him. I told him about Cyrus, and his pharmaceutical holdings, and how he's always on the lookout for something new, and how maybe this was just the thing—can't you see the label?—palm trees, silhouettes of native dancers, and something like 'the new exotic elixir from the South Seas, tested, approved, youth-giving, energy-giving—*Vitality*'—how's that for a name on the package? Vitality!"

Claire squirmed, but Maud rose bravely to the occasion. "Where can I buy some, Lisa?"

"You'll be able to buy some in every drugstore in America next year. I'm working out a tentative deal with Captain Rasmussen right now, subject to Cyrus' approval." She fondled the herb lovingly. "Think of it, this little thing, it's changed my life, it'll help millions of women like me. Oh, I can't wait—my own discovery —there'll be so much to do. I even have ideas for promotion, directing and sending out Polynesian-type dance troupes, or maybe preparing them for television commercials—" She was breathless, as her lively eyes went from Maud to Claire, and back to Maud again. "I mean, I'll have a business, I'll be paying my way, and yet —and yet be helping others. Don't you think it's a stupendous idea?"

Maud inclined her head with the authority the Pope of Rome gave to a blessing. "It's a grand idea, Lisa. I would encourage you to go right ahead."

"I knew you'd be pleased," said Lisa. She returned the herb to the bowl and picked up the bowl. "I'd better finish up with the Captain and fire off a cable and letter to Cyrus." She went to the door, and then paused. "I really owe it all to you, Maud. If you hadn't allowed me to come to The Three Sirens, I wouldn't have had this to look forward to. I should thank you. I will. In fact, you shall have the first shipment of Vitality, gratis and on the house!"

After she had floated out, Maud sat contemplating the one fugitive herb that she still retained in her hand.

Claire lighted a cigarette, and wagged the match until the flame was extinguished. "Is that herb really that good?" she asked.

"No," said Maud.

Claire straightened with surprise. "Did I hear you right?"

"It's a harmless, half-fraud, almost inert, of little therapeutic value, according to Rasmussen's pharmacologists. Field trips are always turning up something—back home, among the Indians, cascara bark as a laxative—or down in these parts, turmeric as a medicine—or stems of the kava plant, marindinum, as a sleeping aid—but most of the stuff is second-rate and really useless. Sometimes a good one comes along. Quinine, for example, from the cinchona bark. We acquired it from the natives of Peru and Bolivia." She shook her head. "But the puai plant—the minute that Paoti mentioned it, I had Sam Karpowicz find some and he knew what it was. It's the most mild form of narcotic stimulant. Its real strength is in its tradition. Truthfully, the magic of suggestion has always been more potent than drugs in primitive societies. The natives have always believed that the puai picks them up, so, needless to say, Claire, it picks them up. But Rasmussen took no chances with selling a tradition, just as the old dispensers of the mandragora herb knew it was too nonvolatile for an anesthetic unless mixed with opium. What Rasmussen did from the beginning, does even now, is mix the ingredients of the puai with ingredients of bêche-de-mer—"

"I think I've heard of that last one. What is it?"

"Bêche-de-mer? It's a sea slug. The natives go into three or four feet of water, pull the slugs off the reefs, cut them open, boil the innards, cure them in the sun. Very popular in Fiji, I remember, where they export the stuff to China. Bêche-de-mer is a stronger stimulant, something that peps up what Morrell used to call 'the immoderate voluptuary.' Sam Karpowicz says we have a hundred better drugs that induce the same results back home. I know nothing about selling a product. I suppose this silly thing has the right label, and it won't hurt anyone, actually. The Hackfelds will make a billion and maybe remember to support other field trips in the future."

"If puai is such a low-grade, ordinary drug, Maud, why did you encourage Lisa to go ahead with the—the half-fraud, as you put it?"

"I repeat, my dear, it won't hurt a soul, and it may do some good. It makes these natives feel younger. It makes Lisa feel younger.

Maybe it'll help others in the same way, too. It could be a psychological boost for its buyers."

"Still, I don't—"

"Another thing, Claire. When a woman reaches forty, and feels forty or more, and is sensible enough to act her age in a society such as ours that is only attentive to those of twenty, I think she should be encouraged to do anything reasonable to make herself busy and active. She should put her mind where her heart is, not where her body is. With Vitality, Lisa will be a young forty, not an old forty, and she'll be a young fifty and sixty, too, and have a place and a way of life. I speak from experience, Claire. One day you'll understand. Lisa is on the right road, and I will encourage her."

Sitting across from Maud, listening to her, Claire drew on her cigarette and began to understand. Maud had found her own puai plant, and it was The Three Sirens. Claire had sympathy for both Lisa and Maud. Claire was twenty-five, and Lisa was fifteen years older than she and Maud was thirty-five years older than she, and yet Claire felt as old as both of them, for age was not only reckoned by years but also by the telltale wood rings of feeling unwanted, neglected, discarded. Claire knew that technically she had the advantage of fewer used-up years of the allotted number, therefore the promise of a longer time on the planet—the one unchallengeable snobbery and arrogance of the almost-young in their twenties and thirties—but this advantage was not enough, for no use was being made of this advantage, and she had no Vitality, no Sirens field trip badge, either.

"Now where were we?" Maud was saying.

Claire retrieved her pad and pencil, but before she could find their place in the dictation, there was a loud voice outside, female, then voices, female and male, some kind of exchange, and Harriet Bleaska came through the door, her face uncharacteristically knotted by some sudden annoyance.

"That Orville Pence, I tell you, Maud," she muttered, and then became aware that there were two in the room. "Oh, hi, Claire." She turned to Maud. "Any chance of seeing you alone sometime today? I need your advice, and I thought—"

"There's no time like the present," said Maud.

Claire stood up immediately. "I'll leave you two alone."

"All right, Claire," said Maud. "Why don't we resume the dictation in—let's say in fifteen minutes?"

*   *   *

After Claire had left the room, Maud gyrated in her chair and gave her entire matriarchal attention to her ugliest duckling. "You were speaking of Orville Pence when you came in," she said. "Does this concern Orville?"

"Orville?" Harriet Bleaska repeated. "Oh, him—" She shook her head, crossed to the bench, and sat down. "He's become nutty as a fruit cake," she said. "I don't get it. He was such a nice guy. Now, he's always making sarcastic remarks to me, and just now, outside, he came bounding up, actually hurt my arm the way he grabbed it, and tried to drag me off somewhere to have a talk. I told him it would have to wait, I had something more urgent on my mind I had to discuss with you, and he got nasty all over again. So I simply turned my back on him and came in."

Through this, Maud had been nodding. "Yes," she said, "these field trips sometimes affect some of the—the members—adversely. The change of environment, trying to perform properly in a totally different culture, this can make some people edgy." She thought of her discussion, during the week, with Sam Karpowicz, and his vehemence at the Sirens teaching curriculum, and his anger over the exposure of Mary to that one study. She also remembered an earlier exchange with Orville himself and the missionary priggishness in his comments on the Sirens society and on Harriet's affair with the native patient who had died. Even Rachel DeJong, usually so remote and objective, had given evidence of being distraught the entire week. And then, thought Maud, there were her own son and daughter-in-law, who presented anything but the picture of connubial bliss when they were publicly together.

Perhaps the time had come, Maud told herself, to assert the authority invested in her as leader of the team, to bring them together, have them air the pressures this study had brought down upon them, and soothe and calm them with learned chapter and verse out of past experiences. But here was Harriet Bleaska, nurse, and the immediacy of her annoyance, and Maud knew that she must meet it now. "I have no idea, Harriet, why Orville is behaving badly with you," Maud lied, "but if it continues, you let me know. I shall find a way to speak to him about it."

"That won't be necessary," said Harriet hastily, somewhat placated. "I'll manage him. He's probably just been getting up on the wrong side of the bed—of the mat, I should have said." Her annoyance had been superficial, and fell away, and she giggled at her joke.

"Was that why you wanted to see me this morning?" asked Maud, trying to repress her impatience at being interrupted in her dictation.

"As a matter of fact, no. I was really coming here to—to have a little confidential talk with you, Maud."

"By all means, Harriet." She hesitated. "Is there something bothering you?"

Harriet had located a cigarette and was nervously lighting it. She was more serious this morning than Maud had known her to be since she had joined the team. "Not exactly bothering me," Harriet said from behind the screen of smoke. "It's just something I wanted to—to discuss with you—I mean, with your background—" She waited, inviting encouragement.

"If there's any way I can be of help—"

"I really want some information from you," Harriet said. "I've been thinking. You've been on many field trips. You know other people who have been on them. You've even been down here in Polynesia before—"

"Yes, all of that is true."

"I—well—have you ever heard—do you know any cases of women, American women on field trips, who've—well—simply stayed behind, decided not to go home?"

Maud suppressed a whistle (now *this* was promising), and her tumid face and ponderous arms remained motionless. "That is an interesting question," Maud said with earnestness. "As I have told you and the others, I have known cases of women who have cohabited with natives and set up households and had children by their native lovers. As for a more permanent arrangement, one of our women staying behind with a native man, or simply staying behind to live in the new society, I can only think of a few such instances. These I do not know about firsthand. I repeat, a few female anthropologists have done this."

"Well, I wasn't really thinking about female anthropologists," said Harriet. "I was just thinking of an ordinary woman—a nobody—I mean, who had no career—that would be easier for her, wouldn't it?"

"I can't say, Harriet. It would very much depend upon the woman. Besides, women present a special case. With men, it is different. I know many cases of men in the field who have gone native—that is, 'stayed behind,' as you put it."

"You do?" said Harriet, eagerly. "Were they happier? I mean, did it work out?"

"One never knows, truly," said Maud. "I would imagine so, I would imagine it has worked out many times."

"You really know such cases?"

"Oh, certainly. Some are legend, still discussed whenever anthropologists gather. There was one anthropologist who went into Outer Asia to study the Buddhist tradition. He became so fascinated by the subject, the people, the life, that he was converted to Buddhism and entered the priesthood. He's probably in some remote lamasery this very day. There was another young man I knew, an anthropologist, who took a field trip to—it was somewhere in Central Africa—and when his study was done, he just stayed on and on, and never returned to America. Still another, he went down to our own Southwest to study the Pueblo Indians. In the end, he renounced his old life and joined the Pueblos. Which reminds me of Frank Hamilton Cushing, an ethnologist from Pennsylvania. He went to New Mexico to study the Zuñi Indians, published a book, *Zuñi Creation Myths*, and was so taken with the life there that he gave up his old life in the East, gave up publishing, and went native. In effect, became a Zuñi until he died in 1900. I'll tell you the best of them—have you ever heard of Jaime de Angulo, who worked up in Berkeley, California?"

"No—no, I don't think so," said Harriet.

"There's a story, not to be believed, but most of it true, I'm sure," said Maud with relish. "Jaime de Angulo was born in Spain, Castilian parentage, reared in a cosmopolitan way, taken to the various spas of Europe by his father. The talk is that he was educated in France, then came over to the United States and acquired his M.D. at John Hopkins. After that, he moved on to California, studied with Kroeber, was a friend of Paul Radin. Anyway, he was a linguist, that was his field, and he could write beautifully in

Spanish, French, English, too. He was a very eccentric person. He —oh, well, that's not what you're interested in—only I was going to mention that he was said to go stark naked often, even around his home and back yard in Berkeley, or he dressed like the natives here on the Sirens, that is, wearing nothing more than an athletic supporter, and this horrified his neighbors. No matter. The important thing is that he would go on field trips, study the Indians of Mexico, study the Indians of California. He wrote an excellent book on the dialects of various American Indian tribes. When he worked among the Indians, he lived as they did, made himself one of them. Eventually, he found their life more compatible than the one he lived away from them. So he changed his way of life. He had a house in Big Sur, but when he decided to go native, he changed this house into something resembling an Indian hogan. He covered the windows of the house, set up a fireplace in the middle of one room, chopped a hole in the roof above it, real Indian style, and then he would roast his meat over this fireplace, go about undressed as a redskin, chanting Indian songs and beating Indian drums. He went native with a vengeance, and I'm sure he was happier for it. Once, when Ruth Benedict wanted to study the Indians, she wrote Jaime de Angulo and asked for an introduction to informants who could give her information on the ceremonials and so forth. Jaime was indignant. He wrote Ruth Benedict, 'Do you realize it is just that sort of thing that kills the Indians?' He meant both spiritually and physically. He wrote her, 'That's what you anthropologists with your infernal curiosity and your thirst for scientific data bring about. Don't you understand the psychological value of secrecy at a certain level of culture?' Then he wrote her, 'I am not an anthropologist but I am half an Indian, or more. Don't forget Cushing killed Zunyi.' There are some cases for you, Harriet."

"The ones you mentioned, I wonder why they changed their lives like that?" said Harriet, thoughtfully.

"I can only give you my view of it, an educated guess. I would suggest that people who go native are people who have no special ties on the outside, that is, back home. The chances are, they are people who are not entirely satisfied with the lives they lived back home or with our civilization. Tom Courtney is a good example of that, a very good example. In a sense he has cut himself off, gone native. You should speak to him."

"I have," said Harriet.

"You have?" Maud was surprised. "And what did he say about the whole subject?"

"He said, 'My case is too personal. Go speak to Maud Hayden. She's more detached. She knows about everything.' So here I am."

"Well, I'm flattered by Mr. Courtney, but I don't know about everything, and in the end this decision comes down to one's own personality. Those anthropologists who stayed behind, I suppose they found more satisfaction in the native life. After all, what is the ideal basic unit for mankind? It is relatively small. If one works in a small unit, like the village on the Sirens, becomes part of it, absorbed by it, it is hard to break away. If a participant observer goes to a foreign society, and stays six weeks or fifty weeks, the odds are he can get away. If he stays two years, leaving is more difficult. If he remains four or five years, like Cushing and de Angulo, the life in the native society becomes his accustomed way of life. So, if his memory of life back home is not too good, what he finds in the field may be more appealing. Also, one grows fond of new friends and hates to leave them. Ideally, an anthropologist should not go native. His loyalty must be to his work. He must tread a narrow line, that is, being part of a people, yet not part of them, learning from them, yet not being blotted up by them. A society like the Sirens is highly seductive. In a place like this, I've got to tell myself that I must maintain my cultural identity. I remind myself that I'm an anthropologist, and a member of a culture tradition of my own, and I must live by the rules of my home society. I remind myself, always, that I simply can't be a good anthropologist unless I do get home with the goods, my material, and analyze it and publish it for the use of my own people. But then, I am an anthropologist, and you are not, and you may not be particularly interested in the duties of my profession."

"I'm not really, no," said Harriet, frankly.

Maud's eyes narrowed, and she studied the homely girl across from her with keen interest. "What you are saying, Harriet, is that you are interested in yourself, how you would react to going native, possibly staying on here? Is that what you are considering?"

"Yes, Maud."

"Well, this is a serious thing. Have you given it a good deal of thought? Have you thought why you are even considering this change?"

"Yes," said Harriet, almost too lightly, "because it's the only game in town."

"I'm sorry, I don't understand you. What does that expression mean?"

Harriet exhaled. "It means, I've found the one place on earth that wants me. Far as I know, there is no other. Certainly, I've found no love, warmth, kindness, no hospitality at home." She paused, went on quickly, "It's rotten at home, Maud, and it's something you've never known. You don't know what it is like to grow up in the United States and be—and be—well, a girl who is unattractive. It's like, you've got to be a movie star, or at least kind of good-looking or nice-looking. Well, who are we kidding? I can say this to you. By the standards the men have at home, I'm zero, less than zero. No man would look at me twice, let alone take me out, let alone—God, even to think of it—marry me. Oh, I haven't withered in the corner, if you know what I mean. When the boys in school, in the hospitals, found out I didn't mind going to bed with them—gosh, I had to do something for companionship—I had dates. Then, they found out I was better than the other girls, in making love I mean. There was no trouble getting men, if I did *that*, but it had to be that, nothing else, never normal relationships. Some men were quite taken by me, that part of me, and it fooled me into thinking they liked me as a woman, might even marry me. But no, in the end it came down to the face and figure, they'd rather have a wife with a face and figure they can showcase, even though she was a lump in bed, than someone like me, even though they enjoyed me more. So, what's my future if I return, what am I going back to? I haven't a close family to speak of. Just lots of relatives in the Midwest, busy with their own headaches. I'm alone, on my own, so what will it be? More dreary hospitals and clinics and lousy, lonely apartments at night, until some fresh intern or young doctor or old doctor finds out I will, I'm easy, and by God, I'm good, and so it's the bed all over again until they're tired or I press them, and then they're off to marry some cold dill pickle. Do you know what I mean, Maud? What am I giving up?"

Somewhat shaken, Maud nodded gravely. "Yes, I understand, Harriet."

"Here—why, here I've been only three weeks—and it's like I'm in paradise. Here my face and figure aren't important, no one gives a damn. What counts here is that I'm warm, and decent, and like to love and be loved, and to those wonderful, wonderful idiots that makes me beautiful. Imagine, Queen of the Festival. Me! And it's not as if I were a nine-day wonder, I thought of that, too; I'm a stranger, white, different, and I'm good at doing what is important here, more important than looks. I've asked myself what it would be like after I was no longer a nine-day wonder, but one of them, day in and day out, year after year. You know what, Maud, I think it would still be good. I watch how the men here treat their women, and also the freedom and fun the women have. It's nothing like at home. It has staying power. It could work."

She caught her breath. "Anyway, I didn't mean to bend your ear like this. I only wanted to tell you something. In the last few weeks I've had a dozen proposals of marriage—yes, truly, for real. Very flattering. But there was one young man here who really impressed me. He's a serious person, whom I thought rather stand-offish and cool, but it turns out he was reticent because he loved me and was afraid he had not enough to offer me. Anyway, the festival got to him, and he sent me his necklace thing, and I met him and we talked and talked, nothing more. You know what, he proposed marriage last night, real big deal, he wants me for his wife, forever. You know who I'm talking about? Vaiuri, the medical practitioner, the head of the infirmary, the fellow I've been working with. He's smart, educated according to Sirens standards, attractive, and he's in love with me and wants me for his wife, wants me not to go home, to stay here for always. Well, it is really something, like learning I've found where I belong and can be happy and appreciated. But I didn't give him an answer because—because why?—because I hate where I came from, what I came from, and still I'm an American girl and this is so strange, here in the middle of nowhere, cut off from civilization as we laughingly call it. So, I don't know, I'm mixed up, rattling around, trying to decide. And I wanted to hear what you would say about the whole native thing in general. I guess nothing can help, nobody can live my life. I've got to make my own decisions."

Maud Hayden was moved as she had not been in a long time. Some instinct in her wanted to make her cry out to this lonely girl: Stay here, for Heaven's sake, stay here and don't go home to the other, stay here and know real acceptance and happiness. Yet, Maud could not cast herself in the role of Miss Lonelyhearts. Her training had made her the observer, the taker-in, not the giver-out, and she had not the daring to enter another's life. She contained herself as best she could.

"Yes, Harriet, I can see where Vaiuri's proposal would be very complimentary, and where life here on the Sirens could possibly be better than life at home. Certainly, you must consider the whole thing realistically and exercise your best judgment. But as you have guessed, I don't dare to advise you. You must come to your own decision about this. I'm sure, for you, it will be the right one. If you decide to stay behind, I will assist you in every way possible. If you decide to return home with us, I will always be available there, too, to help you if I can."

Harriet was standing, and Maud stood, also, out of deference to Harriet's problem and Harriet's drama.

Harriet smiled, and she said, "Thanks, Maud, for playing mother. I'll let you know how I make out."

"You are a sensible person," said Maud. "I know that you will do what is right for you."

Harriet gave a nod of assent, opened the door, stepped through it, closed it with appreciative respect, and walked into the baking compound.

*　*　*

Passing Claire Hayden's quarters, Harriet Bleaska slowed down, thinking that she might see if Claire was inside. Now that Harriet had unburdened herself in privacy, her dilemma was less secret. She wished that she had allowed Claire to remain in the room with Maud. This instant, she had the urge to visit Claire, and share her marriage proposal with one who was of her own years, and hear what Claire might have to say. But Claire had been distant in the past week, and perhaps she had other things on her mind, so Harriet decided to continue on next door to her own hut. Rachel De-Jong just might be in, and if she was, she might lend her professional advice to Harriet's problem.

As Harriet went between Claire's hut and her own, she saw a figure in the shadows, leaning against the side of her house. With her appearance, and recognition of him, Orville Pence quickly left the shadows to advance toward her.

"Harriet, I've got to speak to you." There was a tight scolding in Orville's tone, and his right eye and fussy nose twitched. "You've been trying to avoid me. Nevertheless, I'm going to have my say."

"I haven't been trying to avoid you, but I am now, because you've been sarcastic to me. I don't know what's got into you."

"I'm sorry if I've sounded that way. I only want to help you. I've got to help you."

For the first time, Harriet's interest was aroused. She was seeking advice, and here was someone, despite his bewildering behavior, who was offering to help her. She submitted to curiosity.

"Okay," she said, "but at least, let's get out of the sun, let's get in the shade."

They went between the two huts, and came to a halt facing each other near Harriet's rear window.

Harriet found Orville's eyes fixed on her face, as if examining her for pimples, and automatically her hand went to her forehead and cheek to learn if she had broken out in a rash since breakfast. When his speechless staring began to make her uncomfortable, she took the initiative. "You said you wanted to talk to me, Orville. What about?"

Agitated, he picked at the sunburned bald portion of his head, and then brought his fingers down to his shell-rimmed spectacles and kept trying to set them higher on the moist, slippery bridge of his thin nose. "I know all about you!" he suddenly blurted.

Harriet's bewilderment deepened. How could he know? She had told no one except Maud, and that was scant minutes ago. Another thought occurred to her, that Vaiuri had confided to Orville or perhaps to his native friends, who had in turn told Orville the news. "How do you know?" she asked.

"It's all over the place, that's how. Everyone knows."

"Well," she said defensively, "it's true. I've nothing to be ashamed of. In fact, I'm proud of it."

"Proud of it?" Orville stretched the words out, his voice quavering, his eyes aghast.

"Why shouldn't I be?" Harriet demanded. "He's one of the most educated and important men in the village. He isn't a savage. He respects me. Yes, I'd be proud to be his wife."

Harriet had never seen a man struck by lightning, but she was sure that if she had, he would look as Orville Pence looked this moment. He shuddered as if a stroke of electricity coursed through him. "Wife?" he repeated in stupefaction. "You're going to *marry* one of *them?*"

Harriet's confusion intensified. "Didn't you know? You said everyone is talking about it. I thought you meant Vaiuri's proposal. What do you mean?"

"Vaiuri's proposal?"

"Orville, if you don't stop parroting everything I say I'm leaving you," she said indignantly. "I wish you could hear yourself. What in the devil did you find out about that was so earth-shaking?"

"About you and Uata, your affair with the native who died—"

"Oh, that," she said with a disgusted wave of her hand.

He grabbed her arm in mid-air. "Wait a minute! How dare you dismiss it so—so—like it was nothing at all. It's been the talk of the village. It even got to me, from the natives. I've never been so shocked—that one of us, a decently brought-up girl from the United States—letting herself be seduced by a half-breed and—and—primitive—"

Harriet's surprise had converted to irritation. "He didn't seduce me, you fool, I seduced him. And I enjoyed it and he enjoyed it, and I'd do it over again!"

Orville floundered before her onslaught of words, loosened his grip, and she tore her arm free. His head rattled inside with disbelief, and he leaned against the hut as if it were the Wailing Wall. "You—you don't—you don't know what—what you're saying," he stuttered. "They—they've bewitched you—you don't know—"

That moment, she had a perception about the poor bachelor scholar, and she almost pitied him. "Orville, I'm sorry I've disappointed you so. I had no idea you were that interested in my purity. Even if I had known—I'm sorry, but I still would have slept with him, because he was dying, and he needed someone. Why should it upset you so much?"

"I'm thinking of—of—of the team—our dignity, position here—"

"Well, Maud says I've enhanced our position here, so you need have no concern about that."

Suddenly, his eyes were fixed upon her face again. "And now," he said, "if my ears didn't deceive me, you're going to marry a native—"

"I'm considering it. The medical practitioner I work with, and he's a dear, he proposed, and I must say I'm flattered."

"Harriet, no, you can't. You—you'll lose your American passport!"

What he had chosen to say was so comic to Harriet that she had the urge to laugh. The contorted shape of his pear face suffocated the urge. "Look, Orville, I'll will you my passport. What's it ever gotten me? Has it gotten me a red-blooded American man? A proposal of marriage? A home and children? Love? Has it gotten me love? Nothing, I've gotten nothing out of it except a couple of grand tours with American sexual acrobats who've refused to make an honest woman of me. Well, that's not enough for me. Togetherness is fine, but I don't want it just at night. I want it day and night. I want to be not only a woman, but a wife and mother—"

"I'll marry you!" Orville bellowed.

Harriet Bleaska swallowed the rest of her sentence, and stood gaping at him, her mouth hanging foolishly open.

"I mean it," Orville cried out fervently. "I'll marry you and give you a home and children."

Her pride rose in her throat, and she swallowed that, too. "Why?" she said almost indistinctly. "Do you want to save a soul, rescue a fallen woman?"

"I'm jealous of them," he said with vehemence. "I'm jealous of them and I won't let them have you. I want to take you away, I want you. I—I've never been in love—but I've never felt like this before—so I guess this is love."

She moved closer to him, hollow with compassion. "Orville, do you realize what you are saying?"

"I want to marry you," he insisted, doggedly.

She touched his shirt sleeve, and felt the shiver of his bony arm beneath it. "Orville, we don't even know each other."

"I know enough. I know I won't let you waste yourself on—whatever his name is—the medicine man—and not come back with me. I deserve you more. I can make you happier."

"You want to take me back to—where is it?—yes, Denver. You want to marry me?"

"I've never proposed to any girl before. Almost, but never actually, because of my—my mother—"

"Your mother, family, what would they say?"

"I don't care. That's the point, also. Being away from them, and here, it's made me think. Harriet, I won't let you give yourself to that native, just because he—"

"Wait, stop, Orville. Everything is going too fast. For a quarter of a century I'm a candidate for old-maidhood, and zing, overnight I'm weighing proposals." She considered him, and in the shimmering heat a curious alchemy occurred, and his face looked like the face of someone's mother-in-law. She held her breath, and so many other representations crowded her mind—her role as wife of Vaiuri on the Sirens, her role as Mrs. Pence in Denver—that she felt unstrung. "Orville," she said, and she began to lead him out of the shade and toward her door, "before I can even think of you— we'd better sit down—I'll make some tea and we'll talk—you and I had better talk, a little."

* * *

Usually, when he worked with his three pans, developing negatives, printing them, rinsing them, Sam Karpowicz was oblivious to the outer world's conventions. For him, the darkrooms in his life, be they rude shacks in the Fijis or Mexico, or the more elaborate one behind his home in Albuquerque, or this Iron Maiden in which he was toiling this minute on The Three Sirens, were isolated capsules where Time had been suspended. In his darkrooms, absorbed in the images that he had snatched from God's world, where all was fluid and aging, and pinned to paper in his own world, where all was immobile and immortal, Sam escaped from the urgencies and amenities of survival. In his darkrooms, there were no appointments, social graces, competitions, no groomings, voidings, eatings.

It was therefore unusual, Sam thought, as he ran the contact prints through the clear-water rinse and put them up to dry, that he felt a hunger pang. When he lifted his watch closer to the yellow safety light of the battery-operated lamp, the hour and minute hands confirmed the reminder of his hunger pang. It was already a half-hour after the noon hour, which meant that Estelle was waiting with lunch, and he wanted lunch because, except for the fruit juice he had gulped down as his entire breakfast, he had not had a bite to eat in over fifteen hours.

He had awakened at daybreak, and been unable to fall asleep again, and had left Estelle in her damp slumber, and his troubled Mary behind the continuously closed door of the second rear bedroom, and walked into the hills above the village. He had intended to start taking his plant cuttings, before settling down to the work in the darkroom. But botany tempted him not at all this morning. Instead, alone, he had roamed through the bush, recriminating against the Fates that had sent him to this foul place.

Ever since his eruption in the schoolroom, his daughter had not spoken a word to him, or, at least, not a civil word. And she had spoken to her mother little more. She had kept to her room, to herself, refusing to eat with her parents, refusing to go out with them, appearing only a few times a day to attend the lavatory. Her flimsy door she had kept shut, but behind it, sometimes, Sam could hear her phonograph playing and the pages of a book rustling. If brooding had a sound, Sam was sure that he might have heard that, too.

So confident was he in his rightness that he had poured out justification of his action to Estelle. She had refused to ally herself fully with him. At the same time, in the hope of attaining future family harmony, she had refused to defend Mary's cause, either. Rather, she had represented herself as some kind of neutral institution, ready to accept the two differing camps without judging them, so that they might have a place to reconcile differences. Sam guessed this about Estelle, but he had also guessed that secretly she might be less neutral than she pretended. From little, quiet comments, interjections she made, while Sam inveighed against the educational system on the Sirens, the problems of adolescent girls, his enforced role as paterfamilias, Sam suspected that she had more sympathy for their daughter's hurt than her husband's outrage. Still, he could not be positive about Estelle's feelings, for she had not really given voice to her feelings, nor had he truly invited her to do so.

Through the past festival week, as his initial fury at this erotic society had subsided into greater objectivity, Sam Karpowicz had made the decision that the thing would work itself out. Three weeks hence, he told himself, when they departed from the atmosphere of this island, they would find themselves in a saner region and be able to regain their good senses. Mary, he told himself, would have simmered down, come to some realization that her father had acted in her own best interests, and she would become more subservient. He would reason with her. She would talk to him. It would work out as everything did in what Dr. Pangloss reminded Candide was the best of all possible worlds.

Thus, walking and walking and thinking and thinking through

the early morning, Sam Karpowicz had made truce with his unsettled conscience. Once having accomplished this temporary peace of mind, he had come down from the hills into the village, and, to maintain his partially satisfied state, had bypassed his hut and gone directly into the darkroom.

He had been developing pictures ever since, until his empty stomach reminded him that he was merely mortal. Even then, he might have disregarded his hunger, and stayed on to print a fourth and fifth batch of photographs, had not his stamina begun to crumble under the excessive heat. The darkroom, little larger than a closet, was always hot, hotter than the weather because of the continuously burning lamp kept beneath the storage cabinet containing his pressed plant specimens, but this noon it had become an unbearable oven. Inhaling the steamy air was like swallowing tongues of flame. He had had enough, he decided.

After hanging the last of the curled prints, he turned off the safety lamp, and went outside into the blinding brightness of the day. He recoiled from the sunlight, searching for his green-tinted glasses, finding them in his trouser pocket, and snapping them on over his rimless spectacles. Now, he could see, and although it was sweltering outside too, at last he could breathe.

He started down the path from the darkroom, between Lisa Hackfeld's hut and his own, past Mary's closed window, heading for the compound and his front door. Suddenly, he was startled by the sight of a chunky native boy, no more than Mary's age, leaving his hut; or, to Sam, it appeared that he had come out of the Karpowiczes' front door. Sam jerked off his sunglasses for a better look, and recognized the receding figure as that of Nihau, whom Estelle had told him about and once pointed out—Mary's classmate at the cesspool school.

Instantly, Sam Karpowicz was furious. He had commanded Mary to have nothing further to do with that damned school. He had warned Estelle that neither Mary's instructor nor any of her classmates, let alone Nihau (whose attentions had been definitely corrupting), must ever be permitted to visit Mary or set foot in their household for the remainder of their stay on the Sirens. And here, in flagrant defiance of his edict, Mary or Estelle, or both of them, had slyly conspired to receive the native behind Sam's back.

Sam's initial impulse was to chase after the native intruder, take hold of him, and dress him down good. A tongue-lashing, a verbal

476

no-trespassing, would settle the business of unwanted visitors from now until they were away from this offensive community. Sam controlled his impulse for two reasons: from his position between the huts, he had not seen his front door, and so could not be positive that Nihau had actually emerged from his residence; and, even if Nihau had been inside the Karpowicz hut, Sam could not be certain whether he had been invited or had forced himself upon Mary, or for that matter, if once inside, he had been received with hospitality or hostility. Any confrontation with Nihau, without the proper information in his possession, might weaken Sam's position, make him out the fool. He had better have the facts. If the facts proved that Nihau had, indeed, intruded upon the sanctity of their home, was trying to lure Mary back to the cesspool school, or press some private suit, Sam would break the young buck's neck, or initiate charges against the boy before Maud and Paoti Wright. On the other hand, if Mary or Estelle had sought out the boy, arranged some kind of clandestine meeting, Sam would have it out with either or both of them, and right away.

Aggressively, determined to invoke his authority, Sam entered his hut. His arrival in the room was so impetuous and blind, so physical, that he almost bowled Estelle over, and had to catch her to keep her from falling.

When she recovered, she said, "I was just going out to look for you. Where have you been, Sam?"

"In the darkroom," he said impatiently. "Estelle, I want to—"

"In the darkroom? I've been in there three or four times. You weren't there."

"Quit with the darkroom already. I *was* there—no, wait, I forgot, I got up early and took a long hike—but I've been there over an hour—"

"In the last hour I haven't looked. I've been too busy. Sam, listen—"

"Estelle, you listen," he said, indignant at being sidetracked by her wifely frivolity. "I know why you've been busy the last hour. You've had that goddam native boy in here, against my wishes, and don't deny it. You have, haven't you?"

Estelle's face was pale and drawn. It surprised Sam, in these seconds of truth, how old she looked. "Yes," she was saying, wearily, "Nihau has been here. He just left. Sam, I—"

Sam circled her like an avenging rooster, ready to peck her

down. "I knew it, I knew it," he crowed. "The first chance, you were going to wear the pants of the family. You know what's right, you know what's best. What's in the heads of the mothers of our country? Why are they so sure they always know what is best for the children? Like the father doesn't exist. Like fathers are second-class citizens, the serfs in the fields, to get up dough for this, dough for that, work our fingers to the bone, drag our weary asses back to the house, be permitted a scrap of food and a word or two with our children. I say nuts to that. I say have a vote in this house, and maybe my vote is more important than yours, where Mary comes in. If you could have seen what I saw in that school, that indecency in front of a sixteen-year-old, you'd spit on every one of them from the class, and I mean that Nihau especially; you'd throw him out on his ear, not invite him here to practice on our daughter what they're preaching. I'm going in and tell Mary, too. I've had enough of this soft-pedaling. There's a time for talk and a time for being tough, and I've had enough. I'm going in and I'm going to—"

"Sam—*shut up!*"

Estelle's order penetrated Sam like a bullet at close range. It stopped him dead in his tracks and left him propped there, wounded and wondering, and about to go down. In the long years of their marriage together, through thick and thin, for better or worse, his Estelle had never used such language or such a disrespectful tone of voice to him. The world was coming to an end, and the disintegration was so awesome, he was left speechless.

Estelle was speaking. "You come in here like a raving maniac, not asking, not civilized, not caring what is what and who is where, but just a raving maniac. What's got into you, I don't know. I know only that from the minute you were in that classroom, and saw that your daughter was seeing a man and a woman, decent people, undressed for an anatomy lesson, you've parted from your senses. Such a who-ha about what? About what, Sam?"

He could not reply, because the unexpected rebellion, the *coup d'etat*, had toppled him unexpectedly. Where was his ammunition?

Relentlessly, the she-bandit continued to undermine domestic authority. "Sure, Nihau was here. Do you ask why? Sure, I've been looking for you. Do you think why? No, only a maniac shouting, like maybe somebody kicked you in the testicles. Maybe they should. Maybe I will. You want to give me hell and go in the back room and give your Mary hell. Do you ask if she's even there? Now I'll tell you, you maniac. She's not in her room. She's not in your house. She's gone. Do you hear me straight? She's gone, run away, just like in the magazine stories, she's run away from home. Gone! Do you hear?"

His deeply sunken eyes rolled behind his thick spectacles, and out of his numbness came but one word. "Mary?"

"Our Mary, your Mary, my Mary, she's run away." Estelle's hand was digging into the front pocket of her cotton housedress. She pulled out a scrap of paper and handed it to Sam. "Look at the fancy farewell note." He snatched it, while Estelle recited its contents. " 'I've had enough. You don't understand me and never will. I'm going away. Don't try to find me. I won't come back. Mary.' "

Estelle eased the childish note from her husband's stiff fingers, stuffed it back in her pocket, and glanced at her mate. He still appeared to be in a catatonic state. Nevertheless, she went on, more levelly. "This is what I make of it. She's a baby like you are a baby. She must do something to punish us, you for your foolishness and me for being loyal to you instead of taking her side. So off she goes, after the week of brooding and sulking. I wake up. The note is next to me. Her room is empty. You are gone. After you got up, she must have waited and then run away. Where—what—I don't know. The whole morning I try to find you. No good. So I've got to think. What is there to do? I go to Maud Hayden. She calls Mr. Courtney. We all go to the Chief. He agrees, a searching party. So the last two hours they're searching. The native boy who was here, Nihau—we should have such fine young men in Albuquerque, believe me—he comes here to tell me the progress being made, exactly what is going on. There are four groups of men in four directions looking for her, and he, Nihau, he is looking for her, too."

Sam began to shake his head. He shook his head for ten seconds before speech was restored to him. "I can't believe it," he said.

"Now you can believe it," said Estelle. "She's sixteen, which is one thing and they are all half-here, half-there, capable of anything sometimes. And besides sixteen, she's angry you let her down—her darling father, the one she can turn to—he let her down. So she is getting even."

"So what do we do about it?" said Sam angrily. "Just stand here and gab?"

"Yes, that's what we do, Sam. Where are we going to look? We don't know the place. We'll only get in the way, or get lost and they'll have to send a searching party for us. Besides, I promised everyone we'd be here—if there is some word—"

"What got into her?" interrupted Sam. He began to march up and down the room, "Running away from home, my God—"

"About the running-away part I'm not so worried," said Estelle. "This isn't America. It's a small island. Where can she run to?"

"But she—she can get hurt—fall in a hole—bump into an animal, a wild pig, a mad dog—starve to death—"

"It could happen. Still, I'm not worried about her. The natives know every inch of their island. They'll find her."

"What if they don't?"

"They'll find her," Estelle reiterated, firmly. "Right now I'm less worried about Mary than her father.

He stopped. "What does that mean?"

"It means, God willing, they'll find her sooner or later, and she'll be safe and sound. But will she? What happens when they bring her back to us, and we bring her back to Albuquerque and her fast crowd? Now we've got a rebel who wants to fight us, show us, and will keep on doing so, unless some sense is knocked into her father's head."

"Suddenly, it's me who's all to blame?"

"I don't say you are all to blame. Up to now we shared the good and bad our daughter is, we did our best, and we took credit equally for the good, and for the rest we made the small failures together. But since coming here, Sam, since last week, it's you, it's you and our Mary. You have got to straighten yourself out, Sam, and then we can straighten out Mary."

Sam slammed a fist into a palm. "I still say I did right in the classroom! How could a father act differently? Estelle, again, I swear, if you'd been there—"

Estelle held up a majestic hand, to halt him as Mark Antony had stayed the multitude in the Forum at Julius Caesar's funeral. Hypnotized by the classic gesture, Sam was still.

With controlled intensity, Estelle addressed her husband again. "Sam, give me the floor for once, let me speak, you listen, and what comes after that, let it come." She paused, then went on. "Sam, examine yourself, look deep in your heart. For years you are enlightened, progressive, a liberal. You are so convincing, you have made me be like you, and I am proud we are both this way. We read all magazines, books, nothing banned from our house. We see all movies, all television, go to all lectures, invite over people of every kind. On politics, on sex, on religion, we are liberals. Right? Good. Suddenly, overnight, we are dropped down in a country where it's not talk or books, where it's for real, where a man named Wright, God knows how long ago, said let's practice instead of preach. So here, right or wrong, they do things, community living, early sex education, cooperative children-raising, that for us was always theory. Maybe this is wrong. Maybe theories should stay theories, because when you try them out maybe it's not so good. So here we are, and many things you have always believed, read about, talked about, they do, they try to do. And suddenly, for you, overnight, aha, it's no good. Suddenly, when it comes to sex, and education, and your darling daughter, suddenly it's not so liberal with you and you're acting like a bigoted prude, like Orville Pence. About him, we joke. Are you so different? Still, I can't believe you are behaving like you really are, like the man I married, spent my whole life with. Sam, I remind you, when we were kids in the Village, you were wanting me to sleep with you before we were married—"

His face darkened, and he protested. "Estelle, that was absolutely different and you know it. We knew we would be married. It was just a question of my finishing with school and—"

"Aha, too close to home, eh? The shoe pinches. Sam, we slept together for a year without being married, and what if something went wrong and we didn't marry? So, gone is my virginity, gone is my husband who was not my husband, and me, Estelle Myer, I was somebody's daughter, my papa's daughter, and one time my papa's sixteen-year-old daughter."

"I still say—"

"Say what you want, we were big liberals, not prudes like Orville Pence, and we didn't just talk, we did. So was I so different from our daughter? But here the issue is not even the same. My papa, let him rest in peace, if he found out I was going to a school to be exposed to sex organs and positions yet, he would have pulled me out by the ear, spanked me, punched the principal in the nose, and sued the school system. But if he found out I was in the Village, a virgin, a child, his daughter, letting a young man named Sam Karpowicz, who he never knew, come in my bed all night, and seduce me, he would have killed you and killed me, both of us. I don't say he would have been right. He was old-fashioned, narrow, a little ignorant except for the Old Testament and World Almanac, and we are a generation ahead, and liberal, and should show some improvement. So how does the new papa act to his daughter, not for sleeping with someone, but for going to a school to learn about anatomy and sex and being too bashful to tell him? He humiliates her in front of everyone. He shows her no tolerance. He practically drives her from the house. This is liberal?"

"You're making me out an awful monster—"

"Like my father," Estelle interrupted.

"—when I'm not at all," insisted Sam. "I'm still the things I've tried to be. Despite what happened, I'm broad-minded, progressive, thinking of what's good for everyone—"

"Not with your daughter, Sam. That's where common sense ends and jealousy begins. That's the beginning and the end of it, Sam, and I'll bet Dr. DeJong would back me with every word. You're possessive and you're jealous of our Mary. Think, Sam. Remember way back, not so way back, even, when our Mary was six, maybe seven, always you wanting to hug her, hold her, keep her near you, a kiss for this and a kiss for that. And then for a while she was always slipping away from you, like a little eel, and when you told Dr. Brinley about this and the bed-wetting, he told you off good. Remember? He said she is not running away from you, but from her own feelings toward you, she couldn't trust her own baby sexual feelings, and it made her escape your too much warmth, and it helped make her nervous, and maybe contributed to the bedwetting."

"Estelle, that's not here or there—"

"It's here and it's now, Sam. She's sixteen, half child, half grownup, and me she treats like a stupid stick of wood. If anybody can talk to her, if there's anybody on earth she'll listen to, she trusts, it's her darling father, you. But still she is growing, and sixteen is not six, but you treat her like you did at six and seven and eight because you won't let her go. You're jealous to lose her, have her independent, have her learn about growing up, and what happened here proves it."

"Nonsense."

"Nonsense you say? Truth, I say! It's clear to me now. As long as your self was not at stake, you could be the big, generous liberal. Everything was in our house. Companionate marriage. *New Masses*. Emma Goldman. Sacco-Vanzetti. Henry George. Veblen. Eugene Debs. John Reed. Lincoln Steffens. Bob La Follette. Populists. Spanish Loyalists. New Deal. Kinsey. The whole mishmash. And always I agreed it was good. Make the head broader, the world better. But always around the coffee table, it was liberal. Never did I ask myself what it would be like for real, if there was a test. Every penny you have invested in our house. What would you do if Negroes and Puerto Ricans moved into the neighborhood or tried to? Your whole heart you have invested in your daughter. What if in Albuquerque she started going steady with a Mexican or Indian boy? Would you say that you did not mind about the Negroes, yet maybe exclude them because you know they would be happier elsewhere? Would you say you did not mind about the Mexican boy but he better leave Mary alone for his own sake, because it would not work in the real world? Would you—"

"Cut it out, Estelle!" Sam's face was livid. "What are you trying to make of me anyway? You know how I fought at the university for the ex-Communist who applied. You know I supported the petition to get colored instructors on the staff. And that petition when—"

"Petitions, Sam, petitions are good, a little brave, but not enough. On this island you are faced with the facts of life and yourself, and in the first test, you behave not like a liberal. I don't say I approve of the sex education here, or exposing a sixteen-year-old girl, who has not been prepared for it, to such new things, such radical things, so soon. Of course it might hurt her a little, confuse, or maybe it would not. We don't know. But you have hurt her more, confused her more, this week, than that school could—by not supporting her or backing her, by changing in practice the standards you set for her in theory and big talk. She depended on the Sam Karpowicz she knew, and without warning there was another Sam Karpowicz she did not know. It's not Mary's running away from us that bothers me the worst. It's your running away from us, Sam. That's what I have to say."

He nodded, protesting no more, his face so ashen that she

wanted to hold it in her hands and kiss him and beg his forgiveness, but she did not.

At last, he shrugged, and started for the door.

"Where are you going, Sam?"

"To search," he said.

After he had left, she wondered if he had gone to search for Mary—or for Sam Karpowicz, Liberal.

* * *

In the twenty minutes before three o'clock in the afternoon, when she would have her last appointment of the day, Rachel De-Jong sat in the vacant hut that she used for her office, beside the pile of pandanus mats that served her as psychoanalytical couch, and transcribed her clinical notes on Marama, the woodcutter, and Teupa, the dissatisfied wife. This task completed, she considered the impending arrival of her third patient.

Putting aside the looseleaf notebook confined to professional aspects of her visit to the Sirens, Rachel took up the oblong ledger in which she irregularly confided the personal aspects of her life. Moreturi had been entirely transferred from the first notebook to the second, because his relationship to her (and her thoughts about him) were not for publication.

Opening her diary, Rachel found her last entry, six days old. It was terse, cryptic, and would mean nothing on earth to anyone besides herself. It read:

"First day festival. After daily two sessions, attended swimming meet. Thrilling. One of our team, Marc H., was entry. Performed well until end when performed badly, but in keeping with his personality pattern. In evening went to outdoor dance, in which both Harriet and Lisa participated. Afterwards, late, agreed to accompany a native friend, Moreturi, by canoe to nearby atoll. Romantic like Carmel seashore. We went for swim. I almost drowned. Afterwards rested on sand. Memorable evening."

She examined the passage. What might another, say Joe Morgen, make of it? Nothing, she decided with satisfaction. Not even a Champollion would be able to decipher it. The true history of people was written only in their heads, and went safely, privately, underground with their mortal remains. Everything on paper was only one-tenth of truth. But then, remembering her reading, the cleverness of her predecessors, she was less certain. How little

Sigmund Freud needed of Leonardo da Vinci's life, from what was left on paper, to interpret the truth of that life. And Marie Bonaparte, how little she required to know of Poe to dissect his addled psyche. Still, her own passage committed to paper was bland, offhand, unrevealing, except, perhaps, for the riddle of "Memorable evening." Someone might ask—why memorable? But an evening, especially one in a foreign climate, could be memorable because of the scenery or a mood. Who in the world would ever learn that it had been memorable to its author because it had been the occasion of the first orgasm in her life?

With pleasurable fearlessness, Rachel put her pen to the ledger and began to write:

"Speaking of this native friend, I have seen him but once since our visit to the neighboring atoll. Since I had dismissed him from analysis (see Clinical Notes), I had no reason to receive him at work. Several times, however, he extended social invitations, offering to show me other parts of the main island, and, in fact, the third atoll. These verbal invitations came by messenger, but I had to decline. There has been very little time, what with my patients, my studies of the Social Aid Hut, my investigations of the Hierarchy as an institution of mental help, and my observation of all the festival activity.

"My one consequent encounter with Moreturi occurred early this morning, when I went to call upon his mother, who heads the Hierarchy (see Clinical Notes). He was waiting for me before her door and requested a formal analytical interview. He said my previous work with him had apparently borne some fruit, given him some sort of new insight into himself, and he was bursting to tell me of what I had helped him to accomplish. Naturally, as a psychoanalyst, I found this irresistible, and so I promised him one final session at three o'clock in the afternoon. I cannot imagine what it is he has to reveal to me."

Her watch told her that he would be here in seven minutes. She capped her pen, closed her ledger, and laid both aside. She extracted the hand mirror from her purse, observed herself in it, and then combed her hair and ran a light border of lipstick across her mouth.

She was, she was pleased to see, a young woman, after all. Why had she attempted to be more? What had directed her into becoming a young woman psychoanalyst? Briefly, she concentrated on answering these questions more honestly than she had answered them in her own analysis. In the university, she guessed, she had not wanted to join teeming life. If you went into life as a plain woman, no more, you were defenseless and subjected to too much pain. Your female feelings were buffeted and bruised. You were sometimes laughed at or scorned or humiliated, even emotionally dirtied, and you could not fight back. Of course, as plain woman, you sometimes knew pleasure, even ecstasy, were admired, desired, wanted, but Rachel had set those advantages aside. The dangers of going into life as woman unadorned were too many.

And so, perhaps, as an insurance, a means of self-protection against being humbled or neglected or committed, she had taken on the armor of career. By earning her M.D., becoming a psychoanalyst, she was no longer exposed to the quandaries of being merely mortal. In a way, she was above people, a synthetic goddess sitting on a throne apart from the appalling mainstream of life. The sick and the ailing come to her, the emotional beggars and cripples, and she was their deliverer. There was, too, the other aspect of it. From her high position, behind the magic one-way glass, she lived a hundred lives, enjoyed and suffered a thousand experiences vicariously. Yet, she was above and safe from this erratic life. She could touch it, but it could not touch her. And always, to salve any ache about her noncommitment to life, there was the flag of good purpose that she flew: you led the lame and the blind, you helped, and earned a merit badge from the Creator.

Rachel DeJong returned her compact to her purse. Fine, she thought, so it worked, except when she grew older and wanted it not to work. Joe Morgen could not reach her in her high position, and she no longer had the limbs to come down from it. Marriage meant giving up, for better or worse, that fearful flesh and emotion that she had kept to herself. The question had always been: could she step down, be at eye-level with everyone like her, be jostled in the crowd or bed, be one more member of the people, a woman plain, not a woman psychoanalyst?

But she had stepped down! Six nights ago, on the hospitable sands of a foreign and isolated beach, she had waived the role of voyeur and remote bystander. She had surrendered the part of Deliverer for Deliverance. She had opened herself to an animal man, of another skin and two breeds, and questionable literacy and sensitivity. There had been no immunity. She had been taken as a plain woman, nothing more, and she had given satisfactorily, and she had proved to a man and to herself that she was capable in the role of female.

Yet, even as she glowed with self-congratulation, she was not positive that the major step had been made. There had been too many extenuating circumstances. Moreturi had provoked her into accompanying him by a ridicule and challenge that could only come from a primitive mind. She had responded to his invitation to visit the atoll, to swim in the seminude, because she had been drunk. Not her own free will, but an accident in the water had divested her of garments and resistance. She had not deliberately joined Moreturi in love. She had submitted to his love because she had been too helpless to resist him. In fact, as best she could recall, during the act she had sobered sufficiently to try to resist him. She had resisted him. It was his overpowering masculinity, the christening water washing over them, that had aroused her. Her response had been physical, not mental. There had been no free choice in the act. Therefore, little had been solved. She recognized that she had been afraid to see Moreturi again, curious as her body was (not she, but her body), not out of mortification, but purely because she was still not convinced that she could perform as an ordinary woman. If she was still unsure about herself, she was still unsure about herself and Joe. She would return to California as she had left it—a woman psychoanalyst, with her inner conflicts still unresolved behind her stoical calm.

During the last of her introspection, there was a slight disturbance, and she realized someone was rapping at the door.

Suddenly, she had misgivings about permitting him this final session. It would be an embarrassment for her. And for him. What did he have to say that could be so important? Well, there was nowhere to which she could retreat. Forcibly, she lofted herself to her high position behind the magic one-way glass, and prepared to live another's life, keeping her own in safe seclusion.

"The door's open!" she called out.

Moreturi came into the room, closed the door behind him, and his demeanor was respectful and friendly. None of the familiar self-assurance was evident, as he came toward her, tendering a half-smile.

"It is kind of you to see me once more," he said.

She indicated the layers of matting beside her, "You said I had helped you, and women are nothing if not curious."

"Should I lie down as before?"

"By all means." She watched with fascination the shiftings and displacement of his muscles beneath his tan skin. He stretched himself to a comfortable position on the matting, adjusting the cord that held his white supporter.

For Rachel, the situation in this room, the patient reclining on the couch, the therapist seated on the floor next to him, made their nocturnal encounter unreal. She had been on her back in the dark, and he had been above her on his knees, naked and passionate, and she had allowed him to remove her wet nylon panties, and later, half in the water, she had done crazy things, said crazy things, and now they were six days away from that and a million feelings apart, and she wondered if he was remembering it also.

"Do you want me to talk?" he was asking.

God yes, talk, she wanted to shout. She said, "Please tell me whatever you have on your mind."

He turned his head toward her. "I am in love, at last, Rachel," he said.

The pulses in her wrists jumped, and her throat constricted.

He continued speaking directly at her. "I know you have always regarded me like a man-child, but now I know I have more depth. There is a deepness in me since the festival began. Should I tell you?"

"If—if you feel—"

"I will tell you. You are the only one I can tell this to, because of our intimacy. When I invited the one I speak of to go with me, in the canoe, across the channel, it was only a lark. I confess it. My feelings were not deeper. She resisted me a long time, turned me aside, and I wanted to show her she was as human as me. Also, one enjoys a woman who resists—"

Rachel's cheeks were crimson with humiliation. She had the impulse to slap him.

"—but after the swim, when she gave herself to me, something happened. It had never been like that before between myself and a woman. It was not only below that I felt love, but here, too." He touched his heart. "For once, I was loved as I loved another. This woman who appeared so cold was heated. I was never happier."

She wanted to leave her high throne, kneel over him, kiss him for his sweetness. She wanted to envelop this good person with her gratefulness.

"Rachel, I have thought of what you have said to me and done for me," he went on. "I now see my problem is solved. I will pledge eternal faithfulness, except for the one week of the year that is our custom, and I will be a true husband—"

Rachel's joy turned to alarm. Blindly, she reached out and took his hand. "No, Moreturi, not another word. You are one of the kindest men I have ever met. I'm terribly moved. But a single night, one affair, is no basis for an enduring relationship. Besides, we are worlds apart and it simply would not work. You've done more for me than I've done for you, believe me, but I could never—"

"You?" he said. He sat up with astonishment. "I do not speak of you. I speak of Atetou."

"Atetou?" she gasped.

"My wife. I took her to the atoll last night, and we are changed. There will be no divorce." He peered at her, and saw that she was unable either to close her mouth or speak. "Forgive me if—" he began.

"Atetou!" she repeated shrilly, and she wrapped her arms around herself, and rocked not with mortification but delight. "Oh, my God!"

She began to giggle, and then to laugh, the laughter erupting from her chest and throat. "Oh, Moreturi, this is too delicious!"

She was chortling like a mad fool. She shook with mirth, her entire body convulsed.

She found him beside her, one arm around her, patting her, trying to calm her, but she shook her head, wanting to reassure him that she needed no consolation, that this was rich and wonderful, as tears of merriment rolled down her cheeks.

"Oh, me," she choked. "Oh, Moreturi, this is too much—"

She groped for her purse behind her and pulled out a Kleenex and wiped her eyes, as her laughter subsided to a tittering.

"What is it, Rachel?"

"It's funny, that's what. Old sobersides me, so serious, so pleased and worried when you were talking, positive you were speaking about us—that you were serious about me—"

He looked down into her stained face. "I was serious about you," he said. "I am practical, also. I know it cannot be. You have too much mana at home, you are too wise for a fool like me—"

"Oh, stop it, Moreturi, I'm just a woman like Atetou or any other," she said with relief. Then, with more control, she added, "If you knew there could be nothing between us, why did you take me to that beach, and—and make love to me?"

"For fun," he said simply.

"For fun?" she repeated, and her mouth formed the two words with a kind of new knowledge.

"Is there another reason to make love? To have children, it is the afterthought, not the first and main one. Fun is the important thing in life. It does not make us worse, it always makes us better."

At once, it was Rachel who felt the child before the adult. "For fun," she said once more. "Yes, I see. I suppose I had really never thought of it so—well, so simply before. I've invested it with too much. I've weighted it down. Maybe I've spoiled it, always, for myself."

"What?" he said.

"Never mind." She looked up at him, at his broad young adult face. "Moreturi, was it really fun with me?"

He nodded with great solemnity. "Much pleasure," he said. "You are a woman who gives much pleasure." He hesitated. "Was it not the same for you?"

It surprised her how easy it was to reply to this. "I enjoyed it. Certainly you know."

"I thought so, but—" He shrugged, "You would not see me again. So I was not sure."

"I'm a complicated woman," she said.

"I have not your mind," he said. "I have mine, like my people, and it tells me when there is gladness in love, one does not stop it."

"I'm beginning to see that," she said. "I'm slow, but I'm learning. Forgive my old solemnity, Moreturi. In fact—" She put her hands up, to cup his face in her hands, and she brushed his cheek with a kiss. "—I thank you."

One muscular arm drew her to his naked chest, crushed her against him, and his free hand began to unbutton her skirt. She looked down at his hand, but did not halt it.

"No," she whispered, "really, I can't—it's against the rules, it's never done—I'd be drummed out of the American Psychoanalytical Association—"

"We will have pleasure," he said.

By then, she was on the pile of matting, and her skirt was gone, and as she was divested of the nylon panties, she quickly began to unbutton her blouse. When he caressed her, she giggled once. Her mind had gone to playing a game with the titles of Sigmund Freud. One was Freud's 1905 book, *Three Contributions to the Theory of Sex.* She could name the three, and they were The Three Sirens, and then she had giggled.

"What is it?" Moreturi had asked.

"Don't talk, don't talk."

And don't think, don't think, she told herself, which was gratuitous, for in a moment she could not think. She was a woman, no question now. She was a woman having pleasure for the first time, more fun than she had ever had in her entire life. And later, much later, when the voluptuous pleasure of it was crossed by the intense agony preceding peace, she caught one fluttering thought, and it was of Joe Morgen, good, good Joe—and the thought was, Joe, oh, Joe, you should thank him, this one here—Joe, you'll never know, but you should thank him . . .

And when it was over, and she rested in serenity, she wanted to giggle once more. Her mind had gone back to the Freud title game. It was the title of a book he had published in 1926. She cherished the title. It was called *The Problem of Lay Analysis.*

* * *

Night fell on The Three Sirens between seven-thirty and eight o'clock.

It was during this period, while the torches were being lighted on either side of the compound stream by native boys, that Sam Karpowicz trudged along the path past the Social Aid Hut and into the village.

He had been in hills previously unknown to him all of the afternoon, and what had happened in those hours he could not define in detail. It was like that section of the Gospel of the New Testament that he had read as a young man—read secretly, surreptitiously, to learn how the other half lived (which his parents would not have understood)—where Jesus had gone into the wilderness, alone, to fast, had gone into the mountain and been tempted by the devil and had finally said, Get thee behind me, Satan. Many times during the afternoon Sam had been lost, in more ways than one, but with the end of the afternoon, he had found the right path, and was returning to Galilee.

Quibbling aside, Estelle had been right, and Sam Karpowicz knew it, at last. His duty as father was to raise his daughter to maturity according to his best wisdom and instincts, and give her guidance and support, and make her strong, judicious, independent. His duty was not to suppress his own open-minded principles in order to shelter her and hold her selfishly. It was so clear to him, and what he wanted was to tell her of his self-discovery. But he had not found her, and he was not sure that anyone had. If something had happened to her, he would kill himself.

Once inside the village, he realized his poor physical condition. The back of his neck ached. His arms and calves hurt. He was footsore. His throat was dry and it was difficult to swallow. Perhaps he had called out for her many times, wherever he had been, and he had lost his voice. In the light of the first torch, he could see that from head to toe he was bedraggled, his shirt blotched, his trousers torn at the knees, his shoes caked with dust.

He must hurry on to Estelle, to learn if there was any news of Mary. Then he spied the familiar figure of Tom Courtney, in clean shirt and trousers, on the other side of the stream, striding in the same direction that he was taking.

"Tom!" he shouted.

Courtney halted. Hastily, Sam Karpowicz limped across the first bridge to meet him.

"Tom, has there been any word about my daughter?"

Courtney's features did not conceal his sympathy. "I'm sorry, Sam, but nothing as of a half-hour ago."

"Are the search parties still out?"

"The last I heard, yes. They won't give up. And they'll find her, sooner or later, they'll find her."

"She's just a kid—sixteen—she's never been alone like this. It worries me sick, the things that could happen to her."

Courtney put his hand on Sam's shoulder. "Nothing bad will happen. I have absolute confidence in that, and you must, too. Why don't you get back to your hut and wait? The minute—"

Sam was possessed of a sudden inclination. "Tom, do you know of a native boy, Mary's age, named Nihau? He was her classmate in—"

"Certainly I know Nihau."

"I—I'd like to meet him. I have something to say to him. Where does he live?"

Courtney pointed to the left. "His parents' hut is right up the path there. Of course, he and his father are probably out on the search, but—oh, hell, Sam, let me take you to their place. Come on."

The two of them, Courtney a half-step ahead, swung off the compound and between the thatched huts. It was darker beneath the overhang, but the dim spears of candlenut lights from thinly shielded windows partially illuminated their way.

They had reached a sizable hut, and Courtney said, "Here it is."

Sam removed his spectacles, and then replaced them on his nose again. "Tom, would you introduce me?"

"Of course."

Courtney rapped, and they waited. Courtney rapped a second time. A male voice called out something in Polynesian, and Courtney said to Sam, "He's telling us to come in."

Courtney opened the door, and went inside, followed closely by Sam Karpowicz. The front room, larger than Sam's own, furnished with a stone idol in one corner, was brightly lit by numerous candlenuts. To the rear of the room, a circle of many guests sat, all busily eating and drinking. The air was pungent with the aroma of coconut meat, heated yams, and ripe fruits.

Nihau leaped up from the circle, calling out, "It is Dr. Karpowicz!"

He bounded toward Sam, hand outstretched, to pump Sam's hand, saying happily, "She is safe—we have found her—see—see there—"

He was pointing off, and at first Sam could not find her, and then he did. Mary's back had been to the door, but she had turned, still holding her half-shell of coconut milk. Her dark eyes, and thin sweet face that Sam had known so long and loved so well, appeared frightened. And he was surprised that he had not made her out immediately, for she wore an American dress, a flimsy orange slip of a dress that made her seem smaller than she was.

Nihau was saying, "We found her only an hour ago, high up among the trees. She was only sitting there, and she was unharmed. We led her back, but she preferred to come here first. She was starved, so we are feeding her and the searchers—"

The last of this had been spoken to Courtney, for Sam Karpo-wicz had already left Nihau. He moved toward the circle, and Mary came uncertainly to her feet.

"Mary, I—" He stopped awkwardly, and stared at the native men and women in the circle. "Thank you, all of you, for bringing her back safe and well."

There was a courteous acknowledging bobbing of heads from the diners.

Sam was facing his daughter once more. He removed his specta-cles. "Mary, most often I think I know what is best for you," Sam was saying, "but this time I was wrong, dead wrong, my behavior in the schoolroom. I apologize for it." He had been stiff and stilted as he spoke, but suddenly the reserve crumpled. "God, Mary, I'm glad you're back."

Instantly, her girl's body gave up its defenses, and she cried out, "Oh, Dad, I love you so!" She was in his arms, her hair all over his chest, and he was holding her, caressing her head, and glancing moistly at Courtney.

When they separated, he said to her, "I'd better get home and tell your mother. You come when you're free—"

"I want to come with you now," she said. "First let me thank Nihau and the others."

She had gone to Nihau and the plumpish elder who was his father, and Sam Karpowicz went to Courtney at the door. "Tom, I appreciate this. Maybe you'd like to join the three of us for a bite, American style."

Courtney smiled. "Thanks, but if you've brought rainchecks to the island, I'll take one. Claire and Marc Hayden are expecting me, and Maud will be there, for cocktails. After that we're off to Paoti Wright's, and the feast that closes down this year's festival. I'd bet-ter run right now." He nodded off toward Mary. "I'm glad it worked out."

"More worked out than you can imagine," said Sam.

After Courtney had gone, Sam waited, politely refusing the fruit drinks being tendered him. When Mary joined him, he said, "I thought I'd save myself for some milk and crackers."

"I hope there's enough for me, too, Dad," she said. Then she linked her arm in his, and they went outside, and they went home.

* * *

In the Marc Hayden hut, as he liked to think of it since he had disunited himself (in spirit at least) from his wife that was, Marc quickly rubbed the hair tonic into his scalp. In this barberless, and therefore barbarous, land, his crewcut had given way to a fuller head of hair—unfamiliar but not unattractive, he had come to believe, as he bent to see his reflection in the wall mirror—and quickly he began to slick his hair down with a comb.

He was in a hurry. Fifteen minutes before, while Claire was changing in the rear room, a native boy had materialized at the door with a verbal message for Dr. Hayden. Was he Dr. Hayden, because it could only be given to Dr. Hayden? Yes, he was Dr. Hayden. The message was from Tehura. She must see him briefly, in the next hour, in her hut, before he went to the Chief's party.

The message had, at first, thrilled Marc, for it meant something had happened, finally. Then, because it had been so enigmatic, it had worried him, for perhaps Tehura had suffered a change of heart, or, as bad, a setback in trying to make an arrangement for the craft that would take them away from here. All of this Marc had speculated upon, as the native boy waited. Finally, Marc had said to him in an undertone, "Tell Tehura I am coming."

After that he had hurried with his dressing and grooming, and through it had reviewed the torturous uncertainty of the eventless past week. He had continued to see Tehura daily. Their meetings had been open, for in the eyes of the others, they were still anthropologist and informant. However, their visits were abbreviated. Tehura was too distracted and busy to make sense. At each meeting, he had inquired if there was news, and at each she had said there was none yet, but that she was trying, and he must have patience.

To each meeting, Tehura had brought at least one question, sometimes several, about what her life, their life, would be in the faraway, mammoth continent which was his country and Courtney's, too. Constantly, she had pressed to know of Claire's day-to-day existence there, and had heard out his glowing reports in phlegmatic silence.

Marc's accounts were consistently glowing, because they were, in a sense, sincere, born of a new conviction within him that through Garrity their future would be sublime. It would be a world without a single abyss of failure, a happily-ever-after land in which the air he would breathe, the language he would use, the amenities he would know were all Success. So strongly had he converted himself to this vision of what lay ahead that he was able to impose it convincingly on his past, on Claire's past, on the reality of what life was in America. This sincerity had made Tehura an unwavering confederate. Yet, in their meetings, she had not wanted too much of it, of the fairyland. Her half-primitive mind could accept only a half-vision of civilized perfection at any one time. She would have her fill, and escape their meetings as soon as possible. After each conversation, he would be left wondering how she was translating their mutual ambition into a practical means of attaining it. But tonight, the word had come: she must see him in the next hour.

Having finished with the mirror, Marc realized that he had only one task left. He must tell Claire to go on to the Chief's dinner without him. He must let her know that something had come up, and that he would be a few minutes late. What had come up? Where must he go first? To visit his native informant about a matter important to Matty's work? Possibly. It would slide down well, yet it gave Tehura, at this crucial moment, too much importance. It was risky. He must invent something better. Before he could do so, he was conscious of Claire's presence in the room.

He whirled around to inform her that he would be delayed, but her stance was so improbable, his purpose was deflected. He watched her with detached interest. Claire was stooped low, sometimes almost crouching, as she moved across the matting, examining every crack and fold of the floor covering.

"What in the devil are you doing?" Marc said.

"My diamond," she answered, without looking up, "I can't find it."

He had not been fully attentive, and so he repeated, "Diamond? What diamond?"

She glanced at him, and stood up. "I have only one, Marc, besides my ring. My diamond pendant necklace. I want to wear it to the dinner." She shook her head. "I simply don't know where it is."

Marc tried to hide his reaction, but his heart thudded inside his chest. Easy does it, he told himself. "It's probably somewhere in that junk of yours. Forget it. You have a dozen other things to wear."

"I want the diamond necklace," she persisted. "When I know I have something and can't find it, then it becomes doubly provoking. I can't stand missing things. Like reaching the telephone a split second after the last ring. Things like that drive me insane."

"Have you gone through our luggage?"

"Every inch of it. Not only the jewel box, but everything. I thought maybe I might have dropped it on the floor here . . ." She scanned the floor once more. "No, it's not—"

"It's perfectly obvious what happened," Marc said. "One of the native kids stole it."

"Oh, Marc, really—what a ridiculous notion."

Her condescending dismissal of his suggestion irritated him. "What's so damn ridiculous about my notion? I know these people better than you do—I've been *studying* them—and I wouldn't trust any one of them for a second. Of course, one of them stole it."

"Marc, what in heaven's name would a native locked up on this island do with a diamond necklace, what would he *do* with it?"

He was about to say that the native might give it to his woman, as an ornament and a gift, but he clamped his mouth on this. Instead, carefully, he said, "The native who took it might sell it one day, after we're gone, to that bandit Rasmussen."

"Well, I for one refuse to believe such a thing." She stared at him. "Why is it you always see the worst in everyone?"

He met her stare with his own, which was one of distaste as he remembered how much he despised her. How he would love to see her face with its superior look on the day that she learned he had left her. This reminded him of what he must do, and he determined to bring their pointless haggling to an end. "It's better to know that people have a bad side, too," he said, "than to be gulled, the way you've been, by a bunch of savages and taken in by some beach-comber phony from Chicago." She was about to retort, but he added, hastily, "Hell, let's not go on with this. Okay, no one swiped your precious diamond. So it's here. Find it. I've got to go." He started for the door, then remembered that she did not know he had another appointment. He hesitated. "By the way, I forgot to tell you, I've got to do something first before going to the feast."

"Both of us were invited to dinner, not me alone," she said, coldly.

"Lay off, Claire. We will be there together. I just had word, while you were dressing, that Orville has—has some kind of problem, needs my advice. I promised to see him a few minutes before going to Paoti's palace. Do you mind?"

"Do I have the right to mind anything you do?"

You're goddam right you don't, he wanted to say, but he also wanted to be rid of her, so he said, instead, "Matty'll be here any second, and your friend Mr. Courtney, too, so you'll be escorted in style. I'll be right behind you. Nobody'll miss me. See you there."

He went outside, turning toward Tehura's hut, but after a few steps he slowed down. The frontal lobes of his brain, the ones that anticipated everything, were extraordinarily alert to each action he took now, and these sent down the nerve impulses that inhibited his motion. In his favorite stories, he recalled, great plots and plans were always brought tumbling down because the hero had over-looked some trivial detail, made some minute omission. For Marc, there was too much at stake to fall prey to an insignificant lie. He had told his wife that he was going on to see Orville Pence. What if she ran into Orville and questioned him?

Immediately, Marc reversed his direction, and hurried past his hut and the DeJong hut, until he reached Orville's door. He rapped, and opened the door slightly. Orville was seated in the center of the front room, one hand holding a highball, the other peeling playing cards off a deck.

"Orville, sorry to bust in—"

"Come in, come in, old fellow," Orville said, less formal, more genial than ever before. He tapped the deck of cards. "Telling my fortune. Third time around already. Going to keep doing it till it comes out right. If you'll wait, I'll tell yours, too."

"Thanks, Orville, but I'm in a rush. There's a little favor I want from you.

"Anything, anything."

"No questions, but listen. I have to see someone. Personal busi-ness. Wives are not always tolerant about the someones their hus-bands have to see. So I left Claire saying you needed to talk to me about something urgent."

"As a matter of fact, I do," said Orville. "I may have made a fool-ish commitment today, I'm sure I have, but I feel good about it. I don't know what will happen yet. If you have a little time, I'd like to discuss—"

"Orville, I have no time at all. Can't we talk it over tomorrow?"

"Why, certainly."

"Remember, if you run into Claire, I was with you tonight."

"Well, you were," said Orville, righteously.

"Okay, I'm on my way." He started to leave, then called to Orville. "Let me know how it comes out."

Orville seemed bewildered. "What comes out? You mean you—"

"Your fortune, pal. Let me know what's in the cards."

Marc closed the door, and turned into the compound, when he saw his mother, followed by Courtney, entering his own hut. He flattened into the shadows, until they had disappeared inside. Once it was safe, he hurried to the bridge, crossed to the opposite side of the compound, and continued swiftly in the direction of Tehura's hut.

In less than five minutes, he was at his destination. He put his knuckles to her door, and knocked lightly. He heard her movement behind the door, heard her speak something in Polynesian, and after a moment the door opened several inches. Before he could enter, she slipped outside.

"Someone is with me," she said under her breath. "I do not wish her to know it is you. Come."

She touched his arm and guided him into the passageway between the residences, and then upwards a short distance from her place.

"Who's in there?" he wanted to know.

"Poma," she said in an undertone. "The one who is helping us. She came by to discuss it again, but I did not want her to see you."

"Do you trust her?"

"Yes," said Tehura flatly. "I will explain very quick, and then you must leave."

Marc waited nervously to learn their fate, praying it would be what he wanted, yet uncertain that it could have worked out.

"It was not easy to think of someone, the right one," said Tehura. "If I made one mistake, it would have been bad for both of us. Finally, I thought of Poma. She is a young widow, very beautiful. She is in love with Huatoro. He is in love with me. Because of me, she cannot have him. She volunteered to work with him in the classroom of the school, but he is now indifferent to her because of me. Yet, she knows she could have him for husband, were I not here. Then, in my thinking, there was another reason for Poma. She has a younger brother." Tehura touched her head. "Weak mind, you understand? He is called Mataro—the sailor—because it is all he can do, all he likes to do, like a child."

"But if he's an imbecile, how—?"

"Not important. A good sailor. Also, he has an eighteen-foot-long outrigger canoe with thick pandanus mat sails. It carries a water cask. He sails by his nose, and at night by the star overhead. Always, he admires Captain Rasmussen's compass. Everyone pokes fun at him for that. He must have a big compass, too. This was my thinking, so I took the chance. I spoke to Poma this morning."

To know that their secret was shared by an outsider disturbed Marc. "What did you tell her?"

"I said, 'Poma, it is between us only, but I wish to leave the Sirens and go to Tahiti to live and be like the American women who are here.' She said, 'You cannot, no woman of the Sirens has ever left.' I said, 'Poma, I will be the first if you will help me.' I reminded her that Huatoro has loved us both, but me most. Then I told her I had no love for him. I reminded her if I was forever gone, she would have Huatoro for herself. If I stayed, she would never have him. It pleased her, of course. She is much in love with him. She said, 'I will help you if I can. What must I do?' I said, 'Your brother, Mataro, has two, three times made the feat of sailing his outrigger canoe to other islands. I want him to take me on such a trip. In return, he will have wealth for his compass.' She said, 'How could you give him wealth for his compass?' I said, 'One of the Americans has given me a diamond worth a fortune on the outside. When we are away from here, I will sell it, and have the wealth for Mataro's compass and enough left to take me ahead to Tahiti.' She said, 'When it is known, Paoti will be angry with my brother.' I said, 'Yes, but Paoti will not punish him, for he knows your brother is weak in the head and foolish.' That was our conversation."

"Did she agree to help?"

"Yes, Marc. She will help. In the afternoon, she summoned me and said it would be all right. Tonight she called upon me, for her brother, to see for herself that I did not lie about the diamond. I was showing it to her when you came to my door."

"Good, very good, Tehura, wonderful," Marc said, taking her hands, trying to contain his relief and jubilation. "I love you, Tehura."

"Shhh." She had put her finger to her lips. "There will be time for everything between us."

"Do Poma and her brother know about me?"

She shook her head. "Nothing, not a word. It is better this way."

"Yes. What will her brother say when I show up at the boat with you?"

"Nothing. He will be pleased that one with such wealth will be along, to reward him with a second compass maybe, and even a sextant, too."

"Anything."

Tehura smiled. "It is agreed to happen tomorrow night."

He removed his hands from hers, and knotted them tightly, to keep them from quivering. "So soon?"

"You wanted it soon, did you not?"

"Yes, absolutely—"

"Tomorrow night," she said again. "Come here to my hut, with everything you need, at ten o'clock in the evening. We will rest until the village is asleep. After that, we will go. We will go to the far beach where you came here. Mataro will be there with his canoe and supplies, and we will leave. The voyage to the nearest island will take two days and one night. There, I am told, French planters have some large skiffs. We will pay one to take us to another island where there is a person who has a seaplane like Captain Rasmussen's. That one will fly us to Tahiti. The rest is in your hands."

"My friend from America, Mr. Garrity, will be waiting," said Marc. "Together, the three of us will go to my country."

"Are you pleased, Marc?"

He embraced her. "I've never been happier."

"I am happy, too." She pushed free of him. "Now go."

"Tomorrow night?"

"Yes."

He turned, and departed between the huts. Once, at the edge of the compound, he looked over his shoulder. He could see Tehura opening her door. The light of the candlenuts caught her in profile, and he could see the high curve of her nude breasts. He made a minor memorandum in his head: remind her to bring along some kind of brassière, we're going to California and New York and the new world of the corseted.

Tomorrow! he exclaimed within himself, and he wanted to cry it to all the world and to sing of his defiance and his victory and his prize. He wanted to shatter the equatorial-like calm of the tropical night, to light up the heavy-lidded blackness of the compound, to climb the range of coco palms ahead and to wave their fronds and signal Garrity that he was on his way, on his way at last.

He walked bumpily, so drunk was he with the fever of what was possible and what was to be. Was this how the ragged ones, the oppressed felt, when they burst out of the Bastille? Yes, yes. And was this how they felt, too, later when they sat row upon row behind Madame Defarge watching as Dr. Guillotin's namesake did its work?

And so, finally, the pleasure of it had come to be Madame Defarge's pleasure. He ticked off the heads in the basket: obliterated forever the ghostly head of Adley the father, the slaveholder head of Matty the mother, the reproaching head of Claire the wife. And there would be smaller heads in the basket, too, every one of the taunting savages on the Sirens, and that cocky bastard Courtney with them, for when he and Garrity were through with the exposé of this place, the islands would be found, and become a land of resort motels and restaurants like any other, and every sonofabitch on it would become a servant, grubbing for tips from their betters.

The heads in the basket had sold him short, had conspired through the years and the last weeks to keep him from his true stature as a man. Yet, in the end he was smarter and bigger than any of them. He would have riches and fame. He hummed it to himself: riches and fame, riches and fame. And he would have a bonus besides, that Polynesian piece of ass, Tehura, orifice of orifices, to do with as he pleased.

The thought of Tehura brought his mind to Claire once more, and there was something about Claire's image that would not give him the full satisfaction of victory. By leaving her for another, he would have humiliated her. He knew her uncertainty as a woman. This would cripple her. Yet, it bothered him that it might not humiliate and destroy her entirely. She would always hug the belief that in their relationship she had been more of a woman than he had been a man. Nothing would make that part of her grovel, no flight, no success. Total obliteration of her could only be accomplished by himself, by his taking the wreck of her back one day, or the knowledge of her knowledge would gnaw at him forever as it did this night.

Perhaps later, he thought, he would have to abandon Tehura. She might look dreadful in dresses, stockings, high heels. Native girls always went to fat, and aged early, that was a fact, if not an anthropological fact. Outside her native environment, she might prove more of a social detriment than an asset. Once he had slept with her, and used her on platforms, and on television for several years, she would be tiresome. What could a man talk about to a woman like that? Where could he take her—to LaRue's and Chasen's? To the Plaza Hotel and Twenty-One? No, there was nowhere. Except as an exhibit, she would be useless. In due time, he would have to send her back to the islands. She could join her friend Poma as a waitress in The Three Sirens-Hilton Hotel.

In any case, she would have to make way, sooner or later, for Claire. He had little doubt about Claire. Divorce or no divorce, when he beckoned, she would come running. There would be conditions to his accepting her again, letting her sit on the second throne. She would have to be humble. She would do as he commanded her. She must make no demands, no demands allowed. He would make her eat crow, and she would like it, like anything on his terms. Yes, dammit, she would please him and not taunt him to please her. Crawl, Claire, you bitch, because you are going to have to.

Suddenly, Marc realized, he had arrived at the entrance to Paoti's royal hut. He brought himself up short, and heard the music and the sounds of gaiety inside.

He smiled to himself. Soon the deluge, and they would be heads in a basket. And himself, tomorrow night at almost this time, his new life would begin. How many people on earth, this day, could say that for them tomorrow would bring a new life? How many on earth possessed his secret wizardry?

He had earned a toast to himself. He would have it now. He squared his shoulders, and strutted inside, to have one last pitying look at the doomed.

VIII

EARLY THE FOLLOWING MORNING, Maud Hayden, alone in the bed-room behind her office, interrupted her dressing to place two as-pirins on her tongue and swallow them with water.

Paoti's feast, the night before, had been enlivened by native music, village dancers, and vast quantities of the almost lethal palm juice and kava. Everyone had been mildly intoxicated, even Maud herself (out of deference to her host), and the party had not ended until the small hours of the morning.

Nevertheless, Maud had set her alarm for the customary hour of seven, and at seven she had grimly awakened and grimly gone about her toilet and dressing. Despite only four hours of sleep and a hangover, and her many years, she would not indulge herself. In the field, she was miserly about time. An hour wasted in self-coddling, in toadying to one's bodily demands, meant an hour sub-tracted from the sum of human knowledge. This morning, the only crutches she would permit herself were the two aspirins.

By the time she had finished dressing, and prepared her coffee on the small Coleman stove, the aspirins had begun to do their work. The invisible pincers began to release their grip on her head, and she was able to think more rationally. As always, at this period in the morning, before marching to the day's work (a session with Mr. Manao, the schoolteacher, scheduled for twenty minutes from now), she liked to review her troops in the field.

She reviewed her troops.

She used, as her mental starting point for inspection, the mailbag that had rested in her office late yesterday afternoon and that had been flown back to Tahiti by Captain Rasmussen in the evening.

Lisa Hackfeld had brought in the bulkiest envelope of all, a manila one addressed to her husband, Cyrus Hackfeld, Los Angeles, California, and with it an ordinary airmail envelope addressed to her son, Merrill, who was visiting Washington, D.C., on a conducted tour. Before depositing both in the canvas bag, Lisa had kissed the thick manila envelope with feigned affection. She had explained that her data on the miracle stimulant, the herb known as puai, was in that envelope, as well as Lisa's projected plans for enslaving the entire Western world with Vitality. Cyrus would be proud of her brainstorm, she was positive.

Today, and every day until their departure, Lisa would be occupied from morning until night with her Operation Ponce de Leon, as she now enjoyed referring to it. She would be interviewing dozens of dancers who used the herb, as well as most of the village elders who could relate its history, traditions, and their personal experiences with it.

Of all the people on her team, Maud thought, sipping her coffee, it might be Lisa, rather than one of the professionals, who proved to be the best anthropologist on the trip. Very likely, too, it might be that Lisa would profit most, financially, of those who had come to The Three Sirens. The rich get richer. It was Adley, dear Adley, who liked to say that. And they get younger, too, Maud amended it, richer and younger. Whatever happened with the ridiculous herb, Maud thought, even if it failed commercially, Lisa still would have succeeded for herself. For, on The Three Sirens, she had unwittingly found the antidote against age, the one herb that was anti-death. The ingredient was simple: keeping busy. If anything worked, this was what worked. Maud had no doubt. She *knew*.

Shortly after Lisa had left Rasmussen's mailbag, Rachel DeJong had appeared beside it, more cheerful and amusing than Maud had ever known her to be. Rachel it was who brought in the greatest number of letters, dashed off in the late afternoon. Rachel had been surprisingly talkative. She had shown Maud one envelope addressed to a Miss Evelyne Mitchell, and had explained that this and most of the others were to her patients, announcing her return. Yes, she intended to resume practice, at least for a year. She displayed another letter to one Ernst Beham, M.D., and had added, "And then I'll give up my practice, if Dr. Beham lets me. He's my training analyst." Finally, she had tapped one more envelope addressed,

Maud could see, to a Mr. Joseph Morgen, and she had said, "He's wanted to marry me for some time, and now he's out of luck, because I just wrote him yes."

Today, Maud knew, Rachel would be continuing with her native analysands, and collating their information for her psychiatric paper, and would spend the remainder of her time in her study of the Hierarchy.

Before Rachel had taken her leave, Orville Pence had darted in with a letter, thrown it into the sack, and fled. In a half-hour he had returned, knelt beside the bag, dipped into it, found his letter, and proceeded to tear it up in Maud's presence. "To my mother," he had explained. "I wrote her something I did yesterday. I've just decided it's none of her damn business." With that, and no further explanation, he had gone. But Maud knew what Orville had done, for late yesterday Harriet Bleaska had confided it to both Maud and Claire.

Today, thought Maud, Orville won't do much work. He'll be waiting in a state of harried suspense for Harriet to decide between Vaiuri and himself. He may, she thought, come away from the Sirens with more than he had bargained for, or he may come away with less, with a terrible sense of defeat, should Harriet choose the native, a native, over him. Whatever the outcome, Maud thought, he will leave without his mother.

Then she thought of her own letter, the one she had finished dictating quite late to Claire, the report to Walter Scott Macintosh. Inevitably, the thought of it led her into her near future, the possible separation from Marc and Claire, and her thinking began to center on Marc, but she resisted it. She drank her cooling coffee near the Coleman stove, and moved her inspection of her troops away from the mailbag.

Harriet Bleaska had appeared last night, with her dilemma, as Claire and Maud were parting to dress for dinner. After a short period of discussion—they had been no help, they could not be— Harriet had gone with Claire. Finally, when it was nightfall, and Maud was readying to go to Marc's hut next door, Estelle Karpowicz had stopped in briefly, to say Mary had been found and that all was well between Mary and Sam. Maud's relief had been enormous, for she liked that family and had suffered for both father and daughter. Today, Maud thought, would be a good day for the Karpowiczes. Sam had caught up on his prints, and would be out hunting his plant specimens, and Mary would be in the village with her mother.

Maud had completed her inspection, and her coffee as well, and a new day, the first of the fourth week on The Three Sirens, was about to begin. Yet, going to her desk for her pencils and pad, she was nagged by the fact that as leader she had been remiss, for she had avoided inspecting one member. She had been afraid to look too closely at her son.

For a moment, standing at her desk, she remembered last night seeing Tom Courtney at Claire's, Courtney instead of Marc, who had been called away somewhere, and of the traitorous thought that she had entertained, before evicting it, as the three of them had walked in step to Paoti's dinner. The thought had been that the three of them were more comfortable as three, than if the three had been herself, Claire, and Marc. What a terrible thing.

And so, unhappily, in the early morning, leaning on her desk now, she inspected him and herself. In this minute, she had a deep insight into Marc and herself, but actually it was more herself, and it was this, that Marc was the victim of her selfishness. For she had been selfish, that was unmistakable. She had borne Adley only one child, because Adley had been enough for her and she had been enough for him. And even the one child had suffered from this selfishness. The one son had been treated like no son at all, but rather like a distant relative hopelessly competing for the attention of both a mother and father who were fenced off from him, self-contained, this pair, absorbed in one another, pleased with one another, needing no other person or, indeed, anything else.

The wrongness of it loomed up at her through the far faded years. Now, she thought wretchedly, now so near the end, all that would be left of her on earth would be Marc, her failure. She took the entire blame, absolved Adley completely ("of the dead say nothing but good," amen). If only it could all be relived, those old times, but with her present wisdom superimposed on the past. She would have brought their son into the family, not given all her love to Adley and their career. She would have made the son surer, happier, secure in maternal love, and he would have grown to become a man who in turn could have children he loved, which he had not with Claire.

And, were it possible to do it over again, she would have done so much more. She would have had several children, many, instead of the one automatic basic boy, who lived to mock her failure. But here it was, and here was she, and no matter how much she wished it, how strongly she willed it, there could never be another child on earth, let alone several others, out of her womb, the better to represent her passage through this time on earth. How helpless, how helpless old women are with their old memories. She could stamp on the earth, she could hurl imprecations at the heavens, she could beg of the High Spirit, she could wheedle or sob and curse, and no matter what were the cries from her heart and lungs, there could be no more children, for there was no more Adley and there was no more youth.

She stood there, at her makeshift desk in the filtered sunlight, and she felt enfeebled and lost. Ah, how wrongly she had guessed about the later years. Her young dreams about later years had always been of herself as still young and with Adley and with the perfect son who adored them both, and somehow, with that, one could never imagine loneliness. Once, once, she might have spun the wheel, and spun it again and again, and today had the earnings of that effort, two, three, or four numbers to bet on for the final years. Instead, she had spun the wheel one time, and not even looked, casting all on a single number, and she had lost.

This morning she could admit it: there was no one to blame but herself.

Then she thought of Lisa Hackfeld's legacy that would be taken from the Sirens. Activity. Keep busy, keep occupied, keep going, never stop. That is the single anti-death for old women. It was her mistake of this morning. She had stopped. She had permitted her mind the liberty of a woman's mind and a mother's mind. She was not that at all. She was a social anthropologist, and a busy one, and she vowed that she would never forget that again.

She took up the pencils, the pad, and briskly, she went off to her appointment . . .

* * *

Before ten o'clock in the morning, while his wife still slept, Marc Hayden finished packing his worn canvas knapsack. Into it he had squeezed every necessary article that he would require between here and Tahiti. The rest of his personal belongings, he was forfeiting. It did not matter. From the second he arrived in Tahiti, he could spend as lavishly as Croesus, using his traveler's checks and savings account for his material needs, not needing to worry about depleting his bank balance, for an inexhaustible income awaited him.

During the period that he packed, he had expected Claire to interrupt him. Therefore, when she did, he was prepared for her. She came into the front room, knotting the belt of her pink cotton robe over her white nightgown, just as he picked up the knapsack by its shoulder straps to test its weight.

"Morning," he said. He slung the knapsack over his shoulders, to judge its weight better. "I'm going off on an exploration of the island. Be back after midnight, if I can, or maybe by tomorrow early."

"Since when is all this?" Claire wanted to know. "Whom are you going with?"

"Several of Moreturi's friends. Been planning it for a week. Want to see some of the old stone ruins, the temple put up before Daniel Wright's time. Also, I'm told, there are a few outlying shacks the first Wright erected after landing here from England."

"Have fun," she said, and covered her yawn. She wandered aimlessly about the room, hesitated at the fruit bowl, then knelt and peeled and began slicing a banana for her breakfast. She glanced at him. "You look chipper enough, after last night."

"What was last night?"

"Why, the amount we drank. Whew. You were staggering around, insulting our hosts and Tom—"

"Is this the beginning of another lovely day?"

"Well, you did behave like that. Not that you're any different when you're sober. When we left, your mother apologized to them."

Marc snorted, and settled his knapsack on the floor. "If your report is complete, I'll—"

"As a matter of fact it isn't," Claire said. "You came to the dinner quite late and I had a chance to take Courtney aside and speak to him."

"Naturally."

She ignored his sarcasm. "I mean about my missing diamond pendant. I told him what you said, that you were sure one of the natives had stolen it."

"And he said—" His voice went falsetto and registered pretended horror, "Mercy me, but our people here don't steal, they don't steal at all, they're too busy lovin' and fornicatin'."

She was suddenly furious. "That's right, Marc. He said they positively do not steal. There's never been a case in their history. They know nothing of such misbehavior. They do not covet another's material possessions."

Marc's mind went to Tehura, the fallible, and he felt like throwing her at Claire, but he did not. "Your fuggin' Courtney seems to know everything," he said. "His word is always better than mine."

"About the Sirens, yes. Because he's open-minded and sensible. You're so full of prejudices—"

"Prejudices aren't automatically bad," he snapped. "I have mine, and one of them is that I'm prejudiced against failures who blame their failure on everything but themselves. Your lawyer in Chicago couldn't make it in big time, so he ran away, and here he's a hot-shot frog in a small pond of primitive illiterates. He pontificates against everything we know is good, our country, our system, our customs. But everything here, in this nothing place where he's somebody at last, that's perfect, that's great—"

"Oh, God, stop it, Marc, he's not like that, and you know it."

"And speaking of prejudices, I have another. That's against wives who are so damn hostile to their husbands that they side with everyone else against their husbands, in ideas, discussions, everything. Privately, they take their husbands' money and homes and status, but they chip away at their men in public."

"Are you referring to me?"

"I'm referring to you and plenty of women like you. Thank the Lord they're not the only women on earth. There are other women who are proud of their men."

"Maybe they have reason to be," she said, her voice rising. "Maybe they're married to real men. How do you treat me? How do you behave to me? When was the last time you came to bed with me? Or paid me the least bit of attention? Or treated me like your wife?"

"A woman gets what she deserves," he said, with slurred viciousness. "What do you do for me? A woman—"

"You won't let me—you won't let me be a wife."

"Living with you isn't living with a woman, it's living with an Inquisitor, closing in, shoving, demanding—"

"Marc, I don't do that to you, you do it to yourself. Marc, I want to talk about this. I've been watching you, not only here but at home, and I think you're all mixed up—I won't use the word sick, but mixed up—about yourself, your values, your attitude toward having a family, yourself and women. Just take one thing, the normal practice of a husband and wife sleeping together with some regularity, degree of desire and—"

"So that's it. Well, I'll tell you—I'll tell you—a man wants to sleep with a real woman, not an obsessed little chippy with a whore's mind—"

She teetered on the last brink of self-control. "You mean, a woman who thinks of love, being loved, has a whore's mind? Is that what you think?"

He yanked the knapsack up and over his shoulder with a savage motion. "I think you've been riding me long enough, two years long, and that's enough. You make me want to throw up, and that means throwing you up, too. If I'm sick, it's that I'm sick to the gut of you and the guilts you try to saddle me with—"

"Marc, I'm only trying to work it out."

"You're trying to justify what you've really got in that cheap nooky mind of yours. Have you ever looked at one of the natives here from the waist up? No, you're trying to justify getting into the sack with every big brown—"

"Damn you!" She swung at him, and her palm resounded against his cheek.

Automatically, with his free hand, he struck back, the side of his hand catching her on the mouth and chin. The strength of his blow sent her reeling, but she maintained her balance, rubbing her mouth in mute shock.

"I've had enough of you for the rest of my life!" he shouted. "Just stay out of my way!"

With the knapsack, he strode to the door.

"Marc," she cried after him, "unless you apologize, I'll never—"

But then no one was there. She wavered, eyes full, and made a conscious effort not to dignify the scene and his insanity with her tears. When she removed her hand from her mouth, she saw that there were spots of bright red blood on her fingers.

Slowly, she started for the jar of water in the rear room. Unaccountably, Harriet Bleaska's words of yesterday came to her mind. Harriet, beset by her own dilemma, had said to Claire, "Orville seems to me so much like your Marc, maybe you can tell me what it would be like with such a man. Can you, Claire?" At the time, she could not. This moment, she wished that she had. But perhaps Harriet would not be such a fool as she.

* * *

Harriet Bleaska, in her white nurse's uniform, strode back and forth across the front room of her hut, constantly flicking the ash from her cigarette, constantly wondering if she had been a nincompoop. Heretofore, at this hour, which was the last of the morning, she was always famished. Now, she was not famished at all. Her belly was filled with a gravestone, and it was not clear to her, but quite possibly the stone was etched with the word *folly*.

She had made her decision after breakfast, and hastily written the brief note accepting his proposal of marriage. No more than a minute or two before, she had sent off the note with a native boy. By now it was beyond recall. Momentarily, it would be received, read, and shortly afterwards the recipient would be at her door, in her room—her husband-to-be!—and the die would be cast. Forever after, her life would be a different life, her will bent to another's, her personality and history submerged beneath another's, her single Bleaskaness evaporated into thin air for all eternity. It was the merger and change that she had longed for since adolescence, and yet, now that it was upon her, the mutation struck her with terror.

Then, more coolly, as she lighted a fresh cigarette off the old one, she realized that what engulfed her with terror was not this drastic altering of her life, but rather, the continuing worry about whether she had or had not made her choice wisely and well. How many young women had such radically different suitors from whom to select a legal mate? Did anyone, anywhere, ever have to decide between two men so dissimilar and between living conditions so contrasting?

One last time, before giving up her Bleaskaness along with her isolation behind The Mask, she reviewed the men and what they offered side by side. Roaming the room again, smoking steadily, she examined the good and the bad of being the wife of Vaiuri, half-Polynesian, half-English medical practitioner on The Three Sirens, and of being the wife of Dr. Orville Pence, all-American, all-somebody's-son, ethnologist from Denver, Colorado.

Harriet made her nurse notes with nurse brevity in her head.

Vaiuri's assets: he is physically attractive, he is intelligent, he is interested in what I am interested in, he is probably a good lover like all of them here, he would appreciate my skill at this, he would want many children and so do I, he has a wonderful family and fine friends, he would see that I never starve or need, he loves me.

Vaiuri's liabilities: he is possibly too serious and dogged about everything, he lacks my formal education, he has no high ambition because there is no incentive here, he will cheat on me every year during the festival, he will sometimes feel I'm inferior because I am all white.

The Three Sirens' assets: it is like a perpetual summer resort, I can be myself here, I will have no pressure, I am beautiful here.

The Three Sirens' liabilities: I can't show off my husband to my old friends, no baby showers, no Cokes, no *House Beautiful*, no television programs, it's so far from—from what?

Orville Pence's assets: he is a successful American, he wants me for his wife.

Orville Pence's liabilities: I can't imagine him undressed, he's a spinster type, he's a two-minute man for sure, he has a sister, he has a MOTHER, he'll lecture me, he'll allow us one child maybe, he's something of a bore, he's something of a prude, he'll give me only pin money, he'll make me feel he did me a favor, he'll make me join the Faculty Wives' Club and vote Republican, I can't imagine him undressed.

Denver's assets: it is an American city.

Denver's liabilities: it is an American city. P.S., inhabited by a MOTHER.

Oh, damn, she thought, if only there were a computing machine to solve these problems and guarantee the correctness of the result. There is no such machine, she thought, and there was no one to give me real advice, not Maud, not Claire, not Rachel. It was left to me, and now it is done. Did I do right?

She put a third cigarette between her lips, pressed the butt of the burning one to it, drew, then discarded the butt. She walked. Back and forth she walked. Had she done right? She evoked the bad years, which were most of the years. How ill-used she had been. Always, always, she had offered her body as an apology for The Mask. She had only wanted to belong, but she never had, except now and then, temporarily, but out of sight.

Yes, she decided, yes, yes, yes. She had made the right decision.

She had come to this reassurance, even as she heard the rapping on her cane door.

She crushed her unfinished cigarette into the shell ashtray, quickly patted her impossible hair, licked her endless lips to rid them of any tobacco flake, and called out, "Please come in!"

He bolted into the room, then stood there, eyes wide with nervous uncertainty.

"I got your note," he was saying. "You said to come at once. You said you had good news. Is it what I think it is?"

"I've thought it over, and I've made up my mind. I'll be proud to be Mrs. Orville Pence."

It surprised her a little, and delighted her very much, to see the relief reflected in his face.

"Harriet," he said, "this is the happiest moment of my entire life."

"Mine, too," she said.

"We'll announce it at Maud's luncheon today."

She swallowed. "Orville, aren't you going to kiss the bride?"

As he came stiffly toward her, she remembered, for the last time, the sacrifice that she had made. Forever, she had forsaken the chance to be beautiful—would he ever know that?—because she was the heiress to all those damn shadowed ancestors she had never known, who had shaped the placenta that produced her for this final conformity.

And when he awkwardly embraced her, like a missionary welcoming his flock, she became aware that he smelled of soap and all Presbyterian cleanliness. He kissed her. Liability: she felt no passion. Asset: she felt so safe. Then she kissed him back, perhaps too fervently, for after all, it was no small thing to be Mrs. Pence and to belong.

After a while, she gave an involuntary sigh.

A life of unceasing gratefulness, she knew, had just begun.

* * *

From his place of partial concealment, behind the several coco palm trees that fronted the steep path leading out of the village, Marc Hayden could keep an eye on the comings and goings of the members of the team.

He had observed Claire leave his hut, and disappear into Matty's office. In the fifteen minutes that followed, he had seen Rachel De-

Jong meet Harriet Bleaska and Orville Pence in the compound, and shake their hands, and together the three of them, in obvious high spirits, had gone into Matty's office. Next, Lisa Hackfeld had burst forth from her residence, and hurried to Matty's place. The only ones who had not left their hut were the only ones that he had any interest in at this moment. For some reason, Estelle and Sam Karpowicz, and their girl, had not emerged yet.

Originally, when Marc had walked out on Claire (the bitch) this morning, and taken his knapsack to hide behind Tehura's hut, he had planned to ask Tehura to keep the Karpowiczes occupied at either the lunch or dinner hour. Since he did not dare invade Sam's darkroom earlier, to remove photographs and reels of film, for fear that Sam would have too much time to discover that they were missing, Marc had to plan his borrowing or sharing for today. He would not allow himself to believe that taking the photographs and motion picture film was a theft. He had convinced himself that everything accomplished by members of the team, in the field, was community property, held in common. By this rationalization, Marc owned some share of the product of Sam's cameras. If this were not so, then, at the very least, Marc had a right to borrow the product, and make copies of it for Garrity and himself, and later return the originals to Albuquerque.

Still, Marc could see that Sam Karpowicz might have objections to this arrangement. Sam had recently proved, in his explosion over his daughter's education, how hot-tempered he could be. Not that Sam had been wrong about that. Marc felt that he would have acted in the same way as Sam under the same set of circumstances. If you gave them their heads, little sluts like Mary grew up to become big sluts like Claire. The thing to do was to catch them early, hold the reins tightly. He had been too easy with Claire, even from their lousy honeymoon night, that had been his mistake, and look how she had turned out.

Marc's mind had wandered, and he brought it back to Sam. Yes, Sam could be difficult, and rather than contend with his unreasonableness, Marc had decided to remove what he required from the darkroom in secrecy, and no fuss about it. The problem was getting into the darkroom today when none of the Karpowiczes were home. His morning's plan to have his collaborator, Tehura, invite them to her hut for lunch or dinner had been delayed because Tehura was not in her home and so far was nowhere else to be found. Fortunately, during his search for her, Marc had run into Rachel DeJong, who was on her way to her therapy hut. They had exchanged a few inconsequential words, but in parting, Rachel had said, "Well, see you at your mother's lunch."

Marc had completely forgotten about Matty's luncheon, arranged for twelve-thirty. The luncheon, Marc thought, knowing his mother as he did, would be for the purpose of morale building. The field trip had passed the halfway mark. Adley had said this was always "the critical point," and Matty liked to quote him. This was the time when people became ragged, started to unravel in an alien place and clime. This was the time to gather them together, have them listen while their inspiring leader improved their dispositions, have their leader hear out their grievances and problems, and smooth all down to purring contentment. Oh, how good Matty was at this Kiwanis crap. Thank God that would soon be behind him.

The reminder of this luncheon gave Marc the chance for his visit to the darkroom. He would need nothing more of Tehura until tonight. It was ironic, but Matty was his accomplice in her own downfall. He had never before seen so clearly how he was contributing to her downfall. Once he was gone, and on his way with his Garrity project, Claire (the bitch) would be crushed and Courtney dishonored. But Matty, ah, Matty would be ruined. With Marc and Garrity parading the debauchery of The Three Sirens about the lecture platforms of the United States, Matty would be left with no fresh ammunition for her American Anthropological League meeting. In fact, she would be an object of censure, a disgrace to her profession for her role in betraying a society. She would be lucky to retain her post at Raynor College. Oh, President Loomis, senile fool, would keep her on, and there let her die in the elephant's unknown graveyard, let the two of them, Matty and Claire, grow older and older, wither and shrivel, and disappear together.

Marc awakened from his musings and became alert. He could see that Estelle and Sam Karpowicz had just emerged from their hut. They stood in the glare of the compound discussing something, before they went the five huts down to Matty's office.

The second that they were out of sight, Marc left his concealment behind, and hurried into the compound. The Karpowicz hut was the end hut, and the nearest to him. In less than a minute, sweating, he reached it, and ducked into the side alley to the dark-room in the rear.

Passing the first window, he heard a voice, and froze to his tracks. It was unmistakably Mary Karpowicz' voice. He had quite for-gotten about her. God damn. Why wasn't she at the luncheon? Quietly, he eased alongside the window, so that he could not be seen, and waited, wondering what he should do next. The voices inside, one Mary's, the other a male, and from the slight accent a native male, reverberated upon his ears and infuriated him.

She said, "But if you care for me, why not, Nihau?"

He said, "You are too young."

She said, "I'm older than your Sirens girls here."

He said, "You are not a Sirens girl. You are different. In your country it is different."

She said, "Not so different as you think. Nihau, I don't believe you, I don't believe it is only my age. Tell me why you won't—?"

He said, "You have learned much here, Mary. You have come to adulthood. You are wiser than before. You will have very much to offer the man of your own world you find and love. It will happen soon, two years, three, four. When you find him, you will remem-ber me and thank me. I do not want to spoil you for that. I want you to come to that at the proper time."

She said, "You're the kindest person, Nihau, but I don't under-stand. You are making such a big thing of it, when you yourself said that on this island you are taught, as you have taught me, that it is natural and—"

He said, "Mary, you are not of this island and you will not be with us much longer. You must live and think as your parents and your own people teach you to live and think. I would love to—to engage in this thing—but I will not, because I understand you and care too much for you. That is the end of it. I will not forget you, and you must never forget what you have learned here. Now, come, we will go to my family and have our meal."

Listening, about to mutter an obscenity at the frustration these kids had haltered him with, Marc was profoundly thankful that they had come to their senses. Quickly, he returned to the com-pound, going as far as the bridge. When he turned around, he could see Mary and the native boy leaving the hut. Marc started strolling casually, so that he would pass them, and as he did, he waved cheer-ily, and both of them waved back.

Continuing in the opposite direction from them, he slowed down near the palm trees. He glanced behind him. They had gone over a far bridge and were headed toward the row of houses. Marc watched their receding figures. In seconds, they were out of sight among the huts, and the stifling compound was empty of all life but his own.

Almost on the run, Marc returned to the Karpowicz dwelling. He scurried around it and to the rear.

The cramped, thatched shack, Sam's darkroom, stood in solitary splendor.

Marc tried the flimsy door. It opened easily. On the threshold of riches, his mind leaped ahead. He would take a sampling of the still photographs, the most spectacular of them, and a dozen reels, the most representative of them. He would take enough, but not enough to be missed should Sam happen into the darkroom this afternoon, and not too much to carry out tonight. He would take his booty to his hut, pack and camouflage it, and carry the bundle by a circuitous route toward the Sacred Hut, then double back across the compound to Tehura's hut. He would hide his bundle beside his knapsack, in the thick foliage nearby, until it was evening.

All this must be accomplished swiftly, before Matty's luncheon guests disbanded.

He stepped into the darkroom, shut the door behind him, and was alone, at last, with Ali Baba's riches.

* * *

Inside Maud Hayden's office, an hour and a half had passed and her solidarity luncheon was almost at an end. The guests remained seated on the matting, around the long, low bench which served them as a banquet table. All members of the field team were present, with the exception of Marc Hayden and Mary Karpowicz. The one outsider who had been invited was Tom Courtney, because he was of their world as well as the other world, and he sat at the corner of the improvised table closest the door, and across from Claire.

The luncheon had begun on a note of high celebration. Orville Pence, with Harriet Bleaska on his arm, had arrived with a well-traveled bottle of bourbon. When the team had assembled, he had thumped the heavy bottle on Maud's desk for attention. The moment that the room was stilled, he had announced his engagement to Harriet and said that they would be married and have their honeymoon in Las Vegas, Nevada, the day after returning to the United States.

Everyone, it seemed, had pumped Orville's hand, and kissed Harriet's cheek. Only Claire, except for favoring the pair with a smile, had remained withdrawn. Once, when Orville was pouring the bourbon for the first toast, Claire had caught the nurse's eye. Harriet's face had been aglow with the pleasure of being the center of all this special observance, but when she saw Claire, her smile gave way to uncertainty. Immediately, Claire had been sorry, for she knew that her own expression was one of pity, and that Harriet had read the sorrow in it. To prevent spoiling Harriet's precious moment, Claire had forced upon her features a representation of approval, and she had winked, and made some sort of gesture of genuflection. But the passing moment of truth had not been entirely obliterated: Harriet knew, and plainly sensed that Claire knew she knew, that Claire had wished the bride-to-be had gone native.

After the toasts, there had been the luncheon, served by a lanky, rigid, impassive native woman of indeterminate years. As the woman came from the earth oven, going silently around the table with her dishes, Claire found something familiar about her. Not until the native servant was standing over her did Claire identify her. This was the one named Aimata, condemned to slavery for having murdered her husband some years ago. Aimata's husband had been thirty-five, and since the limit of life was arbitrarily put at seventy, she had been sentenced to thirty-five years of being an outcast drudge. After that, Claire had not been able to take her eyes off the tall brown woman, and throughout the luncheon Claire's food had stuck in her throat.

The luncheon itself had been a success. There had been coconut milk in Maud's plastic cups, the inevitable breadfruit, yams, red bananas, and there had been taro, barbecued chicken, some sort of steamed fish, and finally an incongruous dessert of assorted cookies from Maud's American larder.

All through the meal, as the guests sucked, chewed, swallowed, sipped, smacked their lips, Maud Hayden had talked. She had drawn steadily from her vast storehouse of anecdotes about the

South Seas, about the marvels and pitfalls of anthropology. Always, she had told her stories with humor, although sometimes a moral peeked through. Claire had heard these anecdotes not once, but many times in the last two wordy years, and she was less attentive than the others. Nevertheless, despite her hatred for Maud's progeny, Claire told herself that there was no reason to hate Maud or her anecdotes, and so like the others, like Courtney across from her, all listening, all diverted, she pretended to listen and be regaled.

Maud had told them about the peculiar notions the Marquesan natives had had of America in the early 1800s. In those days, the only knowledge the Marquesans possessed of America was from contact with the whaling men from New England who landed on their shores, and who were interested not in their artifacts or customs or society, but only in their women. With such singleness of purpose did the American sailors concentrate on the Marquesan women that it became an absolute belief in those islands that distant America was a society populated entirely and solitarily by men. In short, from their behavior, it was obvious the visitors had never seen live women before, and now that they had, they were making the most of it.

When Maud had finished, the guests had been entertained. Claire had made the only acid comment. "Maybe the Marquesans were right and are still right," she had said. To this, Rachel DeJong had tapped her cup on the table in applause, and said, "Excellent, Claire, another truth spoken in a jest."

But already, Maud, who was essentially humorless, had embarked on another anecdote about the primitive marriage custom known as couvade. According to this custom, when the wife was pregnant, it was the husband who went to bed. This had led to an uproar of appreciation, and then to a learned discourse on maternity customs among savages by Orville Pence.

By the time the table was cleared, Maud's anecdotes had taken on a more serious theme, beneath their whimsical packaging. She had reminded them all of the teasing wickedness many primitive societies possessed. There had been the instance of Labillardiere, on his visit to the South Seas, trying to compile the native words for numerals. He had made his inquiries among chosen informants, and written down the words, and only after publication had he learned that the word they had given him for one million really meant not one million in their tongue but *nonsense*, and that the word they had given him for a half-million had not been that at all but *fornicate*.

"John Lubbock told the story first," Maud had explained, "because he believed that field workers should keep this sort of disaster in mind when working with native informants. You must check and double check, to know whether you are getting facts or having your leg pulled." Everyone had enjoyed the story, and had got the point. In the final weeks, all of them would be more careful, more wary, in short, more scientific.

During this, Claire had been tempted to add an anecdote of her own. Her bruised lower lip, painted deep carmine, reminded her of her own anthropologist and her exchange with him hours ago. He had said, "I'm sick to the gut of you." Now there was the perceptive, balanced scientific approach demanded by the obese conveyor of anecdotes at the head of the table. What if Claire repeated this. Would it also regale them? She felt weak with disgust of him.

Knowing the relief of deliverance, Claire saw that the others were beginning to rise from the bench-table. She realized that Aimata had disappeared with the last of Maud's tin plates and plastic cups. The horrid luncheon was over, or nearly over, for Sam Karpowicz was calling out, "Would any of you care to see my last week of photographs? I've just printed them."

There was a chorus of assents. Claire found herself standing upright, somewhat removed from the others, between the door and the desk. She watched Sam Karpowicz explaining something to Maud, Orville, and Courtney. Then he came to the desk, opened a manila envelope, and extracted two parcels of photographs, glossy black and whites, five by seven inches, eight by ten inches, and began to remove the rubber bands that bound them. Something about the top picture troubled him, and he laid it aside, then hastily riffling through the others, he laid two more aside, and quickly slipped all three back into the envelope. Aware that Claire had observed him, Sam grinned foolishly. "Diplomacy," he murmured. "I'd taken some of Harriet at the festival dance, you know, the bare-breasted ones—and I think a certain party here whose initials are Orville Pence might take a dim view of them now."

Claire nodded. "Very wise," she said.

Sam weighed his pile of photographs lovingly. "Some really good stuff here. I shot everything, even went a little corny on layouts and picture stories. You know—a typical day in the life of the Chief's son; the development of a festival dance; the home of an average Sirens inhabitant; the eloquent history of the Sacred Hut —everything. Would you like to see some of it?"

"I'd love to," said Claire politely.

He took a fistful of photographs and handed them to Claire. "Here, have a look. I'll pass the others around."

Across the room, Sam gave the rest of his photographs to Maud, who in turn relayed them to the guests grouped around her.

Claire remained where she was, isolated from the others, disinterestedly glancing at each photograph in her stack, and placing it beneath the others. She had finished with the series of posed and candid shots of the Hierarchy in solemn session, and she found herself gazing at a full-length shot of Tehura standing before the open door of her hut. Attired only in her provocative grass skirt, Tehura looked like Everyman's dream of Polynesia. Claire could see that both Maud and Sam would do sensationally well with this set back home.

Claire continued to pick through the photographic layout of Tehura. The home of an average Sirens inhabitant, Sam had labeled this collection. Here was Tehura kneeling beside the massive stone fertility idol in the corner of her front room next to the door. Here was Tehura bent over the earth oven. Here was Tehura posing as if in slumber on the mats of her back room. Here was Tehura laying out three of her grass skirts and two of her tapa-cloth pareus. Here was Tehura proudly pointing at her jewelry and ornaments from suitors. Here was a close-up picture of the jewelry and ornaments laid out in a neat row on the pandanus mat.

Suddenly, Claire had stopped turning over the pictures. Incredulously, she brought the last one closer to her eyes. There could be no mistake, no mistake at all. There it was.

Helplessly, she cast around the room for Courtney, saw him. "Tom," she summoned him.

He came to her, searching her face in an attempt to understand its agitation. "Yes, Claire, what is it?"

"I—I've found my missing necklace, the diamond pendant."

"You have?"

"Here it is." She handed him the two photographs. "Tehura has it."

For a long time, it seemed, he studied the photographs. Frowning, he looked up. "It's a diamond pendant all right, nothing native. You're positive this is the one?"

"Could there be any other?"

"Claire, she couldn't have stolen it. I know Tehura. She wouldn't in a million years."

"Maybe she didn't have to."

Courtney's head jerked toward her, his long face troubled.

"I think I'd better go over and see her," Claire said.

"I'll go with you."

"No," said Claire firmly. "There are some things a woman has to do alone."

* * *

All the afternoon she was tensely poised for her showdown with Tehura, and all the afternoon she was thwarted, because Tehura was not there. Three times, in the clammy heat of the afternoon, Claire had made her way across the endless compound, from her hut to Tehura's hut, and three times Tehura's hut had been empty.

Blindly, in the frustration of waiting between each visit, she had returned to her own quarters, and kept herself occupied with cleaning and laundering. She would not permit herself to anticipate confirmation of the means by which her favorite piece of jewelry had been transported from her luggage to Tehura's possession. She knew, but she would not dwell upon it. She must have the evidence from the native girl's lips.

Now it was after five o'clock, and for the fourth time, Claire was making her way to the hateful hut. If Tehura was still not home, Claire determined to post herself before the door and wait. If she was home, Claire would not waste words. There and then she would finish the last of her unfinished business with Marc.

She reached the hut that had become a dominant site in her life, and when she lifted her fist to knock, she intuitively knew that there would be a response.

She knocked.

The response was instantaneous. *"Eaha?"*

Claire shoved the door, and stepped from the outside heat into the shaded, cooler interior of the front room. Tehura was curled comfortably against the far wall, a bowl of vegetables beside her thigh, and she was in the midst of cutting the vegetables for cooking.

At the sight of Claire, Tehura showed not her customary pleasure but an immediate uneasiness. She did not display her quick smile. She did not offer to rise in the practiced gesture of hospitality. She sat unmoving, in an attitude of watchful waiting.

"I had to speak to you, Tehura," Claire said, still standing.

"Is it so important? I must serve a dinner tonight. Can it not wait until tomorrow?"

Claire stood her ground against the rebuff. "No, Tehura."

The native girl shrugged, and dropped both vegetables and paring bone into the bowl. "Very well," she said with a pout, "you tell me what is so important."

Claire hesitated. Whenever she was in the presence of one of these native women, she felt at a disadvantage. Several weeks ago she had thought it was because of their superiority in sexual activity. When you are in the company of a woman who has known many men, and you have known but one or perhaps none, you feel inferior. But now, Claire understood that it was much more superficial than that. It was exactly what she had perceived her first afternoon in the village, when she had felt like a missionary's wife. It was a matter of clothing, or lack of clothing. There was the native girl, without a stitch on except for the brief grass skirt drawn so high as to almost reveal her private parts. There she was, so female, flaunting every magnificent curve of her tawny brown body. And by contrast, here stood Claire in two binding layers of clothing, announcing in this place her shame of femininity. It gave her the feeling of being constricted, and inhibited. Then, she thought of what she had seen in Sam's photographs, and she forgot her disadvantage.

Claire dropped to her knees, directly before the native girl. She would have to struggle to keep her voice from quavering. "Tehura," she said, "how did you get my diamond necklace?"

Claire had the satisfaction of seeing the girl lose her composure. Tehura flattened against the wall, in the posture of a small house pet at bay. Her slow, vacuous little mind was groping, Claire perceived. In an instant, she would make up some stupid lie.

Claire spoke again. "Don't bother to deny it and embarrass us both. I know you have my necklace. Our photographer took pictures of you—remember? He took pictures of all your possessions. I saw the pictures. And there was my necklace. Tell me how you got it. I'm determined to find out."

Claire waited, and she could see that Tehura was going to brazen it out.

"Ask your husband," Tehura said suddenly. "He gave it to me."

So, thought Claire, that part of it is confirmed. "Yes," she said quietly. "I expected it was Marc."

"A gift," said Tehura quickly, "he gave it to me as a gift for being his informant. He said he would buy you another."

"I don't want another," said Claire, "and I don't want this one back. I only want the truth about what's been going on between you and Marc."

"What truth?" Tehura demanded.

"You know very well what I mean. Let's not play little-girl games. You're grown up and so am I. Marc gave you my most expensive and most sentimental possession, took it from me and gave it to a stranger. I insist on knowing why. For simply being an informant?"

Technically, Tehura could afford to be righteous, and so there was pious righteousness in her voice. "For being what else? What else could there be?" Then, with a thrust of cruelty, she added, "He is your husband, he is not mine."

"He is not mine, either," said Claire.

"That is your business as a woman, not my business," said Tehura.

She is actually being insolent to me, Claire thought, and it is not mere defensiveness, it is from an actual feeling of superiority. There could only be one reason for this, and Claire made up her mind to ferret out an admission.

For seconds, Claire studied the native girl, appalled at how she had changed in these weeks. From her first encounter with Tehura in Paoti's hut, before and during the rite of friendship, she had liked and admired Tehura. The young brown girl had been, to Claire, the perfect symbol of a free soul, gay, amusing, unspoiled. The High Spirit's simple Eve. All that had vanished now. Tehura was as complex, secretive, covetous, inhibited, nervous as any Western woman. When and how had the metamorphosis taken place? Who had put upon her the cankers of outside civilization? What had been the infecting agent? Again, Claire was certain she had the answers, but she had to hear them from Tehura's lips, just as Rachel DeJong always knew the answers, but had to hear them from her patients' lips so that they would come to know, too.

"Tehura, I'm going to ignore your obvious contempt for me," Claire said, slowly. "I'm going to have a short talk with you, I'm going to speak to you honestly, as sincerely as I can, and then you may say what you wish, and after that I'm going to leave you."

"Say whatever you want to say," said Tehura peevishly.

"You've changed, you've changed almost before my eyes. You are not the same young woman I met when I came here. I thought this society was impervious to outside influence. I thought you had progressed far beyond us, in certain ways, and could absorb our visit and throw us off, back to where we came from, without suffering any ill effects. But I see some of you on the Sirens are fallible human beings too, and there must always be one or two in any group who are more susceptible than the rest, more sensitive to outside influences. Something nasty has been at work on you, and that something has warped you. You were a nice person, almost perfect, but you've become something else, too much like many of us outsiders, something imperfect. You've been constantly exposed to only one of us in these last weeks—and so I must suspect him, because I know him so well. Marc has done this to you."

Tehura leaned forward, and there was wrath in her voice. "Marc has done nothing to me—except good. Marc is a good man. You do not appreciate him, that is all. You are the one who is spoiled, and you try to spoil him."

"I see," said Claire. "What do you know about my husband? How do you know he is such a good man?"

"I have been with him every day for weeks in our work. He cannot speak to you, so he speaks to me. I know him well."

"How well, Tehura?"

"Not what you think with your mind."

"I simply asked how well you know him?"

"Better than you do. With me he can speak, be free, he is a man. With you, he is made into nothing but air."

"Is that what he told you?"

"It is what I see with my eyes. He cannot live with you."

Claire bit her lip. "Do you think he can live with any woman? Do you think he can live with you?"

"Yes."

"Well," said Claire, "this is a serious thing. He has really got to you. Let me tell you, Tehura, let me give you a piece of free advice. I don't know what he's told you or planned for you. I don't know if he's merely trying to sleep with you, or has actually talked you into coming to the United States to be his mistress. Or could it be wife?"

"You are saying such things, not Marc."

"No matter what he has in mind, or you have, you listen to me while you can, Tehura. He's a word man, nothing more. That's the cheapest seduction and the worst one, because after the words there is little else, only meanness. Do you understand? Whatever he's said to you, told you these last weeks, about himself, about me, about our life at home, about our country, has been designed to delude and corrupt you."

"No."

"I tell you yes," said Claire forcefully. "We live a dull, monotonous life at home, competing with the Joneses—oh, you don't know what that means, but try to feel what I say—a nervous, restricted, high-tension life, fighting for jobs, status, fighting edginess, ennui—always wondering how we can escape it, make it better. You already have it better here in a thousand ways. Your vocabulary does not even have the words for tranquilizers, campus politics, ambition, frustration, envy, debts, frigidity, loneliness. But these are a great part of our life in my country. I won't say our life is all bad, and yours is all good, but I will say—I have no doubt of it—that Marc has not painted a true picture for you." She caught her breath, and then rushed on. "I will tell you more, Tehura. Marc is not a man for you or for any normal woman. I've learned that on the Sirens. What could he give you that your own men could not? He is intelligent, highly educated, not unattractive, and occasionally he has money for necklaces, that is true, but it is so little, Tehura, so little. He has no strength of tenderness, of understanding, of love. He is stunted, angry, self-centered, too neurotic, sick of mind, to function, behave, as a grown man should behave. He is corroded with envies, hates, self-pity, fantastic prejudices, unrealistic dreams. His values are no more mature than those of a very young boy, less so. I mentioned love. In this place you've treated love as love has never been treated in any society before. You have confessed that you have enjoyed your native men. You will not enjoy an American man in the same way—"

"Tom Courtney was my lover."

"Even Tom, and he's a million years more mature than Marc, even Tom, you told me, you had to teach to be a man. Marc is not

Tom and Marc will not learn, and he is not the men you have known. I haven't experienced a good lover, but Marc, dammit, I can tell you, Marc is the worst. He has no interest in a real woman. He cannot give of himself. He thinks only of himself. Tehura, for your own sake, not mine, I warn you—"

Tehura rose to her feet, trying to maintain some pose of dignity. "I do not believe you," she said.

Claire stood up. "You do not believe me?"

"You are a wife who cannot keep her man. You are jealous and afraid."

"Tehura," Claire pleaded, "how can I reach you, the person you've become, he's made you into?" She saw that it was no use. "All right," she said, "but I hope you will realize it is truly not jealousy. I'm through with Marc. Do as you wish."

She started for the door.

"You can have your necklace," Tehura called out.

"Keep it," Claire said, staring at the door, holding the latch, not turning around. "Keep it, but don't keep him, if you've had that in mind, because if you do, you'll be as much of a fool as I have been."

She went outside, and when she had shut the door behind her, she felt her knees begin to give. As she steadied herself against the hut, she discerned that she was neither tearful nor bitter, only emotionally spent.

It's over, thank God, it's over, she thought. The next time Rasmussen came, she would leave with him. It could not be soon enough.

As for Marc and Tehura, she did not know if there was anything between them, or if ever there would be. She did not care about Marc. But for one moment she had pity for Tehura.

Poor girl, she thought, and then she left her, that native child, to her do-it-yourself purgatory.

* * *

It had been night on The Three Sirens for several hours, and Marc Hayden, returning to the village, was conscious that he was late for his final appointment on the island. When, from the sloping path, he could make out the basket silhouette of the Social Aid Hut directly below, he sagged with relief at having found his way and because what he had done until now had been done so well.

Descending to the village, in the direction of his Tehura's dwelling, he enjoyed a sense of well-being. It was as if, with each step,
he was shedding one more hampering coat of his chrysalis. Soon he
would be free, and in full flight.

He was pleased with himself, with the way he had handled his
last afternoon and evening. After hiding what Rex Garrity called
the "single piece of corroborating evidence, that is, evidence that
The Three Sirens exists and is what you say it is," after covering it
with brush, Marc had slipped into Tehura's empty hut and par-
taken of a filling meal that would carry him until nightfall. When
he was certain that he could not be seen, he had removed himself
from her hut and any chance meeting with wife or team members
by taking one of the few trails out of the village that he had traveled before. He had gone up the rise behind the Social Aid Hut
until he arrived at the clearing where he and Tehura, as anthropologist and informant, had spent so many hours. After resting in
the shade, he had strayed onward until he recognized the scene
of his swimming fiasco, where surely no member of his group
would venture on an ordinary working day.

In the curb of harbor, below the cliff, he had seen several young
native men preparing to launch their long canoes. Believing that he
recognized Moreturi among them, he had made his way carefully down the ladder of rock (conscious, briefly, that here he had
committed his foul on Huatoro and here, plainly, shown the extent
of his love for Tehura). At last, he reached the curved bow of
water. The natives had proved to be fishermen, and their leader was,
indeed, none other than Moreturi.

Much as Marc detested this one in particular, and all the natives
in general, he saw the meeting could provide a means of escaping
introspection. As he had expected, he was invited to join in the
netting of albacore in deeper waters, and gratefully he went along.
He had offered his hand at the paddles, and his volunteering this,
and subsequent amiability, had surprised Moreturi and pleased the
others. The long dugout had been filled with the catch, and by
the time they had returned to the shore, it was evening.

Refreshed by his excursion on the water, Marc had followed the
natives up the terraced rock. At the summit, one who had gone
ahead of the others had prepared a bonfire. Then five or six of them
had stayed on the cliff, and sat around the glowing coals, while fish
and sweet potatoes roasted. Marc could not remember when he had

savored a dinner more. Through the eating, the natives, as a courtesy to their visitor, had limited their conversations to English. There had been some discussion of the sea, and tales told of the exploits of ancestors. By adroitly leading Moreturi on, Marc had got a vague idea of the position of The Three Sirens in relation to other unnamed nearby islands. What he sought to confirm, and had had confirmed to his total satisfaction, was Tehura's claim of an island two days and one night away. His confidence in Poma's brother, the sailor-idiot Mataro, had been bolstered. The escape, he had decided, would present no problems.

Because of his private plans, Marc, thanking the natives profusely, had left them while they still ate around the fire. The trip back to the village, because of the darkness, had taken twice as long. When he had come upon the clearing that he and Tehura had often used, he felt more secure. In that place, for some length of time, he sprawled and rested, dreaming of the glories that were ahead.

Lying there, scanning the starry sky above, the immense and scornful roof that had seen so much of weakness, failure, folly, it gave him satisfaction again that he would not be one of the planet's tramped-down ants. One death fear had always possessed him, that he would make this single passage on earth beneath that sky without achieving distinction. His inarticulated constant prayer had been that he not live and die a mere digit, one of so many statistical digits expiring on earth every new second. To leave this place and time so casually, remembered only as "the son of the eminent" and survived by others as anonymous as he, remembered by only a few friends who would themselves go soon, marked in time by only a few pitiful paid-for obituaries and chiseled engravings on a rock tablet, this had been the terror that haunted him. Now, by sheer strength of character, he had changed all of that. Henceforth, the world would know him as an artistocrat, crowned by celebrity, and thousands and thousands would mourn his passing, and columns would be studded with his pictures and praise of his accomplishments, and he would be alive as long as there were men on earth. Good-by, he thought, good-by old writ on water.

Ah, how good he felt this night.

Then it was that his soaring mind came down to more earthly rewards. One immediate reward was minor, the other major. The minor one was that, after tomorrow, he could abandon anthropology forever. He had gone into it while living under a tyranny. There had been no free and open ballot. A son of Adley and Maud Hayden could have only one party to join, one way to vote. Nine years before, he had received his B.A., and had gone thereafter into the field for a year. This trip was followed by the two years of graduate seminars needed for his doctorate. The field trip with Adley and Maud had been the worst period. He had been in the field with his parents earlier, as a child, but even as an adult fortified with a B.A., the earlier terror haunted him. In the remote high Andes (his parents' second visit there, to accommodate him), cut off from civilization, every fiber of his being had resisted the isolation. He had been obsessed by the possibility of an accident, to himself or to his parents. If it happened to him, he would be left behind. If it happened to them, he would be left alone. He had never fully shaken off these fears, and he dreaded a life in which this periodic isolation was required for advancement. He dreaded it almost as much as he detested a life wasted upon the anonymity of teaching a roomful of nobodys for the possible recompense of —maybe someday—twenty thousand dollars a year.

Now, that terror was exorcised. Enjoying this minor reward, he could also enjoy the major one so near at hand. He conjured up the person of Tehura, whom he had come to know and would soon see. He imagined their reunion. She had promised him herself this night. What had so long been elusive would be his to possess, to possess tonight and for all the nights that he wished it. He envisioned her both as she was, and as he had not yet seen her, his stripped vessel, and the vividness of what he saw so stimulated him, that he roused himself from his rest, and resumed his journey to the village.

It was almost ten o'clock in the evening when he passed the outskirts of the village compound. Except for a few natives strolling in the distance, none of the enemy was in sight. Cautiously, he traversed the area deep beneath the overhang. By counting off the huts, so alike, as he progressed behind them, he was able to locate Tehura's residence in the darkness. He could see the yellow illumination behind the shuttered windows. Nothing had gone wrong. His woman was waiting.

There was one last act before joining her. He burrowed into the tangled foliage, parting the bushes, uncovering his cache, until he had both knapsack and bundle of film. Shouldering one, carrying the other, he moved speedily to Tehura's door, and without knocking, he went inside.

It was a moment before he could see her. She was seated lazily in a shadowed corner of the front room, outside of the circle of burning candlenut lights. She was as provocative as ever, bare-breasted, barelegged, wearing only the short grass skirt, and now, he saw, a lovely white hibiscus in her black hair. She was reposeful, sipping liquid from a half-shell.

"I was worried, Marc," she said. "You are late."

He dropped his knapsack and bundle of film beside the stone idol near the door. "I was in hiding," he said. "I was far from the village. It took time to get back in the dark."

"Anyway, you are here. I am pleased."

"Is there any more news?"

"None. The arrangements are made. Poma's brother will be waiting on the far beach with his outrigger. He will expect us to be there just as the tomorrow's light comes. Soon, we will go. We will be far and safe before we are missed."

"Wonderful."

"We will leave the village at midnight. Everyone will be asleep. We will go behind the huts to the other side, and take the long path by which you first came here."

"Isn't there a shorter route?"

"Yes, but bad in the night. The long way is easier and more certain."

"Fine."

"We have two hours, Marc," she said. "Let us drink to a safe journey. And let us nap a short time to be strong." She offered her half-shell. "Have some of our palm juice. I have just begun."

"Thanks, Tehura," he said, "but not enough kick. I have a couple of pints of Scotch in my sack. That'll go down better."

He opened his knapsack and tugged free a bottle. With a twist, he unscrewed the cap, brought the bottle to his mouth, and took three swallows. The whiskey burned his throat, and fanned hotly through his chest, and was followed by the soothing afterwave of delivery from self.

"What did you do today?" he asked.

"Saw my kin family. It was for farewell, but they did not know it."

"Did you see Huatoro?"

"Of course not."

"Courtney?"

"No. Why do you ask? What is in your head?"

These first drinks always made him uncommonly suspicious and aggressive. He must watch himself. He swallowed from the bottle again, and said, "Nothing is in my head. I just wondered about the people you saw the last time around. Did you see anyone else?"

"Poma, to be certain everything was ready."

"And that was all?"

She hesitated, then said emphatically, "No one else but you."

"Good."

"Who have you seen?" she demanded in turn.

"Since I left my wife this morning, no one. Except, this afternoon I went fishing with some of your friends. Moreturi, and several others." The whiskey had crept up behind his eyes, and he squeezed them to bring her into focus. "You packed?"

"Very little to take. It is in the other room."

"Tehura, where we're going, you can't go around like that."

"I know, Marc. I have learned. I have packed my binding for here—" She touched her breasts. "—and my long tapa skirts, the ones for ceremonies."

He was gulping down whiskey once more. The bottle was almost empty. He set it on the floor, and considered her. "Not that I mind you as you are. You're beautiful tonight, Tehura."

"Thank you."

He went to her, waiting until she had finished with the half-shell and removed it from her lips. He lowered himself beside her, and encircled her naked back with his arm. "I'm in love with you, Tehura."

She nodded, and looked into his face.

His other hand went to her breasts, and slowly he began to stroke them, the curve of one, and then the other.

"I want you, Tehura, right now. I want to begin our love tonight."

"Not tonight," she said, but she did not remove his hand.

"You promised me."

"There is not enough time," she said.

"There's more than an hour."

She peered at him strangely. "That is not enough time for love."

"It is more than enough time."

"Not enough in my country," she persisted.

He laughed without conviction, but felt the fire of the whiskey in his shoulders and groin. "That's big talk for a little girl."

"I do not know what you mean, Marc."

"I mean love is love, and you do it when you feel like it. I feel like it now. I'm sure you do. We'll have time to rest a little afterwards, and then we can go. Look, Tehura, you said we would—"

"I said we would," she agreed flatly.

"I want you here just once. I've got it bad."

Her smooth young face had been stoical. Suddenly, examining his, it reflected a small curiosity. "Yes," she said, "we will make love." With that, she removed his hand from her bosom, and stood up. "In the back room," she said. "It is better."

She went into the rear room. Eagerly, Marc came to his feet, then halted, detoured to his bottle, finished the last of the whiskey, and entered the back room. In the darkness, he could make her out in the middle of the room, still with the flower in her hair and the grass skirt around her torso.

"Let's have at least one light here," he said. "I want to see you."

He handed her his matches, and she struck one, and lighted a wick that had been set in a container of coconut oil. The illumination was low, unsteady, but it overcame all but the deepest shadows.

As she remained standing in the center of the room, he studied her figure possessively. With rising desire, he unbuttoned and discarded his sport shirt. Next, he pulled off his shoes and socks. Watching her, in her immobility, he unbuckled his belt, let his trousers drop, and kicked them aside. Now, he wore only his white jock shorts. He pulled himself to his full height, having pride in the athletic hardness of his body and his obvious virility.

"You look like one of us," she said.

"You'll find me better," he said, smelling the fumes of his own whiskey. "I'm better for you, Tehura."

He moved swiftly to her, wanting to bring her down fast, and took her into his arms and pressed his lips against her mouth. He worked fiercely at her mouth, until it was open, and then he tried to use his tongue, but from the way her head swerved, he sensed that this was repugnant to her. His hands were upon her breasts, caressing them, waiting for the telltale sharpness of the nipples. The nipples remained flaccid, and she remained passive.

He paused, and demanded crossly of her, "What's wrong?"

Her arm snaked around him, and upwards, playing with his hair. "Marc," she said softly, "I have told you that I do not know of kissing, and the breast play does not arouse me. There are other parts to caress, after the dance."

Desire had so consumed him, that he found it almost impossible to speak. "Dance?"

"You will see." She disengaged herself. "Let us both be naked and dance close; do as I do, and we will both be in passion."

He nodded silently, pulled down his jock shorts, threw them away, and straightened. She was taking the flower from her hair, loosening her hair, when she saw him. She smiled. "Our men are not so hairy," she said.

He vibrated with the wanting of her, but waited, for she was untying the band of her skirt. She had freed it, and suddenly she opened the skirt, drew it off her body, and flung it against the wall. "There," she said. "We are as we should be."

He stared at what he had not seen before, and was overcome by the magnificent sheath of her brown skin, all a flawless texture, top to bottom, head to toe.

She was holding out her arms. "Come, Marc, the love dance."

Dazed, he went into her arms, while he embraced her, he felt her arms go around his back, and her fingers play down to his buttocks. He felt her breasts tormenting his chest, and her sweet insinuating voice humming in his ear, and then the slow gyrating of her hips as her large thighs touched his and moved away and touched his again. "Do as I do, Marc," she whispered, and hummed again, and sensuously she revolved her hips toward him and away, toward him and away. Instinctively, he imitated her motions, and gradually he realized that her nipples were hard against his chest.

"Goddammit, honey, let's—" he tried to pull her toward the pile of matting that was her bed, but she resisted.

"No, Marc, we are only beginning. This, and caresses, and after that—"

"No!" he shouted, and with his entire strength, his fingers vises on her arms, he lifted her off her feet, and dumped her on the bedding.

She tried to sit up. "Marc, wait—"

"I'm ready and so are you, and stop the tease, dammit, I've had enough of it."

He shoved her on her back, and laid both of his hands on her thighs.

"Please, Marc—" she protested.

"You'll love me," he said angrily, and without another word, he entered her.

She resigned herself to the act at once. "Yes, Marc, I want to be like you. Love me well, and I will love you."

There was little grace or finesse in his movement. Frenziedly, he pounded at her, as if she were an inanimate mound of flesh.

"Marc, Marc, Marc," she kept calling into his ear, "let us love." He had no idea what she meant, and did not care, for she was not there, and he continued to punish her with all his power.

She tried and tried, but he had no interest in her skill. Her hands were inside his thighs, massaging them, and her fingers pressed firmly over his perineum, so that his virility grew. She was swinging her hips now in wide, rounding rotary motions, as in her erotic dance, and he was despising her for what was happening.

"Another position, Marc," she was calling into his ear. "It is our way—many positions—better—"

"Shut up," he groaned.

He mounted high, and then down and down, and felt all his strength and maleness seep out of him, and he flattened upon her like a great gas balloon suddenly deflated.

"Whew," he said, rolling off her and to his side, "that was something."

She was watching him with bewilderment. "No more?" she asked.

"No more what?"

"It was only a few minutes," she pleaded, "there must be more, more strength from you, or when you are weak, more love after."

He felt his face reddening. Another Claire, the bitch. The world was full of Claires, the bitches. "What the hell are you complaining about?" he demanded. "That was the best humping you ever got, and you know it. You were squealing in my ear every minute. You enjoyed it."

"Marc, you made love alone, you did not make love with me."

He forced a grin, to give himself a face. "I get it, you're having fun, more teasing. I know that's the big sport here. Look, we've both had it. The sample was great and we'll have some big times ahead. Now let's have ourselves some sleep, and we'll hit the road."

He had begun to turn over on his side, away from her, when she sat up, and grasped his arm. Wearily, he came back to her.

There was a naked female urgency about her that nauseated him. "Marc, please Marc, it is not done yet—for you, yes, for me, no—here, when it is not done for both, one tries to make the other happy in other ways, until it is done for both."

"Send a letter to the Social Aid," he said with annoyance.

"You know that I cannot," she said seriously.

"Tehura, relax, will you? I'm whipped. We both need rest. I promise you, as we go along, know each other, our love will get better and better."

She refused to release him. "What if it does not, Marc? I will have no Social Aid Hut in California."

"You'll have my love, that's enough."

"Enough?"

He had turned over to rest again, fatigued by the long day, the fishing, the hiking, the drinking, the orgasm.

She was on her knees over him. "Marc," she beseeched him, "if we are to be lovers, you must learn to love. It is not impossible. Tom Courtney learned. You can learn. Our people learn how to satisfy, and you must try to be like them. I will teach you, I will help you, but we must begin now, right now."

When this insult had penetrated the alcohol and exhaustion upon which he was cradled, his heart went berserk inside its cavity. He pushed himself to a sitting position. "You'll teach me?" he shouted. "Who in the hell do you think you are, you little colored chippy? You're nothing but an ignorant animal, and you're lucky I'm even doing you the favor of trying to make a human being out of you. Now you keep your dirty trap shut, or you're going to be in real trouble with me. If there's any teaching to be done around here, I'll be the one to do it. You remember that. I'll forgive you this once, but there's no second time."

It surprised him that she was already on her feet, going to retrieve her grass skirt, then fastening it to her hips with deliberation as she stared back at him.

"What do you think you're doing?" he demanded.

"I have had enough of you," she said. She had finished with the grass skirt. "Your wife is right about you."

"My wife?" he said. "What in the hell does that mean?"

Tehura was not intimidated by the rising temper in his tone. She stood her ground. "It means that she came here to see me today, late today, and she told me about you."

"Here? She was here?"

"She learned, through some photograph, you had given me the diamond necklace. She came here. She told me about you."

"That silly bitch. And you listened to her?"

"I did not. I thought she was a jealous wife, that is all. I did not even mention it to you. Now I can tell you, Marc. She is right."

He scrambled to his feet, and his manner was ugly. "She's right about what?"

"She did not know if you wanted me for mistress or wife, but she guessed it would be one or the other, and in either way she said it would be bad for me. She said you lied about your life back home. She said you have no interest in anyone but yourself. She said you are incapable of pleasing a woman. She said you are a poor lover. I laughed at her, but tonight I want to weep. Now I know for myself. She is right in everything."

He had lost his faculty of speech. He was nearly blind with rage. He wanted to choke this colored chippy. He wanted to strangle her until she was still forever. What restrained him from violence was a flashing remembrance of Garrity's advice: bring tangible evidence of the Sirens' existence. Tehura was such evidence. Marc knew he dared not lose her.

Relentlessly, she was going on. She would not stop. "Once, I told you that I knew what was wrong with you. I do know now, as your wife has always known. Why were you angry when she showed her breasts the first night? Why are you always angry with what she does? You are angry because you know that some day she might find men who will make her happier than you can, in bed and out of the bed, and you want to prevent it, even to prevent her from thinking about it. You know you cannot give her what other men could, and so you are always afraid. You are ashamed of your sex, so you want to keep it away from your woman and yourself, and to do that you make sex a bad thing, a sin thing. You are always afraid because you are not virile. You do not know that is not wrong. What is wrong is that you could learn, but you will not learn, because that shows someone else and maybe the world you are weak, and you want it to be your secret. It is not a secret to your wife. Now it is not a secret to me. Good-by, Marc."

She turned away and started into the front room, but Marc pursued her, and jumped in front of her, blocking her path to the door. "Where do you think you're going?" he demanded.

"I'm going to Poma," she said, eyes smoldering. "I am going to stay with her."

"And tell her you're not leaving here with me, is that what you are going to do?"

"Yes," she said, "that is what I am going to do."

"And have her hold back her brother and alert the whole village, you little whore?" All hopes of conciliating her had left him. "Do you think I'm going to let you do that?"

"No one will stop you. No one cares about you. Go ahead and do what you want, and leave me alone."

He remained solidly between her and the door. "You are not leaving here alone," he said. "You're going with me to the beach. Once I'm in that outrigger and gone, I'll turn you loose. I never wanted you on the boat anyway. I only wanted the boat, and wanted to fuck you."

"Get out of my way!"

"No, damn you!"

She hurled herself at him, trying to push past him, groping for the door. He had braced himself against her, and now he had her shoulders and thrust her off. She staggered, and then, her face contorted, she tried to force her way past him once more. He intercepted her again, and her nails went to his cheeks and ripped downward.

The pain of his torn skin made him cry out, and he lashed at her with his hand. She sobbed, but kept grinding her nails into his face. He balled his right hand into a fist, even as he tried to fend her off with his left, and then he swung at her face. The smashing blow caught her high on the cheek, lifted her off her feet, and sent her reeling toward the corner. She went over backwards, falling hard, and the impact of the base of her skull on the stone image in the corner sent a cracking sound through the room.

For a split second, lying there, her eyes rolled uncontrollably, and then they closed. She slumped sideways to the matting in the crunched, grotesque posture of so many mummified bodies found in the ruins of Pompeii.

Marc hung over her fallen body, winded, gasping for breath. When his chest had the air he needed, he knelt and bent his head close to her face. She was unconscious, but exhaling faintly.

Good enough, he thought, she'll be out for hours, the ignorant little whore. There was time enough, and he would be well rid of her. He decided that he hadn't needed her person at all. His photographs would be evidence enough of the Sirens. He must go for the beach and the boat as fast as possible.

On unsteady legs, he made his way to the rear room. The impression of her figure was still deep in the matting of her bed. It pleased him. He had had all he ever wanted of her anyway, the means of escape and the piece of tail.

Quickly, he pulled on his shorts, and began to dress. . . .

* * *

It had been one more of those strange evenings for Claire Hayden, one where she lived almost entirely oblivious of her surroundings, and was instead deeply inside that part of herself which was furnished with the bric-a-brac of her past. More and more, since she had become transformed all but officially from Claire Hayden to Claire Emerson, did she go back to remember what had been Claire Emerson's life and not Claire Hayden's. It had not been the perfect life, anything but that, yet it was far, far away and therefore comforting.

This digging into the past—her archeological evenings, she thought wryly—was not healthy, she decided, after an unusually long uncovering of ruins. There was no book or doctor to tell her these retrogressions were bad, but she felt that they were, because they represented some kind of running from reality. This gave her guilts, so similar to the guilts that had been imposed upon her by her mother, when her mother used to say, "Claire, how long are you going to keep your nose in those books? It's not healthy for a growing girl, being a bookworm. You should get out more." Dutifully, she had always left the better world for the worse one. The echo of her mother's voice caught her again, this alone night in the Pacific, and so she removed herself from the better world to the one that she must contend with.

She refused to think of her morning scene with Marc, so mean that scene, or the other, six or seven hours ago with Tehura, so unfortunate. What she hoped, through the evening, was that Tom Courtney would drop by, as he had promised he might. There could be sensible talk, some candor and unburdening, and it would be a more attractive world of reality. She wanted to tell him a little about Marc, and of the entire meeting that she had suffered with Tehura, and afterwards her own feelings and position might be more orderly in her mind.

In fact, she recalled, it was Tom who had suggested that he would try to call upon her. He had known she would see Tehura, and he was anxious about the outcome of their confrontation. He would be busy, he had said, for most of the evening. He had promised to take Sam Karpowicz and Maud to some kind of dinner with the members of the Hierarchy, and he was to help Sam prepare another photographic layout of the Hierarchy holding one of its decision meetings.

Waiting for Tom, wondering if it was already too late for him, she realized that thinking of her mother had created a desire to write her. They corresponded occasionally, but Claire had not written to her mother once from the Sirens.

Thus, with pen and tablet, she used up much of the remaining time before midnight. She wrote three pages to her mother. That finished, she was impelled to write several more letters, to girl friends and married couples she had known before marrying Marc. When her hand began to cramp, and she completed this sudden correspondence, and covered the envelopes with her scrawl, she wondered what had made her write her mother and these old friends. Then she knew. All of them were Claire Emerson's people, and it was Claire Emerson who was reaching out for them, to revive them in her life against the immediate future when she would be single once more.

Finally, it was after midnight, and she gave up on Tom. That was disappointing, but there was tomorrow. She decided that she had better take her sleeping pills now. By the time she had undressed, she would be drowsy and not think too much. Before she could go for the pills, she heard the sounds of conversation in the compound nearby.

She stepped to her front door and opened it, to find Tom Courtney approaching. He waved.

"I didn't think you'd be up," he said. "I was going to see if your light was on."

"I hoped you would come by. Were you with someone just now?"

"I came back with Sam and Maud. Sam got some good shots tonight. He's thrilled as a child." Courtney shook his head. "Wish I had an enthusiasm like that." She still held the door wide, and he said, "Mind if I come in for a few minutes?"

"Please. I'm not a bit sleepy. I'm in the mood to talk."

He went past her into the living room. She remained at the door, then said, "I'll leave it open a little while, to air the room."

He smiled. "And to keep from being compromised."

Claire came away from the door. "I'm in the mood to be compromised," she said. "Take a good look at me." She pirouetted before him, her skirt swinging above her knees. "You see the ex-Mrs. Hayden."

Courtney's eyebrows shot up. "Are you serious?"

"The most ex-Mrs. Hayden the world has ever known."

Courtney fidgeted. "Well—" he said.

"You were a divorce lawyer, you know all the questions, but you don't have to be embarrassed about asking them. In fact, you don't have to ask a thing. I'll be only too glad to tell you, if you are interested."

"I am interested, of course. Is it Tehura?"

"She's the least of it," said Claire. "Let's be social. What'll you drink?"

"I'll have a light Scotch and water, if you will."

"No sooner said than done."

He sat, and watched her thoughtfully as she brought out the bottle of whiskey, the two tin cups, and the pitcher of water. While she made ready the drinks, he said, "You appear quite gay for an ex-anybody. They were never that way when they came to my office. They were always angry."

"I'm just relieved," she said, sitting down. "I'm good and relieved." She handed him his drink, and could see that his face was uncomprehending. "I'll tell you what it's like, Tom," she said, picking up her own drink. "What it feels like, I mean. It's like that ugly meeting you hate to undertake, waiting for the hour to fire someone, or better, to tell someone you've learned the truth about how they've been swindling you, and the anticipation of the meeting gnaws at your nerve ends, drives you crazy, and suddenly there it is, and you have it out, and everything you wanted to say you've said, and it's over and good-by. You are relieved. That's how it *feels*." She lifted her tin cup. "Toast?"

542

"Toast," he said, holding up his cup.

"The fifth freedom," she said. "Freedom from marriage, bad marriage, that is."

They drank, and she observed him over her cup. His eyes would not meet her eyes.

"I've embarrassed you, Tom," she said suddenly. "I see something now. You are very conservative about the holy wedlock—"

"Hardly."

"—and you think I'm being frivolous about it, and you are secretly disappointed, maybe offended."

"Not a bit. I've been the route many times, Claire. I guess I'm surprised, that's all."

"You're better than that. You knew we weren't getting along, you knew that."

"Maybe I—I thought about it, yes."

She took another sip, and she said with earnestness, "Tom, don't make any mistakes about me, not at this late date. Some women are made for careers, and some for being alone, and some for tumbling into a hundred beds, and some are made for being wives and mothers. I'm the last category. I was made to be a wife and have a billion kids and the hearth and home and pumpkin pies and his slippers ready. Maybe that is dull to you, but that is the meaning of life to me. It is all I ever wanted. Small ambition? So I thought. I was wrong. It's wanting too much, I guess."

"Not too much, but a lot."

"It takes two, Tom, to make one wife a wife."

"Yes, I believe that."

"Marc couldn't help. He couldn't help himself, let alone help me. We've been married two years, and we've had no contact. He never grew up, so how could he have children? Or a wife? Well, don't let me go on. I won't give you two years' worth of that. I'll simply say we've been having it out every day, and this morning was the blowup. This morning he said he had enough of me for the rest of his life, and he said more, and I hit him, and he hit me, and the final bell rang. Fight's over. For him it was two years ago. For me, today."

"And Tehura had nothing to do with it?"

"Not really. Had I weakened, that shameful incident would have been the capper. You know I went to see her, don't you?"

"You said you would. I didn't know if you had. What happened?"

"Have you seen her lately, Tom?"

"Not much, no, not actually. I've been too busy."

"I realize she was your girl once, and I know, for myself, what she was less than a month ago. But she's changed. I tell you, she's not recognizable. And I blame it on Marc, her friend Marc. She must have been susceptible, but it took a Marc to transform her into one of us, the worst of us."

"In what way?"

"No more the guileless half-primitive. She's shrewd, she's feline, she's bursting with ambition. In short, civilization's tot. As for my diamond pendant—yes, she has it. She did not steal it. We both knew that. Marc gave it to her. Part of the grand seduction, I suppose. The point is not that he would give it to her, but that she would want it and accept it. I read her the book on Marc. You know what that made me? I quote her. Jealous wife who mistreats and is unable to keep a husband."

"I can't believe it."

"Sorry, Tom."

"It's just that—" He kept shaking his head. "I know her so well. You understand. No one here knows her as well as I do. When you speak of her, I don't recognize the same person."

Claire shrugged. "Your client. See for yourself."

"I may," he said. "In fact, I will. I don't want to tangle with Marc, but I feel a responsibility for her. If she's off the straight and narrow, I'll try to set her right again. I'm troubled by that whole necklace episode. Do you mind if I discuss this openly with her?"

"I told you to see for yourself, go ahead. But if you are thinking you want to pry her away from Marc, to save Marc for me, forget it. You won't be doing me a favor, but a disservice. If you really want to see her for her own sake, to help the poor girl, that's another matter. I'm with you."

"That's all it would be," said Courtney. He rose abruptly, and paced restlessly about the room. "There has to be more to it than a mere affair. I tell you, I know Tehura's mind. She, none of them, make anything of an affair. That's as natural as kissing is to us. But when a girl changes so drastically, wants diamond necklaces that are not her own—I don't know—something is going on, something more than an affair. I'll find out, you can be sure. Tomorrow morning—"

It was then that the interruption came. They were both alarmed by it. The indistinct but harsh sounds of words, as if fired from rifles, rattled across the compound to their open door. Claire leaped up and, with Courtney, she ran outside.

The sight that met their eyes was that of Sam Karpowicz, in a state of dishevelment, gesticulating wildly, pouring out indistinct words at Maud, who stood in her nightdress before the stoop of her hut next door, nodding and nodding.

"Something's wrong," Courtney said to Claire, and the two rushed to find out what it was.

They reached Sam and Maud, just as Maud, touching the botanist's arm, had begun to speak. "Yes, it is terrible, Sam. We'll have to act with dispatch. I would suggest that we consult Paoti—"

"What is it?" Courtney interrupted. "Is there anything I can do?"

Sam Karpowicz, shaking with distress, turned to Courtney. "It's awful, Tom, awful. Somebody's raided my darkroom, stolen at least a third of my printed photographs, negatives, reels of sixteen-millimeter movie film."

"Are you absolutely sure?"

"Positive," Sam asserted, forcefully. "Positive," he repeated. "When I left you a little while ago, I went into the darkroom to develop what I did tonight. I was too busy to notice anything peculiar right off. But I realized, as I worked, that there were funny gaps in the room. I'm very methodical. I pile this here, that there, and suddenly there were no piles. I began to check my layouts and reels against my written inventory—do you want to see?—a third of it gone. It must have happened either this afternoon or this evening."

Maud said, "We simply can't figure out who would do a thing like that."

"That's what beats me," said Sam. "None of us on the team would have to steal film. I mean, here we are together. And the natives. What good would it do them?"

Claire spoke for the first time. "Unless there's some religious fanatic among the natives—the way there is in some societies—

who feels capturing images on paper is capturing the soul, or something like that. Could that be it?"

"I doubt it, Claire," said Maud. "I've found no tabu whatsoever against photography."

Courtney gripped Sam's arm. "Sam, does anyone else know about this?"

"I only discovered the robbery ten minutes ago. I dashed right in the house and woke up Estelle and Mary, to be sure they hadn't been fooling around with the photographs. They were as mystified as I. Then I asked Mary if she'd seen anyone hanging around here today—you know—but she said she was gone most of the day. Earlier in the day, she said, Marc was about—"

"When?" asked Claire sharply.

"When?" said Sam Karpowicz with surprise. "Why, it must have been—it was after we went to Maud's lunch—Mary stayed behind a while, and later went out with Nihau, and that was when she saw your husband."

Claire glanced at Courtney, then back at Sam. "That's odd. He left early this morning to go on an exploration into the hills with some of the villagers. He said he wouldn't be back until after midnight, maybe tomorrow, and now you say—?" Once more, she looked at Courtney. "Tom, are you thinking what I'm thinking?"

"I'm afraid so," said Courtney.

"It would explain a lot of things."

"Yes," said Courtney gravely. "We may be way off, but—"

Maud had elbowed herself closer into the group. "What's going on? If it concerns Marc—"

"It might," said Courtney. He consulted his watch. "Almost one o'clock. Nevertheless, I think I'd better go over and see Tehura."

"Let me go with you," said Claire.

Courtney frowned. "It could be embarrassing."

"I don't care," said Claire.

Sam Karpowicz said, "What's this got to do with the missing film?"

"Maybe nothing," said Courtney, "or maybe everything." He scanned the faces of the other three. "If you all want to come along with me, it's okay. But I'd prefer to see Tehura alone, first. I think I should do this before you go to Paoti."

Without reluctance, Maud Hayden relinquished leadership of

546

the evening to Tom Courtney. She showed her worry as plainly as Sam showed his perplexity. Courtney and Sam had started toward the bridge and, out of some instinct, Maud linked her arm in Claire's before following them.

* * *

In the dim light of Tehura's hut, the three of them, Courtney, Maud Hayden, Sam Karpowicz, stood huddled across the room, their eyes fixed on the limp body of the native girl, broken across the stone fertility idol.

Courtney it was who had come upon her first, sprawled unconscious, her pulse giving up its almost imperceptible beat. He had noted the blood behind her sightless eyeballs, and the blood caked at her eyes, mouth, and ears. He had hurried out and shouted his order to Claire, "Bring Harriet Bleaska, fast!" And when Claire had gone, he had beckoned Maud and Sam into Tehura's room.

Then they had waited.

Once, Maud, in a strained voice, had addressed Courtney. "What is it, Tom? You know more than you've told me."

He had only shaken his head, and stared down at Tehura's figure, remembering the pleasure of their old love, and the pain of this shocking sight, and none of them had spoken again.

It seemed five eternities, but it was no more than five minutes, before they heard the approaching voices and footsteps. Harriet Bleaska, in a robe, carrying a small black medical valise, came in alone. She acknowledged the three of them, and, seeing Tehura's limp body, fell to her knees beside her.

"Better leave me with her for a little while," she called over her shoulder.

Tom guided Maud outside, and Sam was behind them. Beyond the door waited Claire and Moreturi, speaking to one another in undertones. When they looked up, Moreturi came up to Courtney.

"Tom," he said, "how is she?"

"I think she's alive, but—I really don't know."

"I was coming into the village with the others, we had our catch of fish, when Mrs. Hayden and Miss Bleaska told me what happened. Could it be an accident?"

"I honestly don't know, Moreturi."

Claire had joined them. "Tom," she said, "Marc was out in the hills this afternoon. He fished with Moreturi."

"It is true," Moreturi said.

Courtney scratched his head, trying to make something of this, and he suddenly asked, "Did he come back with you?"

"No," said Moreturi. "He ate some food with us, but when it was dark, he left in the middle of our meal."

"Did he speak of Tehura at all?"

"Not that I can remember."

Then they heard Harriet Bleaska's voice, and as one they turned to the open doorway, which she filled. "Tom," she had called out. Now she repeated it, "Tom."

He made a step toward her, when she said, "Tehura is dead. Less than a minute ago it happened. There is nothing to be done."

They stood, all of them, like statues of grief in the semidarkness. The only movement, finally, was by Moreturi, who buried his face in his hands. The only sound, at last, was Maud Hayden's, a kind of wail, and she said, "Poor child."

Harriet had emerged from the doorway toward Tom Courtney. "It was a fracture of the skull, a severe one," she said. "It was too violent, the fall, to be an accident. Her head hit the stone idol, I suppose, and there was brain injury and a torrent of internal bleeding. You saw evidence of the blood. She was unconscious most of the time I think, but dying all the while. She kept trying to say something, even with her eyes closed. I couldn't make it out, really. It might have been—just before she died—there was—" Harriet squinted at Claire, confused, and stopped.

"There was what?" Courtney demanded to know.

"I thought she said 'Marc,' " Harriet said quickly. "I could be wrong."

"You are probably not wrong," said Claire.

"And then," said Harriet, "something I didn't understand—maybe it's Polynesian. First she said, 'ask' and she said this twice, 'Poma.' What is Poma?"

"A person, a girl who is Tehura's friend," said Courtney.

Moreturi had composed himself, and was beside Courtney. "She said, 'Ask Poma'?"

Harriet was troubled. "I think so."

Moreturi and Courtney exchanged some private look. Courtney nodded and Moreturi announced, "I go to Poma, to tell her our Tehura is dead, to ask Poma what she knows of this."

Moreturi sprinted off into the night.

"There was one more thing," Harriet was saying. "I should mention it now. The fracture is behind and above the base of the skull. But there is evidence of some lesser injury in front, on one side of her mouth and cheek. There is swelling and a bruise. It is as if she had been struck, not by an instrument, I don't think, but struck. Maybe someone punched her, knocked her down, and that's how she fell against the stone thing."

Courtney's features revealed no emotion. "Thanks, Harriet." He looked around. "I suppose someone had better notify Paoti. I want to wait here—"

"Let me do it," Harriet volunteered. "It will not be the first time. I want to go inside again, to straighten out, and after that, I'll go to Paoti."

With Moreturi still absent, and Harriet back inside the hut doing whatever nurses did with the dead, those who remained outdoors were drawn more intimately together. There was smoking, and there was continued silence. Sam Karpowicz was completely bewildered. What had begun with a theft of his precious photographs and film had led to this, by what route he could not understand, and he was too sensitive to inquire for an explanation. Maud's dumbness was less grief for the dead girl than for her son, who, it had been made clear, had had some connection with her. Still, she clung to a hidden hope that it was not so. Claire's silence, like Courtney's, was a mourning for Tehura, a flame so bright, so suddenly snuffed out. Yet, overshadowing all their private thoughts, was the wonderment. What had happened? What was behind the mystery?

Ten minutes passed, and then fifteen, and then Moreturi materialized, now less sad than angry, out of the darkness.

There were no questions, no interruptions, to delay the urgency of Moreturi's words.

"At first Poma, after she was awake, would say nothing about today. Then I told her that our Tehura was dead. She wept and she told the truth of it. I will make it brief, for there is much to do this night. Tehura came to Poma, to use her brother and his sailing vessel to leave this island. It was to be tonight and in the morning, at the far beach. Tehura pretended that she was going alone and Poma pretended to believe her. Last night, when Poma was with Tehura here, someone called on Tehura. They stayed outside. Poma was an evil spirit. She could not bear the secrecy. Through the back window, she peeked and listened. The caller was —was Mrs. Hayden's husband—Dr. Marc Hayden." Moreturi paused, then went on. "Dr. Hayden planned to come here tonight, and at midnight he and Tehura were to go to the far beach. There was mention also of one name foreign to Poma, one with the name 'Garrity,' who would be waiting for them in Tahiti."

Maud's voice was hushed. "Marc took your pictures, Sam. He was going to Rex Garrity."

Courtney addressed his native friend. "Did Poma say more, Moreturi?"

"Only that Marc was to be with Tehura tonight, and they were leaving after the midnight hour, to reach the beach when it was light. No more."

They had all forgotten Harriet Bleaska, but now she was with them, holding up an empty Scotch bottle. "I found this."

Courtney accepted it, and looked at Claire. She nodded her head in recognition. "Marc's brand," she said. "He was here."

Courtney turned to Moreturi. "From all the evidence, what has happened is fairly clear. Marc was here tonight with Tehura and he was drinking. He was taking Tehura with him, for whatever reasons he may have had. He was also taking what photographic evidences he could of the Sirens, and he and Garrity were going to sell out the island, exploit it, make a carnival of it. But something happened between Tehura and Marc tonight. Evidently, Marc struck her, and she fell against her stone idol, and died of the injuries. And it is a million to one Marc cleared out with his booty for his partner, Garrity, and is on his way to the beach right now." He stared at Claire and Maud, but there was no softness in him. "I'm sorry. That's the look of it."

"Tom, we must stop him." It was Moreturi speaking.

"Of course we must. If he gets away, these islands are doomed."

"If he gets away," said Moreturi, with no hint of apology for the fineness of his correction, "Tehura will not sleep."

The two men agreed that they must go in pursuit of Marc Hayden immediately. They ignored the others, as they quickly made their plan. Marc had several hours' start on them. Yet he was familiar with only one path to the far beach, the long but safe way, made slower for him by the night. There was the steeper, more difficult short route, along the sea, the one the natives often used. Courtney and Moreturi decided to use it now. They were not certain that they could overtake Marc. They could only try.

Without another word, they were gone.

The others went down into the compound. Harriet left the party to bear the sad news to Chief Paoti. Sam Karpowicz separated from Maud and Claire, somewhat awkwardly, to go to his wife and daughter. Of the party, only Maud and Claire, the two Haydens, stood in the compound, before Maud's hut, absently watching the torches along the stream.

After a while, Claire said, "What if they don't catch him?"

Maud said, "All will be lost."

Claire said, "And if they do catch him?"

Maud said, "All will be lost."

She was pale and old and sorry, as she turned and waddled toward her hut, forgetting to say good night. After Maud had closed the door behind her, Claire walked slowly to her own rooms to wait for morning.

* * *

The morning came to The Three Sirens gradually.

The first of the new day appeared as if through a crack in the horizon. The last of the darkness challenged the expanding light, but halfheartedly, and retreated before the advancing gray shafts of dawn and fled entirely from the incandescent glow of the sun's rim.

The new day would be windless, and the heat would be scalding. In this elevated area, where the two paths to the far beach converged on a spacious boulder ridge, the coconut palms stood straight and calm. Far, far below the eroded cliff, the cobalt sea washed gently against the weathered crags.

The two of them came up out of the sunken gorge, through the dense greenery, to the meeting of the paths, at the point where the paths merged into one crooked footway that led down to the beach. Moreturi's skin was beaded with perspiration mixed with gray dust. Courtney's soiled shirt was glued to his chest and spine, and his trousers flapped where thorns and bush had slashed them.

They rested on the broad, barren boulder, panting like animals who had run all through the night, trying now to regulate their breathing and to regain their physical vigor.

Finally, Moreturi turned, then strode backwards along the wider trail that rose from the plateau. Several times, he knelt to study the oft-trodden path. Courtney watched him with confidence. The villagers were uncanny at tracking, despite the fact that they were not a nomadic, game-hunting people. Their skill at tracking had been developed because it was one of their traditional sports. They had taught Courtney that the tracker's art was in being able to observe something recently out of place. An overturned stone, a pebble even, its moist side turned up and not yet dried by the sun, would indicate feet had displaced it minutes or hours before.

Courtney waited. At last, Moreturi, satisfied, joined his friend. "I think no one has walked here today," Moreturi said.

"You're probably right, but we'd better make sure," Courtney replied. "It's only a half-hour down to the beach. Either the boat is still there, or it's gone off with him."

They had begun to move as one, in the direction of the beach, when suddenly Moreturi's fingers closed tightly on Courtney's shoulder and held him still. Moreturi lifted his flat hand, a gesture requesting silence, and he whispered, "Wait." Quickly, he crouched, listening intently to the earth, and then, after interminable seconds, he straightened. "Something or someone comes," he announced.

"You think so?"

"Yes. Very near."

Automatically, they parted company, Moreturi fading into the inner brush, Courtney finding a station beside a coconut palm, each a sentinel on one side of the trail, waiting and hoping for the one who would come around the bend from the grasslands and ascend the boulder.

A minute passed, and then another, and suddenly he came into full view.

Courtney's eyes narrowed. The approaching figure grew larger. There was the hump of a knapsack on his back, and a shabby bundle carried low, and it was evident that he was at the borderline of fatigue. Gone were the personable visage, now drawn, the trim physique, now cramped, the sartorial neatness, now disheveled.

He did not see them at first, but followed the beaten trail from the plateau to the height of the boulder. Pausing once, to shift the agony of the knapsack's load, he resumed his heavy tread across the high cliff, eyes to the turf, until he reached the meeting of the paths. For an instant, he hesitated, then started doggedly along the single path.

Abruptly, he halted, and astonishment hit his slack mouth and jaw like a giant's blow.

He looked from left to right, first incredulously, then panic-stricken.

He stood swaying in disbelief, as Courtney and Moreturi slowly came together several yards before him.

He licked his lips, hypnotized by the apparition of them. "What are you doing here?" Marc Hayden's voice croaked out of a dry throat, the voice of a man who had spoken to no one all the night and expected to speak to no one all the day.

Courtney took a step toward him. "We came to get you, Marc," he said. "We were waiting for you. The whole sordid mess is out. Tehura is dead."

The pupils of Marc's eyes dilated, and then the eyelids quivered uncomprehendingly. He dropped his ragged bundle, and absently he slipped the knapsack off his back and lowered it to the ground. "She can't be dead."

"She'll never be deader," said Courtney evenly. "You don't have to say a damn thing. Her friend, Poma, told us practically all there is to know. We're taking you back, Marc. You'll have to stand trial before the Chief."

Marc's shoulders flinched, but his face was defiant. "The hell I will!" he burst forth. "It was an accident. She tried to kill me, and —it was self-defense—I had to knock her down. She tripped, fell backwards against that hunk of stone, but she was all right when I left. She was all right. It was an accident, I'm telling you. Maybe somebody else killed her." He gasped, his venomous eyes darting from Courtney to Moreturi. "You've got no right to stop me! I can go where I please!"

"Not now, Marc," said Courtney. "There has to be a hearing. You can have your say there."

"No—"

"You're living in The Three Sirens. You've got to abide by their laws."

"Fat chance I'd have," Marc jeered. "A snowball in hell, that's the chance I'd have. That colored kangaroo court, naked savages, crying and wailing over their little whore, and me, alone—no, never!" His tone took on an edge of cowardly solicitation. "Tom, for Chrissakes, you're one of us, you know better than this. If there's been an accident, and someone wants my version, wants the truth, then see that I get a fair chance—in Tahiti, California, anywhere civilized, among people like us, but not on this Godforsaken pisspot of an island. You know they'll mumble some crap and string me up."

"Nobody strings anybody up here, Marc. If you're not to blame, you won't be found guilty. You'll be freed. If you are guilty—"

"You're crazy, you're one of them," Marc interrupted bitterly. "You want me to stand up there in some shack, alone, against their witnesses, that Poma, her cretin brother, all the other brown bastards, and listen to what they dream up? You want me, a scholar, a scientist, an American, to be judged by them? And what about old Matty and Claire, you want me to stand up in front of them, both of them gloating and hating me as much as the tribesmen? Are you kidding? There'd be the death sentence on me before I opened my mouth. I'm telling you—"

"Marc, control yourself. I repeat, there is no death sentence. Sure, the evidence points strongly against you. But there's still your side of it. Only if that doesn't hold up, if you are judged in any way responsible for Tehura's death, will you be declared guilty and sentenced. But, you'll be allowed to live, except you'll have to remain here, make up Tehura's time to her kin, the time she would have had on earth except for you."

Marc's eyes blazed. "You're asking me to spend fifty years in slavery on this goddam place, you lousy bastard?" he yelled. "The hell with you, both of you, I'm not doing it! Get out of my way!"

Neither Courtney nor Moreturi moved. "Marc," Courtney said, "you can't get past us. You haven't got a chance. There's no place for you to go but back to the village, so listen to reason—"

Even as Courtney spoke, he and Moreturi began to close in on Marc Hayden. It was Courtney's arm reaching for him that galvanized Marc into action. Instinctively, with all his waning power, he slammed out. His fist caught Courtney on the jaw, sending him off balance into Moreturi's arms.

At once, Marc, choking, saliva dribbling down his chin, swerved toward the cliffside, preparing to outflank them and make a dash to the beach. But they had left the path, too, and they were both there, impenetrable, both waiting for him. Marc halted, measuring them, glanced to either side of them, and then the trapped expression in his face showed that he knew: Courtney had been right, there was nowhere to go, nowhere at all.

They were advancing steadily toward him once more, and Moreturi was saying with repressed fury, "I will take him, I will take him back."

Then it was that Marc broke. The sight of the malevolent aborigine drawing near shattered his resistance. Defeat was in his horrified eyes: the civilized wall had come down; the barbarous hordes were engulfing him. His discomposed features seemed to beseech someone not there. "Adley," he choked out. He reeled in retreat, but Moreturi was almost upon him. "No!" Marc shrieked. "No! I'll go to hell first!"

He turned and ran, stumbling across the width of the boulder to the very brink of the towering cliff. His back to the horizon, he faced them, teetering dangerously, shaking his fist, but not at them—how strange, Courtney thought—but at the sky. "Damn you!" he screamed. "For all eternity, damn you!"

Courtney's hand had stayed Moreturi, and Courtney shouted, "Marc, no—don't—!"

Balancing on the cliff's edge, Marc laughed without control, and then he howled, a convulsed lunacy in his twitching face. Suddenly he whirled about, toward the long deep sea, ignoring them, alone with his demons, and for a hanging second he stood poised as a high diver is poised. He did not dive. He took a single grotesque step forward into nothingness, suspended momentarily between heaven and hell, then plummeted downward out of sight, the ribbon of a ghastly, drawn-out, receding groan his last link to the society of men.

"Marc!" Courtney cried out, almost as a reflex, but there was no one there.

They raced toward the spot where he had been, and Courtney fell to his knees, and searched below. The drop was sheer and frightening to the eye, at least two hundred feet downward, until the cliff spread out into a small jutting peninsula of jagged rocks that descended into the ocean.

Moreturi touched Courtney, pointing, and Courtney made out what there was of Marc Hayden. His minute body dangled between two spears of basalt, crushed as an eggshell might be crushed when dropped upon cement, and as they watched, they could see the wash of foamy water nudging his remains, until the tiny corpse began to slide off the slimy stone. In seconds, it had slithered into the green sea, and then it was submerged, until it was gone from view, perhaps forever.

Presently, the two of them rose, not looking at one another until they had returned to the path. Then, Courtney sighed, and shouldered the knapsack, and Moreturi took up the bundle.

Moreturi was the one who spoke. "It is best," he said softly. "Some men are not born to live."

They said no more, but started the long walk back to the village of The Three Sirens.

IX

IT WAS INCREDIBLE to her that they had lived and worked on the islands of The Three Sirens for five weeks and six days, and that this was their last night before departure in the morning.

Claire Hayden, barefooted but still in her thin cotton dress, legs under her, back turned to the dangling lamp for the best light, sat in the front room of her hut and tried to resume reading her portable edition of Hakluyt's *Voyages*.

It was no use. Her eyes and mind strayed. An anthology of sixteenth-century English travel and exploration was too far removed from her needs this night. She had picked up the volume less for self-improvement than for sleep inducement, but it was not working. Her mind preferred to make its own contemporary voyage, over this day, and this week, and the almost three weeks since Marc's death. She was not drowsy, and she lowered the little book to her lap.

Lighting her cigarette, Claire wondered if she had not been mistaken in refusing, several hours earlier, to dine and spend her last evening on the Sirens with her mother-in-law. Her excuse to Maud had been that she needed every moment to pack her belongings. Captain Ollie Rasmussen and Richard Hapai would be arriving in the compound sometime between seven and eight in the morning. All members of the team had been ordered to have their luggage ready for the natives, who would carry it to the far beach. Actually, Claire had declined her mother-in-law's invitation not because of the packing, but because she preferred the independence and comfort of being alone this final evening.

Her colleagues and friends, she knew, had enjoyed a community dinner together. It was as if they were closing ranks, preparing for one front, before returning to the United States. Claire had cooked her own meal, some light native fare, and she had eaten alone, and she had not packed a thing, not yet.

There was little to pack, really, so that task had not bothered her. Several days after Marc's death, she and Maud, both determinedly dry-eyed, had gone through his effects, the shirts, trousers, shorts, socks, shoes, books, cigars, whiskey, ties, and all the rest of the standard issue of civilized man. Maud had wanted to keep several items, the Phi Beta Kappa key, the wafer-thin gold dress watch, the annotated copy of Malinowski's *Crime and Custom in Savage Society*, to remind her that she and Adley had once had a son. Claire had granted her every request, and for herself she had kept nothing, knowing that she had never had a husband. The occasion had been sad only because Claire had tried to understand how the older woman felt and how much of an ordeal this sorting out must be.

When the picking through of Marc's ephemeral estate had been completed, the most poignant moment, for Claire, was the observing of her mother-in-law's wrinkled surprise when she had muttered, "But his work, where is his work?"

There was none of Marc's work in his luggage, and it was evident to both of them, from every blank pad and notebook, that there never had been any. Not only had his luggage and garments produced no single jotting or record made during his stay on The Three Sirens, but the knapsack Courtney had returned produced nothing, either. Even the bundle that Moreturi had carried back to them, once the prints and film had been restored to Sam Karpowicz, offered no evidence of the field anthropologist, save the batch of carbon copies of Maud's own work notes, which Claire had saved to file and which Marc had stolen from her. Except for Rex Garrity's letters to Marc, which had indicated that Marc had written to him, there was no other evidence extant that Marc had done a single thing on the Sirens besides plotting its overthrow. It was this awesome lack of work, of a mind disintegrating, that had pained Maud most deeply, and had made Claire suffer to see her hurt.

That was the worst of it. The belongings of her son that Maud had not kept had been efficiently bound together with hemp and turned over to Captain Rasmussen on his next visit. With Claire's permission, the Captain had been requested to sell the last of Marc's portable possessions in Tahiti, and with the money to purchase some cooking utensils for Tehura's kin and medical supplies for Vaiuri's infirmary.

Tonight, that inventory seemed to have been made so very long ago, to be so dim and unrelated to the present. Claire's wrist watch told her that it was fifteen minutes after ten. Maud and the others would have finished their farewell dinner by now, and gone back to their packing, filled with the kind of happiness and sorrow all travelers experience the night before they leave an alien place to return to their more comfortable familiar homes and disquieting rutted lives. Claire examined her own feelings about leaving. She felt neither happiness nor sorrow. She was in some airless limbo. No emotion moved her.

In her immediate life, everything had changed since coming here, yet nothing had changed. Obviously, she should be feeling like a widow, however widows felt, which probably meant that some important part of her being had been removed, plucked away, taken back, to leave her crippled. Others felt that way about her, but she did not feel that way about herself. She had accepted condolences mechanically, to satisfy those who offered their understandings of grief, but she had felt a pretender and hoax, because she had felt nothing. Maud knew, of course, and possibly Courtney knew, although he may not have believed her. But had she not told Courtney, at the very time Marc was walking out on her, that she was the ex-Mrs. Hayden?

She had always been the ex-Mrs. Hayden, from the honeymoon night to the end. If she had been asked to write intimately of the late Marc Hayden, her page would have had to be as blank as Marc's own work pads. She had not known his inner person, except the festering part of him that was too ill to accept intimacy. Marc had been unable to give of himself to another. There had been no link between them forged of love or hate. Even the obvious part of their union, the corporeal part, had been a sham. Several weeks ago, attempting to sleep, she had played a witless game in her head. She had tried to recollect and count their copulations in two years. She had added eighteen times when she had run out of memory.

Perhaps there had been more times, but she could not remember them or his body. Her mind's biography would always have to be that of the oppressive guest in the house.

What would the others say, not Maud or Courtney, or even Rachel with her psychoanalyst's perceptions, but the others here and at home, if they knew the stark truth? What would anyone say if they knew that she was glad he was finally out of her life?

Uprooting this feeling, even letting it be seen by herself, shocked that part of her raised to conform with sentiment and convention. Oh, she had not wanted Marc to go out of her life in this horrible way. God knows, she could not wish him or any person on earth dead. But the fact of his being gone, ignoring the means, was a relief. The sadism he had imposed upon her the weeks before his death had been almost unbearable. With this remembrance, she could justify her coldheartedness. He had taunted her, insulted her, played vicious games with her weaknesses and fears. And all the tawdry rest of it, the plotting with that pig Garrity, the plotting with Tehura, the readying to run off and leave her a stranded, pitied fool, these she would not forget. Because he had killed himself, instead of escaping, because he was dead, this was by her society's rules enough to exonerate him for all his hideous terrorizing. By the accident of death, he had purged himself, and this impaled her upon widowhood. The devil with convention, she thought, no wound was healed, no years of life salvaged. His one death had not repaired her hundred deaths. To the devil with false conventions, and good-by, good riddance, Marc, you poor sick bastard.

These last weeks on the Sirens, she had wanted to be alone, and her wish had been respected, but for the wrong reasons. Everyone, perhaps even Tom Courtney, who should have known better, thought that she required her period of mourning. She had wanted to be alone only because she had wanted time to ease off the tensions that Marc had brought into her life. The Hadean ordeal was over, and she needed the vacation.

In a desultory way, she had continued working with Maud. Even after Marc had gone to his watery grave, Claire had been strong enough to take Maud's dictation of the flowery obituary notices to the popular press and to anthropological journals. There had been a dozen letters, also, to the faculty at Raynor College and to Maud's professional friends around the country. Everyone important had been notified of Marc's accidental and fatal fall "in the midst of his most valuable effort in the field." What had interested Claire was how all of the formal obituaries and informal letters were somehow focused on what Maud was secretly doing in the field right now and what Maud and Adley had done in the past. How bitter Marc would have been to share even his death with his over-shadowing collaborators.

Rasmussen had taken the news out, and had brought back the condolence cables and press notices. And, in one article datelined Papeete, there was a quotation from the renowned adventurer, Rex Garrity, grieving the untimely loss of the most promising young anthropologist in America, who was his close friend. In the same article, Garrity went on to announce that, after his brief vacation in Tahiti, he was off to Trinidad, and from there to the small isle of Tobago in the British West Indies, where tradition had ship-wrecked Robinson Crusoe. Garrity had been commissioned by the Busch Artist and Lyceum Bureau to emulate Crusoe's twenty-eight years of isolation in twenty-eight days, and Garrity pledged his vast following that he would play castaway honestly, with no more than the food, rum, carpenter's chest, pistols, and gunpowder that Crusoe had possessed.

After the publicity circus, Claire had continued to take dictation of Maud's notes on the Sirens, and Maud's voluminous reports to Walter Scott Macintosh and Cyrus Hackfeld. The dull steno-graphic work had consumed the days. Aside from long walks, only once had Claire ventured outside Maud's office or her own hut. She had attended Tehura's funeral pyre, and found herself weeping beside Tehura's kin, for this was the authentic tragedy. No illness of mind had brought the end to this young thing, only a corruption from the outside, like the old plagues visited upon the islanders by early French explorers.

Claire had seen Tom Courtney almost daily, but always, it seemed to her, in public. Vividly contrasted with memory of Marc's dark illness was Courtney's apparent strength and kindness. She could not explain to herself how she really felt toward Court-ney, but only that his presence, no matter how brief, made her feel reassured and worth while. Always, she had felt abandoned when he took leave of her company. This was curious because, since Marc's death, while Courtney had been friendly enough, he had come to seem more impersonal in his relations with her. She could not engage him, his opinion, his attention, as she had been able to earlier. And she could never find herself alone with him.

She wondered what had made him more remote. Was he conforming to the tiresome shibboleth of respect for the widow? Had his interest in her as a woman waned? Or was it that now, when she was unattached, he was afraid of her need for someone?

All of this week the enigma of Courtney had concerned her. Several times, she had determined to go to him, go straight to his bachelor hut, and sit across from him, and remind him of her feelings about Marc and their marriage, about herself and how she was and what was ahead, about false conventions. They would talk, and there would be a finish to this fakery. Yet, she could not bring herself to do this. She knew women who could go to men, who could telephone them, take them aside, even call upon them. For Claire, such aggressive action was unthinkable, except that she thought about it.

She realized, sitting here before the bright lamp, the book in her lap, three cigarettes stubbed out, that almost an hour had passed in idle reflection. She must be practical and think ahead. Tomorrow she would be in Tahiti. The day after tomorrow she would be in California. There was no immediate problem about money. Marc had little life insurance because he had little interest in any life outside his own, but he had been too embarrassed not to have a policy at all. There was one. And so there was enough money to keep her alive for one year.

Maud, with growing confidence in the results her paper on the Sirens would bring, had invited Claire to live with her in Washington, D.C., if that came through. Claire had been appreciative and vague, but was determined in her heart that she had no wish to remain Maud's secretary and ward. For the time, Claire decided, she would return to the Santa Barbara house, plan nothing, see what would happen for a while, see what life did to her. Eventually, she would take an apartment in Los Angeles, and find a job (there were many friends), and she would have to go through all that other young thing again, the learning to live as a single woman, the joining of this and that, the deciding about dates, ad infinitum, dammit.

The other day, in a different mood, she had considered remaining behind on The Three Sirens to see how that would work. If it did not work, there would always be Rasmussen to rescue her. But it made no sense, absolutely no sense. It was too dramatic for prosaic she, and she had not the bravery for such a change. Oh, if Tom Courtney had suggested it, she fancied that she might have said yes, whatever he meant, whatever she meant, and stayed on to see what would come of it. He had not suggested it, and so she had put the fancy out of her mind.

One more cigarette, she told herself. Then, drawing smoke from it, she drew also from various memories of her life on The Three Sirens. Bred as she had been, raised in a culture so different, there was little that she could take home with her from this island that would be of advantage. What she had appreciated most was utterly unacceptable among those she had grown up with. Yet, these people here, their customs, had reinforced certain secret beliefs that she had held, and that was good. Their behavior had given her more probing insights into herself, and into the life she had lived and to which she must return. Except for the one blight, it had been a good time.

Her wrist watch ticked persistently, and she was nearer to tomorrow. The exactness and inevitability of tomorrow made her feel restless for the first time this evening. She hated leaving the isolated comfort and freedom of this island. Almost overnight, she would be plunged into the strain of counterfeit behavior, the horrid widow pose, while here there was less necessity for that. How terrible to leave a place that had become more home than the home to which she must return. Yet, what was it that she would miss of the Sirens, really, but really, above and beyond the need for no pretense? She had not been close to any of the natives. Then what was it? In her isolation in this room, no one around, no prying, no peering at her, in this privacy, she could be herself and be truthful. So finally she could admit that all she would miss would be one, the one who was Tom Courtney.

This attachment to him, which she knew, and which he did not, made her nervous. She ground out her cigarette, stood up stiffly, flexed her shoulder muscles, and went into the rear room to change for bed, before packing.

Slowly undressing, she found him entering her thoughts again, and she forgave him. What was there about Tom Courtney that made her reluctant to leave him? How could she miss someone who, from his recent behavior, had given no sign that he would miss her the second after she had departed?

The last question lingered as she slipped the pleated white nylon nightgown down over her body. If only he would answer the last question for her this last night. Then she could leave without reservations. If only she was not she, and had the nerve . . .

* * *

The timid knocking on his cane door, in the stillness between the dark and the daylight, seemed to reverberate in the air.

The door came open almost immediately, and there they stood, he in his doorway, she outside it, and they were both surprised. She had never seen him this way before. He was like a white native, attired only in the pubic bag, and she realized that he must be this way in the privacy of his rooms, and that the shirt and trousers he wore outside were a concession to civilization's team. She drew her loose pink robe more tightly across her nightgown, and she stood there, not sure how she had done this or why or what she must say.

"Claire," he said.

"Did I wake you, Tom? I'm sorry. This is crazy. It must be a million hours after midnight."

"I wasn't sleeping," he said. "I was lying in the dark thinking about—well, yes, about you—"

"You were?"

"Come in, come in," he said, and then quickly, realizing the state of his undress, he said, "Hey, wait, let me change—"

"Don't be a child," she said, "because I'm not one, either." She crossed before him into his room.

He closed the door and strode to the bamboo rod of candlenuts. "Let me get some light."

"No, Tom, don't. Leave it this way. It's easier to talk to you. There's enough moonlight from the windows."

She had lowered herself to the pandanus matting. He approached her, his head lost high in the upper darkness, before he came down into sight, and sat a few feet from her.

"I've never called on a man before," she said. "I should have sent you one of those festival shells first. This is The Three Sirens, isn't it?"

"I'm glad you came," he said. "I was going to call on you a dozen times last night, tonight. It's harder for a man."

"Why, Tom? That's the reason I had the courage to—to come

here. I couldn't leave tomorrow, just disappear, without finding out about you. We were so friendly for a while. It was important to me. You have no idea how important. And suddenly, after Marc's death, you weren't there. Why? Respect for the widow?"

"Yes and no. Not for the reasons you seem to think. I was afraid to be alone with you. That's it, really."

"Afraid? Why?"

"Because overnight you were possible. Before, you were not, and all at once you were, and I was afraid of what I might say to you or do. I had strong feelings about you, from the day you arrived, but I had to hide them. Then, all at once, I realized I could express them. And at the same time, I realized that I had no idea how you would feel about my feelings. I'm talking like an idiot, but I mean—before, guarded by a husband, you could afford to show interest in me. Without protection, you might not have the same interest. And if I came in—"

"Tom," she said softly, "thank you."

"For what?"

"For making it possible for me to be here with you without having to blush about it for years after."

"Claire, I'm not saying all of this to—to make you comfortable. I'm speaking to a woman in a way I would not have been able to speak four or five years ago. The fact is, I'm the one who must thank you. Do you want to know why?"

"Yes."

"You made me grow up, and you never knew it. My four years on the Sirens made a man of me. My knowledge of you made a mature man of me. Until today, I was going to stay on here indefinitely. The old reasons. This is an easy, permissive, hedonistic life. You go on in an empty-headed way, and you let your body live. And you're important in this little pool. Going home becomes more and more difficult. If you return, you lose this importance, you become like everyone else. You've got to work too hard for new importance. And you've got to live with your head, too, not just your body. You've got to wear the strait jackets of progress, follow the clock, the law, the conventions like civilized clothes, and what-not. But today I changed my mind. I went to Maud and asked her if I could return to Tahiti and the United States with all of you in the morning. I'm going back with you, Claire."

Claire sat very still, one hand clasping her robe together at the bosom, her flesh pervaded by a weakness and a running warmth. "Why are you leaving here, Tom?"

"Two reasons. Reason one. I've grown up, and I decided that I could come to grips with the outside. Claire, I've been hiding out these last years, hiding from life. It was your presence here, the thoughts you induced, that made me realize my exile was illusory happiness, superficial, shallow, pointless compared to what you represented. Seeing you, perhaps some of the others, made me restless and deeply dissatisfied, even ashamed of myself. That was when I knew I had solved nothing, and never would, unless I solved it in your world, which is my world, too."

He paused, avoiding her eyes, staring down at his hands, and then he looked up at her. "I—I don't want to make a big dramatic speech about returning to a life that most other men take for granted. I only want you to know how I've come to the decision. I fully realize it's not as easy and idyllic at home as it is here. Existence can be more abrasive and troublesome in the States. But I've come to believe that I was set down on this earth, in that place called home, to live my days there and cope with it and do what a man must do. Instead, when the going got rough, I ran. I'm not alone. I'm one of millions. All men have their ways of running. Some run inside themselves. Others act it out, as I did. One bad marriage, one war, one disillusioning job, and I ran for real. I thought the four years here liberated me. They did. Yet, only in small ways. In a big way, I've been a coward. The mature man who does not run, who stays on in the workaday world in which he was born and raised, he is the one who shows a kind of heroism. That's the real unsung heroism, the facing of day-in-and-day-out living, the facing up to conventional work, marriage, procreation, and making of it a good thing. The euphoria of hidden islands and coconut palms and dusky maidens belongs in dreams. If life at home is not up to those dreams, then it is a man's job to make life at home better, improve it, fight for it in his house, neighborhood, community, country. The main thing is to meet life face to face on your own battleground, and this I am going to try to do. That is why I am going back."

He paused, and waited, but Claire said nothing.

"Claire," he said, "you haven't asked the second reason I am going back."

She did not speak.

"It is you, Claire. I am in love with you. I have been in love with you from the moment I set eyes upon you. I want to be near you, be where you will be, if you want it or not."

She could hear herself breathing in the darkness. She was frightened by the thumping of her heart. "Tom—do you—do you mean that?"

"I mean it more than any words I have spoken in my entire life. I am so in love with you that I can't think or speak properly. I've wanted you since you came here, I've wanted you tonight, I've wanted you for my own for the rest of the days of my life. It's—it's all I can say—and what I've been afraid to say until now."

She found that she had covered his hand with her own. "Tom, why do you think I came here tonight?"

"Claire—"

"I want you, too. I need you. I need you tonight and as long as there are nights and the two of us on this earth. I've never—I've never said such things before, to anyone." She had come into his arms, and buried her head against his naked chest. "Maybe it's not right for me to admit these things now."

"What a human being feels about love is right."

"Then, that's what I feel, Tom. Love me always. Love me, and never stop."

* * *

It was eight o'clock in the morning of the last day, and a cooling breeze frolicked with the palm fronds over the village of The Three Sirens.

Through the open front door of her hut, from behind the desk where she sat, Maud Hayden rested from her dictation into the tape recorder and observed the first activity of the morning in the compound. The young native males, the bearers, four or five of them, were carrying the suitcases and crates out to the bank of the stream.

Maud's gaze left the compound, and went to the silver microphone in her hand. In the past half-hour, she had recorded what had remained to be recorded of her factual notes on the Sirens. What had been set down this morning, and during six weeks of mornings, was important and unusual, and she knew the uses to which she could put it and the impact it would make on her colleagues and the nation. For the first time since her grief—that aw-

ful week after, when she had twice wept uncontrollably and secretly—she felt if not completely recovered, at least purposeful.
The blinding puffiness was gone from around her eyes, the knifing
arrow of pain gone from her chest, and in her bones she felt the
healing strength of her accomplishment. Silently, she thanked
them all, Easterday, Rasmussen, Courtney, Paoti, and the distant
Daniel Wright, Esq., too, for giving her back her occupation. No
longer was work a livelihood and a vanity. It was now her husband,
her son, the meaning of her life.

There was hardly any time left. She took in the packings all
around the room, and once more her eyes fell on the microphone
in her hand. What else was there to record?

A final summary would not be amiss. Her forefinger pushed the
recording button on the machine and the spools of tape began to
revolve.

In a low, rasping voice, she spoke aloud.

"One more thought. The practice of love and marriage on The
Three Sirens, which I have observed firsthand, remains for the
most part utterly unlike any other system I have known on earth.
For these natives, schooled to it, adjusted to it across so many
decades, it appears to be perfect. Yet, I am convinced that this pattern of perfection could not be grafted on our own society in the
West. We are heirs of a competitive and restless society, with its
advantages and disadvantages, and we must live within our emotional means. What I have seen work out successfully on The
Three Sirens would probably not work in the United States, Great
Britain, France, Germany, Italy, Russia, or anywhere in the modern world. But this I think, this I think: we can learn from societies
like the Sirens; we can learn a little; we cannot live their life but
we can learn from it."

She allowed the tape to run on a few seconds, before she pressed
the button marked "Stop."

Something else was needed, she felt, some justification for all the
burrowings of the social anthropologists and their colleagues who
participated in these often difficult and unsettling trips into the
field. Whenever she required reassurance of the value of their
work, what they had gone through to garner their scratchy facts,
what they had gone through as individuals, what sacrifices were
offered up, she remembered a statement made by one of her own
whom she admired.

Bending over, she opened her book bag, and examined and returned several titles, until she had located the volume that she wanted. The microphone still in her right hand, she opened Robert Lowie's *Primitive Society* to its introduction, and after turning a dozen pages she found it.

For the last time on this trip, she pressed the recording button, watched the tape unwind, and, reading slowly from Lowie, she addressed the microphone.

" 'The knowledge of primitive societies has an educational value that should recommend its study even to those who are not primarily interested in the processes of culture history. All of us are born into a set of traditional institutions and social conventions that are accepted not only as natural but as the only conceivable response to social needs. Departures from our standards in foreigners bear in our biased view the stamp of inferiority. Against this purblind provincialism there is no better antidote than the systematic study of alien civilizations . . . We see our received set of opinions and customs as merely one of an indefinite number of possible variants; and we are emboldened to hew them into shape in accordance with novel aspirations.' "

A smile had formed itself upon Maud Hayden's large face. With finality, she hit the button that stopped the tape, and knew that all had been said and done.

After returning the book to the bag, and capping the portable tape recorder with its metal top, she looked out the open doorway. The baggage was piled high now, and the Karpowiczes were there, and Harriet and Orville, and Rachel and Lisa. She could see Claire and Tom Courtney together, crossing the compound toward the others.

Captain Rasmussen and Professor Easterday came into sight, greeting the others, and the gathering natives, and now both Rasmussen and Easterday turned toward her hut and were coming to get her.

It was a good time and a bad time, but it was the time to go.

Pressing her palms to the desk, she lifted her bulk from the chair. She made certain to secure the lid of the tape recorder, and she cast about to see if there were any leftover papers. There were none, and she was ready.

Waiting, she wondered if she would ever return to The Three Sirens or if any of them out there would ever return. Or, she wondered, if they wanted to return, and Rasmussen and Courtney were no more, who on earth would there be to guide them to this unknown place?

The Three Sirens, she told herself, is Man's eternal dream of Eden Resurrected. When the world heard of it from her, would the world believe it, and, believing it, seek it out? And then she wondered how long it would take the world to find it, if ever, if ever.

AN AFTERWORD

Off and on, for over four years, I did research on this novel, in order to provide a background, work out customs, develop characters—in short, to create a foundation of factual probability for my fiction.

In an attempt to understand the thinking, methods, personalities of physical and social anthropologists, living and dead, to learn something of their procedures and problems when in the field, to become acquainted with their discoveries and reports of unusual practices in diverse cultures, I read widely among the published writings of the masters of anthropology. For whatever knowledge and insight I have gained, I am primarily indebted to them.

As a supplement to my reading, I was fortunate enough to have the results of firsthand interviews with eleven of America's leading anthropologists. These anthropologists were more than generous in offering their time, energy, wisdom in replying to numerous questions I devised for them, specific questions concerning material I needed for this fictitious narrative.

Where the nature of the information passed on to me in these interviews was highly personal opinions, anecdotes, experiences, I feel it only fair to keep my sources anonymous. However, since these unnamed sources provided suggestions and data that have made portions of this book possible, I thank them now for their courtesy, patience, and frankness.

I am eager to tender my sincerest thanks and appreciation specifically to several prominent anthropologists, who learnedly and candidly replied to my inquiries, and who gave unsparingly of their time and erudition. I wish to acknowledge my debt to Dr.

Frank J. Essene, Head of the Department of Anthropology, University of Kentucky, Lexington, Kentucky; Dr. Leo A. Estel, Associate Professor of Anthropology, Ohio State University, Columbus, Ohio; Dr. John F. Goins, Associate Professor of Anthropology, University of California, Riverside, California; Dr. Gertrude Toffelmier, anthropologist, Oakland, California. Among those outside anthropology, I am most grateful to Dr. Eugene E. Levitt, Chief of the Psychology Section, Indiana University Medical Center, Indianapolis, Indiana, for his cooperation and advice.

I cannot state too strongly that the factual briefings I received through these interviews were used by me in a narrative that is wholly a work of fiction. Not one of the anthropologists who proffered me advice or information had any foreknowledge of the contents of this novel, or had any involvement in its fictional aspects. If I have understood the factual material imparted to me, and used it correctly, if the resultant book has some semblance of accuracy and realism, then a great share of the credit is due to my eminent informants.

For further assistance, I am beholden to Elizebethe Kempthorne, Corona, California; Luise Putcamp Johnson, Dallas, Texas; and Lilo and William Glozer, Berkeley, California. But, as ever, my deepest gratitude goes out to Sylvia Wallace, Wife, for literary advice, for listening, for love.

Needless to say, the characters in this novel are entirely products of my imagination. If similar persons exist in my country, or elsewhere, I am delighted with my perception but quick to insist that the resemblance is coincidental. The strands of plot, too, are born of one author's fancies. As to the customs practiced on the Sirens, these are a mixture of fact and fabrication. Some of the customs described were altered or modified from actual usages in real communities in Polynesia; some were inspired by true traditions of surviving cultures, but have been elaborated upon by my own make-believe; some were originated totally by the author.

Finally, I should like to comment on the authenticity of the novel's locale. While I have crossed the Pacific Ocean twice, I have never physically set foot on The Three Sirens. I have searched for them far and wide, across many years, but their location has always eluded me. Not until recently did I know why. The Sirens had been too near at hand to be seen. It was only when I looked inward that I found them at last. I discovered them one day while musing before my desk, and suddenly there they were, so clear, so familiar, so beautiful—and it came as no surprise at all that where they were, where they existed, had always existed, was in that uncharted region of the imagination which is tabu to all but those who forever seek what life hides from us behind its drab, almost impenetrable curtain of reality.

IRVING WALLACE
LOS ANGELES, CALIFORNIA